# The Marquis de Sade

## The 120 Days of Sodom

### and other writings

# The Marquis de Sade

## The 120 Days of Sodom and other writings

compiled and translated by
*Austryn Wainhouse & Richard Seaver*

with introductions by
*Simone de Beauvoir*
*& Pierre Klossowski*

Grove Press, Inc., New York

ACKNOWLEDGMENTS: The essay by Simone de Beauvoir "Must We Burn Sade?" was originally published in the December 1951 and January 1952 issues of *Les Temps Modernes* as "Faut-il brûler Sade?" and was subsequently reprinted in the collection of the author's essays entitled *Privilèges*. The English translation first appeared in *The Marquis de Sade*, published by Grove Press in 1954, and is here reprinted in a slightly revised translation by permission of the publisher and the translator. "Nature as Destructive Principle," by Pierre Klossowski, served as an introduction to the *Au Cercle du Livre Précieux* edition of *Les 120 Journées de Sodome*. This essay is a slightly revised and condensed version of the chapter entitled "Esquisse du Système" from the author's book, *Sade mon prochain*, published by *Editions du Seuil*, Paris, France, 1947. It is here reprinted by permission of the author and of the editor of *Yale French Studies*. The editors wish especially to thank Miss Marilynn Meeker for her meticulous job of editing, and for the number and diversity of her suggestions.

To the memory of Maurice Heine, who freed Sade from the prison wherein he was held captive for over a century after his death, and to Gilbert Lely, who has unselfishly devoted himself to this same task of liberation and restitution.

# Contents

Chateau et Silas
Psychopathia Sexualis

# *Foreword*

There is an opinion worth pondering, which may perhaps become the prevailing one among Sade's more thoughtful readers: according to it, the immense fragment occupying the better part of the present volume deserves to be considered his crowning achievement, his masterpiece. Certainly, behind that estimate lie "special" criteria. Perverse criteria, one may feel, as one penetrates into a world where, as though in the Château of Silling itself, the appeal to ordinary standards evokes only sardonic silences. Nowhere, indeed, is Sade at such a remove from literature and its reassurances, nowhere does his assault upon ordinary standards reach such a pitch of unpitying absoluteness, nowhere is its violence so categorical or sustained for so long as in *The 120 Days of Sodom*. To this darkest of novels, to this book of purest destruction, to this unsurpassed novel of terror and signal act of terrorism, Sade attached a capital importance. Chronologically, it was his first major work: the year was 1785, he was forty-five and by then had made up his mind about what his writer's task was to consist of. This *psychopathia sexualis* was to be its beginning and end. It was—it would have been—his definitive labor and "crime of love."

In themselves, the details of the manuscript's disappearance and rediscovery make a remarkable story, whose essentials are given in the note preceding the work; here we need only say that the grand event inaugurating the Revolution Sade awaited so impatiently cost him the text in which he had consigned everything of the most intimate and extreme of his own revolt. Over the loss of his *120*

*Days,* which was engulfed in the pillage that followed the Bastille's capture, they were "tears of blood" he wept. "It was, and Sade knew it, his masterpiece that had gone astray," insists Maurice Heine in his preface to the first edition. "The remainder of his literary life was to be dominated by the concern to remedy the consequences of that irreparable accident. With painful perseverance he strove to attain again the mastery that had been his at the supreme height of his solitude and his misanthropy."

The life of the Marquis de Sade was an incredible series of misfortunes, and what is perhaps most incredible of all was his capacity to withstand them. No doubt whatsoever, he invited trouble; it came his way unfailingly. Adversity or, more exactly, the cruel privations of confinement made Sade a writer in the first place—he said so, jubilantly, promising to take a prodigious revenge. Upon the prisoner's fare of eternal anxiety his genius thrived, and the very frailty of words scratched on thin paper, the constant possibility that his persecutors intervene, that authority arbitrarily confiscate or tear to pieces all he had toiled to put together, lent a further dimension to his helpless vulnerability and his rage.

It was thanks to the Revolution that Sade obtained his freedom. Overjoyed at his release, eager to participate in the movement of his times, he soon found himself in another nightmare. His disappointment was almost immediate and withering; but this too he overcame. In prison he had learned patience and cunning and duplicity and the techniques of unfeeling indifference, of what he called apathy; and these were the resources he drew upon to survive in the midst of the Nation and to outlast the Reign of Virtue. When his lawyer Gaufridy wondered about the Marquis' political views, "Citizen Sade" assured him they were just what circumstances demanded, and nothing if not "mobile." Today it requires more than mere naïveté to tax Sade with insincerity. If anyone hated the *ancien régime,* it was he; but he realized at once something it has taken French historians until now to be clear on: that, precious misunderstandings and popular duperies aside, 1789 was a proprietors' uprising calculated to secure and consolidate the position and interests of the bourgeoisie alone. How little he sympathized with the Incorruptible's aim to bring forth a Republic cemented by blood Sade was able to illustrate when, as a judge, and to his mortal peril, he declined to sentence members of the opposition to death, explaining that while one might commit crimes for the sake of pleasure, it was not among his principles to murder in the name of justice.

Elusive, paradoxical figure! On the one hand, *Le Comte Oxtiern ou les Effets du Libertinage,* presented to a public whose approval mattered so deeply to the playwright Sade; on the other hand, that "Theory of Libertinage"[1] Restif de la Bretonne had got wind of and shrilled against in advance of its eventual publication by "the monster-author"—the contrast is extreme and it is strange. What conclusions must one arrive at regarding the man who, while citing Samuel Richardson and the creator of Joseph Andrews as the outstanding explorers of "the human heart, Nature's veritable labyrinth," was filling the more than one hundred notebooks of *Les Journées de Florbelle, ou la Nature dévoilée,* his effort to reconstitute *The 120 Days*?

Again and again we are led back to a fundamental contradiction in Sade; and there, one senses, lies the entire problem of situating him. Introducing the volume that preceded this one, we alluded to the difficulty when we spoke of the two designs corresponding to two drives: to write in order to be read, and to write unreadably, in such a way as to preclude being read, and in answer to a very different but equally real purpose. To be known, and to be unknown; to divulge, and to conceal. To reintegrate society and broad daylight, and to hold to his cell, immuring himself in the night. Sade wanted both, and both at once.

It was he who classified his works as *L (lumière)* or *S (sombre),* or else signed some and refrained from acknowledging others, and even disavowed *Justine,* his spiritual autobiography, so vigorously and so systematically protesting the allegations that the book was his as to establish the solidest grounds for suspicions to the contrary. Thus his "public" and his "clandestine" writings—if they represent

---

[1] This is the name Restif de la Bretonne invented to identify *The 120 Days of Sodom,* whose real title he did not know, but of whose composition he had learned.

antithetical attitudes and intentions—were in a dialectical sense complementary, and in a psychological sense inseparable. The drama of his life, precisely, was their reconciliation.

A.W., R.S.

# The Marquis de Sade

# Part One

# Critical

# Must We Burn Sade?

## by Simone de Beauvoir

### 1

"*I*mperious, choleric, irascible, extreme in everything, with a dissolute imagination the like of which has never been seen, atheistic to the point of fanaticism, there you have me in a nutshell, and kill me again or take me as I am, for I shall not change."

They chose to kill him, first by slow degrees in the boredom of the dungeon and then by calumny and oblivion. This latter death he had himself desired. "The ditch once covered over, above it acorns shall be strewn in order that, the spot become green again and the copse grown back thick over it, the traces of my grave may disappear from the face of the earth as I trust the memory of me shall fade out of the minds of all men. . . ."[1] This was the only one of his last wishes to be respected, though most carefully so. The memory of Sade has been disfigured by preposterous legends,[2] his very name has buckled under the weight of such words as "sadism" and "sadistic." His private journals have been lost, his manuscripts burned—the ten volumes of *Les Journées de Florbelle* at the insti-

---

[1] From Sade's "Last Will and Testament."—*Eds.*

[2] The aging Sade ordering baskets of roses to be brought to him, smelling them voluptuously and soiling them afterward in the mud of the gutters with a sardonic laugh: present-day journalists have taught us how this kind of anecdote is manufactured.

4     THE MARQUIS DE SADE

gation of his own son—his books banned. Though in the latter part of the nineteenth century Swinburne and a few other curious spirits became interested in his case, it was not until Apollinaire that he assumed his place in French literature. However, he is still a long way from having won it officially. One may glance through heavy, detailed works on "The Ideas of the Eighteenth Century," or even on "The Sensibility of the Eighteenth Century," without once coming upon his name. It is understandable that as a reaction against this scandalous silence Sade's enthusiasts have hailed him as a prophetic genius; they claim that his work heralds Nietzsche, Stirner, Freud, and surrealism. But this cult, founded, like all cults, on a misconception, by deifying the "divine marquis" only betrays him. The critics who make of Sade neither villain nor idol, but a man and a writer, can be counted upon the fingers of one hand. Thanks to them, Sade has come back at last to earth, among us.

Just what is his place, however? Why does he merit our interest? Even his admirers will readily admit that his work is, for the most part, unreadable; philosophically, it escapes banality only to founder in incoherence. As to his vices, they are not startlingly original; Sade invented nothing in this domain, and one finds in psychiatric treatises a profusion of cases at least as interesting as his. The fact is that it is neither as author nor as sexual pervert that Sade compels our attention; it is by virtue of the relationship which he created between these two aspects of himself. Sade's aberrations begin to acquire value when, instead of enduring them as his fixed nature, he elaborates an immense system in order to justify them. Inversely, his books take hold of us as soon as we become aware that for all their repetitiousness, their platitudes and clumsiness, he is trying to communicate an experience whose distinguishing characteristic is, nevertheless, a tendency to be incommunicable. Sade tried to make of his psycho-physical destiny an ethical choice; and of this act, in which he assumed his "separateness," he attempted to make an example and an appeal. It is thus that his adventure assumes a wide human significance. Can we, without renouncing our individuality, satisfy our aspirations to universality? Or is it only by the sacrifice of our individual differences that we can integrate ourselves into the community? This problem concerns us all. In Sade the differences are carried to the point of outrageousness, and the immensity of his literary effort shows how passionately he wished to be accepted by the human community. Thus, we find in his work the most extreme form of the conflict from which no individual can escape without self-deception. It is the paradox and, in a sense, the triumph of Sade that his persistent singularity helps us to define the human drama in its general aspect.

In order to understand Sade's development, in order to grasp the share of his freedom in this story, in order to assess his success and his failure, it would be useful to have precise knowledge of the facts of his situation. Unfortunately, despite the zeal of his biographers, Sade's life and personality remain obscure on many points. We have no authentic portrait of him, and the contemporary descriptions which have come down to us are quite poor. The testimony at the Marseilles trial shows him at thirty-two, "a handsome figure of a man, full faced," of medium height, dressed in a gray dress coat and deep orange silk breeches, a feather in his hat, a sword at his side, a cane in his hand. Here he is at fifty-three, according to a residence certificate dated the 7th of March, 1793: "Height: five feet two inches; hair: almost white; round face; receding hairline; blue eyes; medium nose; round chin." The description of the 22nd of March, 1794, is a bit different: "Height: five feet two inches, medium nose, small mouth, round chin, grayish blond hair, high receding hairline, light blue eyes." He seems by then to have lost his "handsome figure," since he writes a few years later, in the Bastille, "I've taken on, for lack of exercise, such an enormous amount of fat that I can hardly move about." It is this corpulence which first struck Charles Nodier when he met Sade in 1807 at Sainte-Pélagie. "An immense obesity which hindered his movements so as to prevent the exercise of those remains of grace and elegance that still lingered in his general comportment. There remained, nevertheless, in his weary eyes an indefinable flash and brilliance which took fire from time to time, like a dying spark on a dead coal." These testimonies, the only ones we possess, hardly enable us to visualize a particular face. It has been said[3] that Nodier's description recalls the aging Oscar Wilde; it suggests

---

[3] Jean Desbordes: *Le vrai visage du marquis de Sade,* Paris, Nouvelle Review Critique, 1939.

Robert de Montesquiou and Maurice Sachs as well, and it tempts us to imagine a bit of Charlus in Sade, but the data is very weak.

Even more regrettable is the fact that we have so little information about his childhood. If we take the description of Valcour for an autobiographical sketch, Sade came to know resentment and violence at an early age. Brought up with Louis-Joseph de Bourbon, his contemporary, he seems to have defended himself against the selfish arrogance of the young prince with such displays of anger and brutality that he had to be taken away from court. Probably his stay in the gloomy château of Saumane and in the decaying abbey of Ebreuil left its mark upon his imagination, but we know nothing significant about his brief years of study, his entry into the army, or his life as an *amiable* man of fashion and debauchee. One might try to deduce his life from his work; this has been done by Pierre Klossowski, who sees in Sade's implacable hatred of his mother the key to his life and work. But he derives this hypothesis from the mother's role in Sade's writings. That is, he restricts himself to a description of Sade's imaginary world from a certain angle. He does not reveal its roots in the real world. In fact, we suspect a priori, and in accordance with certain general notions, the importance of Sade's relationship with his father and mother; the particular details are not available to us. When we meet Sade he is already mature, and we do not know how he has become what he is. Ignorance forbids us to account for his tendencies and spontaneous behavior. His emotional nature and the peculiar character of his sexuality are for us data which we can merely note. Because of this unfortunate gap, the truth about Sade will always remain closed to us; any explanation would leave a residue which only the childhood history of Sade might have clarified.

Nevertheless, the limits imposed on our understanding ought not to discourage us, for Sade, as we have said, did not restrict himself to a passive submission to the consequences of his early choices. His chief interest for us lies not in his aberrations, but in the manner in which he assumed responsibility for them. He made of his sexuality an ethic; he expressed this ethic in works of literature. It is by this deliberate act that Sade attains a real originality. The reason for his tastes is obscure, but we can understand how he erected these tastes into principles, and why he carried them to the point of fanaticism.

Superficially, Sade, at twenty-three, was like all other young aristocrats of his time; he was cultured, liked the theater and the arts, and was fond of reading. He was dissipated, kept a mistress —la Beauvoisin—and frequented the brothels. He married, without enthusiasm and in conformance to parental wishes, a young girl of the petty aristocracy, Renée-Pélagie de Montreuil, who was, however, rich. That was the beginning of the disaster that was to resound—and recur—throughout his life. Married in May, Sade was arrested in October for excesses committed in a brothel which he had been frequenting for over a month. The reasons for arrest were grave enough for Sade to send letters, which went astray, to the governor of the prison, begging him to keep them secret, lest he be hopelessly ruined. This episode suggests that Sade's eroticism had already assumed a disquieting character. This hypothesis is confirmed by the fact that a year later Inspector Marais warned the procuresses to stop giving their girls to the Marquis. But the interest of all this lies not in its value as information, but in the revelation which it constituted for Sade himself. On the verge of his adult life he made the brutal discovery that there was no conciliation possible between his social existence and his private pleasures.

There was nothing of the revolutionary nor even of the rebel about young Sade. He was quite prepared to accept society as it was. At the age of twenty-three he was obedient enough to his father[4] to accept a wife whom he disliked, and he envisaged no life other than the one to which his heredity destined him. He was to become a husband, father, marquis, captain, lord of the manor, and lieutenant-general. He had not the slightest wish to renounce the privileges assured by his rank and his wife's fortune. Nevertheless, these things could not satisfy him. He was offered activities, responsibilities, and honors; nothing, no simple venture

---

[4] Klossowski is surprised by the fact that Sade bore his father no ill will. But Sade did not instinctively detest authority. He admits the right of the individual to exploit and to abuse his privileges. At first, Sade, who was heir to the family fortune, fought society only on the individual, emotional level, through women: his wife and mother-in-law.

interested, amused, or excited him. He wished to be not only a public figure, whose acts are ordained by convention and routine, but a live human being as well. There was only one place where he could assert himself as such, and that was not the bed in which he was received only too submissively by a prudish wife, but in the brothel where he bought the right to unleash his fantasies.

And there was one dream common to most young aristocrats of the time. Scions of a declining class which had once possessed concrete power, but which no longer retained any real hold on the world, they tried to revive symbolically, in the privacy of the bed-chamber, the status for which they were nostalgic: that of the lone and sovereign feudal despot. The orgies of the Duke of Charolais, among others, were bloody and famous. Sade, too, thirsted for this illusion of power. "What does one want when one is engaged in the sexual act? That everything around you give you its utter attention, think only of you, care only for you . . . every man wants to be a tyrant when he fornicates." The intoxication of tyranny leads directly to cruelty, for the libertine, in hurting the object that serves him, "tastes all the pleasures which a vigorous individual feels in making full use of his strength; he dominates, he is a tyrant."

Actually, whipping a few girls (for a consideration agreed upon in advance) is rather a petty feat; that Sade sets so much store on it is enough to cast suspicion upon him. We are struck by the fact that beyond the walls of his "little house" it did not occur to him to "make full use of his strength." There is no hint of ambition in him, no spirit of enterprise, no will to power, and I am quite prepared to believe that he was a coward. He does, to be sure, systematically endow his heroes with traits which society regards as flaws, but he paints Blangis with a satisfaction that justifies the assumption that this is a projection of himself, and the following words have the direct ring of a confession: "A steadfast child might have hurled this giant into a panic . . . he would become timid and cowardly, and the mere thought of even the mildest combat, but fought on equal terms, would have sent him fleeing to the ends of the earth." The fact that Sade was at times capable of extravagant boldness, both out of rashness and generosity, does not invalidate the hypothesis that he was afraid of people and, in a more general way, afraid of the reality of the world.

If he talked so much about his strength of soul, it was not because he really possessed it, but because he longed for it. When faced with adversity, he would whine and get upset and become completely distraught. The fear of want which haunted him constantly was a symptom of a much more generalized anxiety. He mistrusted everything and everybody because he felt himself maladjusted. He was maladjusted. His behavior was disorderly. He accumulated debts. He would fly into a rage for no reason at all, would run away, or would yield at the wrong moment. He fell into every possible trap. He was uninterested in this boring and yet threatening world which had nothing valid to offer him and from which he hardly knew what to ask. He was to seek his truth elsewhere. When he writes that the passion of jealousy "subordinates and at the same time unites" all other passions, he gives us an exact description of his own experience. He subordinated his existence to his eroticism because eroticism appeared to him to be the only possible fulfillment of his existence. If he devoted himself to it with such energy, shamelessness, and persistence, he did so because he attached greater importance to the stories he wove around the act of pleasure than to the contingent happenings; he chose the imaginary.

At first Sade probably thought himself safe in the fool's paradise which seemed separated from the world of responsibility by an impenetrable wall. And perhaps, had no scandal broken out, he would have been but a common debauchee, known in special places for rather special tastes. Many libertines of the period indulged with impunity in orgies even worse. But scandal was probably inevitable in Sade's case. There are certain "sexual perverts" to whom the myth of Dr. Jekyll and Mr. Hyde is perfectly applicable. They hope, at first, to be able to gratify their "vices" without compromising their public characters. If they are imaginative enough to see themselves, little by little, in a dizziness of pride and shame, they give themselves away—like Charlus, despite his ruses, and even because of them. To what extent was Sade being provocative in his imprudence? There is no way of knowing. He probably wished to emphasize the radical separation between his family life and his private pleasures, and probably, too, the only way he could find satisfaction in this clandestine triumph lay in pushing it to the point where it burst forth into the open. His surprise is like that of the child who keeps striking at a vase until it finally breaks. He was playing with fire and still thought himself master, but society was lying in wait. Society wants undisputed possession. It claims each individual unreservedly. It quickly seized upon Sade's secret and classified it as crime.

Sade reacted at first with prayer, humility, and shame. He begged to be allowed to see his wife, accusing himself of having grievously offended her. He begged to confess and open his heart to the priest. This was not mere hypocrisy. A horrible change had taken place overnight; natural, innocent practices, which had been hitherto merely sources of pleasure, had become punishable acts. The young charmer had changed into a black sheep. He had probably been familiar since childhood—perhaps through his relations with his mother—with the bitter pangs of remorse, but the scandal of 1763 revived them dramatically. Sade had a foreboding that he would henceforth, and for the rest of his life, be a culprit. For he valued his diversions too highly to think, even for a moment, of giving them up. Instead, he rid himself of shame through defiance. It is significant that his first deliberately scandalous act took place immediately after his imprisonment. La Beauvoisin accompanied him to the château of La Coste and, taking the name of Madame Sade, danced and played before the Provençal nobility, while the Abbé de Sade was forced to stand dumbly by. Society denied Sade illicit freedom; it wanted to socialize eroticism. Conversely, the Marquis' social life was to take place henceforth on an erotic level. Since one cannot, with any peace of mind, separate good from evil and devote one's self to each in turn, one has to assert evil in the face of good, and even as a function of good.

Sade tells us repeatedly that his ultimate attitude has its roots in resentment. "Certain souls seem hard because they are capable of strong feelings, and they sometimes go to rather extreme lengths; their apparent unconcern and cruelty are but ways, known only to themselves, of feeling more strongly than others."[5] And Dolmancé[6] attributes his vice to the wickedness of men. " 'Twas men's ingrati-

[5] *Aline et Valcour.*
[6] *Philosophy in the Bedroom.*

tude dried out my heart, their perfidy which destroyed in me those baleful virtues for which, perhaps, like you, I was also born." The fiendish morality which he later established in theoretical form was first a matter of actual experience.

It was through Renée-Pélagie that Sade came to know all the insipidity and boredom of virtue. He lumped them together in the disgust which only a creature of flesh and blood can arouse. But he learned also from Renée, to his delight, that Good, in concrete, fleshly, individual form, can be vanquished in single combat. His wife was not his enemy, but like all the wife-characters she inspired, a choice victim, a willing accomplice. The relationship between Blamont and his wife is probably a fairly precise reflection of Sade's with the Marquise. Blamont takes pleasure in caressing his wife at the very moment that he is hatching the blackest plots against her. To inflict enjoyment—Sade understood this 150 years before the psychoanalysts, and his works abound in victims submitted to pleasure before being tortured—can be a tyrannical violence; and the torturer disguised as lover delights to see the credulous lover, swooning with voluptuousness and gratitude, mistake cruelty for tenderness. The joining of such subtle pleasures with the performance of social obligation is doubtless what led Sade to have three children by his wife.

And he had the further satisfaction of seeing virtue become the ally of vice, and its handmaiden. Madame de Sade concealed her husband's delinquencies for years; she bravely engineered his escape from Miolans, fostered the intrigue between her sister and the Marquis, and later lent her support to the orgies at the château of La Coste. She went even so far as to inculpate herself when, in order to discredit the accusations of Nanon, she hid some silverware in Nanon's bags. Sade never displayed the least gratitude. In fact, the notion of gratitude is one at which he keeps blasting away most furiously. But he very obviously felt for her the ambiguous friendship of the despot for what is unconditionally his. Thanks to her, he was able not only to reconcile his role of husband, father, and gentleman with his pleasures, but he established the dazzling superiority of vice over goodness, devotion, fidelity, and decency, and flouted society prodigiously by submitting the institution of marriage and all the conjugal virtues to the caprices of his imagination and senses.

If Renée-Pélagie was Sade's most triumphant success, Madame de Montreuil, his mother-in-law, embodies his failure. She represents the abstract and universal justice which inevitably confronts the individual. It was against her that he most eagerly entreated his wife's support. If he could win his case in the eyes of virtue, the law would lose much of its power, for its most formidable arms were neither prison nor the scaffold, but the venom with which it could infect vulnerable hearts. Renée became perturbed under the influence of her mother. The young canoness grew fearful. A hostile society wormed its way into Sade's household and dampened his pleasures, and he himself yielded to its power. Defamed and dishonored, he began to doubt himself. And that was Madame de Montreuil's supreme crime against him. A guilty man is, first of all, a man accused; it was she who made a criminal of Sade. That is why he never left off ridiculing her, defaming her, and torturing her throughout his writings; he was killing off his own faults in her. There is a possible basis for Klossowski's theory that Sade hated his own mother; the singular character of his sexuality suggests this. But this hatred would never have been inveterate had not Renée's mother made motherhood hateful to him. Indeed, she played such an important and frightful role in the life of her son-in-law that it may well be that she was the sole object of his attack. It is certainly she, in any case, whom he savagely submits to the jeers of her own daughter in the last pages of *Philosophy in the Bedroom*.

If Sade was finally beaten by his mother-in-law and by the law, he was an accomplice to this defeat. Whatever the role of chance and of his own imprudence in the scandal of 1763, there is no doubt that he afterward sought a heightening of his pleasures in danger. We may therefore say that he desired the very persecutions which he suffered with indignation. Choosing Easter Sunday to inveigle the beggar, Rose Keller, into his house at Arcueil meant playing with fire. Beaten, terrorized, inadequately guarded, she ran off, raising a scandal for which Sade paid with two short terms in prison.

During the following three years of exile which, except for a few periods of service, he spent on his estate in Provence, he seemed sobered. He played the husband and lord of the manor most conscientiously. He had two children by his wife, received the homage of the community of Saumane, attended to his park, and read and produced plays, including one of his own, in his theater. But he was ill-rewarded for this edifying behavior. In 1771, he was imprisoned for debt. Once he was released, his virtuous zeal cooled off. He seduced his young sister-in-law, of whom he seemed, for a while, genuinely fond. She was a canoness, a virgin, and his wife's sister, all of which lent a certain zest to the adventure. Nevertheless, he went to seek still other distractions in Marseilles, and in 1772 the "affair of the aphrodisiac candies" took on unexpected and terrifying proportions. While in flight to Italy with his sister-in-law, he and Latour, his valet, were sentenced to death *in absentia,* and both of them were executed in effigy on the town square of Aix. The canoness took refuge in a French convent, where she spent the rest of her life, and he hid away in Savoy. He was caught and locked up in the château of Miolans, but his wife helped him escape. However, he was henceforth a hunted man. Whether roaming through Italy or shut up in his castle, he knew that he would never be allowed a normal life.

Occasionally, he took his lordly role seriously. A troupe of actors was staying on his estate to present *Le Mari cocu, battu et content.* Sade, irritated perhaps by the title, ordered that the posters be defaced by the town clerk, as being "disgraceful and a challenge to the freedom of the Church." He expelled from his property a certain Saint-Denis, against whom he had certain grievances, saying, "I have every right to expel all loafers and vagrants from my property." But these acts of authority were not enough to amuse him. He tried to realize the dream which was to haunt his books. In the solitude of the château of La Coste, he set up for himself a harem submissive to his whims. With the aid of the Marquise, he gathered together several handsome valets, a secretary who was illiterate but attractive, a luscious cook, a chambermaid, and two young girls provided by bawds. But La Coste was not the inaccessible fortress of *The 120 Days of Sodom*; it was surrounded by society. The maids escaped, the chambermaid left to give birth to a child whose paternity she attributed to Sade, the cook's father came to shoot Sade, and the handsome secretary was sent for by his parents. Only Renée-Pélagie conformed to the character assigned to her by her husband; all the others claimed the right to live their own lives, and Sade was once again made to understand that he could not turn the real world of hard fact into a theater.

This world was not content to thwart his dreams; it repudiated him. Sade fled to Italy, but Madame de Montreuil, who had not forgiven him for having seduced her younger daughter, lay in wait for him. When he got back to France, he ventured into Paris, and she took advantage of the occasion to have him locked up, on the 13th of February, 1777, in the château of Vincennes. He was sent back to Aix, was tried and fined there for his Marseilles escapade, and on his way back to Paris, under guard, he escaped and took refuge at La Coste, where, under the resigned eye of his wife, he embarked on the idyl with his housekeeper, Mademoiselle Rousset. But by the 7th of September, 1778, he was back again at Vincennes, "locked up behind nineteen iron doors, like a wild beast."

And now begins another story. For eleven years—first at Vincennes and then in the Bastille—a man lay dying in captivity, but a writer was being born. The man was quickly broken. Reduced to impotence, not knowing how long his imprisonment would last, his mind wandered in delirious speculation. With minute calculations, though without any facts to work on, he tried to figure out how long his sentence would last. He recovered possession of his intellectual powers fairly quickly, as can be seen from his correspondence with Madame de Sade and Mademoiselle Rousset. But the flesh surrendered, and he sought compensation for his sexual starvation in the pleasures of the table. His valet, Carteron, tells us that "he smoked like a chimney" and "ate enough for four men" while in prison. "Extreme in everything," as he himself declares, he became wolfish. He had his wife send him huge hampers of food, and he grew increasingly fat. In the midst of complaints, accusations, pleas, supplications, he still amused himself a bit by torturing the Marquise; he claimed to be jealous, accused her of plotting against him, and when she came to visit him, found fault with her clothes and ordered her to dress with extreme austerity. But these diversions were few and pallid. From 1782 on, he demanded of literature alone what life would no longer grant him: excitement, challenge, sincerity, and all the delights of the imagination. And even then, he was "extreme"; he wrote as he ate, in a frenzy. After

*Dialogue between a Priest and a Dying Man* came *The 120 Days of Sodom, Les Infortunes de la Vertu, Aline et Valcour.* According to the catalogue of 1788, he had by then written thirty-five acts for the theater, half a dozen tales, almost all of *Le Portefeuille d'un homme de lettres,* and the list is probably still incomplete.

When Sade was freed, on Good Friday of 1790, he could hope and did hope that a new period lay open before him. His wife asked for a separation. His sons (one was preparing to emigrate and the other was a Knight of Malta) were strangers to him; so was his "good, husky farm wench" of a daughter. Free of his family, he whom the old society had called an outcast was now going to try to adapt himself to the one which had just restored to him his dignity as a citizen. His plays were performed in public; *Oxtiern* was even a great success; he enrolled in the Piques Section and was appointed President; he enthusiastically wrote speeches and drew up petitions. But the idyl with the Revolution did not last long. Sade was fifty years old, had a questionable past and an aristocratic disposition, which his hatred of the aristocracy had not subdued, and he was once again at odds with himself. He was a republican and, in theory, even called for complete socialism and the abolition of property, but insisted on keeping his castle and properties. The world to which he tried to adapt himself was again an all too real world whose brutal resistance wounded him. And it was a world governed by those universal laws which he regarded as abstract, false, and unjust. When society justified murder in their name, Sade withdrew in horror.

Anyone who is surprised at Sade's discrediting himself by his humaneness instead of seeking a governor's post in the provinces, a post that would have enabled him to torture and kill to his heart's content, does not really understand Sade. Does anyone suppose that he "liked blood" the way one likes the mountains or the sea? "Shedding blood" was an act whose meaning could, under certain conditions, excite him, but what he demanded, essentially, of cruelty was that it reveal to him particular individuals and his own existence as, on the one hand, consciousness and freedom and, on the other, as flesh. He refused to judge or condemn, or to witness anonymous death from afar. He had hated nothing so much in the old society as the claim to judge and punish, to which he himself had fallen victim; he could not excuse the Terror. When murder becomes constitutional, it becomes merely the hateful expression of abstract principles, something without content, inhuman. And this is why Sade as Grand Juror almost always dismissed the charges against the accused. Holding their fate in his hands, he refused to harm the family of Madame de Montreuil in the name of the law. He was even led to resign from his office of President of the Piques Section. He wrote to Gaufridy: "I considered myself obliged to leave the chair to the vice-president; they wanted me to put a horrible, an inhuman act to a vote. I never would." In December, 1793, he was imprisoned on charges of "moderatism." Released 375 days later, he wrote with disgust: "My government imprisonment, with the guillotine before my eyes, did me a hundred times more harm than all the Bastilles imaginable." It is by such wholesale slaughters that the body politic shows only too clearly that it considers men as a mere collection of objects, whereas Sade demanded a universe peopled with individual beings. The "evil" which he had made his refuge vanished when crime was justified by virtue. The Terror, which was being carried out with a clear conscience, constituted the most radical negation of Sade's demoniacal world.

"The excesses of the Terror," wrote Saint-Just, "have dulled the taste for crime." Sade's sexuality was not stilled by age and fatigue alone; the guillotine killed the morbid poetry of eroticism. In order to derive pleasure from the humiliation and exaltation of the flesh, one must ascribe value to the flesh. It has no sense, no worth, once one casually begins to treat man as a thing. Sade was still able to revive his past experience and his old universe in his books, but he no longer believed in them with his blood and nerves. There is nothing physical in his attachment to the woman he calls "The Sensitive Lady." He derived his only erotic pleasures from the contemplation of the obscene paintings, inspired by Justine, with which he decorated a secret chamber. He still had his memories, but he had lost his drive, and the simple business of living was too much for him. Liberated from the social and familial framework which he nevertheless needed, he dragged on through poverty and illness. He quickly ran through the money realized from the unprofitable sale of La Coste. He took refuge with a farmer, and then in a garret, with the son of "The Sensitive Lady," while earning forty *sous* a day working in the theatricals at Versailles.

The decree of the 28th of June, 1799, which forbade the striking of his name from the list of aristocratic *émigrés* on which it had been placed, made him cry out in despair: "Death and misery, this then is the recompense I receive for my everlasting devotion to the Republic." He received, however, a certificate of residence and citizenship; and in December, 1799, he played the part of Fabrice in *Oxtiern*. But by the beginning of 1800, he was in the hospital of Versailles, "dying of cold and hunger," and threatened with imprisonment for debt. He was so unhappy in the hostile world of so-called "free" men that one wonders whether he had not chosen to be led back to the solitude and security of prison. We may say, at least, that the imprudence of circulating *Justine* and the folly of publishing *Zoloé,* in which he attacks Josephine, Tallien, Madame Tallien, Barras, and Bonaparte, imply that he was not too repelled by the idea of another confinement.[7] Conscious or not, his wish was granted; he was locked up in Sainte-Pélagie on the 5th of April, 1801, and it was there, and later at Charenton—where he was followed by Madame Quesnet, who, by pretending to be his daughter, obtained a room near his own—that he lived out the rest of his life.

Of course, Sade protested and struggled as soon as he was shut up, and he continued to do so for years. But at least he was able again to devote himself in peace to the passion which had replaced sensual pleasure: his writing. He wrote on and on. Most of his papers had been lost when he had left the Bastille, and he thought that the manuscript of *The 120 Days of Sodom*—a fifteen-yard roll which he had carefully hidden and which was saved without his knowing it—had been destroyed. After *Philosophy in the Bedroom,* published in 1795, he composed a new opus, a modified and completely developed version of *Justine,* followed by *Juliette.* These two volumes, of which he disclaimed the authorship, appeared

[7] Since the present essay was written, it has been proved that Sade was not actually the author of *Zoloé,* and the French publisher of Sade's complete works, Jean-Jacques Pauvert, has withdrawn the work from his catalogue. None the less, since Napoleon lacked the findings of this recent scholarship, it is very possible that Sade's presumed authorship of the pamphlet did in fact contribute to his reincarceration.—*Eds.*

in a ten-volume edition in 1797. He had *Les Crimes de l'Amour* publicly printed. At Sainte-Pélagie, he became absorbed in an immense ten-volume work, *Les Journées de Florbelle*. The two volumes of *La Marquise de Gange* must also be attributed to him, though the work did not appear under his name.

Probably because the meaning of his life lay henceforth in his work as a writer, Sade now hoped only for peace in his daily life. He took walks with "The Sensitive Lady" in the garden of the retreat, wrote comedies for the patients, and had them performed. He agreed to compose a *divertissement* on the occasion of a visit to Charenton in 1812 by the Archbishop of Paris. On Easter Sunday, 1805, he distributed the holy bread and took up the collection in the parish church. His will proves that he had renounced none of his beliefs, but he was tired of fighting. "He was polite to the point of obsequiousness," says Nodier, "gracious to the point of unctuousness . . . and he spoke respectfully of everything the world respects." According to Ange Pitou, the ideas of old age and of death horrified him. "This man turned pale at the idea of death, and would faint at the sight of his white hair." He expired in peace, however, carried off by "a pulmonary congestion in the form of asthma" on the 2nd of December, 1814.

The salient feature of his tormented life was that the painful experience of living never revealed to him any solidarity between other men and himself. The last scions of a decadent aristocracy had no common purpose to unite them. In the solitude to which his birth condemned him, Sade carried erotic play to such extremes that his peers turned against him. When a new world opened to him, it was too late; he was weighed down with too heavy a past. At odds with himself, suspect to others, this aristocrat, haunted by dreams of despotism, could not sincerely ally himself with the rising bourgeoisie. And though he was roused to indignation by its oppression of the people, the people were nevertheless foreign to him. He belonged to none of the classes whose mutual antagonisms were apparent to him. He had no fellow but himself. Perhaps, had his emotional make-up been different, he might have resisted this fate, but he seems always to have been violently egocentric. His indifference to external events, his obsessive concern with money, the finical care with which he worked out his debauches, as well as the delirious speculations at Vincennes and the schizophrenic character of his dreams, reveal a radically introverted character. Though this passionate self-absorption defined his limits, it also gave his life an exemplary character, so that we examine it today.

2

Sade made of his eroticism the meaning and expression of his whole existence. Thus, it is no idle curiosity that leads us to define its nature. To say with Maurice Heine that he tried everything and liked everything is to beg the question. The term "algolagnia" hardly helps us to understand Sade. He obviously had very marked sexual idiosyncrasies, but they are not easy to define. His accomplices and victims kept quiet. Two flagrant scandals merely pushed aside, for a moment, the curtain behind which debauch usually hides. His journals and memoirs have been lost, his letters were cautious, and in his books he invents more than he reveals about himself. "I have imagined everything conceivable in this sort of thing," he writes, "but I have certainly not done, and certainly never will, all that I have imagined." His work has not unreasonably been compared to the *Psychopathia Sexualis* of Krafft-Ebing, to whom no one would dream of attributing all the perversions he catalogued.

Thus, Sade established systematically, according to the prescriptions of a kind of synthetic art, a repertory of man's sexual possibilities. He certainly never experienced nor even dreamed them all up himself. Not only does he tell tall stories, but most of the time he tells them badly. His tales resemble the engravings that illustrate the 1797 edition of *Justine* and *Juliette*. The characters' anatomy and positions are drawn with a minute realism, but the awkward and monotonous expressionlessness of their faces makes their horrible orgies seem utterly unreal. It is not easy to derive a genuine testimony from all the cold-blooded orgies that Sade concocted. Nevertheless, there are some situations in his novels which he treats with special indulgence. He shows special sympathy with some of his heroes, for example, Noirceuil, Blangis, and Gernande, and particularly Dolmancé, to whom he attributes many of his own tastes and ideas. Sometimes, too, in a letter, an incident, or a turn of dialogue, we are struck unexpectedly by a vivid phrase which we feel is not the mere echo of a foreign voice. It is precisely such scenes, heroes, and texts as these that we must examine closely.

In the popular mind, sadism means cruelty. The first thing that strikes us in Sade's work is actually that which tradition associates with his name: beatings, bloodshed, torture, and murder. The Rose Keller incident shows him beating his victim with a cat-o'-nine-tails and a knotted cord and, probably,[8] slashing her with a knife and pouring wax on the wounds. In Marseilles, he took from his pockets a parchment "cat" covered with bent pins and asked for switches of heather. In all his behavior toward his wife, he displayed obvious mental cruelty. Moreover, he has repeatedly expressed himself on the pleasure to be derived from making people suffer. But he hardly enlightens us when he merely repeats the classical doctrine of animal spirits. "It is simply a matter of jangling all our nerves with the most violent possible shock. Now, since there can be no doubt that pain affects us more strongly than pleasure, when this sensation is produced in others, our very being will vibrate more vigorously with the resulting shocks." Sade does not eliminate the mystery of the conscious pleasure which follows from this violent vibration. Fortunately, he suggests more honest explanations elsewhere.

The fact is that the original intuition which lies at the basis of Sade's entire sexuality, and hence his ethic, is the fundamental identity of coition and cruelty. "Would the paroxysm of pleasure be a kind of madness if the mother of the human race [Nature] had not intended that anger and the sexual act express themselves in the same way? What able-bodied man . . . does not wish . . . to bedevil his ecstasy?" Sade's description of the Duc de Blangis in the throes of orgasm is certainly to be interpreted as a transposition in epic terms of Sade's own practices: ". . . frightful cries, atrocious blasphemies sprang from the Duc's swollen breast, flames seemed to dart from his eyes, he foamed at the mouth, he whinnied like a stallion . . ." and he even strangled his partner. According to Rose Keller's testimony, Sade himself "began to shriek very loud and fearfully" before cutting the cords which immobilized his vic-

---

[8] Sade's confessions do not corroborate Rose Keller's testimony on this point.

tim. The "Vanilla and Manilla" letter proves that he experienced orgasm as if it were an epileptic seizure, something aggressive and murderous, like a fit of rage.

How are we to explain this peculiar violence? Some readers have wondered whether Sade was not, in fact, sexually deficient. Many of his heroes—among them his great favorite, Gernande— are inadequately equipped, and have great difficulty in erection and ejaculation. Sade must certainly have been aware of these problems but such semi-impotence seems rather to have been the result of excessive indulgence, as in the case of many of his debauchees, several of whom are very well endowed. Sade makes frequent allusions to his own vigorous temperament. It is, on the contrary, a combination of passionate sexual appetites with a basic emotional "apartness" which seems to me to be the key to his eroticism.

From adolescence to prison, Sade had certainly known the insistent, if not obsessive, pangs of desire. There is, on the other hand, an experience which he seems never to have known: that of emotional intoxication. Never in his stories does sensual pleasure appear as self-forgetfulness, swooning, or abandon. Compare, for example, Rousseau's outpourings with the frenzied blasphemies of a Noirceuil or a Dolmancé, or the flutters of the Mother Superior in Diderot's *La Religieuse* with the brutal pleasures of Sade's tribades. The male aggression of the Sadean hero is never softened by the usual transformation of the body into flesh. He never for an instant loses himself in his animal nature; he remains so lucid, so cerebral, that philosophic discourse, far from dampening his ardor, acts as an aphrodisiac. We see how desire and pleasure explode into furious crisis in this cold, tense body, impregnable to all enchantment. They do not constitute a living experience within the framework of the subject's psycho-physiological unity. Instead, they blast him, like some kind of bodily accident.

As a result of this immoderation, the sexual act creates the illusion of sovereign pleasure which gives it its incomparable value in Sade's eyes, for all his sadism strove to compensate for the absence of one necessary element which he lacked. The state of emotional intoxication allows one to grasp existence in one's self and in the other, as both subjectivity and passivity. The two partners merge in this ambiguous unity; each one is freed of his own presence and achieves immediate communication with the other. The curse which weighed upon Sade—and which only his childhood could explain—was this "autism" which prevented him from ever forgetting himself or being genuinely aware of the reality of the other person. Had he been cold by nature, no problem would ever have arisen; but his instincts drove him toward outside objects with which he was incapable of uniting, so that he was forced to invent singular methods for taking them by force. Later, when his desires were exhausted, he continued to live in that erotic universe of which, out of sensuality, boredom, defiance, and resentment, he had constructed the only world which counted for him; and the aim of his strategies was to induce erection and orgasm. But even when these were easy for him, Sade needed deviations to give to his sexuality a meaning which lurked in it without ever managing to achieve fulfillment, an escape from consciousness in his flesh, an understanding of the other person as consciousness through the flesh.

Normally, it is as a result of the vertigo of the other made flesh that one is spellbound within one's own flesh. If the subject remains confined within the solitude of his consciousness, he escapes this agitation and can rejoin the other only by conscious performance. A cold, cerebral lover watches eagerly the enjoyment of his mistress and needs to affirm his responsibility for it because he has no other way of attaining his own fleshly state. This behavior, which compensates for separateness by deliberate tyranny, may properly be called "sadistic." Sade knew, as we have seen, that the infliction of pleasure may be an aggressive act, and his tyranny sometimes took on this character, but it did not satisfy him. To begin with, he shrinks from the kind of equality which is created by mutual pleasure. "If the objects who serve us feel ecstasy, they are then much more often concerned with themselves than with us, and our own enjoyment is consequently impaired. The idea of seeing another person experience the same pleasure reduces one to a kind of equality which spoils the unutterable charms that come from despotism." And he declares, more categorically, "Any enjoyment is weakened when shared."

And besides, pleasant sensations are too mild; it is when the flesh is torn and bleeding that it is revealed most dramatically as flesh. "No kind of sensation is keener and more active than that of pain; its impressions are unmistakable." But in order for me to become flesh and blood through the pains I have inflicted, I must recognize my own state in the passivity of the other. Therefore, the person must have freedom and consciousness. The libertine "would really deserve pity if he acted upon an inert, unfeeling object." That is why the contortions and moans of the victim are necessary to the torturer's happiness, which explains why Verneuil made his wife wear a kind of headgear that amplified her screams. In his revolt, the tortured object asserts himself as my fellow creature, and through his intervention I achieve the synthesis of spirit and flesh which was first denied me.

If the aim is both to escape from one's self and to discover the reality of other existences, there is yet another way open: to have one's flesh mortified by others. Sade is quite aware of this. When he used the cat-o'-nine-tails and the switch in Marseilles, it was not only to whip others with, but also to be whipped himself. This was probably one of his most common practices, and all his heroes happily submit to flagellation. "No one doubts nowadays that flagellation is extremely effective in restoring the vigor destroyed by the excesses of pleasure." There was another way of giving concrete form to his passivity. In Marseilles, Sade was sodomized by his valet, Latour, who seems to have been accustomed to render him this sort of service. His heroes imitate him sedulously, and he declared aloud in no uncertain terms that the greatest pleasure is derived from a combination of active and passive sodomy. There is no perversion of which he speaks so often and with so much satisfaction, and even impassioned vehemence.

Two questions immediately arise for those given to labeling individuals. Was Sade a sodomite? Was he basically a masochist? As to sodomy, his physical appearance, the role played by his valets, the presence at La Coste of the handsome, illiterate secretary, the enormous importance which Sade accords to this "fantasy" in his writings, and the passion with which he advocates it, all confirm the fact that it was one of the essential elements of his sexual character. Certainly, women played a great role in his life, as they do in his work. He knew many, had kept Mlle. Beauvoisin and other less important mistresses, had seduced his sister-in-law, had gathered young women and little girls together at the château of La Coste, had flirted with Mademoiselle Rousset, and ended his life at the side of Madame Quesnet, to say nothing of the bonds, imposed by society but reworked in his own fashion, which united him with Madame de Sade. But what were his relations with her? It is significant that in the only two testimonies on his sexual activity, there is no evidence that Sade "knew" his partners in a normal way. In Rose Keller's case, he satisfied himself by whipping her without touching her. He asked the Marseilles prostitute to let herself be "known from behind" by his servant or, if she preferred, by himself. When she refused, he contented himself with fondling her while he was being "known" by Latour.

His heroes amuse themselves by deflowering little girls. This bloody and sacrilegious violence tickled Sade's fancy. But even when they are initiating virgins, they often treat them as boys rather than make them bleed. More than one of Sade's characters feels a deep disgust for women's "fronts." Others are more eclectic in taste, but their preferences are clear. Sade never sang the praises of that part of the female body so joyously celebrated in *The Arabian Nights*. He has only contempt for the poor "unmanly creatures" who possess their wives in conventional fashion. If he had children by Madame de Sade, we have seen under what circumstances; and in view of the strange group orgies at La Coste, what proof is there that it was really he who was responsible for Nanon's pregnancy?

We must not, of course, attribute to Sade the opinions held by the confirmed homosexuals of his novels, but the argument put into the mouth of the Bishop in *The 120 Days of Sodom* is close enough to his heart to be considered as a confession. He says, concerning pleasure, ". . . the boy is worth more than the girl. Consider the problem from the point of view of evil, evil being almost always pleasure's true and major charm; considered thus, the crime must appear greater when perpetrated upon a being of your identical sort than when inflicted upon one which is not, and this once established, the delight automatically doubles." It was easy enough for Sade to write to Madame de Sade that his sole wrong had been "to love women too much"; this was a purely official and hypocritical letter. And it is through a mythical dialectic that he gives them the most triumphant roles in his novels. Their wickedness makes a striking contrast with the traditional gentleness of their sex. When they overcome their natural abjection by committing crime, they demonstrate much more brilliantly than any man that no situation can dampen the ardor of a bold spirit. But if, in imagination, they become first-rate martinets, it is because they are, in reality, born victims.

The contempt and disgust which Sade really felt for these servile, tearful, mystified, and passive creatures run all through his work. Was it his mother whom he loathed in them? We may also wonder whether Sade did not hate women because he saw in them his double rather than his complement and because there was nothing he could get from them. His great female villains have more warmth and life than his heroes, not only for esthetic reasons but because they were closer to him. I do not recognize him at all, as some readers claim to, in the bleating Justine,[9] but there is certainly something of him in Juliette, who proudly and contentedly submits to the same treatment as her sister. Sade felt himself to be feminine, and he resented the fact that women were not the males he really desired. He endows Durand, the greatest and most extravagant of them all, with a huge clitoris which enables her to behave sexually like a man.

It is impossible to tell to what extent women were anything but surrogates and toys for Sade. It may be said, however, that his sexual character was essentially anal. This is confirmed by Sade's attachment to money. Trouble involving embezzlement of inheritances played an enormous role in his life. Theft appears in his work as a sexual act, and the mere suggestion of it is enough to cause orgasm. And though we may refuse to accept the Freudian interpretation of greed, there is the indisputable fact, which Sade openly acknowledged, of his coprophilia. In Marseilles, he gave a prostitute some sugar almonds, telling her that "they would make her break wind," and he looked disappointed when nothing happened. We are also struck by the fact that the two "fantasies" which he tries

---

9 See especially Jean Paulhan: "The Marquis de Sade and His Accomplice," which appears in the introductory section to The Marquis de Sade: *The Complete Justine, Philosophy in the Bedroom, and Other Writings.* New York, Grove Press, 1965.—*Eds.*

to explain most fully are cruelty and coprophagy. To what extent did he practice them? It is a far cry from the practices begun in Marseilles to the excremental orgies of *The 120 Days of Sodom,* but the care with which he describes the latter practices, and particularly the preparations, proves that they were not merely cold and schematic inventions, but emotional fantasies.

On the other hand, Sade's extraordinary gluttony in prison cannot be explained by idleness alone. Eating can be a substitute for erotic activity only if there is still some infantile equivalence between gastrointestinal and sexual functions. This certainly persisted in Sade. He sees a close bond between the food orgy and the erotic orgy. "There is no passion more closely involved with lechery than drunkenness and gluttony," he points out. And this combination reaches a climax in anthropophagous fantasies. To drink blood, to swallow sperm and excrement, and to eat children mean appeasing desire through destruction of its object. Pleasure requires neither exchange, giving, reciprocity, nor gratuitous generosity. Its tyranny is that of avarice, which chooses to destroy what it cannot assimilate.

Sade's coprophilia has still another meaning. "If it is the dirty element that gives pleasure in the act of lust, then the dirtier it is, the more pleasurable it is bound to be." Among the most obvious sexual attractions, Sade includes old age, ugliness, and bad odors. His linking of eroticism with vileness is as original as his linking it with cruelty, and can be explained in like manner. Beauty is too simple. We grasp it by an intellectual evaluation which does not free consciousness from its solitude or the body from its indifference, whereas vileness is debasing. The man who has relations with filth, like the man who wounds or is wounded, fulfills himself as flesh. It is in its misery and humiliation that the flesh becomes a gulf in which consciousness is swallowed up and where separate individuals are united. Only by being beaten, penetrated, and befouled could Sade succeed in destroying its obsessive presence.

He was not, however, masochistic in the ordinary sense of the word. He sneers bitterly at men who become slaves to women. "I leave them to the base pleasure of wearing the chains with which Nature has given them the right to burden others. Let such animals vegetate in the baseness of their abjection." The world of the masochist is a magical one, and that is why he is almost always a fetishist. Objects such as shoes, furs, and whips, are charged with emanations which have the power to change him into a thing, and that is precisely what he wants: to remove himself by becoming an inert object. Sade's world is essentially rational and practical. The objects, whether material or human, which serve his pleasure are tools which have no mystery, and he clearly sees humiliation as a haughty ruse. Saint-Fond, for example, says: "The humiliation of certain acts of debauchery serves as a pretext for pride." And Sade elsewhere says of the libertine that "the degradation which characterizes the state into which you plunge him by punishing him pleases, amuses, and delights him. Deep down he enjoys having gone so far as to deserve being treated in such a way."

Nevertheless, these two attitudes are intimately related. If the masochist wants to lose himself, he does so in order to be entranced by the object with which he hopes to merge, and this effort leads him back to his subjectivity. In demanding that his partner mistreat him, he tyrannizes him; his humiliating exhibitions and the tortures he undergoes humiliate and torture the other as well. And, vice versa, by befouling and hurting the other, the torturer befouls and hurts himself. He participates in the passivity which he discloses, and in wanting to apprehend himself as the cause of the torment he inflicts, it is as an instrument and therefore as an object that he perceives himself. We are thus justified in classing behavior of this kind under the name of sado-masochism. However, we must be careful, for despite the generality of the term, the concrete forms of this behavior may be quite varied. Sade was not Sacher-Masoch. What was peculiar in his case was the tension of a will bent on fulfilling the flesh without losing itself in it. In Marseilles, he had himself whipped, but every couple of minutes he would dash to the mantelpiece and, with a knife, would inscribe on the chimney flue the number of lashes he had just received. His humiliation would immediately be transformed into swagger. While being sodomized, he would whip a prostitute. It was a favorite fantasy of his to be penetrated and beaten while he himself was penetrating and beating a submissive victim.

I have already said that to regard Sade's peculiarities as simple facts is to misunderstand their meaning and implication.

They are always charged with an ethical significance. With the scandal of 1763, Sade's eroticism ceased to be merely an individual attitude: it was also a challenge to society. In a letter to his wife, Sade explains how he has erected his tastes into principles. "I carry these principles and tastes to the point of fanaticism," he writes, "and the fanaticism is the work of my tyrants and their persecutions." The supreme intention that quickens all sexual activity is the will to criminality. Whether through cruelty or befoulment, the aim is to attain evil. Sade immediately experienced coitus as cruelty, laceration, and transgression; and out of resentment he obstinately justified its morbidity. Since society united with Nature in regarding his pleasures as criminal, he made crime itself a pleasure. "Crime is the soul of lust. What would pleasure be if it were not accompanied by crime? It is not the object of debauchery that excites us, but rather the idea of evil." In the pleasure of torturing and mocking a beautiful woman, he writes, "there is the kind of pleasure which comes from sacrilege or the profanation of the objects offered us for worship." It was not by chance that he chose Easter as the day to whip Rose Keller, and it was at the moment that he sardonically suggested that he confess her that his sexual excitement reached its climax. No aphrodisiac is so potent as the defiance of Good. "Our desires for great crimes are always more violent than our desires for small ones." Did Sade do evil in order to feel guilty, or did he escape guilt by assuming it? To reduce him to one or another of these attitudes is to deform him. He never remains at rest in a state either of self-satisfied abjection or of flighty impudence, but keeps oscillating back and forth dramatically between arrogance and a guilty conscience.

Thus, we can perceive the significance of Sade's cruelty and masochism. This man, who combined a violent temperament— though quickly exhausted, it would seem—with an emotional "apartness" almost pathological in character, sought a substitute for anxiety in the infliction of suffering or pain. The meaning of his cruelty is very complex. In the first place, it seems to be the extreme and immediate fulfillment of the instinct of coitus, its total assumption. It asserts the radical separation of the other object from the sovereign subject. It aims at the jealous destruction of what cannot be greedily assimilated. But, above all, rather than crowning the orgasm impulsively, it tends to induce it by premeditation. It enabled him to apprehend through the other person the consciousness-flesh unity and to project it into himself. And, lastly, it freely justified the criminal character which Nature and society had assigned to eroticism. Moreover, by being sodomized, beaten, and befouled, Sade also gained insight into himself as passive flesh. He slaked his thirst for self-punishment and accepted the guilt to which he had been doomed. And this enabled him to revert immediately from humility to pride through the medium of defiance. In the completely sadistic scene, the individual gives vent to his nature, fully aware that it is evil and aggressively assuming it as such. He merges vengeance and transgression and transforms the latter into glory.

There is one act which stands as the most extreme conclusion of both cruelty and masochism, for the subject asserts himself in it, in a very special way, as tyrant and criminal; I am speaking of murder. It has often been maintained that murder was the supreme end of sexuality in Sade. To my mind, this view is based on a misunderstanding. Certainly the vigor with which Sade denied in his letters that he had ever been a murderer was a matter of self-defense, but I think that he was sincerely repelled by the idea. He does, of course, overload his stories with monstrous slaughters. But he does so because there is no crime whose abstract significance is so glaringly obvious as murder. It represents the exacerbated demand for unrestrained and fearless freedom. And besides, by indefinitely prolonging the death throes of his victim, the author can perpetuate on paper the exceptional moment in which a lucid mind inhabits a body which is being degraded into matter. He still breathes a living past into the unconscious remains. But what would the tyrant actually do with this inert object, a corpse?

There is, no doubt, something vertiginous in the transition from life to death; and the sadist, fascinated by the conflicts between consciousness and the flesh, readily pictures himself as the agent of so radical a transformation. But though he may occasionally carry out this singular experiment, it cannot possibly afford him the supreme satisfaction. The freedom that one hoped to tyrannize to the point of annihilation has, in being destroyed, slipped away from the world in which tyranny had a hold on it. If Sade's

heroes commit endless massacres, it is because none of them gives
full satisfaction. They bring no concrete solution to the problems
which torment the debauchee, because pleasure is not his sole end.
No one would seek sensation so passionately and recklessly, even
if it had the violence of an epileptic seizure. The ultimate trauma
must, rather, guarantee by its obviousness the success of an undertaking whose stake exceeds it infinitely. But often, however, this
ultimate trauma puts an end to the undertaking without concluding
it, and though the trauma may be prolonged by murder, such a murder merely confirms its failure.

Blangis strangles his partners with the very fury of orgasm,
and there is despair in the rage wherein desire is extinguished without finding satisfaction. His premeditated pleasures are less wild
and more complex. An episode from *Juliette,* among others, is
significant. Excited by the young woman's conversation, Noirceuil,
who "cared little for solitary pleasures," that is, those in which one
indulges with a single partner, immediately calls in his friends.
"There are too few of us. . . . No, leave me. . . . My passions,
concentrated on a single point, resemble the rays of a sun assembled
by a magnifying glass: they immediately set fire to whatever object
they find in their way. . . ." It is not out of any abstract scruples
that he forbids himself such excesses, but rather because after the
brutal orgasm he would find himself frustrated again. Our instincts
indicate to us ends which are unattainable if we merely act upon our
immediate impulses. We must master them, reflect upon them, and
use our wits in trying to find ways of satisfying them. The presence
of other consciousnesses than our own is what helps us most to get
the necessary perspective on them.

Sade's sexuality is not a biological matter. It is a social fact.
The orgies in which he indulged were almost always collective
affairs. In Marseilles, he asked for two prostitutes and was accompanied by his valet. At La Coste, he set up a harem for himself.
The libertines in his novels form actual communities. The first advantage was the number of combinations for their debauches, but
there were deeper reasons for the socialization of eroticism. In
Marseilles, Sade called his valet "Monsieur le Marquis" and
wanted to see him "know" a prostitute under his name rather than
"know" her himself. The enactment of the erotic scene interested

him more than the actual experience. The fantasies in *The 120 Days of Sodom* are narrated before being carried out. By means of this duplication the act becomes a spectacle which one observes from a distance at the same time that one is performing it. It thus retains the meaning that would otherwise be obscured by solitary animal excitement. For if the debauchee coincided exactly with his movements and the victim with his emotions, freedom and consciousness would be lost in the rapture of the flesh. The flesh would be merely brute suffering, and the rapture merely convulsive pleasure. Thanks, however, to the assembled witnesses, a presence is maintained about them which helps the subject himself remain present. It is through these performances that he hopes to reach out to himself; and in order to see himself, he must be seen. Sade, while tyrannizing, was an object for those who watched him.

Conversely, by witnessing on the flesh to which he had done violence the violence which he himself had borne, he repossessed himself as subject within his own passivity. The merging of the for-oneself and the for-the-other is thus achieved. Accomplices are particularly required in order to give sexuality a demoniacal dimension. Thanks to them, the act, whether committed or suffered, takes on definite form instead of being diluted into contingent moments. By becoming real, any crime proves to be possible and ordinary. One gets to be so intimately familiar with it that one has difficulty in regarding it as blameworthy. In order to amaze or frighten oneself, one must observe oneself from a distance, through foreign eyes.

However precious this recourse to others may be, it is not yet enough to remove the contradictions implied in the sadistic effort. If one fails, in the course of an actual experience, to grasp the ambiguous unity of existence, one will never succeed in reconstructing it intellectually. A spectacle, by definition, can never coincide with either the inwardness of consciousness or the opacity of the flesh. Still less can it reconcile them. Once they have been dissociated, these two moments of the human reality are in opposition to each other; and as soon as we pursue one of them, the other disappears. If the subject inflicts excessively violent pain upon himself, his mind becomes unhinged: he abdicates; he loses his sovereignty. Excessive vileness entails disgust, which interferes with pleasure. In practice, it is difficult to indulge in cruelty, except within very modest limits; and in theory, it implies a contradiction which is expressed in the following two passages: "The most divine charms are as nothing when submission and obedience do not come forth to offer them," and: "One must do violence to the object of one's desire; when it surrenders, the pleasure is greater." But where is one to find free slaves? One has to be satisfied with compromises. With paid and abjectly consenting prostitutes, Sade went somewhat beyond the limits that had been agreed upon. He allowed himself some violence against a wife who maintained a certain human dignity in her docility.

But the ideal erotic act was never to be realized. This is the deeper meaning of the words Sade puts into the mouth of Jérôme: "What we are doing here is only the image of what we would like to do." It was not merely that really heinous crimes were forbidden in practice, but that even those which one could summon up in the midst of the wildest ravings would disappoint their author: "Ah, how many times, by God, have I not longed to be able to assail the sun, snatch it out of the universe, make a general darkness, or use that star to burn the world! oh, that would be a crime . . ." But if this dream seemed satisfying, it was because the criminal projected into it his own destruction along with that of the universe. Had he survived, he would have been frustrated once again. Sadistic crime can never be adequate to its animating purpose. The victim is never more than a symbol; the subject possesses himself only as an imago, and their relationship is merely the parody of the drama which would really set them at grips in their incommunicable intimacy. That is why the Bishop in *The 120 Days of Sodom* "never committed a crime without immediately conceiving a second."

The moment of plotting the act is an exceptional moment for the libertine because he can then be unaware of the inevitable fact, namely, that reality will give him the lie. And if narration plays a primary role in sadistic orgies and easily awakens senses upon which flesh-and-blood objects cease to act, the reason is that these objects can be wholly attained only by their absence. Actually, there is only one way of finding satisfaction in the phantoms created by debauchery, and that is to accede to their very unreality. In choosing eroticism, Sade chose the make-believe. It was only in the imaginary that Sade could live with any certitude and without risk of disappointment. He repeated the idea throughout his work. "The pleasure of the senses is always regulated in accordance with the imagination. Man can aspire to felicity only by serving all the whims of his imagination." It was by means of his imagination that he escaped from space, time, prison, the police, the void of absence, opaque presences, the conflicts of existence, death, life, and all contradictions. It was not murder that fulfilled Sade's erotic nature: it was literature.

### 3

It might seem, at first glance, that by writing Sade was merely reacting as many other prisoners do in the same situation. The idea was not completely new to him. One of the plays presented at La Coste in 1772 was doubtlessly written by him; and his strongbox, forced open by order of Madame de Montreuil, contained certain "leaflets," probably notes on sex, in his own hand. Nevertheless, when he was imprisoned at Vincennes, he waited four years before undertaking a real work. In another cell of the same fortress, Mirabeau, who was also groaning that he was "being buried alive in a tomb," tried to divert himself by doing translations, writing an essay on the *lettres de cachet,* and carrying on a pornographic correspondence. He was trying to kill time, to distract his weary body, and to undermine a hostile society. Sade was driven by similar motives; he set to work; and more than once, while composing his novels, he had to "whip himself up." He also wanted to revenge himself on his torturers. He writes to his wife in a joyous rage: ". . . you fancied you were sure to work wonders, I'll wager, by reducing me to an atrocious abstinence in the article of *carnal sin.* Well, you were wrong: you have produced a ferment in my brain, owing to you phantoms have arisen in me which I shall have to render real."

Although his decision may have been prompted by his confinement, nevertheless it had much deeper roots. Sade had always spun stories for himself around his debauches; and the reality which served as a frame of reference for his fantasies may have given them a certain density, yet it also cramped them by its resistance.

The opacity of things blurs their significance, which is the very quality that words preserve. Even a child is aware that crude drawings are more obscene than the organs and gestures which they represent, because the intention to defile is asserted in all its purity. Blasphemy is the easiest and surest of sacrilegious acts. Sade's heroes talked on and on indefatigably; and in the Rose Keller affair he indulged in endless speechifying. Writing is far more able than the spoken word to endow images with the solidity of a monument, and it resists all argument. Thanks to the written word, virtue maintains her dreary prestige even at the very moment when she is denounced as hypocrisy and stupidity. Crime remains criminal in its grandeur. Freedom may still throb in a dying body.

Literature enabled Sade to unleash and fix his dreams, and also to transcend the contradictions implied by any demonic system. Better still, it is itself a demonic act, since it exhibits criminal visions in an aggressive way. That is what gives Sade's work its incomparable value. Anyone misunderstands Sade who finds it paradoxical that a "solitary" should have engaged in such a passionate effort to communicate. He had nothing of the misanthrope who prefers the company of animals and virgin forests to his own kind. Cut off from others, he was haunted by their inaccessible presence. If he craves for the presence of other persons at the most intimate moments of his life, it is normal that he wish to expose himself to the large public to which a book can aspire.

Did he wish only to shock? In 1795 he wrote: "I am about to put forward some major ideas; they will be heard and pondered. If not all of them please, surely a few will; in some sort, then, I shall have contributed to the progress of our age, and shall be content."[10] And in *La Nouvelle Justine:* "To falsify such basic truths, regardless of their consequences, reveals a fundamental lack of concern for human beings." After presiding over the Piques Section and drawing up speeches and petitions in society's name, he must have liked, in his more optimistic moments, to think of himself as a spokesman for humanity. Of this experience he retained not the evil aspects, but those which were genuinely rewarding. These dreams quickly faded, but it would be too simple to consign Sade to

---

[10] *Philosophy in the Bedroom.*

satanism. His sincerity was inextricably bound up with dishonesty. He delighted in the shocking effects of truth; but if he set himself the duty of shocking, it was because in this way truth might be made manifest. While arrogantly admitting his errors, he declared himself in the right. He wished to transmit a message to the very public he was deliberately outraging. His writings reflect the ambivalence of his relation to the given world and to people.

Even more surprising, perhaps, is the mode of expression he chose. We might expect a man who had so jealously cultivated his singularity to try to translate his experience into a singular form, as, for example, Lautréamont did. But the eighteenth century offered Sade few lyrical possibilities; he hated the mawkish sensibility which the time confused with poetry—the time was not yet ripe for a *poète maudit*. And Sade was in no way disposed to great literary audacity. A real creator should—at least on a certain level and at a given moment—free himself of the yoke of the *given* and emerge beyond other men into complete solitude. But there was in Sade an inner weakness which was inadequately masked by his arrogance. Society was lodged in his heart in the guise of guilt. He had neither the means nor the time to reinvent man, the world, and himself. He was in too much of a hurry, in a hurry to defend himself. I have already said that he sought in writing to gain a clear conscience; and in order to do this, he had to compel people to absolve him, even to approve him. Instead of affirming himself, Sade argued; and in order to make himself understood, he borrowed the literary forms and the tried and tested doctrines of contemporary society. As the product of a rational age, no arm seemed surer to him than reason. He who wrote: "All universal moral principles are idle fancies," submitted docilely to general esthetic conventions and contemporary claims for the universality of logic. This explains both his art and his thought. Though he justified himself, he was always trying to excuse himself. His work is an ambiguous effort to push crime to the extreme while wiping away his guilt.

It is both natural and striking that Sade's favorite form was parody. He did not try to set up a new universe. He contented himself with ridiculing, by the manner in which he imitated it, the one imposed upon him. He pretended to believe in the vain fancies that inhabited it: innocence, kindness, devotion, generosity, and chastity.

When he unctuously depicted virtue in *Aline et Valcour*, in *Justine*, or in *Les Crimes de l'Amour*, he was not being merely prudent. The "veils" in which he swathed Justine were more than a literary device. In order to derive amusement from harassing virtue, one must credit it with a certain reality. Defending his tales against the charge of immorality, Sade hypocritically wrote: "Who can flatter himself that he has put virtue in a favorable light if the features of the vice surrounding it are not strongly emphasized?" But he meant the very opposite: how is vice to be made thrilling if the reader is not first taken in by the illusion of good? Fooling people is even more delicious than shocking them. And Sade, in spinning his sugary, roundabout phrases, tasted the keen pleasures of mystification. Unfortunately, he generally amuses himself more than he does us. His style has often the same coldness and the same mawkishness as the edifying tales he transposed, and the episodes unfold in accordance with equally dreary conventions.

Nevertheless, it was through parody that Sade obtained his most brilliant artistic successes. As Maurice Heine points out, Sade was the precursor of the novel of horror, but he was too deeply rationalistic to lose himself in fantasy. When he abandons himself to the extravagances of his imagination, one does not know which to admire the most, his epic vehemence or his irony. The wonder is that the irony is subtle enough to redeem his ravings: what it does is lend a dry, poetic quality which saves them from incredibility. This somber humor which can, at times, turn on itself, is more than a mere technique. With his shame and pride, his truth and crime, Sade was the very spirit of contentiousness. It is when he plays the buffoon that he is really most serious, and when he is most outrageously dishonest that he is most sincere. His extravagance often masks ingenuous truths while he launches the most flagrant enormities in the form of sober and deliberate arguments; he uses all kinds of tricks to avoid being pinned down; and that is how he attains his end, which is to disturb us. His very form tends to disconcert us. He speaks in a monotonous, embarrassed tone, and we begin to be bored, when all at once the dull grayness is lit up with the glaring brilliance of some bitter, sardonic truth. It is then that Sade's style, in its gaiety, its violence, and its arrogant rawness, proves to be that of a great writer.

Nevertheless, no one would think of ranking *Justine* with *Manon Lescaut* or *Les Liaisons dangereuses*. It was, paradoxically, the very necessity of Sade's work which imposed upon it its esthetic limits. He did not have the perspective essential to an artist. He lacked the detachment necessary to confront reality and re-create it. He did not confront himself; he contented himself with projecting his fantasies. His accounts have the unreality, the false precision, and the monotony of schizophrenic reveries. He relates them for his own pleasure, and he is unconcerned about imposing them upon the reader. We do not feel in them the stubborn resistance of the real world or the more poignant resistance that Sade encountered in the depths of his own heart. Caves, underground passageways, mysterious castles, all the props of the Gothic novel take on a particular meaning in his work. They symbolize the isolation of the image. Perception echoes data's totality and, consequently, the obstacles which the data contain. The image is perfectly submissive and pliant. We find in it only what we put into it. The image is the enchanted domain from which no power whatever can expel the solitary despot. It is the image that Sade was imitating, even while claiming to give it literary opacity. Thus, he disregarded the spatial and temporal coordinates within which all real events are situated. The places he evokes are not of this world, the events which occur in them are *tableaux vivants* rather than adventures, and time has no hold on Sade's universe. There is no future either for or in his work.

Not only do the orgies to which he invites us take place in no particular time or locality, but—what is more serious—no living people are brought into play. The victims are frozen in their tearful abjection, and the torturers in their frenzies. Instead of giving them lifelike density, Sade merely daydreams about them. Remorse and disgust are unknown to them; at most they have occasional feelings of satiety. They kill with indifference; they are abstract incarnations of evil. But unless eroticism has some social, familiar, or human basis, it ceases to be in any way extraordinary. It is no longer a conflict, a revelation, or an exceptional experience. It no longer reveals any dramatic relationship between individuals but reverts to biological crudity. How is one to feel the opposition of others' freedoms or the spirit's descent into the flesh, if all we see

is a display of voluptuous or tortured flesh? Horror itself peters
out in these excesses at which no consciousness is actually present. If
a story like Poe's "The Pit and the Pendulum" is so full of anguish,
it is because we grasp the situation from within the subject; we see
Sade's heroes only from without. They are as artificial and move in
a world as arbitrary as that of Florian's shepherds. That is why
these perverse bucolics have the austerity of a nudist colony.

The debauches which Sade describes in such great detail systematically exhaust the anatomical possibilities of the human body
rather than reveal uncommon emotional complexes. Nevertheless,
though he failed to endow them with esthetic truth, Sade adum-
brated forms of sexual behavior unknown until then, particularly
those which unite mother-hatred, frigidity, intellectuality, "passive
sodomy," and cruelty. No one has emphasized with more vigor the
link between the imagination and what we call vice; and he gives us,
from time to time, insights of surprising depth into the relation of
sexuality to existence.

Are we, then, to admire him as a real innovator in psychology?
It is difficult to decide. Forerunners are always credited with either
too much or too little. How is one to measure the value of a truth
which, to use Hegel's term, has not *become*? An idea derives its
value from the experience it sums up and the methods it initiates.
But we hardly know what credit to give a new and attractive for-
mulation if it is not confirmed by subsequent developments. We are
tempted either to magnify it with all the significance that it acquires
later on or else to minimize its scope. Hence, in the case of Sade,
the impartial reader hesitates. Often, as we turn a page, we come
upon an unexpected phrase which seems to open up new paths, only
to find that the thinking stops short. Instead of a vivid and individual voice, all one hears is the droning drivel of Holbach and La
Mettrie.

It is remarkable, for example, that in 1795[11] Sade wrote:
"Sexual pleasure is, I agree, a passion to which all others are subordinate but in which they all unite." Not only does Sade, in the
first part of this text, anticipate what has been called the "pan-
sexuality" of Freud, but he makes of eroticism the mainspring of

---

[11] *Ibid.*

human behavior. In addition, he asserts, in the second part, that
sexuality is charged with a significance that goes beyond it. Libido
is everywhere, and it is always far more than itself. Sade certainly
anticipated this great truth. He knew that the "perversions" that
are vulgarly regarded as moral monstrosities or physiological defects actually envelop what would now be called an intentionality.
He writes to his wife that all "fancy . . . derives from a principle
of delicacy," and in *Aline et Valcour* he declares that "refinements
come only from delicacy; one may, therefore, have a great deal
of delicacy, though one may be moved by things which seem to exclude it." He understood, too, that our tastes are motivated not by
the intrinsic qualities of the object but by the latter's relationship
with the subject. In a passage in *La Nouvelle Justine* he tries to
explain coprophilia. His reply is faltering, but clumsily using the
notion of imagination, he points out that the truth of a thing lies
not in what it is but in the meaning it has taken on for us in the
course of our individual experience. Intuitions such as these allow
us to hail Sade as a precursor of psychoanalysis.

Unfortunately, he reduces their value when he insists upon
harping, like Holbach, on the principles of psycho-physiological par-
allelism. "With the perfecting of the science of anatomy, we shall
easily be able to show the relationship between man's constitution
and the tastes which have affected him." The contradiction is glaring in the striking passage in *The 120 Days of Sodom* where he
considers the sexual attraction of ugliness. "It has, moreover, been
proved that horror, nastiness, and the frightful are what give
pleasure when one fornicates. Beauty is a simple thing; ugliness is
the exceptional thing. And fiery imaginations, no doubt, always prefer the extraordinary thing to the simple thing." One might wish
that Sade had defined this link between horror and desire which he
indicates only confusedly; but he stops abruptly with a condition
that cancels the question that has been posed: "All these things
depend upon our structures and organs and on the manner in which
they affect one another, and we are no more able to change our
tastes for these things than to vary the shapes of our bodies."

At first glance, it seems paradoxical that this man who was so
self-centered should have given such prominence to theories which
deny any significance to individual peculiarities. He asks that we

make a great effort to understand the human heart better. He tries
to explore its strangest aspects. He cries out: "What an enigma is
man!" He boasts: "You know that no one analyzes things as I do,"
and yet he follows La Mettrie in lumping man together with the
machine and the plant and simply does away with psychology. But
this antinomy, disconcerting though it may be, is easily explained. It
is probably not so easy to be a monster as some people seem to think.
Sade, though fascinated by his own personal mystery, was also
frightened by it. Instead of expressing himself, he wanted to defend
himself. The words he puts into Blamont's mouth[12] are a confession:
"I have supported my deviations with reasons; I did not stop at
mere doubt; I have vanquished, I have uprooted, I have destroyed
everything in my heart that might have interfered with my pleasures." The first of these tasks of liberation was, as he repeated
countless times, to triumph over remorse. And as for repudiating
all feelings of guilt, what doctrine could be surer than that which
undermines the very idea of responsibility? But it would be a big
mistake to try to confine him to such a notion: if he seeks support
in determinism, he does so, like many others, in order to lay claim
to freedom.

From a literary point of view, the commonplace-ridden
speeches with which he intersperses his debauches finally rob them
of all life and all verisimilitude. Here, too, it is not so much the
reader to whom Sade is talking, but himself. His wearisome repetitions are tantamount to a purification rite whose repetition is as
natural to him as regular confession is to a good Catholic. Sade
does not give us the work of a free man. He makes us participate
in his efforts of liberation. But it is precisely for this reason that he
holds our attention. His endeavor is more genuine than the instruments it employs. Had Sade been satisfied with the determinism he
professed, he would have repudiated all his moral anxieties. But
these asserted themselves with a clarity that no logic could obscure.
Over and above the facile excuses which he sets forth so tediously,
he persists in questioning himself, in attacking. It is owing to this
headstrong sincerity that, though not a consummate artist or a coherent philosopher, he deserves to be hailed as a great moralist.

---

[12] *Aline et Valcour.*

4

"Extreme in everything," Sade could not adapt himself to the deist compromises of his time. It was with a declaration of atheism, *Dialogue between a Priest and a Dying Man,* that in 1782 he launched his work. The existence of God had been denied more than once since the appearance in 1729 of *Le Testament du curé de Meslier.* Rousseau had dared to present a sympathetic atheist, Monsieur de Wolmar, in *La Nouvelle Héloïse.* In spite of this, the Abbé Mélégan had been thrown into prison in 1754 for having written *Zoroastre;* and La Mettrie was obliged to take refuge at the court of Frederick II. The atheism vehemently espoused by Sylvain Maréchal and popularized by Holbach's *Le Système de la Nature* in 1770 and by the satires collected under the title *Recueil philosophique,* was none the less a dangerous doctrine in an age which placed the scaffold itself under the aegis of the Supreme Being. Sade, in parading his atheism, was deliberately committing a provocative act. But it was also an act of sincerity. I feel that Klossowski, despite the interest of his study, is misinterpreting Sade in taking his passionate rejection of God for an avowal of need. The sophism which maintains that to attack God is to affirm Him finds a great deal of support these days, but this notion is actually the invention of those to whom atheism is a challenge. Sade expressed himself clearly on the matter when he wrote: "The idea of God is the sole wrong for which I cannot forgive mankind."

And if this is the first mystification he attacks, it is because he proceeds, like a good Cartesian, from the simple to the complex, from the gross lie to the more misleading error. He knows that in order to free the individual from the idols to which society has bound him, one must begin by insuring his independence in the face of heaven. If man had not been terrorized by the great bugbear to which he stupidly pays worship, he would not so easily have surrendered his freedom and truth. In choosing God, he denied himself, and that was his unpardonable offense. Actually, he is responsible to no transcendent judge; there is no heavenly court of appeal.

Sade was not unaware of the extent to which the belief in hell and eternity might inflame cruelty. Saint-Fond toys with such hopes so as to extract pleasure from the limitless suffering of the damned.

He diverts himself by imagining a diabolical demiurge who would embody the diffuse evil of Nature. But not for one instant did Sade consider these hypotheses as anything more than intellectual pastimes. He is not to be recognized in the characters who express them, and he refutes them through his mouthpieces. In evoking absolute crime, his aim is to ravage Nature and not to wound God. His harangues against religion are open to reproach because of the tedious monotony with which they repeat timeworn commonplaces; but Sade gives them still another personal turn when, anticipating Nietzsche, he denounces in Christianity a religion of victims which ought, in his view, to be replaced by an ideology of force. His honesty, in any case, is unquestionable. Sade's nature was thoroughly irreligious. There is no trace of metaphysical anxiety in him; he is too concerned with justifying his existence to speculate on its meaning and purpose. His convictions on the subject were wholehearted. If he served at mass and flattered a bishop, it was because, old and broken, he had chosen hypocrisy. But his testament is unequivocal. He feared death for the same reason that he feared senility: as the dissolution of his individuality; fear of the world beyond the grave is wholly lacking in his work. The fear of the beyond never appears in his work. Sade wished to deal only with men, and everything that was not human was foreign to him.

And yet he was alone among men. The eighteenth century, insofar as it tried to abolish God's reign upon earth, substituted another idol in its place. Atheists and deists united in the worship of the new incarnation of the Supreme Good: Nature. They had no intention of forgoing the conveniences of a categorical, universal morality. Transcendental values had broken down; pleasure was acknowledged as the measure of good; and through this hedonism, self-love was reinstated. For example, Madame du Chatelet wrote: "We must begin by saying to ourselves that we have nothing else to do in this world but seek pleasant sensations and feelings." But these timid egotists postulated a natural order which assured the harmonious agreement of individual interests with the general interest. A reasonable organization, obtained by pact or contract, would suffice to insure the prosperity of society for the benefit of all and each. Sade's tragic life gave the lie to this optimistic religion.

The eighteenth century often painted love in somber, solemn, and even tragic tones; and Richardson, Prévost, Duclos, and Crébil-lon, whom Sade quotes with respect, and, above all, Laclos, whom Sade claimed not to know, created more or less satanic heroes. But their wickedness always has its source, not in spontaneity, but in a perversion of their minds or wills. Genuine eroticism, on the contrary, because of its instinctive character, is reinstated. Natural, healthy, and useful to the species, sexual desire merges, according to Diderot, with the very movement of life, and the passions it brings are likewise good and fruitful. If the characters in *La Religieuse* take pleasure in "sadistic" viciousness, it is because instead of satisfying their appetites they repress them. Rousseau, whose sexual experience was complex and largely unhappy, also expresses this in edifying terms: "Sweet pleasures, pure, vivid, painless, and unalloyed." And also: "Love, as I see it, as I have felt it, grows ardent before the illusory image of the beloved's perfection, and this very illusion leads it to enthusiasm for virtue. For this idea always enters into that of the perfect woman."[13] Even in Restif de la Bretonne, though pleasure may have a stormy character, it is none the less rapture, languor, and tenderness. Sade was the only one to reveal selfishness, tyranny, and crime in sexuality. This would suffice to give him a unique place in the history of the sensibility of his century, but from this insight he derived even more remarkable ethical consequences.

There was nothing new in the idea that Nature is evil. Hobbes, with whom Sade was familiar and whom he quotes freely, had declared that man is a wolf to man and that the state of Nature is one of war. A long line of English moralists and satirists had followed in his steps, among them Swift, whom Sade used and even copied. In France, Vauvenargues continued the puritan and Jansenist development of the Christian tradition which identifies the flesh with original sin. Bayle and, more brilliantly, Buffon, established the fact that Nature is not wholly good; and though the myth of the Noble Savage had been current since the sixteenth century, par-

---

[13] Cf. Sade: ". . . it is horror, villainy, the appalling which pleases; well, where are they more emphatically present than in a vitiated object? if 'tis the filthy thing which pleases in the lubricious act, then certainly the more filthy the thing, the more it should please, and it is surely much filthier in the corrupted than in the intact and perfect object."

ticularly in Diderot and the Encyclopedists, Emeric de Crucé had already attacked it at the beginning of the eighteenth century. Sade had no trouble finding any number of arguments to support the thesis which was implied in his erotic experience and which was ironically confirmed by society's imprisoning him for having followed his instincts. But what distinguishes him from his predecessors is the fact that they, after exposing the evil of Nature, set up, in opposition to it, a morality which derived from God and society; whereas Sade, though rejecting the first part of the generally accepted credo: "Nature is Good; let us follow her," paradoxically retained the second. Nature's example has an imperative value, even though her law be one of hate and destruction. We must now examine more closely the ruse whereby he turned the new cult against its devotees.

Sade conceived the relation of man to Nature in various ways. These variations seem to me not so much the movements of a dialectic as the expressions of the hesitation of a thinking that at times restrains its boldness and at others breaks completely loose. When Sade is merely trying to find hasty justifications, he adopts a mechanistic view of the world. La Mettrie affirmed the moral indifference of human acts when he declared: "We are no guiltier in following the primitive impulses that govern us than is the Nile for her floods or the sea for her waves." Similarly, Sade, in order to excuse himself, compares himself to plants, animals, and the elements. "In her hands I am only a tool that she [Nature] manipulates as she pleases." Although he constantly took refuge in similar statements, they do not express his real thoughts. In the first place, Nature, for him, is not an indifferent mechanism. There is such significance in her transformations that one might play with the idea that she is governed by an evil genius. Nature is actually cruel and voracious, informed with the spirit of destruction. She "would desire the utter annihilation of all living creatures so as to enjoy her power of re-creating new ones." However, man is not her slave.

Sade had already pointed out in *Aline et Valcour* that he can wrest himself free and turn against her. "Let us dare do violence to this unintelligible Nature, the better to master the art of enjoying her." And he declared even more decisively in *Juliette*: "Once man is created, he is no longer dependent upon Nature; once Nature has launched him, she has no further hold on him." He goes further. Man, in his relation to Nature, is comparable to "the froth, the vapor which rises from the rarefied liquid in a heated vessel. The vapor is not created; it is a resultant; it is heterogeneous. It derives its existence from a foreign element. It can exist or not, without detriment to the element from which it issues. It owes nothing to the element and the element owes nothing to it." Though man is of no more value to the universe than a bit of froth, it is this very insignificance which guarantees his autonomy. The natural order cannot control him since he is radically alien to it. Hence, he may make a moral decision, and no one has the right to dictate to him. Why then, with all the paths open to him, did Sade choose the one which led, through the imitation of Nature, to crime? To answer this question, we must understand his system in its totality; the aim of this system was precisely to justify the "crimes" which Sade never dreamed of renouncing.

We are always more influenced than we realize by the ideas we contest. To be sure, Sade often uses naturalism as an *ad hominem* argument. He took sly pleasure in turning to evil account the examples which his contemporaries tried to exploit on behalf of Good, but no doubt he also took for granted that might makes right. When he tries to demonstrate the fact that the libertine has the right to oppress women, he exclaims: "Has not Nature proved, in giving us the strength necessary to submit them to our desires, that we have the right to do so?" One could find many similar quotations. "Nature has made us all equal at birth, Sophie," says la Dubois to Justine. "If Nature wishes to disturb this first stage of general laws, it is for us to correct her caprices." Sade's basic charge against the codes imposed by society is that they are artificial. He compares them, in a particularly significant text, to those that might be drawn up by a community of blind men.[14] "All those duties are imaginary, since they are only conventional. In like manner, man has made laws relative to his petty knowledge, his petty wiles, and his petty needs—but all this has no reality. . . . When we look at Nature we readily understand that everything we decide and organize is as far removed from the perfection of

[14] *Pensée* cited in Maurice Heine: *Le Marquis de Sade,* Paris, Gallimard, 1950.

her views and as inferior to her as the laws of the society of blind
men would be to our own."

Montesquieu had advanced the idea that laws were dependent
on climate, circumstances, and even the arrangement of the "fibers"
of our bodies. It might be concluded that they express the various
aspects assumed by Nature in time and space. But the indefatigable
Sade takes us to Tahiti, Patagonia, and the antipodes, to show us
that the diversity of enacted laws definitively negates their value.
Though they may be related, they seem to him arbitrary. And it
should be noted that for him the words "conventional" and "imaginary" are synonymous. Nature retains her sacred character for
Sade: indivisible and unique, she is an absolute, outside of which
there is no reality.

It is obvious that Sade's thinking on this point was not quite
coherent, that it was not at all times equally sincere, and that it was
constantly developing. But his inconsistencies are not quite so obvious as one might think. The syllogism: Nature is evil, and therefore the society that departs from Nature merits our obedience, is
far too simple. In the first place, society is suspect because of its
hypocrisy. It appeals to Nature's authority even though it is really
hostile to her. And besides, society is rooted in Nature, despite its
antagonism to her. Society manifests its original perversion by the
very way in which it contradicts Nature. The idea of general interest has no natural basis. "The interests of individuals are almost
always opposed to those of society." But the idea was invented in
order to satisfy a natural instinct, namely, the tyrannical will of the
strong. Laws, instead of correcting the primitive order of the world,
only aggravate its injustice. "We are all alike, except in strength,"
that is, there are no essential differences among individuals, and the
unequal distribution of strength might have been offset. Instead, the
strong have arrogated to themselves all the forms of superiority
and have even invented others.

Holbach, and many others along with him, had exposed the
hypocrisy of codes whose sole purpose was to oppress the weak.
Morelly and Brissot, among others, had shown that the ownership
of property has no natural basis. Society has fabricated this harmful institution out of whole cloth. "There is no exclusive ownership
in Nature," wrote Brissot. "The word has been struck from her

code. The unhappy starveling may carry off and devour his bread because he is hungry. His claim is his hunger." In *Philosophy in the Bedroom* Sade uses almost the same terms to demand that the idea of pleasure be substituted for that of proprietorship. How can proprietorship claim to be a universally recognized right when the poor rebel against it and the rich dream only of increasing it by further monopolizing? "It is by complete equality of wealth and condition and not by vain laws that the power of the stronger must be weakened." But the fact is that it is the strong who make the laws for their own profit.

Their presumptuousness is odiously apparent in their arrogation of the right to inflict punishment. Beccaria had maintained that the aim of punishment was to procure redress, but that no one could claim the right to punish. Sade indignantly spoke out against all penalties of an expiatory character. "O slaughterers, jailers, and imbeciles of all regimes and governments, when will you come to prefer the science of understanding man to that of imprisoning and killing him?" He rebels particularly against the death penalty. Society tries to justify it by the *lex talionis,* but this is just another fantasy without roots in reality. In the first place, there is no reciprocity among the subjects; their existences are not commensurable. Nor is there any similarity between a murder committed in a burst of passion or out of need, and coldly premeditated assassination by judges. And how can the latter in any way compensate for the former? In erecting scaffolds, society, far from mitigating the cruelty of Nature, merely aggravates it. Actually, it resists evil by doing greater evil. Its claim on our loyalty is without foundation.

The famous contract invoked by Hobbes and Rousseau is merely a myth; how could individual freedom be recognized in an order that oppresses it? This pact is to the interest of neither the strong, who have nothing to gain in abdicating their privileges, nor the weak, whose inferiority is thereby confirmed. There can be only a state of war between these two groups; and each has its own values, which are irreconcilable with those of the other. "When he took a hundred *louis* from a man's pocket, he was committing what was for him a just act, though the man who had been robbed must have regarded it quite otherwise." In the speech which he puts into the mouth of Coeur-de-fer, Sade passionately exposes the bourgeois hoax which consists in erecting class interests into universal principles. Since the concrete conditions under which individuals live are not homogeneous, no universal morality is possible.

But should we not try to reform society, since it has betrayed its own aspirations? Cannot individual freedom be put precisely to this use? It seems not improbable that Sade may at times have envisaged this solution. It is significant that in *Aline et Valcour* he describes with equal indulgence the anarchic society of cannibals and the communistic society of Zamé in which evil is disarmed by justice. I do not think that there is any irony at all in the latter picture, any more than in the appeal, "Yet Another Effort, Frenchmen . . ." inserted into *Philosophy in the Bedroom*.[15] Sade's activity during the Revolution clearly proves that he wished to be integrated into a collectivity. He suffered bitterly from the ostracism to which he was subjected.

He dreamed of an ideal society from which his special tastes would not exclude him. He really thought that such tastes would not constitute a serious danger to an enlightened society. Zamé assures us that he would not be disturbed by Sade's disciples: "The people you speak of are few; they do not worry me at all." And Sade, in a letter, maintains: "It is not the opinions or vices of private individuals that are harmful to the State, but rather the behavior of public figures." The fact is that the libertine's acts have no real influence; they are not much more than games. Sade takes refuge behind their insignificance and goes so far as to suggest that he would be ready to sacrifice them. Motivated as they are by defiance and resentment, these acts would lose their significance in a world without hatred. If the prohibitions which make crime attractive were abolished, lust itself would be eliminated. Perhaps Sade really longed for the personal conversion that would result from the conversion of other men. He probably expected, also, that his vices would be accepted as something exceptional by a community which respected singularity and which would, therefore, recognize him as an exception. He was sure, in any case, that a man

---

[15] It has been maintained that Sade does not endorse this statement since he puts it into the mouth of Le Chevalier. Le Chevalier, however, merely reads a text of which Dolmancé, Sade's mouthpiece, admits he is the author.

who was content with whipping a prostitute every now and then was less harmful to society than a farmer-general.

The real plagues are established injustice, official abuses, and constitutional crimes; and these are the inevitable accompaniments of abstract laws which try to impose themselves uniformly upon a plurality of radically separate objects. A just economic order would render codes and courts useless, for crime is born of need and illegality and would vanish with the elimination of these grounds. The ideal regime, for Sade, was a kind of reasonable anarchy: "The rule of law is inferior to that of anarchy: the most obvious proof of what I assert is the fact that any government is obliged to plunge itself into anarchy whenever it aspires to remake its constitution. In order to abrogate its former laws, it is compelled to establish a revolutionary regime in which there is no law: this regime finally gives birth to new laws, but this second state is necessarily less pure than the first, since it derives from it." This argument probably does not sound very convincing, but what Sade understood remarkably well was that the ideology of his time was merely the expression of an economic system and that a concrete transformation of this system would put an end to the humbug of bourgeois morality. Very few of his contemporaries developed such penetrating views in such an extreme way.

Nevertheless, Sade did not definitely take the path of social reform. His life and work were not guided by these utopian reveries. How could he have continued to believe in them very long in the depths of his dungeon cells or after the Terror? Events confirmed his private experience. Society's failure was no mere accident. And besides, it was obvious that his interest in its possible success was of a purely speculative nature. He was obsessed by his own case. He cared little about changing himself and much more about being confirmed in his choices. His vices condemned him to solitude. He was to demonstrate the necessity of solitude and the supremacy of evil. It was easy for him to be honest because, maladjusted aristocrat that he was, he had never encountered men like himself. Though he mistrusted generalizations, he ascribed to his situation the value of a metaphysical inevitability: "Man is isolated in the world." "All creatures are born isolated and have no need of one another." If the diversity of human beings could be assimilated—as

Sade himself frequently suggests—to that which differentiates plants or animals, a reasonable society would manage to surmount it. It would be enough merely to respect each one's particularity.

But man does not merely endure his solitude; he demands it *against everyone*. It follows that there is a heterogeneity of values, not only from class to class, but from individual to individual. "All passions have two meanings, Juliette: one, which is very unjust as regards the victim; the other, which is singularly just to the person who exercises it. And this fundamental antagonism cannot be transcended because it is the truth itself." If human projects tried to reconcile themselves in a common quest for the general interest, they would be necessarily unauthentic. For there is no reality other than that of the self-enclosed subject hostile to any other subject which disputes its sovereignty. The thing that prevents individual freedom from choosing Good is that the latter does not exist in the empty heaven or on the unjust earth, or even at some ideal horizon; it is nowhere to be found. Evil is an absolute resisted only by fanciful notions, and there is only one way of asserting oneself in the face of it: to assent to it.

For there is one idea that Sade, throughout his pessimism, savagely rejects: the idea of submission. And that is why he detests the hypocritical resignation which is adorned with the name of virtue. It is a stupid submission to the rule of evil, as re-created by society. In submitting, man renounces both his authenticity and his freedom. It was easy for Sade to show that chastity and temperance are not even justified by their usefulness. The prejudices that condemn incest, sodomy, and all sexual "vagaries" have but one aim: to destroy the individual by imposing upon him a stupid conformism. But the great virtues extolled by the age had a deeper meaning; they tried to palliate the all too obvious inadequacies of the law. Sade raised no objection to tolerance, probably because, so far as he could observe, no one even tried to practice it; but he did attack fanatically what is called humaneness and benevolence. These were mystifications which aimed at reconciling the irreconcilable: the unsatisfied appetites of the poor and the selfish greed of the rich. Taking up the tradition of La Rochefoucauld, he shows that these are merely masks to disguise self-interest.

The weak, in order to check the arrogance of the strong, have

invented the idea of fraternity, an idea which has no solid basis:
"Now I beg of you to tell me whether I must love a human being
simply because he exists or resembles me and whether for these
reasons alone I must suddenly prefer him to myself?" What hypocrisy on the part of privileged persons who make a great to-do
about their philanthropy and at the same time acquiesce in the abject condition of the poor! This false sentimentality was so widespread at the time that even Valmont, in *Les Liaisons dangereuses,*
was moved to tears when he performed an act of charity; and it
was obviously the currency of this mode of feeling that made Sade
unleash all his dishonesty and sincerity against benevolence. He is
certainly joking when he claims that in maltreating prostitutes he
is serving the cause of morality. If libertines were permitted to
molest them with impunity, prostitution would become so dangerous
a profession that no one would engage in it. But he is quite right in
cutting through sophisms and exposing the inconsistencies of a society that protects the very things it condemns, and which, though
permitting debauchery, often pillories the debauchee.

He reveals the dangers of almsgiving with the same somber
irony. If the poor are not reduced to hopelessness, they may rebel;
and the safest thing would be to exterminate all of them. In this
scheme, which he attributes to Saint-Fond, Sade develops the idea in
Swift's famous pamphlet, and he certainly does not identify himself
with his hero. Nevertheless, the cynicism of this aristocrat, who fully
espoused the interests of his class, is more valid to him than the
compromises of guilty-minded hedonists. His thinking is clear—
either do away with the poor or do away with poverty, but do not
use half-measures and thus perpetuate injustice and oppression,[16]
and above all do not pretend to be redeeming these extortions by
handing out a trivial dole to those you exploit. If Sade's heroes let
some poor wretch die of hunger rather than defile themselves by an
act of charity that would cost them nothing, it is because they passionately refuse any complicity with respectable people who appease
their consciences so cheaply.

Virtue deserves no admiration and no gratitude since, far from

---

16 This policy of all or nothing is found among present-day Communists. They re-
pudiate bourgeois charity; and there are many who, on principle, refuse any private
help to the needy.

reflecting the demands of a transcendent good, it serves the interests of those who make a show of it. It is only logical that Sade should come to this conclusion. But after all, if self-interest is the individual's sole law, why despise it? In what respect is it inferior to vice? Sade answered this question often and vehemently. In cases where virtue is chosen, he says: "What lack of movement! What ice! Nothing stirs me, nothing excites me. . . . I ask you, is this pleasure? What a difference on the other side! What tickling of my senses! What excitement in my organs!" And again: "Happiness lies only in that which excites, and the only thing that excites is crime." In terms of the hedonism of his time, this argument carries weight. The only objection one might make is that Sade generalizes from his own individual case. May some people not also be excited by Good? He rejects this eclecticism. *Virtue can procure only an imaginary happiness*; "true felicity lies only in the senses, and virtue gratifies none of them." This statement may seem surprising, since Sade had actually made the imagination the mainspring of vice; but vice teaches us a certain truth through the very fantasies on which it feeds, and the proof is that it ends in orgasm, that is, in a definite sensation; whereas the illusions on which virtue feeds are never concretely recouped by the individual. According to the philosophy that Sade borrowed from his age, sensation is the only measure of reality, and if virtue arouses no sensation, it is because it has no real basis.

Sade explains what he means more clearly in the following parallel between virtue and vice: ". . . the first is illusory, a fiction; the second is authentic, real; the first is founded upon vile prejudices, the second upon reason; the first, through the agency of pride, the most false of all our sensations, may provide the heart with a brief instant's titillation; the other is a veritable mental pleasure-taking, and it inflames every other passion . . ." Virtue, chimerical and imaginary, encloses us in a world of appearances; whereas vice's intimate link with the flesh guarantees its genuineness. Using the vocabulary of Stirner, whose name has rightly been linked with Sade's, we might say that virtue alienates the individual from that empty entity, Man. It is only in crime that he justifies and fulfills himself as a concrete ego. If the poor man resigns himself or vainly tries to fight for his fellows, he is maneuvered and duped, an inert object, a plaything of Nature; he is nothing. He must, like la Dubois or Coeur-de-fer, try to pass over to the side of the strong. The rich person who accepts his privileges passively also exists like an object. If he abuses his power and becomes a tyrant, then he is someone. Instead of losing himself in philanthropic dreams, he will cynically take advantage of the injustice that favors him. "Where would be the victims of our villainy if all men were criminals? We must never cease to keep the people tied to the yoke of error and the lie," says Esterval.

Are we back to the idea that man can only act in obedience to his evil nature? Is he not destroying his freedom with the pretext of safeguarding his authenticity? No, for though freedom may be unable to go counter to given reality, it is able to wrest itself away from it and assume it. This procedure is similar to Stoic conversion which, by deliberate decision, turns reality to its own account. There is no contradiction in Sade's extolling crime and at the same time getting indignant about men's injustice, selfishness, and cruelty.[17] He has only contempt for the timid vice, for the rash crimes which merely reflect passively the heinousness of Nature. One must *make oneself* a criminal in order to avoid *being* evil, as is a volcano or a member of the police. It is not a matter of submitting to the universe, but of imitating it in open defiance.

This is the attitude that Almani, the chemist, assumes at the edge of Mount Etna. "Yes, my friend, yes, I abhor Nature. And the reason I loathe her is that I know her all too well. Knowing her dreadful secrets, I felt a kind of ineffable pleasure in copying her heinousness. I shall imitate her, though I hate her. . . . Her murderous nets are spread for us alone. Let us try to catch her in her own trap. . . . In presenting to me only her effects, she concealed all her causes. I am therefore limited to imitating the former. Unable to guess the motive that put the dagger into her hands, I have been able to take away her weapon and use it as she did." This text has the same ambiguous ring as the words of Dolmancé: " 'Twas men's ingratitude dried out my heart." It reminds us that it was in despair and resentment that Sade devoted himself to evil. And it is in this respect that his hero is distinguished from the

---

17 The similarity with Stirner at this point is striking. Stirner also condemns "vulgar" crime and extols only that which makes for the fulfillment of the ego.

*Sexual
Feeling wsl
R.M*

ancient sage. He does not follow Nature lovingly and joyously. He copies her with abhorrence and without understanding her. And he wills himself to be something without approving himself. Evil is not at one with itself; self-laceration is its very essence.

This laceration must be experienced in a state of constant tension; otherwise, it congeals into remorse and, as such, constitutes a mortal danger. Maurice Blanchot has observed that whenever the Sadean hero, as a result of some scruple, restores to society its power over him, he is doomed to the worst kind of catastrophe.[18] Repentance and hesitation mean that one recognizes that one has judges. It therefore means accepting guilt instead of assuming that one is the free author of one's acts. The man who consents to his passivity deserves all the defeats that the hostile world will inflict upon him. On the other hand: "The genuine libertine likes even the charges that are leveled against him for his execrable crimes. Have we not known men who loved even the tortures appointed by human vengeance, who suffered them gladly, who looked upon the scaffold as a throne of glory? These are men who have attained the highest degree of deliberate corruption."

At this ultimate degree, man is delivered not only of prejudices and shame, but of fear as well. His serenity is that of the ancient sage who regarded as futile "things which do not depend on ourselves." But the sage confined himself to a completely negative self-defense against possible suffering. The dark stoicism of Sade promises positive happiness. Thus, Coeur-de-fer lays down the following alternatives: "Either the crime which makes us happy, or the scaffold which prevents us from being unhappy." Nothing can threaten the man who can transform his very defeats into triumphs. He fears nothing because for him everything is good. The brutal factitiousness of things does not crush the free man because it does not interest him. He is concerned only with their meaning, and the meaning depends only upon him. A person who is whipped or penetrated by another may be the other's master as well as his slave. The ambivalence of pain and pleasure, of humiliation and pride, enables the libertine to dominate any situation. Thus, Juliette can transform into pleasure the same tortures that prostrate Justine.

---

[18] See Maurice Blanchot: "Sade," in the introductory section to The Marquis de Sade, *The Complete Justine.—Eds.*

Fundamentally, the content of the experience is unimportant. The thing that counts is the subject's intention.

Thus, hedonism ends in ataraxia, which confirms the paradoxical relation between sadism and stoicism. The individual's promised happiness is reduced to indifference. "I have been happy, my dear, ever since I have been indulging cold-bloodedly in every sort of crime," says Bressac. Cruelty appears in a new light, as an *ascesis*. "The man who can grow callous to the pains of others becomes insensitive to his own." It is no longer excitement we must seek, but *apathy*. A budding libertine, no doubt, needs violent emotions in order to feel the truth of his individual existence. But once he has possessed it, the pure form of crime will be enough to insure it. Crime has "a character of grandeur and sublimity which prevails and always will prevail over the dull charms of virtue" and which renders vain all the contingent satisfactions one might be tempted to expect. With a severity similar to Kant's, and which has its source in the same puritan tradition, Sade conceives the free act only as an act free of all feeling. If it were to obey emotional motives, it would make us Nature's slaves again and not autonomous subjects.

This choice is open to any individual, regardless of his situation. One of the victims locked up in the monk's harem where Justine is languishing away manages to escape her fate by proving her worth. She stabs one of her companions with a viciousness that arouses the admiration of her masters and makes her the queen of the harem. Those who remain among the oppressed do so because they are poor-spirited, and they must not be pitied. "What can there possibly be in common between the man who can do everything and the one who does not dare do anything?" The contrast of the two words is significant. For Sade, if one dares, one can. Blanchot has emphasized the austerity of this morality. Almost all of Sade's criminals die violent deaths, and it is their merit that transforms their misfortunes into glory. But in fact, death is not the worst of failures, and whatever the fate Sade reserves for his heroes, he assures them a destiny which allows them to fulfill themselves. This optimism comes from an aristocratic vision of mankind, which involves, in its implacable severity, a doctrine of predestination.

For this quality of mind which enables a few elect spirits to rule over a herd of condemned souls appears as an arbitrary dispensation of grace. Juliette was saved and Justine lost from the beginning of time. Even more interesting is the view that merit cannot entail success unless it is *recognized*. The strength of mind of Valérie and Juliette would have been to no avail had it not deserved the admiration of their tyrants. Divided and separated though they be, it must be admitted that they do bow down together before certain values, and they choose reality in the different guises which for Sade are, without question, equivalent to one another: orgasm-Nature-reason. Or, to be more precise, reality imposes itself upon them. The hero triumphs through their mediation. But what saves him finally is the fact that he has staked everything on the truth. Sade believes in an absolute which is beyond all contingencies and which can never disappoint the one who invokes it as a last resort.

It is only out of pusillanimity that everyone does not embrace such a sure ethic, for there can be no valid objection to it. It cannot offend a God who is a mere figment of the imagination; and since Nature is essentially division and hostility, to attack her is to conform to her all the more. Yielding to his naturalistic prejudices, Sade writes: "The only real crime would be to outrage Nature," and adds immediately afterward: "Is it conceivable that Nature would provide us with the possibility of a crime that would outrage her?" She takes unto herself everything that happens. She even receives murder with indifference, since "the life principle of all creatures is death; this death is merely a matter of imagination." Only man attaches importance to his own existence, but he "could completely wipe out his species without the universe's feeling the slightest change." He claims to have a sacred character which makes him untouchable, but he is only one animal among others. "Only man's pride has made a crime of murder."

Indeed, Sade's plea is so forceful that he ends by denying any criminal character to crime. He realizes this himself. The last part of *Juliette* is a convulsive attempt to rekindle the flame of Evil, but despite volcanoes, fires, poison, and plague, if there is no God, man is merely smoke. If Nature permits everything, then the worst catastrophes are a matter of indifference. "To my mind, man's greatest torment is the impossibility of offending Nature!" And if

Sade had staked everything only on the demoniacal horror of crime, his ethic would have ended in radical failure; but if he himself accepted this defeat, it was only because he was fighting for something else, namely, his profound conviction that crime is good.

In the first place, crime is not only inoffensive to Nature, it is useful to her. Sade explains in *Juliette* that if "the spirit of the three kingdoms" were confronted with no obstacles, it would become so violent that it would paralyze the working of the universe. "There would be neither gravitation nor movement." As a result of its inner contradiction, human crimes save it from the stagnation which would also endanger an overly virtuous society. Sade had certainly read Mandeville's *The Grumbling Hive,* which had had a great success at the beginning of the eighteenth century. Mandeville had shown that the passions and defects of individuals served the public welfare, and even that the greatest scoundrels were the ones who worked most actively for the common good. When an inopportune conversion made for the triumph of virtue, the hive was ruined. Sade also declared repeatedly that a collectivity that *fell* into virtue would thereby be pushed into inertia. We have here a kind of presage of the Hegelian theory according to which "the spirit's restlessness" could not be abolished without involving the end of history. But, for Sade, immobility appears not as a static plenitude but as a pure absence. Mankind makes every effort by means of the conventions with which it is armed to cut all its ties with Nature; and it would become a pale phantom were it not for a few resolute souls who maintain within it, in spite of itself, the rights of truth—and truth means discord, war, and agitation.

In the strange text where he compares us all to blind men, Sade says that it is already enough that our limited senses prevent us from attaining the core of reality. Let us, therefore, not spoil our pleasure even more. Let us try to transcend our limits: "The most perfect being we could conceive would be the one who alienated himself most from our conventions and found them most contemptible." In its proper context, this statement recalls both Rimbaud's demand for a "systematic derangement" of all the senses and the attempts of the surrealists to penetrate beyond human artifice to the mysterious heart of the real. But it is as moralist rather than as poet that Sade tries to shatter the prison of ap-

pearances. The mystified and mystifying society against which he
rebels suggests Heidegger's "the one," in which the authenticity of
existence is swallowed up. For Sade, too, it is a question of regaining authenticity by an individual decision. These comparisons are
quite deliberate. Sade must be given a place in the great family of
those who want to cut through the "banality of everyday life" to a
truth which is immanent in this world. Within this framework,
crime becomes a duty: "In a criminal society one must be a criminal." This formula sums up his ethic. By means of crime, the libertine refuses any complicity with the evils of the given situation, of
which the masses are merely the passive, and hence abject, reflection. It prevents society from reposing in injustice and creates an
apocalyptic condition which constrains all individuals to insure their
separateness, and thus their truth, in a state of constant tension.

Nevertheless, it is in the name of the individual that it seems
possible to raise the most convincing objections to Sade's notions;
for the individual is quite real, and crime does him real injury. It is
here that Sade's thinking proves to be extreme: the only thing that
has truth for me is that which is enveloped in my own experience;
the inner presence of other people is foreign to me. Hence, it does
not concern me and cannot dictate any duty to me. "We don't care
a bit about the torment of others; what have we in common with
this torment?" And again: "There is no comparison between what
others experience and what we feel. The strongest pain in other
people is certainly nothing to us, but we are affected by the slightest
tickle of pleasure that touches us." The fact is that the only sure
bonds among men are those they create in transcending themselves
into another world by means of common projects. The only project
that the hedonistic sensualism of the eighteenth century has to offer
the individual is to "procure pleasant sensations and feelings." It
fixes him in his lonely immanence. Sade shows us in *Justine* a surgeon
who plans to dissect his daughter in order to further science and
thereby mankind. Seen in terms of its transcendent future, mankind has value in his eyes; but what is a man when reduced to his
mere vain presence? Just a pure fact, stripped of all value, who
affects me no more than a lifeless stone. "My neighbor is nothing
to me; there is not the slightest relationship between him and myself."

These statements seem contradictory to Sade's attitude in real
life. It is obvious that if there were nothing in common between
the tortures of the victims and the torturer, the latter would derive
no pleasure from them. But what Sade is actually disputing is the
a priori existence of a given relationship between myself and the
other by which my behavior should be guided in the abstract. He
does not deny the possibility of establishing such a relationship; and
if he rejects ethical recognition of other people founded on false
notions of reciprocity and universality, it is in order to give himself
the authority to destroy the concrete barriers of flesh which isolate
human minds. Each mind bears witness only for itself as to the
value it attributes to itself and has no right to impose this value
upon others. But it can, in a singular and vivid manner, demand
recognition of such value in its acts. This is the course chosen by
the criminal, who, by the violence of his self-assertion, becomes real
for the other person and thereby also reveals the other as really
existing. But it should be noted that, quite unlike the conflict
described by Hegel, this process involves no risk for the subject.
His primacy is not at stake; regardless of what happens to him, he
will accept no master. If he is defeated, he returns to a solitude
which ends in death, but he remains sovereign.

Thus, for the despot, other people do not represent a danger
that could strike at the heart of his being. Nevertheless, this outside world from which he is excluded irritates him. He wants to
penetrate it. Paradoxically enough, he is free to make things happen in this forbidden domain, and the temptation is all the more
dizzying in that these events will be incommensurable with his
experience. Sade repeatedly stresses the point that it is not the
unhappiness of the other person which excites the libertine, but
rather the knowledge that he is responsible for it. This is something
very different from an abstract demoniacal pleasure. When he
weaves his dark plots, he sees his freedom being transformed for
others into a destiny. And as death is more certain than life, and
suffering more certain than happiness, it is in persecutions and
murder that he takes unto himself this mystery. But it is not enough
to impose oneself upon the bewildered victim in the guise of destiny.
Duped and mystified as he is, one possesses him, but only from
without. In revealing oneself to the victim, the torturer incites him

to manifest his freedom by his screams or prayers. If it is not revealed, the victim is unworthy of torture. One kills him or forgets about him. He may also escape his torturer by the violence of his revolt, be it flight, suicide, or victory. What the torturer demands is that, alternating between refusal and submission, whether rebelling or consenting, the victim recognize, in any case, that his destiny is the freedom of the tyrant. He is then united to his tyrant by the closest of bonds. They form a genuine couple.

There are occasional cases in which the victim's freedom, without escaping the destiny which the tyrant creates for it, succeeds in getting around it. It turns suffering into pleasure, shame into pride; it becomes an accomplice. It is then that the debauchee is gratified to the full: "There is no keener pleasure for a libertine mind than to win proselytes." To debauch an innocent creature is obviously a satanic act, but in view of the ambivalence of evil, we effect a genuine conversion by winning for it a new adept. The capturing of a virginity, among other things, appears in this light as a ceremony of initiation. Just as we must outrage Nature in order to imitate her, though the outrage is canceled out since she herself demands it, so, in doing violence to an individual, we force him to assume his separateness, and thereby he finds a truth which reconciles him with his antagonist. Torturer and victim recognize their fellowship in astonishment, esteem, and even admiration.

It has rightly been pointed out that there is never any permanent bond among Sade's libertines, that their relationship involves a constant tension. But the fact that Sade systematically makes selfishness triumph over friendship does not prevent him from endowing friendship with reality. Noirceuil is very careful to let Juliette know that he is interested in her only because of the pleasure he finds in her company; but this pleasure implies a concrete relationship between them. Each feels confirmed within himself by the presence of an alter ego; it is both an absolution and an exaltation. Group debauchery produces genuine communion among Sade's libertines. Each one perceives the meaning of his acts and of his own figure through the minds of the others. I experience my own flesh in the flesh of another; then my fellow creature really exists for me. The shocking fact of coexistence eludes our thinking, but we can dispose of its mystery the way Alexander cut through the Gordian knot: we must set ourselves down in it by acts. "What an enigma is man!—Yes, my friend, and that's what made a very witty man say that it's better to f . . . him than to understand him." Eroticism appears in Sade as a mode of communication, the only valid one. We might say, parodying Claudel, that in Sade "the penis is the shortest path between two hearts."

5

To sympathize with Sade too readily is to betray him. For it is our misery, subjection, and death that he desires; and every time we side with a child whose throat has been slit by a sex maniac, we take a stand against him. Nor does he forbid us to defend ourselves. He allows that a father may revenge or prevent, even by murder, the rape of his child. What he demands is that, in the struggle between irreconcilable existences, each one engage himself concretely in the name of his own existence. He approves of the vendetta, but not of the courts. We may kill, but we may not judge. The pretensions of the judge are more arrogant than those of the tyrant; for the tyrant confines himself to being himself, whereas the judge tries to erect his opinions into universal laws. His effort is based upon a lie. For every person is imprisoned in his own skin and cannot become the mediator between separate persons from whom he himself is separated. And the fact that a great number of these individuals band together and alienate themselves in institutions, of which they are no longer masters, gives them no additional right. Their number has nothing to do with the matter. There is no way of measuring the incommensurable. In order to escape the conflicts of existence, we take refuge in a universe of appearances, and existence itself escapes us. In thinking that we are defending ourselves, we are destroying ourselves. Sade's immense merit lies in his taking a stand against these abstractions and alienations which are merely flights from the truth about man. No one was more passionately attached to the concrete than he. He never respected the "everyone says" with which mediocre minds lazily content themselves. He adhered only to the truths which were derived from the evidence of his own actual experience. Thus he went beyond the sensualism of his age and transformed it into an ethic of authenticity.

This does not mean that we can be satisfied with the solution he offers. For if Sade's desire to grasp the very essence of the human condition in terms of his particular situation is the source of his greatness, it is also responsible for his limits. He thought that the solution he chose for himself was valid for everyone else, to the exclusion of any other. Wherein he was doubly mistaken. For all his pessimism, he was, socially, on the side of the privileged, and he did not understand that social injustice affects the individual even in his ethical potentialities. Even rebellion is a luxury requiring culture, leisure, and a certain detachment from the needs of existence. Though Sade's heroes may pay with their lives for such rebellion, at least they do so after it has given their lives a valid meaning; whereas for the great majority of men it would be tantamount to a stupid suicide. Contrary to his wishes, it is chance, and not merit, which would operate in the selection of a criminal elite. If it is objected that he never strove for universality, that he wanted only to insure his own salvation—that does not do him justice. He offers himself as an example, since he wrote—and so passionately! —of his own experience. And he probably did not expect his appeal to be heard by everyone. But he did not think that he was addressing only the members of the privileged classes, whose arrogance he detested. The kind of predestination in which he believed was democratically conceived, and he would not have wanted to discover that it depended upon the economic circumstances from which, as he saw it, it should allow one to escape.

Moreover, he did not suppose that there could be any possible way other than individual rebellion. He knew only two alternatives: abstract morality and crime. He was unaware of action. Though he might have suspected the possibility of a concrete communication among subjects through an undertaking which might unite all men in the common realization of their manhood, he did not stop there. Denying the individual all transcendence, he consigns him to an insignificance which sanctions the use of violence. But this violence in the void becomes absurd, and the tyrant who tries to assert himself by such violence discovers merely his own nothingness.

To this contradiction, however, Sade might oppose another. For the eighteenth century's fond dream of reconciling individuals within their immanence is, in any case, unfeasible. Sade embodied in his own way his disappointment with the Terror. The individual who is unwilling to deny his particularity is repudiated by society. But if we choose to recognize in each subject only the transcendence which unites him concretely with his fellows, we are leading him only to new idols, and their particular insignificance will appear all the more obvious. We shall be sacrificing today to tomorrow, the minority to the majority, the freedom of each to the achievements of the community. Prison and the guillotine will be the logical consequences of this denial. The illusory brotherhood ends in crimes, wherein virtue recognizes her abstract features. "Nothing resembles virtue more than a great crime," said Saint-Just. Is it not better to assume the burden of evil than to subscribe to this abstract good which drags in its wake abstract slaughters? It is probably impossible to escape this dilemma. If the entire human population of the earth were present to each individual in its full reality, no collective action would be possible, and the air would become unbreathable for everyone. Thousands of individuals are suffering and dying vainly and unjustly at every moment, and this does not affect us. If it did, our existence would be impossible. Sade's merit lies not only in his having proclaimed aloud what everyone admits with shame to himself, but in the fact that he did not simply resign himself. He chose cruelty rather than indifference. This is probably why he finds so many echoes today, when the individual knows that he is more the victim of men's good consciences than of their wickedness. To confront this terrifying optimism is to come to his aid. In the solitude of his prison cells, Sade lived through an ethical darkness similar to the intellectual night in which Descartes shrouded himself. He emerged with no revelation but at least he disputed all the easy answers. If ever we hope to transcend the separateness of individuals, we may do so only on condition that we be aware of its existence. Otherwise, promises of happiness and justice conceal the worst dangers. Sade drained to the dregs the moment of selfishness, injustice, and misery, and he insisted upon its truth. The supreme value of his testimony lies in its ability to disturb us. It forces us to re-examine thoroughly the basic problem which haunts our age in different forms: the true relation between man and man.

—Translated by Annette Michelson

# Nature as Destructive Principle
by Pierre Klossowski

> When it wants martyrs, atheism has only to
> speak; my blood is ready to flow.
> —*La Nouvelle Justine*

*I*n Sade's work the uneasy conscience of the debauched libertine
represents a transitional state of mind between the conscience
of social man and the atheistic conscience of the philosopher of
Nature. It offers at one and the same time those negative elements
which Sadean thought, in its dialectical movement, makes great
efforts to eliminate, and the positive elements which will make it
possible to move beyond this intermediary state of mind in order to
get to the atheistic and asocial philosophy of Nature and a moral
system based on the idea of Nature as perpetual motion.

The libertine's conscience maintains a negative relationship
with God on one hand and with his neighbor on the other. Both the
notion of God and the notion of his neighbor are indispensable to
him. The relationship with God is negative because the libertine's
conscience, as we find it in Sade, is not atheistic in a cold-blooded
way; rather its atheism is the result of effervescence and therefore
of resentment; his atheism is only a form of sacrilege. Only the
profanation of religious symbols is able to convince him of his ap-

65

parent atheism, which is thus clearly distinguishable from the conscience of the atheistic philosopher for whom sacrilege has no significance beyond its revelation of the weakness of the individual who indulges in it.

At times the atheism which is affected by the libertine conscience, and the wrong which it projects doing, are meant to be provocations addressed to the absent God, as though scandalous provocations were a way of forcing that God to manifest his existence:

> If there were a God and if that God possessed power, would he allow the virtue which honors him to be sacrificed to vice as you intend to do; would this all-powerful God allow a weak creature like myself who, compared to him, is as the mite in the eye of the elephant, would he, I ask, allow this feeble creature to insult him, scoff at him, stand up to him, and offend him as I take pleasure in doing at every moment of the day?

This kind of impunity adds to the delight of the libertine conscience: the greater the punishment merited by his action, the greater the value which he attributes to crime. His conscience is always activated by remorse; indeed, the remorse seems to provide the energy for his crimes. The debauched libertine does not seek to commit actions which have been rendered indifferent by perpetual motion, as the atheist philosophers claim. What he seeks to commit is evil; the pursuit of evil will be essential to the extension of his sphere of enjoyment: "What animates us is not the object of libertinage, but rather the idea of evil." As a result, the object of libertinage holds no interest unless it leads to the doing of greater evil. Nor does he exclude the possibility of doing evil well; on the contrary, in that possibility he finds the whole value of crime. The conscience of the debauched Sadean keeps its claim on free will and uses its moral categories, all the while maintaining a belief in its ability to do evil. The conscience of the debauched libertine, according to Sade's description, not only appears to be in complete opposition to atheism but also has a relationship with the analysis of evil for evil's sake which we find in Saint Augustine's *Confessions*.

Such a conscience is consequently susceptible to elaborating an entire destructive theology centered about the religion of a Supreme Being of Wickedness, the only Supreme Being that Saint-Fond, the exemplar of the great libertine and debauched lord, is willing to

profess. This religion of evil is not yet ready to deny crime as the
philosophy of perpetual motion does, but prefers to admit it as an
outflow from the existence of an infernal God. Nor is it the refuta-
tion of the dogma found in the first version of *Justine,* that the innocent must be sacrificed for the salvation of the guilty. It is only
the other side of that doctrine; it exalts the necessity of injustice
existing in God. In fact, confronted with the mystery of Revelation,
the astonished reason—if it wishes to articulate the dogma in language which also conveys its sense of scandal—is obliged to substitute the material of blasphemy for the revealed matter. In that way
it gives an exact expression to the impression made by the mystery
on a reasoning faculty which has been abandoned to its own resources. From that point on, when confronted with crime and suffering, it will see in orthodoxy an attempt to legitimate the crimes
of the guilty party through a theory of expiation based on the expiatory virtue of the sufferings of the innocent. Actually, orthodoxy
attributes crime to man's freedom to sin, and attributes the expiatory virtue earned by the innocent party's suffering to the innocent
party's account. What the scandalized reason is imputing to orthodoxy is precisely what reason itself wishes to proclaim as its own
doctrine—a doctrine which, though its conclusions go in a quite
contrary direction, will have the appearance of seeking to set up
its meritorious terms on the basis of a supernatural origin for sin.
All the ills with which God afflicts man can thus be considered
as the ransom God exacts before he allows man the right to inflict
suffering and to be unlimitedly vicious. To the extent that God can
be viewed as the original guilty party who attacked man before
man could attack him, to that extent man has acquired the right
and the strength to attack his neighbor. And if this divine aggression has been of vast proportions, it has thereby legitimized for all
time the impunity of the guilty party and the sacrifice of the innocent.

> If the evils which overwhelm me from the day of my birth to the day
> of my death prove God's indifference to me, then I may very well be
> mistaken about what I call evil. What I characterize as evil where I am
> concerned is apparently a very great good where the being who has
> brought me into the world is concerned. And if I receive evil from others,
> I enjoy the right of returning it, and even the facility of delivering evil

to them first; once I become aware of this, evil becomes good for me as it is for the being who has created me in his dealings with me, and I am pleased by the evil I do to others as God is pleased by the evil he has done to me. . . .

Evil "which is a moral being and not a created being, an eternal being which existed before the world and which formed the monstrous and execrable being who created so bizarre a world," can only sustain that world through evil, can only perpetuate it for evil, and allow other creatures to exist only if they are impregnated with evil:

> This mode which is the very soul of the creator is also that of the creature who is shaped by it. It will exist even after the soul's demise. Everything has to be wicked, barbarous, inhuman—as your God is—and these are the vices which must be adopted if one wishes to please him; not that there is much hope of succeeding, since that evil which always does harm, the evil which is God's essence, could not possibly be susceptible either to love or gratitude. If this God who is the center of evil and ferocity torments man, and has Nature and other men torment him throughout his existence, what reason is there to doubt that he acts in the same way, and perhaps even involuntarily, on this wisp which survives after man and which . . . is nothing other than evil? . . . No matter what his conduct in this world may be, no man can escape this frightful fate because everything which has been brought to life in the womb of evil must return there. That is the law of the universe. Thus the hateful elements of the wicked man are absorbed into the center of the wickedness which is God in order to return and animate still other beings who will be born to similar corruption because they are the fruit of corruption.

What will happen to the good creature?

> The man you call virtuous is not good, or if he is good toward you, he certainly is not toward God, who is nothing other than evil, who desires nothing but evil, who seeks nothing but evil. The man you speak of is simply weak, and weakness is an evil. Such a man, since he is weaker than the absolutely vicious being, . . . will suffer all the more. . . . [But] the more man shall have manifested vices and failures in this world, the closer shall he come to his unchanging goal which is wickedness, and the less will he have to suffer consequently when he is reunited in the home of wickedness which I consider to be the prime matter of the world's formation.

Thus "far from denying God, as the atheist does, or of pardoning Him all his wrongs, as deists do," the conscience of the debauched libertine agrees to admit God with all his vices. The existence of evil in the world affords him the chance to blackmail God, whom he considers the eternal Guilty Party because he is the original Aggressor. To accomplish this goal, the libertine constantly has recourse to traditional moral categories as though to a pact which God has violated. Suffering becomes a promissory note drawn on God.

The libertine conscience also needs to establish an equally negative relationship with its neighbor: "I am pleased with the evil I do to others as God is pleased with the evil he does to me." The libertine's enjoyment comes from the fact of the continuous opposition between this idea and the notion of love for one's neighbor. He makes use of this opposition in establishing his theory of *pleasure through comparison*. One of the four debauchees in *The 120 Days of Sodom* says:

> Only one essential is missing from our happiness—pleasure through comparison, a pleasure which can only be born from the sight of the unhappy, and we see none of that breed here. It's at the sight of the man who isn't enjoying what I have and who is suffering that I know the charm of being able to say: I am happier than he is. Wherever men are equal and where differences do not exist, happiness will never exist; it's quite like the situation of the man who doesn't appreciate the price of good health until he has been ill.

How then are the unfortunate to be comforted?

> The pleasure which comes to me from this pleasant comparison of their state with mine would not exist if I were to comfort them. By withdrawing them from their misery, I would allow them to taste a moment of happiness which, since it draws them closer to me, would remove the whole joy of comparison. . . . In order to establish more firmly this essential difference in happiness, it would be preferable to aggravate their condition. . . .

Thus the conscience of the debauched libertine, though it turns them upside down, is content to remain with those moral categories which the atheist conscience will condemn as structures forged by the weak. But, out of their need for comparisons, the strong put their own strength on trial. By making a comparison of his condition with that of the unfortunate, the fortunate man makes a fatal identification with him. In tormenting the object of his lust in order to derive pleasure from his suffering, and by seeing in the suffering of another his own suffering, he will also see his own punishment. Saint-Fond, after having mistreated a family of poor people outrageously, supposedly has himself assailed by two men whom he has ordered to whip him. This staged whipping is carried off so well that the fear which he inspires in the weak becomes, in this exhibition of strength, his own fear: "I love to make them undergo the sort of thing which troubles and overwhelms my existence so cruelly. . . ." At this stage, his conscience remains riveted to the reality of the others; he hopes to deny that reality but only intensifies it by the love-hatred which he avows for others. The debauched man remains attached to the victim of his lust and to the individuality of that victim whose sufferings he would like to prolong "beyond the bounds of eternity—if eternity has any." The true atheist, to the degree that he really exists, attaches himself to no object; caught in Nature's perpetual motion, he obeys his impulses, looking upon others as no more than Nature's slag. The conscience of the debauched libertine cannot give up its all too human aspirations; perhaps only the stoic atheist would be capable of doing so. The libertine's conscience remains obsessed not only by his neighbor as victim, but also by death. He cannot give up the singular hope of a future and infernal life which amounts to saying that he cannot consent to the annihilation of his "sinning body" precisely because of his senseless desire to work out his fury on the same victim throughout eternity.

In this phase, his conscience none the less betrays a murky need for expiation—an expiation which, if his need could be elucidated, would have no other direction than that of self-liquidation, a freeing of the self by the self. These are the positive particulars of his conscience. The degree to which he seeks expiation is the degree to which his conscience represents one of the moments of Sade's own conscience. His need for expiation seeks satisfaction in his willingness to risk eternal damnation—in order, without doubt, to nourish the sufferings of his victim; but his willingness also implies a continued desire to share that suffering.

Saint-Fond reveals still another characteristic trait of the libertine conscience: pride in his situation, scorn for his fellow man, and, finally, a hatred, mixed with fear, of "that vile low life known as the people." All the elements of this haughty attitude go hand in glove with the exercise of humiliating debaucheries, most of which are planned to deliver a shock to popular morality: "Only minds organized like ours know how well the humiliation imposed by certain wanton acts serves as pride's nourishment." In effect, what the popular or, better, the bourgeois mentality would be incapable either of admitting or of understanding is that those who are supposed to be the guardians of the social order should, by their voluntary degradation, challenge that order and, in so doing, overturn all social values. But in this humiliation—even though it is only a fiction for the Sadean libertine—there is also manifest a desire for voluntary debasement and, in that need, an indication of the libertine's belief that his superior social position gives him special rights. Chief among these rights is his right to revise the notion of what man is. It is an *experimental right,* one which could not be extended to the common run of mortals without danger. It is precisely the exercise of this *right to conduct forbidden experiments* which, born from the libertine conscience, will form one of the fundamental commitments of the Sadean conscience.

Sade's materialistic atheism, when expressed in works published a decade after the *Dialogue between a Priest and a Dying Man,* has lost all the serenity characteristic of that pamphlet. The materialists and Encyclopedists, who were Sade's contemporaries, when they admit matter considered as perpetual motion to the role of the universal agent which excludes any need for God's existence, imply that knowledge of the laws governing this matter may allow for a better individual and social morality, as well as an unlimited rational exploitation of Nature by man. Still, the arguments of La Mettrie, Helvétius, and Holbach undergo an unexpected development when they come into contact with Sadean thought. For Sade *the substitution of Nature in a state of perpetual motion* for God signifies, not the arrival of a happier era for humanity, but only the beginning of tragedy—the tragedy being man's open and conscious acceptance of the change. Here we can detect the Nietzschean theme which opposes to the sufferings of the innocent a consciousness which agrees to endure its guilt because the guilt is the price of feeling alive. This is the hidden sense of the atheism which differentiates Sade so clearly from his contemporaries. To admit matter considered as perpetual motion as the one and only universal agent is equivalent to agreeing to live as an individual in a state of perpetual motion.

> As soon as a body appears to have lost motion by its passage from the state of life to what is improperly called death, it tends, from that very moment, toward dissolution; yet dissolution is a very great state of motion. There is, therefore, no moment when the body of the animal is at rest; it never dies; but because it no longer exists for us, we believe that it no longer exists at all. Bodies are transmuted . . . metamorphosed, but they are never inert. Inertia is absolutely impossible for matter whether matter is organized or not. Weigh these truths carefully and you will see where they lead and what a twist they give to human morality.

Once arrived at this observation, finding himself on the threshold of the unknown, his thought turning back on itself, he withdraws still further, scandalized by the sheer inevitability of his conclusions. Then he takes hold of himself and accepts his discoveries. As a result, the atheistic and materialistic speeches of some of his characters strike us as just so many moments in his thought's effort to get away from moral categories; this is what gives the speeches their quite special dramatic flavor. Matter, which is perpetually in motion and which trembles with pleasure without being able to obtain any pleasure on this side of destruction or dissolution, seems to be neither blind nor without will. Isn't there some purpose in this universal agent?

We become the public at a strange spectacle where Sade insults Nature as he used to insult God; he discovers in Nature the traits of that God who created the greatest number of men with the aim of making them run the risk of eternal tortures "even though it would have conformed more with goodness and with reason and justice to create only stones and plants rather than to shape men whose conduct could only bring endless chastisements." But what a frightful state Nature puts us in,

> since disgust with life becomes so strong in the soul that there is not a single man who would want to live again, even if such an offer were made on the day of his death . . . yes, I abhor Nature; and I detest her because I know her well. Aware of her frightful secrets, I have fallen back on myself and I have felt . . . I have experienced a kind of pleasure in copying her foul deeds. What a contemptible and odious being to make me see

the daylight only in order to have me find pleasure in everything that does harm to my fellow men. *Eh quoi!* I had hardly been born . . . I had hardly quit my cradle when she drew me toward the very horrors which are her delight! This goes beyond corruption . . . it is an inclination, a penchant. Her barbarous hand can only nourish evil; evil is her entertainment. Should I love such a mother? No; but I will imitate her, all the while detesting her. I shall copy her, as she wishes, but I shall curse her unceasingly. . . .

These are the words of the chemist, Almani, a character whose psychology reflects marvelously well one of the positions set forth in Sade's thought. Like the debauched libertine, Almani is still evolving within the sphere of moral categories. Evil strikes him as being Nature's unique element, as it was the unique element of the God who was *absent* to the debauched libertine. And this criminal chemist also believes that the solution to the problem of evil is to be evil. Sade's thought here offers a further attitude of purely human revolt, a revolt which has no hope other than to remain revolt. The reproach directed against Nature, even more than the reproach directed against God, is clearly destined to remain without answer and even without any psychic benefit, since it is addressed to a situation whose very corruption excludes any idea of justification. The atheist mind which launched the anathema against Nature, had wanted its effort to render absurd the reproach which he cannot repress and which escapes from him in spite of himself. His conscience, though it accepts Nature as the supreme instance, has not yet given up the mechanism of moral categories which, in his struggle against God, has been found to be useful and necessary. In God his conscience found vengeance. But once God has been rejected, his maneuver is undone by the discovery of perpetual motion. Since the notion of movement absorbs all idea of annihilation that goes beyond a simple modification of matter's forms, man can no longer reply by outrage to what he considers Nature's outrage; man feels he is unavenged.

We see another factor developing in Almani's statement. Its effect is to show us that evil appears in his speech only as a simple term adequate for translating the effect of the natural dynamism with which the scientist's mind hopes to identify itself. What we see in Almani's resolve to copy the "foul deeds" of Nature is an effort at reconciliation with universal order or, better, with universal disorder. As his indignation expresses its astonishment, curiosity and the desire to know become manifest; the mind tends more and more toward considering itself as an integral part of Nature, which has now become the domain of its investigations. If mind discovers in natural phenomena, not only blind and necessary laws, but also its own purpose—and thereby a coincidence of its purpose with those natural phenomena—then those phenomena will belong to it as so many suggestions which mind must bring into reality.

"Punishments are always proportionate to the crime, and crimes are always proportionate to the amount of information possessed by the guilty party: the Flood presupposes extraordinary crimes, and those crimes presuppose that we possess information infinitely greater than what we really have." These are Joseph de Maistre's comments on original sin. What I should like to emphasize here for later use is the idea of a crime-information relationship, a notion strikingly represented in Sade's thought and even more strikingly in that of certain of his heroes. If knowledge ends by becoming a crime, what we call crime must contain the key to knowledge. As a result, it is only by extending the sphere of crime further and further that mind, reaching those *extraordinary crimes,* will recover its lost knowledge—that knowledge which is infinitely greater than what we have.

Possessed by such dispositions, Sade will push materialistic atheism to a point where it will be invested with the form of a truly transcendental fatalism. We see an example of this in the *System of Nature* set forth by the Pope in his long discussion with Juliette. Here Sade's thought determinedly gets away from its human condition in order to attempt integration with a mythical cosmogony—the only chance it has, apparently, of getting away from the trial where it stands as much accused as it was at the beginning of its efforts. In vain Sade seeks a judge who will acquit him, and does this even though he has withdrawn the judge's competence in the realm of human morality.

Sade first of all admits of the existence of an original and eternal Nature who exists outside the realm of the three kingdoms of species and of creatures [the animal, vegetable, and mineral]. "Were Nature to find herself subject to other laws, the creatures

who are the result of her present laws would no longer exist."
Nature would still exist, though under different laws. "Creatures,
neither beautiful nor good nor valuable," are the result only of
blind laws. Nature creates man in spite of herself; she creates laws
specially applicable to man and, from that point on, she has no
further control over him. At the beginning of the Pope's speech,
this Nature is seen as being entirely distinct from man's nature; but
though man is no longer dependent on this original Nature, he still
cannot escape from the laws which are properly his: the laws of
self-preservation and procreation. These laws, moreover, are in no
way necessary to Nature, and this is the first indication of his ir-
relevance within the core of the universe. He can quadruple his
species or annihilate it completely without the universe's feeling the
slightest change. Here Sade sees Nature becoming aware of the
competitor her own movement has raised up:

> If man multiplies his species, he is right according to his own lights; if
> he destroys his species, he is, by the same lights, wrong; but in Nature's
> eyes all this is changed. If he multiplies, he is wrong because he takes
> away from Nature the honor of a new phenomenon, since the result of
> the laws which govern him is necessarily new creatures. If those who
> have been issued forth do not propagate, Nature will issue forth new
> ones and will enjoy a faculty she no longer has. . . .

In multiplying, man, since he follows a law inherent only to him,
does decided harm to the natural phenomena which are within
Nature's capacity. Foreseeing the conflict, Sade modifies his terminology to render it more accurate for a description of the process
he wishes to dramatize: "If creatures destroy themselves, they are
right as far as Nature is concerned, for they then cease to make
use of a received faculty, but not of an imposed law, and commit
Nature to the necessity of developing one of her most beautiful
faculties. . . ."

   Multiplication of the species is no longer considered to be a
law which the creature cannot get away from; it is only a faculty
which competes with Nature's original faculty. More and more, as
the speech gets more deeply into its description of the conflict,
Nature, first admitted as a force obeying blind laws, reveals herself
as having purpose: she is *creative evolution*. Sade says openly that
man, in propagating or by not destroying himself, binds Nature to

the secondary laws of the species and deprives her of her greatest potential. Nature, if she thereby finds herself the first slave to her own laws, seems only more aware of it and manifests with even greater impetuousness the desire to break the chains of her laws:

> Doesn't she show us to what extent our multiplication disturbs her . . . how much she would like once more to escape by destroying our pro-creative ability . . . doesn't she prove this to us by the afflictions with which she ceaselessly overwhelms us, by the divisions and dissensions she sows in our midst . . . by this tendency toward murder with which she inspires us at every instant. . . . Consequently, those murders which our laws punish so rigorously, those murders which we assume to be the greatest outrage which one can do to Nature, not only, as you can see, do her no wrong but cannot do her wrong; rather they become useful to her outlook, since we see her imitating them so often and since it is certain that she does so only because she hopes for the total annihilation of the creatures she has issued forth in order the better to enjoy her faculty of creating new ones. The greatest scoundrel on earth, the abominable and ferocious and barbarous murderer is thus only the organ of her laws . . . only the motive power of her wishes, and the surest agent of her caprices.

In these pages we see the dimensions of the path which Sadean man has traversed from his theology of a Being supreme in its wickedness to this conception of Nature. We saw him at first accepting the existence of God in order to declare God guilty and to take advantage of God's everlasting guilt; later we saw him confusing this God with a no less ferocious Nature, but still keeping himself on the side of moral categories. But the satanization of Nature was only a preparation for the liquidation of moral categories. The conception of a Nature which aspires to recapture her highest potential signifies in effect the dehumanization of Sade's thought—a dehumanization which now takes on the form of a singular metaphysics. If Sade, in contradistinction to what he habitually affirms, now goes so far as to consider man entirely distinct from Nature, it is primarily in order to emphasize better a profound lack of harmony between the notion of the human being and the notion of the universe. Eager to reclaim his own rights, he is also eager to explain that the extent of Nature's efforts must be measured in direct proportion to that lack of harmony. In Sade's attempt we might also see his will to separate himself from man by imposing on himself the categorical imperative of a cosmic situation which demands the annihilation of all that is human. Without doubt, what Sade is trying to do is declare his separation from a Nature which is the slave of her own laws—and to do so without Nature's knowing about it. But though Nature, as it is said elsewhere in the *System* of Pope Pius VI, uses this means to recover her powers, her work in making populations perish from time to time from illness, cataclysms, wars, and discord, or from crimes of scoundrels, actually works only to the profit of that secondary nature of the three kingdoms which are ruled by the laws of a perpetual metempsychosis. Even were she to send out great criminals or great plagues capable of annihilating the three kingdoms, she would only commit another impotent act. To bring about their disappearance, Nature would have to destroy herself totally, and she does not have that kind of mastery.

> Thus the scoundrel's murders not only help Nature attain goals she would otherwise never fulfill but also aid the laws which the kingdoms received along with their initial impetus. I say at their first impetus in order to facilitate understanding of my system; since there was really no creation, and since Nature is eternal, the impetus is given perpetually and lasts as long as there are beings. The impetus would end when there were no more creatures, and at that point would favor other impetuses which would be those desired by Nature; but Nature will only arrive at that point when there is a total destruction of the goal toward which crimes tend. The result of this situation is that a criminal who might be able to overwhelm the three kingdoms all at once by annihilating them and their productive faculties would be the individual who had best served Nature. . . .

A too perfect harmony would have even more drawbacks than disorder; if war, discord, and crimes were to be banished from the earth, the mind of the three kingdoms, turned to the greatest violence, would then destroy all the other laws of Nature.

> The heavenly bodies would all stop, the influences would be suspended because of the unbalancing dominion of one of them; there would no longer be either the force of gravity or of motion. Thus it is that the crimes of men, disturbing the power of the three kingdoms, prevent that power from arriving at a point of dominance and maintain that perfect equilibrium in the universe which Horace called *rerum concordia discors*. Crime is therefore necessary to the world; and the most useful crimes are those which create the greatest disturbance: a refusal to propagate

> and destruction . . . these are examples of crimes essential to Nature. . . .
> [Yet] enough crimes will never be committed on this earth to satiate
> Nature's burning thirst for them.

Sade soars directly into myth. The philosophy of his century no
longer suffices once it becomes a question of resolving the problem
raised by cruelty. As we have just seen, he would like to *integrate*
cruelty into a universal system where it would be brought to its
pure state by recovering its cosmic function. Henceforth, passions
—from the *simple* passions to the *complex* ones—have a trans-
scendental significance : if man believes he is satisfying himself in
being obedient to them, he is in reality only satisfying an aspiration
which goes beyond his person.

> That murderer believes he is destroying; he thinks that he is absorbing.
> This is sometimes the starting point of his remorse. Let us bring him
> complete tranquillity on that score; and if the system which I have just
> developed is not yet within his grasp, let us prove to him by facts visible
> to his eye that he has not even the honor of destroying, that the annihila-
> tion of which he boasts when he is healthy and which causes him to
> tremble when he is ill, is thoroughly null, and that it is impossible to
> achieve any success in his enterprise.

Let us for a moment compare the principle of life and death, which
will determine Sade's new position on the problem of destruction,
with Freud's death instinct. Freud, opposing this instinct to that of
Eros—the life instinct—uses the two notions as the basis for his
ontological theory. While Freud only envisages life at the organic
level, Sade—much more the metaphysician despite appearances to
the contrary—admits of no difference between life at the organic
and inorganic level; he detaches himself from all considerations
which relate to the species and to the social milieu in order to offer
a single principle :

> The principle of life in all beings is no other than the death principle;
> we receive them both and nourish them both at the same time. At that
> moment we call death, everything appears to dissolve; we believe this
> because of the excessive difference which is then visible in this portion
> of matter which no longer seems alive. But this death is only imaginary;
> it exists only figuratively and has no reality. Matter, deprived of the
> more subtle portion of matter which endowed it with motion, is not
> thereby destroyed; all it does is change form, become corrupt, and that is
> already a proof of the motion it conserves. It nourishes the earth, fertilizes

it, and helps in the regeneration of the other kingdoms as well as in its own. There is, in the end, no difference between the first life we receive and this second life we call death; for the first is made from the matter formed in the woman's womb while the second follows the same process: matter is renovated and reorganized in the earth's entrails. . . . The original creation is an example of this: these laws produce their first progeny through a process of exhaustion; they produce other progeny only through destruction. In the first instance, matter is corrupted; in the second, it is putrefied. In both processes we see the only causes of this immensity of successive creations; they are nothing but the initial principles of exhaustion and annihilation.

Corruption, putrefaction, dissolution, exhaustion, and annihilation: these are aspects of life's phenomena which will have a meaning for Sade that is as moral as it is physical. Only motion is real; creatures are nothing but motion's changing phases. There is a temptation to make a very cautious comparison between this conception of perpetual motion and the Hindu doctrine of samsara. Nature's aspiration to escape from herself in order to recover an unconditioned state would seem to be a dream much like that proposed by the notion of Nirvana—at least to the extent that a Western man has a capacity for such dreams. Sade, rather than setting off on the path which Schopenhauer searched for, thrashes out the one Nietzsche was to follow: the acceptance of samsara, the *eternal return of the same thing*.

Sadean man—having accepted the notion of a Nature which is no more shrewd in wickedness than the Supreme Being, no more voracious than the Minotaur, but rather enslaved from the start by her own laws and the first among the universe's victims—will arrive at a point where he considers himself a microcosm of Nature, suffering, like Nature, from his own activity. That activity, rather than allowing Nature to achieve her highest potential, allows her only to create, to destroy, to create anew, along with her creatures, in a cycle which proves her impotence. The Pope's *System* shows us two competing forces: Nature's aspiration to recover her highest potential, and the principle of the life and death of the three kingdoms which is the principle of perpetual motion bringing about successive creations. In reality, the phenomena are the same. Perpetual motion is blind, but the aspiration to escape from the *laws of this motion* by destruction and crime does no more than show our awareness of motion's role. Sadean man will discover his own conflict in this dualism and perhaps catch glimpses of a final solution. The problem of the cyclic creation and destruction posed by Nature is not much different from the problem of the reality of others as it appears to his conscience. Just as Nature creates obstacles for herself by her will to create, Sadean man creates his neighbor out of a will to create himself. He seems to do this out of a need to destroy the other. Yet he had once aspired to a break with this necessity; through his aspiration toward innocence he had admitted the existence of others and given them reality. Still he remained saddled with the necessity of destroying; and since he wished to prolong the existence of others, he became guilty at that very moment because he had decided to prolong the others' existence only in order to destroy them. Like Nature, which always and simultaneously aspires to and renounces its highest potential, Sadean man faces the question of whether he can renounce others and be prepared to destroy.

If comparison with the unfortunate—a comparison which remains indispensable if the libertine is to know happiness—presupposes the existence of his neighbor, the first step to be taken in the direction of a renaturalization of cruelty will be to deny the reality of his neighbor and to rid the notion of neighbor of its meaning. In implying the neighbor's existence, the pleasure of comparison implies evil. Love of neighbor, the chimera which haunted Sade, is converted by the libertine conscience into a love-hatred of the neighbor. Here the libertine makes a mistake, for love-hatred of his neighbor, while it helps liquidate the reality of the other, liquidates his own reality.

How can Sadean man ever give up his object, which is the other, and accept destruction in all its purity, as he must do if he is faithful to his idea of a Nature freed from the need of creating? To do so, he must renounce, not just the other, but also his individual condition as a self.

In apparently solipsistic terms, a quantity of statements made by Sade's characters implies a doctrine whose conclusions are thoroughly opposed. Under the guise of a *Nature aspiring to its highest potential,* the doctrine takes absolute and sovereign desire as its principle. But in the name of this principle, it establishes between the self and the other a negative reciprocity:

> The false ideas which we have of the creatures who surround us are still the source of an infinite number of judgments whose moral basis is erroneous. We forge chimerical duties for ourselves where our relations with these creatures are concerned, simply because they think they have similar duties toward us. If we have the strength to renounce all that we expect from others, our duties toward them will be immediately annihilated. What, after all, are all the earth's creatures when measured against a single one of our desires? And by what right should I deprive myself of the least of my desires in order to please a creature who is nothing to me and who holds no interest whatsoever for me? . . .

Once the other is nothing, not only am I no longer anything for him, but I am nothing where my own conscience is concerned, and it makes little difference whether the conscience is still mine. For if I break with the other on the moral level, I shall also have broken, on the level of existence, with what I properly am. At any moment I can fall to the mercy of the other who will offer me the same sort of statement as my own: Let us have the strength to renounce all that we expect from others. The wager is pragmatic. Yet, even before this kind of statement is made, the reflective process which leads to it has gone much further in its investigations.

The moral nihilism which tends to suppress awareness of oneself and the other on the level of acts, but which implies no fewer contradictions on Sade's part, appears here as the last consequence of his atheism. In effect Sade could not limit himself to denying the existence of a personal God, the principle of a self who is responsible and who is the guarantor of Sade's own selfhood and privacy; he must also attack him. Just as we saw him attacking the principle of the conservation and propagation of the species, we see him now making an issue of the normative principle of individuation in order to give free scope to the erosive forces he has described: the perversions and abnormalities which indicate the emergence within the individual of a sensitive polymorphism by which conscious individuation has been accomplished within individuals. But far from being satisfied with describing those abnormalities, he lends them the eloquence of his spokesmen who refute the existence of a God, guarantor of the norms, in order to plead, in the language of those very norms, the cause of the abnormalities they bear. Now the supposed abnormalities are abnormalities only to the degree that they are expressed in this language—the language of a conscience which is unable to take account of their positive content, that is, of the positive polymorphism which, in a negative manner and in accordance with Sade's rationalistic terminology, remains tributary. Here we are touching on the singular relationship between Sade and reason, on the constant interaction between the abnormal and thought, and on the contradiction between reason's effort to enunciate universals even as it pleads—and in pleading offers an extreme example of reason reduced exclusively to its own terms—the very special cause of abnormality. But we are at the same time touching on the adventure of a conscience and are seeing its misunderstandings and its snares once it begins to mediate on the meaning of those forces which are hostile to individuation. What it does is invert those forces so that they may be transformed into what the agent most needs in order to give credibility to his speech. Sade elucidates this misunderstanding without really resolving it; and, through his spokesmen, he disguises the snares it contains and thus provides the Sadean conscience with some elasticity.

The dose of cruelty with which Nature has more or less furnished each individual is no more than the other side of desire with which everyone identifies himself, as though he were its only agent, in the moment of initial awareness of the self. For at that point the impulse to cruelty endangers him with destruction just as he endangers others.

The man who asks: what are all the earth's creatures when measured against the least of my desires? is already the victim of the misunderstanding, the plaything of an impulse which raises questions about itself. He is individuated but he resents his individuation. The impulse of desire can lend its absolute character to the individual who, as his part of the bargain, lends his language to desire which has no language. Language borrows desire's violence because violence is scarce in the individual who suffers as much from its lack as he would like to see the other suffer. The result is that he turns against the other the challenge which had been directed against him: *Let us have the strength to renounce what we expect from others*. The formula permits a rupture which compensates his rhetorical solipsism by bringing back into question his awareness of himself.

With this as his point of departure, Sade attempts to find an outlet for the necessity to destroy by a negation of destruction; his concept of a *Nature who destroys her own works* now identifies destruction with the purity of desire. This is the proposal contained in his theory of apathy whose therapeutic value is in its capacity to provoke the renunciation of the other's reality, but as a consequence, of his own reality too.

The practice of apathy, as it is suggested by Sade's characters, presupposed that what we call *soul, conscience, sensitivity, heart,* are only miscellaneous structures brought about by a concentration of the same driving forces. Under pressure from the world of others, these forces can transform the faculties into intimidating influences; but just as readily, when under pressure from our own inner drives, they can become subversive influences; in either instance, their reaction is immediate. What remains constant is the fact that our own inner forces intimidate us at the very moment that they make insurgents out of us.

> Blot out your soul . . . try to find pleasure in everything that alarms your heart; arrive quickly . . . at the perfection of this brand of stoicism; in apathy you will discover a whole host of new pleasures which are delectable in a way quite different from those you think are found in the source of your fatal sensitivity. On the basis of my errors, I have established principles; since that time, I have known felicity.

How does this intimidating insurrection, or this insurrectional intimidation, work its way in us? By images which, seen before we act, incite us either to act or to suffer acts, and also by images of acts which, already committed, come back to us and rekindle the conscience; the conscience they rekindle is, of course, that faculty as it has been reconstructed by dormant drives:

> On one side there is the impossibility of reparations, and on the other the impossibility of figuring out which we should have the greater repentance for. Conscience grows dizzy and is so silent as to make us capable of extending crime beyond the limits of life. This condition indicates that conscience has a very special quality when compared with the other moods of the soul: it can annihilate itself because its operations have been amplified.

Yet elsewhere Sade observes that the same is true of sensitivity: "Any extension of it leads to its annihilation." That observation confirms him in his belief that the same drives are at work in both structures, working either to intimidate or to subvert. Thus our awareness of ourself and of others is the most fragile and the most transparent of functions. As soon as our impulses intimidate us by creating fear or remorse, either on the basis of images of actions performed or actions still to be undertaken, we must substitute acts of any kind each time the images seem on the verge of becoming substitutes for acts or a hindrance to our performing them. Thus Juliette is encouraged

> . . . to do in cold blood the same things which, done in frenzy, are capable of making us remorseful. By doing this we deal from strength each time virtue shows her head again, and this habit of molesting her in a positive way, at the moment when a certain calm in the senses seems to make her reappearance possible and desirable, is one of the surest ways of annihilating her forever. Use this secret, it is infallible; as soon as a moment of calm produces virtue in the guise of remorse—and that is always the guise she uses in order to recapture us—as soon as that happens, immediately do the thing you were thinking about with regret. . . .

How can this practice of apathy become a viable method for the achievement of "voluptuous toughness"? Nothing would seem more contradictory in Sade than this break with others when the result of the abolition of our duties toward others and their consequent exclusion from our sensitivity is translated clearly and constantly by acts which, because of their violence, need the other—acts which by their very nature re-establish the reality of the other and of myself.

If the other is no longer anything for me, and if I am nothing for the other, how can these acts be performed since, in effect, they would turn out to be the acts of a nothing on a nothing?

In order that this nothing never again be filled by my reality and the reality of the other, through the presence either of enjoyment or of remorse, I must disappear in an endless reiteration of acts which I run the danger of regretting because, when they are suspended, the reality of the other imposes itself on me once again. I also run the risk of overestimating them because of the enjoyment they bring me. The risk is there once I take credit for that enjoyment or that regret, or once I give credit for it to the other who may be its source.

Saint-Fond, the perfect type of the perverse libertine who has not got beyond the stage of negative feeling for his fellow men, fails in his fidelity to this necessity by allowing his victim as much reality as he allows himself. In effect, his conscience is intimidated by its own impulses; only this can explain his wish to pursue his victim—always the same victim—throughout eternity. His self-awareness functions in terms of the awareness he continues to have of his victim's self-awareness in moments of suffering, a self-awareness which makes the victim an accomplice in the delights of the torturer.

What is the purpose behind this reiteration of similar acts which is dictated by the moral attitude of apathy? Sade clearly understood the difficulty even in those moments when he was unable to resolve the dilemma: the enjoyment which negative contact with the other procures for me should be anticipated quite as much as remorse. Remorse here is only the other side of enjoyment, and the two are only different forms of behavior which have their sources in the same drives. Henceforth acts should not be informed by that enjoyment which is procured by the particular qualities of a single "victim," but only by the negation of the object which provokes such acts. And in order that this reiteration may validate a negation of destruction itself—to a point where it is emptied of all content—the number of reiterated acts and the quantity of sacrificed objects become of capital importance. Quantity depreciates the value of objects; quantity undermines my reality and that of the other. Thus the moral principle of apathy, which provokes the greatest disturbance in the drives, tries to create a coincidence of the disturbance with an equally strong wariness designed to guarantee the purity of the disturbance. If the habit of apathy is to render the individual capable of doing in cold blood acts which would have brought remorse when done in a moment of frenzy, a similar process could be found for vice; with the result that virtue would never have a chance to make us remorseful. "In virtue's name you will no longer conceive of repenting, because you will have grown accustomed to doing evil in answer to virtue's reappearance, and in order to do evil no longer you would prevent her from ever appearing...."

Could this be the solution to the dialectical drama visible in the Sadean conscience? The answer depends on an answer to a more difficult question: Can the conscience of Sadean man accept any solution? To get beyond the notion of evil, which is always conditioned by the degree of reality he accords to others, we have seen Sadean man carry the exaltation of the ego to its height; yet the height of this exaltation was supposed to be found in apathy where the ego abolished itself simultaneously with the other, where enjoyment disassociated itself from destruction, and where destruction identified itself with desire in its pure form. In this way, the Sadean conscience reproduces in its own operations the perpetual motion of nature which creates but which, in creating, sets up obstacles for herself. The only way she recovers her liberty, even momentarily, is by destroying her own works.

—TRANSLATED BY JOSEPH H. McMAHON

# The Marquis de Sade

# Part Two

# from Les Crimes de l'Amour

# Reflections on the Novel (1800)

*In the Year VIII of the Republic (1800), Sade published a four-volume work which he entitled* Les Crimes de l'Amour *and for which he wrote an introductory text,* Idée sur les romans. *This discursive essay contains much which, a hundred and fifty years later, may seem naive and, considering its author, a trifle conventional. It is none the less a remarkable essay, as Edmund Wilson has rightfully noted, "in which he [Sade] shows a comprehensive knowledge of the history of European fiction from the Greek romances through Boccaccio, Cervantes, Mme. de La Fayette, Marivaux, Richardson and Fielding, to Monk Lewis and Mrs. Radcliffe (who figures as 'Radgliffe'). He lays down some excellent principles, all of which he has more or less violated: that the novelist must not depart from what is probable; that he must not interrupt his story with incidents that are either too frequent or not properly related to the subject; that it should never be the author who moralizes but always one of the characters in his novel, and that he ought not even then to be made to except when he is forced to by circumstances."*[1]

*Sade came to writing relatively late in life. Although the recent discovery of his miscellaneous works (Œuvres diverses) reveals that his initial literary efforts date from a period much earlier than was originally thought, these*

[1] Edmund Wilson: *The Bit Between My Teeth, A Literary Chronicle of 1950–1965.* New York, Farrar, Straus and Giroux, 1965, p. 206.

*are none the less the works of a dilettante, and it is not
unreasonable to assume that Sade, had he remained a free
man throughout his life, might never have become a writer.
Prison fettered the libertine; it made the writer.*

*Sade scholars Maurice Heine and Gilbert Lely both
date the birth of Sade the writer as approximately 1780,
two years after his incarceration in cell No. 6 of the
Vincennes prison. "It was around 1780, in the course of his
fortieth year, that the prisoner of the Royal dungeons began his gigantic labor as a writer. As Maurice Heine notes,
Sade found salvation in his writing, which he came to look
upon as the purpose of his life."[2]*

*Sade was not a man of half measures, and when he
turned to writing he devoted himself to it with the same
total dedication he had earlier shown in his pursuit of libertine pleasures. His letters from prison abound with requests
for and judgments upon literary and philosophical works:
"To refuse me Jean-Jacques' Confessions, now there's an
excellent thing, above all after having sent me Lucretius
and the dialogues of Voltaire; that demonstrates great
judiciousness, profound discernment in your spiritual guides.
Alas, they do me much honor in reckoning that the writings
of a deist can be dangerous reading for me; would that I
were still at that stage." Thus Sade to his wife, in 1783.[3]
When the Bastille was stormed in 1789 and Sade's former
cell sacked—he had been removed ten days before to the
Charenton Asylum at the request of the Bastille authorities, who accused him of inciting the populace to revolt[4]—
the rioters discovered, and looted, Sade's prison library of
some six hundred volumes, "several of which were of great*

---

[2] Gilbert Lely: *La Vie du Marquis de Sade,* Vol. II. Paris, Librairie
Gallimard, 1957, p. 277.

[3] See The Marquis de Sade: *The Complete Justine, Philosophy in the
Bedroom, and Other Writings.* New York, Grove Press, 1965, p. 133.

[4] The Bastille logbook, in its entry for July 2, 1789, notes: "The Count
de Sade shouted several times from the window of the Bastille that the
prisoners were being slaughtered and that the people should come to
liberate them." (*Ibid.,* p. 100.)

92

value."[5] *Having dedicated himself to literature, Sade, in prison, became a voracious reader and student of literatures past and present. His "Reflections on the Novel" reveals the extent of his reading, and if his judgments are not invariably accurate, his literary perception is often acute, as is demonstrated by his preference for the English novelists Fielding and Richardson as opposed to the "fastidious portraits of love's sighs" and the "tedious bedside conversations" of the French novelists of the period.*

*Notable by its absence from Sade's essay on fiction is any mention of Choderlos de Laclos'* Les Liaisons dangereuses. *It cannot be supposed that Sade was unfamiliar with that novel, given the immense success it had enjoyed following its publication in 1782—a success none of Sade's work would ever attain, at least during the author's lifetime. Gilbert Lely has uncovered evidence to show that Sade and Laclos spent seven months together in the same prison— La maison de Santé at Picpus—from the end of March to the middle of October, 1794. From Sade's subsequent silence concerning Laclos' novel, Lely suggests that the two men may have quarreled during their term in Picpus together. The more likely hypothesis is that Sade was, purely and simply, jealous of Laclos—jealous perhaps of his popular success, but doubtless even more because he must have realized (his essay on the novel is too astute for him not to have known it) that Laclos had written a veritable masterpiece of cynicism and evil. Sade's notebooks contain a* Plan d'un roman en lettres *("Outline for an epistolary novel") which is suspiciously reminiscent of* Les Liaisons dangereuses *and lends credence to the theory that Sade regarded Laclos as a rival who had, in Lely's words, "encroached upon a domain he deemed to be exclusively his own."*

*"Reflections on the Novel" also provides evidence of another literary rivalry, that between Sade and Restif de la Bretonne, a writer Sade loathed. The sentiment was mutual.*

---

[5] Lely, *op. cit.*, Vol. II, p. 349.

It was Restif who first referred to Sade as the "monster-author" and who, as an act of revenge against the popularity of Justine, wrote a novel entitled Anti-Justine. Unlike Sade's book, noted Restif, his was one "which wives can read to their husbands," a work which will make the reader "adore women, cherish them, and loathe all the more the vivisector who has just been released from the Bastille." Sade in turn assailed Restif for being a lowly hack who wrote with such speed, in the base pursuit of money, that he had to keep a printing press at the head of his bed.

On 30 Vendémiaire, Year IX (the 22nd of October, 1800), the critic Villeterque published a review of Les Crimes de l'Amour in which he violently attacked the stories themselves, the essay which served as an introduction, and the author, whom he implicitly accused of being the author of the anonymously published Justine. Sade was not one to allow such an indictment or such innuendos to go unanswered; his reply appeared in the form of a pamphlet issued by Sade's publisher Massé in the Year XI (1803). Because of their historical and intrinsic interest, and because the Villeterque-Sade dialogue forms a logical appendix to the essay itself, we have included both in the present volume.

"A note on the cover of the twentieth and final notebook of his autograph manuscript," writes Maurice Heine, "informs us that Sade's work in the form of the novella and short story consists of fifty tales. Sixteen of these, among the shorter or at least the more anecdotal, were intended to be classed as Historiettes and included as part of a two- or three-volume collection of essays entitled Le Portefeuille d'un homme de lettres. Thirty more, so arranged that the somber stories would alternate with the gay, were destined to comprise a four-volume work, with a preface by the author, entitled Contes et Fabliaux du XVIIIᵉ siècle, par un troubadour provençal."[6] All this material was written in

6 Maurice Heine: Le Marquis de Sade. Paris, Librairie Gallimard, 1950, pp. 262–263. Heine relates the fate of the four remaining stories: "One (Les Filous) was reserved for possible inclusion in another work; another

the Bastille during the years 1787 and 1788, and is thus subsequent to the composition of The 120 Days of Sodom.

We find in the manuscript of the projected Contes et Fabliaux du XVIIIᵉ siècle *the following description of the work in Sade's hand:*

> This work comprises four volumes, with an engraving for each tale; these short tales are interspersed in such a manner that an adventure which is gay, and even naughty but well within the limits of modesty and decency, will follow immediately upon a serious or tragic adventure. . . .⁷

Twelve years later, in the Year VIII, Sade published his collection as Les Crimes de l'Amour *in which, abandoning his original plan to alternate the somber with the gay, he included only the "serious or tragic." An article on the work which appeared in the* Journal de Paris *on 6 Brumaire, Year IX (the 28th of October, 1800)—thus barely a week after Villeterque's attack—speculated on the reason for the change in contents. Commenting first upon the "fecundity of the author's imagination" and the "great variety of situations portrayed," the author of the unsigned review went on to observe: "He [Sade] doubtless thought that his somber hue was better suited to us now and for some time to come, since in this realm [of tragedy] reality still continues to surpass fiction."⁸*

Of the thirty stories Sade had planned to include in his Contes et Fabliaux du XVIIIᵉ siècle, *only eleven were retained in* Les Crimes de l'Amour. *One of these,* Eugénie de Franval, *has already appeared in our earlier volume of Sade's writings. In the present volume we include two others:* Florville and Courval, or The Works of Fate *and* Ernestine, A Swedish Tale. *The latter tale will be found in*

---

(Les Infortunes de la vertu) was expanded into a novel; and the two others (Séide, conte moral et philosophique and l'Epoux complaisant) were suppressed by the author."

⁷ D.-A.-F. de Sade: *Historiettes, Contes et Fabliaux/Dorci.* Paris, Jean-Jacques Pauvert, 1957.

⁸ Lely: *op. cit.,* Vol. II, p. 564.

95

*Part Four, together with the play* Oxtiern, or The Misfortunes of Libertinage, *which was adapted from it.* Florville and Courval *is rightly ranked by Lely as among the best of Sade's shorter fiction, on a par with* Eugénie de Franval. *This is the story which especially offended and incensed Villeterque, for in it Sade, relying upon coincidence —or fate—to a degree unusual even for him, renders the heroine guilty of a series of crimes as heinous as they are involuntary. Pierre Klossowski has commented judiciously on this tale:*

> To her future husband, Florville appears an honest and sincere young woman who seems bent on clarifying her strangely burdened past. . . . Not only does Monsieur de Courval not seem jealous of those who have happened to precede him in his intended wife's affections, but is, one might say, immersed in a kind of trance from which he slowly awakens. This unconsciousness has its meaning: Courval seeks happiness in conjugal life—in oblivion, actually. He too is guilty; that is the true source of his sympathy for Florville. When she completes her confession, everything seems to arrange itself: Courval, described to us at the beginning as a man who asks for nothing more than a mild, peaceful calm in wedded life, is only anxious to conclude his marriage in all haste—thanks, it would seem, to the scabrous adventures of his fiancée. It is evident that, under the cover of exceptional generosity, Courval incarnates that Sadean satisfaction derived from possessing Florville's apparently unveiled secret; but actually, Sadean suspicion is incarnated in the heroine. Florville is an enigma to herself, *quite as the human spirit is at the start of its itinerary, before being able to know itself as only God knows it. The author's demon lodges itself in Florville and proceeds to possess her until she is at last exposed to herself for what she is.*[9]

---

[9] Pierre Klossowski: *Sade mon prochain.* Paris, Editions du Seuil, 1947.

# Reflections on the Novel

We give the name "novel" to any work of imagination fashioned from the most uncommon adventures which men experience in the course of their lives.

But why is this kind of literary work called a novel?[1]

Amongst what people did the novel originate, and what are
the most famous examples that history has to offer?

And, finally, what are the rules one must follow in order to
succeed in perfecting the art of writing the novel?

These are the three questions we propose to discuss.

Let us begin with the etymology of the word. There being no
trace of this term, as it relates to this type of composition, amongst
the peoples of antiquity, we must, it would seem to me, concentrate
upon discovering how the term, which we still use today, first came
into our language.

The "Romance" language was, as we know, a mixture of Celtic
and Latin,[2] in use under the first two dynasties of our kings.[3] It is

---

[1] The English term "novel" derives from the French *nouvelle* (short story) and
the Latin *novellus,* the diminutive of *novus* (new). But Sade, in his etymological
and historical ruminations, is referring of course to the French equivalent, that is to
the term *roman.* It might have made more sense, in translating, to use the English
"romance," a cognate of the word around which Sade theorizes. But in English this
word has become too colored, and limited to a certain type of frivolous fiction. Throughout this essay, therefore, for Sade's *roman* the term "novel" has been used.—*Tr.*

[2] Actually, the various Romance languages retain in general only a few words
and expressions from the language native to each region prior to the advent of the
Latin. In French, less than a hundred words can be traced back to the Celtic.—*Tr.*

[3] That is, the Merovingian and the Carolingian.—*Tr.*

reasonable to assume that the works of the kind to which we are referring, written in this language, must have borne the same name, and the term *une romane* must have been used to describe a work in which the emphasis is upon amorous adventures, as the term *romance* was used to describe ballads or lays of the same type. All efforts to discover any other etymological origin for this word come to naught; as common sense offers no alternative, it would seem simplest to adopt the above.

Let us move on then to the second question.

Amongst what people did the novel originate, and what are the most famous examples history has to offer?

The novel is generally thought to have originated with the Greeks, from whom it passed over to the Moors and thence to the Spaniards, who subsequently transmitted it to our troubadours. And they in turn passed it on to our courtly storytellers.

Although I respect this theory of the novel's line of descent, and although there are even parts of it I subscribe to, I none the less can in no wise adopt it literally. Is it not, in fact, difficult to accept without reservation in an era when travel was so infrequent and communication so sporadic? There are customs, habits, and tastes which cannot be transmitted; inherent in all men, they are a part of man's make-up at birth. Wherever man exists, inevitable traces of these customs, habits, and tastes can be discovered.

Let there be no doubt about it: it was in the countries which first recognized gods that the novel originated; and, to be more specific, in Egypt, the cradle of all divine worship. No sooner did man begin to *suspect* the existence of immortal beings than he endowed them with both actions and words. Thereafter we find metamorphoses, fables, parables, and novels: in a word, we find works of fiction as soon as fiction seized hold of the minds of men. Thus we find fabulous works of imagination the moment it becomes a question of imaginary creatures: when whole nations, at first guided by priests, after having slaughtered each other in the name of their chimerical divinities, later take up arms for their king or their country, the homage offered to heroism counterbalances the tribute paid to superstition; not only do they then most rightly substitute these new heroes for their gods, but they also sing their warriors' praises as once they had sung the praises of heaven; they embroider upon the great feats of their lives, or, weary of relating tales about them, they create new characters who resemble them . . . who surpass them, and soon new novels appear, doubtless more probable and far more suitable for man than were those tales that extolled naught but phantoms. *Hercule,*[4] the mighty captain, having valiantly to do battle against his enemies: this is the historical hero; Hercules, destroying monsters, cleaving in twain giants: that is the god . . . the fable, and the origin of superstition; but of reasonable superstition, since its only basis is the reward for heroism, the gratitude due to the liberators of a nation, whereas the superstition that invents uncreated and never perceived beings has no other motive behind it than to provoke fear and hope, and to unsettle the mind.

Every people, therefore, has its gods, its demigods, its heroes, its true stories, and its fables; some part of it, as we have just seen, can have a solid basis in fact, as it pertains to the heroes; all the rest is pure fantasy, incredible; it is all a work of pure invention, a novel, because the gods spoke only through the medium of men who, more or less interested in this ridiculous artifice, did not fail to make up the language of phantoms, from whatever they imagined would be most likely to seduce or terrify, and, consequently, from whatever was most incredible. "'Tis common knowledge," said the scholar Huet, "that the term 'novel' was once applied to history, and that it was later applied to fiction, all of which is proof positive that the one derived from the other."

There were, therefore, novels written in every language and in every country of the world, the events and styles of which were modeled both after the customs of the country and opinions commonly held therein.

Man is prey to two weaknesses, which derive from his existence and characterize it. Wheresoever on earth he dwells, man feels the need *to pray,* and *to love:* and herein lies the basis for all novels. Man has written novels in order to portray beings whom he *implored;* he has written novels to sing the praises of those whom

---

[4] *Hercule* is a generic name, made up of two Celtic words, *Her-Coule,* which means Sir-Captain. *Hercoule* was the name given to a general in the army, and thus there were a goodly number of *Hercoules.* Mythology subsequently attributed the amazing feats of several to one. (See *Histoire des Celtes,* by Peloutier.)

he *loves.* The former, dictated by terror or hope, must have been somber, full of exaggeration, untruths, and fictions, such as those that Esdras composed during the Babylonian captivity. The latter are full of niceties and sentiments, as typified by Heliodorus' *Aethiopica,* a love story about Theagenes and Charicleia. But as man *prayed,* and as he *loved,* wheresoever he dwelled on the face of the earth, there were novels, that is, works of fiction, which at times depicted the fanciful objects of his worship, and at times those more concrete objects of his love.

One should therefore refrain from trying to trace the source of this kind of writing back to one nation in preference to another; one should be persuaded by what we have just said that all nations have more or less employed this form, depending upon the greater or lesser predilection they have had either for love or for superstition.

Let us cast a cursory glance now at those nations which have been most receptive to works of fiction, and at the works themselves and those who have written them. Let us follow the line down to our own day, in order to allow our readers to be in a position to make their own comparisons.

The earliest novelist whereof antiquity speaks is Aristeides of Miletus, but none of his work remains extant. All we know is that his prose romance was called *Milesian Tales.* A reference in the preface of *The Golden Ass* seems to indicate that Aristeides' works were licentious: "I am going to write in this same manner," says Apuleius, in the beginning of *The Golden Ass.*

Antonius Diogenes, a contemporary of Alexander, wrote in a more polished style in *The Loves of Dinias and Dercillis,* a novel full of fabrications, charms, and spells, of voyages, and of most remarkable adventures—a work that le Seurre copied in 1745, in a short, even more extraordinary work; for, not content to take his heroes through familiar lands, as had Diogenes, le Seurre at times takes them to the moon, and at times down into the bowels of hell.

Next come the loves of Rhodanes and Sinonis, written by Iamblichus of Syria; the loves of Theagenes and Charicleia which we have already mentioned; Xenophon's *Cyropaedia;* the loves of Daphnis and Chloë, by Longus; the loves of Ismene and Ismenia;

and a whole host of others, some translated, others totally forgotten today.

The Romans, more critically minded and more given to spite and malice than to love and prayer, confined themselves to a few works of satire, such as those by Petronius and Varro, which should in no wise be classed as novels.

The Gauls, more inclined to these two weaknesses, had their bards, whom we can consider as the first novelists in that part of Europe wherein we dwell today. The occupation of these bards, says Lucan, was to render in verse the immortal acts of their nation's heroes, and to sing them to the accompaniment of an instrument which resembled a lyre; very few of these works have come down to us today.

Then we have the words and deeds of Charlemagne, attributed to Archbishop Turpin of Reims, and all the tales of the Round Table—Tristram, Lancelot, Perceval—all written with a view toward immortalizing known heroes or inventing others modeled after them but who, embellished by the imagination, surpass them by the wonderment of their deeds. But what a great gulf separates these long, boring, and superstition-laden works from the Greek novels which had preceded them! What barbarity, what coarseness followed after those tasteful and pleasing works of fiction whereof the Greeks had given us the models; for though there were doubtless others before them, these are the earliest with which we are familiar today.

The troubadours were next to appear, and although we ought to class them as poets rather than as novelists, the multitude of agreeable tales in prose that they composed is none the less reason enough for us to grant them a rightful place amongst the writers of whom we are speaking. Let anyone who doubts this claim cast his eyes upon their *fabliaux*—written in the Romance language during the reign of Hugh Capet[5]—which Italy hastened to emulate.

This beautiful part of Europe, still groaning beneath the yoke of the Saracens and still far removed in time from that period when she was to become the birthplace of the Renaissance in the arts, boasted almost no novelists prior to the tenth century. They ap-

---

[5] Founder, in 978 A.D., of the Capetian dynasty, the third dynasty of French kings which ruled, through fourteen kings in direct succession, until 1328.—*Tr.*

peared more or less at the same time as did our troubadours in France, and indeed imitated them. But let us be quite candid concerning this glory: it was not the Italians who became our masters in this art, as Laharpe contends (page 242, vol. III), but, on the contrary, on our own soil in France that they received their training: 'twas at the school of our troubadours that Dante, Boccaccio, Tasso, and even to some degree Petrarch, sketched out their compositions; almost all of Boccaccio's tales can be found as well in our own *fabliaux*.

The same cannot be said for the Spanish, versed in the art of fiction by the Moors, who themselves derived it from the Greeks, having the entire body of Greek fiction translated into Arabic; they wrote delightful novels, much imitated by our writers; of which more later.

As gallantry took on a new aspect in France, the novel improved, and 'twas then, that is to say at the beginning of the previous century, that Honoré d'Urfé wrote his novel *Astrée,* which led us to prefer—and most deservedly so—his charming shepherds of the Lignon to those foolish knights of the eleventh and twelfth centuries. From that time forth, the rage to emulate seized all those whom Nature had endowed with a taste for this kind of writing. The astonishing success of *Astrée,* which was still being widely read midway through the present century, had completely captured people's fancies, and the work was widely imitated, though never improved upon. Gomberville, La Calprenède, Desmarets, and Scudéry all thought to surpass the original by substituting princes and kings for the Lignon shepherds, and they slipped back into the error which their model had managed to avoid. Scudéry's sister made the same mistake as her brother: like him, she wanted to ennoble d'Urfé's manner and style and, like her brother, she substituted boring heroes for charming shepherds. Instead of portraying, in the person of Cinna, a prince such as Herodotus had painted him, she composes an Artamène more insane than all the characters in *Astrée,* a lover who can do naught but weep from morn till night, and whose languors, instead of becoming an object of interest to us, only tax our patience. The same drawbacks in her *Clélie,* wherein she endows the Romans, whom she badly distorts, with all the absurd qualities of the models she was following, which have never been better depicted.

If I may be permitted to go back for a moment, I should like to keep the promise I made to take a cursory look at Spain.

To be sure, if knighthood had served as a source of inspiration for our novelists, to what extent had it not also influenced writers on the other side of the Pyrenees? The contents of Don Quixote's library, amusingly catalogued by Miguel Cervantes, clearly demonstrate it; but, however that may be, the renowned author of the memoirs of the greatest madman that any novelist has ever conceived most certainly has no rival worthy of the name. His immortal work, known throughout the world, translated into every language, and perforce considered the foremost novel ever written, doubtless possesses, more than any other novel, the art of storytelling, of blending agreeably the various adventures, and especially of being edifying and amusing. "This book," said Saint-Evremond, "is the only one I reread without getting bored, and the only book I should like to have written." The twelve stories by the same author, highly interesting and full of wit and refinement, definitely place this renowned Spanish novelist in the front rank; without him we might possibly not have had either Scarron's charming work or the greatest part of Lesage's.

After d'Urfé and his imitators, after the Ariadnes and the Cleopatras, the Pharamonds and the Polixandres—all those works, in short, wherein the hero, after languishing throughout nine volumes, was happy indeed to marry in the tenth—after, I say, all this hodgepodge unintelligible today, there appeared Madame de La Fayette who, albeit beguiled by the languorous tone she found in the works of her predecessors, none the less shortened them considerably. And in becoming more concise she became more interesting. It has been said that, because she was a woman (as though this sex, naturally more delicate, more given to writing novels, could not aspire in the realm of fiction to many more laurels than we), it has been claimed, I say, that Madame de La Fayette was aided a great deal, and was able to write her novels only with the help of La Rochefoucauld with what regards the reflections and of de Segrais with what regards the style; be that as it may, there is nothing more interesting than *Zayde,* nor any work more agreeably written than *La Princesse de Clèves*. Gracious and charming lady, though the graces may have held your brush, is love not sometimes allowed to guide it?

Fénelon appeared on the scene and thought to make his mark by poetically offering guidance to sovereigns who never paid him any heed. Voluptuous lover of Guyon, your soul had need to love, your mind felt the need to paint; if only you had forsaken pedantry or your pride in teaching kings how one ought to rule, we would have had from your pen more than one masterpiece, rather than a single book which no one reads any longer. The same cannot be said for you, delightful Scarron: till the end of time, your immortal novel will provoke laughter, your scenes will never grow old or out-dated. Telemachus, who had but one century to live, will perish beneath the ruins of this century which already is no more; and your actors from Le Mans, gracious and beloved child of madness, will amuse even the most serious readers, so long as men shall dwell upon the face of the earth.

Toward the end of the same century, the daughter of the cele-brated Poisson (Madame de Gomez), penned works in a manner far different from the writers of her own sex who had preceded her, but they were no less pleasant; and her *Journées amusantes,* as well as her *Cents nouvelles,* will, despite their shortcomings, always form the nucleus of the library for those who enjoy this kind of writing. Gomez understood her art, 'twould be impossible to refuse her this rightful encomium. Mademoiselle de Lussan, Mesdames de Tencin and de Graffigny, Elie de Beaumont, and Riccoboni vied with her; their writings, full of refinement and taste, are most assuredly an honor to their sex. De Graffigny's *Lettres d'une Péruvienne* will always remain a model of tenderness and sentiment, and those of Mylady Catesby, by Riccoboni, could serve eternally as a model to those who aspire to naught but grace and lightness of touch.

But let us return to the century we left, urged on by the desire to render homage to the gracious women who held sway in this kind of writing, wherefrom the men could learn most excellent lessons.

The Epicureanism of writers such as Ninon de Lenclos, Marion Delorme, the Marquise de Sévigné and the Messieurs La Fare, de Chaulieu, de Saint-Evremond—in short of all that charm-ing group which, awakening from the languors of the goddess of

Cytherea, began to come around to Buffon's opinion "that there is naught that is good in love save the physical"—soon changed the tone of the novel.

The writers who emerged thereafter sensed that earlier insipidities would no longer amuse a century perverted by the Regency, a century which had recovered from the follies of chivalry, the absurdities of religion, and the adoration of women, and which, finding it simpler to amuse or to corrupt these women than to serve them or shower fulsome praise upon them, created scenes, situations, and conversations more in keeping with the spirit of the times: they clothed cynicism and immorality in a pleasant, bantering, and sometimes even philosophical style, and at least gave pleasure if they did not edify.

Crébillon wrote *Le Sopha, Tanzaï, Les Egarements de coeur et d'esprit,* etc.—all novels which indulged vice and strayed from virtue but which, when they were offered to the public, were greeted with great success.

Marivaux, more original in his manner of portraying, and terser in style, at least offered convincing characters, captivated the heart and made his public weep. But how, with all that energy, could anyone possess a style so precious and mannered? He is proof positive that Nature never accords the novelist all the gifts required to perfect his art.

Voltaire's goal was quite different: having no other purpose in mind than to insert philosophy into his novels, he gave up everything else in exchange. And with what skill he succeeded in attaining his goal! And, despite all the criticisms, *Candide* and *Zadig* will always remain pure masterpieces!

Rousseau, to whom Nature had granted in refinement and sentiment what she had granted only in wit to Voltaire, treated the novel in another way altogether. What vigor, what energy in *La Nouvelle Héloïse!* While Momus was dictating *Candide* to Voltaire, love was etching with its flaming torch every burning page of *Julie,* and we can safely assert that this sublime book will never be bettered; may that truth cause the pen to fall from the hands of that legion of ephemeral writers who, for the past thirty years, have continued to pour out poor imitations of that immortal original; let them be made to feel that, in order to equal that work, they would have to possess a fiery soul like Rousseau's and a philosophic mind such as his—two traits Nature does not bring together in a single person more than once a century.

Athwart all that, Marmontel offered us what he called *Moral Tales,* not because he was teaching morality (as one esteemed man of letters has said), but because the tales portrayed our customs, albeit a trifle too much in the mannered style of Marivaux. What, in fact, do these tales add up to? Puerilities, written solely for women and children, and indeed 'twould be hard to conceive that they came from the same hand as *Bélisaire,* a work which in itself would be enough to assure the author's fame; did he who had written the fifteenth chapter of this book have to aspire to the petty fame of having given us these rosy-hued tales?

Finally, the English novels, the vigorous works of Richardson and Fielding, arrived to teach the French that 'tis not by portraying the fastidious languors of love or the tedious conversations of the bedchamber that one can obtain any success with the novel, but by depicting robust and manly characters who, playthings and victims of that effervescence of the heart known as love, reveal to us both its dangers and its misfortunes; only by so doing can this evolution be shown, this portrayal of passions so carefully traced in the English novels. 'Tis Richardson, 'tis Fielding, who have taught us that the profound study of man's heart—Nature's veritable labyrinth—alone can inspire the novelist, whose work must make us see man not only as he is, or as he purports to be—which is the duty of the historian—but as he is capable of being when subjected to the modifying influences of vice and the full impact of passion. Therefore we must know them all, we must employ every passion and vice, if we wish to labor in this field. From these works we also learn that 'tis not always by making virtue triumph that a writer arouses interest; that we most certainly ought to tend in that direction, insofar as it is possible, but that this rule, which exists neither in Nature nor in the works of Aristotle, is simply one that we should like all men to follow for our own sake and happiness, and is in no wise essential in the novel, nor is't even the one most likely to awaken the reader's interest. For when virtue triumphs, the world is in joint and things as they ought to be, our tears are stopped even, as it were, before they begin to flow. But if, after

severe trials and tribulations, we finally witness virtue overwhelmed by vice, our hearts are inevitably rent asunder, and the
work having moved us deeply, having, as Diderot was wont to say,
"smitten our hearts in reverse," must inevitably arouse that interest
which alone can assure the writer of his laurels.

Imagine for a moment: if the immortal Richardson, after
twelve or fifteen volumes, had *virtuously* concluded by converting
Lovelace, and by having him *peacefully* marry Clarissa, would the
reader, when the novel was thus turned round, have shed the delightful tears it now wrings from every sensitive soul?

'Tis therefore Nature that must be seized when one labors in
the field of fiction, 'tis the heart of man, the most remarkable of her
works, and in no wise virtue, because virtue, however becoming,
however necessary it may be, is yet but one of the many facets of
this amazing heart, whereof the profound study is so necessary to
the novelist, and the novel, the faithful mirror of this heart, must
perforce explore its every fold.

Learned translator of Richardson, Prévost, you to whom we
are indebted for having rendered into our language the beauties of
that renowned author, do you yourself not also deserve an equal
share of praise for your own work? And is't not only fair and right
that you are called the *French Richardson*? You alone had the
ability to hold the reader's attention for a long period by complex
and intricate fables, by always sustaining one's interest though
dividing it; you alone were sparing enough of your episodes that
interest in your main plot waxed rather than waned as they grew
more numerous and more complex. Thus that multitude of events
wherewith Laharpe reproaches you is not only the source in your
work of the most sublime effects, 'tis also what proves most clearly
both the quality of your mind and the excellence of your talent.
Finally (to add to our own opinion of Prévost what others have
thought as well), *"Les Mémoires d'un homme de qualité, Cleveland, L'Histoire d'une Grecque moderne, Le Monde moral,* and
above all *Manon Lescaut*[6] are filled with touching and terrible

---

[6] What tears one sheds upon reading this delightful work! How beautifully is
Nature portrayed therein, and how interest is not only sustained but successively
heightened! How many difficulties are overcome! Think of all the philosophers it
would take to provoke that interest in a ruined girl. Would it be too much of an

scenes which invincibly affect and involve the reader. The situations
in these works, so beautifully arranged, derive from those moments
when Nature shudders with horror," etc. And this, then, is what is
called writing a novel; these are the qualities which will assure
Prévost a posterity his rivals can never hope to attain.

Thereafter follow the writers of the middle of the present century: Dorat, as mannered as Marivaux, as cold and amoral as
Crébillon, but a more pleasing writer than either of the two with
whom we have compared him: the frivolity of his century excuses
his own, and he had the ability to depict it vividly.

Will the charming author of the *Reine de Golconde* allow me
to offer him a toast to his talent? We have rarely encountered a
more agreeable wit, and the loveliest tales of the century are not
the equal of the tale whereby you gained immortality; at once more
charming and more felicitous than Ovid, since the Hero-Saviour of
France proves, by recalling you to the bosom of your country, that
he is as much the friend of Apollo as of Mars: respond to the hope
of this great man by adding yet a few more roses to fair Aline's
breast.

D'Arnaud, a disciple of Prévost, can often claim to surpass
him; both dip their pens into the waters of the Styx, but d'Arnaud
oft tempers his upon the flanks of Elysium. Prévost, more vigorous,
never altered the tones wherewith he painted *Cleveland.*

R***[7] floods the public with his works; he needs a printing
press at the head of his bed. Fortunately, one press alone will groan
beneath the weight of his *terrible output;* his is a vile, pedestrian
style, his adventures are disgusting, inevitably taken from the lowest, meanest milieux; a gift of prolixity his sole merit, for which
only the pepper merchants are grateful to him.

Perhaps at this point we ought to analyze these new novels in
which sorcery and phantasmagoria constitute practically the entire
merit: foremost among them I would place *The Monk,* which is

exaggeration to dare suggest that this work deserves the title of our finest novel?
'Twas therein Rousseau saw that, despite imprudences and oversights, a heroine could
still manage to touch our hearts; and perhaps we would never have had *Julie* without
*Manon Lescaut.*

[7] Sade here refers to Restif de la Bretonne, whom he loathed personally as much as
he loathed his works.—*Tr.*

superior in all respects to the strange flights of Mrs. Radcliffe's brilliant imagination. But that would take us too far afield. Let us concur that this kind of fiction, whatever one may think of it, is assuredly not without merit: 'twas the inevitable result of the revolutionary shocks which all of Europe has suffered. For anyone familiar with the full range of misfortunes wherewith evildoers can beset mankind, the novel became as difficult to write as monotonous to read. There was not a man alive who had not experienced in the short span of four or five years more misfortunes than the most celebrated novelist could portray in a century. Thus, to compose works of interest, one had to call upon the aid of hell itself, and to find in the world of make-believe things wherewith one was fully familiar merely by delving into man's daily life in this age of iron. Ah! but how many disadvantages there are in this manner of writing! The author of *The Monk* has avoided them no more than has Mrs. Radcliffe. Here, there are perforce two possibilities: either one resorts increasingly to wizardry—in which case the reader's interest soon flags—or one maintains a veil of secrecy, which leads to a frightful lack of verisimilitude. Should this school of fiction produce a work excellent enough to attain its goal without foundering upon one or the other of these two reefs, then we, far from denigrating its methods, will be pleased to offer it as a model.

Before broaching our third and final question ("What are the rules one must follow in order to succeed in perfecting the art of the novel?"), we must, it would seem to me, reply to the constant objection of certain melancholy minds who, to give themselves a gloss of morality wherefrom their hearts are often far distant, persist in asking: "Of what use are novels?"

Of what use, indeed! hypocritical and perverse men, for you alone ask this ridiculous question: they are useful in portraying you as you are, proud creatures who wish to elude the painter's brush, since you fear the results, for the novel is—if 'tis possible to express oneself thuswise—the representation of secular customs, and is therefore, for the philosopher who wishes to understand man, as essential as is the knowledge of history. For the etching needle of history only depicts man when he reveals himself publicly, and then 'tis no longer he: ambition, pride cover his brow with a mask which portrays for us naught but these two passions, and not the man.

The novelist's brush, on the contrary, portrays him from within . . . seizes him when he drops this mask, and the description, which is far more interesting, is at the same time more faithful. This, then, is the usefulness of novels, O you cold censors who dislike the novel: you are like that legless cripple who was wont to say: and why do artists bother to paint full-length portraits?

If 'tis therefore true that the novel is useful, let us not fear to outline here a few principles which we believe necessary to bring this kind of literature to perfection. I realize full well that it is difficult to accomplish this task without supplying my enemies with ammunition they can use against me. Shall I not become doubly guilty of not *writing well* if I prove that I know how one must proceed in order to *write well*? Ah! let us put these vain conjectures aside, let us offer them up as sacrifices to the love of art.

The most essential requirement for the novelist's art is most certainly a knowledge of the human heart. Now, every man of intelligence will doubtless second us when we assert that this important knowledge can only be acquired through an intimate acquaintance with *misfortune* and through *travel*. One must have seen men of all nations in order to know them well, and one must have suffered at their hands in order to learn how to judge and evaluate them; the hand of misfortune, by ennobling the character of him whom she crushes, places him at that proper perspective from which it is essential to study men; from this perspective, he views them as a traveler perceives the wild waves crashing against the reefs whereon the tempest has tossed him. But no matter what the situation wherein Nature or destiny has placed him, let the novelist, would he know the hearts of men, be sparing of his own conversation when he is with them. One learns nothing when one speaks; one only learns by listening. And that is why the garrulous and the gossips are generally fools.

O you who wish to venture upon this difficult and thorny career, bear ever in mind that the novelist is the child of Nature, that she has created him to be her painter; if he does not become his mother's lover the moment she gives birth to him, let him never write, for we shall never read him. But if he feels that burning need to portray everything, if, with fear and trembling he probes into the bosom of Nature, in search of his art and for models to discover, if he possesses the fever of talent and the enthusiasm of genius, let him follow the hand that leads him; once having divined man, he will paint him. If his imagination is held in check, let him yield to it, let him embellish what he sees: the fool culls a rose and plucks its petals; the man of genius smells its sweet perfume, and describes it. This is the man we shall read.

But in counseling you to embellish, I forbid you to stray from verisimilitude: the reader has a right to become incensed when he observes that the author is asking too much of him. He can see that he is being deceived, his pride is hurt, he no longer believes anything he reads the moment he suspects he is being misled.

What is more, let no barrier restrain you; exercise at will your right to attack or take liberties with any and all of history's anecdotes, whenever the rupture of this restriction demands it in the formation of the pleasures you are preparing for us. Once again, we do not ask that you be true, but only that you be convincing and credible. To be too demanding of you would be harmful to the pleasure we expect from you. None the less, do not replace the true by the impossible, and let what you invent be well said; you shall be forgiven for substituting your imagination for the truth only when this is done for the express purpose of adorning or impressing; one can never be forgiven for expressing oneself poorly when one has complete freedom of expression. If, like R***, you write *only what everyone already knows,* were you, like him, to give us four volumes a month, better not to put pen to paper at all. No one obliges you to exercise this as your profession; but if you undertake it, do it well. Above all do not choose it merely as a crutch to your existence; your work will reflect your needs, you will transmit your weakness into it; it will have the pallor of hunger: other professions will offer themselves to you: make shoes, but refrain from writing books. We shall not think any the less of you, and since you will not be a source of annoyance to us, we may even like you all the more.

Once you have your outline down on paper, work zealously to enlarge and improve upon it, without however respecting the limitations it seems initially to impose upon you: were you to adhere strictly to this method, your work would be cold and lack breadth. We want outbursts from you, flights of fancy rather than rules.

Transcend your drafts, vary them, elaborate upon them: work is the surest source of inspiration. What makes you believe that the inspiration you receive while working is any poorer than that dictated by your outline? Basically, all I ask of you is this one thing: to sustain interest throughout, to the very last page. You shall miss the mark if you punctuate your tale by incidents either repeated too often or which stray too far afield from the main subject. Let those you do make so bold as to indulge in be as well polished as the main plot. You must make amends to the reader when you oblige him to leave something which interests him in order to begin a secondary plot. He may allow you to interrupt him, but he will not forgive you if you bore him or tax his patience. Therefore let your side plots derive from and return to the main plot. If you make your heroes travel, be familiar with the country whereto you take them, carry your magic to the point of identifying me with them; remember that I am walking close beside them in every region to which you take them. Remember too that I may be better informed than you; I shall not forgive a lack of verisimilitude with what regards customs or a slip with what regards dress, and even less an error in geography: as no one compels you to embark upon these escapades, 'tis essential that your local color be exact, else you must remain back home by your fireside. 'Tis the only case in your work when we will not tolerate the make-believe, unless the country you take me to be imaginary; and even in that case, I shall always demand verisimilitude.

Avoid the affectation of moralizing: it has no place in a novel. If the characters your plot requires are sometimes obliged to reason, let them always do so without affectation, without the pretension of doing so. 'Tis never the author who should moralize but the character, and even then you should only allow him to do so when forced by the circumstances.

When you arrive at the denouement, let it occur naturally, let it never be stiff or contrived, but always born of the circumstances. I do not require of you, as do the authors of the *Encyclopédie,* that the denouement be in accordance with the wishes of the reader: what pleasure is there left to him when he has divined everything? The denouement must be the logical result of a threefold demand: the events that lead up to it, the requirements of verisimilitude, and the imagination's inspiration. And if, then, with these principles wherewith I charge your mind, and with your tendency to elaborate, you do not write well, you will at least perform better than we.

For we must confess, in the stories that you are about to read, the audacious effort we have been so bold as to make does not always adhere strictly to the rules of the art. But we trust that extreme verisimilitude of the characters will perhaps compensate for it. Nature, even stranger than the moralists portray it to us, continually eludes the restricting limitations which their policy would like to impose. Uniform in her framework, unpredictable in her effects, Nature's constantly troubled bosom resembles the depths of a volcano, whence there rumble forth in turn either precious stones serving man's needs or fire balls which annihilate them; mighty when she peoples the earth with such as Antonius and Titus; frightful when she spews forth an Andronicus or a Nero; but always sublime, always majestic, always worthy of our studies, of our brush strokes, and of our respectful admiration, because her designs are unknown to us, because 'tis never upon what those designs cause us to feel that we, slaves to her whims or needs, should base our feelings toward her, but upon her grandeur, her energy, no matter what the results may be.

As minds grow increasingly corrupt, as a nation grows older, by virtue of the fact that Nature is increasingly studied and better analyzed, in order for prejudice to be increasingly eradicated, all these things must be made more widely known. This holds equally true for all the arts; 'tis only by advancing that any art moves nearer to perfection; the goal can only be reached by successive attempts. Doubtless we could not have advanced so far in those trying times of ignorance when, weighed down beneath the yoke of religion, whosoever valued the arts risked the penalty of death for his efforts; when talent had as its reward the stakes of the Inquisition. But in the state wherein we live today, let us always start from this principle: when man has weighed and considered all his restrictions, when, with a proud look his eyes gauge his barriers, when, like the Titans, he dares to raise his bold hand to heaven and, armed with his passions, as the Titans were armed with the lavas of Vesuvius, he no longer fears to declare war against those who in times past were a source of fear and trembling to him, when his *aberrations* now seem to him naught but errors rendered legitimate by his studies —should we then not speak to him with the same fervor as he employs in his own behavior? In a word, is eighteenth-century man therefore identical with the man of the eleventh century?

Let us conclude with a positive reassurance that the stories we are presenting today are absolutely new and in no wise a mere reworking of already oft-told tales. This quality is perhaps not without some merit in an age when everything seems already to have been written, when the sterile imaginations of authors seem incapable of producing anything new, and when the public is offered naught save compilations, extracts, and translations.

Still, we should mention that *La Tour enchantée* and *La Conspiration d'Amboise* have some basis in historical fact. We mention this to show the reader, by our candor, how far we are from wishing to deceive him on this score. In this type of fiction, one must be original or refrain from indulging in it.

Regarding the one and the other of these two stories, here is what the reader will find in the sources indicated below.

The Arab historian Abul Kasim Terif ibn-Tariq, whose work is little known amongst our men of letters today, relates the following in connection with *La Tour enchantée:* "Out of sensual pleasure, the effeminate prince Rodrigue enticed to his court his vassals' daughters, and abused them. Amongst them was Florinde, the daughter of Count Julian. Rodrigue violated the girl. The girl's father, who was in Africa, learned of the news from a letter, couched in the form of an allegory, sent him by his daughter. He roused the Moors to revolt and returned to Spain at the head of a Moorish army. Rodrigue is at a loss what to do: his treasury is empty. Hearing there is an immense fortune buried in the Enchanted Tower near Toledo, Rodrigue goes there. He enters the tower, and there sees a statue of Time, which strikes with its staff and, by means of an inscription, enumerates to Rodrigue the list of misfortunes which await him. The prince advances and sees a large tank of water, but no money. He retraces his steps and orders the tower to be sealed. The edifice vanishes in a clap of thunder, and not a trace of it remains. In spite of the dire predictions, Rodrigue amasses an army, wages war for eight days hard by Cordova, and is killed. No trace of his body was ever found."

So much for the historical facts. If one will now read our work, he will see whether or not the multitude of events wherewith we have surrounded this dry historical event merits our considering the anecdote as properly our own invention.[8]

As for *La Conspiration d'Amboise,* let the reader consult Garnier and he will see how little indebted we are to history in this story.

No guide has broken ground for us in the other stories: plot, style, episodes—all are our own invention. It may be said that these are not what is best in our work. No matter; we have always believed, and we shall continue to believe, that 'tis better to invent, albeit poorly, than to translate or copy. The inventor can lay claim to talent or genius, and has at least that much in his favor; what claim can the plagiarist make? I know of no baser profession, nor do I conceive of any avowal more humiliating than that which such men are obliged to make to themselves, namely, that they are totally lacking in wit, since they are obliged to borrow the wit of others.

Regarding the translator, God forbid that we fail to give him his due. But all he does is add to the luster of our rivals; and if only for the honor of the Nation, were it not best to say to these proud rivals: *and we too know how to create.*

Finally, I must reply to the reproach leveled at me when *Aline et Valcour* was published. My brush, 'twas said, was too vivid. I depict vice with too hateful a countenance. Would anyone care to know why? I have no wish to make vice seem attractive. Unlike Crébillon and Dorat, I have not set myself the dangerous goal of enticing women to love characters who deceive them; on the contrary, I want them to loathe these characters. 'Tis the only way whereby one can avoid being duped by them. And, in order to suc-

---

8 This anecdote is the one which opens the Brigandas episode in that section of the novel *Aline et Valcour* which bears the title: *Sainville et Léonore,* and interrupts the episode of the body discovered in the tower. Those who have plagiarized this episode word for word have likewise not neglected to copy verbatim the first four lines of this anecdote, which is spoken by the chief of the Bohemians. It is therefore essential for us here to point out to those who buy novels that the works currently on sale at Pigoreau and Leroux's bookshop under the title *Valmor et Lidia,* and at Clérioux and Moutardier's under the title *Alzonde et Koradin,* are absolutely one and the same, and both have been plagiarized verbatim from the *Sainville et Léonore* episode, which forms approximately three volumes of my work entitled *Aline et Valcour.*

ceed in that purpose, I painted that hero who treads the path of vice with features so frightful that they will most assuredly not inspire either pity or love. In so doing, I dare say, I am become more moral than those who believe they have license to embellish them. The pernicious works by these authors are like those fruits from America beneath whose highly polished skins there lurk the seeds of death. This betrayal of Nature, the motive of which 'tis not incumbent upon us to reveal, is not done for man. Never, I say it again, never shall I portray crime other than clothed in the colors of hell. I wish people to see crime laid bare, I want them to fear it and detest it, and I know no other way to achieve this end than to paint it in all its horror. Woe unto those who surround it with roses! their views are far less pure, and I shall never emulate them. Given which, let no one any longer ascribe to me the authorship of J......;[9] I have never written any such works, and I surely never shall. They are naught but imbeciles or evildoers who, despite the authenticity of my denials, can still suspect me of being the author of that work, and I shall henceforth use as my sole arm against their calumnies the most sovereign contempt.

---

[9] Sade is, of course, alluding to *Justine.—Tr.*

# Villeterque's Review of
# Les Crimes de l'Amour[1]

*A* detestable book by a man suspected of having written one even more horrible. I do not know, nor do I wish to know, to what extent this suspicion has any foundation in fact. A journalist has the right to pass judgment on books, and not the right to make accusations. I shall go even further: he ought to feel sorry for him over whose head there hovers so terrible a suspicion, until such time as, having been found guilty, he is denounced for public execration.

In a piece entitled "Reflections on the Novel" which serves as a preface to *Les Crimes de l'Amour,* the author raises three questions, which he proposes to answer: Why is this kind of literary work called a "novel"? Amongst what people did the novel originate, and what are the most famous examples history has to offer? And, finally, what are the rules one must follow if one wishes to succeed in writing well?

I shall not bother with the first two questions, which have been discussed frequently and in sufficient detail by others, except to remark that the author, in discussing these first two questions, makes a great show of his erudition, which is actually riddled with errors, and prates on irrelevantly about them at great length. I shall move on to what he calls, with respect to the novel, "perfecting the art of writing."

"It is not," says the author, "by making virtue triumph that we arouse interest. This is no wise essential in the novel. Nor is't

[1] This article appeared in *Le Journal des Arts, des Sciences, et de la Littérature* on 30 *Vendémiaire,* Year IX (October 22, 1800), 2° année, No. 90, pp. 281–284.—*Tr.*

even the rule most likely to arouse interest on the part of the reader. For when virtue triumphs, the world being in joint and things as they ought to be, our tears cease to flow even, as it were, before they have begun. But if, after severe trials and tribulations, we finally witness 'virtue overwhelmed by vice,' our hearts are inevitably rent asunder and, the work having moved us deeply, it must indubitably arouse the interest which alone can assure a writer of his laurels."

Is this not tantamount to reducing into principles the plot of the infamous work which the author disclaims? Do we not run the risk, by simply repudiating and disassociating ourselves from the notoriety connected with the execrable form of this work, do we not run the risk of seeming to embrace its basic premises, which in the final analysis are none other than to portray "virtue overwhelmed by vice"?

Why else would anyone paint scenes in which crime reigns triumphant? Such scenes awaken evil tendencies in the wicked; from the virtuous man, who is ever steadfast in his principles, they provoke cries of indignation; and in him whose heart is willing but whose flesh is weak, they incite despondent tears. These horrible portraits of crime do not even serve the purpose of rendering crime more odious; therefore, they are both useless and dangerous. These calamitous principles are so patently false that even those persons who subscribe to them in private disown them in public.

In the tale entitled *Eugénie de Franval,* the author declares:

> By leaving [crime] in the darkness it seeks, have we not as it were annihilated it? Scandal noised abroad is certain scandal, and the recital of it awakens the passions of those who are inclined toward the same kind of crime.

Here we see the author contradicting his own views, a not uncommon practice when one holds to erroneous opinions.

I was unable to read these four volumes, full of the most revolting atrocities, without a feeling of indignation. Nor does the author's style in any wise compensate the reader for the disgust inspired by the stories themselves. In the present work, that style is pitiful, constantly lacking in any sense of proportion, teeming with sentences in bad taste, filled with contradictions and trivial reflections. Now and then, in a few pages, one finds a smattering of reflections which are reasonable and based upon principles of justice, but 'tis as though they were tacked onto the work as an afterthought. One feels they do not relate at all to anything which has preceded or to anything that follows.

Nor should the reader believe for a moment that a single crime for every story is sufficient for the author, for such is not the case; he crams them in: 'tis a tissue of horrors. In one tale, a woman is violated by her son, she kills him, subsequently she sends her own mother to the gallows and marries her father. In another, we observe a father who raises his daughter according to the most despicable principles, lives in sin with her, persuades her to poison her mother, etc. And these are examples of what the author is so bold as to term "perfecting the art of writing."

You who write novels, 'tis no longer in the world around you, in the realm of reality whose events either trouble or embellish life, nor is it any longer in the more complete and perfect understanding of the human heart, that you must look for your subjects. Rather must you delve into the history of poisoning, debauchery, and murder, and draw therefrom. And you must portray villains as being happy—all for the greater glory and encouragement of virtue.

Rousseau, Voltaire, Marmontel, Fielding, Richardson, et al., you have not written novels. You have painted customs, you should have painted crimes. You make virtue appear attractive by proving to us that virtue alone is the way to happiness. You are all wrong. You should show us "virtue overwhelmed by vice"; 'tis thus one instructs and holds the reader's interest. But you were not among the select few whom Nature has created to paint her; you did not become her "lover the moment she gave you birth." Nor have you "opened her bosom with fear and trembling, therein to seek your art." You were not endowed with the "burning zeal to describe absolutely everything," nor were you blessed with the ability to know how to strike home a dozen times straight and true with the dagger's blade. In your insipid works, we do not observe mothers strangling their children or children who poison their mothers; nor do we find sons who rape their own mothers. Adieu, Rousseau, Voltaire, Marmontel, Fielding, and Richardson: you will be read no more.

VILLETERQUE

# The Author
## of
# Les Crimes de l'Amour
## To Villeterque,
## Hack Writer[1]

*I* have long been of the opinion that insults dictated by jealousy, or by any other motive even more abject, which eventually reach our ears via the foul breath of a hack writer, should have no more effect upon a man of letters than the early morning sounds in the farmyard—the barking and the cackling—would have upon a sensible, peaceable traveler. Consequently filled with naught but contempt for the impertinent diatribe written by Villeterque-the-hack, I would most assuredly not bother my head about replying to it were it not for my desire to alert the public to the constant danger of being slandered at the hands of these gentlemen.

From the stupid account Villeterque gave *Les Crimes de l'Amour* 'tis obvious he has not read the book. If he had, he would never have put words into my mouth that have never even crossed my

[1] We apply the term "journalist" to an educated man, a man capable of discussing a work reasonably, of analyzing and giving an account of it with sufficient clarity to render it familiar to the reader. But whosoever has neither the intelligence nor the judgment necessary to exercise that honorable calling, whosoever compiles, prints, slanders, lies, vilifies, rants and raves—all of which he does to earn a living—that man, I say, is naught but a *hack;* and that man is Villeterque. (See his article of 30 *Vendémiaire,* Year IX.)

mind; nor would he quote out of context isolated phrases—which someone no doubt dictated to him—in order that, by twisting them to fit his purpose, he might give them a meaning they were never intended to have.

And yet, without having read the book (as I have just shown), Villeterque begins by labeling my work DETESTABLE and by CHARITABLY declaring that this DETESTABLE *work comes from the hand of a man suspected of having penned one even more* HORRIBLE.[2]

At this point, I challenge Villeterque to do two things he cannot refuse me: 1) To publish not isolated, truncated, and mutilated phrases, but complete passages which prove my book to be DETESTABLE, although those who have read it are in agreement that it is, on the contrary, a work solidly based upon a refined and heightened sense of morality. 2) I challenge him to prove that I am the author of that even more HORRIBLE book.

'Tis only a vile slanderer who thus casts wild aspersions upon a person's integrity without offering the slightest proof to buttress them. The truly honest man offers proof, cites facts, and refuses to deal in hearsay. Villeterque, however, denounces without proving; he makes a most odious allegation against me but fails to specify what it is. Therefore, Villeterque is a slanderer; what is more, Villeterque is not ashamed to reveal that he is a slanderer even before he commences his diatribe.

Be that as it may, I state and affirm that I have never written any *immoral books,* and that I never shall. I repeat it again here, not for the sake of the hack writer Villeterque—'twould be seeming to ascribe too much weight to his opinion—but for the sake of the public, whose judgment I respect as much as I despise Villeterque's.[3]

---

[2] Here again, of course, Sade is referring to the allegation that he is the author of *Justine.—Tr.*

[3] 'Tis this same contempt that compels me to remain silent with what regards that idiotic, slanderous rhapsody by one *Despaze* by name, who also claimed I was the author of that infamous book which, out of deference to our moral code, we must ever refrain from mentioning. Full aware that this mischief-maker was naught but a swindler spewed forth by the Garonne and, for some ridiculous reason, come to disparage in Paris arts whereof he was completely ignorant, works he had never read, and worthy persons who ought to have joined forces and bludgeoned him to death; perfectly aware that this obscure individual, this ne'er-do-well, had with great pain given birth to a few detestable verses, solely with this perfidious object in mind, for whose results the beggar waited as though for a crust of bread, I resolved to

After that initial act of generosity, the sixpenny hack broaches the substance of the matter. Let us follow him, if we are not overcome by a feeling of disgust; for 'tis difficult to follow Villeterque without experiencing a feeling of revulsion: his opinions are a cause for disgust, and his writings—or rather his plagiarisms—inspire it. . . . No matter; let us be brave.

In my "Reflections on the Novel," Villeterque-the-ignoramus assures us that I am guilty of an infinite number of errors, despite all my seeming erudition. Here again should the charge not be backed up by proof? But in order to recognize errors of *erudition,* one must have a smattering of erudition oneself, and Villeterque, who is soon going to demonstrate that he does not have even a nodding acquaintance with scholarly works, is far from possessing the erudition it would require to prove my errors. Therefore he limits himself to declaring that I commit them, without having the courage to specify what they are. To be sure, this kind of criticism is not difficult, and I am no longer surprised that there are so many critics and so few good works. This is the reason why most of the literary journals, Villeterque's first and foremost, would be completely unknown if their publishers did not slip them furtively into people's pockets, like the addresses of those charlatans that are dropped in the streets.

My errors clearly established, clearly proven, as we have seen, by the word of the scholar Villeterque, who none the less does not have the courage to cite a single one, the worthy hack then proceeds to an examination of my principles, and 'tis here he is profound: 'tis here that Villeterque rants and raves: the subtlety and sagacity of his reasoning drive all before them; his words are as thunder and lightning, and woe unto anyone who remains unconvinced once Aliboron-Villeterque has spoken!

---

let him languish shamefully in the humiliation and opprobrium into which his sorry scribbling had straightway cast him, fearing lest my ideas, were they to linger for even a minute upon so loathsome a creature, might be defiled. But as these gentlemen have chosen to emulate those asses which, when they are hungry, bray in unison, I have been obliged to strike out indiscriminately against them all, in order to still the racket. This, then, is what compels me to lift them for a moment, by their ears, from the slough wherein they lay expiring, so that the public may recognize them by the seal of shame upon their foreheads; after which, having rendered this service to humanity, I boot them both back into the foul sewer wherein their baseness and degradation will keep them wallowing forever.

Yes, learned and profound *Vile stercus,* I have said before and I say again that the study of the great masters has proven to me that 'twas not through the constant triumph of virtue that a writer could claim to hold the public's interest in a novel or a tragedy; that this rule, whether it applies to Nature herself or to the works of Aristotle or those of any of our poets, is one whereunto all men must conform for the common weal, without its being absolutely essential in a dramatic work of whatever kind. But what I am expounding here are not my own principles; I am inventing nothing new: read my works and you will see not only that what I am saying here is but the result of the impact upon me of a close study of the great masters, but also that I have not even adhered to this maxim, however excellent or wise I deem it to be. For, in the final analysis, what are the two principal mainsprings of dramatic art? Have all the authors worthy of the name not declared that they are *terror* and *pity*? Now, what can provoke *terror* if not the portrayal of crime triumphant, and what can cause *pity* better than the depiction of virtue a prey to misfortune? One therefore has either to forego interest or submit to these principles. That Villeterque is not widely enough read to appreciate the truth of this statement, so be it, this will be a source of surprise to no one. It is useless to be familiar with the rules of any art when one's only ambition is to write soporific bedtime stories, or to copy some insipid tales out of *A Thousand and One Nights* with a view toward proudly passing them off as one's own. But if Villeterque-the-plagiarist is unaware of these principles, for the simple reason that he is unaware of practically everything, at least he does not dispute them. And when, for the account of his newspaper, he manages to filch some tickets to a play and, ensconced in one of the seats reserved for the non-paying public, he is treated, in return for his pittance, to the masterpieces of Racine and Voltaire, let him then learn—when, for example, he goes to see *Mahomet*—that Palmire and Seide both die virtuous and innocent, whilst Mohammed triumphs; let him also be ever mindful that in *Britannicus* the young prince and his mistress likewise die innocent and virtuous, whilst Nero continues to reign; let him note the same thing in *Polyeucte* and in *Phèdre,* and in a great many other dramatic works. And when he has returned home, let him open Richardson and note to what degree the celebrated Englishman sustains a high degree of interest by portraying virtue's misfortunes. These are the truths whereof I should like Villeterque to be convinced, and if indeed he were, then he would be less *cholericly,* less *arrogantly,* less *stupidly* inclined to levy criticism against those who put them into practice, after the example of our great writers. But the problem is that Villeterque, who is not a great writer, is not even acquainted with the works of the great masters; the problem is that, the moment the axe is removed from Villeterque-the-irascible, the dear man is completely lost. None the less, let us hearken to this eccentric when he speaks of the manner wherein I put these principles into practice. Ah! 'tis on this point the *pedant* is a pleasure to hear.

I say that, in order to sustain interest, there are times when vice must offend virtue; I further declare that this is a sure way to hold attention, and upon this axiom Villeterque launches an attack upon my morality. *Verily, verily,* I say unto you, Villeterque, that you are as *stupid* a judge of men as you are of works. What I am prescribing here is perhaps the highest compliment it is possible to pay to virtue; and indeed, were virtue not so beautiful, would people ever weep so over her misfortunes? If I myself did not believe virtue to be man's most respected idol, would I say to playwrights: Whenever you wish to inspire a feeling of pity in your public, have the courage to assail, if only for a moment, what is most beautiful in heaven above or on earth below, and you will see what bitter tears your sacrilege will provoke. Therefore, I pay virtue a compliment when Villeterque accuses me of rebelling against its worship. But Villeterque, who is doubtless not virtuous, has no idea how one pays homage to virtue. Only to the votaries of a divinity is granted access to her temple, and Villeterque, who perhaps has no sense of the divinity or any form of worship, hasn't the faintest notion of what we are talking about. But when on the following page Villeterque makes the allegation that for me to think the way our great masters do, to pay homage to virtue as they do, constitutes proof positive that I am the author of that book wherein virtue suffers the worst humiliations—'tis at this point, the reader will have to admit, that Villeterque's logic explodes in all its blinding clarity. I prove that without bringing virtue into the picture, it is impossible to write any dramatic work worthy of the name; I offer this truth, since I believe and affirm that indignation, anger, and tears must be the result of the insults whereof virtue is the object and the misfortunes wherewith it is afflicted. And from this, if one is to believe Villeterque, it follows that I am the author of that execrable book wherein one finds the exact opposite of everything I set forth and profess! Yes, quite the exact opposite, for the author of that work appears to make vice triumph over virtue only out of spite . . . or out of libertinage. A perfidious scheme, from which he has no doubt not deemed it necessary to derive the least dramatic interest, whilst the models I cite have always taken the opposite tack, and whilst I, insofar as my poor powers have enabled me to emulate these masters, have depicted vice in my works only in those colors most likely to make it forever detested; and if upon occasion I have allowed vice some modicum of triumph over virtue, it was never for any other reason than to make virtue appear more interesting or more beautiful. My taking the opposite tack from that taken by the author of the book in question does not mean, therefore, that I accept or sanction that author's principles. Since I loathe these principles and shun them in my works, I therefore cannot have adopted them. And Villeterque-the-irresponsible, who imagines he will prove my guilt by in fact citing the very evidence which exonerates me from it, is in consequence naught but a cowardly *slanderer,* whom it behooves us to unmask.

"But, pray tell, what is the purpose of all these scenes of crime triumphant?" asks the hack. The purpose, Villeterque, is to have them act as a foil for the opposite scenes, and that in itself is quite enough to prove their usefulness. Furthermore, where precisely does crime emerge triumphant in those stories you attacked so *stupidly* and with such *effrontery*? I trust the reader will kindly allow me a brief analysis, in order to prove to him that Villeterque does not know whereof he speaks when he claims that, in these tales, I grant the greatest ascendancy to vice over virtue.

Where is virtue better rewarded than in the tale entitled *Juliette et Raunai*?

If virtue is chastised in *La Double Épreuve,* does crime, even so, triumph therein? Assuredly not, as there is not a single criminal character in this entirely sentimental story.

Virtue, I admit, succumbs in *Miss Henriette Stralson,* as it does in Richardson's *Clarissa Harlowe.* But in this tale, is crime not punished by the very hand of virtue?

In *Faxelange,* is crime not even more severely punished, and virtue not freed from its fetters?

In *Florville et Courval,* does the hand of fate allow crime to triumph? All the characters who involuntarily perpetrate these crimes are but the pawns of that fate wherewith the Greeks endowed their gods. Do we not daily witness the same events as the misfortunes of Oedipus and his family?

Where is crime more wretched, and more severely punished, than in *Rodrigue?*

In *Laurence et Antonio,* does crime not succumb, and is virtue not crowned by the sweetest hymen imaginable?

In *Ernestine,* is't not by the hand of the heroine's virtuous father that the villain Oxtiern is punished?

Is crime not brought to the gallows in *Dorgeville?*

Does the remorse which leads La Comtesse de Sancerre to the grave not avenge the virtue which she outraged?

Finally, in *Eugénie de Franval,* does the monster I painted not run himself through with his own sword?

Villeterque . . . Villeterque-the-hack, where in the name of all that is holy does crime emerge victorious in my stories? Ah! the truth of the matter is that the only thing I see triumphing here is your own ignorance and your cowardly desire to slander.

Now, I ask my *reprehensible censor* upon what grounds he dares to describe such a work as "a compilation of revolting atrocities," when none of his reproaches proves to be well founded? And once having proved that much, what remains of the criticism leveled by that inept *phrase-maker?* Nothing but satire without a trace of wit, of criticism without the slightest discernment, and of spleen without provocation—all because Villeterque is a fool, and from fools there never stems aught but foolish things. I contradict myself, the pedagogue Villeterque goes on to say, whenever I put into the mouth of one of my protagonists thoughts in any wise contrary to those enunciated in my preface. Loathsome ignoramus: have you not yet learned that every character in any dramatic work must employ a language in keeping with his character, and that, when he does, 'tis the fictional personage who is speaking and not the author? and that, in such an instance, 'tis indeed common that the character, inspired by the role he is playing, says things completely contrary to what the author may say when he himself is speaking? Imagine what a man Crébillon would have been were he always to have spoken in the accents of Atrée; or what a person Racine, if his thoughts had been only those of Nero. Fancy what a monster Richardson would have been had his principles been only those of Lovelace! Ah, Monsieur Villeterque, what a fool you are! This is one truth concerning which both I and my characters will always be in complete agreement whenever we have the occasion to exchange views regarding your prosaic existence. But what a show of weakness on my part! Must I then resort to reason when 'tis contempt that is called for? And, indeed, what more does a lout deserve, one who dares to say to him who at every turn has castigated vice: "Show me some villains who are happy, 'tis what is required for one to perfect one's art: the author of *Les Crimes de l'Amour* will prove it to you!" No, Villeterque, I neither claimed nor proved any such thing; and in my defense I appeal from your stupidity to the enlightenment of the public. I said quite the contrary, Villeterque, and my works are constructed upon the opposite bases.

A splendid invocation finally brings our hack scribbler's vile diatribe to an end:

> Rousseau, Voltaire, Marmontel, Fielding, Richardson, you have not written novels [he exclaims]. You have painted *customs,* you should have painted *crimes!*

—as though crime did not constitute a part of our customs, and as though there were not *criminal customs* and *virtuous customs.* But this is too much for Villeterque, whose mind is incapable of embracing so vast a concept.

Actually, should such reproaches have even been leveled at me in the first place, I who have the highest regard for all those authors whom Villeterque cites, and who have never ceased to extol their merits in my "Reflections on the Novel"? And, furthermore, have these mortals for whom I have never had anything but the highest regard—these same authors to whom Villeterque refers in his article—have they not described and painted crimes in their works? Is Rousseau's *Julie* such a virtuous girl? Is the hero of *Clarissa Harlowe* a man of such impeccable moral standards? Is there all that much virtue in *Zadig* and in *Candide*? And these are but a few I could name.

Ah! Villeterque, I have somewhere written that when one aspires to write without having the good fortune to be endowed with any talent for it, it would be infinitely preferable to fashion ladies' dancing pumps or boots; at the time I wrote these words, I did not realize they were meant for you. Follow that advice, my good fellow, pray do; you may perhaps turn out to be a tolerable good shoemaker, but as sure as I'm alive you will never be anything but a wretched writer. But, Villeterque, you may find comfort in the thought that Rousseau, Voltaire, Marmontel, Fielding, and Richardson will always be read. Your ridiculous jokes on this score will not convince anyone that I disparage these great writers, when on the contrary I have never ceased to cite them as examples. But one thing of which you may be quite certain, Villeterque, is that you will never be read, first because you have never written anything which could possibly ever survive you; but even assuming that someone should one day stumble upon one of your literary plagiarisms, he will certainly prefer to read it in the original, in its pristine state rather than sullied by a pen as coarse as yours.

Villeterque, you have ranted and raved, you have lied, you have piled stupidity upon slander, ineptitude upon chicanery—all in order to avenge your *mirror*-authors, in whose camp your boring anthologies so rightly place you.[4] I have taught you a lesson, and I stand ready to teach you another, if ever you should happen to insult me again.

D.-A.-F. DE SADE

---

[4] The only work we have, thank God! from this scribbler's pen is his *Veillées,* a work he describes as *philosophic,* though all it really is, is *soporific.* A disgusting, monotonous, wearisome collection of debris wherein the pedant, ever on his high horse, desires nothing more than to have us—stupid creature that he is—mistake his drivel for elegance, his turgid style for wit, his plagiarisms for imagination. But alas, upon reading him, all we discover are platitudes when he is himself, and bad taste when he plagiarizes others.

# Florville and Courval, or The Works of Fate

## (1788)

# Florville and Courval,
## or
## The Works of Fate

*M*onsieur de Courval had just turned fifty-five; a vigorous man, in excellent health, he could look forward to another twenty years of life. Having known nothing but unpleasantness with a first wife, who had long ago left him to devote herself to a life of libertinage, and having good reason to believe, on the basis of the most reliable testimony, that this creature was now in her grave, he was seriously considering the possibility of remarrying, this time a person who, by the kindness of her character and the excellence of her morals, would help him to forget his earlier misfortunes.

As unlucky with his children as with his wife, Monsieur de Courval, who had had only two—a girl who had died while still very young, and a boy who, at the age of fifteen had, like his wife, abandoned him, unfortunately to follow the same principles of debauchery—Monsieur de Courval, I repeat, did not believe that any ties could ever bind him to this monster, and planned to disinherit him and bequeath his possessions to the children he hoped to have by the new wife he wished to marry. He had an income of fifteen thousand francs: formerly engaged in business, his fortune was the fruit of his labors, and he had lived well within his means, as decent men will, surrounded by a handful of friends who loved and esteemed him, who visited him either in a handsome apartment which he occupied on the rue Saint-Marc or, more often, on a charming little estate near Nemours, where Monsieur de Courval spent two-thirds of the year.

133

This worthy man disclosed his plan to his friends, and seeing that they approved of it, he bade them make immediate inquiries amongst their acquaintances to discover whether in their circle there were someone between the ages of thirty and thirty-five, whether a widow or spinster, who might serve his purpose.

Two days later, one of his former colleagues came to inform him that he believed he had found exactly the person Monsieur de Courval was seeking.

"The young lady I am recommending to you," his friend said to him, "has two things against her which I must first reveal, so that I can subsequently console you by giving an account of her good qualities. 'Tis quite certain that neither her father nor mother is alive, but we have no idea who they were or where she lost them. All we do know," the intermediary went on, "is that she is the cousin of Monsieur de Saint-Prât, a man of considerable reputation who acknowledges her, esteems her, and who will freely sing her praises to you, which is no more than she deserves. Her parents left her nothing, but she has an income of four thousand francs from Monsieur de Saint-Prât, in whose house she was reared and wherein she spent her entire childhood. This is her first fault," said Monsieur de Courval's friend, "let us move on to the second: an affair that occurred when she was sixteen years old, a child who died; she has never seen the father again. So much for the debit side; now a word about the things in her favor.

"Mademoiselle de Florville is thirty-six years old, though she looks but twenty-eight, if that; it would be difficult to conceive of a more attractive and interesting face: her features are gentle and delicate, her skin has the whiteness of a lily, and her chestnut-brown hair reaches down to her ankles. Her mouth is fresh, most pleasantly adorned, the very image of a springtime rose. She is rather tall, but she has such a lovely figure, there is so much grace in her movements, that her height, which otherwise might make her appear somewhat hard, is of no consequence. Her arms, her neck, her legs, are all pleasingly molded, and hers is a kind of beauty that will long resist the onset of age.

"As for her conduct, her extreme regularity may perhaps not please you. She is not much given to mundane activities and leads a most secluded life. She is extremely pious, assiduous in her devotion to the duties of the convent in which she lives, and if she is a source of edification to all those around her by her religious qualities, she also is a source of delight to all who behold her, because of her mind and the charms of her character. . . . In a word, she's an angel on earth, whom Heaven has reserved for the happiness of your later years."

Monsieur de Courval, delighted at the prospect of such an encounter, urged his friend to arrange for him to see the person in question without further delay.

"The matter of her birth concerns me not in the least," he said. "So long as her blood is pure, what does it matter to me who transmitted it to her? And her affair when she was sixteen daunts me just as little; she has made up for the lapse by many years of modesty and discretion. I shall marry her as though I were marrying a widow. Having set my mind on a woman between thirty and thirty-five, 'twould have been difficult indeed for me to add to that demand the foolish requirement that she be a virgin. Thus, nothing about your proposals displeases me; all that remains is for me to urge you to let me see the object herself."

Monsieur de Courval's friend was not long in satisfying his desire. Three days later he gave a dinner at his house, with the lady in question as one of the guests. It was difficult not to be captivated at first sight by this charming person: her features were those of Minerva herself, disguised beneath those of love. Since she was privy to the matter, she was even more reserved, and her decorum, her circumspection, and the nobility of her bearing, together with so many physical attributes and so gentle a nature, and with so judicious and well-developed a mind, soon had poor Courval so enamored that he begged his friend to hasten matters to their conclusion.

They met again two or three times, once at the same house, another time at Monsieur de Courval's, or at Monsieur de Saint-Prât's, and finally, in response to his most earnest entreaties, Mademoiselle de Florville declared to Monsieur de Courval that nothing could flatter her more than the honor he was bestowing upon her but that, in all fairness, she could in no wise accept before she herself had discovered to him the adventures of her life.

"You have not been told everything," said this charming girl, "and I cannot consent to be yours until you know more about me. Your esteem means too much to me to put myself in a position whereby I might lose it, and I assuredly would not deserve it if, taking advantage of your illusions, I were to consent to become your wife, without your first judging whether I am worthy to be."

Monsieur de Courval assured her that he was aware of everything, that 'twas he rather than she who should be evincing the concern she was showing, and that if he were fortunate enough to please her, then she should no longer trouble her head about it. Mademoiselle de Florville was firm; she insisted that she would not give her consent to anything until Monsieur de Courval had been thoroughly instructed with regard to her; and so he had to give in to her. The only concession he was able to wrest from her was that Mademoiselle de Florville would come to his estate near Nemours, that all preparations would be made for the marriage he desired, and that, as soon as he had heard her story, she would become his wife forthwith.

"But Monsieur," said that gracious girl, "if all these preparations come to naught, why make them? . . . What if I convince you that I was not born to be yours? . . ."

"That, Mademoiselle, is something I defy you ever to convince me of," said the worthy Courval. "Let us proceed, I beg of you, and do not stand in the way of my plans."

On this last point he was not to be swayed; all the arrangements were made, and they left for Courval's estate. There, however, they were alone, as Mademoiselle de Florville had requested; the things she had to say were only for the ears of the man who wished to marry her; hence no one was admitted. The day after her arrival, this beautiful and interesting girl, having asked Monsieur de Courval to listen closely, related the events of her life in the following terms:

## MADEMOISELLE DE FLORVILLE'S STORY

Your intentions concerning me, Monsieur, no longer allow that you be kept in ignorance of certain things. You have seen that Monsieur de Saint-Prât, to whom you have been told I was related, has himself attested to this fact. And yet, on this point, you have been completely misled. My origins are a total mystery to me, and I have never had the satisfaction of knowing who my parents were. When I was only a few days old, I was found in a green taffeta bassinet on Monsieur de Saint-Prât's doorstep; to the canopy of the bassinet was attached an anonymous letter, which simply said:

*Since after ten years of marriage you have no children, and since your constant desire is to have one, adopt this infant; her blood is pure; she is the issue of a chaste marriage and not of libertinage; her birth is honorable. If the child is not to your liking, take her to an orphanage. Make no inquiries, they will come to naught. It is impossible to tell you anything more.*

The worthy people on whose doorstep I had been left straightway took me in, raised me, and tendered me every possible care. I can say that I owe them everything. As there was no indication of my name, it pleased Madame de Saint-Prât to call me *Florville*.

I had just turned fifteen when I had the misfortune of seeing my protectress die. Nothing can express the pain I felt at that loss. I had become so dear to her that on her deathbed she besought her husband never to abandon me and to settle on me an income of four thousand francs. Both requests were punctually granted, and to these kindnesses Monsieur de Saint-Prât added that of acknowledging me as a cousin of his wife and of arranging for me, in this capacity, the bequest with which you are familiar. Yet I could no longer remain under his roof; Monsieur de Saint-Prât explained to me why.

"I am a widower, and still young," this virtuous man said to me. "To live under the same roof might give rise to suspicions that we do not deserve. Your happiness and your reputation are dear to me; I do not want to compromise either one. We must part company, Florville; but as long as I live I shall not abandon you; nor do I even want you to leave the fold of my family. I have a sister in Nancy; I am going to commend you to her. Her friendship will be no less steadfast than my own, of that I can assure you. And there, with her, still as it were before my eyes, I can continue to watch over anything you may require to complete your education or establish your situation in the world."

I did not learn this news without breaking down into tears.

This latest sorrow further intensified the grief I had felt upon the death of my benefactress. None the less convinced that Monsieur de Saint-Prât was right, I decided to follow his advice, and I set off for Lorraine, in the company of a lady from that region into whose care I had been entrusted. She delivered me to Madame de Verquin, Monsieur de Saint-Prât's sister, with whom I was to live.

Madame de Verquin's house bespoke an orientation quite different from that of Monsieur de Saint-Prât. If in the latter I had seen decency, religion, and morality reign supreme, in this other frivolity, the taste of pleasure, and independence were ensconced as though 'twas their sanctuary and refuge.

Before many days had elapsed after my arrival, Madame de Verquin informed me that my prudish air displeased her, saying that it was incredible for someone to arrive from Paris with such awkward manners . . . with so ludicrous a strain of modesty, and that if I wished not to offend her I would have to adopt another tone. This beginning alarmed me; I shall not attempt to make myself out to you any better than I am, Monsieur; but all my life I have been deeply displeased by anything which departs from the straight and narrow paths of morality and religion, I have been the avowed enemy of whatsoever offends virtue, and the sins into which I have been led in spite of myself have caused me so much remorse that 'tis not, I assure you, doing me a service to bring me back into contact with the world. I am not made to live in it; and when I am forced into contact with the world, I become shy and unsociable. What best befits the state of my soul and the inclinations of my mind is the most obscure seclusion.

These reflections, still imperfectly formulated, not fully ripened at such a tender age, did not protect me either from Madame de Verquin's poor counsel or from the evil into which her enticements were to plunge me. The constant company I saw, the boisterous pleasures with which I was surrounded, the example set and the conversation heard—all combined to lure me into error. I was told that I was pretty, and I was foolish enough to believe it.

The Normandy regiment was at that time garrisoned in Nancy. Madame de Verquin's house was the officers' meeting place. 'Twas also the trysting place for all the young women in town, and there all the amorous intrigues of the town were begun, broken off, and re-formed.

It is likely that Monsieur de Saint-Prât was unaware of at least a part of his sister's conduct. How, in the light of his austere morality, could he have agreed to send me there if indeed he had known her well? This consideration made me hesitate, nay kept me from complaining to him. Should I be perfectly honest? Perhaps I did not even want to complain to him. The impure air I was breathing began to defile my heart and, like Telemachus on Calypso's island, perhaps I might not have listened to Mentor's advice.

The shameless Madame de Verquin, who for a long time had been trying to corrupt me, asked me one day if it was indeed true that I had brought a pure heart with me to Lorraine, and whether I was not languishing over some lover left behind in Paris?

"Alas, Madame," I said to her, "I have never even dreamt of the misdeeds you impute to me, and your brother can answer to you concerning my conduct. . . ."

"Misdeeds?" Madame de Verquin broke in. "If you are guilty of any, 'tis to be yet so naive at your age. I trust you'll take steps to correct this."

"Oh, Madame, is this the kind of language I should be hearing from such a respectable lady?"

"Respectable? . . . Ah, not another word! I assure you, my dear, that of all the sentiments I would like to inspire, respect is the one I care least about. 'Tis love I wish to inspire. . . . But respect—I am not yet of an age to cultivate that sentiment. Follow my example, my dear, and you will be happy. . . . By the way, have you noticed Senneval?" added that siren, referring to a young officer of seventeen who was wont to frequent her house.

"Not particularly, Madame," I replied. "I can assure you that I look upon them all with equal indifference."

"That is precisely what you must not do, my dear young friend. From now on, I want us to share our conquests. . . . You must have Senneval. He is my handiwork, 'tis I who took the trouble to form him. He loves you; you *must* have him. . . ."

"Oh! Madame, I would appreciate your excusing me from such plans. Truly, I don't care for anyone."

"You must. The arrangements have already been made with his colonel, who, as you have seen, is my present lover."

"I beg of you not to involve me in your designs. I am not by nature inclined toward the pleasures you cherish."

"Oh, that will change! Someday you will love them, as I do. 'Tis all too easy not to appreciate things whereof one is still ignorant. But 'tis inadmissible not to want to know something which was meant to be adored. In a word, the plans have already been set: this evening, Mademoiselle, Senneval will declare his passion to you. You had better not keep him languishing too long or I shall be angry with you . . . extremely angry."

At five o'clock the group gathered. As it was very warm, card parties were arranged outside in the groves, and everything was so well organized that Monsieur de Senneval and I, being the only ones who were not playing, found ourselves obliged to engage in a conversation.

It would be useless to conceal from you, Monsieur, that no sooner had this charming and witty young man revealed his love to me than I felt myself drawn to him as though by some irresistible force. And when later I tried to analyze this attraction, I found that it was all very obscure. It seemed to me that this inclination was not the result merely of some ordinary feeling; what distinguished it was concealed by a veil before my eyes. On the other hand, at the very moment my heart would fly out to him, an invincible force seemed to hold it back, and in this tumult, in this ebb and flow of incomprehensible ideas, I could not make up my mind whether I was doing right to love Senneval, or whether I should flee from him forever.

He was given ample time to declare his love to me . . . alas, he was allowed more than enough! I had time to appear responsive, in his eyes, to his declaration and, taking advantage of my confusion, he demanded that I confess my feelings toward him. I was weak enough to tell him that he was far from displeasing me and, three days later, guilty enough to let him taste the fruits of victory.

'Tis a truly extraordinary thing, the malicious joy of vice in its triumphs over virtue. Nothing could match Madame de Verquin's transports of pleasure as soon as she learned that I had fallen into the trap she had set for me. She laughed at me, poked fun at me, and in the end assured me that what I had done was the simplest, most reasonable thing in the world. She said I could receive my lover every night in her house, without fear, for she would not even be aware of what I did, being too occupied for her own part to pay any attention to such trifles. She added that she would still have as high a regard for my virtue, since in all likelihood I would limit myself to this one, whilst she, obliged to contend with three, was most assuredly far from possessing my qualities of modesty and reserve. When I took the liberty of telling her that such promiscuous conduct was odious, that it showed a lack of sensitivity and feeling, that it was demeaning to our sex and reduced it to the level of the basest of animals, Madame de Verquin burst out laughing.

"You Gallic heroine," she said. "I admire you and do not blame you. I am well aware that at your age sensitivity and feeling are the twin gods to whom one sacrifices pleasure. At my age, 'tis not quite the same. Completely disillusioned concerning these phantoms, we accord them slightly less sway. We prefer pleasures of a more concrete sort than the silly things about which you wax ecstatic. Why, pray tell, should we be faithful to men who have never been faithful to us? Is it not bad enough to be the weaker sex, without being the more gullible as well? Any woman who lets herself be guided by the principle of sensitivity in such matters is quite foolish. . . . Believe me, my dear, vary your pleasures whilst your age and your charms allow you to, and cast aside your chimerical faithfulness, your sad, shy virtue, which is never satisfying in itself and never makes any impression on others."

These words made me shudder, but I realized that I no longer had the right to dispute them. The criminal help of that immoral woman was now necessary to me, and I had to treat her with circumspection. 'Tis a fatal disadvantage of vice, for it places us, as soon as we are in its clutches, in bondage to people whom we would otherwise scorn. And so I accepted all of Madame de Verquin's complaisances. Each night Senneval gave me new proof of his love, and thus six months passed in such a state of intoxication that I scarcely had time to reflect.

The baleful consequences soon opened my eyes. I became pregnant, and I thought I would die of despair upon finding myself in a condition which Madame de Verquin merely found amusing.

"Still in all," she said, "we must save appearances, and since it would not be very seemly for you to have your child in my house, Senneval's colonel and I have made some arrangements. He is going to give the young man a leave. You will depart a few days ahead of him for Metz, and he will follow shortly behind. There, with his help, you'll give birth to this illicit fruit of your tenderness. Afterward, you will both return here, one after the other, the same way you have gone."

I had no choice but to obey. As I told you, Monsieur, once one has had the misfortune to commit a sin, one places oneself at the mercy of all men and all situations; the whole world has a claim upon us, we become the slaves of anything that breathes the moment we forget ourselves to the point of becoming a thrall to our passions.

Everything happened just as Madame de Verquin had said. On the third day, Senneval and I were once again together, in Metz, at the house of a midwife whose address I had obtained before leaving Nancy, and there I gave birth to a boy. Senneval, who had never ceased to display the most tender and delicate sentiments, seemed to love me even more after I had, to use his own words, doubled his existence. He showed me every possible consideration, begged me to leave his son to him, swore to me that he would receive every possible care throughout his life, and said that he would not return to Nancy until his debt with regard to me had been fulfilled.

It was not until he was on the verge of leaving that I dared to mention how unhappy the sin he had caused me to commit was bound to make me, and to propose that we atone for it by consecrating our union at the foot of the altar. Senneval, who had not been expecting this proposal, was much disturbed by it. . . .

"Alas," he said to me, "am I free to do as I like? I am still not of age; would I not therefore require my father's consent? And what would our marriage be without this formality? Besides, I am far from a suitable match for you; as Madame de Verquin's niece —for in Nancy I was considered as such—you can aspire to a much better match. Believe me, Florville, let us forget our past mistakes. You can count on my discretion."

These words, which I had not at all expected, made me cruelly aware of the enormity of my transgression. My pride kept me from responding, but as a result my sorrow was all the greater. If anything had been concealing the full horror of my conduct from my own eyes, it was, I confess, the hope of one day atoning for it by marrying my lover.

What a credulous girl I was! I did not imagine—although Madame de Verquin's perverse ways should have opened my eyes —I did not believe that one could make sport of seducing a poor miserable girl and then abandon her. Nor did I realize that honor, this sentiment so highly respected amongst men, was so empty and ineffective with regard to us, and that our weakness could justify an insult which men would never dare subject one another to except at the risk of their lives. Thus I saw myself at once the victim and the dupe of the man for whom I gladly would have laid down my life. This frightful realization came very close to sending me to my grave. Senneval did not leave me. The cares he proffered me were the same as ever, but never again did he allude to my proposal, and I was far too proud to reveal to him a second time the reason for my despair. He disappeared as soon as I was fully recovered.

My mind made up never to return to Nancy, and knowing full well that I was seeing my lover for the last time in my life, I felt all my old wounds reopening when I bade him farewell. None the less, I had the strength to endure this final blow. . . . What a heartless creature! He left, tore himself from my breast, which was wet with tears, without shedding a single tear himself!

Such then is the consequence of those vows of love we are foolish enough to believe! The more sensitive we are, the more our seducers forsake and abandon us. . . . Perfidious creatures! The greater the means we employ to hold them, the greater their tendency to leave us.

Senneval had taken his child and had placed him somewhere in the country where it was impossible for me to find him. . . . He wanted to deprive me of the joy of loving and raising this tender fruit of our union. One would have thought that he wanted me to forget everything which might still bind us to each other, and so I did; or, rather, I thought I did.

I determined to leave Metz immediately and not return to Nancy. Yet I did not want to quarrel or break off relations with

Madame de Verquin. In spite of her failings, it was enough that she was such a close relative of my benefactor to make me treat her with consideration throughout my life. I wrote her a most courteous letter, using as an excuse for not returning to Nancy that my shame over the sin I had committed there was too great, and requesting her permission to return to her brother's house in Paris. She answered me straightway that I was mistress of my own destiny and free to do as I pleased, and said that I could always count on her friendship. She added that Senneval had not yet come back to Nancy, that no one knew whither he had gone, and that I was a foolish girl to worry my head over all these trifles.

After I had received this letter, I returned to Paris and hastened to cast myself at Monsieur de Saint-Prât's knees. My silence and my tears soon revealed my wretchedness to him; but I was careful to blame no one but myself and never to mention the role his sister had played in my seduction. Monsieur de Saint-Prât, like all souls in whom good predominates, in no wise suspected his relative's dissolute ways; he judged her the most worthy of women. I did nothing to dissuade him or destroy his illusions; Madame de Verquin was aware of this act of loyalty, because of which her friendship for me did not wither.

Monsieur de Saint-Prât felt sorry for me . . . made me truly feel the wrong I had done, and eventually forgave me.

"Ah, my child," he said to me with that gentle gravity of a worthy soul, so different from the odious frenzy of crime, "oh, my beloved daughter, now you see the price one must pay for straying from the path of virtue. 'Tis so necessary to follow that path, virtue is so intimately bound up with our existence that, the moment we abandon it, nothing but misfortune awaits us. Contrast the tranquillity of your state of innocence when you departed this house with the frightful anxiety wherewith you are afflicted upon your return. Do the meager pleasures you may have experienced in your fall from virtue compensate for the torments which now assail your heart? Happiness, therefore, is to be found solely in the exercise of virtue, my child, and all the sophistries of its detractors will never bring a single one of its enjoyments or rewards. Ah! Florville, those who deny or combat these sweet enjoyments do so out of jealousy and nothing more, of that you can be certain, or from the barbarous pleasure of making others as guilty and as wretched as they. They blind themselves, and seek to blind everyone else; they have lost their way, and seek to lead everyone else astray as well. But were you able to read deep into their hearts, you would discover naught but sorrow and remorse. All these apostles of crime are but miserable, desperate creatures. There's not a single one of them who, were he sincere, would not avow, assuming he were capable of telling the truth, that his foul words and dangerous writings were in fact motivated solely by his passions. And indeed, what man can seriously maintain that the foundations of morality can be undermined without risk? Who would dare to claim that to do good, and to desire good, must not perforce be the veritable goal of man in life? And how can the man who does naught but evil expect to be happy in a society whose most vital interest is to see good multiply and flourish? But will this apologist for crime not tremble constantly himself when he has uprooted from every heart the very thing to which of necessity he owes his preservation? What will prevent his servants from bringing about his ruin if they have ceased to be virtuous? What will keep his wife from dishonoring him if he has convinced her that virtue is worthless? Who will restrain the hands of his children if he has dared to destroy the seeds of good implanted in their hearts? How will his freedom, and his possessions, be respected if he has said to the high and mighty: *Act with impunity, virtue is naught but a fantasy*? Therefore, no matter what this poor wretch's condition, be he rich or poor, father or husband, master or slave, on all sides dangers will spring up for him, from all directions daggers will be poised at his heart. Let there be no mistake: if he has dared destroy in man the only duties which offset man's perversity, then sooner or later the unfortunate creature will perish, a victim of his own frightful systems.[1]

"Let us leave religion aside for the moment, if you like, and consider only man. Who would ever be foolish enough to believe

---

[1] *"Ah, my friend, never try to corrupt the person you love, the situation may get out of hand,"* a sensitive woman once said to the friend who was bent upon seducing her. Adorable woman, allow me to quote thine own words, they describe so aptly the soul of the woman who, a short while later, saved this same man's life, that I should like to engrave these touching words in the temple of memory, wherein thy virtues assure thee a place.

that, were a person to break every law society has formulated, this society which he outrages will allow him to go unpunished? Is it not in the interest of man, and of the laws he makes for his safety, always to try and destroy whatsoever obstructs it or is harmful to it? Influence of some kind, or wealth, may provide the evildoer with a fleeting glimmer of prosperity. But how brief will be its reign! Recognized for what he is, unmasked, and soon turned into a hated object of public scorn, will he then find any apologists for his conduct? will any partisans appear to comfort or console him? No one will admit to knowing him; as he no longer has anything to offer them, all will cast him aside as they would a burden. Misfortune will beset him on every side; he will languish in shame and adversity, and, no longer having even his own heart as a refuge, he soon will die of despair. What, then, is this absurd reasoning on the part of our adversaries? What is this impotent effort to attenuate virtue, to dare say that whatsoever is not universal is therefore chimerical, and that, virtues always being local, none of them can be said to have any absolute validity? What! there is no virtue because each people has had to forge its own? because different climes and temperatures have necessitated different kinds of restraints, because, in one word, virtue has multiplied in a thousand guises—because of all this there is no virtue on the face of the earth? One might as well doubt of the existence of a river because it forks off into a thousand different tributaries and branches. Well, what better proof both of the existence and necessity of virtue is there than man's need to adapt it to his various moral codes and to use it as the basis for them all? Show me a single people that lives without virtue, a single one for whom benevolence and human kindness are not the fundamental bonds—I shall go even further: show me a band of villains which is not bound together by some principles of virtue, and I shall cease defending its cause. But if, on the contrary, virtue is demonstrated to be useful everywhere, if there is no nation, no state, no society, no individual that can do without it, if, in one word, man cannot live happily or securely without it, would I then be wrong, my child, to exhort you never to stray from it?

"You see, Florville," my benefactor went on, enfolding me in his arms, "you see where your initial deviation from virtue has brought you. And if error should beckon to you again, if seduction or your own weakness should lay new snares for you, dwell then upon the unhappiness this first lapse has caused you, think of the man who loves you as he would his own daughter . . . whose heart is broken by your lapses from righteousness, and in these reflections you will find all the strength required for a devotion to virtue, which I would inculcate in your heart forever."

Monsieur de Saint-Prât, in keeping with these same principles, did not offer me the hospitality of his own house. Rather, he suggested I go and live with one of his relatives, a woman as renowned for the great piety of her ways as Madame de Verquin was for her faults. I was delighted by this arrangement. Madame de Lérince accepted me gladly and graciously, and within a week after my return to Paris, I was installed in her house.

Ah, Monsieur, what a difference between this woman and the one I had lately left! If vice and depravity had established their reign in Madame de Verquin's, it was as though Madame de Lérince's heart was the sanctuary of every virtue. As much as I had been frightened by the former's depravity, so I was equally consoled by the edifying principles which governed the latter. In hearkening to Madame de Verquin, I had found only bitterness and remorse; in abandoning myself to Madame de Lérince, I found naught but kindness and comfort.

Ah, Monsieur, allow me to describe for you this adorable woman, whom I shall cherish always. 'Tis a tribute my heart owes to her virtues, and I am powerless to resist it.

Madame de Lérince, who was about forty years of age, was still possessed of a freshness of youth; an air of candor and modesty embellished her features even more than did the divine proportions wherewith Nature had endowed them. A trifle too much nobleness and majesty rendered her, in the eyes of some, awesome at first glance, but what they might have mistaken for pride softened the moment she opened her mouth to speak. Hers was a soul so pure and beautiful, she was so gracious and of a candor so entire that one gradually felt an increasing tenderness for her, in spite of oneself and in addition to the veneration she inspired upon first meeting her. There was nothing strained or superstitious about Madame de Lérince's religion. The principles of her faith were dictated by an extreme sensibility. The notion of the existence of God, the worship due this Supreme Being: such were this loving soul's most lively pleasures. She confessed openly that she would be the most miserable creature alive if any perfidious enlightenment should ever force her mind to destroy in her the respect and love she reserved for her worship. Even more strongly attached—if such were possible—to the sublime morality of that religion than to its ceremonies and practices, she made this excellent morality the guide for her every act. Never had slander sullied her lips; she did not indulge in even the slightest jest which might afflict or offend another human being. Brimful of tenderness and sensibility for her fellow man, finding them interesting even unto their failings, Madame de Lérince's sole concern was either carefully to conceal their faults or gently to reprove them. Were they unhappy, she found no greater pleasure than in succoring them; nor did she wait for the poor to come and implore her help: she sought them out . . . she sensed them, and her face could be seen to light up with joy whenever she had brought comfort to a widow or provided for an orphan, whenever she had arranged materially to help a destitute family, or, with her own hands, had broken the chains of adversity. There was nothing harsh, nothing austere in all this: if the pleasures proposed were chaste, she partook of them with great delight, indeed she invented some of her own, for fear that people might find her company boring. Wise . . . enlightened with the moralist . . . profound with the theologian, she inspired the novelist and smiled upon the poet, she astonished the lawmaker and politician, and directed the games of the child. Her mind was brilliant in a number of ways, but the facet that shone brightest in her was the special care she took, the charming effort she made, to bring out the intelligence in others, or to show her appreciation of that quality in them. By inclination living withdrawn from society, cultivating her friends out of choice rather than necessity, Madame de Lérince was, in one word, a model for either sex, endowing everything around her with this tranquil happiness . . . this celestial delight promised to the honest, decent man by the Holy God of Whom she was the living image.

I shall not weary you, Monsieur, with the monotonous details of my life during the seventeen years I had the good fortune to live with this adorable creature. Discussions concerning morality and piety, as many charitable acts as 'twas possible for us to perform: such were the duties that occupied our days.

"Men are frightened away from religion, my dear Florville," Madame de Lérince used to say to me, "solely because clumsy, unskillful guides have made them aware of naught save religion's restrictions, without offering them its sweet rewards. Can there exist a man so absurd that, when first his eyes open and view the universe, he still refuses to admit that so many wonders can only be the handiwork of an omnipotent God? Once this prime truth has been admitted—and what more is required for his heart to be convinced of it—what kind of cruel and barbarous creature would he have to be still to refuse to pay homage to the benevolent God by Whom he was created?

"The diversity of religions is also cited as an embarrassment: one thinks to prove them false by their very multiplicity. What sophistry! Is not the existence of this Supreme God proved by this very unanimity of all peoples to recognize and serve Him in some guise, is this tacit avowal which is engraved in the hearts of all men not a proof even more irrevocable—if indeed such be possible —than the sublimities of Nature? What! man cannot live without a God, he cannot question himself without finding proofs within himself, he cannot open his eyes without discovering traces of this God everywhere, and still he dares to doubt! No, Florville, there are no sincere atheists; pride, obstinacy, passion: these are the destructive weapons of this God Who ceaselessly revivifies himself in the heart and mind of man. And when every beat of this heart, every luminous trait of this mind and reason offers me this indubitable Being, shall I refuse to pay Him my homage? Shall I not humble myself before His grace, that I might endure the miseries of life, and someday partake of His glory? Should I not aspire to the favor of spending eternity in His bosom, or should I rather run the risk of spending this eternity in a frightful abyss of torture, for having refused to accept the indubitable proofs this mighty Being has vouchsafed me with what regards the certitude of His existence! My child, does this awful choice allow for even a moment's reflection? O you who stubbornly refuse to recognize the fiery letters this God has traced even in the very depths of your hearts, at least be just for a moment and, if only out of pity for yourselves, yield to Pascal's invincible argument: 'If indeed there is no God, what does it matter whether you believe in Him, what harm is there in this allegiance? And if there is a God, what dangers do you not run by refusing Him your faith?'

"You say, unbelievers, that you are at a loss to know what homage to pay to this God, the multitude of religions beclouds your judgment. Very well then, examine them all, I have no objection whatsoever, and afterward come and say in good faith in which of them you find more grandeur and more majesty. Deny, if you can, O Christians, that the religion into which you were fortunate enough to be born, appears to be the one whose characteristics are holiest and most sublime. Seek elsewhere such great mysteries, dogmas as pure, a morality as comforting. Find in some other religion the ineffable sacrifice of a God for His creatures; find in another promises more beautiful, a future more pleasing, a God greater and more sublime! No, you cannot, ephemeral philosopher; you cannot, pleasure's thrall, you whose faith changes with the physical state of your nerves; blasphemous at the height of your passion, a believer as soon as your fires have cooled, you cannot, I say. Sentiment constantly acknowledges this God Whom your mind resists, He always exists beside you, even in the midst of your errors. Break the chains wherewith you are bound to crime, and never will this Holy, Almighty God desert the temple He has erected in your heart. 'Tis in the farthest depths of your heart, my dear Florville, even more than in your reason, that the necessity must be discovered for this God Whom everything reveals and proves to us; 'tis in this same heart we must also discover the necessity for the worship we devote to Him, and 'tis this heart which will soon persuade you, my dear friend, that the noblest and purest of all religions is the one into which we have been born. Let us therefore practice this sweet religion with joy and exactitude, let it fill our most beautiful moments here below and, cherishing it the while, as step by step we move toward the term of our days, let it be by the path of love and delight that we go to offer up unto the bosom of the eternal Father this soul which emanated from Him, was formed solely to know Him, and which we have enjoyed and delighted in only insofar as we have believed in and worshiped Him."

'Twas in this wise Madame de Lérince used to speak to me,

and from her counsel my mind drew strength, and my soul was purified beneath her saintly wing. But, as I have said before, I shall spare you the minor details of my daily life in this house and rather concentrate upon what is essential. 'Tis my sins I must reveal to you, generous and sensitive man, and as for those times when Heaven has vouchsafed to let me dwell in peace on the path of virtue, I shall simply offer up a prayer of thanks and pass them over in silence.

I had not ceased writing to Madame de Verquin; twice a month I likewise received letters from her. And although I doubtless should not have continued this correspondence, and although the fact that my reformed ways and improved principles incited me to break it off, still my debt to Monsieur de Saint-Prât, the hope that I might someday receive word of my son, and above all —let me confess it—a secret feeling which yet drew me ineluctably toward the site of so many past pleasures—all these things led me to keep up a correspondence which Madame de Verquin, on her end, was good enough to maintain on a regular basis.

I tried to convert her, I lauded the life I was presently leading and wrote her of its sweet solace, which she dismissed as a figment of my imagination; she constantly laughed at or combated my resolutions and, ever firm in her own, assured me that nothing in the world would ever be able to weaken them. She wrote me of the new girls whom she had, for her own amusement, won over to her cause, and claimed they were far more docile than I had been. This toppling of so many virtues was, the perverse woman claimed, but a small triumph, so many little victories she always enjoyed winning, and the pleasure of luring these young hearts into evil consoled her for being unable to realize all that her imagination incited her to undertake.

I was wont to ask Madame de Lérince to lend me her eloquent pen in order to unsettle my opponent, and she was happy to oblige. Madame de Verquin answered us, and her sophisms, oftentimes extremely convincing, obliged us to resort to even more compelling arguments of a sensitive soul, wherein, so Madame de Lérince rightly maintained, was everything necessary to destroy vice and confound incredulity.

From time to time I asked Madame de Verquin for news of

the man I still loved, but either she could not or would not deign to give me any.

The time has come, Monsieur; I must tell you of the second catastrophe of my life, a tale so cruel and bitter it breaks my heart each time I call it to mind. Hearing it, you will learn of the terrible crime of which I am guilty and will no doubt abandon the flattering plans you have regarding me.

Madame de Lérince's house, however orderly I may have portrayed it to you, was none the less accessible to a handful of friends: Madame de Dulfort, a woman well along in years who was formerly attached to the household of the Princesse de Piémont, and who came very often to see us, one day asked Madame de Lérince for permission to introduce to her a young man who came to her most highly recommended, and whom she would be pleased to bring into a house wherein the examples of virtue to which he would constantly be exposed could only contribute to mold his heart. My benefactress apologized, saying that she never received young men, but later, hard pressed by her friend's urgent entreaties, she consented to meet the Chevalier de Saint-Ange.

He made his appearance. Whether out of presentiment . . . or whatever you care to name it, Monsieur, when first I laid eyes upon this young man, I was seized with a trembling that shook me from head to foot, the cause of which 'twas impossible to conceal. . . . I almost fainted. . . . As I did not search for the reason for this strange reaction, I imputed it to some strange disposition, and Monsieur de Saint-Ange ceased to preoccupy me. But if this young man had, at first sight, been such a source of agitation to me, he too had been the victim of a similar disturbance; he later admitted this to me himself. Saint-Ange was filled with so great an admiration for the house into which he had been granted access that he did not dare forget himself so far as to reveal what flame was inwardly consuming him. Thus three months went by before he found the courage to say anything to me; but I noted such a vivid expression in his eyes that it soon became impossible for me not to understand what they were saying. My mind firmly made up not to fall prey again to the kind of error which had been the cause of all my suffering, and strengthened now by better principles, I was upon twenty different occasions on the verge of informing Madame de

Lérince of the feelings I thought I discerned in the young man. Subsequently restrained by the fears I thought I might arouse in her, I chose to remain silent. A baleful resolution, it would appear, since it resulted in the frightful calamity whereof I shall shortly apprise you.

We were wont to spend six months each year on a lovely country estate Madame de Lérince owned ten leagues from Paris. Monsieur de Saint-Prât often used to come and visit us there. Unfortunately for me, this particular year he was down with a siege of gout, which prevented him from joining us. I say unfortunately for me, Monsieur, because, quite naturally having a greater confidence in him than in his relative, I would have confessed to him certain things I could never bring myself to discover to others, the avowal of which would no doubt have warded off the fatal accident which befell me.

Saint-Ange requested permission to join us on our journey, and as Madame de Dulfort also interceded in his behalf, his request was granted.

All of us in our little group were concerned to know who this young man really was. Nothing very precise or substantial seemed to be known of his background or origins; Madame de Dulfort passed him off as the son of a provincial gentleman to whom she was related, whilst he, now and again forgetting what Madame de Dulfort had said, referred to himself as a native of Piedmont, a claim further reinforced by the manner in which he spoke Italian. He was of an age to embark upon a career, but thus far had not done so, nor did he seem so inclined. He had, moreover, a very pretty face, full worthy of being portrayed by an artist's brush, had excellent manners, a conversation which was exceeding decent, and also appeared to be very well educated; but behind all this there lurked a prodigious vitality, a kind of impetuosity of character which at times frightened us.

No sooner had we arrived at Madame de Lérince's country estate than Monsieur de Saint-Ange, whose feelings had only grown more intense because of his efforts to curb them, found it impossible to conceal them any longer from me. I trembled . . . and yet managed to maintain sufficient composure to show him naught but pity.

"In truth, Monsieur," I said to him, "you must have a false opinion of your own worth, or else time must weigh heavy indeed upon your hands if you have enough to devote to someone twice your age. But even assuming I were foolish enough to hear you out, what foolish plans might you dare entertain regarding me?"

"Plans to bind myself to you by the holiest of ties, Mademoiselle. How little esteem you must have for me, if you could even suspect I had any others!"

"To be quite candid with you, Monsieur, I do not intend to offer the public the odd spectacle of a woman thirty-four marrying a child of seventeen."

"Ah! cruel woman, could you even conceive of such insignificant differences if in your heart there was a flame even one-thousandth as strong as the one that consumes mine?"

" 'Tis certain indeed, Monsieur, that, for my part, I am quite calm. . . . I have been so for many a year, and I trust I shall so remain for as long as God sees fit to prolong my days here on earth."

"You deprive me even of the hope that I might one day move your heart to pity."

"I shall go even further: I dare forbid you to speak to me any further of your mad projects."

"Ah! Florville, beautiful Florville, so you wish to make my life miserable?"

"I wish it to be peaceful and happy."

"It can be so only with you."

"Yes . . . as long as you fail to rid yourself of the foolish sentiments you should never have conceived in the first place. Try to vanquish them, try to control yourself, and your tranquillity and composure will return."

"I cannot."

"You don't want to; to succeed in the effort, we must separate. Let two years go by without seeing me, this agitation will disappear, you will forget me, and you will be happy."

"Ah, never, never . . . For me there will never be any happiness save at your feet. . . ."

And as the other guests rejoined us at this moment, our first conversation concluded on this note.

Three days later, Saint-Ange, having again contrived to see

me alone, attempted to renew the conversation in the same vein as that of the earlier evening. This time, I was so stern in admonishing him to remain silent that tears rushed to his eyes. He turned from me abruptly, declaring that I was driving him to despair and that, if I continued to treat him in this manner, he would soon put an end to his life. . . . Then, retracing his steps like a man possessed:

"Mademoiselle," he said to me, "you do not know the soul you are outraging. . . . No, truly you do not. You must know that I am capable of resorting to the most extreme measures . . . measures which you perhaps cannot even imagine. . . . Yes, I shall resort to them a thousand times over rather than forgo the happiness of being yours."

And he withdrew in a state of dreadful agitation.

I had never been more tempted than I was at that moment to confide in Madame de Lérince, but, I repeat, I was restrained by the fear of compromising this young man, and I said nothing.

Saint-Ange spent the following week fleeing my presence; he scarcely addressed a word to me, and avoided me at table . . . in the salon . . . during our walks, probably in order to see whether this change in his conduct would make any impression upon me. Had I shared his feelings, this stratagem would surely have worked, but this was so far from the case that I scarcely seemed to be aware of his tactics.

At last he accosted me in a remote corner of the garden. . . .

"Mademoiselle," he said, his words ill concealing the violence of the feelings behind them, "I have finally managed to regain my self-composure . . . your counsels have had upon me the effect you desired and expected. . . . As you can see, I am again in complete control of myself. . . . My only purpose in getting you alone is to bid you my final adieu. . . . Yes, I'm going to leave you forever, Mademoiselle. . . . I'm going to flee from you . . . never again will you set eyes upon the man you loathe . . . oh! no, no, you will never see him again!"

"I am pleased to hear of your plan, Monsieur, and would like to believe that you have at last come to your senses again. But," I added, smiling, "your conversion appears to me as yet far from accomplished."

"Well, how would you have me be then, Mademoiselle, in order for me to convince you of my indifference?"

"Quite different from the way I see you now."

"But at least after I have left . . . when my presence is no longer a painful burden to you, then will you perhaps believe in my return to that reason toward which all your efforts have been urging me?"

"It is true that 'tis only your departure which will persuade me of your return to reason, and I shall never cease counseling you to adopt that course."

"Am I then such a frightful object for you?"

"You, Sir, are a most amiable man, who ought to be devoting his time to conquests of another sort, and to leave in peace a woman for whom it is impossible to hear your pleas."

"And yet you will hear me," he then said, in an absolute rage, "yes, cruel woman, no matter what you may say, you shall hear the sentiments of my inflamed heart, and you may rest assured that there is nothing in the world I shall not do, either to deserve you or to obtain you. . . . Nor should you believe in my departure," he went on in great heat, "or my pretended departure. I dreamt that up merely to test you. . . . Me, leave you! Do you for one moment believe I could tear myself away from this place where you dwell? . . . Hate me, falsehearted creature, hate me, since such is my unhappy fate, but never hope to vanquish the love for you which burns within me. . . ."

And as he spoke these last words, Saint-Ange was in such a state that, by some turn of fate I have never been able to understand, he succeeded in touching my heart, and I was obliged to turn away my head to hide my tears. I left him there in the thicket where he had managed to corner me. He made no effort to follow me; I heard him throw himself to the ground and give way to a fit of sobbing both frightful and completely uncontrolled. . . . And Monsieur, I must admit that, although I was quite certain that I did not entertain any feelings of love for this young man, I could not contain myself, and I in turn burst out sobbing, whether out of commiseration for him or from the memory of my own earlier experiences.

"Alas," I said to myself, yielding to my sorrow, "those were the same words Senneval used. 'Twas in these very terms that he expressed his burning love for me . . . also in a garden . . . in a garden just like this one . . . did he not tell me he would love me forever . . . and did he not deceive me cruelly? Merciful Heaven! he was even the same age. . . . Ah! Senneval . . . Senneval . . . is't you who are trying once again to destroy my peace of mind? Have you reappeared in this seductive guise only to drag me down again into the abyss? . . . Away, you coward! . . . away . . . I now loathe even your memory!"

I wiped away my tears, and went to lock myself in my room till dinner time. Then I went downstairs . . . but Saint-Ange did not appear, but sent word that he was ill. The following day he was clever enough to reveal to me a face which seemed completely untroubled. I was taken in by appearances; I really believed that he had mustered sufficient strength to overcome his passion. I was mistaken; the treacherous scoundrel! . . . Alas, what am I saying, Monsieur? I owe him no more invectives. . . . All I owe him are my tears, and my remorse.

Saint-Ange appeared so calm because he had laid his plans. Two days passed, and toward the evening of the third he publicly announced his departure. With Madame de Dulfort, his benefactress, he made arrangements concerning their common affairs in Paris.

We all went to bed. . . . Forgive me, Monsieur, for the commotion this frightful tale arouses within me even before I have finished relating it: I can never call it to mind without trembling with horror.

As it was exceeding warm, I had gone to bed almost naked. My maid had just left the room, and I had snuffed out the candle. . . . Unfortunately, a sewing basket had remained open on my bed, for I had just cut some material I was going to need the following day. Scarcely had my eyes begun to close than I heard a noise. . . . I quickly sat up . . . I felt myself seized by a hand. . . .

"This time you'll not escape me, Florville," said Saint-Ange, for 'twas he; "forgive the immoderation of my passion, but make no effort to elude it: I must make you mine!"

"Vile seducer!" I cried out, "leave this room immediately, or suffer the effects of my wrath. . . ."

"The only thing which will make me suffer is not to have you, cruel girl," the ardent young man went on, throwing himself upon me so skillfully and with such fury that before I knew what he was about the damage was done. . . .

Incensed by his excessive audacity, and determined to resort to any measures rather than submit to it any longer, I threw him off me and seized a pair of scissors I had at the foot of the bed. My anger notwithstanding, I maintained control of myself and sought to wound him in the arm, much more in order to frighten him by this display of resolution on my part than to punish him as he deserved to be; feeling my movement, his own became redoubled in intensity.

"Out, traitor!" I cried, thinking to strike him in the arm, "get out this minute, and blush at the crime you have committed! . . ."

Oh! Monsieur, a fatal hand had guided my blows. . . . The poor young man uttered a piercing cry and fell to the floor. . . . I straightway lighted my candle and bent over him. . . . Merciful Heaven! I had struck him in the heart! He was dying! I threw myself on the bloody body . . . I pressed him to my troubled breast . . . my lips, pressed against his, tried to breathe life back into the expiring soul. I washed his wound with my tears. . . .

"O you! whose only crime was to love me overmuch," I said, despair having driven me to a state of frenzy, "did you deserve such punishment? Should you have lost your life at the hand of her for whom you would have sacrificed it gladly? Oh, poor, poor young man . . . the image of him whom I adored, if to love you would undo what I have done and restore you to life, know then, at this cruel moment, when unhappily you can no longer hear me, know, if there is still a breath of life left in your soul, that I would gladly sacrifice my own life if 'twould suffice to bring back yours. . . . Know that I was never indifferent to you . . . that I never saw you without a feeling of intense emotion, and that my feelings for you were perhaps far superior to those of the tender love which burned in your heart."

With these words, I collapsed upon the body of this unfortunate young man, and fell unconscious. My maid, having heard the commotion, entered the room, and revived me, then joined me in my efforts to bring Saint-Ange back to life. But it was all to no avail, alas! We left this fatal room, carefully locked the door behind us, we took the key with us and straightway fled to Paris, to Monsieur de Saint-Prât's. . . . I had him awakened, handed him the key of this baleful room, and recounted to him my horrible adventure. He offered me sympathy, comforted me, and, despite his illness, immediately set out for Madame de Lérince's house. As it was but a short distance from Paris to her country estate, all this transpired before the night was out. My protector reached his relative's estate just as everyone was getting up, and before anyone knew what had happened during the night. Never have any friends, or any relatives, conducted themselves more nobly than in this circumstance: far from imitating those stupid or ferocious persons who, in such crucial moments, find pleasure only in making known whatever can damage or render unhappy those around them as well as themselves, in this instance the servants scarcely knew what had happened.

"Well, now, Monsieur," said Mademoiselle de Florville, breaking off her tale at this point because of the tears which were choking her, "will you now marry a girl capable of such a murder? Will you suffer in your arms a creature who deserves the full punishment of the law, a sorry creature who is constantly tormented by her crime and who, since the cruel moment when she committed it, has not spent a single peaceful night? No, Monsieur, not a single night has gone by that my poor victim has not appeared to me covered with the blood I caused to flow from his heart."

"Don't be so upset, Mademoiselle, I beg of you," quoth Monsieur de Courval, mingling his tears with those of that charming girl. "Given the sensitive soul wherewith Nature has endowed you, I understand your remorse. But there is not even the shadow of a crime in this fatal adventure. 'Tis without question a most terrible misfortune, but nothing more. There is nothing premeditated, nothing atrocious about it; simply the desire to ward off a most odious assault . . . in a word, a murder committed quite by chance, in self-defense. . . . Dismiss it from your mind, Mademoiselle, this I beg of you, nay, I demand it. The most rigorous tribunal would have done naught but wipe away your tears. Oh! how mistaken you were if you feared for a moment that an event such as this would deprive you of the rights to my heart which your qualities have assured you. No, fair Florville, no indeed: far from dishonoring you, this whole affair tends but to accentuate your virtues all the more brilliantly, it renders you ever more worthy of finding a comforting hand to help you forget your sorrows."

"The kind words you have just offered me," Mademoiselle de Florville went on, "are the same as those Monsieur de Saint-Prât has expressed. But the great goodness both of you have shown me can in no wise stifle the pangs of my own conscience. No matter, Monsieur; let us proceed with our story; you must be anxious to learn how all this turns out."

Madame de Dulfort was no doubt deeply grieved: not only was this young man a most attractive person, he had come to her too highly recommended for her not to deplore his loss. None the less, she understood the wisdom of silence, she saw that scandal, though it would mean my ruin, would not bring her protégé back to life; and she said not a word.

Despite the severity of her principles and the extreme probity of her morals, Madame de Lérince behaved even more admirably, if such were possible, for prudence and humanity are the distinctive characteristics of true piety. First she informed the household that during the night I had been foolish enough to wish to ride up to Paris, in order to take advantage of the pleasant weather; she added that she had been privy to this innocent caprice, that she had in fact approved of my act, as she herself had planned to drive to Paris to dine that same evening. Using this as a pretense, she sent all her servants up to Paris. Once she was alone with Monsieur de Saint-Prât and her friend Madame de Dulfort, she sent for the priest. Madame de Lérince's spiritual guide must have been as wise and enlightened as she: without further ado, he gave Madame de Dulfort an official certificate and, with the help of two of his servants, secretly and humanely interred the poor victim of my rage.

Once this had been taken care of, everyone reappeared and was sworn to secrecy. Monsieur de Saint-Prât came to comfort me, revealing to me all that had just been done to bury my misdeed in the most profound oblivion. He seemed to want me to resume my life with Madame de Lérince as though nothing had happened. . . . She was fully disposed to receive me. . . . I could not bring myself to do it. Then he counseled me to seek distraction and amuse myself.

Madame de Verquin, with whom, as I have mentioned before, I had never stopped corresponding, was still urging me to come and spend a few months with her. I mentioned this plan to her brother, he approved it, and a week later I set out for Lorraine. But the memory of my crime pursued me everywhere; nothing succeeded in restoring my peace of mind.

I used to awake from a deep sleep and fancy I could still hear the moans and cries of poor Saint-Ange. I would see him lying at my feet covered with blood, he would reproach me for being cruel and assure me that the memory of this frightful act would haunt me to my dying day, and that I did not know the heart I had destroyed.

One night, among many, I dreamt of Senneval, that wretched lover I had never forgotten, since he alone was still enticing me back to Nancy. . . . In my dream, Senneval showed me two corpses at the same time, the body of Saint-Ange and that of a woman unknown to me.[2] He shed bountiful tears upon both of them, and showed me nearby a coffin, bristling with thorns, which seemed to open for me. I awoke in a state of terrible agitation, my soul besieged by a thousand unclear and conflicting sentiments, and a secret voice seemed to say to me: "Yes, so long as thou shalt live, this wretched victim will wring tears of blood from thine eyes, tears more burning and bitter every day; and thy remorse, like the knife's edge, shall not be dulled but grow increasingly sharper."

Such, then, was my state upon arriving at Nancy, Monsieur, and there a thousand new sorrows awaited me: once the heavy hand of fate descends upon us, the blows rain down with renewed fury until they have crushed us.

I alighted at Madame de Verquin's. In her last letter she had invited me to come and stay with her; it would be a great pleasure for her, so she wrote, to see me again. But, Merciful Heaven,

---

[2] Let the reader keep in mind the phrase: *a woman unknown to me,* in order to avoid any confusion. Florville still has further losses to endure before the veil is lifted and discovers to her the woman she saw in her dream.

under what conditions were we to share this joy! I arrived to find her on her deathbed. Were it possible, Good Lord! She had written me no more than a fortnight before . . . telling me of her present pleasures and her plans for those yet to come. Thus is't, then, with mortal man's plans: 'tis at the very moment they are being laid that pitiless death comes, in the midst of his amusements, and cuts the thread of all his days; whilst he, living without the least concern for that fatal moment, acting as though he would live forever, then vanishes into the dark cloud of immortality, uncertain of the fate which awaits him there.

Allow me, Monsieur, to interrupt my story for a moment to speak of her death and to picture the appalling stoicism that accompanied this woman to the grave.

Madame de Verquin, who was no longer young—she was then fifty-two—after some escapade quite mad for her age, jumped into a pond to cool off. She straightway felt indisposed, was borne home in a terrible state, and the following day pneumonia set in. On the sixth day she was informed she had no more than twenty-four hours left to live. This news did not daunt her; she knew I was en route to see her, and she instructed her servants to receive me. I arrived the same evening which, according to the doctor's prognosis, was to be her last here on earth. She had had herself taken into a room furnished with all possible elegance and taste. She was lying there, casually attired, on a voluptuous bed whose heavy lilac-colored curtains contrasted pleasantly with garlands of freshly cut flowers: bunches of roses, carnations, jasmine, and tuberoses embellished every corner of her room. She was plucking the petals of the flowers and putting them into a basket, then covering her bed and the rest of the room with them. The moment she saw me, she extended her hand in greeting.

"Come over here, Florville," she said to me, "embrace me on my bed of flowers. . . . How tall and lovely you have grown. . . . Ah, by my faith! virtue indeed agrees with you. . . . They've informed you of my condition, I'm sure they have, Florville. . . . I'm full aware of it myself. . . . In a few hours I'll be gone. . . . I did not expect our reunion would be so brief. . . ." And as she saw my eyes filling with tears: "Come, now, my silly chit," she went on, "don't be a child. . . . Do you then think me so wretched? Have I not enjoyed myself as much as any woman on the face of this earth? I lose naught save those years when I would have had to give up all my pleasures, and how would I have managed without them? In truth, I in no wise regret not having lived any longer; in a short while, no man would have deigned to give me a second look, and I have never aspired to live to an age when I would inspire naught but feelings of repulsion and disgust. Death, my child, is an object of fear only to those who believe. Constantly torn between the images of heaven and hell, never certain which of the two will open to receive them, they are ravaged by anxiety, whilst I, who expect nothing, who am certain of being no more miserable after my death than I was before I was born, shall go peacefully to sleep, with no regrets and, likewise, with no sentiments of pain or sorrow, with no remorse and no misgivings. I have asked that I be laid to rest beneath my bower of jasmine, they have already prepared me a grave there, Florville, and there shall I lie. And the atoms emanating from this decaying body will help to nourish and sustain this flower which, of all flowers, I most loved. Think," she went on, stroking my cheeks with a bouquet of jasmine, "next year when you smell these flowers, you will be breathing the soul of your former friend; and as the scent rises to the fibers of your brain, it will implant in your mind some pleasant thoughts and force you to think of me."

Again tears welled up in my eyes. . . . I pressed this poor woman's hands tightly in mine, and I searched for a way to persuade her to give up these dreadful, materialistic ideas for some less impious philosophy. But scarcely had I begun to give voice to this thought than she pushed me away in alarm. . . .

"Oh, Florville," she cried, "I beg of you, do not poison my final moments with your false beliefs, and let me die in peace. I did not loathe them my whole life through only to embrace them on my deathbed. . . ."

I fell silent. What effect would my feeble eloquence have had, pitted as it was against such steadfastness of purpose? I would only have grieved Madame de Verquin without converting her; out of humanity, I desisted.

She rang; straightway I heard a sweet, melodious music which seemed to emanate from a neighboring room.

"This is how I intend to die, Florville," said that Epicurean. "Is't not preferable to being surrounded by a bevy of black-robed priests, who would only fill my last moments with confusion, threats, and despair? . . . No, I wish to teach your pious souls that one can, without emulating them, die in peace; I wish to persuade them that 'tis not religion that's needed for one to die with an untroubled soul, but simply courage and reason."

The hour was growing late. A notary, whom she had sent for, entered the room. The music ended, she dictated a few final wishes: childless, a widow for many years, and, consequently, mistress of many things, she made bequests to her friends and to her servants. Then she took a small coffer from a secretary near the bed.

"This is all I now have left," she said. "A little cash and a few jewels. Let us enjoy ourselves the rest of the evening. There are six of you here in the room, I shall divide all this into six parts, and we shall hold a lottery. We'll have a draw, and each of you shall keep whatever he wins."

I marveled at the woman's self-possession. It seemed to me incredible that one could have so many things wherewith to reproach oneself and yet arrive at one's final moments in a state of utter calm—'twas the baleful result of her lack of belief. If the horrible deaths of some evil people cause us to shudder, how much more frightened ought we to be by such steadfast obduracy!

None the less, her desires were carried out. A magnificent meal was served, in conformance with her orders. She ate heartily several courses, drank a number of Spanish wines and quaffed several different liqueurs, the doctor having told her that, in her condition, it made no difference.

The lottery was held, each of us won about a hundred *louis,* either in gold or in jewels. No sooner was this little game over than she was seized with a violent attack.

"Well, Doctor, is this the end?" she said, maintaining her perfect calm.

"Madame, I fear it is."

"Come hither then, Florville," she said to me, stretching out her arms, "come receive my last farewell, I wish to expire on the bosom of virtue. . . ."

She clasped me in a tight embrace, and her lovely eyes closed forever.

A stranger in that house, no longer having any reason to remain there, I straightway departed. . . . I leave it to your imagination to fancy the state I was in . . . and how much this spectacle had darkened my thoughts even further.

Madame de Verquin's manner of thinking and mine were too utterly opposed for me ever to love her sincerely. Had she not, in fact, been the prime cause of my disgrace, and all the misfortunes resulting therefrom? Yet this woman, the sister of the only man who had really ever cared for me, had always treated me with consideration and kindness, even unto her dying breath. My tears, therefore, were quite sincere, and became all the more bitter as I reflected that, with all her excellent qualities, that poor creature had been the unwilling cause of her own perdition and that, already cast forth from the bosom of the Almighty, she was doubtless even now suffering the punishments exacted for a life so depraved. God in His infinite wisdom and goodness vouchsafed to comfort me and help me banish these troubling thoughts from my heart. I fell to my knees and dared pray to Him that He might forgive that unfortunate soul. I, who so sorely needed Heaven's grace, dared to implore it for others, and to move it as much as 'twere in my power I added ten *louis* of my own to what I had won at Madame de Verquin's, and straightway had it distributed among the poor of her parish.

Moreover, this unfortunate woman's wishes were scrupulously carried out; the arrangements she had made were too meticulous for them not to be. She was buried in her bower of jasmine, and on her tombstone was engraved the one word: VIXIT.

Thuswise did the sister of my dearest friend meet her end: a fountain of intelligence and knowledge, possessed of great grace and talent, Madame de Verquin, had she chosen to live a different life, would have been deserving of the love and esteem of all who knew her; all she garnered was contempt. Her licentious habits increased with age—one is never more dangerous, when one has no principles, than at the age when one has ceased to blush. Depravity sits like gangrene upon the heart, one hones one's initial misdeeds to a finer edge and, imperceptibly, one begins to commit the most heinous crimes, still fancying they are but harmless misdemeanors.

I was amazed by the incredible blindness of Madame de Verquin's brother. 'Tis the distinctive characteristic of candor and goodness; decent people never suspect the evil whereof they themselves are incapable, and this explains why they are so easily duped by the first rogue who chances along to take advantage of them, and why 'tis so easy, and so inglorious, to deceive them. The insolent rogue who attempts it is working only to debase himself and, without even proving his talent for vice, merely manages to make virtue seem all the more brilliant.

In losing Madame de Verquin, I had lost all hope of ever learning any news of my son and my lover—you can imagine that, given the frightful condition in which I had found her, I had not dared to broach the subject.

Completely crushed by this catastrophe, utterly exhausted by a voyage made in a most painful state of mind, I resolved to rest for a while in Nancy—at an inn where I had previously put up—seeing absolutely no one, since Monsieur de Saint-Prât had seemingly wished that I conceal my real name. 'Twas from there I wrote my dear protector, determined not to leave until I had received his reply.

*A miserable girl, who is nothing to you, Monsieur,* I wrote to him, *whose only claim upon you is for your pity, endlessly upsets your life; instead of writing to you of the grief you must be feeling over the loss you have just suffered, she dares speak to you of herself, ask you what you would have her do, and awaits your orders,* etc.

But it was ordained that misfortune would stalk me wheresoever I went, and that I would be either the eternal victim of or witness to its sinister effects.

One evening I was returning to the inn rather late, having ventured out for a breath of fresh air, accompanied by my chambermaid and a footman I had hired upon my arrival in Nancy. Everyone else had already retired for the night.

As I was about to go up to my room, a tall and still very handsome woman about fifty years of age, whom I recognized from having seen her since I had moved into the inn—this woman, I say, suddenly emerged from her room, which was adjacent to mine, and, armed with a dagger, burst into a room across the corridor. My natural reaction was to see. . . . I hastened forward, with my maid and footman trailing close behind. In the twinkling of an eye, before we even had time to call to her or come to her aid, we saw the poor creature throw herself upon another woman and, twenty times over, drive the dagger into her heart, then cross back over to her own room, so completely distraught that she even failed to notice our presence. Our first thought was that the poor creature had gone stark raving mad. We could not understand a crime for which we could detect no motive. My maid and footman were on the verge of crying out. For reasons I was unable to fathom, some pressing urgency caused me to command them to remain silent. Taking them both by the arm, I herded them with me into my room and immediately closed the door behind us.

A frightful commotion was soon heard. The woman who had just been stabbed somehow managed to stagger out onto the stairs, screaming horribly, and, before she breathed her last, named her assailant. And as we were known to be the last to enter the inn before the murder was committed, we were arrested at the same time as the culprit.

None the less, the dying woman's accusation freed us from any taint of suspicion, and the authorities merely ordered us not to leave the inn until after the trial.

Cast into prison, the murderess refused to admit her guilt, and steadfastly maintained that she was innocent. There were no other witnesses save me and my servants. We were summoned to testify; I had great difficulty concealing the uneasiness wherewith I was being devoured . . . I who deserved death fully as much as this woman whom my forced testimony would surely send to the gallows, for, although the circumstances were somewhat different, I was guilty of the same crime. I have no idea to what lengths I would have gone to avoid making this cruel deposition. It was as though each word I uttered in testimony were another drop of blood wrung from my heart. Still, there was no way around it, the testimony had to be given: we confessed to what we had seen.

However convinced were the authorities, moreover, that 'twas this woman who had committed the crime—her motive, apparently, was to rid herself of a rival—however convinced they were, I say, that she was the guilty party, we later learned beyond any shadow of a doubt that without our testimony it would have been impossible to convict her. There was, it seems, a man somehow implicated in the affair, who had fled following the murder and who might otherwise have been a likely suspect. But our testimony, and especially that of my footman—who was attached to the inn where the crime had taken place—these cruel depositions which we had no choice but to make or run the risk of implicating ourselves, sealed the poor woman's doom.

The last time I confronted her, this woman examined me in considerable amazement and asked how old I was.

"Thirty-four," I told her.

"Thirty-four? . . . And you're a native of this region? . . ."

"No, Madame."

"Your name is Florville?"

"Yes, 'tis thus I am called."

"I do not know you," she went on, "but you are highly esteemed in this town and considered a most respectable young lady. That, unfortunately for me, is quite enough."

Then, in a state of considerable agitation, she continued:

"Mademoiselle, in the depths of this frightful situation wherein I find myself, you appeared to me in a dream. You were there with my son . . . for I am a mother and, as you see, a most unhappy one . . . your face was the same . . . you were wearing the same dress . . . and the scaffold loomed before my eyes. . . ."

"A dream," I cried, "a dream, Madame!" immediately recalling my own dream; I was struck by this woman's features, I recognized her as the woman who had appeared with Senneval in my own dream, near the coffin bristling with thorns. . . . Tears flowed from my eyes . . . the more I examined this woman, the more I was tempted to retract my testimony. . . . I wanted to request that I be put to death in her place. . . . I wanted to flee, but could not tear myself away. . . .

When the authorities saw the terrible state this confrontation had put me in, they confined themselves—since they were persuaded of my innocence—to separating us. I returned home in a state of complete despair, prey to a whole host of confused sentiments the cause of which I was unable to discover. The following day, that poor woman was put to death.

That same day, I received the reply from Monsieur de Saint-Prât. He urged me to return to Paris. As Nancy was anything but a pleasant place for me after the baleful scenes I had witnessed there, I left it without a moment's delay and headed for the capital, pursued by the fresh ghost of that woman, who seemed with every passing moment to be crying out to me:

*'Tis thou, wretched girl,'tis thou who hast sent me to my death, and thou knowest not whom thy hand has brought low, even unto the grave.*

Overwhelmed by such an accumulation of calamities, persecuted by as many sorrows, I besought Monsieur de Saint-Prât to find me some retreat where I might finish out my days in the most complete solitude, and in the strictest observance of my religious duties. He suggested the one wherein you discovered me, Monsieur; I entered it that same week and did not leave it save twice a month to visit my dear protector, and to spend a few moments with Madame de Lérince. But Heaven, which seemed intent upon raining down ever new afflictions upon me, denied me the pleasure of long enjoying my friend's company: I had the misfortune to lose her last year. Because of her tender feelings for me, she claimed my presence during those cruel moments, and 'twas also in my arms that she breathed her last.

But—and who would have believed it, Monsieur?—her death was not as peaceful as that of Madame de Verquin. The latter, expecting nothing, had no fear of losing everything; the former seemed to tremble at the thought of seeing the certain object of her hope disappear. In the woman who should have been beset by remorse from all quarters, there was none, so far as I could see; Madame de Lérince, who had never had any cause for remorse, was filled with it. In dying, Madame de Verquin had but one regret, and that was that she had been unable to do enough evil. Madame de Lérince died lamenting the good she had left undone. The former, deploring naught save the loss of her pleasure, covered herself with flowers; the latter wished to die upon a cross of ashes, full of regret at the memory of those many hours she had not devoted to virtue.

This contrast made a profound impression upon me; my conscience weakened. "And why?" I asked myself, "why should the practice of virtue not result in a feeling of peace at such moments, when it seems granted to the partisans of evil?" But just then, strengthened by a heavenly voice which seemed to thunder forth from the depths of my heart, I cried out: "Is't for me to try and fathom the will of the Almighty? What I saw only assures me all the more of the value of righteousness: Madame de Lérince's fears are virtue's anxiety and concern; whilst Madame de Verquin's cruel apathy is but the final aberration of crime. Ah, if 'tis given to me to choose at my final moments, may God grant me the grace rather to be afraid like Madame de Lérince than benumbed like Madame de Verquin."

Such, then, is the last of my adventures, Monsieur. For the past two years I have been living in the Convent of the Assumption, where my benefactor placed me. Yes, Monsieur, for two years now I have lived there, without having known a single moment's repose, without having spent a single night without the image of poor Saint-Ange and that of the unfortunate woman who, by my testimony, was condemned in Nancy, appearing to me. 'Twas thus you found me; these are the secrets I had to reveal to you. Was it not my bounden duty to relate them to you before yielding to the sentiments wherewith you are deluded? Will you now consider whether 'tis possible for me to be worthy of you? . . . Ponder whether she whose soul is so overcome with affliction can ever bring into your life any moments of joy. Oh! Monsieur, rid yourself of your illusions; let me return to the harsh retreat which alone befits me. Were you to wrench me from it, you would only have before you the constant spectacle of remorse, pain, and misfortune.

Mademoiselle de Florville could not help finishing her story in a state of considerable agitation. By nature quick-witted, sensitive, and delicate, she could not avoid being deeply affected by the recital of her woes.

Monsieur de Courval, who saw no more plausible reason in

the later events described than in the former which might alter his plans, did all in his power to reassure the woman he loved.

"I repeat to you, Mademoiselle," he said to her, "there are indeed some singular and fateful things in what you have just told me. But I fail to see a single one which should trouble your conscience or harm your reputation. . . . An affair when you were sixteen . . . so be it, but think how excusable it was: your age; the blandishments of Madame de Verquin; a young man, perhaps quite charming, whom you have never laid eyes on again, isn't that so, Mademoiselle?" Monsieur de Courval added with a trace of concern in his voice, "and whom you may reasonably expect never to see again?"

"Oh, never, most assuredly never!" Florville replied, suspecting the reasons for Monsieur de Courval's anxiety.

"Well, then, Mademoiselle, let us conclude our arrangements," Monsieur de Courval resumed. "Let us complete them, I beg of you, and let me persuade you, without wasting another moment, that there is nothing in your story which can ever diminish in the heart of an honest man either the extreme consideration due to such a paragon of virtue or the homage demanded by so many charming qualities."

Mademoiselle de Florville asked permission to return again to Paris to consult with her protector one last time, firmly promising that, so far as she were concerned, no further obstacle would be raised in view of the proposed match. Monsieur de Courval could not very well refuse her permission to fulfill this worthy obligation.

She departed, and a week later returned with Monsieur de Saint-Prât. Monsieur de Courval showered him with courteous attentions; he made him full aware how flattered he was to ally himself with the person to whom Monsieur de Saint-Prât had vouchsafed his love and protection, and he urged him to continue to acknowledge that charming creature as his relative and ward. Saint-Prât replied to Monsieur de Courval's attentive remarks in the manner expected of such a gentleman, and went on to add even further encomiums to his assessment of Mademoiselle de Florville's character.

At last the day that Monsieur de Courval had so desired arrived; the ceremony was performed, and when the marriage contract was read, he was amazed to learn that Monsieur de Saint-Prât, without having told a soul, had added, in consideration of this marriage, four thousand pounds' income to the pension of like amount which Mademoiselle de Florville was already receiving from him, and a legacy of a hundred thousand francs payable to her after his death.

Upon seeing these newest proofs of her protector's generosity, this interesting girl could not restrain her tears, which flowed abundantly, and, in her heart of hearts, was delighted to be able to offer the man who had deigned to marry her, a fortune at least the equal of his own.

Sentiments of cordiality and unfettered joy, and assurances of mutual esteem and attachment marked the celebration of this marriage . . . this fateful marriage whose torches the Furies secretly extinguished.

Monsieur de Saint-Prât, as well as the bridegroom's friends, spent a week with Courval, but the newlyweds did not return to Paris with them. They decided to remain in the country until the onset of winter, to put some necessary order into their affairs and thus start off on the right foot when they set up housekeeping in Paris. Monsieur de Saint-Prât was entrusted with the task of finding them a pleasant house not far from his own, in order that they might see each other often.

With the pleasing prospect of these arrangements before them, Monsieur and Madame de Courval had already been at their country residence for three months, and had already good reason to believe a child was on the way—a piece of news they lost no time in communicating to kindly Monsieur de Saint-Prât—when an unexpected event cruelly occurred to dash the couple's happiness, turning the tender roses of hymen into the frightful cypresses of mourning.

Here my pen pauses. . . . I should spare the reader, ask him to proceed no further. . . . Yes, let him break off the story at this point, if he prefers not to shudder with horror. . . . Sad condition of man here on earth . . . cruel twists of unpredictable fate. . . . Why must Florville, the most virtuous, charming, and sensitive creature alive, find herself, through a most incredible chain of circumstances, the most abominable monster Nature has ever conceived?

One evening, this tender and loving wife was sitting next to her husband reading an unbelievably gloomy English novel which at the time was being much discussed.

"I must confess," she said, dropping her book, "here is a creature almost as miserable as I."

"As miserable as you," quoth Monsieur de Courval, clasping his beloved wife in his arms, "O Florville, I thought I had helped you to put all your tribulations behind you. . . . I see now I was mistaken. . . . But did you have to tell me in such brutal terms? . . ."

But Madame de Courval seemed oblivious to his entreaties; nor did she respond to his caresses with a single word, but mechanically pushed him away from her in terror and threw herself down upon the sofa on the far side of the room, where she burst into tears. In vain did her worthy husband come and cast himself at her feet, in vain did he beg this woman whom he adored to calm herself, or at least apprise him of the cause of such a fit of despair. Madame de Courval continued to push him away, to turn aside when he essayed to dry her tears, to such a degree that Monsieur de Courval, by then being thoroughly persuaded that some distressing memory of Florville's earlier passion had returned to inflame her heart anew, could not refrain from chiding her about it.

Madame de Courval listened to his reproaches, but when he was finished she rose to her feet.

"No, Monsieur," she said to her husband, "you are wrong in judging in this way the fit of depression wherewith I have just been overwhelmed. 'Tis not memory that alarms me, but forebodings which terrify me. . . . I see myself happy with you, Monsieur . . . yes, very happy . . . and I was not born to be happy. 'Tis impossible that I remain so very long, for it is ordained that the dawn of my happiness will never be aught but the lightning which precedes the thunderbolt. 'Tis this thought which caused me to tremble: I fear we are not destined to live together. Today your wife, perhaps tomorrow I shall no longer be. Deep in my heart, a secret voice cries out, saying that for me all this happiness is but a shadow, which will vanish like the flower which blooms and withers in the space of a single day. Therefore, do not accuse me of being capricious, nor say that I am growing cold or indifferent, Monsieur. My own guilt is an excess of sensibility, an unfortunate tendency to see things in the most sinister light possible, the cruel result of my reverses of fortune. . . ."

Monsieur de Courval was still at his wife's feet, trying unsuccessfully by his words and caresses to allay her fears, when suddenly—it was just before seven o'clock of an October evening—a servant entered to say that a man he had never seen before most urgently requested to have a word with Monsieur de Courval. . . . Florville shuddered . . . in spite of herself, tears streamed down her cheeks, she stumbled and almost fell; she tried to say something, but the words died on her lips.

More concerned about his wife's condition than with what he had just learned, Monsieur de Courval replied somewhat testily that the stranger should wait, and turned back to aid his wife. But Madame de Courval, fearing to succumb to the secret emotion wherewith she was gripped, and desiring to conceal her deepest feelings in the presence of the stranger who had just been announced, found the strength to struggle to her feet, and said:

" 'Tis nothing, Monsieur, nothing. Show the gentleman in."

The servant left, to return a moment later with a man about thirty-seven or thirty-eight, whose charming countenance bore the telltale signs of some deep-rooted sorrow.

"Father! . . ." cried the stranger, casting himself at Monsieur de Courval's feet. "Will you recognize a miserable son who has been separated from you for twenty-two years, a son more than punished for his cruel sins by the reverses of fortune he has suffered constantly since then?"

"What! You, my son! . . . Great God! . . . What circumstance . . . thankless creature . . . caused you to recall my existence?"

"My heart . . . this heart which, though guilty, has none the less never ceased to love you. . . . Listen to me, Father . . . pray do. I have greater misfortunes than my own to discover to you; please sit down and hear me out. Pray forgive me, Madame," continued young Courval, turning to his father's wife, "if I am obliged, though 'tis the first time in my life I have had the opportunity to pay you my respects, to reveal in your presence some terrible family misfortunes, which I can no longer conceal from my father."

"Speak then, Monsieur, speak," Madame de Courval managed to stammer, casting a wild glance at this young man. "Misfortune's language is not new to me; I have known it since childhood."

Then our traveler, in a state of uncontrollable uneasiness, stared fixedly at Madame de Courval, and said to her:

"You, unhappy, Madame! . . . Oh, Merciful Heaven, can you be as unhappy as we?"

They sat down. Madame de Courval's state would be difficult to describe. . . . She glanced at the visitor . . . quickly she lowered her eyes to the floor. . . . She gave a deep, racking sigh. Monsieur de Courval was weeping, and his son tried to calm him, beseeching him to listen closely to what he had to say. Finally the conversation became somewhat more orderly.

"I have so many things to tell you, Monsieur," said young Courval, "that I trust you will allow me to gloss over the details and go straight to the heart of the matter. And I ask that both you and Madame give your word not to interrupt me before I have reached the end of my tale.

"I left you when I was fifteen, Monsieur; my first impulse was to follow my mother, whom I was blind enough to prefer to you. You and she had been separated for many years. I rejoined her in Lyon, where her riotous living so frightened me that I found myself obliged to leave her, were I to preserve whatever sentiments I had left for her. I went to Strasbourg, where the Normandy regiment was stationed. . . ."

Madame de Courval gave a start, but kept control of herself.

"The colonel seemed interested in me," young Courval went on. "I made myself known to him, and he gave me a commission as a second lieutenant. The following year, I accompanied the regiment to Nancy, where it was transferred, and there I fell in love with a young relative of Madame de Verquin. I seduced this young girl, had a son by her, and cruelly abandoned her."

At these words, Madame de Courval trembled, a low sigh welled from her breast, but she otherwise managed to maintain her composure.

"This unhappy affair was the cause of all my misfortunes. I placed the poor girl's child with a woman near Metz, who promised to take care of him, and a short while later rejoined my regiment.

I was condemned for my conduct: since the girl had not been able to return to Nancy, I was accused of having been the cause of her ruin. Too charming and likable a creature not to have caught the fancy of the entire town, she did not lack for defenders, who were bent upon avenging her honor. I fought a duel and killed my opponent. I then fled to Torino with my son, whom I had returned to fetch near Metz.

"For twelve years I served the King of Sardinia. I shall spare you the detailed description of my tribulations during this period. Suffice it to say they were infinite. 'Tis upon leaving France that one learns to miss it. Still, my son was growing into manhood, and a most promising young man he was too. In Torino I had met a French woman who had accompanied that Princess of France who had married into the Court of Sardinia, and that worthy person having taken a sympathetic interest in my misfortunes, I dared ask her to take my son with her to France, in order to complete his education. I promised to put my affairs sufficiently in order that I would be able to come and reclaim the boy from her care within six years. She consented, took my poor child to Paris with her, spared no effort to bring him up properly, and kept me fully and regularly informed of his progress.

"I appeared a year earlier than I had promised. I arrived at the lady's house, full of the sweet expectation of embracing my son, of clasping in my arms this token of a love betrayed . . . but which still burned in my heart. 'Your son is dead,' quoth the worthy friend, her eyes overbrimming with tears. 'He was the victim of the same passion which was the cause of his father's misfortunes. We had taken him to the country with us; there he fell in love with a charming girl whose name I have promised not to divulge. Carried away by the violence of his passion, he tried to ravish by force what had been denied him by virtue. . . . A blow, struck solely with the intention of frightening him off, went straight into his heart, and killed him outright.' "

At this point, Madame de Courval fell into a sort of trance, which for a moment made them fear she had suddenly been struck dead: her eyes were wide and staring fixedly; the blood had frozen in her veins. Monsieur de Courval, who had realized all too clearly the fatal connections binding together these adventures, interrupted his son and hastened to his wife's side. She came back to her senses and, with an heroic display of courage, managed to say:

"Let your son continue, Monsieur. Perhaps I have not yet reached the end of my trials."

All the while, young Courval, though he failed to understand why this lady was so disturbed about events which seemed to relate to her but indirectly, but discerning something incomprehensible for him in the features of his father's wife, looked at her intently, deeply moved.

Monsieur de Courval took his son's hand and, distracting his attention from Florville, commanded him to continue, but to concentrate on essentials and eliminate the details, because his tales were the repository of mysterious circumstances which were of the gravest import.

"In a state of utter despair over the death of my son," the traveler continued, "and having no further reason to remain in France—save for you, Father, whom I did not dare to face and whose wrath I greatly feared—I resolved to travel in Germany. . . . Ill-starred author of my days, I now come to the cruelest part of my story," said young Courval, bathing his father's hands with his tears. "Summon your courage, I beseech you.

"When I arrived at Nancy, I learned that a Madame Desbarres—that was the name which my mother, as soon as she had led you to believe she was dead, had assumed in her disorderly life—I learned, I say, that this same Madame Desbarres had just been cast into prison for having stabbed her rival, and that she was perhaps going to be executed the following day."

"Oh, Monsieur," poor Florville cried out at this point, burying herself in her husband's breast, her body racked with sobs, "Oh, Monsieur, do you now see the full measure of my miseries?"

"Yes, Madame, I do indeed," said Monsieur de Courval. "I see everything, Madame, but I beg you to let my son finish."

Florville contained herself, but she was scarcely breathing, her every feeling was impaired, her nerves were stretched to the breaking point.

"Go on, my son, go on," quoth the unhappy father. "In a moment I shall explain everything to you."

"Very well, Monsieur," young Courval went on. "I inquired

whether there were not some mistake in names, but unfortunately it was only too true that the criminal was my mother. I asked permission to see her, the request was granted. I threw myself in her arms. . . . 'I am guilty of the crime for which I am going to die,' this unhappy creature said to me, 'but there is a terrible quirk of fate in the affair which is responsible for my death. There was another person under suspicion; all evidence pointed to him. But a woman and her two servants who, as chance would have it, were residing in the inn, witnessed my crime, though I was so distraught that I failed to notice them. Their testimony alone is responsible for my death. No matter, let us not waste our last moments together in useless regrets. I have some secrets of great consequence to divulge: now listen closely to what I have to say, my boy.

" 'The moment my eyes have closed forever, go and seek out my husband. Tell him that, amongst my many crimes, is one whereof he is ignorant and which I must finally confess. You have a sister, Courval. . . . She was born a year after you. . . . I doted on you, and was afraid this girl might be a menace to you, that her father, at the time of her marriage, might settle a dowry upon her, using part of the inheritance which should have been yours alone. In order to keep your legacy intact, I resolved both to get rid of this girl and to make certain that in the future my husband would cull no further fruits from our marital bonds. My disorders led me into other sins, and prevented me from feeling the effects of these new crimes by causing me to commit even more terrible ones. But as for my daughter, I determined absolutely to murder her. I was about to put this infamous plan into effect, in concert with the wet nurse, whom I had amply compensated, when this woman told me that she knew a man who, married for years, was childless, though he wanted nothing more than to have children. Why didn't I kill two birds with one stone, she said to me: get rid of my daughter and perhaps make the man happy?

" 'I straightway accepted her suggestion. That same evening, my daughter was placed on this man's doorstep, with a letter in her cradle.

" 'The minute I am dead, fly to Paris and ask your father's forgiveness for me, beg him not to curse my memory and to go fetch that child and bring her back home into his own house.'

"With these words, my mother embraced me . . . and tried to calm the frightful agitation into which I had been plunged by all she had revealed to me. . . . Oh, Father, the following day she was executed. I was felled by a terrible illness, which reduced me to the edge of the grave, where I hovered for two years between life and death, with neither the strength nor the courage to write you.

"Upon recovering my health, my initial act was to come and cast myself at your feet, to beg forgiveness for your poor, unfortunate wife, and to discover to you the name of the person who can give you news of my sister: Monsieur de Saint-Prât."

Monsieur de Courval faltered, his senses began to fail him and grow benumbed, he was nigh unto unconscious . . . his condition became truly alarming.

As for Florville, who had been suffering the tortures of hell for the past quarter hour, she arose with the tranquillity of someone who has just come to a decision.

"Very well, Monsieur," she said to Courval, "do you now believe there exists somewhere in the world a criminal more atrocious than poor Florville? . . . Let me tell you then who I am, Senneval: at once your sister, the girl you seduced in Nancy, the murderer of your son, and the loathsome creature who dispatched your mother to the gallows. . . . Yes, gentlemen, these are my crimes: no matter which of you I cast my eyes upon, I see only an object of horror. Either I see my lover as my brother, or I see my husband as the author of my days. And if I look at myself, I see naught but the execrable monster who stabbed her own son and was the instrument of her mother's death. Do you think Heaven can have a sufficient store of torments for me? Do you think, given the tortures wherewith my heart is laden, that I can go on living a moment longer? No, there remains but one further crime to commit, a crime which will avenge all the others."

And so saying, the poor girl leapt forward, snatched up one of Senneval's pistols, and blew out her brains before either of them had time to realize what she was about. She died without uttering another word.

Monsieur de Courval fainted. His son, stunned by the scenes he had just witnessed, called for help as best he could. Florville was beyond all help: already the shadows of death were overspreading her bloodstained face, whose features were now convulsed not only because of her violent end but also because of the sentiments of despair which filled her heart at the moment of her death.

Monsieur de Courval was transported to his bed, where for two months he lingered close to the grave. His son, in an equally cruel state, none the less was fortunate enough to see his tenderness and loving care rewarded by his father's recovery.

Both of them, however, after having suffered such cruel and manifold blows of misfortune, resolved to withdraw from the world. A rigorous, self-imposed solitude has removed them forever from the eyes of their friends, and there, in the bosom of piety and virtue, they are peacefully living out the thread of their sad and painful days, of their lives which were given them only to convince both them and all who read this unhappy tale that 'tis only in the darkness of the grave that man can find the peace which the wickedness of his fellow men, the disorder of his passions, and above all the fate decreed unto him, will deny him eternally here upon this earth.

# The Marquis de Sade

# Part Three

# The 120 Days of Sodom (1785)

$O_n$ the 22nd of October, 1785, Donatien-Alphonse-
François de Sade, for more than seven years a prisoner of
the Royal dungeons, and since February of 1784 confined
in the Bastille, began the final revision of his first major
work, which he entitled The 120 Days of Sodom. There are
those who consider it his masterpiece; there can be no doubt
that it is the foundation upon which the rest of his achievement reposes.

If this was the first major work, it was also the decisive step: three years earlier Sade had written the Dialogue
between a Priest and a Dying Man in which the ferocity of
his atheism and the rigor of his vision were evident, but
with The 120 Days he moved further, much further, into
a realm of philosophic absolutism from which there could
be no retreat. Sade was here declaring all-out war on the
society that had judged and imprisoned him, and on that
virtue which it preached as the ultimate good. If, up to
this time, he had been drawn instinctively to the twin poles
of pleasure and vice, now the full power of his intellect
entered into the fray. Henceforth he would do all he could
to "outrage the laws of both Nature and religion." Sade
was out to shock, as no writer had ever tried to shock his
readers before in the history of literature. He was fully
aware of what he was about. After describing his main

183

*characters and his plan of action in the opening pages of*
The 120 Days, *the author warns:*

> *I advise the overmodest to lay my book aside at once*
> *if he would not be scandalized, for 'tis already clear*
> *there's not much of the chaste in our plan, and we dare*
> *hold ourselves answerable in advance that there'll be*
> *still less in the execution. . . . And now, friend-reader,*
> *you must prepare your heart and your mind for the*
> *most impure tale that has ever been told since our*
> *world began, a book the likes of which are met with*
> *neither amongst the ancients nor amongst us mod-*
> *erns. . . .*

*If Sade was cognizant of the importance of the work*
*he was undertaking, he was also aware of the dangers of*
*seizure to which such a manuscript was constantly subject,*
*given the conditions and place of its composition. He there-*
*fore devised a method which, he thought, would at least*
*minimize the chances of having the manuscript lost or taken*
*from him. Using sheets of thin paper twelve centimeters*
*wide, he pasted them together into a kind of scroll just*
*over twelve meters long, which he thought would be rela-*
*tively easy to conceal. From the 22nd of October on, he*
*worked for twenty consecutive evenings, from seven till*
*ten, at the end of which time he had covered one side of the*
*scroll with a microscopic writing; he then continued on the*
*other side, until he had completed the manuscript[1] by the*
*28th of November. But all his precautions were in vain:*
*when the Bastille was stormed, most of the manuscripts*
*Sade had left behind were lost or destroyed, and neither the*
*notes nor the roll itself ever came into the author's hands*
*again. It must have been especially to the scroll of* The 120
Days *that Sade was referring when he wrote to his steward,*
*Gaufridy, in May, 1790, that its loss had caused him to*
*shed "tears of blood":*

---

[1] Prior to transferring the final draft to the scroll, Sade had prepared
copious notes; this doubtless explains the speed with which he transcribed
the material onto the roll of paper.

184

*There are moments when I am moved by a wish to join the Trappists, and I cannot say but what I may go off some fine day and vanish altogether from the scene. Never was I such a misanthrope as since I have returned into the midst of men; and if in their eyes I now have the look of a stranger, they may be very sure they produce the same effect upon me. I was not idle during my detention; consider, my dear lawyer, I had readied fifteen volumes for the printer; now that I am at large, hardly a quarter of those manuscripts remains to me. Through unpardonable thoughtlessness, Madame de Sade let some of them become lost, let others be seized; thirteen years of toil gone for naught! The bulk of those writings had remained behind in my room at the Bastille when, on the fourth of July, I was removed from there to Charenton; on the fourteenth the Bastille is stormed, overrun, and my manuscripts, six hundred books I owned, two thousand pounds worth of furniture, precious portraits, the lot is lacerated, burned, carried off, pillaged: a clean sweep, not a straw left: and all that owing to the sheer negligence of Madame de Sade. She had had ten whole days to retrieve my possessions; she could not but have known that the Bastille, which they had been cramming with guns, powder, soldiers, was being prepared either for an attack or for a defense. Why then did she not hasten to get my belongings out of harm's way? my manuscripts?—my manuscripts over whose loss I shed tears of blood! Other beds, tables, chests of drawers can be found, but ideas once gone are not found again. . . . No, my friend, no, I shall never be able to figure to you my despair at their loss, for me it is irreparable. . . .*[2]

Justine, Juliette, Philosophy in the Bedroom, *and* La Nouvelle Justine *all represent attempts by Sade to recon-*

---

[2] The Marquis de Sade: *The Complete Justine, Philosophy in the Bedroom, and Other Writings.* New York, Grove Press, 1965, p. 144.

*stitute, in one form or another, the elements he had ex-*
*pounded in* The 120 Days of Sodom, *which he assumed lost*
*forever. But, though Sade would never know it, the precious*
*roll had not been destroyed. It was found, in the same cell*
*of the Bastille where Sade had been kept prisoner, by one*
*Arnoux de Saint-Maximin, and thence came into the posses-*
*sion of the Villeneuve-Trans family, in whose care it re-*
*mained for three generations. At the turn of the present*
*century, it was sold to a German collector, and in 1904 it*
*was published by the German psychiatrist, Dr. Iwan Bloch,*
*under the pseudonym of Eugene Dühren. Bloch justified his*
*publishing the work by its "scientific importance . . . to*
*doctors, jurists, and anthropologists," pointing out in his*
*notes the "amazing analogies" between cases cited by Sade*
*and those recorded a century later by Krafft-Ebing. Bloch's*
*text, however, as Lely notes, is replete with "thousands of*
*errors" which hopelessly denature and distort it.*

*After Bloch's death, the manuscript remained in Ger-*
*many until 1929, when Maurice Heine, at the behest of the*
*Viscount Charles de \*\*\*, went to Berlin to acquire it. From*
*1931 to 1935, Heine's masterful and authoritative text of*
*the work appeared in three quarto volumes, in what must*
*be considered the original edition of the work.*[3] *This is what*
*Heine had to say of* The 120 Days:

> *It is a document of singular value, as well as the first*
> *positive effort (aside from that of the father-confes-*
> *sors) to classify sexual anomalies. The man responsi-*
> *ble for having undertaken this methodical observation,*
> *a century before Krafft-Ebing and Freud, fully deserves*
> *the honor bestowed upon him by scholars of having*
> *the gravest of these psychopathic conditions known by*
> *the term "sadism."*[4]

*And Lely, on* The 120 Days:

---

[3] *Les 120 Journées de Sodom, ou l'Ecole du Libertinage, par le marquis*
*de Sade. Edition critique établie sur le manuscrit original autographe par*
*Maurice Heine, A Paris, par S et C, aux dépens des bibliophiles souscrip-*
*teurs, 1931–1935.*
[4] *Ibid.*

186

*Despite the reservations one has to make,*[5] The 120 Days *contains some of the most admirable pages the Marquis de Sade ever wrote. The texture, the breadth, the sweep of the sentences, all seem more allied to his correspondence . . . than to his other works. The Introduction, wherein we see deployed to full advantage the resources of his art, in its newest and most spontaneous form, is without doubt Sade's masterpiece. . . .*[6]

*There are other works more finished, of greater literary merit and with a philosophic content more developed, but Messrs. Heine and Lely are correct:* The 120 Days of Sodom *is the seminal work in all Sade's writing. It is perhaps his masterpiece; at the very least, it is the cornerstone on which the massive edifice he constructed was founded.*

---

[5] Lely's reservations center around the exaggerated emphasis Sade placed, in *The 120 Days,* upon the coprophilic aberration.

[6] Lely, *op. cit.,* Vol. II, p. 334.

# TABLE OF CONTENTS

## PART THE FIRST

THE 150 SIMPLE PASSIONS COMPOSING THE NARRATION
OF MADAME DUCLOS FOR THE MONTH OF NOVEMBER

# INTRODUCTION

*T*he extensive wars wherewith Louis XIV was burdened during his reign, while draining the State's treasury and exhaust-
ing the substance of the people, none the less contained the secret
that led to the prosperity of a swarm of those bloodsuckers who are
always on the watch for public calamities, which, instead of appeasing, they promote or invent so as, precisely, to be able to profit from
them the more advantageously. The end of this so very sublime
reign was perhaps one of the periods in the history of the French
Empire when one saw the emergence of the greatest number of
these mysterious fortunes whose origins are as obscure as the lust
and debauchery that accompany them. It was toward the close of
this period, and not long before the Regent sought, by means of the
famous tribunal which goes under the name of the *Chambre de
Justice,* to flush this multitude of traffickers, that four of them conceived the idea for the singular revels whereof we are going to give
an account. One must not suppose that it was exclusively the low-
born and vulgar sort which did this swindling; gentlemen of the
highest note led the pack. The Duc de Blangis and his brother the
Bishop of X***, each of whom had thuswise amassed immense fortunes, are in themselves solid proof that, like the others, the nobility neglected no opportunities to take this road to wealth. These
two illustrious figures, through their pleasures and business closely
associated with the celebrated Durcet and the Président de Curval,
were the first to hit upon the debauch we propose to chronicle, and
having communicated the scheme to their two friends, all four
agreed to assume the major roles in these unusual orgies.

For above six years these four libertines, kindred through their wealth and tastes, had thought to strengthen their ties by means of alliances in which debauchery had by far a heavier part than any of the other motives that ordinarily serve as a basis for such bonds. What they arranged was as follows: the Duc de Blangis, thrice a widower and sire of two daughters one wife had given him, having noticed that the Président de Curval appeared interested in marrying the elder of these girls, despite the familiarities he knew perfectly well her father had indulged in with her, the Duc, I say, suddenly conceived the idea of a triple alliance.

"You want Julie for your wife," said he to Curval, "I give her to you unhesitatingly and put but one condition to the match: that you'll not be jealous when, although your wife, she continues to show me the same complaisance she always has in the past; what is more, I'd have you lend your voice to mine in persuading our good Durcet to give me his daughter Constance, for whom, I must confess, I have developed roughly the same feelings you have formed for Julie."

"But," said Curval, "you are surely aware that Durcet, just as libertine as you . . ."

"I know all that's to be known," the Duc rejoined. "In this age, and with our manner of thinking, is one halted by such things? do you think I seek a wife in order to have a mistress? I want a wife that my whims may be served, I want her to veil, to cover an infinite number of little secret debauches the cloak of marriage wonderfully conceals. In a word, I want her for the reasons you want my daughter—do you fancy I am ignorant of your object and desires? We libertines wed women to hold slaves; as wives they are rendered more submissive than mistresses, and you know the value we set upon despotism in the joys we pursue."

It was at this point Durcet entered. His two friends related their conversation and, delighted by an overture which promptly induced him to avow the sentiments he too had conceived for Adelaide, the Président's daughter, Durcet accepted the Duc as his son-in-law, provided he might become Curval's. The three marriages were speedily concluded, the dowries were immense, the wedding contracts identical.

No less culpable than his two colleagues, the Président had

admitted to Durcet, who betrayed no displeasure upon learning it, that he maintained a little clandestine commerce with his own daughter; the three fathers, each wishing not only to preserve his rights, but noticing here the possibility of extending them, commonly agreed that the three young ladies, bound to their husbands by goods and homes only, would not in body belong more to one than to any of them, and the severest punishments were prescribed for her who should take it into her head not to comply with any of the conditions whereunto she was subject.

They were on the eve of realizing their plan when the Bishop of X***, already closebound through pleasure shared with his brother's two friends, proposed contributing a fourth element to the alliance should the other three gentlemen consent to his participation in the affair. This element, the Duc's second daughter and hence the Bishop's niece, was already more thoroughly his property than was generally imagined. He had effected connections with his sister-in-law and the two brothers knew beyond all shadow of doubt that the existence of this maiden, who was called Aline, was far more accurately to be ascribed to the Bishop than to the Duc; the former who, from the time she left the cradle, had taken the girl into his keeping, had not, as one may well suppose, stood idle as the years brought her charms to flower. And so, upon this head, he was his colleagues' equal, and the article he offered to put on the market was in an equal degree damaged or degraded; but as Aline's attractions and tender youth outshone even those of her three companions, she was unhesitatingly made a part of the bargain. As had the other three, the Bishop yielded her up, but retained the rights to her use; and so each of our four characters thus found himself husband to four wives. Thus there resulted an arrangement which, for the reader's convenience, we shall recapitulate:

The Duc, Julie's father, became the husband of Constance, Durcet's daughter;

Durcet, Constance's father, became the husband of Adelaide, the Président's daughter;

The Président, Adelaide's father, became the husband of Julie, the Duc's elder daughter;

And the Bishop, Aline's uncle and father, became the husband of the other three females by ceding this same Aline to his friends, the while retaining the same rights over her.

It was at a superb estate of the Duc, situated in the Bourbonnais, that these happy matches were made, and I leave to the reader to fancy how they were consummated and in what orgies; obliged as we are to describe others, we shall forego the pleasure of picturing these.

Upon their return to Paris, our four friends' association became only the firmer; and as our next task is to make the reader familiar with them, before proceeding to individual and more searching developments, a few details of their lubricious arrangements will serve, it seems to me, to shed a preliminary light upon the character of these debauchees.

The society had created a common fund, which each of its members took his turn administering for six months; the sums, allocated for nothing but expenses in the interests of pleasure, were vast. Their excessive wealth put the most unusual things within their reach, and the reader ought not be surprised to hear that two million were annually disbursed to obtain good cheer and lust's satisfaction.

Four accomplished procuresses to recruit women, and a similar number of pimps to scout out men, had the sole duty to range both the capital and the provinces and bring back everything, in the one gender and in the other, that could best satisfy their sensuality's demands. Four supper parties were held regularly every week in four different country houses located at four different extremities of Paris. At the first of these gatherings, the one exclusively given over to the pleasures of sodomy, only men were present; there would always be at hand sixteen young men, ranging in age from twenty to thirty, whose immense faculties permitted our four heroes, in feminine guise, to taste the most agreeable delights. The youths were selected solely upon the basis of the size of their member, and it almost became necessary that this superb limb be of such magnificence that it could never have penetrated any woman; this was an essential clause, and as naught was spared by way of expense, only very rarely would it fail to be fulfilled. But simultaneously to sample every pleasure, to these sixteen husbands was joined the same quantity of boys, much younger, whose purpose was to assume the office of women. These lads were from twelve to eighteen years old, and to be chosen for service each had to possess a freshness, a face, graces, charms, an air, an innocence, a candor which are far beyond what our brush could possibly paint. No woman was admitted to these masculine orgies, in the course of which everything of the lewdest invented in Sodom and Gomorrah was executed.

At the second supper were girls of superior class who, upon these occasions forced to give up their proud ostentation and the customary insolence of their bearing, were constrained, in return for their hire, to abandon themselves to the most irregular caprices, and often even to the outrages our libertines were pleased to inflict upon them. Twelve of these girls would appear, and as Paris could not have furnished a fresh supply of them as often as would have been necessary, these evenings were interspersed with others at which were admitted, only in the same number as the well-bred ladies, women ranging from procuresses up through the class of officers' wives. There are above four or five thousand women in Paris who belong to one or the other of the two latter classes and whom need or lust obliges to attend soirees of this kind; one has but to have good agents to find them, and our libertines, who were splendidly represented, would frequently come across miraculous specimens. But it was in vain one was honest or a decent woman, one had to submit to everything: our Lordships' libertinage, of a variety that never brooks limits, would overwhelm with horrors and infamies whatever, whether by Nature or social convention, ought to have been exempt from such ordeals. Once one was there, one had to be ready for anything, and as our four villains had every taste that accompanies the lowest, most crapulous debauch, this fundamental acquiescence to their desires was not by any means a matter of inconsequence.

The guests at the third supper were the vilest, foulest creatures that can possibly be met with. To him who has some acquaintance with debauchery's extravagances, this refinement will appear wholly understandable; 'tis most voluptuous to wallow, so to speak, in filth with persons of this category; these exercises offer the completest abandon, the most monstrous intemperance, the most total abasement, and these pleasures, compared with those tasted the evening before, or with the distinguished individuals in whose company we have tasted them, have a way of lending a sharp spice to earlier activities. At these third suppers, debauch being more thorough, nothing was omitted that might render it complex and piquant. A hundred whores would appear in the course of six hours, and only too often something less than the full hundred would leave the games. But there is nothing to be gained by hurrying our story or by broaching subjects which can only receive adequate treatment in the sequel.

As for the fourth supper, it was reserved for young maids; only those between the ages of seven and fifteen were permitted. Their condition in life was of no importance, what counted was their looks: they had to be charming; as for their virginity, authentic evidence was required. Oh, incredible refinement of libertinage! It was not, assuredly, that they wished to pluck all those roses, and how indeed could they have done so? for those untouched flowers were always a score in number, and of our four libertines only two were capable of proceeding to the act, one of the remaining two, the financier, being absolutely incapable of an erection, and the Bishop being absolutely unable to take his pleasure save in a fashion which, yes, I agree, may dishonor a virgin but which, however, always leaves her perfectly intact. No matter; the twenty maidenheads had to be there, and those which were not impaired by our quartet of masters became, before their eyes, the prey of certain of their valets just as depraved as they, whom they kept constantly at beck and call for more than one reason.

Apart from these four supper parties there was another, a secret and private one held every Friday, involving many fewer persons but surely costing a great deal more. The participants were restricted to four young and high-born damsels who, by means of strategy and money, had been abducted from their parents' homes. Our libertines' wives nearly always had a share in this debauch, and their extreme submissiveness, their docile attentions, their services made it more of a success each time. As for the genial atmosphere at these suppers, it goes without saying that even greater profusion than delicacy reigned there; not one of these meals cost less than ten thousand francs, and neighboring countries as well as all France were ransacked so that what was of the rarest and most exquisite might be assembled together. Fine and abundant wines and liqueurs were there, and even during the winter they had fruits of every season; in a word, one may be certain that the table of the world's greatest monarch was not dressed with as much luxury nor served with equal magnificence.

But now let us retrace our steps and do our best to portray one by one each of our four heroes—to describe each not in terms of the beautiful, not in a manner that would seduce or captivate the reader, but simply with the brush strokes of Nature which, despite all her disorder, is often sublime, indeed even when she is at her most depraved. For—and why not say so in passing—if crime lacks the kind of delicacy one finds in virtue, is not the former always more sublime, does it not unfailingly have a character of grandeur and sublimity which surpasses, and will always make it preferable to, the monotonous and lackluster charms of virtue? Will you protest the greater usefulness of this or of that, is it for us to scan Nature's laws, ours to determine whether, vice being just as necessary to Nature as is virtue, she perhaps does not implant in us, in equal quantity, the penchant for one or the other, depending upon her respective needs? But let us proceed.

The *Duc de Blangis,* at eighteen the master of an already colossal fortune which his later speculations much increased, experienced all the difficulties which descend like a cloud of locusts upon a rich and influential young man who need not deny himself anything; it almost always happens in such cases that the extent of one's assets turns into that of one's vices, and one stints oneself that much less the more one has the means to procure oneself everything. Had the Duc received a few elementary qualities from Nature, they might possibly have counterbalanced the dangers which beset him in his position, but this curious mother, who sometimes seems to collaborate with chance in order that the latter may favor every vice she gives to those certain beings of whom she expects attentions very different from those virtue supposes, and this because she has just as much need of the one as of the other, Nature, I say, in destining Blangis for immense wealth, had meticulously endowed him with every impulse, every inspiration required for its abuse. Together with a tenebrous and very evil mind, she had accorded him a heart of flint and an utterly criminal soul, and these were accompanied by the disorders in tastes and irregularity of whim whence were born the dreadful libertinage to which the Duc was in no common measure addicted. Born treacherous, harsh, imperious, barbaric, selfish, as lavish in the pursuit of pleasure as miserly when it were a question of useful spending, a liar, a gourmand, a drunk, a dastard, a sodomite, fond of incest, given to murdering, to arson, to theft, no, not a single virtue compensated that host of vices. Why, what am I saying! not only did he never so much as dream of a single virtue, he beheld them all with horror, and he was frequently heard to say that to be truly happy in this world a man ought not merely fling himself into every vice, but should never permit himself one virtue, and that it was not simply a matter of always doing evil, but also and above all of never doing good.

"Oh, there are plenty of people," the Duc used to observe, "who never misbehave save when passion spurs them to ill; later, the fire gone out of them, their now calm spirit peacefully returns to the path of virtue and, thus passing their life going from strife to error and from error to remorse, they end their days in such a way there is no telling just what roles they have enacted on earth. Such persons," he would continue, "must surely be miserable: forever drifting, continually undecided, their entire life is spent detesting in the morning what they did the evening before. Certain to repent of the pleasures they taste, they take their delight in quaking, in such sort they become at once virtuous in crime and criminal in virtue. However," our hero would add, "my more solid character is a stranger to these contradictions; I do my choosing without hesitation, and as I am always sure to find pleasure in the choice I make, never does regret arise to dull its charm. Firm in my principles because those I formed are sound and were formed very early, I always act in accordance with them; they have made me understand the emptiness and nullity of virtue; I hate virtue, and never will I be seen resorting to it. They have persuaded me that through vice alone is man capable of experiencing this moral and physical vibration which is the source of the most delicious voluptuousness; so I give myself over to vice. I was still very young when I learned to hold religion's fantasies in contempt, being perfectly convinced that the existence of a creator

is a revolting absurdity in which not even children continue to believe. I have no need to thwart my inclinations in order to flatter
some god; these instincts were given me by Nature, and it would be
to irritate her were I to resist them; if she gave me bad ones, that is
because they were necessary to her designs. I am in her hands but a
machine which she runs as she likes, and not one of my crimes does
not serve her: the more she urges me to commit them, the more of
them she needs; I should be a fool to disobey her. Thus, nothing
but the law stands in my way, but I defy the law, my gold and my
prestige keep me well beyond reach of those vulgar instruments of
repression which should be employed only upon the common sort."

If one were to raise the objection that, nevertheless, all men
possess ideas of the just and the unjust which can only be the product of Nature, since these notions are found in every people and
even amongst the uncivilized, the Duc would reply affirmatively,
saying that yes, those ideas have never been anything if not relative,
that the stronger has always considered exceedingly just what the
weaker regarded as flagrantly unjust, and that it takes no more
than the mere reversal of their positions for each to be able to
change his way of thinking too; whence the Duc would conclude that
nothing is really just but what makes for pleasure, and what is unjust is the cause of pain; that in taking a hundred *louis* from a
man's pocket, he was doing something very just for himself, although the victim of the robbery might have to regard the action
with another eye; that all these notions therefore being very arbitrary, a fool he who would allow himself to become their thrall. It
was by means of arguments in this kind the Duc used to justify his
transgressions, and as he was a man of greatest possible wit, his
arguments had a decisive ring. And so, modeling his conduct upon
his philosophy, the Duc had, from his most tender youth, abandoned
himself unrestrainedly to the most shameful extravagances, and to
the most extraordinary ones. His father, having died young and, as
I indicated, left him in control of a huge fortune, had however
stipulated in his will that the young man's mother should, while she
lived, be allowed to enjoy a large share of this legacy. Such a condition was not long in displeasing Blangis: poison appearing to be the
only way to avoid having to subscribe to this article, the knave
straightway decided to make use of it. But this was the period

when he was only making his first steps in a vicious career; not daring to act himself, he brought one of his sisters, with whom he was carrying on a criminal intrigue, to take charge of the execution, assuring her that if she were to succeed, he would see to it that she would be the beneficiary of that part of the fortune whereof death would deprive their mother. However, the young lady was horrified by this proposal, and the Duc, observing that this ill-confided secret was perhaps going to betray him, decided on the spot to extend his plans to include the sister he had hoped to have for an accomplice; he conducted both women to one of his properties whence the two unfortunate ones never returned. Nothing quite encourages as does one's first unpunished crime. This hurdle once cleared, an open field seemed to beckon to the Duc. Immediately any person whomsoever showed opposition to his desires, poison was employed forthwith. From necessary murders he soon passed to those of pure pleasure; he was captivated by that regrettable folly which causes us to find delight in the sufferings of others; he noticed that a violent commotion inflicted upon any kind of an adversary is answered by a vibrant thrill in our own nervous system; the effect of this vibration, arousing the animal spirits which flow within these nerves' concavities, obliges them to exert pressure on the erector nerves and to produce in accordance with this perturbation what is termed a lubricious sensation. Consequently, he set about committing thefts and murders in the name of debauchery and libertinage, just as someone else would be content, in order to inflame these same passions, to chase a whore or two. At the age of twenty-three, he and three of his companions in vice, whom he had indoctrinated with his philosophy, made up a party whose aim was to go out and stop a public coach on the highway, to rape the men among the travelers along with the women, to assassinate them afterward, to make off with their victims' money (the conspirators certainly had no need of this), and to be back that same night, all three of them, at the Opera Ball in order to have a sound alibi. This crime took place, ah, yes: two charming maids were violated and massacred in their mother's arms; to this was joined an endless list of other horrors, and no one dared suspect the Duc. Weary of the delightful wife his father had bestowed upon him before dying, the young Blangis wasted no time uniting her shade to his mother's, to his sister's, and to those of all his other victims. Why all this? to be able to marry a girl, wealthy, to be sure, but publicly dishonored and whom he knew full well was her brother's mistress. The person in question was the mother of Aline, one of the figures in our novel we mentioned above. This second wife, soon sacrificed like the first, gave way to a third, who followed hard on the heels of the second. It was rumored abroad that the Duc's huge construction was responsible for the undoing of all his wives, and as this gigantic tale corresponded in every point to its gigantic inspiration, the Duc let the opinion take root and veil the truth. That dreadful colossus did indeed make one think of a Hercules or a centaur: Blangis stood five feet eleven inches tall, had limbs of great strength and energy, powerful sinews, elastic nerves, in addition to that a proud and masculine visage, great dark eyes, handsome black eyelashes, an aquiline nose, fine teeth, a quality of health and exuberance, broad shoulders, a heavy chest but a well-proportioned figure withal, splendid hips, superb buttocks, the handsomest leg in the world, an iron temperament, the strength of a horse, the member of a veritable mule, wondrously hirsute, blessed with the ability to eject its sperm any number of times within a given day and at will, even at the age of fifty, which was his age at the time, a virtually constant erection in this member whose dimensions were an exact eight inches for circumference and twelve for length over-all, and there you have the portrait of the Duc de Blangis, drawn as accurately as if you'd wielded the pencil yourself. But if this masterpiece of Nature was violent in its desires, what was it like, Great God! when crowned by drunken voluptuousness? 'Twas a man no longer, 'twas a raging tiger. Woe unto him who happened then to be serving its passions; frightful cries, atrocious blasphemies sprang from the Duc's swollen breast, flames seemed to dart from his eyes, he foamed at the mouth, he whinnied like a stallion, you'd have taken him for the very god of lust. Whatever then was his manner of having his pleasure, his hands necessarily strayed, roamed continually, and he had been more than once seen to strangle a woman to death at the instant of his perfidious discharge. His presence of mind once restored, his frenzy was immediately replaced by the most complete indifference to the infamies wherewith he had just indulged himself, and of this indifference, of this kind of apathy, further sparks of lechery would be born almost at once.

In his youth, the Duc had been known to discharge as often as eighteen times a day, and that without appearing one jot more fatigued after the final than after the initial ejaculation. Seven or eight crises within the same interval still held no terrors for him, his half a century of years notwithstanding. For roughly twenty-five years he had accustomed himself to passive sodomy, and he withstood its assaults with the identical vigor that characterized his manner of delivering them actively when, the very next moment, it pleased him to exchange roles. He had once wagered he could sustain fifty-five attacks in a day, and so he had. Furnished, as we have pointed out, with prodigious strength, he needed only one hand to violate a girl, and he had proved it upon several occasions. One day he boasted he could squeeze the life out of a horse with his legs; he mounted the beast, it collapsed at the instant he had predicted. His prowess at the table outshone, if that is possible, what he demonstrated upon the bed. There's no imagining what had come to be the quantity of the food he consumed. He regularly ate three meals a day, and they were all three exceedingly prolonged and exceedingly copious, and it was as nothing to him to toss down his usual ten bottles of Burgundy; he had drunk up to thirty, and needed but to be challenged and he would set out for the mark of fifty; but his intoxication taking on the tinge of his passions, and liqueurs or wines having heated his brain, he would wax furious, and they would be obliged to tie him down. And despite all that, would you believe it? a steadfast child might have hurled this giant into a panic; true indeed it is that the spirit often poorly corresponds with the fleshly sheath enveloping it: as soon as Blangis discovered he could no longer use his treachery or his deceit to make away with his enemy, he would become timid and cowardly, and the mere thought of even the mildest combat, but fought on equal terms, would have sent him fleeing to the ends of the earth. He had nevertheless, in keeping with custom, been in one or two campaigns, but had acquitted himself so disgracefully he had retired from the service at once. Justifying his turpitude with equal amounts of cleverness and effrontery, he loudly proclaimed that his poltroonery being nothing other than the desire to preserve himself, it were perfectly impossible for anyone in his right senses to condemn it for a fault.

Keep in mind the identical moral traits; next, adapt them to an entity from the physical point of view infinitely inferior to the one we have just described; there you have the portrait of the *Bishop of X\*\*\**, the Duc de Blangis' brother. The same black soul, the same penchant for crime, the same contempt for religion, the same atheism, the same deception and cunning, a yet more supple and adroit mind, however, and more art in guiding his victims to their doom, but a slender figure, not heavy, no, a little thin body, wavering health, very delicate nerves, a greater fastidiousness in the pursuit of pleasure, mediocre prowess, a most ordinary member, even small, but deft, profoundly skilled in management, each time yielding so little that his incessantly inflamed imagination would render him capable of tasting delight quite as frequently as his brother; his sensations were of a remarkable acuteness, he would experience an irritation so prodigious he would often fall into a deep swoon upon discharging, and he almost always temporarily lost consciousness when doing so.

He was forty-five, had delicate features, rather attractive eyes but a foul mouth and ugly teeth, a hairless pallid body, a small but well-shaped ass, and a prick five inches around and six in length. An idolater of active and passive sodomy, but eminently of the latter, he spent his life having himself buggered, and this pleasure, which never requires much expense of energy, was best suited to the modesty of his means. We will speak of his other tastes in good time. With what regards those of the table, he carried them nearly as far as the Duc, but went about the matter with somewhat more sensuality. Monseigneur, no less a criminal than his elder brother, possessed characteristics which had doubtless permitted him to match the celebrated feats of the hero we painted a moment ago; we will content ourselves with citing one of them, 'twill be enough to make the reader see of what such a man may be capable, and what he was prepared and disposed to do, having done the following:

One of his friends, a man powerful and rich, had formerly had an intrigue with a young noblewoman who had borne him two children, a girl and a boy. He had, however, never been able to wed her, and the maiden had become another's wife. The unlucky girl's lover died while still young, but the owner howbeit of a tremendous fortune; having no kin to provide for, it occurred to him to bequeath all he had to the two ill-fated children his affair had produced.

On his deathbed, he made the Bishop privy to his intentions and entrusted him with these two immense endowments: he divided the sum, put them in two purses, and gave them to the Bishop, confiding the two orphans' education to this man of God and enlisting him to pass on to each what was to be his when they attained their majority. At the same time he enjoined the prelate to invest his wards' funds, so that in the meantime they would double in size. He also affirmed that it was his design to leave his offsprings' mother in eternal ignorance of what he was doing for them, and he absolutely insisted that none of this should ever be mentioned to her. These arrangements concluded, the dying man closed his eyes, and Monseigneur found himself master of about a million in banknotes, and of two children. The scoundrel was not long deliberating his next step: the dying man had spoken to no one but him, the mother was to know nothing, the children were only four or five years old. He circulated the intelligence that his friend, upon expiring, had left his fortune to the poor; the rascal acquired it the same day. But to ruin those wretched children did not suffice; furnished with authority by their father, the Bishop—who never committed one crime without instantly conceiving another—had the children removed from the remote pension in which they were being brought up, and placed them under the roof of certain people in his hire, from the outset having resolved soon to make them serve his perfidious lust. He waited until they were thirteen; the little boy was the first to arrive at that age: the Bishop put him to use, bent him to all his debauches, and as he was extremely pretty, sported with him for a week. But the little girl fared less well: she reached the prescribed age, but was very ugly, a fact which had no mitigating effect upon the good Bishop's lubricious fury. His desires appeased, he feared lest these children, left alive, would someday discover something of the secret of their interests. Therefore, he conducted them to an estate belonging to his brother and, sure of recapturing,

by means of a new crime, the sparks of lechery enjoyment had just
caused him to lose, he immolated both of them to his ferocious
passions, and accompanied their death with episodes so piquant and
so cruel that his voluptuousness was reborn in the midst of the torments wherewith he beset them. The thing is, unhappily, only too
well known: there is no libertine at least a little steeped in vice who
is not aware of the great sway murder exerts over the senses, and
how voluptuously it determines a discharge. And that is a general
truth whereof it were well the reader be early advised before undertaking the perusal of a work which will surely attempt an ample
development of this system.

Henceforth at ease in the face of whatever might transpire,
Monseigneur returned to Paris to enjoy the fruit of his misdeeds,
and without the least qualms about having counteracted the intentions of a man who, in his present situation, was in no state to
derive either pain or pleasure therefrom.

The *Président de Curval* was a pillar of society; almost sixty
years of age, and worn by debauchery to a singular degree, he offered the eye not much more than a skeleton. He was tall, he was
dry, thin, had two blue lusterless eyes, a livid and unwholesome
mouth, a prominent chin, a long nose. Hairy as a satyr, flat-backed,
with slack, drooping buttocks that rather resembled a pair of dirty
rags flapping upon his upper thighs; the skin of those buttocks was,
thanks to whipstrokes, so deadened and toughened that you could
seize up a handful and knead it without his feeling a thing. In the
center of it all there was displayed—no need to spread those cheeks
—an immense orifice whose enormous diameter, odor, and color
bore a closer resemblance to the depths of a well-freighted privy
than to an asshole; and, crowning touch to these allurements, there
was numbered among this sodomizing pig's little idiosyncrasies that
of always leaving this particular part of himself in such a state of
uncleanliness that one was at all times able to observe there a rim
or pad a good two inches thick. Below a belly as wrinkled as it was
livid and gummy, one perceived, within a forest of hairs, a tool
which, in its erectile condition, might have been about eight inches
long and seven around; but this condition had come to be most rare

and to procure it a furious sequence of things was the necessary preliminary. Nevertheless, the event occurred at least two or three times each week, and upon these occasions the Président would glide into every hole to be found, indiscriminately, although that of a young lad's behind was infinitely the most precious to him. The head of the Président's device was now at all times exposed, for he had had himself circumcised, a ceremony which largely facilitates enjoyment and to which all pleasure-loving persons ought to submit. But one of the purposes of the same operation is to keep this privity cleaner; nothing of the sort in Curval's case: this part of him was just as filthy as the other: this uncapped head, naturally quite thick to begin with, was thus made at least an inch ampler in circumference. Similarly untidy about all the rest of his person, the Président, who furthermore had tastes at the very least as nasty as his appearance, had become a figure whose rather malodorous vicinity might not have succeeded in pleasing everyone. However, his colleagues were not at all of the sort to be scandalized by such trifles, and they simply avoided discussing the matter with him. Few mortals had been as free in their behavior or as debauched as the Président; but, entirely jaded, absolutely besotted, all that remained to him was the depravation and lewd profligacy of libertinage. Above three hours of excess, and of the most outrageous excess, were needed before one could hope to inspire a voluptuous reaction in him. As for his emission, although in Curval the phenomenon was far more frequent than erection, and could be observed once every day, it was, all the same, so difficult to obtain, or it never occurred save as an aftermath to things so strange and often so cruel or so unclean, that the agents of his pleasures not uncommonly renounced the struggle, fainting by the wayside, the which would give birth in him to a kind of lubricious anger and this, through its effects, would now and again triumph where his efforts had failed. Curval was to such a point mired down in the morass of vice and libertinage that it had become virtually impossible for him to think or speak of anything else. He unendingly had the most appalling expressions in his mouth, just as he had the vilest designs in his heart, and these with surpassing energy he mingled with blasphemies and imprecations supplied him by his true horror, a sentiment he shared with his companions, for everything that smacked of religion. This disorder of mind, yet further augmented by the almost continual intoxication in which he was fond of keeping himself, had during the past few years given him an air of imbecility and prostration which, he would declare, made for his most cherished delight.

Born as great a gourmand as a drunk, he alone was fit to keep abreast of the Duc, and in the course of this tale we will behold him to perform wonders which will no doubt astonish the most veteran eaters.

It had been ten years since Curval had ceased to discharge his judicial duties; it was not simply that he was no longer fit to carry them out, but I even believe that while he had been, he may have been asked to leave these matters alone for the rest of his life.

Curval had led a very libertine life, every sort of perversion was familiar to him, and those who knew him personally had the strong suspicion he owed his vast fortune to nothing other than two or three execrable murders. However that may be, it is, in the light of the following story, highly probable that this variety of extravagance had the power to stir him deeply, and it is this adventure, which attracted some unfortunate publicity, that was responsible for his exclusion from the Court. We are going to relate the episode in order to give the reader an idea of his character.

There dwelled in the neighborhood of Curval's town house a miserable street porter who, the father of a charming little girl, was ridiculous enough to be a person of sensibility. Twenty messages of every kind had already arrived containing proposals relating to the poor fellow's daughter; he and his wife had remained unshaken despite this barrage aimed at their corruption, and Curval, the source of these embassies, only irritated by the growing number of refusals they had evoked, knew not what tack to take in order to get his hands upon the girl and to subject her to his libidinous caprices, until it struck him that by simply having the father broken he would lead the daughter to his bed. The thing was as nicely conceived as executed. Two or three bullies in the Président's pay intervened in the suit, and before the month was out, the wretched porter was enmeshed in an imaginary crime which seemed to have been committed at his door and which got him speedily lodged in one of the Conciergerie's dungeons. The Président, as one would expect, soon took charge of the case, and, having no desire to permit it to drag on, arranged in the space of three days, thanks to his knavery and his gold, to have the unlucky porter condemned to be broken on the wheel, without the culprit ever having committed any crime but that of wishing to preserve his honor and safeguard his daughter's.

Meanwhile, the solicitations were renewed. The mother was brought in, it was explained to her that she alone had it in her power to save her husband, that if she were to satisfy the Président, what could be clearer than that he would thereupon snatch her husband from the dreadful fate awaiting him. Further hesitation was impossible; the woman made inquiries; Curval knew perfectly well to whom she addressed herself, the counsels were his creatures, and they gave her unambiguous replies: she ought not waste a moment. The poor woman herself brought her daughter weeping to her judge's feet; the latter could not have been more liberal with his promises, nor have been less eager to keep his word. Not only did he fear lest, were he to deal honorably and spare the husband, the man might go and raise an uproar upon discovering the price that had been paid to save his life, but the scoundrel even found a further delight, a yet keener one, in arranging to have himself given what he wished without being obliged to make any return.

This thought led to others; numerous criminal possibilities entered his head, and their effect was to increase his perfidious lubricity. And this is how he set about the matter so as to put the maximum of infamy and piquancy into the scene:

His mansion stood facing a spot where criminals are sometimes executed in Paris, and as this particular offense had been committed in that quarter of the city, he won assurance the punishment would be meted out on this particular square. The wretch's wife and daughter arrived at the Président's home at the appointed hour; all windows overlooking the square were well shuttered, so that, from the apartments where he amused himself with his victims, nothing at all could be seen of what was going on outside. Apprised of the exact minute of the execution, the rascal selected it for the deflowering of the little girl who was held in her mother's arms, and everything was so happily arranged that Curval discharged into the child's ass the moment her father expired. Instantly he'd completed his business, "Come have a look," quoth he, opening a window looking upon the square, "come see how well I've kept my bargain," and one of his two princesses saw her father, the other her husband, delivering up his soul to the headsman's steel.

Both collapsed in a faint, but Curval had provided for everything: this swoon was their agony, they'd both been poisoned, and nevermore opened their eyes. Notwithstanding the precautions he had taken to swathe the whole of this exploit in the most profound mystery, something did indeed transpire: nothing was known of the women's death, but there existed a lively suspicion he had been untruthful in connection with the husband's case. His motive was half-known, and his eventual retirement from the bench was the outcome. As of this moment, no longer having to maintain appearances, Curval flung himself into a new ocean of errors and crimes. He sent everywhere for victims to sacrifice to the perversity of his tastes. Through an atrocious refinement of cruelty, but one, however, very easily understood, the downtrodden classes were those upon which he most enjoyed hurling the effects of his raging perfidy. He had several minions who were abroad night and day, scouring attics and hovels, tracking down whatever of the most destitute misery might be able to provide, and under the pretext of dispensing aid, either he envenomed his catch—to give poison was one of his most delectable pastimes—or he lured it to his house and slew it upon the altar of his perverse preferences. Men, women, children: anything was fuel to his rage, and at its bidding he performed excesses which would have got his head between block and blade a thousand times over were it not for the silver he distributed and the esteem he enjoyed, factors whereby he was a thousand times protected. One may well imagine such a being had no more religion than his two confreres; he without doubt detested it as sovereignly as they, but in years past had done more to wither it in others, for, in the days when his mind had been sound, it had also been clever, and he had put it to good use writing against religion; he was the author of several works whose influence had been prodigious, and these successes, always present in his memory, still constituted one of his dearest delights.

The more we multiply the objects of our enjoyments . . .[1]

(a) . . . the years of a sickly childhood.


(b) *Durcet* is fifty-three; he is small, short, broad, thickset; an agreeable, hearty face; a very white skin; his entire body, and principally his hips and buttocks, absolutely like a woman's; his ass is cool and fresh, chubby, firm, and dimpled, but excessively agape, owing to the habit of sodomy; his prick is extraordinarily small, 'tis scarcely two inches around, no more than four inches long; it has entirely ceased to stiffen; his discharges are rare and uneasy, far from abundant and always preceded by spasms which hurl him into a kind of furor which, in turn, conducts him to crime; he has a chest like a woman's, a sweet, pleasant voice and, when in society, the best-bred manners, although his mind is without question as depraved as his colleagues'; a schoolmate of the Duc, they still sport together every day, and one of Durcet's loftiest pleasures is to have his anus tickled by the Duc's enormous member.


And such, dear reader, are the four villains in whose company I am going to have you pass a few months. I have done my best to describe them; if, as I have wished, I have made you familiar with even their most secret depths, nothing in the tale of their various follies will astonish you. I have not been able to enter into minute detail with what regards their tastes—to have done so now would have been to impair the value and to harm the main scheme of this work. But as we move progressively along, you will have but to keep an attentive eye upon our heroes, and you'll have no trouble discerning their characteristic peccadillos and the particular type of voluptuous mania which best suits each of them. Roughly all we can say at the present time is that they were generally susceptible

---

[1] Place here the portrait of Durcet as it is in notebook 18, the one that's bound in pink, then, after having concluded this portrait with the words under (a) in the notebooks, continue with (b).

of an enthusiasm for sodomy, that the four of them had themselves buggered regularly, and that they all four worshiped behinds.

The Duc, however, relative to the immensity of his weapon and, doubtless, more through cruelty than from taste, still fucked cunts with the greatest pleasure.

So also did the Président, but less frequently.

As for the Bishop, such was his supreme loathing for them the mere sight of one might have kept him limp for six months. He had never in all his life fucked but one, that belonging to his sister-in-law, and expressly to beget a child wherewith some day to procure himself the pleasures of incest; we have seen how well he succeeded.

As regards Durcet, he certainly idolized the ass with as much fervor as the Bishop, but his enjoyment of it was more accessory; his favorite attacks were directed toward a third sanctuary—this mystery will be unveiled in the sequel. But on with the portraits essential to the intelligence of this work, and let us now give our reader an idea of these worthy husbands' four wives.

What a contrast! *Constance,* the Duc's wife and the daughter of Durcet, was a tall woman, slender, lovely as a picture, and modeled as if the Graces had taken pleasure in embellishing her, but the elegance of her figure in no way detracted from her freshness, she was not for that the less plumply fleshed, and the most delicious forms graced by a skin fairer than the lily, often induced one to suppose that, no, it had been Love itself who had undertaken her formation. Her face was a trifle long, her features wonderfully noble, more majesty than gentleness was in her look, more grandeur than subtlety. Her eyes were large, black, and full of fire; her mouth extremely small and ornamented by the finest teeth imaginable, she had a narrow, supple tongue, of the loveliest pink, and her breath was sweeter still than the scent of a rose. She was full-breasted, her bosom was most buxom, fair as alabaster and as firm. Her back was turned in an extraordinary way, its lines sweeping deliciously down to the most artistically and the most precisely cleft ass Nature has produced in a long time. Nothing could have been more perfectly round, not very large, but firm, white, dimpled; and when it was opened, what used to peep out but the cleanest, most winsome, most delicate hole. A nuance of tenderest pink had shaded this ass, charming asylum of lubricity's sweetest pleasures, but, great God! it was not for long to preserve so many charms! Four or five attacks, and the Duc had spoiled all those graces, how quickly had they gone, and soon after her marriage Constance was become no more than the image of a beautiful lily wherefrom the tempest has of late stripped the petals away. Two round and perfectly molded thighs supported another temple, in all likelihood less delicious, but, to him inclined to worship there, offering so many allurements it would be in vain were my pen to strive to describe them. Constance was almost a virgin when the Duc married her, and her father, the only man who had known her, had, as they say, left that side of her perfectly intact. The most beautiful black hair—falling in natural curls to below her shoulders and, when one wished it thus, reaching down to the pretty fur, of the same color, which shaded that voluptuous little cunt—made for a further adornment I might have been guilty of omitting, and lent this angelic creature, aged about twenty-two, all the charms Nature is able to lavish upon a woman. To all these amenities Constance joined a fair and agreeable wit, a spirit somewhat more elevated than it ought to have been, considering the melancholy situation fate had awarded her, for thereby she was enabled to sense all its horror and, doubtless, she would have been happier if furnished with less delicate perceptions.

Durcet, who had raised her more as if she were a courtesan than his daughter, and who had been much more concerned to give her talents than manners, had all the same never been able totally to destroy the principles of rectitude and of virtue it seemed Nature had been pleased to engrave in her heart. She had no formal religion, no one had ever mentioned such a thing to her, the exercise of a belief was not to be tolerated in her father's household, but all that had not blotted out this modesty, this natural humility which has nothing to do with theological chimeras, and which, when it dwells in an upright, decent, and sensitive soul, is very difficult to obliterate. Never had she stepped out of her father's house, and the scoundrel had forced her, beginning at the age of twelve, to serve his crapulous pleasures. She found a world of difference in those the Duc imbibed with her, her body was noticeably altered by those formidable dimensions, and the day after the Duc had despoiled her of her maidenhead, sodomistically speaking, she had fallen dangerously ill. They believed her rectum had been irreparably damaged; but her youth, her health, and some salutary local remedies soon restored the use of that forbidden avenue to the Duc, and the luckless Constance, forced to accustom herself to this daily torture, and it was but one amongst others, entirely recovered and became adjusted to everything.

*Adelaide*, Durcet's wife and the daughter of the Président, had a beauty which was perhaps superior to Constance's, but of an entirely different sort. She was twenty, small and slender, of an extremely slight and delicate build, of classic loveliness, had the finest blond hair to be seen. An interesting air, a look of sensibility distributed everywhere about her, and above all in her features, gave her the quality of a heroine in a romance. Her exceptionally large eyes were blue, they expressed at once tenderness and decency; two long but narrow and remarkably drawn eyebrows adorned a forehead not very high but of such noble charm one might have thought this were modesty's very temple. Her nose, thin, a little pinched at the top, descended to assume a semi-aquiline contour; her lips inclined toward the thin, were of a bright, ripe red; a little large, her mouth was the unique flaw in this celestial physiognomy, but when it opened, there shone thirty-two pearls Nature seemed to have sown amidst roses. Her neck was a shade long, attached in a singular way and, through what one judged a natural habit, her head was ever so faintly bent toward her right shoulder, especially when she was listening; but with what grace did not this interesting attitude endow her! Her breasts were small, very round, very firm, well-elevated, but there was barely enough there to fill the hand. They were like two little apples a frolicking Cupid had fetched hither from his mother's garden. Her chest was a bit narrow, it was also a very delicate chest, her belly was satin smooth, a little blond mound not much garnished with hair served as peristyle to the temple in which Venus seemed to call out for an homage. This temple was narrow to such a point you could not insert a finger therein without eliciting a cry from Adelaide; nevertheless, two lustrums had revolved since the time when, thanks to the Président, the poor child had ceased to be a virgin, either in that place or in the delicious part it remains for us to sketch. Oh, what were the attractions this second sanctuary possessed, what a flow in the line of her back, how magnificently were those buttocks cut, what whiteness there, and what dazzling rose blush! But all in all, it was on the small side. Delicate in all her lines, she was rather the sketch than the model of beauty, it seemed as though Nature had only wished to indicate in Adelaide what she had so majestically articulated in Constance. Peer into that appetizing behind, and lo! a rosebud would offer itself to your gaze, and it was in all its bloom and in the most tender pink Nature wished you to behold it; but narrow? tiny? it had only been at the price of infinite labors the Président had navigated through those straits, and he had only renewed these assaults successfully two or three times.

Durcet, less exacting, gave her little affliction in this point, but, since becoming his wife, in exchange for how many other cruel complaisances, with what a quantity of other perilous submissions had she not been obliged to purchase this little kindness? And, furthermore, turned over to the four libertines, as by their mutual consent she was, how many other cruel ordeals had she not to undergo, both of the species Durcet spared her, and of every other.

Adelaide had the mind her face suggested, that is to say, an extremely romantic mind, solitary places were the ones she preferred, and once there, she would shed involuntary tears—tears to which we do not pay sufficient heed—tears apparently torn from Nature by foreboding. She was recently bereft of a friend, a girl she idolized, and this frightful loss constantly haunted her imagination. As she was thoroughly acquainted with her father, as she knew to what extents he carried his wild behavior, she was persuaded her young friend had fallen prey to the Président's villainies, for he had never managed to induce the missing person to accord him certain privileges. The thing was not unlikely. Adelaide imagined the same would someday befall her; nor was that improbable. The Président, in her regard, had not paid the same attention to the problem of religion Durcet had in the interests of Constance, no, he had allowed all that nonsense to be born, to be fomented, supposing that his writings and his discourses would easily destroy it.

He was mistaken: religion is the nourishment upon which a soul such as Adelaide's feeds. In vain the Président had preached, in vain he had made her read books, the young lady had remained a believer, and all these extravagances, which she did not share, which she hated, of which she was the victim, fell far short of disabusing her about illusions which continued to make for her life's happiness. She would go and hide herself to pray to God, she'd perform Christian duties on the sly, and was unfailingly and very severely punished, either by her father or by her husband, when surprised in the act by the one or the other.

Adelaide patiently endured it all, fully convinced Heaven would someday reward her. Her character was as gentle as her spirit, and her benevolence, one of the virtues for which her father most detested her, went to the point of extreme. Curval, whom that vile class of the poverty-stricken irritated, sought only to humiliate it, to further depress it, or to wring victims from it; his generous daughter, on the other hand, would have foregone her own necessities to procure them for the poor, and she had often been espied stealing off to take to the needy sums which were intended for her pleasures. Durcet and the Président finally succeeded in scolding and pounding good manners into her, and in ridding her of this corrupt practice by withholding absolutely all the means whereby she could resume it. Adelaide, having nothing left but her tears to bestow upon the poor, went none the less to sprinkle them upon their woes, and her powerless howbeit staunchly sensitive spirit was incapable of ceasing to be virtuous. One day she learned that some poor woman was to come to prostitute her daughter to the Président because extreme need bade her do so; the enchanted old rake was already preparing himself for the kind of pleasure-taking he liked best. Adelaide had one of her dresses sold and immediately got the money put in the mother's hands; by means of this small assistance and some sort of a sermon, she diverted the woman from the crime she was about to commit. Hearing of what she had done, the Président proceeded to such violences with her—his daughter was not yet married at the time—that she was a fortnight abed; but all that was to no avail: nothing could put a stop to this gentle soul's tender impulses.

*Julie,* the Président's wife, the Duc's elder daughter, would have eclipsed the two preceding women were it not for something which many behold as a capital defect, but which had perhaps in itself aroused Curval's passion for her, so true is it that the effects of passions are unpredictable, nay, inconceivable, and that their disorder, the outcome of disgust and satiety, can only be matched by their irregular flights. Julie was tall, well made although quite fat and fleshy, had the most lovely brown eyes in the world, a charming nose, striking and gracious features, the most beautiful chestnut brown hair, a fair body of the most appetizing fullness, an ass which might easily have served as a model to the one Praxiteles sculpted, her cunt was hot, strait, and yielded as agreeable a sensation as such a locale ever may; her legs were handsome, her feet charming, but she had the worst-decked mouth, the foulest teeth, and was by habit so dirty in every other part of her body, and principally at the two temples of lubricity, that no other being, let me repeat it, no other being but the Président, himself subject to the same shortcomings and unquestionably fond of them, nay, no one else, despite her allurements, could have put up with Julie. Curval, however, was mad about her; his most divine pleasures were gathered upon that stinking mouth, to kiss it plunged him into delirium, and as for her natural uncleanliness, far from rebuking her for it, to the contrary he encouraged her in it, and had finally got her accustomed to a perfect divorce from water. To these faults Julie added a few others, but they were surely less disagreeable: she was a vast eater, she had a leaning toward drunkenness, little virtue, and I believe that had she dared try it, whoredom would have held little by way of terror for her. Brought up by the Duc in a total abandon of principles and manners, she adopted a whore's philosophy, and she was probably an apt student of all its tenets; but, through yet another very curious effect of libertinage, it often happens that a woman who shares our faults pleases us a great deal less in our pleasures than one who is full of naught but virtues: the first resembles us, we scandalize her not; the other is terrified, and there is one very certain charm the more.

Despite his proportions, the Duc had sported with his daughter, but he had had to wait until she was fifteen, and even so had not been able to prevent Julie from being considerably damaged by the adventure, indeed, so much so that, eager to marry her off, he had been forced to put a term to pleasure-taking of this variety and to be content with delights less dangerous for her, but at least as fatiguing. Julie gained little by gaining the Président, whose prick, as we know, was exceedingly thick and, furthermore, however much she was dirty from neglect of herself, she could not in any wise keep up with a filthiness in debauch such as the one that distinguished the Président, her beloved spouse.

*Aline,* Julie's younger sister and really the daughter of the Bishop, possessed habits and defects and a character very unlike her sister's.

She was the most youthful of the four, she had just become eighteen; she had a fetching, exuberantly healthy, and almost pert little countenance; a little turned-up nose; brown eyes full of expression and vivacity; a delicious mouth; a most shapely though somewhat tall figure, well-fleshed; the skin a bit dark but soft and fine; the ass rather on the ample side but well-molded, a pair of the most voluptuous buttocks that ever a libertine eye may behold, the love mound brown-haired and pretty, the cunt a trifle low or, as they say, *à l'anglaise,* but as tight as one might wish, and when she was presented to the assembly she was thoroughly a maid. And she still was at the time the party we are to chronicle got under way, and we shall see in what manner her maidenhead was annihilated. As for the first fruits of her ass, the Bishop had been peacefully plucking them every day for the past eight years, but without, however, arousing in his dear daughter much of a taste for these exercises: she, despite her mischievous and randy air, only cooperated out of obedience and had never hinted that she shared the slightest pleasure in the infamies whose daily victim she was. The Bishop had left her in the most profound ignorance, scarcely did she know how to read or write, and she had absolutely no idea of religion's existence; her mind was natural, it was that of a child, she would give droll replies, she liked to play, she loved her sister a great deal, detested the Bishop out of all measure, and feared the Duc as she dreaded fire. On the wedding day, when she discovered herself naked and surrounded by the four men, she wept, and moreover did all that was asked of her, acting without pleasure as without ill-temper. She was sober, very clean, and having no other fault but that of laziness, nonchalance reigned in all her movements and doings and everywhere about her person, despite the liveliness announced by her bright eyes. She abhorred the Président almost as much as she hated her uncle, and Durcet, who treated her with no excess of consideration, nevertheless seemed to be the only one for whom she appeared to have no repugnance.

These then were the eight principal characters in whose company we are going to enable you to live, good reader. It is now time to divulge the object of the singular pleasures that were proposed.

It is commonly accepted amongst authentic libertines that the sensations communicated by the organs of hearing are the most flattering and those whose impressions are the liveliest; as a consequence, our four villains, who were of a mind to have voluptuousness implant itself in the very core of their beings as deeply and as overwhelmingly as ever it could penetrate, had, to this end, devised something quite clever indeed.

It was this: after having immured themselves within everything that was best able to satisfy the senses through lust, after having established this situation, the plan was to have described to them, in the greatest detail and in due order, every one of debauchery's extravagances, all its divagations, all its ramifications, all its contingencies, all of what is termed in libertine language its passions. There is simply no conceiving the degree to which man varies them when his imagination grows inflamed; excessive may be the differences between men that is created by all their other manias, by all their other tastes, but in this case it is even more so, and he who should succeed in isolating and categorizing and detailing these follies would perhaps perform one of the most splendid labors which might be undertaken in the study of manners, and perhaps one of the most interesting. It would thus be a question of finding some individuals capable of providing an account of all these excesses, then of analyzing them, of extending them, of itemizing them, of graduating them, and of running a story through it all, to

provide coherence and amusement. Such was the decision adopted.
After innumerable inquiries and investigations, they located four
women who had attained their prime—that was necessary, experience was the fundamental thing here—four women, I say, who,
having spent their lives in the most furious debauchery, had reached
the state where they could provide an exact account of all these
matters; and, as care had been taken to select four endowed with
a certain eloquence and a fitting turn of mind, after much discussion, recording, and arranging, all four were ready to insert,
each into the adventures of her life, all the most extraordinary
vagaries of debauch, and to do so in such an order and at such a
pace that the first, for example, would work into the tale of her life's
activities the one hundred and fifty simple passions and the least
esoteric or most ordinary deviations; the second, within the same
framework, an equal number of more unusual passions involving
one or more men with one or several women; the third was also
to introduce into her narration one hundred and fifty of the most
criminal whimsies and those which most outrage the laws of both
Nature and religion; and as all these excesses lead to murder and
as these murders committed through libertinage are infinitely various and are just as numerous as the occasions upon which the
libertine's inflamed imagination adopts different tortures, the fourth
was to adorn the events of her life with a meticulous report upon
one hundred and fifty assorted examples of them. In the meantime,
our libertines, surrounded, as at the outset I indicated, by their
wives and also by other objects in every kind, were to pay close
heed, were to be mentally heated, and were to end by extinguishing,
by means of either their wives or those various objects, the con-
flagration the storytellers were to have lit. There is surely nothing
more voluptuous in this project than the luxurious manner whereby
it was carried out, and they are both this manner and these several
recitations which are to compose this work; wherewith, having said
this much, I advise the overmodest to lay my book aside at once if
he would not be scandalized, for 'tis already clear there's not much
of the chaste in our plan, and we dare hold ourselves answerable
in advance that there'll be still less in its execution. Insomuch as
the four actresses we have been speaking of play a most essential
role in these memoirs, we believe, even were we to have to beg the

reader's forgiveness therefor, we should still feel obliged to describe them; they will narrate, they will act: such being the case, is it possible that they remain unknown? Banish all expectation of beauties portrayed, although there were doubtless in the plans provisions for employing these four creatures physically as well as morally; be that as it may, neither their charms nor their years were the deciding factors, but rather their minds and their experience only that counted, and with what regards the latter, our friends could not possibly have made better choices.

*Madame Duclos* was she to whom they entrusted the relating of the one hundred and fifty simple passions; the woman who went by this name was forty-eight years of age, still in fairly good condition and preserving the vestiges of beauty; she had very handsome eyes, an exceedingly fair skin, and one of the most splendid and plumpest asses that could ever favor your gaze; a mouth both clean and fresh, superb breasts, and pretty brown hair, a heavy figure but a noble one, and all the looks and the tone of a brilliant whore. She had spent her life, as shall be observed, in places and under circumstances where indeed she had been obliged to study what she is going to relate, and to see her was to realize she must have gone to the task with wit and verve, with ease and interest.

*Madame Champville* was a tall woman of about fifty, slender, well made, having the most voluptuous quality in her look and bearing; a faithful devotee of Sappho, she had that kind of expression even in her slightest movements, in her simplest gestures, in her least words. She had ruined herself for the sake of keeping girls and, had it not been for this predilection to which she generally sacrificed everything she was able to earn abroad, she might have been comfortably well to do. For a long time she had been in public service, and during recent years had been making her way as an outfitter in her turn, but had confined herself to a limited practice, her clients being reliable rakehells of a certain age; never did she receive young men, and this prudent conduct was lucrative and did something to improve her affairs. She had been blond, but a more venerable tint, and that of wisdom, was beginning to color her hair; her eyes were still exceedingly attractive, blue, and they contained a most agreeable expressiveness. Her mouth was lovely, still fresh, missing no teeth as yet, she was flat-chested but had a belly which was good, but had never aroused envy, her mound was rather prominent, and her clitoris protruded three inches when well warmed; tickle this part of her and one was certain to see her fly into an ecstasy in no time, and especially if the service were rendered by a female. Her ass was very flabby and worn from use, entirely soft, wrinkled, withered, and so toughened by the libidinous customs she in recounting her history will explain to us, that one could do everything one wished without her feeling anything there. One strange and assuredly very rare thing, above all in Paris: she was as much a maid on this side as a girl emerging from a convent, and perhaps, had it not been for the accursed part she put to use, and put to use with people who cared for nothing but the extraordinary and whom, consequently, that side pleased, perhaps, I say, had it not been for that part, this singular virginity might have perished with her.

*Madame Martaine,* a portly matron of fifty-two, very well preserved and very healthy and blessed with the biggest and most beautiful rump one could wish for, boasted the precise opposite by way of adventure. She had devoted her life to sodomitical debauch, and was so well familiarized therewith she tasted absolutely no joy save therefrom. A natural deformity (she had also been blessed with an obstruction) having prevented her from knowing any other, she had given herself over to this kind of pleasure, led to it both by her inability to do anything else and by early habit, in consideration of which she clung fast to this lubricity wherein 'twas declared she was yet delicious, ready to brave come what might, dreading nothing. The most monstrous engines were as naught to her, in fact such were the ones she preferred, and the sequel to these papers will perhaps reveal her still giving valorous fight beneath the standards of Sodom, as the most intrepid of buggresses. Her features were gracious enough, but signs of languor and of decline were beginning to mar her attractions, and but for the plumpness sustaining her yet, she might have been thought time-worn and frayed.

As for *Madame Desgranges,* she was vice and lust personified; tall, thin, fifty-six, ghostly pale and emaciated, dead dull eyes, dead lips, she offered an image of crime about to perish for lack of strength. She had once upon a time been brunette, there were some who even maintained she'd had a beautiful body; not long thereafter it had become a mere skeleton capable of inspiring nothing but disgust. Her ass, withered, worn, marked, torn, more resembled marbled paper than human skin, and its hole was so gaping, sprung, and rugose that the bulkiest machines could, without her knowing a thing, penetrate it dry. By way of crowning graces, this generous Cytherean athlete, wounded in several combats, was missing one nipple and three fingers. She limped, and was without six teeth and an eye. We may perhaps learn by what order of attacks she had been so mistreated; but one thing is certain: nothing she had suffered had induced her to mend her ways, and if her body was the picture of ugliness, her soul was the depository of all the most unheard of vices and crimes: an arsonist, a parricide, a sodomite, a tribade, a murderess, a poisoner, guilty of incest, of rape, of theft, of abortions, and of sacrileges, one might truthfully affirm that there is not a single crime in the world this villain had not committed herself, or had others commit for her. Her present calling was procuring; she was one of society's most heavily titled furnishers, and as to much experience she joined a more or less agreeable prattle, she had been chosen to fill the role of fourth storyteller, that is to say, the one in whose story the greatest number of infamies and horrors were to be combined. Who better than a creature who had performed them all could have played this part?

These women once found, and found in every article to be such as was desired, the friends turned their attentions to accessories. They had from the outset planned to surround themselves with a large number of lust-inspiring objects of either sex, but when it was

brought to their attention that the only setting in which this lubricious roister could conveniently be held was that same château in
Switzerland belonging to Durcet, the one in which he had dispatched little Elvire, when, I say, it was remarked that this château
of only moderate size would not be able to lodge so great a throng
of inhabitants, and that, what was more, it might well prove unwise or dangerous to bring along such a host, the list of subjects
was trimmed to thirty-two in all, the storytellers included: to wit:
four of that class, eight young girls, eight young boys, eight men
endowed with monstrous members, for the delights of passive
sodomy, and four female servants. But thoroughness went into the
recruiting of all that; a year was devoted to these details, an
enormous amount of money too, and these are the measures they
employed to obtain the most delicious specimens of all France
could offer in the way of eight little girls: sixteen intelligent procuresses, each accompanied by two lieutenants, were sent into the
sixteen major provinces of France, while a seventeenth was occupied with the same work in Paris only. Each of these outfitters
was given a rendezvous at one of the Duc's estates on the outskirts of Paris, and all of them were to appear there, during the
same week, exactly ten months after the date of their departure
—this was the period they were given for searching. Each was to
bring back nine subjects, which came to a total of one hundred and
fifty-three girls, from which one hundred and fifty-three a choice
of only eight was to be made.

The procuresses were instructed to emphasize high birth, vir-
tuousness, and the most delicious visage possible; they were to
conduct their researches so as to draw material chiefly from eminent families, and were not to hand over any girl without being
able to prove that she had been forcibly abducted from either a
convent housing *pensionnaires* of quality, or from the home of a
family, and that a family of distinction. Whatever was not superior
to the class of bourgeoisie, and what from these upper classes was
not both very virtuous and wholly virgin and impeccably beautiful,
would be refused without mercy; spies were posted to survey these
women's proceedings and to supply the society with exhaustive and
prompt reports of what they were doing.

For each suitable subject found, they were paid thirty thousand francs, the agents assuming all expenses. The costs were incredible. With respect to age, it was fixed at from twelve to fifteen; anything above or below was pitilessly rejected. At the same time, under identical circumstances, with the same means, at the same expense, seventeen agents of sodomy likewise scoured the capital and the provinces in search of little boys, and their rendezvous was set for a month after the selection of the girls. As for the young men whom we propose henceforth to designate as fuckers, the size of the member was the sole criterion: nothing under ten or eleven inches long by seven or eight around was acceptable. Eight men labored throughout the kingdom to supply this demand, and their rendezvous was scheduled to fall a month after the little boys'. While the story of how these selections were made and received is not our foremost concern, it might not be inappropriate at this point to insert a word on the subject in order to bring out yet a little more of our four heroes' genius; it seems to me that nothing which serves to enlarge the reader's understanding of these figures and to shed light upon a party as extraordinary as the one we are going to describe, can be judged irrelevant.

The time for the assembling of the little girls having arrived, everyone converged upon the Duc's estate. Some few procuresses having been unable to fill their quota of nine, some others having lost their charges en route, either by illness or flight, only one hundred and thirty of them were present at the rendezvous, but what charms, great God! never, I believe, have so many charms been seen gathered together in one place. Thirteen days were given over to this examination, and each day ten of them were inspected. The four friends gathered in a circle, and in its middle was placed the little girl, dressed as she had been at the moment she had been seized; the procuress responsible for her capture recited her history. If something of the conditions of high birth or virtue were wanting, the inquiry went no deeper, the child was forthwith rejected, without appeal, and sent on her way, and the purveyor lost all that she had spent in connection with her. Next, having provided all the vital particulars, the procuress was asked to retire, and the child was interrogated in order to determine whether what had just been alleged were true. If all seemed well, the procuress was called in again, and she lifted the girl's skirts from behind, so as to expose her buttocks to the group; this was the first thing it wished to examine. The slightest defect in this part was grounds for immediate rejection; if on the contrary naught were amiss here, she was ordered to strip, or was stripped, and, naked, she passed and passed again, five or six times over, from one of our libertines to the other, she was turned about, she was turned the other way, she was fingered, she was handled, they sniffed, they spread, they peeped, they examined the state of the goods, was it new, was it used, but did all this coolly and without permitting the senses' illusion to upset any aspect of the examination. This done, the child was led away, and beside her name inscribed upon a ballot, the examiners wrote *passed* or *failed* and signed their names; these ballots were then dropped into a box, the voters refraining from communicating their opinions to one another; all the girls examined, the box was opened: in order to be accepted, a girl had to have our four friends' names in her favor. The absence of one name was enough to exclude her instantly and, in every instance, inexorably, as I have said: the unsuitable ones were kicked directly out, set at large, alone and without a guide, save when, as happened with perhaps a dozen, our libertines frolicked with them after the choices had been made and before turning them over to their procuresses.

This round resulted in the exclusion of fifty candidates, the other eighty were gone over afresh, but with much greater exactitude and severity; the least defect warranted instantaneous dismissal. One, lovely as the day, was weeded out because one of her teeth grew a shade higher from the gum than the rest; more than twenty others were refused because they were daughters of nothing better than bourgeois. Thirty were eliminated during this second round, hence only fifty were left. The friends resolved not to continue to the third round until having first been relieved of some fuck through these fifty aspirants' own ministry, this in order that the senses' perfect calm could insure saner and sounder choice. Each of the quartet encompassed himself by a team of twelve or thirteen children; members of each team adopted varying attitudes, teams were shifted, everything was directed by the procuresses, and everything was brought off with such dexterity, there was, in a word, so much lubricity in the doing that sperm flew, temperatures subsided, and another thirty disappeared from the race. Twenty remained; that was still a dozen too many. Further expedients to procure calm were resorted to, every means wherefrom one would suppose disgust could be born was employed, but the twenty still remained, and how might one have subtracted from a number of creatures so wonderfully celestial you would have declared they were the very work of a divinity? Equal in beauty, something else had to be discovered which could at least award eight of them some kind of superiority over the twelve others, and what the Président then proposed was worthy indeed of all the disorder of his mind. That made no difference; the suggestion was accepted: it had to do with finding out which of them would best do something the chosen eight would be often called upon to do. Four days sufficed amply to decide this question, and at last twelve were given their leave, but not blankly as in the case of the others; they provided a week's complete and exhaustive amusement, then were put into the keeping of the procuresses who soon made a pretty penny from the prostitution of creatures as distinguished as these. As for the successful eight, they were installed in a convent to keep until the day of departure, and in order to reserve until the designated period the pleasure of enjoying them, the four colleagues did not touch them before then.

I'll not be so foolhardy as to attempt to describe these beauties: they were all of them superior in an equal degree: my brush strokes would necessarily be monotonous; I shall be content to give their names and to affirm that upon my word it is perfectly impossible to obtain an idea of such an assemblage of graces, of attractions, of perfections, and that had Nature wished to give Man an idea of what her greatest and wisest art can create, she would not have presented him with other models.

The first was named *Augustine:* she was fifteen, the daughter of a Languedoc baron, and had been kidnaped from a convent in Montpellier.

The second was named *Fanny:* she was the daughter of a counselor to the parliament of Brittany and had been abducted from her father's own château.

The third was named *Zelmire:* she was fifteen years old, she was the Comte de Terville's daughter, and he idolized her. He had taken her hunting with him on one of his estates in Beauce and, having left her alone in the forest for a moment, she had been pounced upon at once. She was an only child and, with a dowry of four hundred thousand francs, was the following year to have married a very great lord. It was she who most wept and grieved at the horror of her fate.

The fourth was named *Sophie:* she was fourteen and was the daughter of a rather well-to-do gentleman who lived on his estate in Berry. She had been seized while on a walk with her mother, who, seeking to defend her, was flung into a river, where she expired before her daughter's eyes.

The fifth was named *Colombe:* she was from Paris, the child of a counselor to Parliament; she was thirteen and had been kidnaped while returning in the evening to her convent with a governess, after leaving a children's ball. The governess had been stabbed to death.

The sixth was named *Hébé:* she was just twelve, the daughter of a cavalry captain, a nobleman who lived in Orléans. The youngster had been enticed and carried away from the convent where she was being brought up; two nuns had been bought. You could not hope to find anything more seductive or sweeter.

The seventh was named *Rosette:* she was thirteen and was the child of the Lieutenant-General of Chalon-sur-Saône. Her father had just died, she was with her mother in the countryside near the city, and was captured within sight of her relatives by agents disguised as thieves.

The last was named Mimi or *Michette:* she was twelve, she was the daughter of the Marquis de Sénanges and had been kidnaped on her father's estate in the Bourbonnais while on a carriage drive which she had been allowed to take with two or three women from the château. The women were murdered. It will be remarked that the preparations for these revels cost much money and many crimes; to such people, treasure means exceedingly little, and as for crime, one was then living in an age when it was not by any means probed and punished the way it is nowadays. Hence everything succeeded, and so prettily that, the inquests amounting to virtually nothing at all, our libertines were never troubled by consequences.

The time drew nigh for the examination of the little boys. Easier to obtain, their number was greater. The pimps produced one hundred and fifty of them, and it will surely be no exaggeration if I affirm that they at least equaled the little girls, as much in their delicious faces as in their childhood graces, their candor, their innocence, and their elevated rank. Thirty thousand francs were paid for each of them, the same sum given for the girls, but the entrepreneurs risked nothing, because this game being more delicate and far more to the taste of our epicures, it had been decided that no one would be put in danger of losing his expenses, that while the lads with whom it was impossible to come to terms would be rejected, as they would be put to some use they would also be paid for.

Their examination was conducted like that of the girls, ten were verified each day, but with the very wise precaution which had been a little too much neglected with the girls, with the precaution, I say, of always preceding the examination by a discharge arranged with the aid of the ten who were under present scrutiny. The others were half of a mind to bar the Président from the ceremony, they were wary of the depravation of his tastes; they had feared, in the selection of the girls, being made the dupes of his accursed predilection for infamy and degradation: he promised to keep himself in check, and if he kept his word, it is unlikely he did so without difficulty, for when once a damaged or diseased imagination becomes accustomed to these species of outrages against good taste and Nature, outrages which so deliciously flatter it, it is no easy matter to restore such a person to the path of righteousness: it seems as if the desire to satisfy his longing displaces reason in his judgments. Scorning what is truly beautiful, no longer cherishing but what is frightful, desire's pronouncements correspond to its criteria, and the return to truer sentiments would appear to him to be a wrong done those principles whence he should be most sorry to stray. One hundred hopefuls were found unanimously approved when the initial séances were over, and these decisions had to be five times reconsidered in order to arrive at the small group alone to be accepted. Thrice in succession fifty survived the balloting, and then, to reduce that number to the stipulated eight, the jurors were compelled to resort to unusual measures in order somehow to lessen the appeal of idols still glamorous despite everything they had been able to do to them. The idea occurred to them to dress the boys as girls: twenty-five were eliminated by this trick which, lending to a sex they worshiped the garb of one to which they had become indifferent, depreciated their value and ruined almost all the illusion. But nothing could alter the voting on the twenty-five that were left. 'Twas all in vain, in vain they spattered their fuck about, in vain they wrote their names upon the ballots at the same moment they discharged, in vain they put to use the expedient adopted with the little girls, the twenty-five proved irreducible every time, and at last they agreed to have them draw lots. Here are the names they gave the lucky ones who remained, their age, their birth, and a word or two about their adventures; their portraits? I cry off: Cupid's own features were surely no more delicate, and the models Albani sought from which to choose traits for his divine angels must certainly have been inferior by far.

*Zélamir* was thirteen years old: he was the only son of a gentleman out of Poitou who had been bringing him up with the greatest care. Escorted by a single domestic, he had been sent to Poitiers to visit a kinsman; our rogues ambushed them, slew the domestic, and made off with the child.

*Cupidon* was the same age: he had been a pupil in a school at La Flèche, and was the son of a gentleman dwelling in the vicinity of that town. A trap was laid for the boy, he was kidnaped while on an outing the students used to take on Sundays. He was the prettiest pupil in the entire *collège*.

*Narcisse* was twelve; he was a Knight of Malta. He had been abducted in Rouen, where his father filled an honorable post compatible with his nobility; the boy was en route to the Collège de Louis-le-Grand at Paris, he was waylaid and seized while on the road.

*Zéphyr,* the most delicious of the eight, it being supposed that their excessive beauty might allow the possibility of a choice, was from Paris; he was pursuing his studies there, in a famous pension. His father, a ranking officer, did all in his power to get his son back, and failed; money had seduced the headmaster of the school, who delivered seven specimens, of whom six were refused. Zéphyr had set the Duc's head to spinning, and the latter protested that were it to have cost a million to bugger the boy he would have paid it in cash on the spot. He reserved to himself the lad's initiation, and it was generally granted him. O tender and delicate child, what disproportion and what a dreadful fate were in store for you!

*Céladon* was the son of a magistrate of Nancy; he was captured at Lunéville, whither he had gone to visit his aunt. He had just attained his fourteenth year. In this case a girl was used to bait the trap. Céladon and she were introduced, the little wench drew him into the snare by feigning love for him; he was negligently chaperoned, the stroke was successful.

*Adonis* was fifteen; he was ravished at Plessis, where he was enrolled in school. He was the son of a judge of the assize courts who raised a great hue and cry, but all to no avail, the capture had been so nicely planned no one knew a thing about it. Curval, who had been mad about the child for two years, had made his acquaintance at his father's house, and it was he who had supplied the means and information necessary to debauch him. The others were greatly surprised to find such sensible good taste in a head so depraved as Curval's, and he, most proud, profited from the event to show his colleagues that, as was plainly to be seen, he still could boast a sometimes fine palate. The child recognized him and fell to weeping, but the Président consoled him with the assurance it would be to him would befall the deflowering, and while uttering these comforting words, he wobbled his enormous engine against those frail little buttocks. Curval asked the assembly for the boy; his request was unopposed.

*Hyacinthe* was fourteen years old; he was the son of a retired officer living in a small city in Champagne. He adored hunting and was taken while afield, his father having been so imprudent as to allow him to set out alone.

*Giton* was twelve; he was kidnaped at Versailles from amidst the page boys at the King's stables. He was the son of a man of consequence from the Nivernais, who not six months prior had brought him to Versailles. He was very simply abducted while walking alone on the avenue de Saint-Cloud. He became the Bishop's passion, and to the Bishop was the prize decreed.

Those, thus, were the masculine deities our libertines prepared for their lubricity; we will see in due time and place the use to which they were put. One hundred and forty-two subjects remained, but whereas there had been much trifling over the eight, there was none with this game: not one of the defeated candidates was dismissed until he had served some purpose.

Our libertines spent a month with them at the Duc's château. As they were on the eve of setting forth, as all the practical arrangements were completed, the company had little else to do but amuse itself until the day of departure. When at last they were thoroughly fed up with their sport, they fell upon a pleasant means for disposing of what had provided it: that was to sell the boys to a Turkish pirate, a scheme whereby no trace of them would be left and a part of the costs would be recovered. They were sent in small groups to a place near Monaco, the Turk came to get them and lead them off into slavery, doubtless a dreadful fate, but one whereby, none the less, our four villains were hugely entertained.

And now came the moment for choosing the fuckers. Those of this class who failed to meet the standards were the cause of no embarrassment; being mature and reasonable men, it was enough to pay them for their trouble, their traveling expenses, and send them home. The eight experts who had contracted to furnish the fuckers had, furthermore, many fewer obstacles to surmount, since the specifications were by and large concrete and the conditions made no difference at all. Thus it was fifty came to the rendezvous; from amongst the twenty biggest, the eight youngest and most attractive were singled out, and since in the sequel mention will almost never be made save of the four biggest of the eight, I shall restrict myself to naming these.

*Hercule,* with a body hewn in the image of the god whose name he had been given, was twenty-six years of age and was endowed with a member eight and one-quarter inches around by thirteen long. Nothing more beautiful nor more majestic has ever been seen; this tool was almost always upright, and with only eight discharges, so tests revealed, it could fill a pint measure to the brim. Hercule was also very gentle, very sweet, and had an interesting countenance.

*Antinoüs,* so named because, like Hadrian's favorite, he had, together with the world's prettiest prick, its most voluptuous ass, and that is exceedingly rare. Antinoüs wielded a device measuring eight inches in circumference and twelve in length. He was thirty and had a face worthy of his other features.

*Bum-Cleaver* lugged a club so amusingly shaped it was nearly impossible for him to perform an embuggery without splitting the ass, whence came the name he bore. The head of his prick resembled the heart of an ox, it was eight and three-eighths inches around; behind it, the shaft measured only eight, but was crooked and had such a curve it neatly tore the anus when penetrating it, and this quality, very precious to libertines as jaded as ours, had made him singularly sought after.

*Invictus,* so named because, no matter what he did, his erection was perpetual, was furnished with an engine eleven inches long and seven and fifteen-sixteenths inches around. Greater ones, who had difficulty stiffening, had been turned away to make room for him who, regardless of the quantity of discharges he produced in a day, rose heavenward at the slightest touch.

The other four were of about the same dimensions and the same shape. The forty-two rejected candidates provided a fortnight's entertainment and, after the friends had put them through their paces and worn them to the bone, they were well rewarded and bidden adieu.

Nothing now remained but the choice of the four ladies-in-waiting, and this final stage was without doubt the most picturesque. The Président was not the only one whose tastes were depraved; his three friends, and especially Durcet, were indeed a little tainted by his accursed, crapulous, and debauched mania which causes one to find a greater, more piquant attraction in an old, disgusting, and filthy object than in what Nature has fashioned most divinely. Explaining this fancy would probably be difficult, but it exists in many people; Nature's disorder carries with it a kind of sting which operates upon the high-keyed sort with perhaps as much and even more force than do her most regular beauties; it has been proven, moreover, that when one's prick is aloft, it is horror, villainy, the appalling, that pleases; well, where are they more emphatically present than in a vitiated object? If 'tis the filthy thing which pleases in the lubricious act, then certainly the more filthy the thing, the more it should please, and it is surely much filthier in the corrupted than in the intact and perfect object.

No, as to that there's no doubt. Furthermore, beauty belongs to the sphere of the simple, the ordinary, whilst ugliness is something extraordinary, and there is no question but that every ardent imagination prefers in lubricity the extraordinary to the commonplace. Beauty, health never strike one save in a simple way; ugliness, degradation deal a far stouter blow, the commotion they create is much stronger, the resultant agitation must hence be more lively; in the light of all this, there should be no cause for astonishment in the fact that an immense crowd of people prefer to take their pleasure with an aged, ugly, and even stinking crone and will refuse a fresh and pretty girl, no more reason to be astonished at that, I say, than at a man who for his promenades prefers the mountains' arid and rugged terrain to the monotonous pathways of the plains. All these matters depend upon our constitutions, our organs, upon the manner whereby they are affected, and it is no more in our power to change our tastes in this connection than it is in our power to alter the form of our bodies.

Be that as it may, such, as I have said, was the dominating taste of the Président and, to tell the truth, the taste which came near to predominating in his three confreres, for when it came to choosing female servants, their views were identical, and we are about to see from this choice that its making bespoke the constitutional disorder and depravation to which we have just alluded.

The most painstaking search was initiated in Paris; the four creatures needed were finally located; however loathsome may be their portraits, the reader will none the less permit me to draw them: that I do so is essential to that aspect of manners the elucidation of which is one of the principal aims of this work.

*Marie* was the name of the first one; she had been the servant of a notorious brigand quite recently put to death on the wheel, whipping and branding had been her penalty. She was fifty-eight years old, had almost no hair left, her nose stood askew, her eyes were dull and rheumy, her mouth large and filled with her thirty-two teeth, yes, they were all there, but all were yellow as sulphur; she was tall, raw-boned, having whelped fourteen children, all fourteen of whom, said she, she'd strangled from fear they'd turn out ne'er-do-wells. Her belly rippled like the waves of the sea, and one of her buttocks was devoured by an abscess.

The second was known as *Louison;* she was sixty, stunted, hunchbacked, blind in one eye, and lame, but she had a fine ass for her age and her skin was still in fairly good repair. She was as wicked as the devil and forever ready to commit any horror and every extravagance one could possibly demand of her.

*Thérèse* was sixty-two; she was tall, thin, looked like a skeleton, not a hair was left on her head, not a tooth in her mouth, and from this opening in her body she exhaled an odor capable of flooring any bystander. Her ass was peppered with wounds, and her buttocks were so prodigiously slack one could have furled the skin around a walking stick; the hole in this splendid ass resembled the crater of a volcano what for width, and for aroma the pit of a privy; in all her life, Thérèse declared, she had never once wiped her ass, whence we have proof positive that the shit of her infancy yet clung there. As for her vagina, it was the receptacle of everything ungodly, of every horror, a veritable sepulcher whose fetidity was enough to make you faint away. She had one twisted arm and limped in one leg.

The fourth was called *Fanchon;* six times she had been hanged in effigy, and not a crime exists in this world she had not committed. She was sixty-nine, she was flat-nosed, short, and heavy; she squinted, had almost no forehead, had nothing but two old teeth in her stinking maw, and they were ready to fall out, an erysipelas blazed all over her ass and hemorrhoids the size of your fist hung from her anus, a frightful chancre consumed her vagina, and one of her thighs had been entirely burned. She was dead drunk three-quarters of the year, and in that condition, her stomach being very weak, she vomited over everything. Despite the batch of hemorrhoids adorning it, her asshole was naturally so large that all unawares she blew driblets and farts and often more besides. Apart from acting as servants in the luxurious recreation palace the four friends had in mind, these women were also to lend a hand at all the convocations and render all the lubricious services and ministrations that might be required of them.

As soon as all these matters had been decided and the summer having already begun, they turned their thoughts to the transporting of the various objects which were, during the four months' sojourn on Durcet's estate, to render its inhabitation comfortable and agreeable. A vast store of furniture and mirrors, of viands and wines and liqueurs of all kinds were ordered borne thither, workmen were sent there, and little by little the numerous subjects were conducted to the château where Durcet, who had gone ahead, received, lodged, and established them as they arrived.

But the moment has come to give the reader a description of the renowned temple appointed for so many luxurious sacrifices throughout the projected four-month season. He will observe with what great care they had chosen a remote and isolated retreat, as if silence, distance, and stillness were libertinage's potent vehicles, and as if everything which through these qualities instills a religious terror in the senses had necessarily and evidently to bestow additional charm upon lust. We are going to picture this retreat not as once it was, but in the state of embellishment and yet more perfect solitude that resulted from the four friends' efforts.

To reach the place one had first to get to Basel; at that city you crossed the Rhine, beyond which the road became steadily narrower until you had to abandon your carriage. Soon afterward you entered the Black Forest, you plunged about fifteen leagues into it, ascended a difficult, tortuous road that, without a guide, would be absolutely impracticable. By and by you caught sight of a sinister and mean hamlet of charcoal burners and gamekeepers;

there began the territory Durcet owned, and the hamlet was his; as this little village's population was composed almost entirely of thieves or smugglers, Durcet easily befriended it, and his first order to the inhabitants was expressly to enjoin them under no circumstances to allow anyone whomsoever to pass on toward the château after the 1st of November, the date by which the entire society was to be assembled in it. He distributed weapons to his faithful vassals, granted them certain privileges they had been long soliciting, and the barrier was lowered. That done, and the gates tightly sealed, one will see by the following description how difficult of access was Silling, the name Durcet's château bore.

Having passed the village, you begin to scale a mountain almost as high as the Saint-Bernard and infinitely more difficult to ascend, for the only way to reach the summit is by foot; not that the route is forbidden to pack mules, but such are the precipices which everywhere border the one so very narrow path that must be followed, that you run the greatest danger if you ride; six of the mules used to transport supplies and food perished, taking with them two laborers who had thought to mount astride them. Five full hours are required to reach the top of the mountain, and there you come upon another extraordinary feature which, owing to the precautions that had been taken, became a new barrier so insurmountable that none but birds might have overcome it: the topographical accident we refer to is a crevice above sixty yards wide which splits the crest into northern and southern parts, with the result that, after having climbed up the mountain, it is impossible, without great skill, to go back down it. Durcet had united these two parts, between which a precipice fell to the depth of a thousand feet and more, by a fine wooden bridge which was destroyed immediately the last of the crew had arrived, and from this moment on, all possibility of communicating with the Château of Silling ceased. For, cross the bridge and you come down into a little plain about four acres in area; the plain is surrounded on all sides by sheer crags rising to the clouds, crags which envelop the plain within a faultless screen. The passage known as the bridge path is hence the only one by which you may descend into or communicate with the little plain; the bridge removed or destroyed, there is not on this entire earth a single being, of no matter what species you may imagine, capable of gaining this small plot of level land.

And it is in the center of this flat space so well surrounded, so solidly protected, that one finds Durcet's château. Yet another wall, thirty feet high, girds it; beyond the wall a moat filled with water and exceedingly deep defends a last tall and winding enclosure; a low and strait postern finally leads into the great inner court around which all the living quarters are built, and they are very capacious, very well furnished thanks to the arrangements latterly concluded; one discovers a long gallery on the first floor. I would have it remarked that the description I am about to give of the apartments corresponds not to what in former times they may have been, but to the manner in which they had just been rearranged and distributed in accordance with our libertines' common conception. From the gallery you moved into a very attractive dining hall provided with buffets shaped like towers which, communicating with the kitchen, made it possible to serve the company its food hot, promptly, and without the help of any waiters. From this dining hall, hung in tapestries, warmed by heating devices, furnished with ottomans, with excellent armchairs, and with everything which could make it both comfortable and pleasing to the eye, you passed into a large living room or salon, simple, plain, but exceedingly warm and equipped with the very best furniture; adjacent to this room was an assembly chamber intended for the storytellers' narrations. This was, so to speak, the lists for the projected jousts, the seat of the lubricious conclaves, and as it had been decorated accordingly, it merits something by way of a special description.

Its shape was semicircular; set into the curving wall were four niches whose surfaces were faced with large mirrors, and each was provided with an excellent ottoman; these four recesses were so constructed that each faced the center of the circle; the diameter was formed by a throne, raised four feet above the floor and with its back to the flat wall, and it was intended for the storyteller; in this position she was not only well before the four niches intended for her auditors, but, the circle being small, was close enough to them to insure their hearing every word she said, for she was placed like an actor in a theater, and the audience in their niches found themselves situated as if observing a spectacle in an amphitheater. Steps led down from the throne, upon them were to sit the objects of debauchery brought in to soothe any sensory irritation provoked by the recitals; these several tiers, like the throne, were upholstered in black velvet edged with gold fringe, and the niches were furnished with similar and likewise enriched material, but in color dark blue. At the back of each niche was a little door leading into an adjoining closet which was to be used at times when, having summoned the desired subject from the steps, one preferred not to execute before everyone the delight for whose execution one had summoned that subject. These closets were provided with couches and with all the other furnishings required for every kind of impurity. On either side of the central throne an isolated column rose to the ceiling; these two columns were designed to support the subject in whom some misconduct might merit correction. All the instruments necessary to meting it out hung from hooks attached to the columns, and this imposing sight served to maintain the subordination so indispensable to parties of this nature, a subordination whence is born almost all the charm of the voluptuousness in persecutors' souls.

One could walk from this semicircular room directly to a chamber which formed the end of this part of the living quarters. This chamber was a kind of boudoir, it was soundproof and secluded, but very warm within, very dark during the day, and its purpose was for private interviews and secluded contests, or for certain other secret delights which will be unveiled in the sequel. To reach the other wing, one had to retrace one's footsteps, and once in the gallery, at the end of which an exceedingly handsome chapel was visible, one entered the opposite wing which completed the circuit of the inner courtyard. You discovered a splendid antechamber adjoined by four superb apartments, each having a boudoir and wash cabinets; splendid Turkish beds canopied in three-colored damask with matching furniture adorned these suites whose boudoirs offered everything and more of the most sensual that lubricity might fancy. These four units, exceptionally well-heated and comfortable, were intended for the four colleagues, who were perfectly lodged therein. In that the protocols stipulated that their wives

were to occupy the same quarters, no separate space was set aside
for them.

Upstairs, the second story contained about the same number
of apartments, but they were otherwise divided; you first came
upon, to one side, a vast room bordered by eight niches, each having a little bed—these were the girls' quarters, and beside them
were two small chambers for the old women who were to have
charge of them. Further along, a pair of pretty rooms had been
set aside for two of the storytellers. Now turning about and going
in the other direction, you found a similar eight-niched room for
the little boys; by it were two rooms for the duennas appointed to
supervise them; and beyond these were two more rooms, also
alike, for the two other storytellers. Eight cheerful rooms, as fine
as anything you have yet seen, formed the eight fuckers' quarters,
although these individuals were destined to do very little sleeping
in their own beds. Below, on the ground floor, were the kitchens
and, near them, six small chambers for the six persons to whom
the preparation of food had been confided; amongst them were
three cooks renowned for their art; they were all females, women
having been preferred for a pleasure outing like this one, and I
believe the decision was just. The cooks were assisted by three
robust young scullery maids, but none of the kitchen staff was to
appear at the revels, that was not its purpose, and if the rules
imposed in this connection were violated, 'tis merely because libertinage stops at nothing, and the true way of extending and multiplying one's desires is to attempt to impose checks upon them. One
of these three underlings was to look after the numerous livestock
which had been fetched to the château—with the exception of the
four aged ladies who were meant for household duties, there were
no domestics save for these three cooks and their seconds. But
depravity, cruelty, disgust, infamy, all those passions anticipated or
experienced, had erected another locality whereof it is a matter of
urgency that we give a sketch, for the laws essential to the proper
unfolding of our tale demand that we depict it with thoroughness
now.

A fatal stone there was which, cunningly made, could be raised
from below the step of the altar in the little Christian temple we
discerned from the gallery; beneath that stone one beheld a spiral

stairway, very narrow and very steep, whose three hundred steps could convey you down into the bowels of the earth, to a kind of vaulted dungeon, closed by triple doors of iron, and in which was displayed everything the cruelest art and the most refined barbarity could invent of the most atrocious, as much for gripping one with terror as for proceeding to horrors. And there below, what tranquillity! to what degree might not the villain be reassured who brought his victim there! What had he to fear? He was out of France, in a safe province, in the depths of an uninhabitable forest, within this forest in a redoubt which, owing to the measures he had taken, only the birds of the air could approach, and he was in the depth of the earth's entrails. Woe, a hundred times woe to the unlucky creature who in the midst of such abandonment were to find himself at the mercy of a villain lawless and without religion, whom crime amused, and whose only interest lay in his passions, who heeded naught, had nothing to obey but the imperious decrees of his perfidious lusts. I know not what will transpire in that nether place, but this I may say without doing our tale a disservice, that when a description of the dungeon was given the Duc, he reacted by discharging three times in succession.

Everything being ready at last, everything perfectly disposed, the subjects installed, the Duc, the Bishop, Curval, and their wives, with the four second-ranking fuckers in their train, set off (Durcet and his wife, together with all the rest, having arrived beforehand, as we have previously noted), and not without infinite difficulty, finally reached the château on the evening of the 29th of October. Immediately they had crossed it, Durcet had the bridge cut. But that was not all: having inspected the place, the Duc decided that, since all the provisions were within the fortress, and since therefore they had no need to leave it, it were necessary, in order to forestall external attack, which was little dreaded, and escapes from within, the possibilities of which were less unlikely, it were necessary, I say, to have walled shut all the gates, all the passages whereby the château might be penetrated, and absolutely to enclose themselves inside their retreat as within a besieged citadel, without leaving the least entrance to an enemy, the least egress to a deserter. The rec-

ommendation was put into effect, they barricaded themselves to
such an extent there was no longer any trace left of where the exits
had been; and then they settled down comfortably inside.

After the provisions we have just cited had been taken, the
two days still remaining before the 1st of November were devoted
to resting the subjects, that they might make a fresh appearance at
the scenes of debauchery soon to begin, and during this interval the
four friends labored over a code of laws which, as soon as it was
brought to perfection and signed, was promulgated to those concerned. Before advancing to the matter, it is essential that these
articles of government be made known to the reader who, after
the exact description we have given him of everything, will now
have no more to do than follow the story, lightly and voluptuously,
his mind impeded by nothing, his memory embarrassed by no unexpected intrusions.

## STATUTES

*The company shall rise every day at ten o'clock in the morning,
at which time the four fuckers who have not been on duty during
the night shall come to pay the friends a visit and shall each bring a
little boy; they shall pass from one bedchamber to another, successively. They shall perform as bidden by the friends' likings and
desires, but during the preliminaries the little boys shall serve only
as a tempting prospect, for it has been decided and planned that the
eight maidenheads of the little girls' cunts shall remain intact until
the month of December, and their asses shall likewise remain in
bond, as shall the asses of the eight little boys, until the month of
January, at which times the respective seals shall be broken, and
this in order to allow voluptuousness to become irritated by the
augmentation of a desire incessantly inflamed and never satisfied, a
state which must necessarily lead to that certain lascivious fury the
friends shall strive to provoke, considering it one of lubricity's most
highly delectable situations.*

*At eleven o'clock, the friends shall repair to the quarters ap-
pointed for the little girls. In that place will be served breakfast*

consisting of chocolate, or of roasts cooked in Spanish wine, or of
other appropriate restoratives. This breakfast shall be served by
the eight little girls, naked, aided by the two elders, Marie and
Louison, assigned to the seraglio of girls, the other two elders
being assigned to that of the boys. If, during this breakfast, the
friends are moved to commit impudicities with the little girls, before or after, the latter shall lend themselves thereunto with the
resignation prescribed to them, and wherein they shall not be found
wanting without severe punishment being the consequence. But it is
agreed that at this hour there shall be undertaken no secret or
private exercises, and that if a moment's wantonizing be desired,
it shall be conducted openly and before the public present at the
morning meal.

These little girls shall adopt the general custom of kneeling at
all times whenever they see or meet a friend, and they shall remain
thus until told to stand; they, the wives, and the elders shall alone
be subject to these regulations, wherefrom the others are dispensed,
but everyone shall be bound never to address the friends save as
my Lord.

Before leaving the girls' apartments, that one of the friends
who is invested with the month's stewardship (it being intended that for the space of a month one friend shall be in general
supervision of everything, each friend acceding to the office in his
turn and in the following order: Durcet during November, the
Bishop during December, the Président during January, the Duc
during February), he, then, who is the month's presiding officer,
before leaving the girls' quarters, shall inspect them all, to determine whether they are in the state wherein they have been instructed to maintain themselves, whereof the elders shall be each
morning apprised and which will be determined by the need that
exists for them to keep in such and such a state.

As it is strictly forbidden to relieve oneself anywhere save
in the chapel, which has been outfitted and intended for this purpose, and forbidden to go there without individual and special
permission, the which shall be often refused, and for good reason,

*the month's presiding officer shall scrupulously examine, immediately after breakfast, all the girls' water closets, and in the case of a contravention discovered in the one above-designated place or in the other, the delinquent shall be condemned to suffer the penalty of death.*

*The friends shall move from there into the little boys' apartments in order to perform the same inspections and similarly to pronounce capital punishment against offenders. The four little boys who have not been that morning with the friends, shall now receive them when they enter their chamber and shall untrouser themselves before them, the other four shall remain standing at attention, awaiting the orders which are given them. Messieurs may or may not indulge in lewd byplay with the four they have not until now seen during the day, but whatever they do shall be done publicly; no intimate commerce shall be held at this hour.*

*At one o'clock, those of the girls or the boys, of mature and of young years, who have obtained permission to satisfy urgent needs, that is to say, the heavier sort, and this permission shall never be but most sparingly accorded, and at the most to a third of the subjects, those, we repeat, shall betake themselves to the chapel where everything has been artistically arranged for the voluptuous delights falling under this head. In this place they will find the four friends who shall wait for them until two o'clock and never any longer, and who shall distribute and adjust them as they judge proper to the delights of this order which they may be moved to taste.*

*From two to three the first two tables shall be served: they shall dine simultaneously, one in the girls' large apartment, the other in that of the young boys: the three kitchen servants shall serve these two tables. At the first shall sit the eight little girls and the four elders; at the second the four wives, the eight little boys, and the four storytellers. During their meal, Messieurs will be pleased to gather in the living room where they will chat together until three o'clock. Just before this hour, the eight fuckers shall make their appearance here, as well clothed and as well adorned as it is in their power to be.*

*At three shall be served the masters' dinner, and the honor to be present there shall be enjoyed by none but the eight fuckers; this meal shall be served by the four wives, entirely naked, aided by the four elders, clad as sorceresses; to the latter shall fall the task of bringing the plates from the towers into which the servants, on the other side, shall have put them, and the plates shall be handed to the wives, who shall deposit them on the table. The eight fuckers, in the course of the dinner, will be at liberty to handle and touch the unclothed bodies of the wives in whatever manner and to whatever extent they please, without the said wives being permitted to refuse or defend themselves; the fuckers will even be able to go to the point of employing insults and of thickening their sticks by apostrophizing them with all the invectives they may see fit to pronounce.*

*The friends shall rise from table at five, at which time these Messieurs only (the fuckers shall retire until the hour of general assembly), these Messieurs only, I say, shall pass into the salon, where two little boys and two little girls, who shall be changed daily, shall, in a state of nudity, serve them coffee and liqueur; nor shall it be at this point in the day's activities Messieurs shall permit themselves diversions which might enervate them; conversation shall be limited to simple jesting.*

*Shortly before six o'clock, the four children who have been serving, shall withdraw and go promptly to dress themselves. At exactly six, Messieurs shall pass into the assembly chamber heretofore described. They shall each of them repair to their respective alcoves, and the following distribution shall be observed by the others: upon the throne shall be the storyteller, the tiers below the throne shall be occupied by the sixteen children, so arranged that four of them, that is to say, two girls and two boys, shall be situated directly opposite each niche; each niche shall have before it a like quatrain; this quatrain shall be specially allocated to the niche before which it is placed, the niches alongside being ex-*

cluded from making any claims upon it, and these quatrains shall
be diversified each day, never shall the same niche have the same
quatrain. Each child in each quatrain shall have one end of a chain
of artificial flowers secured to his arm, the other end of the chain
leading to the niche, so that when the niche's proprietor wishes any
given child in his quatrain, he has but to tug the garland, and the
child shall come running and fling himself at the master's feet.

Above the quatrain shall be situate an elder, attached to the
quatrain, and responsive to the orders of the chief of that quatrain's niche.

The three storytellers who are not on active service as
raconteurs during the month shall be seated upon a bench at the
foot of the throne, assigned to no one but yet ready to do anyone's
bidding. The four fuckers appointed to spend the night with the
friends may be absent from the assembly; they shall be in their
rooms, busy grooming themselves for the coming night, at which
time great feats shall be regularly expected of them. With respect
to the four others, they shall be each one at the feet of one of the
friends, who shall be in his niche and upon his couch beside that
one of the wives whose turn it is to be with any given husband. This
wife shall be at all times naked, the fucker shall wear a closefitting
singlet and shorts of taffeta, pink in color, the month's storyteller
shall be attired as an elegant courtesan, as shall be her three companions, the little boys and the little girls of the quatrains shall
always be differently and splendidly costumed, one quatrain in
Asiatic style, one in Spanish, another in Turkish garb, a fourth in
Greek, and on the following day otherwise; but all these costumes
shall be of taffeta or of lawn; at no time shall the lower half of
the body be discomfited by any raiment, and the removal of a pin
shall suffice to bare it completely.

As for the elders, they shall alternately interpret the Graeae,
nuns, fairies, sorceresses, and upon occasion, widows. The doors
to the closets contiguous to the niches shall be half opened at all
times, and the closets shall be kept at a warm temperature by stoves,
and shall be garnished with all the appurtenances required for vari-

*ous debauches. Four candles shall burn in each of the closets, and fifty in the auditorium.*

*Punctually at six o'clock, the storyteller shall begin her story, which the friends may interrupt at any point and as frequently as they please; this narration shall last until ten o'clock in the evening, and during this time, as its object is to inflame the imagination, every lubricity will be permitted, save however for those which might be prejudicial to the approved schedule of deflowerings, which shall be at all times rigorously observed; apart from this, Messieurs may do what they like with their fucker, wife, quatrain, quatrain elder, and even with the storytellers if this whim move them, and that either in their niche or in the adjacent closet. The narration shall be suspended for as long as the pleasures of him whose needs interrupt it continue, and when he shall have done and be sated, the tale shall be resumed.*

*The evening meal shall be served at ten. The wives, the storytellers, and the eight little girls shall without delay proceed to dine by themselves, women never being admitted to the men's supper, and the friends shall sup with the four fuckers not scheduled for night duty, and with four little boys. Aided by the elders, the four other boys shall serve.*

*The evening meal concluded, Messieurs shall pass into the salon for the celebration of what are to be called the orgies. Everyone shall convene there, both those who have supped apart and those who have supped with the friends, the four fuckers chosen for the night's service being excepted.*

*The salon shall be heated to an unusual temperature, and illuminated by chandeliers. All present shall be naked: storytellers, wives, little girls, little boys, elders, fuckers, friends, everything shall be pell-mell, everyone shall be sprawled on the floor and, after the example of animals, shall change, shall commingle, entwine, couple incestuously, adulterously, sodomistically, deflowerings being at all times banned, the company shall give itself over to every excess and to every debauch which may best warm the mind. When 'tis time for these deflowerings, it shall be at this moment and in these circumstances that those operations shall be performed, and once a child shall be initiate, it shall be available for every enjoyment, in all manners and at all times.*

*The orgies shall cease at precisely two in the morning, the four fuckers designated for nocturnal exercise shall come, in elegant undress, to lead away each of them the friend wherewith he is to bed, each friend shall be provided also with one of the wives or with a deflowered subject, when deflowered subjects there be, or with a storyteller, or with an elder to pass the night 'twixt her and his fucker, and all this according to his disposition, whereunto but one clause is put, that he submit himself to prudent arrangements whence it may result that each friend varies his companions every night, or is able so to do.*

*Such shall be the daily order of procedure. In addition, each week of the seventeen prescribed as the period of the sojourn at the château shall be marked by a festival. There shall be, first of all, marriages, full particulars relating to which shall be made available in due time and place. But as the first of these matches shall be made between the youngest of the children, who are not able to consummate them, they will in no wise disturb the schedule established for the deflorations. Marriages between adults being all post-defloratory, their consummation will damage nothing since, in acting, the friends shall be enjoying only what has been enjoyed already.*

*The four elders, to be held answerable for the behavior of their four children, shall, when it is faulty, report it to the month's presiding officer, and each Saturday there shall take place a common meting out of punishments, at the time of the orgies. An exact list of accumulating delinquencies shall be kept until then.*

*With what regards misbehavior on the part of the storytellers, their punishments shall be one-half that of the children, because their talents are to some purpose, and talent must always be respected. As for errors in the conduct of the wives, they shall always be rewarded by punishment double that given the children.*

*Should any subject in some way refuse anything demanded of him, even when incapacitated or when that thing is impossible, he shall be punished with utmost severity; 'tis for him to provide, for him to discover ways and means.*

*The least display of mirth, or the least evidence given of disrespect or lack of submission during the debauch activities, shall be esteemed one of the gravest of faults and shall be one of the most cruelly punished.*

*Any man taken* flagrante delicto *with a woman shall be punished by the loss of a limb when authorization to enjoy this woman has not hitherto been granted him.*

*The slightest religious act on the part of any subject, whomsoever he be, whatsoever be that act, shall be punished by death.*

*Messieurs are expressly enjoined at all gatherings to employ none but the most lascivious language, remarks indicative of the greatest debauchery, expressions of the filthiest, the most harsh, and the most blasphemous.*

*The name of God shall never be uttered save when accompanied by invectives or imprecations, and thus qualified it shall be repeated as often as possible.*

*With respect to their tone, it shall at all times be exceedingly brutal, exceedingly harsh, and exceedingly imperious when addressing the wives and the little girls, but wheedling, whorish, and depraved when addressing the men whom the friends, by adopting with them the role of women, should regard as their husbands.*

*Any friend who fails to comply with any one of these articles, or who may take it into his head to act in accordance with a single glimmer of common sense or moderation and above all to spend a single day without retiring dead drunk to bed, shall be fined ten thousand francs.*

*Whenever a friend experiences the need to relieve himself heavily, a woman from that class he considers fitting shall be obliged to accompany him, to attend to those duties he shall during this activity indicate to her.*

*No subject, whether male or female, shall be allowed to fulfill duties of cleanliness whatsoever they may be, and above all those consequent upon the heavy need relieved, without express permission from the month's presiding officer, and if it be refused him, and if despite that refusal he surrender to this need, his punishment shall be of the very rudest.*

*The four wives shall have no prerogatives of any kind over the other women; on the contrary, they shall at all times be treated with a maximum of rigor and inhumanity, and they shall be frequently employed upon the vilest and most painful enterprises, such as for example the cleaning of the private and common privies established in the chapel. These privies shall be emptied only once every week, but always by them, and they shall be severely punished if they resist the work or accomplish it poorly.*

*Should a subject attempt evasion while the assembly is sitting, he shall be punished by death instantly, whomsoever he be.*

*The cooks and their assistants shall be respected, and those of the friends who violate this article shall pay a fine of one thousand gold louis. With regard to these fines, they shall all be specially employed, upon the return to France, for the initial expenses incidental to a new party, either in this same kind, or in another.*

These affairs being settled and these regulations published on the 30th, the Duc spent the morning of the 31st inspecting everything, having the statutes repeated aloud, and scrupulously examining the premises to see whether they were susceptible to assault or favorable to escape.

Having concluded that one would have to have wings or the devil's powers to get out or in, he reported his findings to the society and devoted the evening to haranguing the women. By his order they were all convoked in the auditorium, and having mounted that kind of tribune or throne intended for the storyteller, here more or less is the speech he delivered to them:

"Feeble, enfettered creatures destined solely for our pleasures, I trust you have not deluded yourselves into supposing that the equally absolute and ridiculous ascendancy given you in the outside world would be accorded you in this place; a thousand times more subjugated than would be slaves, you must expect naught but humiliation, and obedience is that one virtue whose use I recommend to you: it and no other befits your present state. Above all, do not take it into your heads to rely in the least upon your charms; we are utterly indifferent to those snares and, you may depend upon it, such bait will fail with us. Ceaselessly bear in mind that we will make use of you all, but that not a single one of you need beguile herself into imagining that she is able to inspire any feeling of pity in us. Roused in fury against the altars that have been able to snatch from us some few grains of incense, our pride and our libertinage shatter them as soon as the illusion has satisfied our senses, and contempt almost always followed by hatred instantly assumes the pre-eminence hitherto occupied by our imagination. What, furthermore, might you offer that we do not know by heart already? what will you tender us that we shall not grind beneath our heels, often at the very moment delirium transports us?

"Useless to conceal it from you: your service will be arduous, it will be painful and rigorous, and the slightest delinquencies will be requited immediately with corporal and afflicting punishments; hence, I must recommend to you prompt exactness, submissiveness, and a total self-abnegation that you be enabled to heed naught but our desires; let them be your only laws, fly to do their bidding, anticipate them, cause them to be born. Not that you have much to gain by this conduct, but simply because, by not observing it, you will have a great deal to lose.

"Give a thought to your circumstances, think what you are, what we are, and may these reflections cause you to quake—you are beyond the borders of France in the depths of an uninhabitable forest, high amongst naked mountains; the paths that brought you here were destroyed behind you as you advanced along them. You are enclosed in an impregnable citadel; no one on earth knows you are here, you are beyond the reach of your friends, of your kin: insofar as the world is concerned, you are already dead, and if yet you breathe, 'tis by our pleasure, and for it only. And what are the persons to whom you are now subordinated? Beings of a profound and recognized criminality, who have no god but their lubricity, no laws but their depravity, no care but for their debauch, godless, unprincipled, unbelieving profligates, of whom the least criminal is soiled by more infamies than you could number, and in whose eyes the life of a woman—what do I say, the life of a woman? the lives of all the women who dwell on the face of the earth, are as insignificant as the crushing of a fly. There will, doubtless, be few excesses to which we will not be carried; let not one of them dismay you, without the flutter of an eyelash lend yourselves to them all, and faced with whatever it may be, show patience, submission, and courage. If, unhappily, some amongst you succumb to our passions' intemperance, let her adjust bravely to her fate: we are not going to exist forever in this world, and the most fortunate thing that can befall a woman is to die young. Our ordinances have been read to you: they are very wise and well-designed for your safety and for our pleasures; obey them blindly, and expect the worst from us should we be irritated by your misbehavior. Several amongst you have ties with us, I know, and perhaps they embolden you, and perhaps you hope for indulgence on this account; you would be most gravely mistaken were you to put much store by them: no blood attachment is sacred in the view of people like ourselves, and the more they seem so to you, the more their rupture will stimulate the perversity in our spirits. Daughters, wives, it is to you, then, I address myself at present: expect us to grant you no prerogative, you are herewith advised that you will be treated with an even greater severity than the others, and that specifically to point out to you with what scorn we view the bonds whereby you perhaps think us constrained.

"Moreover, do not simply wait for us to specify the orders we would have you execute: a gesture, a glance, often simply one of our internal feelings will announce our desire, and you will be as harshly punished for not having divined it as you would be were you, after having been notified, to ignore that desire or flout it. It is up to you to interpret our movements, our glances, our gestures, to interpret our expressions, and above all not to be mistaken as to our desires. Let us suppose, for example, this desire were to see a particular part of your body and that, through clumsiness, you were to exhibit some other—you appreciate to what extent such contempt would be upsetting to our imaginations, and you are aware of all that one risks by chilling the mind of a libertine who, let us presume, is expecting an ass for his discharge, and to whom some fool presents a cunt.

"By and large, offer your fronts very little to our sight; remember that this loathsome part, which only the alienation of her wits could have permitted Nature to create, is always the one we find most repugnant. And relative to your ass itself, there are precautions to observe: not only would you be well-advised, upon presenting it, to hide the odious lair which accompanies it, but it behooves you to avoid the display, at certain moments, of an ass in that certain state wherein other folk desire always to find it; you probably understand me; and furthermore, the four duennas will furnish you later on with instructions which will complete the explanation of everything.

"In short: shudder, tremble, anticipate, obey—and with all that, if you are not very fortunate, perhaps you will not be completely miserable. No intrigues amongst you, no alliances, none of that ridiculous friendship between girls which, by softening the heart in one sense, in another renders it both more ill-tempered and less well-disposed to the one and simple humiliation to which you are fated by us; consider that it is not at all as human beings we behold you, but exclusively as animals one feeds in return for their services, and which one withers with blows when they refuse to be put to use.

"You have seen with what stringency you are forbidden anything resembling any act of religion whatsoever. I warn you: few crimes will be more severely punished than this one. It is only too well known that in your midst there are yet a few fools unable to bring themselves to abjure this infamous God and abhor his worship; I would have you know that these imbeciles will be scrupulously examined, and there is no extremity they will not suffer who are so unlucky as to be taken in the act. Let them be persuaded, these stupid creatures, let them henceforth be convinced that in all the world there are not twenty persons today who cling to this mad notion of God's existence, and that the religion he invokes is nothing but a fable ludicrously invented by cheats and impostors, whose interest in deceiving us is only too clear at the present time. In fine, decide for yourselves: were there a God and were this God to have any power, would he permit the virtue which honors him, and which you profess, to be sacrificed to vice and libertinage as it is going to be? Would this all-powerful God permit a feeble creature like myself, who would, face to face with him, be as a mite in the eyes of an elephant, would he, I say, permit this feeble creature to insult him, to flout him, to defy him, to challenge him, to offend him as I do, wantonly, at my own sweet will, at every instant of the day?"

This little sermon concluded, the Duc descended from the chair and, with the exception of the four elders and the four narrators, who knew very well they were there as sacrificers and priestesses rather than as victims, except for those eight individuals, I say, everyone burst into tears, and the Duc, not much touched by the scene, left those enacting it to conjecture, jabber, and complain to each other, in perfect certainty the eight spies would render a thorough report of everything; and off he went to spend the night with Hercule, the member of the troupe of fuckers who had become his most intimate favorite in the capacity of a lover, little Zéphyr still having, as a mistress, the first place in his heart. In that upon the following morning everything was to begin, the mechanism was to start functioning, everyone accordingly completed final arrangements, went soundly to sleep, and on the morrow at the stroke of ten, the curtain rose upon a scene of libertinage which was to continue unimpeded, in strict compliance with prescription, until and including the 28th day of February.

And now, friend-reader, you must prepare your heart and your mind for the most impure tale that has ever been told since our world began, a book the likes of which are met with neither amongst the ancients nor amongst us moderns. Fancy, now, that all pleasure-taking either sanctioned by good manners or enjoined by that fool you speak of incessantly, of whom you know nothing and whom you call Nature; fancy, I say, that all these modes of taking pleasure will be expressly excluded from this anthology, or that whenever peradventure you do indeed encounter them here, they will always be accompanied by some crime or colored by some infamy.

Many of the extravagances you are about to see illustrated will doubtless displease you, yes, I am well aware of it, but there are amongst them a few which will warm you to the point of costing you some fuck, and that, reader, is all we ask of you; if we have not said everything, analyzed everything, tax us not with partiality, for you cannot expect us to have guessed what suits you best. Rather, it is up to you to take what you please and leave the rest alone, another reader will do the same, and little by little, everyone will find himself satisfied. It is the story of the magnificent banquet: six hundred different plates offer themselves to your appetite; are you going to eat them all? No, surely not, but this prodigious variety enlarges the bounds of your choice and, delighted by this increase of possibilities, it surely never occurs to you to scold the Amphitryon who regales you. Do likewise here: choose and let lie the rest without declaiming against that rest simply because it does not have the power to please you. Consider that it will enchant someone else, and be a philosopher.

As for the diversity, it is authentic, you may be sure of it; study closely that passion which to your first consideration seems perfectly to resemble another, and you will see that a difference does exist and that, however slight it may be, it possesses precisely that refinement, that touch which distinguishes and characterizes the kind of libertinage wherewith we are here involved.

We have, moreover, blended these six hundred passions into the storytellers' narratives. That is one more thing whereof the reader were well to have foreknowledge: it would have been too monotonous to catalogue them one by one outside the body of the story. But as some reader not much learned in these matters might perhaps confuse the designated passions with the adventure or simple event in the narrator's life, each of these passions has been carefully distinguished by a marginal notation: a line, above which is the title that may be given the passion. This mark indicates the exact place where the account of the passions begins, and the end of the paragraph always indicates where it finishes.[2]

But as numerous personages participate in a drama of this kind, notwithstanding the care we have taken in this introduction to describe and designate each one . . . we shall provide an index which will contain the name and age of every actor, together with a brief sketch of them all; so that should the reader, as he moves along, encounter what seems to him an unfamiliar figure, he will have merely to turn back to this index, and if this little aid to his memory suffice not, to the more thorough portraits given earlier.

## THE ROMANCE OF THE SCHOOL FOR LIBERTINAGE
### DRAMATIS PERSONAE

The *Duc de Blangis,* fifty, built like a satyr, endowed with a monstrous member and prodigious strength; he may be regarded as the depository of every vice and every crime. He has killed his mother, his sister, and three of his wives.

The *Bishop of X\*\*\** is his brother; forty-five years old, more slender and more delicate than the Duc; a nasty mouth. He is deceitful, adroit, a faithful sectary of sodomy, active and passive, he has an absolute contempt for all other kinds of pleasure, he has brought about the cruel deaths of the two children whose sizable fortune was left in trust with him; he is a nervous type, so sensitive he nearly swoons upon discharging.

The *Président de Curval,* sixty; a tall, thin, lank man, with sunken, dead eyes, an unhealthy mouth, the walking image of low

2 In spite of what Sade says regarding the marginal notations intended to distinguish a particular passion described from the recital of a simple event in the life of the narrator, he apparently never made them. The first complete French edition, prepared for publication by Maurice Heine from Sade's original manuscript, does not contain them; nor does the 1953 Pauvert edition, which follows Heine scrupulously. In the latter, from which the present translation was made, the storytellers' narrations, in which the recital of the various passions is presented, are given in italics. We have here followed the example of the 1953 French edition.—*Tr.*

license and libertinage, frightfully dirty about his body and attaching voluptuousness thereto. He has been circumcised, his erection is rare and difficult, it does take place however, and he ejaculates almost every day. His tastes induce him to prefer men; all the same, he has no scorn for a maid. For singularities in his tastes, he has a fondness for old age and whatever is kin to him in filthiness. He is endowed with a member practically as thick as the Duc's. In late years he has seemed as though unstrung by debauchery, and he drinks a great deal. He owes his fortune solely to murders and is nominally guilty of one, a dreadful one, whose details are contained in his biography previously given. When discharging, he experiences a sort of lubricious rage; it drives him to cruel deeds.

*Durcet,* banker, fifty-three, a great friend of the Duc, and his schoolmate; he is short, squat, and chubby, but his body looks healthy, pretty, and fair. He has the figure of a woman and all a woman's tastes: by his little firmness deprived of giving women pleasure, he has imitated that sex and has himself fucked at any time of day or night. He is also rather fond of a good mouthing, 'tis the only expedient which is able to afford him an agent's pleasures. His pleasures are his only gods, and he is constantly prepared to sacrifice everything to them. He is clever, adroit, and has committed a profusion of crimes; he poisoned his mother, his wife, and her niece in order to assure his inheritance. His spirit ·is stoical, stalwart his heart, and absolutely insensible to pity. He no longer stiffens, his ejaculations are most rare; his instants of crisis are preceded by a kind of spasm which hurls him into a lubricious fury dangerous for those who are serving his passions.

*Constance,* the Duc's wife, Durcet's daughter; twenty-two years of age, she is a Roman beauty, with more majesty than finesse, plump but well-constructed, a superb body, a unique ass, a model ass, hair and eyes very dark. She is not without brains or wit, and but too well senses the horror of her fate. A great fund of native virtue nothing has been able to destroy.

*Adelaide,* Durcet's wife, the Président's daughter; a pretty little object, she is twenty, blond, very tender eyes of a lovely, animated blue, she has about her everything of the romantic heroine. A long, well-attached neck, her one defect is her mouth, which is a shade large. Small breasts and a little ass, but all that, though delicate, is fair and well-molded. A mind given to fantasy, a tender heart, excessively virtuous and believing; she secretly performs her Christian duties.

*Julie,* the Président's wife, elder daughter of the Duc; she is twenty-four, fat, fleshy, with fine brown eyes, a pretty nose, striking and agreeable features, but an appalling mouth. She has little virtue and even pronounced tendencies to uncleanliness, alcoholism, gluttony, and whoredom. Her husband loves her for her defective mouth; this singularity appeals to the Président's tastes. She has never been given either principles or religion.

*Aline,* her younger sister, supposed daughter of the Duc, really one of the Duc's wives and the Bishop's child; she is eighteen, has a very agreeable and fetching countenance, abounding health, brown eyes, an upturned nose, a mischievous air although she is profoundly indolent and lazy. She seems as yet to have no temperament and most sincerely detests all the infamies she is victim of. The Bishop baptized her behind at the age of ten. She has been left in crass ignorance, knows neither how to read nor write, she abhors the Bishop and greatly fears the Duc. She is much attached to her sister, is sober and tidy, speaks oddly and like a child; her ass is charming.

*Duclos,* the first storyteller; forty-eight, preserves her looks, is in good physical health, has the finest ass to be seen. Brunette, full figure, very well fleshed.

*Champville* is fifty; she is slender, well made, has lascivious eyes, she is a tribade, and everything about her proclaims it. Her present trade is pimping. She was once fair-haired, has pretty eyes, is long in the clitoris and ticklish in that part, has an ass much worn from service, but is none the less untupped in that place.

*Martaine* is fifty-two; she's a procuress too, a matronly dame, hale and hearty; inner obstructions have prevented her from ever knowing any but Sodom's delights, for which indeed she seems to have been specially created, for, her age notwithstanding, she has the world's noblest ass; it is both broad and big and so habituated to introductions that she can accommodate the weightiest engines without the flutter of an eyelash. She has pretty features still, but they are beginning to fade.

*Desgranges* is fifty-six; she is even now the greatest villain who has ever lived; she is tall, slender, pale, and was once dark-haired, she is crime's personification. Her withered ass resembles marbled paper, or parchment, and its orifice is immense. She is one-dugged, is missing three fingers and six teeth, *fructus belli.* There exists not a single crime she has not perpetrated or engineered, her prattle is pleasing to the ear, she has wit, and is currently one of the outfitters most highly respected by society.

*Marie,* the first of the duennas, is the youngest at fifty-eight; she has been whipped and branded, and was a servant to thieves. Her eyes are lackluster and running, her nose crooked, her teeth yellow, one buttock's gnawed by an abscess. She has borne and killed fourteen children.

*Louison,* the second duenna, is sixty; she is small, lame, one-eyed, and hunchbacked, but for all that she has yet a very pretty ass. She is always ready for crime and is extremely wicked. She and Marie are appointed as governesses to the girls, and the two following to the boys.

*Thérèse,* aged sixty-two, looks like a skeleton, has no hair, no teeth, a stinking mouth, an ass seamed with scars, its hole is of excessively generous diameter. Filthy and fetid to an atrocious degree; she has a twisted arm, and she limps.

*Fanchon,* sixty-nine years old, has been six times hanged in effigy and has perpetrated every crime under the sun; she squints, is flat-nosed, short, heavy, has no forehead, two teeth only. An erysipelas covers her ass, a bunch of hemorrhoids hangs from her hole, a chancre is eating her womb, she has a burnt thigh, and a cancer gnaws her breast. She is constantly drunk and vomits, farts, and shits here, there, and everywhere all the time, and all unawares she is doing it.

## HAREM OF LITTLE GIRLS

*Augustine,* daughter of a Languedoc baron, fifteen years old, alert and pretty little face.

*Fanny,* daughter of a Breton counselor, fourteen, a sweet and tender air.

*Zelmire,* daughter of the Comte de Terville, seigneur of Beauce, fifteen, a noble look and a very sensitive soul.

*Sophie,* daughter of a gentleman from Berry, charming features, fourteen years.

*Colombe,* daughter of a counselor to the Parliament of Paris, thirteen years old, exuberant health.

*Hébé,* daughter of an Orléans officer, a very libertine air, charming eyes, she is twelve.

*Rosette* and *Michette,* both look like lovely virgins. The first is thirteen and is the daughter of a Chalon-sur-Saône officer, the other is twelve and is a daughter of the Marquis de Sénanges; she was abducted from her father's estate in the Bourbonnais.

Their figures, the rest of their features and chiefly their asses are beyond all description. They were chosen from amongst one hundred and thirty.

## HAREM OF LITTLE BOYS

*Zélamir,* thirteen, son of a Poitou squire.

*Cupidon,* same age, son of a gentleman from near La Flèche.

*Narcisse,* twelve, son of a nobleman situated in Rouen, Knight of Malta.

*Zéphyr,* fifteen, son of a general living in Paris. He is destined for the Duc.

*Céladon,* son of a Nancy magistrate. He is fourteen.

*Adonis,* son of a judge of a Paris assize court; fifteen, destined for Curval.

*Hyacinthe,* fourteen, son of a retired officer dwelling in Champagne.

*Giton,* page to the King, twelve, son of a gentleman from the Nivernais.

No pen is capable of representing the graces, the features, and the charms of these eight children superior also to all the tongue is empowered to say, and chosen, as you know, from amongst a very large number.

## EIGHT FUCKERS

*Hercule,* twenty-six, very pretty, but also a very mean character, the Duc's favorite; his prick measures eight and one-quarter inches around and thirteen in length. Plentiful discharge.

*Antinoüs* is thirty. A fine specimen of a man, his prick is eight inches around and twelve inches long.

*Bum-Cleaver,* twenty-eight years old, has the look of a satyr; his majestic prick is bent saber fashion, its head, or glans, is enormous, it is eight and three-eighths inches in circumference and the shaft eight in length. A fine curve to this majestic prick.

*Invictus* is twenty-five, he is exceedingly ugly, but healthy and vigorous; the great favorite of Curval, he is continually aroused, and his prick is seven and fifteen-sixteenths inches around by eleven inches long.

The four others measure from nine to ten and fifteen-sixteenths inches long, by from seven and a half to seven and five-eighths inches around, and they are from twenty-five to thirty years of age.

---

End of the Introduction. Omissions I have made in it:

1. I must say that Hercule and Invictus are, the one a very mean character and the other very ugly, and that not one of the eight has ever been able to enjoy either a man or a woman.

2. That the chapel is used for a toilet, and give details of this usage.

3. That the outfitters, male and female, had cutthroats with them and under their orders during their forays.

4. Give some few more details about the elders' breasts and speak of Fanchon's cancer. Also a few more touches to the descriptions of the children's faces.

# PART THE FIRST

THE 150 SIMPLE PASSIONS, OR THOSE BE-
LONGING TO THE FIRST CLASS, COMPOSING
THE THIRTY DAYS OF NOVEMBER PASSED
IN HEARING THE NARRATION OF MADAME
DUCLOS; INTERSPERSED AMONGST WHICH
ARE THE SCANDALOUS DOINGS AT THE
CHÂTEAU DURING THAT MONTH; ALL BE-
ING SET DOWN IN THE FORM OF A JOURNAL.

# THE FIRST DAY

*T*he company rose the 1st of November at ten o'clock in the morning, as was specified in the statutes which Messieurs had mutually sworn faithfully to observe in every particular. The four fuckers who had not shared the friends' couches, at their waking hour brought Zéphyr to the Duc, Adonis to Curval, Narcisse to Durcet, and Zélamir to the Bishop. All four children were very timid, even more awkward, but, encouraged by their guides, they very nicely carried out their tasks, and the Duc discharged. His three colleagues, more reserved and less prodigal with their fuck, had as much of it deposited in them as did the Duc, but distributed none of their own.

At eleven o'clock they passed into the women's quarters where the eight young sultanas appeared naked, and in this state served chocolate, aided and directed by Marie and Louison, who presided over this seraglio. There was a great deal of handling and colling, and the eight poor girls, wretched little victims of the most blatant lubricity, blushed, hid behind their hands, sought to protect their charms, and immediately displayed everything as soon as they observed that their modesty irritated and annoyed their masters. The Duc rose up like a shot and measured his engine's circumference against Michette's slender little waist: their difference did not exceed three inches. Durcet, the month's presiding officer, conducted the prescribed examinations and made the necessary searches; Hébé and Colombe were found to have lapsed, their punishment was pronounced at once and fixed for the following Saturday at orgy hour. They wept. No one was moved.

They proceeded to the boys' apartments. The four who had not appeared that morning, namely Cupidon, Céladon, Hyacinthe, and Giton, bared their behinds in accordance with orders, and the sight provided an instant's amusement. Curval kissed them all on the mouth, and the Bishop spent a moment frigging their pricks while the Duc and Durcet were doing something else. The inspections were completed, no misconduct was discovered.

At one o'clock Messieurs betook themselves to the chapel where, as you know, the sanitary conveniences were installed. The calculation of requirements for the coming soiree having led to the refusal of a good number of requests, only Constance, Duclos, Augustine, Sophie, Zélamir, Cupidon, and Louison appeared; all the others had asked permission and had been instructed to hold back until evening. Our four friends, ranged around the same specially constructed seat, had these seven subjects take their seat one after another, and then retired when they had enough of this spectacle. They descended to the salon where, while the women dined, they gossiped and tattled until the time came for them to be served their meal. Each of the four friends placed himself between two fuckers, pursuant to the imposed rule that barred all women from their table, and the four naked wives, aided by the elders costumed as the Graeae, served them the most magnificent and the most succulent dinner it were possible to concoct. No one more delicate, more skilled than the cooks they had brought with them, and they were so well paid and so lavishly provided that everything could not fail to be a brilliant success. As the midday fare was to be less heavy than the evening meal, they were restricted to four superb courses, each composed of twelve plates. Burgundy wine arrived with the hors d'oeuvres, Bordeaux was served with the entrees, champagne with the roasts, Hermitage accompanied the entremets, Tokay and madeira were served with dessert.

Spirits rose little by little; the fuckers, whom the friends had granted every liberty with their wives, treated them somewhat untenderly. Constance was even a bit knocked about, rather beaten for having dawdled over bringing a dish to Hercule who, seeing himself well advanced in the Duc's good graces, fancied he might carry insolence to the point of drubbing and molesting his wife; the Duc thought this very amusing. Curval, in an ugly humor by the time dessert arrived, flung a plate at his wife's face, and it might have clove her head in two had she not ducked. Spying one of his neighbors stiffen, Durcet, though they were still at table, promptly unbuttoned his breeches and presented his ass. The neighbor drove his weapon home; the operation once concluded, they fell to drinking again as if nothing had happened. The Duc soon imitated his old friend's little infamy and wagered that, enormous as Invictus' prick might be, he could calmly down three bottles of wine while lying embuggered upon it. What effortlessness, what ease, what detachment in libertinage! He won what he had staked, and as they were not drunk on an empty stomach, as those three bottles fell upon at least fifteen others, the Duc's head began gently to swim. The first object upon which his eye alighted was his wife, weeping over the abuse she had sustained from Hercule, and this sight so inspired the Duc he lost not an instant doing to her things too excessive for us to describe as yet. The reader will notice how hampered we are in these beginnings, and how stumbling are our efforts to give a coherent account of these matters; we trust he will forgive us for leaving the curtain drawn over a considerable number of little details. We promise it will be raised later on.

Our champions finally made their way into the salon, where new pleasures and further delights were awaiting them. Coffee and liqueurs were distributed by a charming quartet made up of Adonis and Hyacinthe, two appealing little boys, and two pretty maids, Zelmire and Fanny. Thérèse, one of the duennas, supervised them, for it was decreed that wherever two or more children were gathered, a duenna was to be on hand. Our four libertines, half-drunk but none the less resolved to abide by their laws, contented themselves with kisses, fingerings, but their libertine intelligence knew how to season these mild activities with all the refinements of debauch and lubricity. It was thought for a moment that the Bishop was going to have to surrender his fuck in exchange for the extraordinary things he was wringing from Hyacinthe, while Zelmire frigged him. His nerves were already aquiver, an impending crisis was beginning to take possession of his entire being, but he checked himself, the tempting objects ready to triumph over his senses were sent spinning and, knowing there was yet a full day's work ahead of him, the Bishop saved his best for the evening. Six different kinds of liqueur were drunk, three kinds of coffee, and the hour sounding at last, the two couples withdrew to dress.

Our friends took a fifteen minute nap, then moved into the throne room, the place where the auditors were to listen to the narrations. The friends took their places upon their couches, the Duc having his beloved Hercule at his feet, near him, naked, Adelaide, Durcet's wife and the Président's daughter, and for quatrain opposite him, and linked to his niche by a chain of flowers, as has been explained, Zéphyr, Giton, Augustine, and Sophie costumed as shepherds, supervised by Louison as an old peasant woman playing the role of their mother.

At Curval's feet was Invictus, upon his couch lay Constance, the Duc's wife and Durcet's daughter, and for quatrain four little Spaniards, each sex dressed in its costume and as elegantly as possible: they were Adonis, Céladon, Fanny, and Zelmire; Fanchon, clad as a duenna, watched over them.

The Bishop had Antinoüs at his feet, his niece Julie on his couch, and four little almost naked savages for quatrain. The boys: Cupidon and Narcisse; the girls: Hébé and Rosette; an old Amazon, interpreted by Thérèse, was in charge of them.

Durcet had Bum-Cleaver for fucker, near him reclined Aline, daughter of the Bishop, and in front of him were four little sultanas, the boys being dressed as girls, and this refinement to the last degree emphasized the enchanting visages of Zélamir, Hyacinthe, Colombe, and Michette. An old Arab slave, portrayed by Marie, presided over this quatrain.

The three storytellers, magnificently dressed as upper-class Parisian courtesans, were seated below the throne upon a couch, and Madame Duclos, the month's narrator, in very scanty and very elegant attire, well rouged and heavily bejeweled, having taken her place on the stage, thus began the story of what had occurred in her life, into which account she was, with all pertinent details, to insert the first one hundred and fifty passions designated by the title of *simple passions:*

*'Tis no slight undertaking, Messieurs, to attempt to express oneself before a circle such as yours. Accustomed to all of the most*

subtle and most delicate that letters produce, how, one may wonder, will you be able to bear the ill-shaped periods and uncouth images of a humble creature like myself who has received no other education than the one supplied her by libertinage. But your indulgence reassures me; you ask for naught but the natural and true, and I dare say what of these I shall provide you will merit your attention.

My mother was twenty-five when she brought me into the world, and I was her second child; the first was also a daughter, by six years my elder. My mother's birth was not distinguished. She had been early bereft of both her father and mother, and as her parents had dwelled near the Récollet monastery in Paris, when she found herself an orphan, abandoned and without any resources, she obtained permission from these good fathers to come and ask for alms in their church. But as she had some youth and health, she soon attracted their notice, and gradually mounted from the church below to the rooms above, whence she soon descended with child. It was as a consequence of one such adventure my sister saw the light, and it is more than likely that my own birth might rightly be ascribed to no other cause.

However, content with my mother's docility and seeing how she did make the community to prosper and flourish, the good fathers rewarded her works by granting her what might be earned from the rental of seats in their church; my mother no sooner obtained this post than, with her superiors' leave, she married one of the house's water carriers who straightway, without the least repugnance, adoped my sister and me.

Born into the Church, I dwelled so to speak more in the House of God than in our own; I helped my mother arrange the chairs, I seconded the sacristans in their various operations, I would have said Mass had that been necessary, although I had not yet attained my fifth year.

One day, returning from my holy occupations, my sister asked me whether I had yet encountered Father Laurent. . . .

I said I had not.

"Well, look out," said she, "he's on the watch for you, I know he is, he wants to show you what he showed me. Don't run away, look him straight in the eye without being afraid, he won't touch *you, but he'll show you something very funny, and if you let him do it he'll pay you a lot. There are more than fifteen of us around here whom he's shown it to. That's what he likes best, and he's given a present to us all."*

*You may well imagine, Messieurs, that nothing more was needed, not only to keep me from fleeing Father Laurent, but to induce me to seek him out; at that age the voice of modesty is a whisper at best, and its silence until the time one has left the tutelage of Nature is certain proof, is it not, that this factitious sentiment is far less the product of that original mother's training than it is the fruit of education? I flew instantly to the church, and as I was crossing a little court located between the entrance of the churchyard and the monastery, I bumped squarely into Father Laurent. He was a monk of about forty, with a very handsome face. He stopped me.*

*"Whither are you going, Françon?" he asked.*

*"To arrange the chairs, Father."*

*"Never fear, never fear, your mother will attend to them," said he. "Come, come along with me," and he drew me toward a sequestered chamber hard by the place. "I am going to show you something you have never seen."*

*I follow him, we enter, he shuts the door and, having posted me directly opposite him:*

*"Well, Françon," says he, pulling a monstrous prick from his drawers, an instrument which nearly toppled me with fright; "tell me," he continues, frigging himself, "have you ever seen anything to equal it? . . . that's what they call a prick, my little one, yes, a prick . . . it's used for fucking, and what you're going to see, what's going to flow out of it in a moment or two, is the seed wherefrom you were created. I've shown it to your sister, I've shown it to all the little girls of your age, lend a hand, help it along, help get it out, do as your sister does, she's got it out of me twenty times and more. . . . I show them my prick, and then what do you suppose I do? I squirt the fuck in their face. . . . That's my passion, my child, I have no other . . . and you're about to behold it."*

*And at the same time I felt myself completely drenched in a white spray, it soaked me from head to foot, some drops of it had leapt even into my eyes, for my little head just came to the height of his fly. However, Laurent was gesticulating. "Ah! the pretty fuck, the dear fuck I am losing," he cried, "why, look at you! You're covered with it." And gradually regaining control of himself, he calmly put his tool away and decamped, slipping twelve sous into my hand and suggesting that I bring him any little companions I might happen to have.*

*As you may readily fancy, I could not have been more eager to run and tell everything to my sister; she wiped me dry, taking the greatest care to overlook none of the spots, and she who had enabled me to earn my little fortune did not fail to demand half of my wages. Instructed by this example, I did not fail, in the hope of a similar division of the spoils, to round up as many little girls for Father Laurent as I could find. But having brought him one with whom he was already familiar, he turned her away, the while giving me three sous by way of encouragement.*

*"I never see the same one twice, my child," he told me, "bring me some I don't know, never any of those who say they've already had dealings with me."*

*I managed more successfully; in the space of three months, I introduced Father Laurent to more than twenty new girls, with whom, for the sake of his pleasure, he employed the identical proceedings he had with me. Together with the stipulation that they be strangers to him, there was another relative to age, and it appeared to be of infinite importance: he had no use for anything younger than four or older than seven. And my little fortune could not have been faring better when my sister, noticing that I was encroaching upon her domain, threatened to divulge everything to my mother if I did not put a stop to this splendid commerce; I had to give up Father Laurent.*

*However, my functions continued to keep me in the neighborhood of the monastery; the same day I reached the age of seven I encountered a new lover whose preferred caprice, although very childish, was nevertheless somewhat more serious. This one was named Father Louis, he was older than Laurent, and had some unidentifiable quality in his bearing that was a great deal more libertine. He sidled up to me at the door of the church as I was entering it, and made me promise to come up to his room. At first*

*I advanced a few objections, but once he had assured me that three years ago my sister had come for a visit and that he received little girls of my age every day, I went with him. Scarcely were we in his cell when he closed and bolted the door and, having poured some elixir into a goblet, made me swallow it and then two more copious measures too. This preparatory step taken, the reverend, more affectionate than his confrere, fell to kissing me and, chattering all the while, he untied my apron and, raising my skirt to my bodice, he laid hands, despite my faint strugglings, upon all the anterior parts he had just brought to light; and after having thoroughly fingered and considered them, he inquired of me whether I did not desire to piss. Singularly driven to this need by the strong dose he had a few moments earlier had me drink, I assured him the urge so to do was as powerful as ever it could be, but that I did not want to satisfy it in front of him.*

*"Oh, my goodness, do! Why yes, my little rascal," quoth the bawdy fellow, "by God yes, you'll piss in my presence and, what's worse, you'll piss upon me. Here it is," he went on, plucking his prick from his breeches, "here's the tool you're going to moisten, just piss on it a little."*

*And thereupon he lifted me up and set me on two chairs, one foot on one chair, the other foot on the other, he moved the chairs apart as far as was possible, then bade me squat. Holding me in this posture, he placed a container beneath me, established himself on a little stool about as high as the pot; his engine was in his hand, directly under my cunt. One of his hands supporting my haunches, he frigged himself with the other, and my mouth being at a level with his, he kissed it.*

*"Off you go, my little one, piss," cried he, "flood my prick with that enchanting liquid whose hot outpouring exerts such a sway over my senses. Piss, my heart, care not but to piss and try to inundate my fuck."*

*Louis became animated, excited himself, it was easy to see that this unusual operation was the one which all his senses most cherished; the sweetest, gentlest ecstasy crowned that very moment when the liquids wherewith he had swollen my stomach, gushed most abundantly out of me, and we simultaneously filled the same pot, he with fuck, I with urine. The exercise concluded, Louis de-*

*livered roughly the same speech to me I had heard from Laurent, he wished to make a procuress of his little whore, and this time, caring precious little for my sister's threats, I boldly guided every child I knew to dear Louis. He had every one of them do the same thing, and as he experienced no compunction upon seeing any one of them a second or third time, and as he always gave me separate payment, which had nothing to do with the additional fee I extracted from my little comrades, before six months had passed I found myself with a tidy little sum which was entirely my own; I had only to conceal knowledge of it from my sister.*

"Duclos," the Président interrupted at this point, "we have, I believe, advised you that your narrations must be decorated with the most numerous and searching details; the precise way and extent to which we may judge how the passion you describe relates to human manners and man's character is determined by your willingness to disguise no circumstance; and, what is more, the least circumstance is apt to have an immense influence upon the procuring of that kind of sensory irritation we expect from your stories."

"Yes, my Lord," Duclos replied, "I have been advised to omit no detail and to enter into the most minute particulars whenever they serve to shed light upon the human personality, or upon the species of passion; have I neglected something in connection with this one?"

"You have," said the Président; "I have not the faintest notion of your second monk's prick, nor any idea of its discharge. In addition, did he frig your cunt, pray tell, and did he have you dandle his device? You see what I mean by neglected details."

"Your pardon, my Lord," said Duclos, "I shall repair these present mistakes and avoid them in the future. Father Louis possessed a very ordinary member, greater in its length than it was around and in general of a most common shape and turn; indeed, I do recall that he stiffened rather poorly and that it was not until the crisis arrived he took on a little firmness. No, he did not frig my cunt, he was content to enlarge it with his fingers as much as possible, so as to give free issue to the urine. He brought his prick very close two or three times, and his discharge was rapid, intense, and brief; nothing came from his mouth but the words: 'Ah, fuck! piss, my child, piss the pretty fountain, piss, d'ye hear, piss away, don't you see me come?' And while saying that, he intermittently sprinkled kisses on my mouth. They were not excessively libertine."

"That's it, Duclos," said Durcet, "the Président was right; I could not visualize a thing on the basis of your first telling, but now I have your man well in view."

"One moment, Duclos," said the Bishop, upon seeing that she was about to proceed. "I have on my own account a need rather more pressing than to piss, it's had me in its grip for an age and I have the feeling it's got to go."

So saying he drew Narcisse to his alcove. Fire leapt from the prelate's eyes, his prick stood up against his belly, foam flecked his lips, it was confined fuck that wished absolutely to escape and which could not be liberated save by violent means. He dragged his niece and the little boy into his closet. Everything came to a pause; a discharge was regarded as something far too portentous not to suspend everything the moment someone was about to produce one; all was to concur to make it delicious. But upon this occasion Nature's will did not correspond with the Bishop's wishes, and several minutes after having retired to the closet, he emerged from it, furious, in the same state of erection and, addressing himself to Durcet, presiding officer for November:

"Put that odd little fellow down for some punishment on Saturday," he said, flinging the child ten feet away from him, "and make it severe, if you please."

It was apparent that the boy had not been able to satisfy Monseigneur, and Julie whispered in her father's ear what had happened.

"Well, by God, then take another," cried the Duc, "choose something from one of our quatrains if nothing in yours suits you."

"Ah, my satisfaction now would be far beyond the damned little that would have been sufficient a moment ago," said the prelate. "You know to what we are led by a thwarted desire; I'd prefer to restrain myself, but no undue leniency with that poor little fool," he continued, "that's what I recommend...."

"But be at ease, my dear Bishop," said Durcet, "I promise you he'll get a good scolding, 'tis a fine idea to provide the others

with an example. I'm sorry to see you in such a state; try something
else; have yourself fucked."

"Monseigneur," spoke up Martaine, "I feel myself greatly
disposed to satisfy you, were Your Excellency to wish it. . . ."

"No, no, Christ, no!" the Bishop cried, "don't you know that
there are a thousand occasions when one does not want a woman's
asshole? I'll wait, I'll wait . . . let Duclos continue, I'll get rid of
it tonight, I'll have to find the one I want. Proceed, Duclos."

And the friends having laughed right heartily at the Bishop's
libertine frankness—"there are a thousand occasions when one
does not want a woman's asshole"—the storyteller resumed in these
terms:

*It was not long after I had attained the age of seven that one
day, following my custom of bringing one of my little comrades to
Louis, I found another monk with him in his cell. As that had never
happened before, I was surprised and wanted to leave, but Louis
having reassured us, my little friend and I went boldly in.*

*"Well there, Geoffrey," Louis said to his companion, pushing
me toward him, "did I not tell you that she was nice?"*

*"Why yes indeed, she is," said Geoffrey, taking me upon his
knees and giving me a kiss. "How old are you, my little one?"*

*"Seven, Father."*

*"Just fifty years younger than I," said the good father, kissing
me anew.*

*And during this little dialogue, the sirup was being prepared
and, as was customary, each of us swallowed three big glasses of it,
but, as it was not customary for me to drink when I brought Louis
a toy, because he only expected a sprinkling from the girl I brought,
because I did not usually stay for the ceremony but used to leave
at once, for all these reasons I was astonished by their actions, and
in a tone of the most naive innocence I inquired:*

*"And why do you have me drink, good Father? do you want
me to piss?"*

*"To be sure, we do, my child," quoth Geoffrey, who still had
me squeezed between his thighs and whose hands were already
straying over my front, "yes, you're to piss, and the adventure is
to take place with me; it will be, perhaps, a little different from*

*the other one you experienced here. Come into my cell, let's leave Father Louis with your little friend, and let's get to business ourselves; we'll return when all our needs are satisfied."*

*We left; before going, Louis told me in a whisper to be very obliging with his friend, and said I'd not regret it if I were. Geoffrey's cell was not far from Louis', and we reached it without being seen. No sooner inside than Geoffrey, having barricaded the door, told me to get rid of my skirts. I obeyed, he himself pulled my shift above my navel and, having seated me on the edge of his bed, he spread my thighs as wide as it were possible, at the same time thrusting me back in such a way my belly came into full view and my weight rested entirely upon the base of my spine. He besought me to keep in that position and to begin to piss immediately he gave one of my thighs a little slap with his hand. Then, scrutinizing me for a moment in this attitude, with one hand he separated the lips of my cunt, with the other he unbuttoned his breeches and with quick and energetic movements began to shake a dark, stunted little member which seemed not much inclined to respond to what was required of it. To give it some encouragement, our man set about doing his duty and proceeded to his chosen custom, the one which procured him the greatest possible titillation—down he went on his knees, I say, between my legs, spent another instant peering into the little orifice I presented to his eye, several times applied his mouth to it, between his teeth muttering certain luxurious phrases I cannot remember because at the time I did not understand them, and continued to agitate that sullen little member, which, though fearfully bullied, did not budge. Finally, he sealed his lips to those of my cunt, I received the signal, and instantly draining what my bladder contained into the gentleman's mouth, I flooded him with a stream of urine he swallowed as fast as I launched it into his gullet. Whereupon his member unfurled, and its proudly lifted head throbbed against one of my thighs: I felt it bravely spray his debilitated manhood's sterile issue. Everything had been so well managed he swallowed the final drops at the same moment his prick, confused by his victory, wept bloody tears over it. Trembling in every limb, Geoffrey got to his feet, and I observed that he no longer had for his idol, once the incense had been extinguished, the same religious fervor he had while delirium, inflaming his homage,*

*still sustained its glory: he rather abruptly gave me twelve sous,*
*opened the door without asking me, as had the others, to bring him*
*girls (he was evidently furnished by someone else) and, pointing*
*the way to his friend's cell, told me to go there, said that he was in*
*a hurry, that he had his offices to perform, that he could not con-*
*duct me himself, and then shut his door without affording me the*
*chance to answer him.*

"Oh yes indeed!" said the Duc, "unnumbered are they who
absolutely cannot bear the instant when the illusion is shattered. It
seems as if one's pride suffers when one lets a woman see one in
such a state of feebleness, and disgust would appear to be the result
of the discomfiture one experiences at such moments."

"No," said Curval, whom Adonis, kneeling, was frigging,
and whose hands were wandering over Zelmire, "no, my friend,
pride has nothing to do with it, but the object which is in the profoundest sense devoid of all value save the one our lust endows it
with, that object, I say, shows itself for what in truth it is once
our lubricity has subsided. The more violent has been the irritation,
the more this object is stripped of its attraction when this irritation
ceases to sustain it, just as we are more or less fatigued after
greater or lesser exertion, and this aversion we thereupon sense is
nothing but the sentiment of a glutted soul whereunto happiness is
displeasing because happiness has just wearied it."

"But from this aversion, all the same," spoke up Durcet, "is
often born a plan for revenge, whose fatal consequences have often
been observed."

"Yes, but that's another matter," Curval replied, "and as the
aftermath of these recitals will perhaps afford us examples of what
you're saying, let's not anticipate through dissertations what will be
naturally produced of itself."

"Président, be frank," said Durcet: "on the verge of running
amuck yourself, I believe that at the present moment you prefer
to prepare yourself to feel how one enjoys than to discuss how one
becomes disgusted."

"Why, not at all, not a bit of it," said Curval, "I am as cool
as ice. . . . To be sure, yes," he continued, kissing Adonis' lips, "this
child is charming . . . but he's not to be fucked; I know of nothing

worse than your damnable regulations . . . one must reduce oneself to things . . . to things . . . Go on, Duclos, go on, continue, for I have the feeling I might perpetrate something foolish, and I want my illusion to remain intact at least until I go to bed."

The Président, perceiving his engine beginning to rebel, sent the two children back to their posts and, lying down beside Constance, who, pretty as she was, doubtless failed to stimulate him as much, he a second time besought Duclos to resume her story; she did at once, as follows:

*I rejoined my little comrade. Louis had been serviced; not very well pleased, we both left the monastery, I almost resolved not to return again. Geoffrey's tone had wounded my little pride, and without probing further to determine the origins of my displeasure, I liked neither its apparent cause nor its consequences. However, it had been written in my destiny that I was to have yet a few more adventures in that pious retreat, and the example of my sister, who had, so she told me, done business with fourteen of its inhabitants, was to convince me that I was still far from the end of my tour. Three months after this last episode, I became aware of overtures being made to me by another one of these reverend fathers, this one a man of about sixty. He invented every kind of ruse to lure me to his room; one of them succeeded, so well in fact that one fine Sunday morning I found myself there, without knowing why or how it had happened. The old rascal, known as Father Henri, shut and locked the door as soon as I had crossed the threshold, and embraced me with exceeding warmth.*

*"Ah, little imp!" cried he, transported with joy, "I've got you now, you'll not escape me this time, ha!"*

*The weather was extremely cold at the time, my little nose was running as children's usually do in the winter; I drew out a handkerchief.*

*"What's this? What's this? Be careful there," warned Henri, "I'm the one who'll attend to that operation, my sweet."*

*And having stretched me out upon his bed with my head a little to one side, he sat down next to me and raised my head upon his lap. He peered avidly at me, his eyes seemed ready to devour the secretion oozing from my nose. "Oh, the pretty little snotface," said he, beginning to pant, "how I'm going to suck her." Therewith bending down over me, and taking my nose in his mouth, not only did he devour all the mucus between my nose and mouth, but he even lewdly darted the tip of his tongue into each of my nostrils, one after the other, and with such cleverness he provoked two or three sneezes which redoubled the flow he desired and was consuming so hungrily. But ask me for no details bearing upon this fellow, Messieurs, nothing appeared, and whether because he did nothing, or because he did it all in his drawers, there was nothing to be seen, and amidst the multitude of his kisses and lecherous lickings there was nothing outstanding which might have denoted an ecstasy, and consequently it is my opinion that he did not discharge. All my clothes were in place, even his hands stayed still, and I give you my word that this old libertine's fantasy might be performed upon the world's most respectable and least initiated girl without her being able to suppose there was anything lewd in it at all.*

*But the same could not be said of the one that chance presented to my consideration the same day I turned nine years old. Father Etienne, that was the libertine's name, had several times asked my sister to bring me to him, and she had got me to promise to go alone, for she was unwilling to accompany me, fearing lest my mother, who already scented something in the wind, might find out; well, I was planning to pay him a visit when, one day, I ran directly into him in a corner of the church, near the sacristy. His manner was so gracious, he argued so persuasively that he had no need to drag me away by main force. Father Etienne was about forty, a healthy, robust, strapping fellow. We were no sooner closeted together than he asked whether I knew how to frig a prick.*

*"Alas!" said I, blushing to the ears, "I don't even know what you're talking about."*

*"Well then I'll explain, my chit," said he, bestowing heartfelt kisses upon my mouth and eyes, "my unique pleasure in this world is to educate little girls, and the lessons I give are so excellent they prove unforgettable. Begin by removing your skirts, for if I am to teach you how you must proceed in order to give me pleasure, 'tis only fair that at the same time I teach you what to do in order to receive it, and that lesson cannot be a success if anything hinders us.*

*Here we go. We shall begin with you. What you behold down here,"* said he, placing his hand on my mound, *"is called a cunt, and this is what you must do in order to awaken very felicitous sensations in it. With one finger—one will do—lightly rub this little protuberance you feel here. It, by the way, is called the clitoris."*

*I followed instructions.*

*"There, you see, that way, my little one, while one hand is busy there, let one finger of your other hand gradually work its way into this delicious crack. . . ."*

*He adjusted my hands.*

*"That's the way, yes . . . Well! Don't you feel anything?"* he asked, keeping me to my task.

*"No, Father, I truly don't,"* I answered most naively.

*"Ah, that's because you are still too young, but two years from now you'll see the pleasure it gives."*

*"Wait,"* I interrupted, *"I think something's happening."*

*And with all imaginable vigor I rubbed the places he had pointed out. . . . Yes, sure enough, a few faint titillations convinced me that what I'd begun was worth continuing, and the extensive use I have made ever since of this relief-providing exercise has more than once persuaded me of my master's competence.*

*"And now 'tis my turn,"* said Etienne, *"for your pleasures arouse my desires, and I simply must share them, my angel. Here we are; take this,"* he said, inviting me to grip a tool so monstrous my two little hands were scarce able to close around it, *"take this, my child, 'tis called a prick, and this movement here,"* he went on, guiding my wrist in rapid jerks, *"this action is called frigging. Thus, by means of this action you frig my prick. Go to it, my child, put all your strength into it. The more rapid and persistent your movements, the more you will hasten a moment which, believe me, I cherish. But bear one essential thing in mind,"* he added, all the while directing my flying hands, *"be careful at all times to keep the tip uncovered. Never allow this skin, we call it the prepuce, to cover it over; were this prepuce to happen to cover this part, which we call the glans, all my pleasure would vanish. That's it; we're shortly going to see something, my little one,"* my teacher continued, *"watch me do on you what you did on me."*

*And pressing himself against my chest as he spoke and as I kept in motion, he placed his hands so adroitly, he wriggled his fingers with such high art that pleasure rose at last to grip me, and it is without a shadow of a doubt to him I owe my initiation. And then, my head reeling, I abandoned my task, and the reverend, not yet ready to complete it, consented to forget his pleasure for a moment in order to devote himself exclusively to cultivating mine; and when he had caused me to taste it all, he had me resume the work my ecstasy had obliged me to interrupt, and very expressly enjoined me to keep my mind strictly on what I was about and to care for naught but him. I did so with all my soul. It was only just: I surely owed him my thanks. I went so merrily to work, and I observed all his instructions so faithfully that the monster, vanquished by such rapid vibrations, finally spewed forth all its rage and covered me with its venom. Thereupon Etienne seemed to go out of his mind, borne aloft in the most voluptuous delirium; ardently he kissed my mouth, he fondled and frigged my cunt, and the wildness in his speech still more emphatically declared his disorder. Gross expressions, mingling with others of the most endearing sort, characterized this transport, which lasted quite a while, and whence at last the gallant Etienne, so unlike his piss-swallowing colleague, emerged to tell me that I was charming, that he greatly hoped I would come back to see him, and that he would treat me every time as he was going to now: pressing a silver coin into my hand, he conducted me back to the place he had brought me from and left me wonderstruck, thrilled and enchanted with this latest good fortune. Feeling much better about the monastery, I decided to return to it often in the future, persuaded that the more I advanced in age, the more agreeable adventures I would meet with there. But destiny called me elsewhere; more important events awaited me in a new world, and upon returning to my house I learned news which was soon to sober the elation produced in me by the happy outcome of my latest experience.*

Here a bell was heard struck in the salon; it announced supper. Whereupon Duclos, generally applauded for the auspicious little beginnings she had made, descended from the stage, and, after having made a few adjustments to repair the disorder all four of them seemed to be in, the friends turned their thoughts to new pleasures and hastened to find out what Comus held in store for them.

This meal was to be served by the eight little girls, naked. Having been wise enough to leave the auditorium a few minutes early, they stood ready the moment the masters entered these fresh surroundings. The table companions were to be twenty in number: the libertine quartet, the eight fuckers, the eight little boys. But, still furious with Narcisse, the Bishop wished to veto his presence at the banquet, and as it was perfectly natural that they make allowances for one another's whims and observe a mutual tolerance, no one raised his voice to contest the sentence, and the poor little simpleton was confined alone in a dark closet to await that stage in the orgies when perhaps Monseigneur might be inclined to make friends with him again. The wives and the storytellers, dining apart, had concluded their meal in great haste in order to be ready for the orgies, the elders directed the movements of the eight little girls, and dinner was begun.

This meal, much heavier than the one which had been eaten earlier in the day, was served with far greater opulence and splendor. It began with a shellfish soup and hors d'oeuvres composed of twenty dishes; twenty entrees came on next, and soon gave way to another twenty lighter entrees made up entirely of breasts of chicken, of assorted game prepared in every possible way. This was offset by a serving of roasts; everything of the rarest imaginable was brought on. Next arrived some cold pastry, soon afterward twenty-six entremets of every description and form. The table was cleared, and what had just been removed was replaced by a whole array of cold and hot sugared pastries. Dessert finally appeared: a prodigious number and variety of fruits, though the season was winter, then ices, chocolate, and the liqueurs which were taken at table. As for the wines, they varied with each service: Burgundy accompanied the first; two kinds of Italian wine came with the second and third; Rhine wine with the fourth; with the fifth, Rhône wines; sparkling champagne with the sixth; two kinds of Greek wine with the other two courses. Spirits were prodigiously roused, for, as distinct from lunch, one was not granted permission during dinner to take the waitresses to task, or with that same severity; these creatures, being the very quintessence of what the company had to offer, had to be treated rather more sparingly but, on the other hand, the friends indulged in a furious round of impurities with them.

Half-drunk, the Duc said he would not touch another drop, from now on it was Zelmire's urine or nothing, and he drained two large glasses of it which he obtained by having the child climb upon the table and squat over his plate. "Why, there's nothing to drinking weak young piss," said Curval and, calling Fanchon to him: "Come hither, venerable bitch, I'd slake my thirst at the very source." And thrusting his head between the old crone's legs, he greedily sucked up the impure floods of poisonous urine she darted into his stomach. And now their words grew heated, they argued various philosophical problems and considered several questions relating to manners; I leave it to the reader to imagine the purity of those discourses and the loftiness of their moralizing. The Duc undertook an encomium of libertinage, and proved that it was natural, and that the more numerous were its extravagances, the better they served the creator of us all. His opinion was generally acclaimed, enthusiastically applauded, and they rose to go and put into practice the doctrines which had just been established. Everything was ready in the orgy salon: the women were there, already naked, lying upon piles of pillows on the floor, strewn promiscuously amongst the young catamites who had hastened away from table a little after dessert. Our friends reeled in; two elders undressed them, and they fell upon the flock like wolves assailing a sheepfold. The Bishop, whose passions had been cruelly irritated by the obstacles they had encountered of late, laid hands on Antinoüs' sublime ass while Hercule skewered him, and vanquished by this latest sensation and by the important and doubtless so much desired service Antinoüs was rendering him, he finally spat out streams of semen so hard driven and so pungent he swooned in ecstasy. Bacchus' wiles had spellbound senses glutted from excess, numbed from luxury; our hero passed from his faint to a sleep so profound he had to be carried to his bed. The Duc was having a marvelous time. Curval, recollecting what Martaine had offered the Bishop, stuffed her while he got his own ass stoppered. A thousand other horrors, a thousand other infamies accompanied and succeeded those, and our three indomitable champions—for the Bishop no longer was of this

world—our valorous athletes, I say, escorted by the four night-toil-
ing fuckers who had not been at the revels but who now came to
fetch them, retired with the same wives who had shared their
couches during story time. Luckless victims of their brutality, upon
whom it is only too likely they showered more outrages than
caresses and who, it is equally probable, inspired in them more
disgust than pleasure. . . .

Such were the events that transpired on the first day.

# THE SECOND DAY

*T*he company rose at the customary hour. The Bishop, entirely recovered from his excesses, and who, waking at four in the morning, was deeply shocked to find they had let him go to bed unaccompanied, had summoned Julie and his fucker for the night to come and occupy their posts. They answered the call instantly, and in their arms the libertine plunged back into the thick of new impurities.

When, in keeping with regulations, breakfast had been taken in the girls' quarters, Durcet went on his rounds, and, notwithstanding all the arguments he heard, further delinquencies appeared to his eyes. Michette was guilty of one kind of fault and Augustine, whom Curval had ordered to keep herself throughout the day in a certain state, was found in the absolutely opposite state; she declared she had forgotten, made a hundred apologies, and promised it would not happen again, but the quadrumvirate was inexorable, and both names were inscribed on the list of punishments to be executed come the first Saturday.

Highly dissatisfied with all these little girls' ineptness in the art of masturbation, annoyed by the effects of this awkwardness with which he had been obliged to put up the previous evening, Durcet proposed that one hour in the morning be set aside for giving them lessons, and that the friends take turns rising an hour early, the exercise period being set from nine until ten—one friend would rise at nine every morning, I say, to participate in the training. It was decided that the supervisor would be seated comfortably in a chair in the middle of the harem and that each little girl, led

283

forth and guided by Duclos, the best frigger in the castle, would demonstrate upon the friend, would direct the little girl's hand, her motion, would explain the intricacies of tempo, how much and how little speed was required and how that depended on the patient's condition, would also explain what attitudes and postures were most conducive to the operation's success; furthermore, punishments were fixed for her who at the end of a fortnight, despite the lessons, should fail of perfect proficiency in this art. It was emphasized to the little girls that, pursuant to the good ecclesiastic's doctrines, the glans was to be kept uncovered at all times, and that the hand not in action was meanwhile continually to be employed exciting the adjacent areas, this in keeping with the particular fancy of the patient.

The financier's proposal pleased everyone; Duclos was informed, she accepted her appointment, and that same day she set up a frigging dummy upon which, in their spare time, the little girls could exercise their wrists and maintain the necessary degrees of agility and suppleness. Hercule was given the same instructorship in the boys' chamber; they being, as always, more skilled in this technique than the girls, because in the case of boys it is merely a question of doing for others what they do unto themselves, a week was ample time to turn them into the most delicious corps of friggers you could ever hope to meet with. On this particular morning, not one of them was found at fault, and Narcisse's behavior of the previous day having brought about the refusal of all permissions, the chapel was empty save for Duclos, a pair of fuckers, Julie, Thérèse, Cupidon, and Zelmire. Curval was stiff as a ramrod, Adonis had inspired an astonishingly high temperature in him when, that morning, he had visited the boys, and it was generally thought he would erupt while watching Thérèse and the two fuckers manage their affairs; but he kept a grip upon himself.

The midday meal was the usual affair, but the dear Président, having drunk a singular amount and frolicked about even more while eating, became inflamed all over again when coffee was served by Augustine and Michette, Zélamir and Cupidon, directed by old Fanchon, whom out of whimsy they had commanded to be as naked as the children. From this contrast Curval's new lubricious furor was born, and he gave himself over to some choice extravagances at the expense of Zélamir and the duenna; this riotous conduct finally cost him his fuck.

The Duc, pike aloft, closed in upon Augustine; he brayed, he swore, he waxed unreasonable, and the poor little thing, all atremble, retreated like a dove before the bird of prey ready to pounce upon it. He limited himself, however, to a few libertine kisses, and was content to give her an introductory lesson in advance of the ones she was to begin the following morning. The two others, less animated, having already started their naps, our two champions imitated them, and the quartet did not wake until six o'clock, the hour when the storytelling began in the throne room.

All the previous day's quatrains had been altered with respect to both subjects and dress, and our friends had these couch companions: the Duc shared his niche with Aline, the Bishop's daughter and consequently his own niece; beside the Bishop lay his sister-in-law, Constance, the Duc's wife and Durcet's daughter; Durcet was with Julie, the Duc's daughter, the Président's wife; that he might be roused from sleep and roused to more, Curval had with him Adelaide, Durcet's wife, one of the creatures in this world it gave him the greatest pleasure to tease because of her virtue and her piety. He opened up with a few scurrile jests and low pranks, and having ordered her throughout the séance to maintain a posture that sorted well with his tastes, but which the poor woman found very tiresome to maintain, he threatened her with all his anger might produce were she to budge or give him a moment's inconvenience. Everything being ready, Duclos ascended the platform and resumed her narration in this wise:

*Three days having elapsed since my mother had appeared at the house, her husband, far more uneasy about his belongings and his money than about her, took it into his head to enter her room, where it was their custom to hide their most precious possessions; and what was his astonishment when, instead of what he was seeking, he found nothing but a note, written by my mother, advising him to make the best of his loss because, having decided to leave him forever, and having no money of her own, she had been forced to take all she had been able to make off with. As for the rest, he was to blame himself and his hard use of her for her departure and for her having left him with two daughters who were, however, certainly worth as much as and possibly more than what she had removed. But the old gaffer was far from judging equal what now he had and what he had just lost, and the dismissal he graciously gave us, together with the request we not even sleep in the house that night, was convincing evidence some discrepancy existed between his way of reckoning and my mother's.*

*Not much afflicted by a compliment which gave us full liberty to launch forth unimpeded into the little mode of life that was beginning to please us so much, my sister and I thought only to collect our few belongings and to bid as swift a farewell to our dear stepfather as he had seen fit to bid us. Without the loss of a minute, we withdrew, and while waiting to decide how best to come to grips with our new destinies, we took lodgings in a small room in the neighborhood. Our first thoughts turned to what might be our mother's fate and whereabouts; we had not the least doubt but that she had gone to the monastery, having decided to live secretly with some father, or that she was being kept somewhere in the vicinity, and this was the opinion we held, without being unduly concerned, when a friar from the monastery brought us a note that bore out our conjectures. The substance of the note was that we would be very well advised, immediately night had fallen, to come to the monastery and speak to the Father Superior, who was the note's author; he would wait for us in the church until ten o'clock and would lead us to the place presently occupied by our mother, whose actual happiness and peace he would gladly have us share. He very energetically urged us not to fail to come, and above all to conceal our movements with all possible care; for it was essential our stepfather know nothing of what was being done in behalf of both our mother and ourselves. My sister, fifteen years old at the time and hence more clever and more reasonable than I, who was but nine, after having dismissed the bearer of the letter and given him the reply that she would ponder its contents, admitted she found all these maneuvers very peculiar indeed.*

*"Françon," says she, "let's not go. There's something wrong with it. If this were an honest proposal, why wouldn't Mother have either added a few words or made some kind of sign. Father Adrien, her best friend, left there almost three years ago, and since*

*then she's only dropped in at the monastery while passing by, and hasn't had any other regular intrigue there. What would have led her to choose this place for hiding? The Father Superior isn't her lover and never has been. I know, it's true she has amused him two or three times, but he's not the man to lose his head over a woman for that slender reason: he's even more inconstant and brutal to women once his caprice is satisfied. And so why would he have taken such an interest in our mother? There's something queer about it, I tell you. I never liked that old Superior; he's wicked and harsh, and he's a brute. Once he got me into his room, there were three more of them there, and after what happened to me then I swore I'd never set foot in the place again. If you take my advice, you'll leave all those nasty monks alone. There's no reason why I shouldn't tell you so now, Françon, I have an acquaintance, a good friend, I dare say; her name is Madame Guérin, I've been going to her place for the past two years, and in all that time not one week has gone by without her arranging something nice for me. But none of those six-penny fucks like the ones at the monastery; I get at least three crowns from every one. Here, there's proof of it," my sister continued, showing me a purse containing more than ten louis, "you can see I'm able to make my own way in the world. Well, my advice to you is to do what I do. Guérin will take you on, I'm sure of it, she got a glimpse of you a week ago when she came to fetch me for a party, and she told me to make you a proposal, and she said that, young as you are, she'd always find some way of placing you. Do like me, I tell you, and we'll be well off in no time. Now, that's all I've got to say to you; I'll pay your expenses for tonight, but from then on don't count on me, little sister. Each for himself in this world. That's what I say. I've earned that money with my body and my fingers, do the same yourself. And if you have any qualms, go talk it over with the devil, but don't come looking for me; well, I've told you what I think, and I'll tell you now that I'd sooner stick my tongue two feet out than give you even a glass of water for nothing. As for Mother, I don't care what's happened to her, as a matter of fact, even if it's the worst I'm perfectly delighted, and all I hope is that the whore is far enough away so I'll never see her again for the rest of my life. I know all the things she did to prevent me from getting anywhere in the trade, and all the while she* was giving me that fine advice, the bitch was doing things three times worse. So, may the devil take her and above all not bring her back, that's all I care."

Not having, to tell you the truth, a heart more tender, nor a soul much more generous than my sister's, it was in all good faith I echoed the invectives wherewith she pilloried that excellent mother, and thanking my sister for the helpful words she promised to speak in my behalf, I in my turn promised to follow her to this woman's house and, once I had been adopted, to put an end to my reliance on her. As for refusing to go to the monastery, we were fully agreed.

"If indeed she is happy, so much the better for her," I commented, "and in that case we can look out for our own welfare without having to go and submit to the same fate. And if it is a trap they're setting for us, we've got to avoid it."

Whereupon my sister embraced me.

"Splendid," said she, "I see you're a good girl. Don't worry, we're going to make a fortune. I'm pretty, so are you; we'll earn as much as we want, my chit, but don't become attached to anyone, remember that. One today, another tomorrow, you've got to be a whore, a whore in body and soul. As for myself," she went on, "I'm one now, such as you see me, and there isn't any confessional, or priest, or counsel, or threat that could ruin things for me. By Jesus, I'd go show my ass on the sidewalk as calmly and coolly as I'd drink a glass of wine. Imitate me, Françon, be amenable and you can get anything out of men; the trade's a little hard in the beginning, but you'll get along and things get better. So many men, so many tastes. At first you've got to expect it, one of them wants one thing, another wants something else. But that doesn't matter, you're there to please and give them service; the customer is always right. It doesn't take long, and then the money's in your pocket."

I admit I was amazed to hear such wild remarks from a girl so young, who had always seemed to me so decent. But as my heart beat in harmony with the spirit of what she said, I let her know at once that I was not only disposed to duplicate all her actions, but even prepared to go a great deal further if necessary. Delighted with me, she fell to embracing me again, and as it was growing late, we sent out for a chicken and some good wine and *supped and slept together, having decided to present ourselves the very next morning at the establishment of Madame Guérin and to ask her to include us amongst her* pensionnaires.

It was during that supper my sister taught me all I still did not know about libertinage. She showed herself naked to me, and I can warrant that she was one of the prettiest creatures there was in Paris at the time: the fairest of skin, the most agreeable plumpness, yet the most supple and intriguing figure, the loveliest blue eyes, and all the rest correspondingly fine. I also learned for how long Guérin had been promoting her interests, and with what great pleasure she procured her clients who, never tired of her, asked for her constantly. No sooner were we in bed than it occurred to us we had managed very badly in failing to give the Father Superior a reply, for our negligence might annoy him, and while we remained in this quarter of town it was important to humor him at least. But what was to be done? Eleven o'clock had struck; we resolved to let things take their course.

The adventure probably meant a great deal to the Superior, we supposed, and hence it was not difficult to surmise that he was laboring more in his own behalf than in that of the alleged happiness he had mentioned in his communication; at any rate, midnight had just sounded when we heard a soft knocking at our door. It was the Superior himself; he had been waiting for us, said he, since two in the afternoon, we should at least have given him a response, and, seating himself at our bedside, he informed us that our mother had decided to spend the rest of her days in a little secret apartment they had at the monastery and in which she was having the world's most cheerful time, improved by the company of all the house's bigwigs who would drop in to spend half the day with her and with another young woman, our mother's companion; it was simply up to us to come and increase the number, but, in that we were a little too young to stay on permanently, he would only contract us to a three-years' stint, at the end of which he swore we would be granted our freedom and a thousand crowns apiece; he added that he had been charged by our mother to assure us that we would be doing her a great kindness were we to come to share her solitude.

"Father," my sister said most impudently, "we thank you for

*your proposal. But at our age we have no inclination to have our-
selves locked up in a cloister in order to be whores for priests,
we've had enough of that already."*

The Superior renewed his arguments, he spoke with a heat
and energy which illustrated his powerful desire to have the thing
succeed; finally observing that it was destined to fail, he hurled
himself almost in a fury upon my sister.

"Very well, little whore," he cried, "at least satisfy me once
again before I take my leave."

And unbuttoning his breeches, he got astride her; she offered
no resistance, persuaded that by allowing him to have his way she'd
be rid of him all the sooner. And the smutty fellow, pinning her
between his knees, began to brandish and then to abuse a tough and
rather stout engine, advancing it to within a quarter of an inch of
my sister's face.

"Pretty face," he gasped, "pretty little whore's face, how I'll
soak it in my fuck, by sweet Jesus!"

And therewith the sluices opened, the sperm flew out, and the
entirety of my sister's face, especially her nose and mouth, were
covered with evidence of our visitor's libertinage, whose passion
might not have been so cheaply satisfied had his design in coming to
us met with success. More complacent now, the man of God's only
thoughts were of escape; after having flung a crown upon the table
and relit his lantern:

"You are little fools, you are little tramps," he told us. "You
are ruining your chances in this world; may Heaven punish your
folly by causing you to fall on evil days, and may I have the pleasure of seeing you in misery; that would be my revenge, that is what
I wish you."

My sister, busy wiping her face, paid him back his stupidities
in kind, and, our door shutting behind the Superior, we spent the
remainder of the night in peace.

"You've just seen one of his favorite stunts," said my sister.
"He's mad about discharging in girls' faces. If he only confined
himself to that . . . but the scoundrel has a good many other eccentricities, and some of them are so dangerous that I do indeed
fear . . ."

But my sister was sleepy, she dozed off without completing her *sentence, and the morrow bringing fresh adventures with it, we gave no more thought to that one.*

*We were up early; having prettied ourselves as much as possible, we set out for Madame Guérin's. That heroine lived in the rue Soli, in a very neat ground-floor apartment she shared with six tall young ladies between the ages of sixteen and twenty-two, all in splendid health, all very pretty. But, Messieurs, you will be so kind as to allow me to postpone giving their descriptions until the proper moment in my story arrives. Delighted by the project which brought my sister to her for a long stay, Madame Guérin greeted us cordially and with the greatest pleasure showed us our rooms.*

*"Young as you may find this child to be," my sister said as she introduced me, "she will serve you well, I guarantee it. She is mild-tempered, thoughtful, has a very good character, and the soul of a thoroughgoing whore. You must have a number of old lechers amongst your acquaintances who are fond of children; well this is just what they're looking for . . . put her to work."*

*Turning in my direction, Guérin asked me if I was willing to undertake anything.*

*"Yes, Madame," I answered with something of an indignant air, and it pleased her, "anything provided it pays."*

*We were introduced to our new companions, who already knew my sister very well and out of friendship for her promised to look after me. We all sat down to dine together, and such, in a few words, Messieurs, was how I became installed in my first brothel.*

*I was not to remain long unemployed; that same evening, an old businessman arrived wrapped up in a cloak; Guérin selected him for my first customer and arranged the match.*

*"Ah, this time," said she to the old libertine, leading me forth, "if it's still hairless you like them, Monsieur Duclos, you'll be delighted with the article, or your money back. Not a hair on her body."*

*"Indeed," said the old original, peering down at me, "it looks like a child, yes indeed. How old are you, little one?"*

*"Nine, Monsieur."*

*"Nine years old! . . . Well, well! that's how I like them, Madame Guérin, that's how I like them, you know. I'd take them*

*even younger if you had any around. Why, bless my soul, they're
ready as soon as they're weaned."*

*And laughing good-naturedly at his remarks, Guérin with-
drew, leaving us alone together. Then the old libertine came up and
kissed me upon the mouth two or three times. With one of his
hands guiding mine, he had me pull from his fly a little device that
could not have been more limp; continuing to act more or less in
silence, he untied my skirts, lay me upon the couch with my blouse
raised high upon my chest, mounted astride my thighs which he had
separated as far as possible; with one hand he pried open my little
cunt while with the other put all his strength into manipulating his
meager machine. "Ah, pretty little bird," he said as he agitated
himself and emitted sighs of pleasure, "ah, how I'd tame you if I
were still able to, but I can't anymore. There's no remedy for it, in
four years' time this bugger of a prick will have ceased to get stiff.
Open up, open up, my dearest, spread your legs." And finally after
fifteen minutes of struggle, I observed my man to sigh and pant
with greater energy. A few oaths lent strength to his expression,
and I felt the area surrounding my cunt inundated with the hot,
scummy seed which the rascal, unable to shoot it inside, was attempting to tamp down with his fingertips.*

*He had no sooner done so than he was gone like a flash of
lightning, and I was still cleaning myself when my gallant passed
out the door and into the street. And so it was I came, Messieurs,
to be named Duclos; the tradition in this house was for each girl to
adopt the name of her firstcomer. I obeyed the custom.*

"One moment there," said the Duc. "I delayed interrupting you
until you came to a pause; you are at one now. Would you provide
further information upon two matters: first, have you ever had any
news of your mother, have you ever discovered what became of
her? Secondly, was there any cause for the antipathy you and your
sister had for her, or would you say these feelings were naturally
inculcate in you both? This relates to the problem of the human
heart, and 'tis upon that we are concentrating our major efforts."

"My Lord," Duclos replied, "neither my sister nor I have
ever heard the slightest word from that woman."

"Excellent," said the Duc, "in that case it's all very clear, wouldn't you say so, Durcet?"

"Incontestably," answered the banker. "Not a shadow of a doubt, and you are very fortunate you did not put your foot in that one. Neither of you would ever have got out."

" 'Tis incredible," Curval commented, "what headway that mania has made with the public."

"Why, no; after all, there's nothing more delicious," the Bishop replied.

"And the second point?" asked the Duc, addressing the story-teller.

"As for the second point, my Lord, that is to say, as for the reason for our antipathy, I'm afraid I should be hard pressed to account for it, but it was so violent in our two hearts that we both made the avowal that we would in all probability and very easily have poisoned her had we not managed, as it turned out, to be rid of her by other means. Our aversion had reached the ultimate degree of intensity, and as nothing overt occurred to give rise to it, I should judge it most likely that this sentiment was inspired in us by Nature."

"What doubt of it can there be?" said the Duc. "It happens every day that she implants the most violent inclination to commit what mortals call crimes, and had you poisoned her twenty times over, this act would never have been anything but the result of the penchant for crime Nature put in you, a penchant she wishes to draw to your attention by endowing you with such a powerful hostility. It is madness to suppose one owes something to one's mother. And upon what, then, would gratitude be based? is one to be thankful that she discharged when someone once fucked her? That would suffice, to be sure. As for myself, I see therein naught but grounds for hatred and scorn. Does that mother of ours give us happiness in giving us life? . . . Hardly. She casts us into a world beset with dangers, and once in it, 'tis for us to manage as best we can. I distinctly recall that, long ago, I had a mother who aroused in me much the same sentiments Duclos felt for hers: I abhorred her. As soon as I was in a position to do so, I dispatched her into the next world; may she roast there; never in my life have I tasted a keener delight than the one I knew when she closed her eyes for the last time."

At this point dreadful sobs were heard to come from one of the quatrains. It proved to be the Duc's; upon closer examination it was discovered that young Sophie had burst into tears. Provided with a heart unlike those villains', their conversation had brought to mind the cherished memory of her who had given her life, and who had perished in an effort to protect her while she was being abducted; this cruel vision offered itself to her tender imagination, a flood of tears ensued.

"Ah, by God, now!" said the Duc, "that's splendid. It's for mama you're crying, is it, my little snotface? Come here, come along, let me comfort you."

And the libertine, warmed by what had been happening, by these words of his, and by the effects they produced, displayed a thunderous prick which was apparently speeding toward a discharge. Marie, the quatrain's duenna, led the child forward all the same. Her tears flowed abundantly down her cheeks, the novice's dress she was wearing that day seemed to lend yet more charm to the sorrow which embellished her looks: it were impossible for a creature to be lovelier.

"By the Holy Bugger," quoth the Duc, springing up like one gone out of his mind, "what a pretty mouthful we have here. I'm going to do what Duclos has just described . . . smear some fuck on her cunt. . . . Undress her."

And everyone silently awaited the issue of this little skirmish.

"Oh! my Lord, my Lord!" cried Sophie, casting herself at the Duc's feet, "at least respect my sorrow, I groan for my mother's fate, she was dear to me, she died defending me, I shall never see her again. Have pity upon my tears, grant me this one evening of respite."

"Why, fuck my eyes!" the Duc exclaimed, fondling his heaven-threatening prick, "I'd never have believed this scene could be so voluptuous. Off with her clothes, I tell you to take them off," he roared at Marie, "she should already be naked."

And Aline, lying upon the Duc's couch, shed warm tears, so did Adelaide, who was heard to utter a moan in Curval's alcove; the latter, in no wise partaking of that lovely creature's grief, violently scolded his playmate for having shifted from the position he had commanded her to keep, and, that done, turned an appreciative gaze upon the delicious scene whose outcome interested him exceedingly.

Sophie's clothes are removed without the faintest regard for her feelings, she is placed in the posture Duclos has just described, the Duc announces that he is about to discharge. But how is the thing to be done? What Duclos has just related had been performed by a man virtually incapable of an erection, and he had been able to direct his flabby prick's discharge wherever he wished. Such was not the case here: the threatful head of the Duc's engine had not the least inclination to lower the awful stare whereby it seemed bent on cowing heaven; it appeared necessary, so to speak, to place the child on high. No one knew what to do, and the more obstacles were encountered, the more the enraged Duc fumed and blasphemed. Desgranges finally came to the rescue; nothing that pertained to libertinage was unknown to that sage old dame. She caught up the child and set her so skillfully upon her knees that, whatever the stance the Duc might adopt, the end of his prick was sure to nudge her vagina. Two servants came up to hold Sophie's legs, and had it been her deflowering hour, never might she have displayed the merchandise to better advantage. But there was yet more to attend to: a clever hand was needed to cause the torrent to leap its banks and to direct the flood fairly to its destination. Blangis had no desire to entrust so important a matter to an untutored child.

"Take Julie," Durcet suggested, "she'll suit you; she's beginning to frig like an angel."

"Bah," muttered the Duc, "I know the clumsy bitch. And she knows her father. No, she'd be panic-stricken, she'd fumble it."

"Upon my soul, I do recommend a boy for the job," said Curval; "why not Hercule? His wrist is like a whip."

"I won't have anyone but Duclos," the Duc answered, "she's the best of our friggers, allow her to quit her post for a moment or two."

Duclos steps forward, beaming with pride to have been accorded so distinguished a preference. She rolls her sleeve to the elbow and grasps the nobleman's enormous instrument, she sets to rattling that spear, keeps the foreskin snapped broadly back, she moves it with such art, she agitates it by means of strokes so swift and simultaneously so perfectly attuned to the state she observes her patient to be in, that the bomb finally explodes upon the very hole it is to cover, inundating it. The Duc shrieks, swears, storms. Duclos is disconcerted not in the least, she gauges her movements by the degree of pleasure they produce. Antinoüs, properly situated for this function, delicately works the sperm into the vagina as proportionally it flows from the spigot, and the Duc, vanquished by the most delicious sensations, dying from joy, sees grow gradually slack, between his frigger's fingers, that high-spirited, mettlesome member whose ardor has just been so powerfully communicated to the rest of himself. He flings himself back upon his sofa, Duclos strides back to her throne, the child wipes herself, is consoled, and regains her quatrain, and the recital continues, leaving the spectators convinced of a truth wherewith, I believe, they have already been penetrated for a long time: that the idea of crime is able always to ignite the senses and lead us to lubricity.

*I was greatly surprised,* said Duclos, taking up the thread of her narrative, *to see all my companions laugh when I returned, and ask me if I had wiped myself, and say a thousand other things which proved they knew perfectly well what had just happened. I was not long left in my quandary; leading me into a room adjacent to the one in which the parties ordinarily took place and in which a short while before I had been at work, my sister showed me a hole which looked squarely upon the couch and from which it was easy to see everything that transpired there. She told me that the young ladies found it diverting to watch what men did to their colleagues; I could come and do some spying whenever I wished, provided there was not someone already at the hole. For it not infrequently occurred, said she, that this respectable hole had a part in mysteries which would be disclosed to me later on. The week was not out before I took advantage of my opportunities: one morning someone came and asked for a girl named Rosalie, one of the most lovely blondes it were possible to behold; I was curious to see what was to be done to her. I hid myself and witnessed the following scene.*

*The man with whom she had to cope was no older than twenty-six or thirty. Immediately she entered, he had her sit down on a very high stool used especially for this ceremony. As soon as she was settled, he removed all her combs and hairpins and down all the way to the floor floated in a cloud the superb golden hair that adorned Rosalie's head. He drew a comb from his pocket, combed her hair, took handfuls of it, tangled it, kissed it, everything he did was accompanied by remarks praising the beauty of that hair in which he took such a keen and exclusive interest. At last, from out of his trousers he pulled a smart little prick, already quite stiff, and he promptly enveloped it in his Dulcinea's hair; once well wrapped, he began to fondle his dart and discharged, at the same time passing his other arm around Rosalie's neck and applying his lips to her mouth. He extricated his defunct engine, I saw that my companion's hair was matted with glistening fuck; she cleaned it, put it up again, and our lovers separated.*

*A month later, someone came in quest of my sister; this personage, I was told by the others, merited observing, for he had a most baroque specialty. He was a man of about fifty. Straightway he entered, without any preamble, without a caress, he exhibited his behind to my sister, who knew her part to perfection; he has her take her place on the bed, he backs toward her, she seizes that flaccid and wrinkled old ass, drives her five fingers into the orifice, and begins to struggle and battle and worry it with such force the bed creaks. Be that as it may, without bringing anything else to light, our man wriggles, twitches, follows my sister's movements, lends himself luxuriously to this fearful abuse, cries he is coming, comes, and affirms this is the greatest of all pleasures. He had indeed taken a furious buffeting, my sister was in a sweat; but what mild stuff! what lack of imagination!*

*Although the gentleman with whom I had to do not long afterward was hardly more difficult to satisfy, he at least seemed more voluptuous and, in my view, his mania had more of the libertine tincture. He was a heavy-set man of about forty-five, short, sturdy, but energetic and hearty. Never having met a person with his predilection, my first act, as soon as we were alone together, was to hoist my skirts to the navel: a dog confronted by a hickory stick could not have looked more unhappy: "Good God, dearie, let's not have any of your cunt, please put it away." So saying, he snatched down my skirts even more hastily than I had raised them. "These poor little whores," he mumbled, screwing up his face in a pout, "never have anything but cunts to show you. I may not be able to discharge this evening, thanks to that exhibition . . . unless I can succeed in getting the accursed image of that cunt out of my head." Whereupon he turned me about and methodically raised my petticoats from behind. Guiding me himself, and keeping my skirts raised at all times, he moved me about in order to observe how my buttocks bounced when I walked, and then he had me approach the bed, upon which he had me lie belly down. Next, with the most scrupulous attention he examined my ass, with one hand screening his eyes to avoid any glimpse of my cunt whereof, it appeared, he was in mortal terror. At last, having warned me to do all in my power to conceal that unworthy (I employ his expression) part from his sight, he brought both hands to bear on my ass and manipulated it lewdly and at length: he opened it, he closed it again, spread and squeezed it, sometimes he applied his mouth to it, and once or twice I even felt him press his lips to the hole; but he still had not touched himself, nothing could be discerned. None the less, he must have felt hidden pressures mount and readied himself for the denouement of his little ritual. "Lie down," he told me, tossing a few pillows on the floor, "yes, down there, that's it, that will do . . . with your legs well spread, the ass a shade higher, and the hole stretched as wide open as it will go; come now, wider still," he continued, noticing my docility. And then, taking a stool and placing it between my legs, he sat down in such a way that his prick, which he now dragged from his breeches and began to vibrate, was as it were at a level with the hole upon which he was to offer a libation. His movements now grew more rapid, with one hand he frigged himself, with the other he separated my buttocks, and a few adulatory commendations seasoned with a quantity of hard language constituted his speech. "Ah, bugger the Almighty, here 'tis, the lovely ass," he cried, "the sweet little hole, and how I'm going to wet it." He kept his word. I felt myself soaked; his ecstasy seemed to annihilate the libertine. Ah, how true it is that the homage rendered at this temple is always more ardent than the incense which is burned at the other; and my worshiper left after promising to re-*

*turn to see me again, for he averred I satisfied his desires very well.*
*He did indeed come back the next day, but was untrue to me, his*
*inconstancy led him to my sister's asshole; I observed them, saw*
*everything: every aspect of the rite was absolutely the same, and*
*my sister lent herself to it with the same good will.*

"Did your sister have a handsome ass?" Durcet inquired.

"You may judge by one fact, my Lord," Duclos replied. "A
famous painter commissioned to do a Venus with a magnificent behind asked her the following year to be his model after having, he
said, consulted every procuress in Paris without finding anything
to equal her."

"Well now, since she was fifteen and since we have a few girls
of the same age here, compare her ass," the financier continued,
"with some of the asses you see in the room."

Duclos' eyes came to rest upon Zelmire, and she told Durcet
that it would be impossible, not only with respect to the ass, but
even with respect to the face, to find anyone who bore a closer
resemblance to her sister.

"In that case," said Durcet, "come here, Zelmire, present your
cheeks."

She did indeed belong to his quatrain; the charming girl approached all atremble. She was placed at the foot of the couch,
made to lie upon her belly, her rump was raised by means of
cushions, the little hole was in plain sight. The lecher's prick begins
to rise, he falls to kissing and fondling what lies under his nose.
He orders Julie to frig him, she sets to work, his hands stray
hither and yon, snatching at divers objects, lust heats his brain,
under Julie's voluptuous treatment his little prick looks as if it were
about to stiffen, the lecher swears, the fuck flows, and the bell sounds
for dinner.

As the same profusion reigned at every meal, to have described
one is to have described them all; but as almost everyone had discharged, there was a general need to recuperate strength, and therefore the friends drank a great deal at this supper. Zelmire, to
whom they gave the sobriquet of Duclos' sister, was to an uncommon degree regaled during the subsequent orgies, and everyone

simply had to kiss her ass. The Bishop left a puddle of fuck thereon, the three others restiffened over it, and they went to bed as they had the night before, that is to say, each with the wife he had had upon his couch, and with one of the four fuckers who had not appeared since the midday meal.

# THE THIRD DAY

*T*he Duc was abroad at nine o'clock. 'Twas he who volun-
teered to be the first to lend a hand in the lessons Duclos was to
administer to the little girls. He installed himself in an armchair
and for one long hour submitted to various fondlings, masturbations, pollutions, and to a wide variety of tricks performed by each
of those little ones who, throughout it all, were guided and supervised by their mistress; and as may be readily imagined, his
spirited temperament was furiously aroused by the ceremony. He
was obliged to make unbelievable efforts to preserve his fuck from
loss, but, more or less in control of himself, he managed to contain
himself and returned to his friends in triumph, boasting that he'd
just weathered an assault he defied any one of them to beat off
as phlegmatically. That brought on considerable wagering, the
stakes were high, a fine of fifty *louis* was ultimately imposed upon
whoever discharged during the lessons.

Instead of taking breakfast and conducting searches, this
morning was employed in drawing up a program for the seventeen
orgies planned for the end of each week, in this way definitively to
fix the dates of the deflowerings now that, after having become
better acquainted with the subjects than they had been previously,
they were able to pass legislation. In that this timetable in the
most decisive manner regulated all the operations to be executed
during the campaign, we have deemed it necessary to provide the
reader with a copy: it seems to us that, once he has perused it and
familiarized himself with the subjects' several destinies, he will be
able to take a keener interest in their individual persons.

301

## SCHEDULE OF WORKS TO BE ACCOMPLISHED
## DURING THE REMAINDER OF THE PARTY

On the 7th of November, at which time the first week will have drawn a close, Messieurs shall proceed in the morning to the marriage of Michette and Giton, and those two wedded individuals, whose age forbids them from conjoining, as is true in the cases of the three following couples, shall be separated on their marriage night, for to closet them together would be as futile as this ridiculous ceremony which will serve only to create diversion during the day. That same evening, punishments which have accumulated and been entered on the list kept by the month's presiding officer shall be meted out.

On the 14th, Messieurs shall in the same way effect the marriage of Narcisse and Hébé, with the same clauses as those cited above.

On the 21st, in the same way, Colombe and Zélamir shall be married.

On the 28th, Cupidon and Rosette.

On the 4th of December, Champville's narrations having prepared the way for the following enterprises, the Duc shall deflower Fanny.

On the 5th, the said Fanny shall be wedded to Hyacinthe who, in the presence of the company assembled, shall take his pleasure with his young wife. In such will consist the fifth week's festival, and the corrections shall take place in the evening as usual, because the marriages shall be celebrated in the morning.

On the 8th, Curval shall deflower Michette.

On the 11th, the Duc shall deflower Sophie.

On the 12th, to celebrate the sixth week's festival, Sophie shall be married to Céladon, and the clauses cited for the above-mentioned marriage shall be made to apply to this one; this shall not be repeated for those to follow.

On the 15th, Curval shall deflower Hébé.

On the 18th, the Duc shall deflower Zelmire, and on the 19th, in order to celebrate the seventh week's festival, Adonis shall marry Zelmire.

On the 20th, Curval shall deflower Colombe.

On the 25th, Christmas Day, the Duc shall deflower Augustine, and on the 26th, for the eighth week's festival, Zéphyr shall marry Augustine.

On the 29th, Curval shall deflower Rosette, and all the foregoing arrangements have been made to insure that Curval, less well membered than the Duc, be provided with more youthful girls.

On the 1st of January, the first day of the year and the one upon which Martaine's newly begun narration will influence imaginations to consider new pleasures, the sodomistic deflorations shall be inaugurated, and shall proceed in the following order:

On the 1st of January, the Duc shall sound Hébé's ass.

On the 2nd, in celebration of the ninth week, Hébé, having been plumbed fore by Curval, from behind by the Duc, shall be turned over to Hercule, who, before the company assembled, shall employ her for purposes to be specified upon the occasion.

On the 4th, Curval shall embugger Zélamir.

On the 6th, the Duc shall embugger Michette; on the 9th, in celebration of the tenth week's festival, the said Michette, who will have been deflowered fore by Curval, and whose ass will have been tried by the Duc, shall be turned over to Bum-Cleaver, that he may enjoy her, etc., etc.

On the 11th, the Bishop shall sodomize Cupidon.

On the 13th, Curval shall sodomize Zelmire.

On the 15th, the Bishop shall sodomize Colombe.

On the 16th, for the eleventh week's festival, Colombe, whose cunt will have been deflowered by Curval, her ass by the Bishop, shall be turned over to Antinoüs, who shall enjoy her, etc.

On the 17th, the Duc shall embugger Giton.

On the 19th, Curval shall embugger Sophie.

On the 21st, the Bishop shall embugger Narcisse.

On the 22nd, the Duc shall embugger Rosette.

On the 23rd, for the twelfth week's festival, Rosette shall be turned over to Invictus.

On the 25th, Curval shall march into Augustine's behind.

On the 28th, the Bishop shall enter Fanny's.

On the 30th, for the thirteenth week's festival, the Duc shall take Hercule for his husband and Zéphyr for his wife, and the marriage shall be both accomplished and consummated before the eyes of everyone, as shall be the three others which follow.

On the 6th of February, for the fourteenth week's festival, Bum-Cleaver shall become Curval's husband, Adonis his wife.

On the 13th of February, for the fifteenth week's festival, Antinoüs shall be made husband to the Bishop, to him shall Céladon be made a wife.

On the 20th of February, for the sixteenth week's festival, Invictus shall as a husband be wedded to Durcet, Hyacinthe as a wife.

As for the festival of the seventeenth week, due to fall on the 27th of February, upon the eve of the narrations' conclusion, it shall be celebrated by sacrifices for which Messieurs reserve themselves *in petto* the choice of victims.

These arrangements provide for the obliteration of all maidenheads by the 30th of January, with the exception of those of the four young boys whom Messieurs are to marry as wives, and whom they are eager to preserve intact until their weddings, in order that their amusement be made to last until the end of the party.

As the objects are progressively depucelated, they shall take the place of the wives upon the couches at storytelling time, and, at nighttime, they shall lie with Messieurs, alternately, and at Messieurs' choice, together with the last four fairies Messieurs will take to themselves as wives during the final month.

From the moment a girl or a depucelated boy shall have replaced a wife upon the couch, the said wife shall be repudiated. From this moment onward, she shall be in general discredit, and shall be ranked lower than the servants.

With regard to Hébé, aged twelve, Michette, aged twelve, Colombe, aged thirteen, and Rosette, aged thirteen, as progressively they are surrendered to the fuckers and exercised by the latter, they too shall fall into discredit, shall henceforth be used for none but harsh and brutal purposes, shall rank with the repudiated wives, and shall be treated with the utmost rigor. And as of the 24th of January, all four of them will have descended to the same inferior level.

This schedule affirms that unto the Duc shall fall nine pucelages: the first encuntments of Fanny, Sophie, Zelmire, Augustine, the original embuggeries of Hébé, Michette, Giton, Rosette, and Zéphyr.

Unto Curval shall fall the cunt-pucelages of Michette, Hébé, Colombe, Rosette, the ass-pucelages of Zélamir, Zelmire, Sophie, Augustine, and Adonis, being in all nine deflorations.

Unto Durcet, who does not fuck at all, is reserved the ass-pucelage of Hyacinthe, who in the capacity of a wife shall be wedded to him.

And unto the Bishop, who fucks naught but asses, are reserved the sodomistical depucelations of Cupidon, of Colombe, of Narcisse, of Fanny, and of Céladon.

The entire day having been spent preparing this program and chatting about it, and no one having been found at fault, all went uneventfully ahead, the storytelling hour arrived; everyone took his place, the illustrious Duclos mounted the stage. She proceeded in this wise:

*A young man, whose mania, although not in my opinion very libertine, is none the less curious enough, appeared at Madame Guérin's shortly after the adventure I spoke of yesterday. He had to have a young and healthy wet nurse; he suckled the good woman's teat and leaked his seed over her thighs while gorging himself on her milk. His prick struck me as paltry and mean, all his person rather puny, and his discharge was as mild as his proceedings were benign.*

*Another one appeared in the same room the next day; his mania will doubtless prove more entertaining to you. He insisted upon having his woman enveloped in a sheet so that her face and breast would be entirely hidden from him, the single part of her body he wanted to see, and which had to be of the highest degree of excellence, was her ass, all the rest meant nothing to him, and he assured Madame Guérin that a glimpse of anything else would anger him exceedingly. Guérin had a woman brought in from the outside: she was ugly to the point of bitterness and almost fifty years old, but her buttocks were molded like those of Venus, nothing more beautiful could ever bewitch one's gaze.*

*I was eager to see this operation; the old duenna, well wrapped up, was told at once to lie belly down on the edge of the bed. Our libertine, a man of about thirty and who seemed to me a gentleman of the cloth, lifts her skirts above her loins, is thrilled by what greets his eyes and flatters his tastes. He touches, he spreads this superb breech, showers passionate kisses upon it, and, his imagination fired by what he supposes rather than by what he would actually have seen had the woman been unveiled and even had she been attractive, he fancies he is holding commerce with Aphrodite herself, and at the end of a fairly brief career, his engine hardens thanks to the jerks and jolts, and unlooses a warm rain over the ensemble of the sublime ass exposed to his view. His discharge was sharp and impetuous. He was seated facing the adored idol; one of his hands opened it while with the other he polluted it, and he cried ten times in succession: "Ah, what a beautiful ass! Ah, what a delight to drown such an ass in fuck!" He rose when done, and left without indicating the least desire to find out with whom he had been dealing.*

*A young abbot called for my sister a short time afterward. He was youthful and handsome, but one could scarcely discern his prick, so minute and soft it was. He stretched his almost naked partner on a couch, knelt down between her thighs, supporting her buttocks with both hands, with one of them tickling the pretty little hole in her behind. Meanwhile, he conveyed his mouth to my sister's cunt. He tickled its clitoris with his tongue, and managed so cunningly, so harmoniously synchronized the two activities, that within the space of three minutes he had plunged her into a delirium; I saw her head toss about, her eyes begin to roll, and heard the rascal cry: "Ah, my dear Reverend Father, you're slaying me with pleasure!"*

*The abbot's custom was simply to swallow the liquid his libertine dexterity made flow; and this he did not now fail to do, shaking himself the while, agitating himself as he bore down upon my sister: I saw him spatter indubitable evidence of his virility upon the floor. My turn came the next day, and I believe I can assure you, Messieurs, that it was one of the sweetest operations to which in all my life I have ever been exposed: that scoundrel of an abbot had my first fruits, and it was into his mouth I shed my first fuck. More eager than my sister to give him pleasure in return for what he had caused me, I unthinkingly seized his drooping prick, and my little hand replied to what his mouth had made me feel with such delight.*

The Duc could not prevent himself from interrupting at this point. To a remarkable degree excited by the pollutions he had undergone that same morning, he had an idea that this species of lubric sport executed with the fascinating Augustine, whose sparkling, roguish eyes announced the most precocious temperament, would deliver him of a charge of fuck that was stinging his balls in a dreadful way. She was a member of his quatrain, he found her likeable, she was destined to be deflowered by him, he summoned her. On this particular evening she had a kerchief tied round her head, was clad in peasant guise, and seemed charming beneath that costume. The duenna hoisted her skirts and established her in the posture Duclos had represented. The Duc first of all lay hands on her buttocks, knelt, brought a finger to the anus and lightly titillated its rim, seized up the clitoris this amiable child already had in considerable growth, and sucked it. The people of Languedoc are highspirited, they say, and Augustine proved them right; fire leapt into her pretty eyes, she sighed and panted and moaned, her thighs rose mechanically, and the Duc was pleased to sip a gush of young fuck which in all likelihood had never flowed before.

But joy is seldom succeeded by joy. There are libertines so hardened in vice that the simpler, the more delicate and banal be the thing they do, the less effect it has upon their execrable minds. Of their number our beloved Duc was one, he swallowed that delicious child's sperm without his own contriving to flow; all present beheld the moment arrive, for no one is more illogical than a libertine, the moment appeared at hand, I say, when he would blame his unresponse upon the poor little wretch who, all a dither at having yielded to Nature, was hiding her face in her hands and struggling to get free and return to her place.

"Get me another one," thundered the Duc, casting furious glances at Augustine, "I'll suck every last one of them if that's required to lose my fuck."

Zelmire, the second girl in his quatrain, was brought to the fore, she too was the Duc's by escheat. Though equal in years to Augustine, the grief for her plight robbed her of the power to taste a pleasure which, who knows, had it not been for that, Nature might have allowed her to relish. Up rose her skirts, up above two little thighs whiter than alabaster, a chubby little mons veneris hove into view, it was upholstered by a fluffy down just beginning to appear. She is adjusted, obliged to yield, she obeys automatically, but sweat, strain, suck though he does, nothing happens to the Duc. Fifteen minutes of this and he rises in a fury, and, flinging himself into his closet with Hercule and Narcisse:

"Ah, by fuck!" he roars. "It's very clear to me that's not the game I'm hunting"—'tis to the two little girls he alludes—"and that I'll only have a fair shot at this."

It is not known to what excesses he surrendered himself, but ere an instant had passed screams and shouts declared he had carried the day, and proved that boys are always the far more certain implements to a discharge than the most adorable girls. In the meantime, the Bishop had likewise enchambered himself with Giton, Zélamir, and Invictus, and the outbursts which accompanied his discharge having struck the assembly's ears, the two brothers, who had probably resorted to similar expedients, returned, more calmly to listen to the rest of the story our heroine took up again in these terms:

*Nigh unto two years passed by during which time no one of particular interest arrived at Madame Guérin's; the gentlemen who called either had tastes too ordinary to warrant description, or had tastes analogous to those I have already described; and then one day I was told to prepare myself, and above all to wash out my mouth. A heavy, thickset man of about fifty stood beside the mistress of the house.*

*"Well, there she is," said Madame. "She's only twelve, Monsieur, just as clean and tidy as if she'd come this morning out of her mother's belly, and you can take my word for that."*

*The customer inspects me, has me open my mouth, he examines my teeth, sniffs my breath, and evidently satisfied that all is in order, he goes with me into the sanctuary intended for pleasure. We sit down face to face and very near to one another. No one could be more solemn than my gallant nor more phlegmatic. He stares coldly at me, then appraises me with narrowed eyes, I have no idea where all this is leading when, finally breaking his silence, he bids me collect a mouthful of saliva. I obey, and as soon as he fancies my mouth must be full, he throws himself upon my neck, passionately puts his arm around my head, thereby immobilizing it, and gluing his lips to my mouth, he pumps, sucks, eagerly swallows all the bewitching fluid I have collected, and it seems enough to put him in an overwhelming ecstasy. He sucks my tongue into his mouth with identical fervor, and when he senses it is dry, perceives my mouth is empty, he commands me to repeat the operation. He reiterates his, then I do, then he does, and so on eight or ten times over.*

*He sucked up my saliva with such furious avidity it discomfited my chest and lungs. I thought that at least a few sparks of pleasure were going to climax his transports; I was mistaken. His apathy, whence he emerged only for brief instants during his most intense suckings, compassed him again immediately he had drained me, and when at last I told him I could do no more, he fell to eyeing me distantly, to staring at me as he had at the beginning, then got up without a word, paid Guérin, and left.*

"Ah, God's prick and balls!" cried Curval, "I'm happier than he, for I'm coming."

Everyone raised his head, everyone saw the dear Président doing to Julie, his wife, whom that day he had for couch companion, the same thing Duclos had just been relating. That this passion appealed admirably to his tastes was generally well known; Julie by and large procured him abundant pleasure in this manner, Duclos had no doubt done less well by her gallant. But that was in all likelihood his own fault; failing to appreciate what certain mouths, in certain conditions, may offer, he got nothing from Duclos', whereas the Président obtained satisfaction from Julie's.

*A month later,* said Duclos, who had been invited to continue, *I had dealings with a sucker who assailed what one might term the same fort but from an entirely different angle. This latter was an elderly abbot who, after having previously kissed and caressed my bum for above half an hour, introduced his tongue into its hole, made it penetrate deep, dart to left and right, turn this way, turn that way, all with such surpassing art I thought I felt it drive nigh to the depths of my entrails. But this abbot of mine, much less phlegmatic, as he used one hand to spread my buttocks, used the other to frig himself very voluptuously, and as he discharged he drew my anus to his face with such violence and tickled it so lubriciously that my ecstasy coincided with his. When he was finished, he spent another moment scrutinizing my buttocks, staring at that hole he'd just reamed wider, and couldn't prevent himself from gluing his mouth to it one last time; then he hastened off, assuring me he would be back frequently, would ask for me, and that he was most content with my ass. He kept his promise, and for six months he came to visit me three or four times a week, regularly performing the same operation to which I became so thoroughly accustomed that each time he executed his little project, I all but expired with delight—an aspect of the rite about which he appeared to care very little, for, as best I could judge, he had no inclination to find out whether or no my work pleased me; that did not seem to matter to him. And indeed, who can tell? Men are extraordinary indeed; had he known of it, my pleasure might even have displeased him.*

And now Durcet, whom the story had inflamed, like the old priest was moved to suck some asshole or other, but would not have a girl's. He called for Hyacinthe, who of them all pleased him the most. He placed the little chap, kissed his ass, frigged his prick and sucked it. By the nervous shuddering of his body, by the spasm which ordinarily heralded his discharge, it was thought the evil little anchovy that Aline was thumping and pulling as best she could, was finally going to disgorge its seed, but no, the financier was penurious when it came to parting with his fuck, he simply could not, or would not, stiffen. It occurs to them all that his object ought to be changed, Céladon is substituted for Hyacinthe, but all's at a standstill, not the least improvement is apparent. The opportune tolling of a bell announcing supper saves the banker's honor.

"Why," says he, laughing with his confreres, "it's not my fault, you saw I was about to win a victory; this damned supper will have to delay it. Well, by God, let's go and have a fling at the table, I'll return all the more ardent to Cupid's tourney after having been crowned by Bacchus."

The evening meal was equally succulent and gay, quite as lubricious as ever, and was followed by orgies in the course of which an abundance of little infamies were perpetrated. Many were the mouths sucked and the asses, but one of the most engaging drolleries of all was the game in which they hid the face and chest of each little girl and gambled upon recognizing her on the basis of a study of her ass. The Duc was occasionally misled, but not so the others, for they were too well accustomed to the use of the bum. The friends retired for the night, and the morrow brought further and new pleasures, and a few reflections.

# THE FOURTH DAY

*B*eing full eager to be able to distinguish immediately which of the youngsters in either sex was, in a depucelatory sense, to belong to each of their number, the friends decided to have them wear, regardless of their costume and, in that other extreme, even when undressed, a hair ribbon, which would indicate of whom the individual child was the property. Colors were thereupon chosen: the Duc adopted pink and green: whosoever should wear a pink ribbon to the fore, would be his by the cunt; similarly, whosoever wore a green ribbon to the rear, would be his by the ass. And so Fanny, Zelmire, Sophie, and Augustine straightway affixed a pink ribbon on one side of their coiffures; Rosette, Hébé, Michette, Giton, and Zéphyr attached a green favor to their hair where it fell toward the neck, this clue attesting the rights the Duc enjoyed to their asses.

Curval chose black for the front, yellow for the rear; thus Michette, Hébé, Colombe, and Rosette were in future constantly to wear a black ribbon forward; Sophie, Zelmire, Augustine, Zélamir, and Adonis pinned a yellow one above their nape.

Durcet identified his Hyacinthe with a lilac ribbon hanging to the rear, and the Bishop, who owned title to but five assholes to be deflowered sodomistically, ordered Cupidon, Narcisse, Céladon, Colombe, and Fanny to wear a violet one in the rear.

Never, regardless of the subject's posture, chore, or dress, were these ribbons to be neglected or improperly worn, and so it was that by this simple arrangement each friend was always able to tell at a glance what property was his, and in what way.

312

Curval, who had passed the night with Constance, had bitter complaints to lodge against her in the morning. It was not entirely clear what lay at the root of the trouble, nor what precisely the trouble was; so little is needed to displease a libertine. But there was more than enough to the thing to cause him to have her listed for Saturday punishment, and he was formulating charges when that lovely creature declared that she was pregnant; Curval, apart from her husband the only one whom it was possible to suspect as the agent in this affair, had effected no carnal juncture with her save at the beginning of this party, that is to say, four days previously. Our libertines were gladdened by these tidings, seeing in the event much possibility of clandestine delight, and the Duc exulted over this stroke of fortune. In any event, the declaration earned her exemption from the punishment she would otherwise have had to undergo in return for having displeased Curval. She was to be spared: they preferred to leave the fruits on the branch to ripen, a gravid woman diverted them, and what they promised themselves for later on even more lewdly entertained their perfidious imaginations. Constance was dispensed from service at table, from chastisements, and from a few other little odds and ends the accomplishment of which her state no longer rendered voluptuous to observe, but she was still obliged to appear upon the couches and until further orders to share the bed of whoever wished to choose her for the night.

It was Durcet who, that morning, contributed his presence to the pollution exercises, and as his prick was extraordinarily small, he gave the pupils rather more of a problem than had been posed by the Duc's massive construction. However, they fell earnestly to work. But the little banker, who had been plying a woman's trade all night long, could never bear a man's. He was adamant, intractable, and the skill of these eight charming students combined with that of their deft instructress was unable, when all was said and done, even to get him to raise his nose. He left the classroom in triumph, and as impotence always provokes that kind of mood called a teasing one in the idiom of libertinage, his inspections were astonishingly severe. Rosette amongst the girls, Zélamir amongst the boys were the victims of his thoroughness: one was not as she had been told to be—this enigma will be explained—the other, unfortunately, had rid himself of what he had been ordered to keep.

Those present at the public latrines were only seven in number: Duclos, Marie, Aline, and Fanny, two second-class fuckers, and Giton. Curval, who did considerable stiffening that day, grew very excited over Duclos. Dinner, at which his conduct and remarks were very libertine indeed, calmed him not one whit, and the coffee served by Colombe, Sophie, Zéphyr, and his dear friend Adonis, set his brain all afire. He laid hands on this selfsame Adonis, tumbled him onto a sofa, and while spewing forth oaths slid his enormous member between the lad's thighs (approaching him from behind), and as that outsized tool protruded a fair six inches beyond, he commanded Adonis vigorously to frig what emerged, and himself set to frigging the boy above the morsel of flesh upon which Adonis was spitted. Meanwhile, he presented the assembly with an ass no less filthy than broad, whose impure orifice began to exert a potent attraction upon the Duc. Seeing this ass within reach, he trained his vivacious prick on the hole while continuing to suck Zéphyr's mouth, an operation he had begun before this new idea had occurred to him.

Curval, who had not been expecting such an attack, emitted blasphemous paeans of joy. He danced with delight, spread himself wider, braced himself; at the same instant, the fresh young fuck of the charming boy he was frigging started to drip out upon the enormous head of his own aroused instrument. That warm fuck he feels wetting him, the reiterated blows of the Duc who is also beginning to discharge, it all quickens his warrior's soul, the weapon is primed, off goes the gun, floods of foamy sperm splash against Durcet's ass, for the banker has just posted himself there within easy range lest, says he, something be wasted, and Durcet's plump white buttocks are submerged beneath a spellbinding liquor he would have by far preferred as a rinse for his bowels.

Nor was the Bishop idle; he was one after the other sucking clean the divine assholes of Colombe and Sophie. But doubtless fatigued by some nocturnal exercise, he showed not one spark of life, and like all other libertines rendered unjust by caprice and disgust, he lashed out furiously against these two delicious children, blaming them for the only too well merited shortcomings of his debilitated frame. Messieurs nap for a few minutes; then 'tis storytelling time, and in they troop to listen to the amiable Duclos, who resumes her tale in the following manner:

*There had been a few changes in Madame Guérin's house,* said our heroine. *Two very pretty girls had just found dupes who were only too willing to keep them and whom they deceived just the way we all do. To fill the gaps in the ranks, our dear mother had scouted around and set her sights upon a rue Saint-Denis tavern-keeper's daughter, thirteen years old and one of the most fetching creatures in all the wide world. But the little lady, quite as well-behaved as she was pious, was successfully resisting all enticements when Guérin, having one day employed the cleverest stratagem to lure her to her house, immediately put her in the hands of the unusual person whose mania I propose to describe next. He was an ecclesiastic of fifty-five or fifty-six, but so youthful and vigorous you'd have thought him under forty. No man in Europe had such a singular talent for drawing young girls into vice, and as it was his one art, developed to a sublime degree, he had turned it into his one and only pleasure. The whole of his fleshly delight consisted in extirpating childhood prejudices and unnatural terrors, in cultivating scorn for virtue, in decking vice in the most dazzling colors. He neglected nothing: seductive images, flattering promises, delicious examples, he would press everything into service, everything would be brilliantly manipulated, his artistry being faultlessly attuned to the child's age and cast of mind, and never did he miss the mark. Granted a mere two hours of conversation, he was sure to make a whore of the best-behaved and most reasonable little girl; for thirty years he had been conducting his missionary labors in Paris, and, he had once assured Madame Guérin, who counted herself one of his best friends, he had to his credit more than ten thousand girls whom he had personally seduced and plunged into libertinage. He rendered similar services to at least fifteen procuresses, and whenever he was not coping with a particular problem at someone else's behest, he was busy doing research for its own sake and for his professional pleasure, energetically corrupting whatever he came across and then packing it off to his outfitters. Now, the most extraordinary aspect of the entire thing, and the one which, Messieurs, prompts me to cite the example of this uncommon individual, was that he never enjoyed the fruit of his labors. He would encloset himself alone with the child, but, despite his vast understanding, his mind's agility, his eloquent persuasiveness, he used always to emerge from conference greatly inflamed. One could be perfectly certain the operation irritated his senses, but it was impossible to discover where or when or how he satisfied them. Closest scrutiny had never revealed anything but a prodigious blaze in his stare when once he had concluded his speeches, a few twitching movements of his hand upon the front of his breeches, within which one could tell there was a definite erection, produced by the diabolic work he was doing; but that was all.*

*He came to the house, was accorded a private interview with the young barmaid, I watched the proceedings: the consultation was prolonged, the seducer's language was amazingly pathetic, the child wept, got hot, seemed to enter into a kind of enthusiastic fit; it was at this moment the orator's eyes flamed brightest, and it was now we remarked the gestures in the neighborhood of his fly. Not long afterward, he rose, the child stretched forth her arms as if seeking to embrace him, he kissed her in a grave and fatherly manner, without any trace of lechery. He left, and three hours later the little girl arrived with her baggage at Madame Guérin's.*

"And the man?" asked the Duc.

"He disappeared once his sermon was over," Duclos replied.

"Without coming back to see the results of his work?"

"No, my Lord, there was no doubt in his mind. He had never once failed."

"Now there is a most extraordinary personage," Curval admitted. "What does your Grace make of it?"

"I suspect," the Duc answered, "that the seduction provided all the heat necessary and that he discharged in his breeches."

"No," quoth the Bishop, "I think you underestimate the man: all this was simply by way of preparation for his debauches, and upon leaving I wager he went off to consummate greater ones."

"Greater ones?" cried Durcet. "And what more delicious, more voluptuous delight could one hope to procure oneself, than that of enjoying the object one creates?"

"I have it!" spoke up the Duc, "I dare say I've found him

out: all this, just as you say, was merely preparatory in character, corrupting girls would heat his imagination, then off he'd go to dip his tool in boys. . . . I'll wager he was a bugger, yes, 'tis plain."

Duclos was asked whether she had any evidence to support that conjecture, and did he or did he not also seduce little boys? Our narrator replied that she had no proof of the thing, and despite the Duc's exceedingly likely allegation, everyone remained more or less in suspense as to the character of that strange preacher; after it had been unanimously agreed that his mania was truly delicious, but that one had either to consummate the work or do worse afterward, Duclos went on with her story:

*The day after the arrival of our young novice, who was named Henriette, there came to the establishment an eccentric old lecher who put us both, Henriette and I, to work at the same time. This latest libertine had no other pleasure than that of observing through a hole all the voluptuous activities transpiring in an adjoining room, he adored spying on them, thus found in others' pleasures the divine aliment of his own lubricity. He was installed in the room I mentioned to you, the same one to which I and my companions often repaired for the diversion of watching libertines in action. I was assigned the task of amusing him while he looked through the hole, and young Henriette entered the arena together with the asshole-sucker I described to you yesterday. The management considered that rascal's very voluptuous antics just the kind of spectacle my onlooker would relish, and in order better to arouse the actor, and in order that he render the scene yet more lascivious and more agreeable to see, he was told he was being given an apprentice and that it was with him she was to make her debut. The little barmaid's air of modesty and childishness speedily convinced him of it; and so he was as hot and as lewd in his nasty stunts as 'twere possible to be; nothing could have been further from his mind than that he was being observed. As for my old buck, his eye glued to the hole, one hand on my bum, the other on his prick, which he gently agitated, he seemed to be keeping the progress of his ecstasy abreast the one he was watching. "Ah, what a sight!" he said now and again; "what a fine ass that little girl has, and how well that bugger in there is tonguing it." At last, Henriette's lover having dis-*

*charged, mine folded me in his arms and, after a moment's kissing, he turned me over, fondled, kissed, lewdly licked my behind, and squirted evidence of his virility over my cheeks.*

"While frigging himself?" the Duc asked.

"Yes, my Lord," answered Duclos, "and frigging a prick whose incredible littleness, I assure you, isn't worth the bother describing."

*The gentleman with whom I had to do next, Duclos continued, would not perhaps deserve to be included in my report were it not for one element, a rather unusual one, I should say, which distinguished his otherwise quite routine pleasures, and this little circumstance will illustrate to what point libertinage is able to degrade all a man's feelings of modesty, virtue, and decorum. This person did not want to see; he wished to be seen. Knowing that men exist whose whim it is to spy upon the pleasure-takings of others, he bade Guérin find him one such fellow, conceal him, and said he would enact a drama for him. Guérin at once got in touch with the man I had entertained a few days previously behind the partition, and without telling him that the performer he was about to see knew that he was going to be seen—this would have interfered with his passion's fulfillment—she gave him to believe he was to observe a very arcane mystery indeed.*

*The inspector and my sister were put in the room with the hole, the actor and I went into the other one. He was a young man about twenty-eight years old, handsome and strong. Informed of the hole's location, he not too pointedly moved to where he could be perfectly viewed and had me take my place beside him. I frigged him. When his prick held a good slope, he got to his feet, exhibited his tool to the inspector, turned around, displayed his ass, raised my skirts and showed mine, knelt before me, teased my anus with the tip of his nose, spread heartily, displayed everything with as much thoroughness as delight, and discharged by frigging himself, the while keeping my hinder skirts high and my ass squarely opposite the spy hole, in such wise that he who stood posted on the other side of the wall simultaneously beheld, at this decisive moment, both my bum and my lover's wrathful device. If the latter*

*was in seventh heaven, God knows what was going on in the next
room; my sister later told me she had had a madman on her back
who had sworn he'd never had as fine a time as this, and after that
her buttocks had been washed by a tide no less fierce than the one
that had burst over mine.*

"If that young man of yours truly had a good prick and a
pretty ass," Durcet opinioned, "there was ample in the situation to
provoke a generous discharge."

"It must then have been delicious," returned Duclos, "for his
engine was very long, quite thick, and his ass as soft, as sweetly
plump, as attractively formed as the god of love's."

"Did you spread his cheeks?" the Bishop inquired. "Did you
show his vent to the inspector?"

"Yes, your Lordship," said Duclos, "he displayed mine, I
displayed his, he presented it with incomparable suggestiveness."

"I've been witness to a dozen such scenes," Durcet announced,
"which have cost me a fortune in fuck; there is nothing more
delicious to see or do. I refer to both: for it is just as pleasant to
spy upon someone as to want to be observed."

*Another individual, with approximately the same tastes,* Duclos
went on, *took me to the Tuileries some few months later. He
wanted me to accost men and frig them six inches from his face
while he hid under a pile of folding chairs; and after I had frigged
seven or eight passers-by, he settled himself upon a bench by one of
the most frequented of the paths, lifted my skirts from behind, and
displayed my ass to all and sundry, put his prick in the air and
ordered me to frig it well within view of half of Paris, the which,
although it was at night, created such a scandal that by the time
he most cynically unleashed his fuck, more than ten people had
gathered around us, and we were obliged to dash away to avoid
being publicly covered with shame.*

*When I related this adventure to Guérin, she laughed approv-
ingly and said she had once known a man in Lyon (where panders
enter into the trade at an early age), a man, I say, whose mania
was certainly just as unusual. He would disguise himself as a public
mercury, himself fetch in visitors to dally with the two girls he paid*

*and maintained for no other purpose, then he would conceal him-*
*self in a corner to watch his client go to work; the girl, whose hire*
*depended upon her skill in these moments, would guide the libertine*
*she had in her arms and unfailingly give her employer a view of his*
*prick and ass, the sight of which constituted the one pleasure that*
*agreed with our false pimp's palate, the one that was able to loosen*
*his fuck.*

Duclos having brought her recital to an early conclusion that evening, the time that remained until supper was devoted to a few choice lubricities, and as the example of the cynic had fired their four daring brains, the friends did not isolate themselves in their closets, but disported within clear view each of the other. The Duc had Duclos strip off her clothes, had her bend and lean upon the back of a chair and commanded Desgranges to frig him upon her comrade's buttocks, in such wise that the head of his prick might graze Duclos' asshole with each stroke. To that one was added a number of other episodes which the proper presentation of our material forbids us from disclosing at this stage; but the fact remains that the chronicler's inferior vent was completely sprayed and that the Duc, handsomely served and entirely surrounded, discharged to the tune of bellowings and shouts which indicated to what a point his mind had been stimulated. Curval had himself fucked, the Bishop and Durcet for their part did passing strange things with both sexes; then supper was served.

After it, dances were held: the sixteen youngsters, the four fuckers, and the four wives were able to perform three quadrilles, but all the participants at the ball were naked, and our roués, indolently reclining upon sofas, were deliciously amused by all the different beauties one after another offered them by the divers attitudes the dancers were obliged to strike. Messieurs had the storytellers at their side, and these ladies manualized them rapidly or slowly, depending upon the pleasure they were experiencing; but, somewhat fatigued by the day's frolickings, no one discharged, and each went to bed to acquire the strength needed for all the following day's new infamies.

# THE FIFTH DAY

*T*hat morning it was Curval's duty to lend his presence at the academy of masturbation, and as the little girls were beginning to make tangible progress, he was hard put to resist the multiplying thumps and jerks and the variegated but universally lubricious postures of these eight charming little maids. Wishing to keep his weapon charged, he withdrew without firing it, lunch was announced, and at table the friends decreed that Messieurs' four young lovers, to wit: Zéphyr, the Duc's favorite; Adonis, beloved of Curval; Hyacinthe, friend to Durcet; and Céladon, unto whom the Bishop was plighted, were henceforth to be admitted to all meals, would dine beside their lovers in whose bedchambers they were, as well, regularly to sleep, a favor they would share with the wives and fuckers; the which eliminated a ceremony customarily performed, as the reader is aware, every morning, this ceremony consisting in the fetching of the four lads by the four off-duty fuckers. They were now to come of their own accord, and when from now on Messieurs were to pass into the little boys' chambers, they were to be received, in accordance with prescribed regulation, by the remaining four only.

The Duc, who for the past two or three days had been head over heels in love with Duclos, whose ass he found superb and language pleasing, demanded that she also sleep in his bedroom, and this precedent having been established, Curval similarly introduced Fanchon, of whom he was passionately fond, into his. The two others decided to wait yet a little longer before deciding who was to fill this fourth post of privilege in their chambers.

It was that same morning ruled that the four young lovers who had just been chosen would have by way of ordinary dress, whenever they were not obliged to wear characterizing costumes, as when formed in quatrains, would have, I say, the clothing and style I am going to describe: it was a little jerkin, tight-fitting, of light cloth, tailored like a Prussian uniform with a slit tail, but much shorter, scarcely reaching to halfway down the thigh; this jacket, like all uniforms buttoned across the chest and at the vent, was of pink satin lined with white taffeta, the cuffs and trim were white satin, underneath was to be worn a kind of short vest or waistcoat, also of white satin, and the breeches were to match; but these breeches were provided with a heart-shaped rear flap under which one could slip one's hand and grasp the ass without the slightest difficulty; the flap was held up by a ribbon tied in a big bow, and when one wished to have the child completely exposed in this part, one had merely to undo the bow, which was of the color selected by the friend to whom the pucelage belonged. Their hair, carelessly arranged so that a few curls fell to either side, floated absolutely free behind, and was simply knotted by a ribbon of the appropriate color. A highly-scented powder, in color between gray and pink, tinted their hairdress, their eyebrows were carefully plucked and emphasized by black pencil, a light touch of rouge applied to the cheeks, all this heightened their natural beauty; their heads were never covered, black silk stockings brocaded in rose covered their legs, they were agreeably shod in gray slippers attached by a pink bow. A cream-colored gauze cravat, very voluptuously tied, blended prettily with a little lace ruffle; when the four of them were clad in this style, you may rest assured that nothing in all the world was as charming to behold as these little fellows.

Immediately they were granted their new privileges, a few others were abolished: all permissions, of the kind they had upon occasion been accorded in the morning, were absolutely refused now, but they were given all the rights over the wives the fuckers enjoyed: they could maltreat the women as they saw fit and not only at mealtime, no, but at any time of the day, all the time, if they chose, and they could be confident that in any dispute arising 'twixt the wives and themselves, their side would be heard with sympathy.

These matters attended to, the usual searches were conducted;

the lovely Fanny, whom Curval had ordered to be in such and such a state, was found in the contrary one (the sequel will provide elucidation of this obscure point) : her name was set down in the punishment ledger. Amongst the young gentlemen, Giton had done what he had been forbidden to do; down went his name. After the chapel functions had been completed by the very few subjects who were on hand to execute them, the friends went to dinner.

This was the first meal at which the four lovers joined the friends at table. They took their places, each sitting to the right of the friend who doted upon him, the friend's favorite fucker being seated to the friend's left. These four additional guests lent a further charm to the meal; they were all four very gentle, very sweet, and were beginning to accommodate themselves very well to the general tone of the household. The Bishop, in the liveliest spirits that day, kissed Céladon virtually without interruption throughout the course of the meal, and as that child was a member of the quartet chosen to hand around the coffee, he left table a little before dessert. When Monseigneur, who had worked himself into a splendid sweat over the boy, saw him entirely naked in the salon, he lost all self-control.

"By Jesus!" he cried, his face purple, "since I cannot tup his ass, I can at least do what Curval did to his bardash yesterday."

And so saying he seized the good-natured little rascal, laid him on his belly, and slipped his prick between his thighs. The libertine was lost in the clouds, his weapon's hair rubbed the cute little hole he would fain have perforated: one of his hands fondled this delicious little cupid's buttocks, with the other he frigged Céladon's prick. What was more, he glued his mouth to the lovely child's, pumped the air from his lungs, swallowed his saliva. In order to excite his brother, the Duc created a libertine spectacle by placing himself in front of the Bishop and proceeding to lick out the asshole of Cupidon, the other of the two boys serving coffee that day. Curval moved to within close range and had himself frigged by Michette, and Durcet offered the prelate the sight of Rosette's widespread buttocks. Everyone toiled to procure him the ecstasy to which he plainly aspired; it occurred, his nerves trembled, his teeth chattered, his eyes shone, he would have been a terrifying object for anyone save those three who knew full well the terrible effects joy had upon that man of God. The fuck finally broke forth and flowed over Cupidon's buttocks, for that quick-witted little aide had at the last moment wriggled his way beneath his comrade so as to receive the treasure which might otherwise have gone entirely to waste.

The storytelling hour came, they readied themselves. By an unusual stroke of circumstance, all the fathers found their daughters beside them on their couches. But Messieurs were not alarmed. Duclos began to speak.

*In that you have not required me, Messieurs, to give you an exact day by day account of everything that happened to me at Madame Guérin's establishment, but simply to relate the more out of the ordinary events which highlighted some of those days, I shall omit mention of several not very interesting episodes dating from my childhood, for they would be naught but tedious repetitions of what you have heard already. And so I shall tell you that I had just reached the age of sixteen, not without having acquired a wealth of experience in my métier, when it fell to my lot to have a libertine whose daily caprice merits to be cited. He was a sober, very grave judge of nearly fifty years, a man who, if one is to believe Madame Guérin, who told me she had known him for many years, regularly exercised every morning the whimsicality wherewith I shall entertain you. His ordinary pimp had reached the age of retirement and recommended that the judge put himself in our dear mother's hands; this was his first call at the house, and he began with me.*

*He stationed himself, alone, in the room with the spy hole, I entered the other with a hod carrier, a Savoyard, I believe; well, he was a common fellow, but a healthy strapping one: those qualifications were enough for the judge, who cared nothing for age or looks. I was, within clear view and as near as possible to the hole, to frig my honest churl, who knew what was expected of him and reckoned this a very pretty way indeed to earn his supper. After having unreservedly complied with all the instructions the good judge had given me, after having done all my sweet country buck could desire of me, I had him discharge into a porcelain dish, and having wrung the last drop from his prick, I dashed into the adjoining room. My man is awaiting me in an ecstasy, he pounces upon the dish, swallows the hot fuck, his own erupts; with one hand I encourage his ejaculation, with the other I collect in my hand every precious dram that falls and, between jets, quickly raising my hand to the old prankster's mouth, with great dexterity and nimbleness I see to it that he swallows his own fuck quite as fast as he squirts it out.*

*That was all there was to it; no fingerings, no kisses, he didn't even lift my skirts, and rising from his chair with just as much aplomb as a moment before he had been aroused, he took his cane and left, saying that I frigged very skillfully, so he considered, and that I had very well grasped his character. A new workman was brought in the next day, for they had to be changed daily, as had the women. My sister operated for him, he left content, returned again on the morrow, and during my entire stay at Madame Guérin's I never saw a single day go by without him arriving punctually at nine, and never did he raise a single skirt, although he was ministered by some charming girls.*

"Had he any inclination to see the commoner's ass?" Curval wanted to know.

"He had indeed, Monsieur le Président," Duclos replied. "While amusing the man whose fuck he ate, one had to take great care to turn him this way and that, and the man had also to turn the girl around in every direction."

"Well, now," said Curval, "that makes sense. But for that I'd not have understood a thing."

*Shortly afterward,* continued Duclos, *the harem's strength was increased by the arrival of a girl of about thirty, attractive enough, but with hair as red as Judas'. At first we thought she was a new recruit, but no, she quickly disabused us by explaining that she had come for only one party. The man for whom this latest heroine was intended soon arrived also: he was an important financier of prepossessing appearance, and his singularity of taste, since the girl set aside for him would doubtless not have been wanted by anyone else, this singularity, I say, gave me the greatest desire to observe them come to grips. No sooner had they entered the room than the girl removed every stitch of her clothing and displayed a very fair and very plump body.*

*"Very well, be off, jump about, skip," said the financier, "you know perfectly well I like them in a sweat."*

*And thereupon the redhead falls to cutting capers, running around the room, leaping like a young goat, and our man keeps his eye fixed on her while he frigs himself; these activities continued a great while and there was no telling to what they were leading. When the girl was swimming in perspiration, she approached the libertine, raised an arm, and had him smell her armpit where sweat was dripping from every hair.*

*"Ah, that's it, that's it!" cried the tycoon, staring with furious approval at that sticky arm she held a centimeter from his nose, "what an odor! ravishing!"*

*Then slipping to his knees before her, he sniffed the interior of her vagina, inhaling deeply, and then breathed in the scent emergent from her asshole, but he returned constantly to her armpits, whether because those parts flattered him the most, or because he found the bouquet superior, it was always there his mouth and nose betook themselves with the greatest fervor. At last a rather lengthy but not very thick device, a device he had been buffeting in vain for above an hour, decided to wake and have a look about. The girl takes her place, the financier comes up from behind and lodges his anchovy under her armpit, she squeezes her arm, exerting what I judged must have been a powerful grip; meanwhile, her posture enables the gentleman to enjoy the sight and odor of her other armpit, he lays hands on it, buries his snout under it and discharges while licking, while devouring this part which affords him such delight.*

"And the creature had to have red hair?" asked the Bishop. "That was a *sine qua non*?"

"Absolutely," Duclos replied. "Those women, as you are not unaware, Monseigneur, exude an infinitely more violent underarm aroma, and his sense of smell once stung, no question of it, by ripe odors, his pleasure organs would be aroused at once."

"Of course," the Bishop agreed. "But, by God, it seems to me

I'd have preferred smelling that woman's asshole to sniffing under her arms."

"Ah, ha!" spoke up Curval, "there is much to be said in favor of the one and the other, and let me assure you that if you'll but give the arms a try, you'll find them perfectly delicious."

"Which is to say, I take it," said the Bishop, "that Monsieur le Président finds that stew to his taste?"

"Why yes, I've sampled it," Curval replied, "and apart from a few occasions when I added other episodes to that one, I protest to you that all by itself it has always been able to get some fuck out of me."

"Oh yes, those episodes, I fancy what they were," the Bishop broke in, "you smelled the ass . . ."

"One moment there," interrupted the Duc. "Don't oblige him to make his confession, Monseigneur, he'd tell us things we are not yet to hear; go on, Duclos, don't let these chatterers encroach upon your domain."

*I recall the period,* our narrator resumed, *when for more than six weeks Guérin absolutely forbade my sister to wash, requiring her, on the contrary, to keep herself in the rankest and most impure state she could contrive to be in; we had no inkling of the Madame's designs until one day there arrived a grog-blossomed old rake who, in a half-drunken and most uncouth tone, asked Guérin whether the whore was ready. "Oh, my goodness, you may be sure she is," Guérin replied. They are brought together, put in the room, I fly to the hole; scarcely am I there than I see my naked sister astride a capacious bidet filled with champagne and there is our man, armed with a great sponge, busily washing her and carefully recovering every bit of dirt that rolls from her body.*

*It had been so long since she had cleaned any part of herself, for she had been strictly ordered not to wipe her behind, that the wine immediately took on a brown and dirty hue, and probably an odor which could not have been very agreeable. But the more the wine became corrupted by the filth streaming into it, the more delighted our libertine grew. He sipped a little, found it exquisite, provided himself with a glass and, filling it to the brim six or seven times, he downed the putrid and disgusting wine in which he'd just* finished washing a body laden for so long with impurities. When he had drunk his fill, he seized my sister, laid her down flat upon the bed, and upon her buttocks and well-opened hole, spewed floods of immodest semen brought to a boil by the unclean details of his unpleasant mania.

But another visitor, a far nastier one, was time and again to attract my regard. We had in the house one of those women who are called street scouts or trotters, to employ the bordello term, and whose function is to run abroad night and day and dig up new recruits. Over forty years old, this creature had, as well as very faded charms which had never been very winning, the dreadful defect that consists in stinking feet. And such, no other, was the fair sort whereof the Marquis de L*** was enamored. He arrives, Dame Louise—for such was her name—is introduced to him, he finds her superb, and once he has conducted her into the pleasure sanctuary, "Pray remove your shoes," says he. Louise, who had been explicitly enjoined to wear the same stockings and slippers for a month, offers the Marquis a foot that would have made a man of less fine discrimination puke straight off; but, as I say, that foot's very filth and nauseous quality was precisely what our nobleman cherished most. He catches it up, kisses it with fervor, with his mouth he spreads each toe, one after the other, with his tongue he gathers from each space, and gathers with incomparable enthusiasm, the blackish and fetid scum Nature deposits there and which, with a little encouragement, easily increases by itself. Not only does he draw this unmentionable stuff into his mouth, but he swallows it, savors it, and the fuck he loses while frigging himself stands as unequivocal proof of the excessive pleasure he takes in this fare.

" 'Tis beyond me," was the Bishop's simple comment.

"Then I suppose I'd best explain it to you," Curval said.

"What? You've a taste for that?"

"Observe," the Président replied.

The others rose, came from their niches, surrounded him, and beheld that peerless libertine, in whom were met all the tastes of the most crapulous lewdness, embrace the indescribable foot tendered him by Fanchon, that aged and foul servant we described earlier. Curval was in half a swoon as he sucked.

"There's nothing to be wondered at there," said Durcet, "one need but be mildly jaded, and all these infamies assume a richer meaning: satiety inspires them in the libertinage which executes them unhesitatingly. One grows tired of the commonplace, the imagination becomes vexed, and the slenderness of our means, the weakness of our faculties, the corruption of our souls lead us to these abominations."

*Such must surely have been the case,* Duclos went on, *with the elderly General C\*\*\*, one of Guérin's most reliable clients. The women he required had to be damaged either by Nature, by libertinage, or by the effects of the law; in a word, he accepted none who were not one-eyed or blind, lame, hunchbacked, legless cripples, or missing an arm or two, or toothless, or mutilated in their limbs, or whipped and branded or clearly marked by some other act of justice, and they always had to be of the ripest old age.*

*At the scene I witnessed he had been given a woman of about fifty, bearing the brand of a public thief, and who was, in addition, missing an eye. That double degradation figured as a treasure in his view. He closeted himself with her, had her strip away her clothes, ecstatically kissed the indubitable signs of crime on her shoulders, ardently sucked each ridge and furrow of those scars he called honorably won. That accomplished, he transferred his avid attentions to her asshole, he spread open her buttocks, appreciatively kissed the withered hole they defended, sucked it for what seemed an age, and then planting himself astride the old girl's back, he rubbed his prick on the wounds that attested the triumph of justice, and as he rubbed, he praised her for having gone down in exemplary defeat; and then, bending over her bum, he showered further kisses upon the altar at which he had rendered such a lengthy homage, and squirted an abundance of fuck upon the inspiring marks which had so fired his own warrior's spirit.*

"Oh, by God!" cried Curval, whose brain was in a lubricious ferment that day, "look my friends, behold by the sign of this risen prick what a flame that passion described ignites in me."

And calling out to Desgranges:

"Hither, impure buggress," he continued in the same strain,

"come, you who so resemble what we have just heard described; come, beget me the same pleasure the general got by her."

Desgranges approaches. Durcet, his friend in these excesses, helps the Président strip her. She raises a few objections at first; they are the more certain and pursue their way, scolding her for wishing to hide something whereby she may be cherished all the more by the society. Her branded back comes to light at last, and there are a "T" and a "P" which affirm she has twice undergone the dishonoring ordeal whose vestiges nevertheless completely ignite our libertines' impudicious urges.

The rest of that worn and wasted body—that ass of parchment or ancient leather, that ample, noxious hole glistening in its center, this mutilated tit, those three vanished fingers, this short leg that causes her limp, that mouth destitute of teeth—everything combines to stimulate our libertine pair. Durcet sucks her from in front, Curval posteriorly, and even though objects of the greatest beauty and in the best condition are there before their eyes and ready to brave anything in order to satisfy the least of their desires, even so it is with what Nature and villainy have dishonored, have withered, it is with the filthiest and least appetizing object our two rakes, presently beside themselves, are about to taste the most delicious pleasures. . . . Ah, now give me your explanations of man— here are two men who seem as if they were disputing what is nigh to a cadaver, like two savage mastiffs wrangling over a corpse; here, I say, we have two eminent citizens who, after having given themselves over to the foulest excesses, finally erupt their fuck, and notwithstanding the exhaustion caused by these feats, would very possibly go on to perform other ones of the same crapulous and infamous kind, and perform them without an instant's delay, were it not for the supper bell announcing other pleasures well worth their consideration.

The Président, made desperate by his loss of fuck, and who in such cases could never be revived save by excessive feeding and swilling, flew to work and stuffed himself like a pig. Adonis frigged Invictus and gave him some fuck to drink, but hardly content with this latest outrage, which had been executed at once, Curval rose, said his imagination proposed a few rather more delicious stunts, and without further explanation, led Fanchon, Adonis, and Hercule away with him to the further boudoir and did not reappear until the orgies; but then conducted himself so brilliantly that he was again able to commit a thousand fresh horrors, each more extraordinary than the other, but not, we regret, to be described to the reader, or rather not yet, for the structure of our tale obliges us to defer them.

And then to bed. Curval, the unfathomable Curval to whom that night the divine Adelaide, his daughter, befell, Curval, who could have spent a most delightful night with her, was found the next morning squirming over the body of the disgusting Fanchon, with whom he had performed additional abominations all night long, whilst Adonis and Adelaide, driven from his couch, were, one of them, in a little bed far away, and the other lying on a mattress upon the floor.

# THE SIXTH DAY

*I*t was Monseigneur's turn to assist at the masturbations; he presented himself. Had Duclos' disciples been males, Monseigneur would probably not have been able to resist them. But a little crack below the navel was a frightful blemish in his eyes, and had the Graces themselves encircled him, once he had caught sight of that imperfection nothing more would have been needed to calm him. And so he put up an indomitable defense, I even believe his prick remained limp, and the operations were continued.

Nothing could be plainer than that Messieurs were extremely eager to find fault with the eight little girls so as to procure themselves the following day, which was the fatal Saturday of retribution, so as, I say, at this time to procure themselves the pleasure of punishing all eight. They had six already on the list; the sweet and beautiful Zelmire made the seventh; did she in all good faith really merit correction? or was it simply that the pleasure of inflicting the proposed penalty won out in a struggle with strict equity? we leave the question to be decided by the wise Durcet's conscience; our task is simply to record events. One very fair dame further swelled the miscreants' ranks: 'twas the gentle Adelaide. Durcet, her husband, appeared anxious to set an example by pardoning less in her than in the others, and it was he himself she happened to disappoint. He had led her to a certain place where the services she had been forced to render him, after certain of his functions, were something less than absolutely clean or palatable; not everyone is as depraved as Curval, and although Adelaide was his daughter, she had none of his tastes. She may have balked. Or she may have managed poorly. Or, again, it might only have been some teasing on Durcet's part. Whatever the cause, she was inscribed upon the punishment list, to the vast satisfaction of nearly all concerned.

The examination of the boys' quarters having unearthed nothing, the friends moved on to the arcane pleasures of the chapel, pleasures all the more piquant and all the more extraordinary in that even those who besought permission to come and procure them, were usually refused admittance. Constance, two subaltern fuckers, and Michette were the only ones to attend that morning's party.

At dinner, Zéphyr, of whom they were becoming prouder every day, what for the charms which seemed more and more to embellish him and the voluntary libertinage wherein he was making great strides, Zéphyr, I say, insulted Constance who, although no longer a waitress, nevertheless always appeared at the midday meal. He called her a baby-maker and struck her several blows in the belly to teach her, said he, to lay eggs with her lover, then he kissed the Duc, caressed him, gave his prick a few affectionate tugs, and managed so successfully to fire that hero's brain that Blangis swore the afternoon would not pass without his moistening Zéphyr with fuck; and the little rascal nagged the Duc, daring him to do it at once. As Zéphyr was to serve coffee, he left at dessert time and reappeared naked with the Duc's cup. Instantly they were settled in the salon, the Duc, very animated, began with one or two smutty remarks; then sucked the child's mouth and prick, set him on a chair, his ass at the level of his mouth, and earnestly pumped at his hole for fifteen minutes. His prick rebelled at last, dressed its lofty head, and the Duc saw very clearly that the homage required some incense after all. However, their contract forbade everything save the expedient employed the day before; the Duc resolved therefore to emulate his associates. He had Zéphyr crouch on a sofa, drove his engine between the lad's thighs, but what had befallen Curval happened also to the Duc: his device protruded half a foot beyond.

"You'd best do as I did," Curval advised, "frig the child against your prick, water your glans with his fuck."

But the Duc found it more pleasant to impale two at the same time. He besought his brother to fit Augustine in place, her buttocks were pressed flush against Zéphyr's thighs and the Duc, thus simultaneously fucking a boy and a girl, as it were, to put yet a little more of the lubricious into the thing, frigged Zéphyr's prick on the pretty, round and fair buttocks of Augustine, and soaked them with that child-fuck which, as may easily be imagined, was mightily warmed by such treatment and soon spattered abundantly out.

Curval, who found the general perspective very inviting, and who spied the Duc's ass, open wide and fairly yawning for a prick— as does the ass of every bugger at those instants his prick is up— Curval, I say, drew up to repay him in kind for what he had received the previous evening, and the dear Duc no sooner felt the voluptuous joltings occasioned by this intromission, than his fuck, taking wing at almost the same time Zéphyr's departed him, splashed the lower edges of the temple whose columns Zéphyr was wetting. But Curval did not discharge, and withdrawing his proud and mettlesome engine from the Duc's bum, he menaced the Bishop, who was likewise frigging himself between Giton's thighs, threatening to make him undergo the fate the Duc had just experienced. The Bishop hurls a challenge, 'tis accepted, battle is joined, the Bishop is embuggered and, between the thighs of the pretty child he is caressing, goes on deliciously to lose a draught of libertine fuck most deliciously wheedled out of him. However, a benevolent spectator to it all, Durcet, having no one but Hébé and the duenna to attend to his needs, and although nearly dead drunk, was by no means wasting his opportunities and was quietly perpetrating infamies the proper time has not yet come to disclose. But calm finally descended over the field, the warriors slumbered, and woke again at six, the hour when Duclos' gifted tongue was to lay the foundation for new pleasures.

The quatrains that evening featured certain sexual changes: that is to say, all the girls were costumed as sailors, the little boys as tarts; the effect was ravishing, nothing quickens lust like this voluptuous little reversal; adorable to find in a little boy what causes him to resemble a girl, and the girl is far more interesting when for the sake of pleasing she borrows the sex one would like her to have. Each friend had his wife on his couch that day; they exchanged congratulations upon that very religious arrangement, and everyone being ready to listen, Duclos resumed her lewd stories.

*There was, at Madame Guérin's, a certain girl of about thirty, blond, rather heavy-set, but unusually fair and healthy; her name was Aurore, she had a charming mouth, fine teeth, and a voluptuous tongue, but—and who would believe such a thing?—whether because of a faulty education, or owing to a weak stomach, from that adorable mouth there used constantly, incessantly to erupt prodigious quantities of wind, and above all after she had eaten a hearty meal, she was capable, for the space of an hour, of blowing a stream of belches powerful enough to turn a windmill. But they are right who declare no fault exists that is not a little appreciated by someone, and our fine lass, thanks to this one, had one of the most ardent suitors: he was a learned and grave professor of Scholasticism at the Sorbonne who, tired of wasting his time proving the existence of God in his school, would sometimes come to our brothel to convince himself of the existence of his dear God's creatures. He would send prior notice of his intended arrival, and Aurore would feed like one dying of hunger. Curious to see that pious colloquy, I fly to the spy hole: my lovers greet one another, I observe a few preliminary caresses all directed upon the mouth, then most delicately our rhetor seats his companion in a chair, seats himself opposite her and, taking her hands, deposits his relics between them, sad old vestiges they were, in the most deplorable state.*

*"Act," he enjoins her, "act, my lovely one. Act; you know by what means I may be drawn from this languid condition, I beg you to adopt them with all dispatch, for I feel myself pressed mightily to proceed."*

*With one hand she fondles the doctor's flabby tool, with the other she draws his head to hers, glues her lips to his mouth and in no time at all she has, one after another, shot sixty great belches down his gullet. Impossible to represent the ecstasy of this servant of God; he was in the clouds, he inhaled, he swallowed everything that came his way, you'd have thought the very idea of losing the least puff of air would have distressed him, and whilst all this was going on, his hands roamed inquiringly over my colleague's breasts and under her petticoat, but these fingerings were no more than episodic; the unique and capital object was that mouth overwhelming him with sighs and digestive rumblings. His prick finally en-*

larged by the voluptuous vibrations the ceremony caused to be born in him, he discharged into my companion's hand, and ran off to deliver a lecture, protesting as he went that never had he enjoyed himself more.

Some time after this, a rather more extraordinary man came to the house with a particular problem in mind, and it well deserves to be mentioned in this catalogue of natural wonders. Guérin had, that day, urged me to eat, had all but forced me to eat as copiously as, not long before, I had seen Aurore dine. Guérin took care to have me served everything she knew I liked best, and having forewarned me, as we rose from table, of everything I should have to do for the elderly libertine with whom she intended to match me, she had me swallow down three grains of emetic dissolved in a glass of warm water. The old sinner arrived, he was a brothel-hound I had seen dozens of times before without bothering to find out what he came to do. He embraces me, drives a dirty and disgusting tongue into my mouth, and the action of the emetic I'd drunk is complemented by his stinking breath. He sees my stomach's about to rise, he's in an ecstasy. "Courage, dearie," he cries, "be brave, never fear, I don't propose to lose a drop of it." Being foreadvised of all he expects of me, I seat him on the couch, lay his head to rest on the edge of it; his thighs are separated, I unbutton his breeches, drag out a slack, stunted instrument that betrays no sign of stiffening, I shake, squeeze, pull it, he opens his mouth: all the while frigging him, all the while receiving the touches of his impudicious hands which stray over my buttocks, at point-blank I launch into his mouth the imperfectly digested dinner that vomitive has fetched up from my stomach. Our man is beside himself, he rolls his eyes, pants, bolts down the spew, goes to my lips to seek more of the impure ejaculation that intoxicates him, he does not indeed miss a drop, and when it seems to him the operation is in danger of ending, he provokes a repetition of it by dexterously inserting his appalling tongue into my mouth, and his prick, that prick I've scarcely been able to touch because of my convulsive retchings, that prick doubtless warmed by nothing but such infamies, grows purple, rises up of itself, and weeps into my fingers the unsuspected proof of the impressions these foul activities have made upon it.

"Ah, by God's balls," said Curval, "that's a very delicious passion indeed, but none the less susceptible of improvement."

"And how?" asked Durcet in a voice broken by signs of lubricity.

"How?" Curval repeated, "why, by the choice of food and of partner."

"Partner? Oh, but of course. You'd prefer a Fanchon."

"To be sure!"

"And the food?" Durcet continued, while Adelaide frigged him.

"Food?" the Président murmured, "why, I think I'd force her to give me back, and in the same manner, what I'd just introduced into her."

"That is to say," stammered the financier, beginning to lose all control of himself, "you'd spew into her mouth, she'd swallow and then have to blow it back at you?"

"Precisely."

And each rushing into his closet, the Président with Fanchon, Augustine, and Zélamir; Durcet with Desgranges, Rosette, and Invictus: proceedings were halted for roughly thirty minutes. Then the two lechers returned.

"Ah," the Duc said chidingly to Curval, the first to reappear, "you've been up to some nastiness or other."

"Ah, a little of this, a little of that," the Président replied, "it's my life's happiness, you know. I've not much patience with mild or tidy pleasures"

"But I trust you were also purged of a little fuck?"

"Enough of that nonsense," the Président said, "do you suppose everyone is like you, flinging fuck this way and that every six minutes? Why no, I leave those efforts and that unconscionable prodigality to you and to vigorous champions like Durcet," he went on, watching the financier stagger wearily from his closet.

"Yes," said Durcet, "yes, it's true, there was no resisting the girl. Desgranges is so filthy in word, deed, and body, she is so adroit, so suitable in every way . . ."

"Well, Duclos," the Duc said, "go on with your story, for if we don't quiet him down, the indiscreet little fellow will tell us everything he did, and never once consider what a dreadful breach

of good manners it is to boast of the favors one has received from
a pretty woman."

And Duclos obediently returned to her tale.

*Since,* said our chronicler, *these gentlemen are so fond of
that kind of drollery, I greatly regret they were unable to restrain
their enthusiasm yet another minute, for the effects of what I have
still to relate this evening might, it seems to me, have better found
their mark. Precisely that which Monsieur le Président declared to
be lacking to the perfection of the passion I have just described
was entirely present in the one that follows; what a pity, I repeat,
that I was unable to get to it in time. The example of the elderly
Président de Saclanges affords, in every particular and word for
word, all the singularity Monsieur de Curval appeared to desire.
By way of a partner for him, Guérin had chosen the dean of our
chapter: a tall, sturdy lass of about thirty-six, a great and chronic
drunk, loutish, foul-mouthed, rather a fishmonger's wife, although
by no means unattractive; the good Président arrives, they are
served supper, both get blind drunk, both become unreasonable, one
vomits in the other's mouth, the one swallows the stuff, then the
other vomits into the mouth of the first, now he swallows, and so
forth and so on, and they finally collapse into the supper's debris,
that is to say, into the filth they've just splashed all over the floor.
And then I am sent into the fray, for my co-worker has not an
ounce of strength left, indeed she has lost consciousness. But this,
however, is the crucial moment from the libertine's point of view:
I find him prone, his prick straight and hard as a crowbar; I seize
his instrument, the Président stammers, swears, draws me to him,
sucks my mouth, and discharges like a bull, the while twisting and
turning and continuing to wallow in his ordure.*

*The same girl, somewhat later, participated in a drama which
was surely not much less filthy; a monk of some consequence, who
paid her very liberally, threw himself astride her belly after having
spread and immobilized my companion's thighs by tying them to
heavy articles of furniture. Several kinds of food were brought in
and served the monk, who had the dainties placed on the girl's
naked belly. The merry fellow then picks up the morsels he is to
eat, and dips them one by one in his Dulcinea's open cunt, and only*

consumes them after they have been completely impregnated with
the spices the vagina secretes.

"Ha !" cried the Bishop, "an entirely novel manner of dining."
"And one which wouldn't suit you, eh, my Lord ?" said Duclos.
"By God's belly, no !" replied the man of the Church, "I'm not
that fond of the cunt."

*Very well,* our storyteller replied, *lend an ear to the item
with which I am going to close this evening's narrations, I am persuaded it will amuse you more.*

*I had been with Madame Guérin for eight years—had just
reached the age of seventeen—and during this period not a day
had passed without my seeing a certain farmer-general arrive at
the house every morning and be received with the warmest welcome. He was thought very highly of by the management; a man of
roughly sixty, rotund, short, he resembled Monsieur Durcet in a
good many points. Like Monsieur, he had an air of freshness and
youth, and was also plump; he required a different girl every day,
and those of the house were never used save in emergencies or
when someone contracted abroad failed to meet her appointment.
Monsieur Dupont, so was our financier called, was just as dis-
criminating in his choice of girls as he was fastidious in his tastes,
he simply would not have a whore to attend to his needs except in
the rare and extreme cases I mentioned; he had to have, on the
contrary, working women, shopgirls, especially milliners or seam-
stresses. Their age and coloring also had to meet specification: they
had to be between fifteen and eighteen, neither more nor less, and,
most important of all, they needed to have a sweetly molded ass,
an ass so absolutely clean that the least blemish, a mere grain of
matter clinging at the hole was sufficient grounds for rejection.
When they were maids, he paid twice as much.*

*They had made plans for, and were that day actually expect-
ing the arrival of, a young lacemaker of sixteen whose ass was generally acclaimed by connoisseurs as a true model of what an ass
should be; Monsieur Dupont did not know the treasure that was to
be offered him, and as it turned out the young lady had word sent
that on this particular morning she was unable to leave her parents'*

*house and that matters would have to proceed without her. Guérin, knowing Dupont had never set eyes on me, ordered me to dress in a shopgirl's costume at once, to go out, take a cab at the end of the street, and alight again at the brothel, all this fifteen minutes after Dupont entered the house; I was to play my role with care and pass myself for a milliner's apprentice. But the most important consideration of all was the anise water: I was to fill my stomach at once with half a quart of it, and directly afterward I was to drink the large glass of balsamic liqueur she gave me; you shall shortly learn for what its effect was intended. Everything went forward very smoothly; fortunately, we had been given several hours' notice, and in this time were able to make thorough preparations. I arrived at the house with a very silly air, I was presented to the financier who directly scrutinized me very closely, but as I was keeping a sharp eye on my conduct, he could discover nothing about my person which might contradict the story that had been invented for him.*

*"Is she a maid?" Dupont asks.*

*"Not in that place," says Guérin, pointing to my belly, "but I will answer for the other side."*

*And it was a most impudent lie she told. Little does it matter; our man believed her, and that alone was necessary.*

*"Lift your skirts, hurry it up," says Dupont.*

*And Guérin raises my skirts from behind, drawing me toward her as she does so and thus entirely exposing the temple at which the libertine performed his worship. He stares, for a moment he fingers my buttocks, he spreads them with both hands, and evidently satisfied, he announces that the ass is suitable for his purposes. Next, he asks me several questions relating to my age, my trade, and content with my feigned innocence and the look of having been born yesterday that I affect, he has me accompany him to his apartment, for there was one reserved exclusively for him at Guérin's: he did not like being observed while at work, he was certain not to be in this place. Both of us having entered, he carefully shuts and secures the door, considers me for a moment, then in a rather brutal fashion—brutality characterized him throughout the scene—he inquired whether it were indeed true that I had never been fucked in the ass. As my role called for total ignorance of the meaning of such an expression, I had him repeat it, declared I still understood nothing, and when by means of the most unambiguous gestures he conveyed what he wished to say, I replied, with a simulated look of fright and modesty, that I should be a very unhappy girl indeed if ever I had lent myself to such infamies. Whereupon he told me to remove my skirts, but only my skirts, and once I had obeyed him, leaving my blouse down to hide my front, he raised it above my buttocks to the height of my bodice; but while he was undressing me my neckerchief slipped down, revealing my breasts. He became incensed.*

*"Devil take those damned tits of yours," he cried; "who asked you for tits? That's what I can't bear about these creatures, every single impudent one of them is wild to show you her miserable bubs."*

*Hastening to cover them over, I approached him to beg his pardon, but observing that I was going to exhibit my cunt thanks to the posture I was about to assume, he lost his temper a second time:*

*"But, sweet Jesus! Can't you stay put?" he demanded, seizing my haunches and turning me so that there was no danger he would catch a glimpse of anything but my ass, "stay that way, fuck your eyes, I don't care any more for your cunt than I do for your chest, your ass is all you need with me."*

*So saying, he stood up and guided me to the edge of the bed upon which he installed me in such wise the upper half of my body rested on the bed, then, seating himself on a very low stool, he found himself situated between my wide-flung legs and his head on a level with my ass. He peers at me for another instant, then, deciding I am not yet adjusted as I ought to be, up he gets, fetches a cushion, fits it under my belly, thus arching my ass more sharply; he sits down again, examines, and goes about everything with the sang-froid and confidence of the seasoned and mature libertine. A moment passes, then he grasps my two buttocks, spreads them, poses his open mouth upon the hole, fastens his lips hermetically to it, and immediately, pursuant to the signal he gives me and in obedience to the considerable pressure that has built up within me, I unleash a booming fart, possibly the most explosive one he has received in all his life; it shoots down his gullet and he backs away, furious.*

*"What the devil!" he cries, "so you are so bold as to fart into my mouth, are you?"*

*And he straightway claps his mouth to my asshole again.*

*"Yes, Monsieur," I say as I release a second stifler, "that's how I deal with gentlemen who kiss my ass."*

*"Very well then! fart, if you must, you little rascal, since you can't help it, fart, I say, fart as hard as you like and as often as you can."*

*From this moment onward I cast off all restraint, nothing can express the urgency of my desire to give vent to the boisterous winds produced by the potion I had drunk earlier; our man is thrilled by them, he receives some in his mouth, the others in his nostrils. After fifteen minutes of this exercise, he lies down upon the couch, draws me to him, his nose still wedged between my buttocks, orders me to frig him and meanwhile to continue a ceremony which gives rise in him to such exquisite pleasures. I fart, I frig, I manipulate a slack little prick neither much longer nor much thicker than my finger, but by dint of buffets, jerks, and farts the instrument finally stiffens. The augmentation of our gentleman's pleasure, the critical instant's approach is announced by a new iniquity: it is now his tongue that provokes my farts, 'tis his tongue that, like a flail, darts deep into my anus in order to stir up the winds, 'tis against his tongue he wants me to blow those zephyrs, he becomes unreasonable, he is no longer in possession of his wits, 'tis clear, and his wretched little engine sadly sprinkles seven or eight drops of watery, brownish sperm upon my fingers; and now he is restored to his senses. But as his native brutality fomented his distraction, so now it replaces it at once, and he barely gives me enough time to readjust myself. He scolds, he mutters and swears, in one word he offers me the abhorrent image of vice that has slaked its thirst, and I am made the butt of that unthinking indelicacy which, once its glitter has paled, seeks to find revenge in scorn for the worshiped object that latterly captivated the senses.*

"Now that's a man I prefer to all the others," said the Bishop. "And do you know if he had his little sixteen-year-old apprentice the next day?"

"Yes, Monseigneur, he did indeed, and the day after that a

maid of fifteen far prettier yet. As few men used to pay as much, few were better served."

This passion having stimulated heads so well acquainted with that species of disorder, and having put them in mind of a taste they all relished, Messieurs simply could not bear waiting any longer to make use of it. Each of them plucked what windy fruits there were to be had, neglecting no likely sources, then supper arrived, with their gourmandizing pleasures they blended nearly all the infamies they had just heard described, the Duc got Fanchon tipsy and had the befuddled old thing vomit into his mouth, Durcet had the whole harem fart, and in the course of the evening swallowed at least threescore mouthfuls of unwholesome air. As for Curval, in whose brain all kinds of extravagances danced gaily, he declared he was moved to perform some solitary orgies and went off to the remote boudoir, accompanied by Fanchon, Marie, Desgranges, and thirty bottles of Champagne wine. Later on, all four had to be carried back into society, for they were discovered floating in a very tide of their own ordures, and the Président was found asleep, his mouth fastened to that of Desgranges, who was still wearily retching into it. The three other friends aquitted themselves no less brilliantly, performing feats in like kind or somewhat different; they too had spent their orgy period drinking, they had besotted their little ministers and lapped up their vomit, they had got the little girls to fart, I truly haven't space to tell you all they did, and had it not been for Duclos, who coolly kept her wits about her, who when it was abandoned by the others assumed the government of the revels, preserved order, and put the merrymakers to bed, I repeat that had it not been for Duclos, it is very probable indeed that rosy-fingered Dawn, opening the gates of Apollo's palace, would have found them lying still plunged in their excrements, rather more after the example of swine than like heroes.

Needful only of rest, each lay by himself that night, and cradled in Morpheus' arms, recovered a little strength for the strenuous new day ahead.

# THE SEVENTH DAY

*T*he friends had ceased to participate in Duclos' nine o'clock lessons. Wearied from the night's riot, fearing, furthermore, lest some operation might result in loss of fuck at that very early hour, and esteeming, finally, that this ceremony was accelerating their indifference to joys and to objects whose interest and integrity it was surely to their advantage to preserve for a while, they agreed that instead of one of themselves, one of the fuckers would hereafter take his turn at the morning exercises.

The inspection and searches were conducted, only one little girl was wanting to make all eight of them eligible for correction, and she was the lovely and intriguing Sophie, a child accustomed to fulfilling all her duties; however ridiculous they may have seemed to her, she respected them none the less, but Durcet, who had earlier conferred with Louison, her governess, so artfully caused her to tumble into the snare that she was declared to be at fault and was as a consequence added to the fatal register. The sweet Aline, equally subjected to close scrutiny, was also judged guilty, and so it was that the evening's list contained mention of the eight little girls, four of the little boys, and two from among the wives.

These tasks accomplished, Messieurs concentrated their thoughts upon the marriage highlighting the festival that marked the end of the first week. No chapel permissions were granted that day, Monseigneur clad himself pontifically, they betook themselves to the altar. The Duc, representing the bride's father, and Curval, who represented the young groom's, led forth Michette and Giton. Both were extraordinarily arrayed in the most formal

344

dress, but also reversedly, that is to say, the little boy was costumed as a girl, the little girl wore boy's clothes. We regret to say that the sequence we originally established for the treatment of our matter obliges us to postpone yet a little longer the pleasure the reader will doubtless take in learning the details of this religious ceremony; but the appropriate moment for disclosing them will surely arrive, and probably fairly soon.

Messieurs passed into the salon. It was while awaiting the hour of dinner our four libertines, encloseted with that charming little couple, had them remove their clothing, and obliged them mutually to perform everything in the sphere of matrimonial ritual their age permitted, with the single exception of the introduction of the virile member into the little girl's vagina, which introduction could perfectly well have been effected, for the boy stiffened very satisfactorily, but he was held in check in order that nothing might happen to spoil a flower destined for plucking by others. But, apart from that, they were allowed to finger and caress one another; young Michette polluted her little husband and Giton, aided by his masters, frigged his little wife as nicely as you please. However, they were both beginning to realize full well the bondage they were in, and this recognition prevented voluptuous joy, even that joy their young years permitted them to experience, from being born in their little hearts.

They dined, the bride and groom assisted at the wedding feast, but at coffee, heads having waxed hot over them, they were stripped naked, as were Zélamir, Cupidon, Rosette, and Colombe, who were serving coffee. Thigh-fuckery having become fashionable at this time of day, Curval laid hands on the husband, the Duc captured his bride, and the two men enthighed the couple on the spot. The Bishop, who since coffee had been brought in had taken a liking to him, now fell ravenously upon the charming Zélamir's behind, which he tongued, sucked, and whence he elicited farts, and he soon managed to transpierce the little fellow in the same way, while Durcet committed his preferred little villainies upon Cupidon's charming behind. Our two principal athletes did not discharge; one of them soon had Rosette in his clutches, the other Colombe, they slipped their pricks between the children's legs and, just as they had with Michette and Giton, ordered them to frig, with their pretty little hands and in accordance with the instruction they had been receiving, those monstrous prick ends thrusting beyond their crotches and out into space; and while the youngsters toiled away, the libertines comfortably fingered their helpers' delicious, fresh little assholes. And still no fuck shed; Messieurs knew full well what delicious chores lay ahead that evening, they proceeded circumspectly. The young couple's privileges were abrogated, their marriage, although made in keeping with every formality, became no more than a jest; they each of them returned to their quatrains, and the company established itself in the auditorium. Duclos took up her story.

*A man with more or less the same predilections as the financier whose exploits terminated yesterday evening's recital shall be the athlete with whom, may it please your Lordships, today's shall begin. He was a crown attorney of some sixty years and not only were his eccentricities unusual, but for practicing them he would have none but women older than he. Guérin gave him one of her friends, an aged procuress whose withered buttocks bore a powerful likeness to a crumple of old parchment being used to keep tobacco moist. Such, notwithstanding, was to be the object employed for our libertine's offerings. He knelt down before that decrepit bum and kissed it lovingly; farts were blown up his nose, he waxed ecstatic, opened his mouth, the lady opened her vent, his tongue went enthusiastically in quest of the mellow winds soughing in that tunnel. He could not resist the delirium into which the operation was plunging him. From his breeches he has brought out an ancient, pale, shriveled little device, an object as ill-favored as the one he deifies. "Ah! Fart, my old sweetie, fart thoughtlessly, fart abundantly," he cries, frigging himself with all his strength. "Fart, my love, for only thy little farts will break the spell binding this slumbering prince." The procuress redoubles her efforts, and, drunk with joy, the libertine surrenders his burden: between his goddess' legs fall two or three unhappy droplets of the sperm responsible for the whole of his delight.*

O terrible effect of example! Who would have believed it? At the very same instant, and quite as if they had received a signal, all four of our libertines individually summon the duenna of their quadrilles. They lay eager hands upon those foul and rammy asses, solicit farts, obtain them, and are fully prepared to be just as happy as the crown attorney, but restrain themselves, for they remember the pleasures awaiting them at the orgies; whereupon they dismiss each his Venus, and Duclos continues:

*I shall lay little emphasis upon the following passion,* said that amiable creature, *for I realize that there are not many in your midst, Messieurs, who are its votaries; however, you have commanded me to tell everything, and I obey. A very young man, a young man with a very handsome face, used to find it vastly amusing to lick out my cunt once a month, and at a certain period. I would be lying on my back, my legs flung wide, he used to kneel in front of me and suck, with both hands lifting my flanks so as to bring my cunt to within easy reach. He swallowed both fuck and blood, for he managed so adroitly, worked with such good will, and was such a pretty lad I used to discharge. He would frig himself, would be in seventh heaven, nothing evidently could afford him so much pleasure, and the hottest, the most ardent discharge, performed while in action, used always to convince me of his high humor. The following day he would usually see Aurore, not long afterward it would be my sister, and in the course of the month he would pass us all in review, and he doubtless made the rounds of every other whorehouse in Paris at the same time.*

*But, Messieurs, I believe you will concur in my judgment when I say that the aforementioned caprice is no more singular than that of another gentleman, an old friend of Guérin, who had been furnishing him for years. She assured us that all his joy consisted in eating expelled ovulations and in lapping up miscarriages; he would be notified whenever a girl found herself in that case, he would rush to the house and swallow the embryo, half swooning with satisfaction.*

"I knew that particular man," said Curval. "His existence and his tastes are as authentic as anything else in the world."

"Perhaps," said the Bishop. "And I know something just as certain as your man, and that is I'd not imitate him."

"And why, pray tell?" asked the Président. "I am convinced it would produce a lively discharge, and were Constance to grant me her kind permission, for I hear she's gravid now, why, I can promise her I'll fetch Monsieur her son along before he's fully done, and I'll toss him off like a sardine."

"Oh, all the world knows your horror of pregnant women," cried Constance, "and everyone also knows you only got rid of Adelaide's mother because she conceived a second time, and if Julie were to take my advice, she'd be careful."

"Why yes, 'tis perfectly true that I am not fond of progeny," quoth Curval, "and that when the beast is laden it quickens a furious loathing in me, but to imagine I killed my wife on that account is to be gravely mistaken. Bitch that you are, get it into your head that I have no need of reasons in order to kill a woman, above all a bitch that, were she mine, I'd very surely keep from whelping."

Constance and Adelaide fell to weeping, and this brief dialogue revealed something of the secret hatred the Président bore for the charming wife of the Duc who, for his part, very far from supporting her in the discussion, replied to Curval, saying that he ought perfectly well to know that he, Blangis, was equally ill-disposed to offspring, and that although Constance was pregnant, she had not yet given birth. And at this point Constance's tears flowed all the faster; she was on her father's couch, and Durcet, not taxing himself to comfort her, advised his daughter that if she did not cease her blubbering that instant, her state notwithstanding, he was going to boot her ass out of the auditorium. The hapless creature shed inwardly upon her heart the tears wherewith she was reproached, and was content to say: "Alas, Great God! very wretched am I, but 'tis my fate, I must endure it." Adelaide, who had also been weeping away on the Duc's couch and whose distress the Duc had been moving heaven and earth to increase, also managed to dry her tears, and this scene, somewhat tragical although very mirthful to our four libertines' villainous souls, ground to an end, and Duclos resumed her tale:

*In Guérin's establishment there was a room most curiously constructed, and it was always used by one man. It had a double floor, and this narrow between-stories area, where there was only space enough to lie down, served to lodge the uncommon breed of libertine in the interests of whose passion I had regular employment. He would take a girl and, descending through a trap door, would lie down and arrange himself in such a manner his head was directly below a hole that had been bored in the floor above; the girl accompanying him had the single chore of frigging him, and I, located above, had simply to do the same thing for a second man. The hole, obscure and seemingly a natural flaw in the planks, remained uncovered as if through negligence, and I, acting at the behest of tidiness, eager to avoid spotting the floor, would while manualizing my man direct his fuck so that it fell through the hole and, consequently, upon the face of the gentleman below. It was all managed with such skill nothing seemed out of place, and the operation would be a success each time: at the moment the fuck frigged from the person above splashed upon the nose of the person being frigged below, the latter would unleash his own, and that was all there was to it.*

    *However, the elderly dame I mentioned not long ago reappeared, but she was to be pitted against a different champion. This new one, a man of about fifty, had her remove her clothes and then licked out every orifice in her old corpse: ass, cunt, mouth, nostrils, armpits, ears, he omitted nothing, and with each sucking the rascal swallowed whatever he obtained. And he went further still, he had her chew slices of pastry which he would then have out of her mouth and into his, and swallow. He would have her keep mouthfuls of wine she had gargled or swished about, he would have them from her, and drink them too; and all the while his prick would be so furiously erected that the fuck seemed ready to fly all unaided. Finally he would sense the crucial instant's arrival and, hurling himself upon the crone, he would thrust his tongue at least six inches into her asshole and discharge like a madman.*

    "Ah, by God!" said Curval, "will you now say that youth and pretty looks are indispensable to an elicitation of fuck? Why, once again 'tis the filthy act that causes the greatest pleasure: and the filthier it be, the more voluptuously fuck is shed."

    "Those are the piquant salts," Durcet concurred, "which as they are exhaled from the object serving our lust, enter us and irritate our animal spirits, put them in a commotion; well now, who is it doubts that everything derelict, maculate, or stinking secretes a greater quantity of these salts and hence has a greater capacity for stimulating and determining our discharge?"

This thesis was soberly discussed for a little while; as there was a quantity of work to be done after supper, it was served earlier than was customary, and at dessert the little girls, every one of them condemned to do penance, departed for the salon where they were to be corrected together with the four boys and the two wives who also lay under sentence. That made fourteen victims: the eight girls, whose names the reader knows, Adelaide and Aline, and four youths: Narcisse, Cupidon, Zélamir, and Giton. Already drunk with anticipation of the particular delight that was awaiting them and of which they were incredibly fond, they completed their intoxication by imbibing a prodigious amount of wine and liqueurs, and then removed to the salon where the patients were awaiting them, and such was Messieurs' common state, so besotted were they, in such lecherous fury did they enter, that there is surely no one in the wide world who would have wished to exchange places with those unlucky culprits.

Attendance at the orgies was that day confined to the delinquents and the four elders who were there as servants; everyone was naked, everyone trembled, everyone was weeping and wondering what to expect when the Président, taking his seat in a tall armchair, bade Durcet announce the name of each criminal, and cite his offense. Durcet's face was as wrathful as his colleague's, he took up the register and undertook to read from it, but encountered difficulties and was unable to proceed; the Bishop came to his rescue, and although quite as drunk as the banker, held his wine with greater success and in a loud voice read one after the other the names of the guilty and their faults; and after each citation the Président pronounced sentence in keeping with the physical faculties and age of the criminal, but the punishment decreed was in every instance severe all the same. This ceremony concluded, punishment was inflicted. We are in despair, for here we are once again forced by the design of our history to make a little detour: yes, we must for the time being omit describing those lubricious corrections, but our readers will not hold it against us; they appreciate our inability to give them complete satisfaction at the present moment; but they can be sure of it, their time will come.

The ceremony lasted a very long time. There were fourteen subjects to punish, and some very pleasant episodes interrupted the proceedings. No doubt of it, everything was delicious, for our scoundrels discharged, all four of them, and retired so weary, so drunk with wine and pleasure, that had it not been for the four fuckers who came to fetch them, they might not have reached their chambers where, despite all they had just accomplished, further lewd exploits were performed.

The Duc, who had Adelaide for his bed companion that night, did not want her. She had been one of the delinquents punished, and punished so well by him that he, having poured out every drop of his fuck in her honor, had no more need of her that evening and, relegating her to a mattress on the floor, he gave her place to Duclos, more firmly installed in his good graces than ever.

# THE EIGHTH DAY

*T*he previous day's examples having made a deep impression, no one was found, no one could be found wanting the next day. The lessons continued, they were executed upon the fuckers, and as the day produced no outstanding event until coffee, we will begin our account with that little rite. Coffee was served by Augustine, Zelmire, Narcisse, and Zéphyr. The thigh-fuckeries began again, Curval laid hands on Zelmire, the Duc on Augustine, and after having admired and kissed their pretty buttocks which, I truly don't know why, that day possessed a charm, an attraction, a blush of vermilion the friends had not hitherto remarked, after, I say, our libertines had thoroughly kissed and caressed those exquisite little asses, farts were elicited from them; the Bishop, who had Narcisse in his grip, had already procured himself some, Zéphyr's could be heard spluttering into Durcet's mouth—why not imitate them? Zelmire succeeded, but Augustine had striven with might and main, the Duc had threatened her with another Saturday martyrdom, with punishment as severe as what she had just suffered the day before, but strains and struggles, menaces and imprecations were all in vain, nothing emerged from the poor little creature, she was already in tears when a driblet at length appeared and satisfied the Duc who inhaled the aroma and, highly pleased with this mark of docility in the pretty child of whom he was so fond, he camped his enormous engine between her thighs, then withdrew it as he was about to discharge, and totally inundated her two buttocks. Curval had done the same to Zelmire, but the Bishop and Durcet contented themselves with what is known as

352

the little goosing; later, their nap over, they passed into the auditorium, where the splendid Duclos, arrayed that day in everything that could most successfully cause an observer to forget her age, appeared even lovelier under the candlelight, and our libertines, grown very hot with much looking at her, were loath to allow her to ascend to the platform without first having her exhibit her buttocks to the assembly.

"A magnificent ass, upon my soul," said Curval.

"Oh, indeed, my friend," said Durcet, "I warrant there are few better to be seen."

These encomiums heard, our heroine lowered her skirts, took her seat, and resumed her story in such wise as the reader shall observe, if he be pleased to continue, which we advise that he do for the sake of his pleasure.

*A reflection and an event were responsible, Messieurs, for the shift in battlefields; the digladiations I shall from now on relate were performed in other surroundings. The reflection was a most simple one: I remarked the lamentable condition of my purse, and straightway was set to thinking. I had been nine years at Madame Guérin's, and although, during that time, I had disbursed very little, I now found myself without even a hundred louis; that woman, extremely clever and never once deaf to the pleading of her own welfare, always found a way to pocket two-thirds of the house's receipts and to impose additional deductions upon the remainder. These practices displeased me and, subject to repeated solicitations from another procuress, Madame Fournier, who wanted nothing more than to have me settle down with her, and knowing that this Fournier received elderly debauchees of a higher tone and greater means than Guérin's clientele, I decided to take my leave of the one and throw in my lot with the other. As for the event which lent support to my ideas, it was the loss of my sister: I had grown very attached to her, and I could no longer remain in a house where everything reminded me of her but whence she was absent.*

*For nearly six months that dear sister had been receiving visits from a tall, dark, and silent man whose face I found exceedingly disagreeable. They would retire together, and I do not know how they passed their time, for never did my sister want to discuss what they did, and never did they cavort in a place where I could view their commerce. In any event, she came into my room one fine morning, embraced me, and said that her fortune was made, she was to be the mistress of the tall man I disliked, and I learned only that the deciding factor in her conquest was the beauty of her buttocks. And with that she gave me her address, settled her accounts with Guérin, gave each of us a farewell kiss, and left. You may be sure that I did not fail to go to the indicated address, for I wished to see her. It was two days after her departure; I arrived, asked for my sister, and my request was answered by shrugs and blank expressions. I saw perfectly clearly that my sister had been duped, for I could not imagine she would have deprived me of the pleasure of her company. When I related the thing to Guérin and complained of what had happened, a malign smile crept over her face. She refused to explain herself; hence I concluded she was embroiled in this mysterious adventure but did not want me to become involved in it. It all had a deep effect upon me and brought a swift end to my unresolve; as, Messieurs, I shall have no occasion to speak of that beloved sister in future, I may say now that, notwithstanding the inquiries I had made and the lengths to which I went to find her, I was never able to discover what had become of her.*

"I dare say not," Desgranges observed, "for, twenty-four hours after having left you, she was no longer alive. No, she did not deceive you; rather, she was herself deceived. But, as you surmised, Guérin knew what was afoot."

"Merciful Heavens! what are you telling me?" cried Duclos. "Alas! though deprived of the sight of her, I still imagined she was alive."

"Most erroneously," Desgranges replied. "She told you the strict truth: it was indeed the beauty of her buttocks, the astonishing superiority of that memorable ass that procured her the adventure in which she flattered herself a fortune was to be earned, but wherein she gained death only."

"And the tall silent man?" Duclos asked.

"He was no more than the courtier in the story, he was working for another."

"Yet, I tell you, he saw her assiduously for six months."

"In order to deceive her," Desgranges answered; "but go on with your tale, these clarifications might prove tedious to their Lordships, and should they wish to hear more of the matter, they may rest assured the anecdote will figure in my depositions."

"And spare us any emotional demonstrations, Duclos," the Duc said dryly, upon noticing that it was all she could do to keep back a few involuntary tears, "we don't much care for regrets and grievings, you know; as a matter of fact, all the works of Nature could be blown to hell and we'd not emit so much as a sigh. Leave tears to idiots and children, and may they never soil the cheeks of a clearheaded, clear-thinking woman, the sort we esteem."

With these words, our heroine took herself in hand and resumed her narrative at once.

*Owing to the two reasons I have just presented to your Lordships, I made up my mind to leave; Fournier offered me better accommodations, a far more interesting table, much more remunerative although more arduous work, an equal share in the receipts, and no service charges. I went to her at once. At that time she occupied an entire house, and five pretty young girls composed her seraglio; I made the sixth. You will allow me to proceed again as earlier I did when describing Guérin's establishment: I will not portray my companions-at-arms until one by one they step into the arena.*

*On the morrow of my arrival, I was given a project, for Fournier ran a bustling house, people came and went all the time, each of us would often receive five or six clients in the space of a day; but I shall continue, as I have until now, to select none but those who, by dint of singularity or piquancy, are apt to arrest your attention.*

*The first man I welcomed in my new habitation was a disbursing official, aged about fifty. He had me kneel by the bed with my chin resting on its edge; he established himself on the bed, kneeling also, and above me. He frigged his prick squarely into my mouth, commanding me to keep it wide open; I lost not a drop, and the bawdy fellow was prodigiously amused by the contortions and efforts to vomit this disgusting mouthwash caused in me.*

*You will perhaps prefer me to group the four other adven-*

*tures in this category I had at Madame Fournier's, although you understand, Messieurs, that these encounters were separated in time. I am certain the telling will be far from displeasing to Monsieur Durcet, and perhaps very opportune, and for the rest of the evening he will most kindly permit me to entertain him with accounts of a passion for which he has enthusiasm, and which procured me the honor of making his acquaintance.*

"What's this?" exclaimed Durcet; "you are going to have me play a role in your story?"

"With your gracious leave, my Lord," Duclos replied. "I shall simply advise Messieurs when I reach the point where you make your entrance."

"But my modesty . . . oh dear, oh dear! Before these little girls, do you mean you intend to disclose all my turpitudes to their innocent hearing?"

And everyone having chuckled over the financier's whimsical fears, Duclos resumed her narrative.

*Another libertine, much older and in a different way disgusting, succeeded the one I mentioned a moment ago, and came to give me a second representation of the same mania; he had me stretch out naked upon a bed, stretched out himself, his head to my toe, popped his prick in my mouth and his tongue in my cunt, and having adopted this attitude, bade me make return for the voluptuous titillations he declared his tongue was very certainly going to procure for me. I sucked as best I could; he had my pucelage, he licked, bubbled, splashed about and, without doubt, in all these maneuvers, labored infinitely more in his own behalf than in mine. Whatever may have been the truth, I felt nothing, and was exceedingly happy not to be horribly revolted by the whole affair; there ensued the roué's discharge, an operation which, in accordance with Fournier's earnest wishes, for she had given me foreknowledge of everything, an operation, I say, which I strove to make as lubricious as possible by sucking, by wringing the juice from his prick with my lips, by swishing it about in my mouth, and by running my hand over his buttocks and tickling his anus, which last detail, he indicated, pleased him very much, and which he performed on me in turn as best he could. . . . The business completed, our man beat his retreat, assuring Madame Fournier that never yet had he been outfitted with a girl who gave him more satisfaction than I.*

*Shortly after this latest of my exploits, an old witch of about seventy came to our house; I was curious to know what brought her to us, she seemed to have an expectant air, and, yes, I was told that she was awaiting a customer. Extremely eager to see to what purpose the old bag of bones was going to be put, I asked my companions whether there were not a room from which one might have a view of the bouts, as had been possible at Guérin's. One of my friends replied that indeed such facilities were available and led me to a chamber equipped with not one, but two holes; we took our posts, and this is what we saw and heard, for the wall was no more than a thin partition, and sound traversed it so easily we lost not a word. The old dame arrived first. She looked at herself in a mirror, primped, made adjustments, as if she fancied her charms were yet capable of conquering. A few minutes later, in walked this Chloë's Daphnis; he was sixty at the most, a tax commissioner, a man who was very comfortably well off and who preferred spending his money upon worn-out sluts, old trash like this, rather than upon pretty girls; and why? 'Twas a singularity of taste you say that you understand, Messieurs, and indeed you explain the thing admirably. He advances, surveying his Dulcinea; she makes him a bow of deepest respect.*

*"No nonsense, you old bitch," says the rake, "I don't care for elegant manners. Get out of your clothes. . . . But wait just one moment. Have you any teeth?"*

*"No, Sire, not a one is left in my head," quoth the lady, opening her foul old mouth. "See for yourself, may it please your Lordship."*

*Whereupon up steps his Lordship and, grasping her head, he deposits upon her lips one of the most passionate kisses I have seen in all my life; not merely did he kiss, but he sucked, he devoured, most amorously he darted his tongue far, far into that putrid gullet, and the dear old grandmother, of whom not so much had been made in many a long year, replied with a tenderness which . . . I should have much difficulty describing to you.*

"*Very well,*" *said the official,* "*that will do. Off with your clothes.*"

*Meanwhile, he too undoes his breeches and brings out a little dark and wrinkled member about which there is nothing at all that promises an early erection. However, the old girl is naked, and with unimaginable effrontery comes up to offer her lover the sight of an ancient, yellow, and shriveled body, dry, shapeless, and unfleshed, the full description whereof, irrespective of your particular fancies in such matters, would so fill you with horror it were better for me to say no more; but far from being disgusted, repelled, upset by what greets his eye, our libertine is positively enchanted; ecstatic, he seizes her, draws her to where he is seated in a chair, manualizes her while waiting for her to remove a last stitch of clothing, again darts his tongue into her mouth and, turning her around, for a moment pays his respects to the other side of the coin. I very distinctly saw him fondle her buttocks—but what am I saying? buttocks? rather, I saw him manipulate the two wrinkled rags which fell in waves and little ripples from her haunches and lay flapping on her thighs. Well, such as they were he drew them apart, voluptuously fastened his lips upon the infamous cloaca they enclosed, drove his tongue repeatedly thereinto, and while he sweated happily over this ruin, she struggled to give some firmness to the moribund device she was rattling.*

"*Let's get to the heart of the matter,*" *said her beloved;* "*without my favorite stunts, all your attempts will be useless. You've been told?*"

"*Yes, Monsieur, I have been told.*"

"*And you know you've got to swallow?*"

"*Yes, my dearie, I'll swallow, oh yes, my little cabbage, my pet, down it'll go, I'll devour every little drop my duckling makes.*"

*And therewith the libertine deposits her on the bed, her head lying toward its foot, he straightway pops his limp engine between her gums, drives doughtily in up to the balls, wriggles about until, seizing his delight's legs and perching them upon his shoulders, his snout is nicely lodged between the old creature's buttocks. His tongue wanders deep into that exquisite hole; the honeybee going in quest of the rose's nectar sucks not more voluptuously; the lady sucks too, our hero begins to stir. "Ah, fuck!" he cries after a* quarter of an hour of this libidinous calisthenic, "*suck me, suck me, suck and swallow it, you filthy buggress, swallow, for it's coming, by Jesus' sweet face, it's coming, don't you feel it?*" *And flinging kisses here and there, scattering kisses upon everything in sight, thighs, vagina, buttocks, anus, everything gets licked, everything is sucked, the old bitch gulps, and the poor old wreck, who withdraws as slack a device as the one he inserted, and who has apparently discharged unerected, goes tottering out all ashamed of his transports, and as promptly as ever he can gains the door in order to avoid the sobering sight of the appalling object which has just seduced him in his weakness.*

"And the old bitch?" inquired the Duc.

*The old bitch coughed, spat, blew her nose, dressed with all possible dispatch, and left.*

*A few days later, the same companion thanks to whom I had been able to enjoy witnessing this scene had her turn. She was a blond girl of about sixteen, with the world's most interesting physiognomy; I eagerly seized the opportunity to see her at work. The man with whom she was to hold conference was at least as old as the tax commissioner. He had her kneel between his legs, immobilized her head by catching hold of her ears, and snapped into her startled mouth a prick which looked to me to be dirtier and more unappetizing than a rag left to soak in the gutter. Observing that frightful morsel approaching her clean healthy lips, my poor colleague was moved to back away, but it was not for nothing our gentleman held her like a spaniel by the ears.*

"*What the devil's this?*" *he muttered.* "*Are you going to be difficult?*"

*And threatening to summon Fournier, who had doubtless recommended the most conciliatory attitude to her, he triumphed over her hesitations. She opens her lips, retreats, opens them again and finally, gagging and spluttering, accepts into that sweetest of mouths that most infamous of relics; from this point onward, the villain's speech was exceedingly rude.*

"*Ah, little slut!*" *he shouted in a rage,* "*you've got scruples, have you, about sucking the finest prick in France? You suppose, do you, that one's got to wash one's balls just for your sake? Well, fuck you, bitch: suck, do you hear? suck the sweetmeat."*

*Waxing very hot thanks to these sarcasms and the revulsion he noticed he was inspiring in my companion, for true it is, Messieurs, that the loathing you quicken in us becomes the gadfly that arouses your pleasure, stings your lust; waxing most ardent, I say, the libertine plunged into an ecstasy and left in the poor girl's mouth the most definite evidence of his virility. Less complaisant than the old woman, she swallowed nothing, and far more revolted, a moment later she retched her stomach empty, and our libertine, readjusting himself without paying much attention to what she was about, laughed sneeringly between his teeth, amused by his libertinage's cruel consequences.*

*My turn came next. But more fortunate than my two predecessors, it was to Cupid himself I was turned over, and after having satisfied him I was left with nothing but wonder to find tastes so peculiar in a young man so well framed to please. He arrives, he has me take off what I am wearing and lies down upon the bed, orders me to squat above his face and with my mouth proceed to try to wring a discharge from a very mediocre prick, for which however he has words of praise and whose fuck he entreats me to swallow as soon as I feel it flow.*

*"But don't waste the occasion to idleness," the little libertine added, "meanwhile, I'd have that cunt of yours flood urine into my mouth, I promise you I'll swallow it as you shall my fuck, and I'd be delighted to sniff a few farts from that splendid ass."*

*I fell to the task and simultaneously executed my three chores with such skill and grace that the little anchovy soon vomited all its fury into my mouth; I swallowed heartily, my Adonis likewise made short shrift of the piss that poured out of my crack and, while he drank, he inhaled the fragrance that a continual stream of farts bore to his nostrils.*

"Forsooth, Mademoiselle," murmured Durcet, "you could surely have dispensed with disclosures that portray all my youthful childishness."

"Ha!" said the Duc with a merry laugh, "well indeed! You

who scarcely dare look at a cunt today, do you mean to say you used to have 'em piss in the old days?"

" 'Tis true," said Durcet, "I blush to admit it, for what could be more dreadful than to have such turpitudes upon one's conscience? Oh, I presently feel the heavy weight of remorse, my friend. . . . O delicious asses!" he exclaimed, in his enthusiasm kissing Sophie's which he had drawn close for a minute's fondling, "O divine asses! how I reproach myself for the incense I deprived you of! O delicious fundaments, I promise you an expiatory sacrifice, I swear upon your altars never again while I live to stray from the paths of rectitude."

And that splendid behind having heated him somewhat, the libertine placed the novice in what was doubtless an exceedingly indecent posture but one in which he was able, as has been seen above, to give his little anchovy to be sucked while sucking the tidiest, freshest, most voluptuous of asses. But Durcet, become now too blasé, too surfeited with that pleasure, only very rarely found it invigorating; one could suck all one wished, he could do the same till his lips cracked, 'twas always the same: he would withdraw in the same collapsed state and, cursing and swearing at the girl, would regularly postpone until some happier moment the pleasures Nature denied him then.

Not everyone was so unfortunate; the Duc, who had passed into his closet with Zélamir, Bum-Cleaver, and Thérèse, emitted shouts and bellows which attested to his happiness, and Colombe, hawking and spitting in great earnestness, left precious little doubt about the temple at which he had done his worshiping. As for the Bishop, reclining upon his couch in the most natural manner, Adelaide's buttocks pinching his nose and his prick in her mouth, he was in seventh heaven, for he was having a wealth of farts out of the young woman; Curval, in an extremely upright state, plugged Hébé's little mouth with his outsized stopper, and yielded up his fuck as he resorted to other stunts.

Mealtime arrived. The Duc wished to advance the thesis that if happiness consisted in the entire satisfaction of all the senses, it were difficult to be happier than were they.

"The remark is not a libertine's," said Durcet. "How can you be happy if you are able constantly to satisfy yourself? It is not in desire's consummation happiness consists, but in the desire itself, in hurdling the obstacles placed before what one wishes. Well, what is the perspective here? One needs but wish and one has. I swear to you," he continued, "that since my arrival here my fuck has not once flowed because of the objects I find about me in this castle. Every time, I have discharged over what is not here, what is absent from this place, and so it is," the financier declared, "that, according to my belief, there is one essential thing lacking to our happiness. It is the pleasure of comparison, a pleasure which can only be born of the sight of wretched persons, and here one sees none at all. It is from the sight of him who does not in the least enjoy what I enjoy, and who suffers, that comes the charm of being able to say to oneself: 'I am therefore happier than he.' Wherever men may be found equal, and where these differences do not exist, happiness shall never exist either: it is the story of the man who only knows full well what health is worth after he has been ill."

"In that case," said the Bishop, "you would maintain as a real source of pleasure the act of going and contemplating the tears of persons stricken by misery?"

"Most assuredly," Durcet replied. "In all the world there is perhaps no voluptuousness that more flatters the senses than the one you cite."

"What? You would not succor the lowly and wretched?" exclaimed the Bishop who took the most genuine delight in engaging Durcet to expatiate upon a question whose examination was so much to the taste of them all and upon which, they knew, the financier was able to deliver some very sound opinions.

"What is it you term succor?" Durcet responded. "For the voluptuousness I sense and which is the result of this sweet comparison of their condition with mine, would cease to exist were I to succor them: by extricating them from a state of wretchedness, I should cause them to taste an instant's happiness, thus destroying the distinction between them and myself, thus destroying all the pleaure afforded by comparison."

"Well then, following that," reasoned the Duc, "one should in one way or another, so as the better to establish that distinction indispensable to happiness, one should, I say, rather aggravate their plight."

"There is no doubting it," said Durcet, "and that explains the infamies of which I have been accused all my life. Those who are in perfect ignorance of my motives," the banker continued, "call me harsh, ferocious, barbaric, but, laughing at these divers denominations, I go merrily on; I cause, I dare say, what fools describe as atrocities, but thereby I have created pleasure-giving distinctions and have made many a delectable comparison."

"Come now," said the Duc, "confess, my dear fellow: admit that upon more than a score of occasions you have engineered the ruin of some poor folk, simply by that means to serve the perverse tastes you have just acknowledged."

"More than a score?" said Durcet. "More than ten score, my friend, and, without the slightest exaggeration, I could enumerate above four hundred families reduced to beggardom, a state in which they'd not now be languishing had it not been for me."

"And," said Curval, "I fancy you have profited from their ruin?"

"Why yes, that has very frequently been the case, but I must also confess that often enough I have acted not to gain, but purely to undo, at the behest of that certain wickedness which almost always awakens the organs of lubricity in me; my prick positively jumps when I do evil, in evil I discover precisely what is needed to stimulate in me all of pleasure's sensations, and I perform evil for that reason, for it alone, without any ulterior motive."

"Upon my soul," declared the Président, "I own I fancy nothing better than that taste. When I was in Parliament I must have voted at least a hundred times to have some poor devil hanged; they were all innocent, you know, and I would never indulge in that little injustice without experiencing, deep within me, a most voluptuous titillation: no more was needed to inflame my balls, nothing used to heat them more certainly. You can imagine what I felt when I did worse."

"It is certain," said the Duc, whose brain was beginning to warm as he fingered Zéphyr, "that crime has sufficient charm of itself to ignite all the senses, without one having to resort to any other expedient; no one understands better than I that enormities and malpractices, even those at the most extreme remove from libertine misbehavior, are quite as capable of inciting an erection as those which lie directly within the sphere of libertinage. The man who is addressing you at this very instant has owed spasms to stealing, murdering, committing arson, and he is perfectly sure that it is not the object of libertine intentions which fires us, but the idea of evil, and that consequently it is thanks only to evil and only in the name of evil one stiffens, not thanks to the object, and were this object to be divested of the power to cause us to do evil, our prick would droop, 'twould interest us no more.''

"What could be more certain than that?" the Bishop demanded. "And thence is born another certitude: the greatest pleasure is derived from the most infamous source. The doctrine which must perpetually govern our conduct is this: the more pleasure you seek in the depths of crime, the more frightful the crime must be; as for myself, Messieurs," added the Bishop, "if I may be permitted to speak personally, I affirm that I have reached the point of no longer being susceptible of this sensation you have been discussing, of no longer experiencing it, I say, as a result of lesser or minor crimes, and if the one I perpetrate does not combine as much of the atrocious, of the base, of the vicious, of the deceitful, of the treacherous as may be possibly imagined, the sensation is not merely faint, there is no sensation at all."

"Very well," said Durcet, "is it possible to commit crimes such as these our minds yearn after, crimes like those you mention? For my part, I must declare that my imagination has always outdistanced my faculties; I lack the means to do what I would do, I have conceived of a thousand times more and better than I have done, and I have ever had complaint against Nature who, while giving me the desire to outrage her, has always deprived me of the means."

"There are," said Curval, "but two or three crimes to perform in this world, and they, once done, there's no more to be said; all the rest is inferior, you cease any longer to feel. Ah, how many times, by God, have I not longed to be able to assail the sun, snatch it out of the universe, make a general darkness, or use that star to burn the world! oh, that would be a crime, oh yes, and not a little misdemeanor such as are all the ones we perform who are limited in a whole year's time to metamorphosing a dozen creatures into lumps of clay."

Whereupon, their minds having waxed gay and hot, as two

or three young girls had already had cause to remark, and their pricks beginning to rise, they left the table and went in search of pretty mouths, thereinto to pour the floods of that liquor whose too insistent throbbings promoted the utterance of so many horrors. That evening they confined themselves to mouth pleasures, but invented a hundred manners of varying them, and when they had run, all four of them, each a magnificent race, in a few hours of repose they sought to find the strength necessary to starting out afresh.

# THE NINTH DAY

*T*hat morning Duclos expressed her opinion, saying she held it prudent either to offer the little girls new patients to replace the fuckers then being employed in the masturbation exercises, or to terminate their lessons, for she believed their education sufficiently advanced. Duclos very astutely pointed out that by continued use of the young men known by their title of fucker, there might result that species of intrigue Messieurs wished especially to prevent; moreover, she added, for such exercises these young men were worth nothing at all; since they were prone to discharge immediately they were touched, their skittishness or incontinence ought certainly be better exploited, Messieurs' asses had only to lose if the program remained unchanged. It was therefore decided that the lessons would cease; they had generally succeeded, there were already amongst the little girls a few who frigged masterfully: Augustine, Sophie, and Colombe could easily have been matched, what for skill and nimbleness of wrist, against the capital's most famous friggers. Of them all, Zelmire was least adept: not that she lacked agility or that considerable science was not conspicious in all her motions, no, but it was her tender and melancholic character which stood in her way, she seemed unable to forget her sorrows, she was sad and pensive at all times. At that morning's breakfast inspection tour, her duenna affirmed she had the previous evening caught the child in a prayerful attitude, flagrantly on her knees before retiring; Zelmire was summoned, questioned, she was asked the subject of her prayers; she at first refused to answer, then, threats having been employed, she fell to

366

weeping and admitted she had besought God to deliver her from
the perils wherewith she was beset, and had above all prayed
that help would come before her virginity were lost. The Duc
thereupon declared she deserved to die, and made her read the
articles which dealt specifically with this subject.

"Very well," she sighed, "kill me, at least the God I invoke
shall have pity upon me, kill me before you dishonor me, and that
soul I have devoted to Him will at least fly in purity to His breast.
I shall be delivered of the torment of seeing and hearing so many
horrors every day."

A reply wherein reigned such a quantity of virtue, of candid
innocence, and of gracious amenity caused our libertines prodigiously to stiffen. There were voices that called out for her instantaneous depucelation, but the Duc, reminding his cohorts of the
inviolable contract they had subscribed to, was content to propose
—and his suggestion was unanimously approved—that she be condemned to be punished very violently the following Saturday and
that, in the meantime, she kneel and for fifteen minutes take into
her mouth and suck each friend's prick, and that she be given by
way of warning the assurance that, were she to repeat her error, it
would decidedly cost her her life, for she would be judged and
punished to the fullest extent of the law. The poor little thing
crawled up to accomplish the first part of her penance, but the
Duc, whom the ceremony had aroused, and who after having pronounced sentence had prodigiously fondled her ass, like the villain
he was, shot all his boiling seed into that pretty little mouth, in so
doing threatening to strangle her if she spat out a drop, and the
poor little wretch swallowed it all, not without furious repugnances.
The three others were similarly sucked one after the other, but
yielded nothing, and after the usual visit to the boys' quarters and
the excursion to the chapel, which that morning produced little because almost everyone had been refused permission to join the
party, the meal was served, and then Messieurs entered the salon for
coffee.

It was served by Fanny, Sophie, Hyacinthe, and Zélamir;
Curval fancied he might thigh-fuck Hyacinthe, and obliged Sophie
to post herself in such a way as to be able to suck that length of his
prick which protruded beyond Hyacinthe's tightly squeezed legs.

The scene was pleasant and inspiriting, he frigged the little chap he held hugged to his belly, and Hyacinthe discharged upon Sophie's face; the Duc, who owing to the dimensions of his prick was the only other one who could imitate this performance, likewise arranged himself with Zélamir and Fanny, but the lad had not yet reached the discharging age, and thus the nobleman had to do without the very agreeable episode Curval considered so enjoyable. After they had finished, Durcet and the Bishop took charge of the four children and had themselves sucked, but no one discharged, and after a brief nap, the company moved into the auditorium where, everyone having assumed his place, Duclos went on with her disclosures.

*Before any other audience,* said that amiable girl, *I might shrink at broaching the subject of the narratives wherewith this entire week we shall be occupied, but however crapulous that subject, I am too well acquainted with your tastes, Messieurs, to be in any wise apprehensive. No, I believe you'll not be displeased; quite the contrary, I am convinced you will find my anecdotes agreeable. I ought however to advise you that you are about to hear of abominable, filthy goings on; but whose ears could be better made to appreciate them? your hearts love and desire them, hence I enter into the matter without further delay or ambages.*

*At Madame Fournier's we had a trusty old client who was known as the Chevalier, I don't know why, or whence the title came; his custom was to pay us a visit every evening, and the little rite that we regularly performed with him was equally simple and bizarre: he would unbutton his breeches, and we were required to form a queue and one by one drop a turd into them. Once we had all done our duty, he would button up again and go off in great haste, taking that freight with him. While he was being supplied he would frig himself for an instant or two, but he was never seen to discharge, and no one knew where he went or what he did with his breechload of shit.*

"Oh, by Jesus!" muttered Curval, who never heard anything he had not a desire to do on the spot, "I'll have someone shit in my breeches, and I'll keep the treasure the whole evening."

And ordering Louison to come render him that service, the old libertine provided the assembly with a full-blown dramatization of the whimsy whereof account had just been delivered.

"Well, go on," he said phlegmatically, nodding to Duclos and settling down on his couch again, "there's nothing to it, and I expect it will only be the lovely Aline, my charming companion for the afternoon, who'll find something inconvenient about it. As for myself, a pound of shit in the vicinity suits me perfectly."

And Duclos resumed her story.

*Forewarned,* said she, *of all that was destined to take place at the home of the libertine to whom I was being sent, I dressed myself as a boy, and as I was only twenty, with pretty hair and a pretty face, that costume very well became me. Before leaving, I took care to do in my breeches what Monsieur le Président has just had done for him in his. My man was awaiting me in bed, I approach him, he kisses me very lewdly two or three times, he tells me I'm the prettiest little boy he's ever set eyes upon, and while praising me he undertakes to unbutton my breeches. I put up a faint resistance with the single purpose of inflaming his desires all the more, he entreats me, urges me, he has his way, but how am I to describe to you the ecstasy that possesses him when he perceives the package I have brought along, and the colorful mess it has made of my two buttocks.*

*"Why, what's this?" cries he. "You've shit in your breeches, have you? But, my little rascal, 'tis very nasty, you know. How could you have done such a thing?"*

*And quick as a shot, holding me with my back turned to him and my breeches pulled down, he sets to frigging and rattling himself, presses against me, and spurts his fuck upon my beshitted behind, the while driving his tongue into my mouth.*

"Do you mean to say," exclaimed the Duc, "he refrained from touching anything? Didn't he handle it?"

"No, your Lordship," Duclos made him answer, "I recount all that transpired, I conceal no detail; but have a little patience, Sire, and we will gradually reach more entertaining circumstances."

"*Come,*" *said one of my companions,* "*let's go watch a truly humorous fellow. He doesn't need a girl, he amuses himself all alone.*"

*We repaired to the hole, having been informed that in the adjoining room, the one selected for his activities, there was a pierced chair and beneath it a chamber pot we had been busy filling for four days and in which there must have been at least a dozen large turds. Our man arrives. He was an elderly tax-farmer of about seventy years. He shuts the door, goes straight to the pot he knows to be brimming with the goodies he has ordered for his sport. He takes up the vessel and, seating himself in an armchair, passes a full hour gazing lovingly at all the treasure whereof he has been made the proprietor; he sniffs, inhales, he touches, he handles, seems to lift one turd out after another in order to contemplate them the better. Finally become ecstatic, from his fly he pulls a nasty old black rag which he shakes and beats with all his might; one hand frigs, the other burrows into the pot and scoops out handfuls of divine unction. He anoints his tool, but it remains as limp as before. There are moments, after all, when Nature is so stubborn that even the excesses we most delight in fail to awake a response. He did all in his power, and unavailingly, for nothing resulted or rose gloriously up, but by dint of abuse meted out by the same hand that had just been steeped in the ordure, the ejaculation occurred, he trembled, thrilled, fell backward, smelled, breathed deeply, rubbed his prick, and discharged upon the heap of shit which had just so inspired him.*

*Another gentleman dined with me one evening. We were alone together, and twelve large plates heaped with the same meats were brought in and combined with the remnants of an earlier course. He sniffed these new dishes, sampled their aromas, and after he had finished eating, bade me frig him upon the one that had struck him as the most handsome.*

*A young crown attorney used to pay according to the number of enemas one was willing to receive at his hands; when I crossed swords with him, I agreed to accept seven, he administered them all himself; thus, seven times over had I to mount a little stepladder, while he, stationed underneath me, frigged himself*

*until I spewed out over his prick the entire charge with which he*
*had lubricated my bowels.*

As may be readily imagined, the entire evening was devoted
to unclean activities of roughly the same species that had been
treated in story, and that Messieurs turned to this kind of sport
will be all the more easily understood in the light of their general
enthusiasm for this passion; it was of course Curval who carried
matters the furthest, but his three colleagues were scarcely less infatuated with the novelties laid out before them. The little girls'
eight steaming turds were arranged amidst the supper's dishes, and
at the orgies the competition was doubtless even keener for those
of the little boys; and thus ended the ninth day whose term they
saw arrive with the greatest pleasure, for they had high expecta-
tions for the morrow, which was destined to provide them with
more amply detailed anecdotes treating a subject they adored.

# THE TENTH DAY

(Remember to be more guarded in the beginning and more gradually to disclose what is to be clarified here.)

The farther we advance, the more thoroughly we may inform the reader about certain facts we were obliged to no more than hint at in the earlier part of our story. We are able, for example, presently to advise him of the purpose of the morning visits and searches conducted in the children's quarters, the cause of their punishment when in the course of these inspections delinquents were found, and just what were the delights Messieurs tasted in the chapel: the subjects were expressly forbidden to go to the toilet or in any other place to move their bowels without individual and particular permission, this in order that there be held in reserve matters which could, as the occasion arose, be doled out to those who desired them. The visit served to determine whether anyone had neglected to comply with this order; the officer of the month carefully inspected all the chamber pots and other receptacles, and if he found any that were not empty, the subject concerned was immediately inscribed in the punishment register. However, provision had been made for those who could hold back no longer: they were, a little before the midday meal, to betake themselves to the chapel Messieurs had converted into a privy so designed that our libertines were able to enjoy the pleasure which the satisfaction of these pressing needs had the power to procure them, and the others, who had been allowed, or who had been able, to keep their loads, had the opportunity to be rid of them at some time or another

372

during the day and in that manner which most pleased the friends, and above all in that particular manner upon which full details will subsequently be provided, for these details will compass all the manners of indulging in this voluptuous delight.

And there was yet another cause which led to the distribution of punishment, and it was the following one: what is called in France the bidet ceremony did not exactly please our friends; Curval, for example, could not bear to have the subjects with whom he came to grips wash themselves; Durcet's attitude was identical, and so it was that the one and the other would notify their duennas of the subjects with whom they planned to amuse themselves the next day, and these subjects were forbidden to wipe, rub, or wash themselves in any way and under any circumstances, and the two other friends, who did not share this abhorrence of tidiness and for whom dirt was not by any means essential, nevertheless concurred with Curval and Durcet, aided in maintaining an agreeable state of affairs, and if after having been told to be impure a subject took it into his head to be clean, he was straightway added to the fatal list.

That is what happened that morning to Colombe and Hébé; they had shitted during the previous night's orgies and, knowing that they were listed to serve coffee on the following day, Curval, who planned to amuse himself with both of them and who had even advised them that they would be expected to fart, had recommended that things be left just as they were. The children did nothing to themselves before going to bed. Inspection arrived, and Durcet, aware of the instructions Curval had given, was perfectly amazed to find them as neat as a pin; forgetfulness was the excuse they offered, but their names went down in the register nevertheless.

No chapel permissions were granted that morning. (We should like the reader to make a particular effort to remember what we mean by such an expression; this will dispense us from having to repeat our explanations.) Calculations of what would be required during the storytelling period forbade any prodigality until that time.

Upon this day the boys' masturbation lessons were suspended, for they had entirely served their purpose, and every one of the little lads frigged as expertly as the cleverest whore in Paris. Zéphyr and Adonis led the pack in skill, speed, and deftness, and there are few pricks which would not ejaculate nigh to bleeding were they to be ministered by little hands as nimble and delicious as theirs.

Nothing worth citing occurred until coffee; it was served by Giton, Adonis, Colombe, and Hébé; these four children had, by way of preparation, been stuffed with every decoction which is best able to provoke winds, and Curval, who had proposed to be treated to farts, received a generous quantity of them. The Duc had himself sucked, or rather licked, by Giton, whose little mouth simply could not manage to engulf the enormous machine tendered him. Durcet performed some choice little horrors with Hébé, the Bishop thigh-fucked Colombe. Six o'clock sounded, they moved into the auditorium where, everyone having taken his post, Duclos began to recount what you shall read:

*A new companion had very recently come to Madame Fournier's; owing to the role she is going to play in the account of the passion which follows, I believe I should give you at least a rough sketch of her. She was a young seamstress, debauched by the seducer I earlier mentioned having observed at Guérin's, and she also worked for Fournier. She was fourteen, had chestnut-brown hair, sparkling brown eyes, the most voluptuous little face in all the world, skin lily white and satin smooth, very trimly made she was, although rather inclining to fleshiness, from which slight disadvantage there resulted the sweetest, cutest, the plumpest ass, the fairest, oh 'twas possibly the finest ass in Paris. I was stationed at the hole in the partition and soon beheld the man who was to deflower her, for she was yet a maid on either side, nothing could be plainer. Such a tidbit could only have been fed to someone very much beloved of the house: he was the venerable Abbé de Fierville, equally renowned for his wealth and his debauchery, and he had the gout to his very fingertips. He arrives swathed to the eyes in a mantle, installs himself in the chamber, examines all the equipment he is about to use, prepares everything, and then the little girl arrives; her name is Eugénie. Somewhat frightened by her first lover's grotesque face, she lowers her gaze and blushes.*

"*Come hither, come hither,*" *says the libertine,* "*and show me your behind.*"

"*Oh, Monsieur . . .*" *murmurs the shy little thing.*

"*Come, come,*" *fumes the old roué,* "*nothing worse than these novices; she just can't imagine anyone should wish to look at an ass. Well, by the Saviour, get your damned skirts up.*"

*And, stepping closer for fear of displeasing Fournier, whom she has promised to be very obedient, she finally pulls her skirt halfway up from behind.*

"*Higher, do you hear, higher,*" *cries the pleasant old rascal.* "*Do you suppose I'm going to bother to do it myself?*"

*And in due time the beautiful ass is completely exposed. The man of God scrutinizes it, has her stand straight, has her bend forward, has her squeeze her legs tight together, has her separate them and, leaning her over the bed, spends a moment crudely, nay, uncouthly rubbing all his frontward privities, which he has brought to light and with which he now prods and pushes Eugénie's matchless bum, as if to electrify himself, as if to attract to himself some of that lovely child's essential heat. From this he passes to kisses, he falls to his knees in order to be more at his ease, and with both hands holding those superb buttocks as far apart as possible, both his tongue and lips rummage about in search of treasure.*

"*They're right,*" *says he,* "*you do have a passably fine ass. Have you been shitting recently?*"

"*Just a little while ago, Father,*" *the little one answers.* "*Madame had me do that before coming up.*"

"*Why, that's nice . . . and so there's nothing left in your bowels,*" *says the lecher.* "*Well, we're going to see.*"

*And catching up the syringe, he fills it with milk, returns to behind his object, brandishes the nozzle, plunges it into the vent, and shoots out the fluid. Having been told what to expect, Eugénie submits to everything; no sooner is the remedy in her entrails than he lies down on the bed and orders Eugénie to come at once and straddle him.* "*Now,*" *says he,* "*if you've got anything to do, have the kindness to do it in my mouth.*" *The timid creature has taken her place as she has been told to do, she pushes, the libertine frigs himself, his mouth, sealed hermetically to her asshole, catches every drop of the precious liquid that leaps out of it. He swallows*

376 ❦ THE MARQUIS DE SADE

it all, giving evidence of the greatest scrupulousness in this matter, and just when he swills down the final mouthful, his fuck escapes and he is hurled into a delirium. But what is this strange mood, this cloud of loathing which, as in the case of almost every other libertine, comes to darken a mind whence the entire illusion has fled? Brutally casting the little girl far from him once he has done, the saintly man readjusts his cleric's garb, says that he has been cheated, deceived, for this child, he swears, had not priorly shitted, no, they'd lied, she'd come to him full of shit, and he'd swallowed half her turd, fie upon them. It is to be noted that Monsieur l'Abbé wanted milk only, not shit. He grumbles, he curses, he storms, says he won't pay, won't ever come back, says he'll be damned if he'll stir himself for little snotfaces like this one, and goes off shouting a thousand other invectives I'll surely have occasion to report to you in connection with another passion in which they play a major role rather than, as in this instance, a very subordinate one.

"Well, by God," Curval remarked, "there you have a very fastidious man who'll get upset over swallowing a little shit when there are I don't know how many who feast upon it."

"Patience, Sire, patience," said Duclos, "allow my recitals to succeed each other in the order you yourselves dictated and you shall see the superior libertines you allude to achieve wonders on the stage."

My turn came two days later. Instructions had been given me, and I stayed away from the water closet for thirty-six hours. My hero was an elderly ecclesiastic who served as chaplain to the King; like the aforementioned athlete he too was crippled with gout: he was only to be approached if one were naked, but one's front and breast had to be very thoroughly covered; much emphasis had been placed upon this latter article, and I had been warned that were he to catch the least glimpse of those parts, it would prove a heavy misfortune, I'd never be able to get him to discharge. I approach, he studies my behind with extreme attentiveness, asks my age, asks whether it is true I have a great urge to shit, inquires as to the kind of shit I ordinarily produce, is it soft?

is it hard? and a thousand other questions the asking of which, it seems to me, has the effect of animating him, for, as he chatters away his prick gradually lifts its head and leans toward me. That prick, approximately four inches in length by two or three around, had, despite its brilliant sheen, something of so humble and so pitiful an air that one all but needed spectacles to be certain of its existence. Solicited by my man thus to do, I laid firm hands on it, and noticing that my motions were rather well irritating his desires, he made ready to consummate the sacrifice.

"But is it a truly authentic desire, my child," says he, "this desire to shit you mention? For I don't care to be deceived; come, let's see whether you do indeed have shit in your ass."

And so saying, he buries his right hand's longest finger in my fundament, while with his left hand he sustains the erection I have excited in his desire. That plummeting finger had no need to search far, the chaplain was swiftly persuaded I had, quite as I said, the sincerest wish to shit, and when his gropings contacted the object of our mutual concern, he flew into a perfect ecstasy:

"Ah, by God's belly," he cries, "she tells the truth, the chicken is about to lay, and I feel the egg."

Enchanted, the bawdy old priest passes a moment kissing my bum, and observing the haste I am in and that I shall soon be unable to restrain the insurgent turd, he has me climb aboard an apparatus quite similar to the one your Lordships have here in the chapel; once seated, my behind perfectly exposed to his view, I was able to lodge my complaint in a receptacle located two or three inches from his nose. This apparatus had been built expressly for the chaplain, and he employed it frequently, for scarcely a day went by without him coming to Fournier's to assist in delivering either some girl attached to the house or some other from outside it. An armchair drawn close allowed him to observe the process from a point of vantage situated just below the ring supporting my ass.

When we had taken our positions upon our respective thrones, he ordered me to commence the operation. For prelude, I release a series of farts; he inhales them. The turd hoves into sight at last; he begins to pant.

"Shit, my little one, shit away, my angel," he cries, all afire. "Show me the turd coming forth out of your lovely ass."

*And he aids the delivery, pressing his fingers about my anus, he facilitates the eruption; he frigs himself, he observes, he is drunk with lust, pleasure's excess finally transports him completely, he loses his head; his cries, his sighs, his fingerings, everything convinces me he is nearing the final stage and, turning my head toward him, I find I have judged correctly, for there is his miniature engine spattering a few drops of sperm into the same pot I have just filled. The chaplain left in a good humor, and even assured me he expected he would honor me with another visit, which promise I knew very well to be false, for it was common knowledge he never saw the same girl twice.*

"Well, I appreciate his feelings in the matter," declared the Président, who was kissing Aline's ass. "One must be in our deplorable situation, one must be reduced to rack and ruin in order to be able to bear having the same ass shit twice."

"Monsieur le Président," spoke up the Bishop, "there is a certain halting tone in your voice which leads me to suspect your prick is in the air."

"Tush," Curval replied, "I'm merely kissing the buttocks of Mademoiselle your daughter, who hasn't even the courtesy to let fly one wretched little fart."

"I am then enjoying better luck than you," the Bishop announced, "for Madame your wife, lo and behold! has just presented me with the most beautiful and the bulkiest turd. . . ."

"Silence, gentlemen, silence, I say!" came from the Duc, whose voice seemed muffled as if by something covering his head. "Silence, by Jesus! we are here to listen, not to act."

"Which is therefore to say, I take it, that you are doing nothing," inquired the Bishop, "and is it in order to listen that you are wallowing under three or four assholes?"

"Well, you know, he's right. Go on, Duclos, it were wiser that we hear about foolish acts than commit them. We must save our strength."

And Duclos was on the point of resuming when they all heard the usual shouts and customary blasphemies that accompanied the Duc's discharges; surrounded by his quatrain, being frigged by Augustine who, said he, did it deliciously, his fuck was escaping him as with Sophie, Zéphyr, and Giton he performed countless little wantonries of a kind very analogous to those Duclos had been describing.

"Great God!" Curval exclaimed, "I can't tolerate these bad examples; there's nothing that makes me discharge like a discharge, and would you believe it? here's that little whore," he added, referring to Aline, "who only a moment ago could accomplish nothing at all and who is presently doing everything one could ask for . . . but no matter, I'll keep my grip. Ah, you bitch, shit away, shit your head off, it will get you nowhere, I don't intend to give up my seed."

"I see very well, Messieurs," said Duclos, "that after having perverted you it is my responsibility to restore you to reason, and to do so I am going to resume my story without waiting for your command."

"No, don't you do it," cried the Bishop, "I am not as continent as Monsieur le Président, not I, my fuck's itching me, and it's got to be shed."

Wherewith, he was seen very publicly to perform things the structure of this very complex fiction prevents us from revealing at this stage, but things whose delightful influence very rapidly brought leaping forth the fuck whose mounting pressure had discomfited the Bishop's thrice-blessed balls. As for Durcet, absorbed in Thérèse's ass, nothing was heard from him, and in all likelihood Nature refused him what she lavishly granted the others, for he was not as a rule mute when accorded her favors. Seeing that now at last calm had been restored, Duclos went on with her lubricious exploits.

*A month later, I came to grips with a man whom one had almost to violate in order satisfactorily to carry out an operation somewhat akin to the one I related several minutes ago. I shit upon a dish, I bring it to him and thrust it under his nose while he sits in an armchair quietly reading a book, seemingly unaware of my presence. He looks up, falls to swearing, asks how the devil can the girl have the insolence to do such a thing in his presence, but all the same it's a queer turd she's got there, he contemplates it, handles it; I ask forgiveness for the liberty I have taken, he con-*

*tinues to mumble incoherencies at me, and then discharges with his eyes fixed on the morsel of shit; and in so doing he says he'll find me again someday, that sooner or later he'll see to it that I get what I deserve.*

*A fourth gentleman employed none but women of seventy or more in practices which were quite similar; I watched him enact his rite with an old creature who could not have been less than eighty. He was reclining upon a sofa, the matron was straddling him; she deposited her strange old package on his belly while frigging a wrinkled, shriveled prick which scarcely discharged at all.*

*At Fournier's establishment we had another curious article of furniture: a kind of toilet chair, provided with the usual hole and set against the wall; things were so arranged that a man could lie in such a way that while his body extended into the neighboring room, his shoulders passed through an opening and his head occupied the place usually reserved for the chamber pot. I had been appointed to the task, and kneeling between his legs, I sucked his prick as best I could throughout the operation. Well, this extraordinary ceremony consisted in having a workman, who was paid to act a part whose full consequences he neither knew nor divined; in having, I say, a man of the people enter the room containing the chair, climb upon it, and do his business squarely upon the face of the patient over whom I was toiling; but the shit bearer had absolutely to be a poor drudge fetched in from the humblest milieu, he had as well to be old and ugly, he was inspected before being put to work, and were he to lack any of these qualities, our libertine would have nothing to do with him. During all this, I saw nothing but heard rather a lot: the instant of collision was also that of my man's discharge, his fuck sprang down my throat the same moment the turd splashed upon his face, and when he emerged from beneath the chair and got to his feet, I saw by the state he was in that he had been handsomely served. By chance, after the exercise was over, I happened to meet the fellow who had performed so brilliantly; he was from the Auvergne, a good honest chap who earned his livelihood working with stonemasons; he seemed delighted to earn a crown by doing naught but ridding himself of what he would have had one way or another to expel from his bowels, and this little chore struck him as infinitely less arduous than carrying his*

*hod. He was, what for his looks, quite dreadful to behold and must
have been over forty.*

"Faith," muttered Durcet, "I think that should do it."

And passing into his closet with the eldest of the fuckers, with
Thérèse and Desgranges, he was heard braying and whinnying
some minutes later; he returned but was disinclined to inform the
company of the precise nature of the excesses whereunto he had
surrendered himself.

Supper was announced; it proved at least as libertine as ever,
and after the meal, the four friends having been moved to spend
the evening away from one another instead of frolicking together
as they customarily did, the Duc went off to the boudoir at the end
of the corridor, taking with him Hercule, Martaine, his daughter
Julie, Zelmire, Hébé, Zélamir, Cupidon, and Marie.

Curval commandeered the auditorium, providing himself with
what companionship Constance could afford him, for she fell to
trembling every time she found herself with him, and he did
exceedingly little to allay her fears; he also took Fanchon, Desgranges, Bum-Cleaver, Augustine, Fanny, Narcisse, and Zéphyr.

The Bishop went into the drawing room with Duclos who,
that evening, revenged herself upon the fickle Duc, who had led
Martaine away with him; Aline, Invictus, Thérèse, Sophie, the
charming little Colombe, Céladon, and Adonis completed the prelate's entourage.

Durcet remained in the dining room. It was cleared, rugs and
cushions were brought in and strewn all about. He encloseted himself, I say, with Adelaide, his beloved wife, with Antinoüs, Louison,
Champville, Michette, Rosette, Hyacinthe, and Giton.

More the redoubling of lecherous appetites than any other
reason had doubtless dictated this arrangement, for brains were
heated to such a point that evening that it was unanimously agreed
no one would go to bed; it was perfectly incredible what was
achieved in each room by way of infamies and impurities.

Toward dawn, their Lordships decided to return to table,
although they had taken abundant drink throughout the night;
everyone trooped into the dining room, there was an indistinct,
promiscuous pell-mell, the cooks were awakened and soon sent in

scrambled eggs, toast, onion soup, and omelettes. Drinking was resumed, the company grew very merry, all save Constance who was plunged in inconsolable sadness. Curval's hatred was growing just as certainly as was her poor belly; she had that night during the orgies experienced the effects of his hostility, she had suffered everything but blows, for Messieurs had agreed to leave the pear to ripen; she had, I say, blows excepted, undergone every imaginable mistreatment; she thought to complain to Durcet and to her husband, the Duc: they both bade her go to the devil and remarked that she must surely have been guilty of some fault which was hidden from their eyes, yes, surely, else how could she thus ever have displeased that most virtuous and most gentle of mortals; they wagged their heads and walked away. And then they all went to bed.

# THE ELEVENTH DAY

*T*hey did not rise till late that day, and dispensing with all the usual ceremonies, went directly to table once they had got up from their beds. Coffee, served by Giton, Hyacinthe, Augustine, and Fanny, was largely uneventful, although Durcet could not do without some farts from Augustine, and the Duc thrust his brave instrument between Fanny's lips. Now, as from the desire to what the desire causes 'tis ever but a single step with personages such as our heroes, they went unswervingly toward satisfying themselves; happily, Augustine was prepared, she blew a steady breeze into the little financier's mouth, and he came nigh to stiffening; as for Curval and the Bishop, they confined themselves to fondling the two little boys' behinds, and then our champions moved to the auditorium.

*One day little Eugénie, who was becoming more familiar with the rest of us and whom six months in the whorehouse had only rendered all the prettier, Eugénie, I say, one day accosted me and, lifting her skirts, bade me look at her ass. "Do you see, Duclos, how Fournier wants me to keep my behind today?"*

*An inch-thick patch of shit covered her sweet little asshole.*

*"And why does she want you to wear that?" I asked her.*

*"It's for the sake of an old gentleman who is coming this afternoon," she explained, "and he expects a beshitted ass."*

*"Well, well," said I, "he'll be very pleased with you I'm sure, for yours couldn't possibly be more thickly encrusted."*

*And she told me that Fournier's was the hand that had*

383

*smeared her thus. Curious to witness the impending scene, I flew to the spy hole as soon as dear little Eugénie was summoned. The principal actor was a monk, but one of those monks we call gros bonnets, a Cistercian, tall, heavy, vigorous, and nearing sixty. He caresses the child, kisses her upon the mouth, and demanding to know whether she is neat and clean, he hoists her petticoats personally to verify a constant state of cleanliness whereof Eugénie gives him full assurance, although knowing nothing could be further from the truth; but she had been instructed so to speak to him.*

*"What's this, my little rascal?" exclaims the monk upon catching sight of that formidable mess. "What? Do you dare tell me you are neat and tidy when your ass is as filthy as this? Why, by the Virgin, I'm sure 'tis a fortnight since this bum's been wiped. 'Tis very troubling indeed, for I like things to be clean, I do, and it truly looks as if I had better look into the situation."*

*While speaking he had deposited Eugénie upon a bed, knelt behind her buttocks, and begun to pry them apart with both his hands. One would have thought that, at the outset, he purposed simply to observe the state of affairs, which caused him great surprise, but little by little he becomes accustomed to things as they are, sees here a virtue where he had seen only a fault before, sticks out his tongue and moves his head closer, sets to polishing the gem, the clods and spots he removes, the pristine object they conceal inflames his senses, his prick gets up, his nose, mouth, and tongue seem simultaneously to be at work, his ecstasy appears so delicious he is all but deprived of the power to speak, his fuck finally mounts —he grasps his prick, frigs it, and as he discharges, finishes cleaning that anus, which is now so fresh and pure one would scarcely suppose it had been nasty no more than a minute or two before.*

*But the libertine was not yet ready to bring the affair to a conclusion, this voluptuous mania of his constituted a mere preliminary; he gets to his feet, bestows further kisses upon his little partner, exposes to her view a great ass of very evil aspect and very unclean, and he orders her to give it a thorough shaking, to socratize it; this brings his prick up furiously again, he now returns to Eugénie's ass, overwhelms it with renewed caresses, lickings, and so forth, but what he did after that it is not for me to relate, nor would it properly figure in these introductory narrations; you will,*

*Messieurs, have the great kindness to allow Madame Martaine to tell you of the behavior of a villain with whom she was only too well acquainted; and in order to avoid all questions, my Lords, which your own regulations forbid me to treat, or resolve, I continue on to another episode.*

"Just one word, Duclos," said the Duc, who then queried the storyteller in an indirect language which enabled her to make lawful reply. "Was it big with the monk? Was this Eugénie's first time?..."

"Yes, Sire, the first, and the monk's was about the size of yours."

"Ah, fuck my eyes!" muttered Durcet; "ะ damned pretty demonstration, I'd like to have seen that."

*You would perhaps have been equally curious,* Duclos said as she picked up the thread of her narrative, *about the individual who, a few days later, passed into my hands. Outfitted with a vessel containing eight or ten great turds gathered from all quarters and whose authors he would have been very distressed to have identified, I was with my own hands to rub him from head to toe with this fragrant pomade. Not an inch on his body was neglected, not even his face, and when I had massaged his prick, which I frigged at the same time, the infamous pig, who all the while stared contentedly at himself in a mirror, left evidence of his humble virility between my palms.*

*And at last, gentlemen, we have arrived; I can now advise you that the homage is about to be made in the veritable temple. I had been told to hold myself in readiness, I kept my bowels closed for two long days. It was a commander of the Order of the Knights of Malta with whom I was to break a lance; he used to see a different girl every morning for these exercises; the following scene transpired at his home.*

"*Very fair buttocks,*" *was his opinion as he embraced my behind. "However, my child," he continued, "there's more to it than simply having a comely ass, you know. That comely ass must know how to shit. Tell me, have you the urge?"*

"*Such an urge I'm dying to satisfy it, Monsieur,*" *I confessed.*

"*Well, by Jesus, that's delicious!*" exclaimed the commander, "*that's what is called excellent service to society, but look here, my little duck, would you like to shit in this chamber pot I'm offering you?*"

"*In faith, Monsieur,*" I made answer, "*what with the need I have to shit, I'd do it anywhere, I'd even shit in your mouth.*"

"*No! In my mouth, you say? Why, bless me, that is delicious, and that's precisely the place I myself had in mind for you,*" he added, setting the pot aside.

"*Well, Monsieur, let's make haste, bring up your mouth,*" said I, "*for indeed I'll not be able to hold back much longer.*"

*He places himself on the couch, I climb astride him, while operating I frig him, he supports my haunches with his hands and receives, piece by piece, everything I deposit in his avid mouth. He is thrilled by it all, nears his ecstasy, my wrist is hardly needed to bring forth the floods of semen which salute my performance; I frig, conclude my shitting, our man loses himself and his seed altogether, and I leave him delighted with me, or at least so he has the kindness to say to Fournier, at the same time requesting the services of another girl for the morrow.*

*The personage who came next employed more or less the same approach to the problem, but simply kept the morsels in his mouth for a longer period. He reduced them to a fluid, rinsed his mouth with them for a quarter of an hour, and spat out little more than dingy water.*

*Yet another had, if that is possible, a still more bizarre eccentricity; he liked to find four turds in the pot beneath a pierced chair, but those four turds could not be mixed with so much as a single drop of urine. He would be shut up alone in the room containing this treasure, never did he allow a girl with him, and every precaution had to be taken to insure his solitude, he could not bear the thought he might be observed, and when at last he felt secure he went into action; but I am absolutely unable to tell you what he did, for no one had ever seen him; all that is known is that when he had left the room, the pot was discovered perfectly empty and as tidy as can be. But what he did with his four turds only the devil can tell you, if indeed he knows. He may perhaps have thrown them away somewhere, but, then again, he could also have done something else with them.*

*However, what would lead one to suspect he did not do that something else with them is that he left the procuring of those four turds entirely up to Fournier, and never made the least inquiry about their origin. One day, in order to observe whether what we were about to say would alarm him—for his alarm might have provided us with a clue about the fate of those turds—we told him that the ones he had been served that day had come from several persons suffering from syphilis. He laughed good-naturedly with us, was not in the slightest disturbed, which reaction was not to be expected from someone who had employed rather than cast away the turds. When we sought, upon one or two occasions, to push our questions a little further, he bade us be silent, and never were we to learn more of the matter.*

*That concludes what I have to tell you this evening,* said Duclos; *tomorrow I propose to relate my new mode of life, or rather the new turn my same mode of life took, when I met Monsieur d'Aucourt; and as for the charming passion you so heavily favor, I hope to have the honor to entertain you with examples of it for at least another two or three days.*

Opinions were divided about the fate of the turds in the episode Duclos had just recounted, and while arguing and reasoning about them, Messieurs had a few produced for themselves; and the Duc, eager to make everyone aware of the taste he was developing for Duclos, exhibited to the entire assembly his libertine manner of amusing himself with her, and the dexterity, aptitude, and promptness, accompanied by the most stirring language, wherewith she knew so artfully how to satisfy him.

Supper and the orgies transpired without any unusual incident, nothing of importance took place before the afternoon of the next day, and so we may move directly to the recitations wherewith Duclos brightened the 12th of November.

# THE TWELFTH DAY

*T*he new mode of life I was about to begin, said Duclos,
obliges me to draw your attention, Messieurs, to my personal
appearance and character at the time; one is better able to figure
the pleasures being described if one is first acquainted with the object that procures them. I had just attained my twenty-first year.
My hair was brown, but nevertheless my skin was of a most agreeable whiteness. The abundance of hair covering my head fell in
floating and perfectly authentic curls to just above my knees. I had
the eyes you behold me now to have, and they have always been
judged lovely. My figure was rather full although tall, supple, and
gracious. With what regards my behind, that part of the anatomy
in which libertines today take such a keen interest, it was by common consent superior to the most sublime specimens one is likely
ever to see, and there were few women in Paris who had an ass as
deliciously molded; it was full, round, very plump, and exceedingly
soft, generous, I say, but without its ampleness detracting anything
from its elegance, the least gesture immediately discovered that
heavenly little rosebud you so cherish, Messieurs, and which, I do
indeed like yourselves believe, is a woman's most magical attraction. Although I had been for a long season active in libertinage,
my ass could not have been healthier or looked more untried; its
splendid condition was in part owing to the good constitution
Nature had granted me and in part to the extreme prudence I
exercised on the battlefield, scrupulously avoiding encounters capable of damaging my most precious asset. I had very little love for
men, I had never had but one attachment; I had a libertine mind,

but it was extraordinarily libertine, and after having described my charms it is only fitting that I say a word or two about my vices. I love women, Messieurs, I don't deny it. Not however to the uncommon degree my good colleague, Madame Champville, loves them; she will very probably tell you that she has ruined herself for them; I have simply always preferred them to men in my pleasures, and those they have procured me have always exerted a more powerful sway over my senses than masculine delights. Apart from this fault, I have had another of adoring to steal: I have refined this mania to an unbelievable point. Entirely convinced that all possessions should be equally distributed in the world and that it is only strength and violence which are opposed to this equality, foremost law of Nature, I have striven to rectify the actual scheme and to do my utmost to re-establish the proper balance. And had it not been for this accursed compulsion I might perhaps still be with the benevolent mortal of whom I shall speak next.

"You say you have done considerable stealing?" said Durcet.

"An astonishing amount, Monsieur; had I not always spent what I filched, I would be wealthy today."

"But was there not more to it than that?" the financier pursued. "Some aggravating detail, such as, for instance, forced entry, abuse of confidence, manifest deceit?"

"Everything under the sun," Duclos assured him. "I did not think it worth dwelling on these matters which would also have disturbed the smooth unfolding of my history, but since it is evident they might amuse you, in future I'll not forget to cite my thefts.

"As well as that fault, I have always been reproached for another: I am said to have a hard heart, a very bad one indeed; but is that fault really mine? or is it not rather from Nature we have our vices as well as our perfections? and is there anything I can do to soften this heart she caused to be insensible? I don't believe I have ever in all my life wept over my troubles, and I can safely assure you I have never dropped a tear for the afflictions of others: I loved my sister, and I lost her without the least twinge of grief, you were witness to the stoic indifference with which I greeted

news of her undoing; I would, by God, see the universe perish
without a sniffle or a sigh."

"That is how one must be," said the Duc, "compassion is a
fool's virtue. Close examination reveals that it is never anything
but compassion which costs us delights. But with that toughened
heart of yours, you must have committed crimes, for, you know,
insensibility leads straight to nothing else."

"My Lord," Duclos replied, "the regulations prescribed for
our narrations prevent me from apprising you of a great many
things; my companions will supply what you have ordained I omit.
I do have one word to say, however: when later on they attempt to
represent themselves to you as villains, you may be perfectly sure I
have never been any better than they."

"That, I should say, is doing justice to oneself," Blangis observed. "Well, go on with your tales; we'll have to be content with
what you tell us, for we have ourselves set bounds to your discourses; but remember that when we, you and I, have a little chat
together, I'll insist upon hearing of your various peccadillos."

"And I shall conceal none of them from you, Sire. May it be
that after having heard me out you shall have no cause to repent
of your indulgence toward one of the King's worst subjects."
Wherewith she lifted up her voice and addressed the assembly
again:

*Despite all these defects, and above all that of being thoroughly
unappreciative of the value of the humiliating sentiment of gratitude, which I consider as naught but an injurious burden to humanity
and one which completely degrades the pride and self-respect implanted in us by Nature, with all these deficiencies, I say, my
companions were nevertheless very fond of me, and of them all I
was the most sought after by men.*

*Such was my situation when a rich landowner named d'Aucourt
came to have a party at Fournier's; as he was one of her steadfast
clients, but one who preferred girls brought in from outside the
house to those residing in it, he was held in the highest esteem, and
Madame, who felt I had absolutely to make his acquaintance, gave
me notice two days beforehand not to waste an ounce of the precious
matter for which he had a greater passion than any of the other*

men I had met with until then; but from the details you will be able to judge of all this for yourselves. D'Aucourt arrived, and having eyed me up and down, he scolded Madame Fournier for having waited so long to supply him with this pretty creature. I thanked him for his gallantry, and up we went together. D'Aucourt was about fifty years of age, heavy-set, fat, but his face was pleasant to see, there was animation in his features, he was witty and, what pleased me most of all about him, he had a gentleness and honesty of character which enchanted me from the first moment.

"You must have the world's loveliest ass," said he, drawing me to him and burrowing his hand beneath my skirts. His hand went directly to my behind. "I am a connoisseur, and girls of your figure and general look almost invariably possess striking asses. Why, look here, didn't I tell you so?" he continued, after briefly palpating the object, "how fresh and round it is!"

And nimbly turning me around as with one hand he lifted my skirts to my waist and with the other fondled the article, he fell to work examining the altar to which he addressed his prayers.

"Jesus!" he cried, "by the Saviour, 'tis really one of the finest asses I have clapped eyes on in all my days and, believe me, I have studied many. . . . Spread . . . Great God, behold that strawberry! . . . allow me to suck it . . . devour it . . . 'tis really a beautiful ass indeed, this one . . . eh, tell me, dearie, have they given you the instructions?"

"Yes, Monsieur."

"They told you I have them shit?"

"Yes, Monsieur."

"But your health?" went on the capitalist, "there's nothing amiss?"

"Never fear, good sir."

"It's simply, d'ye see, that I carry things rather far," he went on, "and if you have the least illness or symptom, then I run a great risk."

"Sir," said I, "you can do absolutely anything you please, I guarantee you I am as fit and sound and safe as a newborn babe; you may act in confidence."

After this preamble, d'Aucourt had me bend around toward him and, all the while keeping my buttocks spread wide, and gluing *his mouth to mine, he sucked my saliva for fifteen minutes or so; he withdrew his mouth in order to expectorate a little "fuck," and then returned to his amorous mouth pumping.*

*"Spit into my mouth, spit," he repeated, "from time to time, fill it with saliva."*

*And then I felt his tongue run over my gums, drive as far as possible into my mouth, and I had the impression it was endeavoring to draw everything out of me.*

*"Excellent," said he, "I'm getting stiff. Let's go to work."*

*Then he fell to contemplating my buttocks again, ordering me to encourage the rise of his prick. I pulled out a strange little engine three inches thick and only five long; it was as hard as a cobblestone and full of fire.*

*"Remove your skirts," d'Aucourt told me, "while I take off my breeches; your buttocks and mine too have to be thoroughly at their ease for the ceremony we are about to execute."*

*Then, once I had obeyed him:*

*"Lift your blouse further up, that's it, close to your corset," he continued, "and see to it your behind is absolutely disencumbered. . . . Lie on your stomach upon the bed."*

*He fetched up a chair and seated himself by the bed, then returned to caressing my bum, the mere sight of which appeared to intoxicate him; he spread my buttocks for a moment and I felt his tongue sound deep into my entrails, this, said he, in order beyond any shadow of equivocation to verify whether indeed the hen were inclined to lay; I report his own expressions to you. All this while, I was not touching him, nor at that stage, he was himself lightly stroking the dry little member I had just brought from its lair.*

*"Are you ready, my child?" he asked. "For it is high time we undertake our task; your shit seems to me as it should be, I've established that, remember to shit gradually, a little at a time, and always to wait until I have consumed one morsel before pushing out the next. My operation takes quite a while, so don't be in haste. A light slap on your ass will notify you that I'm ready for more, but see to it that I get no more than a bite."*

*Having then adopted the most comfortable position, he glued his mouth to the object of his worship, and in less time than it takes to tell I delivered a gobbet of shit the size of a pigeon's egg. He sucked it, turned it a thousand times about in his mouth, chewed it, savored it, at the end of three or four minutes I distinctly saw him swallow it; I push again, the same ceremony is repeated, and as I had a prodigious charge to be rid of, ten times over he filled his mouth and emptied it, and even after all was done he seemed famished still.*

*"That is all, Monsieur," I said when I had finished, "I'm pushing in vain now."*

*"It's all over, is it, my little dear? Why, then I believe I'll discharge, yes, discharge while paying my respects to this superb ass. Oh, Great God, what pleasure you give me! I've never eaten more delicious shit, I'd swear to that before any jury. Give it to me, bring it hither, hither, my angel, bring me your matchless ass to suck, let me devour it."*

*And thrusting what seemed to be twelve inches of tongue through my anus and while doing so manualizing himself, the libertine spatters his fuck over my legs, not without uttering a host of obscene words and oaths necessary, apparently, to the crowning of his ecstasy.*

*When at last it was all over, he sat down, invited me to sit beside him and, regarding me with great interest, asked whether I were not tired of the life of the brothel and if I should not be pleased to come across someone who would extricate me from it; seeing he had taken a fancy to me, I began to demur, and to spare you a long story which could not possibly be of any interest to you, after an hour of debating I let myself be won over, and it was decided that on the following day I would take up quarters in his home in return for twenty louis per month and board; that as he was a widower, I could conveniently occupy a large apartment in his town house; that I would have a maid to wait upon me and the society of three of his friends and their mistresses with whom he got together for libertine suppers four times each week, sometimes at his own establishment, sometimes at one of theirs; that my one obligation, and occupation, would be to eat a great deal, and always the fare he had served to me, because, doing what he did, it were essential I be fed on a diet which accorded with his taste—to eat a great deal, I say, to sleep long and soundly in order that my digestion be good and thorough, to purge myself regularly once a month,* and to shit into his mouth twice every day; that this rate of shit consumption, or rather of shit production, ought not to frighten me because, by stuffing me with food, as he planned to do, I would perhaps hear the call not twice but three times a day. The capitalist presented me with a very pretty diamond in token of his eagerness to conclude the bargain; then he embraced me, told me to settle my affairs with Fournier and to be ready the following morning, at which time he would come to fetch me himself. My farewells were quickly said; my heart regretted nothing, for it knew nothing of the art of forming attachments, but my pleasures regretted the loss of Eugénie, with whom for six months I had enjoyed an exceedingly intimate liaison; I left. D'Aucourt received me with wonderful graciousness and himself took me to the very pretty suite which was to be my new habitation; I was soon fully installed. I was expected, indeed condemned, to eat four meals whence were excluded a great number of things I should have adored having: I had to go without fish, oysters, salted meat, eggs, and every kind of dairy product; but on the other hand I was so well recompensed that in truth I had no real grounds for complaint. The basis of an ordinary repast consisted of an immense quantity of breast of chicken, of boned fowl prepared and presented in every imaginable fashion, little beef or other red meat, nothing that contained grease, very little bread or fruit. I had to eat these foods even for breakfast in the morning and, in the afternoon, at tea; at these hours, they were served me without bread, and d'Aucourt gradually induced me entirely to abstain from bread; ever since then I've not eaten it at all, and I've also given up heavy soups. The result of this diet, as my lover had calculated, was two bowel movements per day, and the stools were very soft, very sweet, somewhat small but, so d'Aucourt maintained, of an exquisite taste which could not be obtained by ordinary nourishment; and d'Aucourt was a man whose opinion deserved to be accorded some weight, for he was a connoisseur. Our operations were performed when he awoke and when he retired for the night. Their details were more or less what I have already given you: he would always begin with a prolonged sucking of my mouth, which I had always to present to him in its natural state, that is to say, unwashed: I was only allowed to rinse it out afterward. He would not, furthermore, discharge every time he dined,

*our arrangement did not in any way bind him to fidelity. D'Aucourt
kept me as the* pièce de résistance, *I was the roast beef, as it were,
but that did not prevent him from sallying forth every morning for
a nibble of lunch somewhere else.*

*Two days after I had arrived, his comrades in debauch came
for an evening at his home, and as each of the three boasted, in the
taste we are presently analyzing, a superficially different although
fundamentally identical passion, by your leave, Messieurs, every
little example adding to our collection, I shall devote a few words
to the fantasies in which they indulged themselves.*

*The guests arrived. The first was an elderly parliamentarian,
in his sixties, and named d'Erville; his mistress was a woman of
forty, exceedingly handsome, and having no visible defect other
than a certain excess of flesh: her name was Madame du Cange.
The second was a retired military officer of between forty-five and
fifty, he was called Desprès, his mistress was an attractive young
person of twenty-six, blond, and having as lovely a body as you
may hope to find: her name was Marianne. The third was an abbot, sixty years old, Du Coudrais by name; his mistress was a lad
of sixteen, pretty as a star, whom the good ecclesiastic passed off as
his nephew.*

*The table was laid in that part of the house near my cham-
bers; the meal was festive, the fare delicate, and I remarked that
the young lady and the youth were on a diet very similar to mine.
Characters declared themselves while we dined; it was impossible
to be more a libertine than d'Erville; his eyes, his speech, his gestures, everything about him proclaimed debauchery, libertinage was
painted in his every line; there was more of the restrained, the
deliberate in Desprès, but lust was none the less the soul of his
existence; as for the abbot, he was the world's most arrant, boldest
atheist: blasphemies flew from his lips with virtually every word he
pronounced; with regard to the ladies, they emulated their lovers,
tattled and chattered a blue streak but in a rather agreeable tone;
the young boy struck me as being as great a fool as he was a pretty
one, and du Cange, who seemed smitten by him, cast a series of
tender glances toward him, every one of which he failed even to
notice.*

*All propriety had vanished by the time dessert arrived, and the conversation had become as filthy as the goings on: d'Erville congratulated d'Aucourt upon his latest acquisition and begged to know whether my ass had any merit, and if I shitted pleasantly.*

*"Oh, by God," my capitalist replied with a smile, "you've only to establish the facts for yourself; we hold our goods in common, you know, and lend one another our mistresses quite as willingly as we do our purses."*

*"Why," d'Erville murmured, "I believe I will have a peek."*

*Taking me by the hand at once, he proposed that we repair to a closet together. As I was hesitating, du Cange raised her brows and said in a rude voice:*

*"Be off with you, Mademoiselle, we don't stand on ceremony here. I'll look after your lover while you're away."*

*And d'Aucourt, whose eyes I consulted, having made a sign of approbation, I followed the old legislator. 'Tis he, Messieurs, and the other two as well, who are going to offer you the three demonstrations of the taste we are currently studying and which should compose the better part of today's narration.*

*As soon as I was closeted with d'Erville, he, very much warmed by the drink he had imbibed, kissed me upon the mouth with extreme enthusiasm, and in so doing belched a few hiccups into my mouth, which nearly made me eject from that orifice what, a few minutes later, he seemed to have the most pressing desire to see emerge from another. He lifted my skirts, examined my behind with all the lubricity of a consummate libertine, then informed me he was not at all surprised at d'Aucourt's choice, for indeed, said he, I had one of the most beautiful asses in Paris. He besought me to commence with a few farts, and after he had absorbed a half dozen of them, he returned to kissing my mouth, the while fondling me and vigorously spreading my buttocks.*

*"Are you beginning to feel the need?" he asked.*

*"I feel little else," I replied.*

*"Very well, my pretty child, be so good as to shit upon this dish."*

*He had brought with him one of white porcelain, he held it while I pushed, and scrupulously examined the turd as it emerged from my behind, a delicious spectacle which, so he maintained, intoxicated him with pleasure. When I had finished, he picked up the* plate, ecstatically inhaled the voluptuous product it contained, handled, kissed, sniffed the turd, then telling me he could bear it no longer, and that it was now lust wherewith he was drunk thanks to this, the most sublime piece of shit he had ever seen, he bade me suck his prick; although there was nothing in any way agreeable about this operation, fear of angering d'Aucourt by not cooperating with his friend induced me to accede to everything. He settled himself in an armchair, or rather sprawled sideways in it, having deposited the plate on a neighboring table upon which he also rested half his body, his nose buried in the shit; he extended his legs, and I, having drawn up a low chair and having pulled from his fly a mere suspicion of a very soft prick instead of a real member, despite my repugnance I fell to sucking this miserable relic, hoping that a mouthing would give it at least a little consistency. It did not: once I had taken the wretched object into my mouth, the libertine started his operation and thrust into his the pretty little egg, all bright and new, which I had just laid for him; he did not eat it, he battened upon it: the game lasted three minutes, during which his squirmings, shudderings, contortions, declared a very ardent and a very expressive delight. But it was all in vain, not a trace of solidity appeared in that ugly little stub of a tool which, after having wept tears of chagrin into my mouth, withdrew itself more ashamed than ever and left its master in that prostration, in that abandon, in that exhaustion which is the certain consequence of a potent draught of pleasure.

"Ah," said the parliamentarian, "I forswear my faith; never have I seen anyone shit like that."

Upon returning to the dining room we found only the abbot and his nephew, and as they were operating, I can give you the essential particulars at once. Whereas the others exchanged mistresses in this little society, nothing could induce Du Coudrais to do so: always content with what he had, he never accepted a substitute for it; he would not have been able, I was informed, to amuse himself with a woman; but in every other respect, he and d'Aucourt were alike. He went about his ceremony in the same way, what was more, and when we entered the room the youngster was lying belly down upon the edge of a divan, presenting his ass to his dear uncle who, kneeling before it, was lovingly receiving into his mouth and steadily consuming all the lad was producing, the while frigging an exceedingly small prick we observed dangling between his thighs. The abbot discharged, our presence notwithstanding, and swore that the boy was shitting better with every day that passed.

Marianne and d'Aucourt, who were amusing themselves together, soon reappeared and were followed by Desprès and du Cange who, they said, had only been cuddling and volleying while waiting for me.

"Because," said Desprès, "she and I are old acquaintances, whereas you, my lovely queen, you whom I see for the first time, inspire in me the most ardent desire for a more thorough amusement."

"But," I objected, "Monsieur d'Erville has taken it all; I have nothing more to offer you."

"Why indeed!" he said with a merry laugh, "indeed, I ask nothing from you, I'll furnish all that is needed. I merely require your fingers."

Curious to learn the meaning of this enigma, I accompany him, and as soon as we are alone together, he asks to kiss my ass for a brief minute. I raise it toward him and after two or three licks and sucks at the hole, he unbuttons his breeches and bids me do unto him what he has just done in my behalf. His posture excited my suspicions: he was seated facing the back of a chair, by clinging to which he kept his balance, and beneath him was a pot waiting to be filled; and so, observing he was ready to perform all by himself, I asked why it were necessary for me to kiss his ass.

"Nothing could be more necessary, my heart," he replied; "for my ass, in all of France the most capricious of asses, never shits save when kissed."

I obeyed, but took care to stay clear of danger; perceiving my cautious maneuvering:

"Closer, for God's sake, get closer, sweetie," he said in an imperious tone. "Are you afraid of a little shit?"

And so at last, in order to be friendly, I brought my lips to the vicinity of the hole; but he no sooner felt them there than he tripped the spring, the eruption was so violent one of my cheeks was splashed from temple to chin. He needed but one shot to submerge the plate; never in my life had I seen such a turd: all by itself it would easily have filled a very deep salad bowl. Our man snatches it up, takes it with him, and lies down on the edge of the bed, presents his entirely beshitted ass, and orders me to play with it while he feasts upon what has just darted out of his entrails. Filthy as his bum was, I had to obey. "His mistress doubtless does as much," I said to myself; "I must be as obliging as she." I plunge three fingers into the murky aperture pleading for my attentions; our man is beside himself with joy, he falls upon his own excrements, daubs his face with them, wallows in them, feeds upon them, one of his hands holds the plate, the other jostles his prick rising up majestically between his thighs; I redouble my efforts, they are not in vain, I feel his anus contract around my fingers, this reports that his erector muscles are about to launch the seed, the prospect delights me, the plate is licked clean, and my partner discharges.

Once again back in the salon, I find my inconstant d'Aucourt with the lovely Marianne; the rascal had also made use of her. The only one who remained was the page boy, with whom, I believe, he might also have come to terms had the jealous abbot only consented to relinquish him for half an hour. When everyone had returned, they all spoke of removing their clothes and of performing a few extravagances in front of each other. The idea struck me as excellent, for it would enable me to see Marianne's body, which I had the greatest desire to examine; it proved delicious, firm, fair, splendidly proportioned, and her ass, which I fondled several times in a joking manner, seemed to me a veritable masterpiece.

"What do you want with such a pretty girl?" I asked Desprès. "For the pleasure you appear to cherish places no emphasis upon looks."

"Ah," said he, "you don't know all my mysterious little ways."

I was absolutely unable to learn more about them, and although I lived for more than a year with d'Aucourt, and was present at every get-together, neither Desprès nor Marianne wished to clarify anything to me, and I remained in entire ignorance of their secret intelligences which, of whatever kind they may have been, did not prevent the taste her lover used to satisfy with me from being an authentic and distinct passion worthy in every respect of inclusion in our anthology. Whatever he did with Marianne, I sup-

*posed, must have been merely episodic and either has been or cer-*
*tainly will be related at some one of our sessions.*

*After some rather indecent libertine stunts, some farts, yet a*
*few more little turds or turdlets, we had considerable talk and*
*sounding impieties on the part of the abbot, who seemed to locate*
*one of his most perfect lecheries in ungodly conduct and discourse;*
*after all this, everyone put on his clothes again and went off to bed.*
*The next morning, as usual, I appeared in d'Aucourt's room as he*
*was preparing to arise, and neither of us reprimanded the other for*
*our little infidelities of the evening before. He said that, with the*
*exception of myself, he knew of no girl who shitted better than did*
*Marianne; I put several questions to him, asking what she did with*
*a lover who was so admirably self-sufficient, and d'Aucourt replied*
*that all this was a secret between the two of them and they had*
*never seemed willing to disclose it. And we, my own lover and I,*
*went on with our usual little tricks.*

*I was not as confined at d'Aucourt's house as I had been be-*
*fore; I sometimes ventured abroad; he had complete faith, he told*
*me, in my honesty. I could very well see what danger I would be*
*exposing him to were I to impair my health, and he left me to*
*my own devices. With what regarded the health in which, most*
*selfishly, he took such a keen interest, I did nothing to betray his*
*trust, but as for the rest, I considered myself free to do just about*
*everything that would earn me any money. And so, being repeat-*
*edly solicited by Fournier who was eager to arrange parties for me*
*at her establishment, I lent my talents to every project wherefrom*
*I was assured an honorable profit. I was no longer one of her crew,*
*I was a young lady kept by a farmer-general; would I have the*
*great kindness to give Madame Fournier an hour of my valuable*
*time and pass at her establishment on such and such a day, etc., etc.*
*You may fancy how well that paid. It was in the course of these*
*brief distractions that I encountered the new shit worshiper I'll dis-*
*cuss next.*

"Just one instant," put in the Bishop. "I did not want to interrupt you until you reached the end of a chapter; you seem to be at
one now. Would you therefore have the kindness to shed some
additional light upon two or three essential points in this latest

party? When you celebrated the orgies after your interview with Desprès, did the abbot, who until then had been caressing his bardash only, commit acts of infidelity? In a word, did he lay hands upon you? did the others desert their women for the boy?"

"Monseigneur," said Duclos, "the abbot never once left his little boy; he scarcely so much as glanced at us even though we were naked and all but on top of him. But he toyed with d'Aucourt's ass and Desprès' and also d'Erville's: he kissed them, sucked them, d'Aucourt and d'Erville shitted into his mouth and he swallowed the better part of each of those two turds. But he would not touch the women. The same was not true of the three other friends relative to his youthful bardash; they kissed him, licked his asshole, and Desprès went off alone with him for I have no idea what exercise."

"Excellent," said the Bishop. "You observe that you failed to mention everything, and that what you have just recounted forms still another passion, since it figures the taste of a man who has other men shit in his mouth, and quite mature men at that."

"That is true, Monseigneur," Duclos admitted, "I confess my error but am not sorry for it, because the soiree has drawn to a close and has indeed been overlong. The bell we are about to hear struck would have indicated that I did not have sufficient time to end the story I was preparing to begin, and with your gracious leave we will postpone it until tomorrow."

The bell did indeed ring and as no one had discharged during the sitting and as every prick was, however, mightily aloft, they only betook themselves to supper after promising to make good their loss at the orgies. But the impetuous Duc was never able to postpone important business and having ordered Sophie to present her buttocks, he had that lovely child shit, and he swallowed her turd for dessert. Durcet, the Bishop, and Curval, all similarly occupied, concluded the same operation, the first with Hyacinthe, the second with Céladon, the third with Adonis. The last named, having failed to give ample satisfaction, was inscribed in the punishment book, and Curval, swearing like a trooper, revenged himself upon Thérèse's ass, which exploded, at point-blank range, the most ponderous turd imaginable. The orgies were eminently libertine and Durcet, forsaking youthful turds, said that for the evening's games he would have none but what his three old friends could yield him. They humored him with passing fair performances, and the little libertine discharged like a stallion while devouring Curval's shit. Night came at last to restore some measure of calm to so much intemperance, and to restore as well our libertines' desires and faculties.

# THE THIRTEENTH DAY

*T*he Président, who that night lay with Adelaide, his daughter, having sported with her until he felt sleep about to claim him, had therewith relegated her to the pallet beside his bed in order that Fanchon might have her place, for he was ever eager to have the old duenna by his side when lust awoke him, which occurred almost every night; toward three in the morning, he opened his eyes with a start and fell to swearing and blaspheming like the true rascal he was. He would at such times be gripped by a lubric furor which now and again became dangerous. That is why he was so fond of having that trusty old Fanchon near him, for no one was so skillful at calming him, whether by offering herself or by immediately bringing him one of the objects lying in his bedchamber.

On that particular night, the Président, instantly recollecting some infamies he had perpetrated upon his daughter just before falling asleep, called for her at once with the intention of repeating them; but she was not there. Imagine the consternation and the commotion created by such an incident. Curval springs from bed in a towering rage, asks where his daughter is; candles are lit, everyone hunts about, the place is ransacked, nothing's to be found; the last place searched is the girls' apartments. Every bed is examined, and at last the interesting Adelaide is discovered seated in her nightgown near Sophie's cot. Those two charming girls, united by their similarly tender natures, their piety, virtuous sentiments, candor, and absolutely identical amenity, had been seized by the most beautiful affection for each other and they were exchanging comforting words, consoling one another for the dreadful fate that had

403

been reserved for them. No one had perceived their commerce until then, but what followed proved that this was not the first time they had got together, and it was discovered as well that the elder of the two was cultivating the other's finer sentiments, and had especially pleaded with her not to stray from her religion and her duties toward God, Who would one day comfort and console them for all their woes.

I leave it to the reader to picture Curval's fury and stormy reaction when he located the lovely missionary; he seized her by the hair and, overwhelming her with invectives, all very harsh, dragged her to his chamber, where he tied her to his bedpost and left her until the next morning to ponder over her indiscretion. All of the friends having rushed to the scene, it will also be readily imagined with what haste and decision Curval had the two delinquents' names written down in the register. The Duc argued passionately in favor of instantaneous correction, and what he proposed was not by any means mild; but the Bishop having countered with a very reasonable objection to what his brother was urged to do, Durcet was content simply to include them on the agenda. There was no way of attacking the duennas; they were all four bedded in Messieurs' chambers that night. This fact accounted for the imperfect administration of the household, and arrangements were made whereby, in future, there would always be at least one duenna in the girls' quarters and another in the boys'. Their lordships retired to bed again, and Curval, whom anger had rendered more than cruelly impudicious, did things to his daughter we cannot yet describe, but which, by precipitating his discharge, at least put him quietly to sleep.

All the hens in the chicken coop had been so terrified that, on the morrow, no misbehavior was discovered, and amongst the boys, only Narcisse, whom, the evening before, Curval had forbidden to wipe his ass, wishing to have it nicely beshitted at coffee, which this child was scheduled to serve, and who had unfortunately forgot his instructions, only Narcisse, I say, had cleaned his anus and he had done so with extreme care. It was in vain the little chap explained that his mistake could be repaired, since, said he, he wanted to shit there and then; he was told to keep what he had, and that he would be none the less inscribed in the fatal book; which inscription the redoubtable Durcet instantly performed before his eyes, thus to make him sense all the enormity of his fault, a veritable sin and possibly by itself capable of upsetting or, who knows? of preventing Monsieur le Président's discharge.

Constance, whom they did not hinder because of her state, Desgranges, and Bum-Cleaver were the only ones who were granted chapel permission; everyone else received the order not to draw the cork until the evening toasts.

The preceding night's events provided the dinner's conversation; they made game of the Président for permitting the bird to fly from its cage, etc.; some champagne restored his gay spirits, and the company sallied forth to coffee. Narcisse, Céladon, and Zelmire distributed it, so did Sophie, who was greatly ashamed of herself; she was asked how often the thing had happened, she replied that it had occurred only twice, and that Madame de Durcet gave her such good counsel that indeed she thought it most unjust to punish them both for it. The Président assured her that what she called good counsel was, in her situation, the very worst, that the devotion wherewith Madame de Durcet had been filling her head would serve no purpose save to get her punished every day, and that, in her present circumstances, she was to have no masters and no gods save his three confreres and himself, no religion save that of blindly serving and obeying them in everything. And, all the while he was delivering this sermon, he had her kneel between his legs and bade her suck his prick, which the poor little thing did all atremble. As always partisan to thigh-fuckery, the Duc, obliged as he was to abstain from the capital practice, impaled Zelmire in this style, meanwhile having the little girl shit in his cupped hand and gobbling it up as quickly as it was received, and all that while Durcet was inducing Céladon to discharge into his mouth, and the Bishop was industriously extracting a turd from Narcisse. A few minutes, no more, were set aside for the nap that they found such an aid to digestion; then, having taken up their posts in the auditorium, Duclos faced the gathering and began the day's narrative.

*The gallant octogenarian Fournier had in mind for me, Messieurs, was an official from the auditing bureau, short, pudgy, and with an extremely unpleasant face. He set a pot between us, we*

*squatted down back to back and shitted simultaneously; he seizes
up the pot, with his fingers stirs the two turds, mixes them, swallows the batter while I promote his discharge, an eruption which
takes place in my mouth. He barely even glanced at my behind.
Nor did he do any kissing, but his ecstasy was very sharp and compelling all the same: he pranced all about the room, swearing while
he gulped and ejaculated, and then took himself off, giving me four*
louis *for this strange ceremony.*

*However, my landowner became more fond of me with each
passing day, and more trusting too, and this trust, which I lost no
time in abusing, soon became the cause of our eternal separation.
. . . One day when he had left me alone in his library, I noticed
that, before going out for the day, he had filled his purse with
money taken from a deep drawer entirely filled with gold. "Ah,
what a capture!" I said to myself, and having from that very instant conceived the idea of making off with this sum, I set to watching for the means and opportunity whereby to appropriate it:
d'Aucourt never locked the drawer, but he carried with him the key
to his library, and having discovered that this door and lock were
both very frail, I fancied it would take little effort to break the
one and the other. Having adopted the plan, I concentrated upon
nothing but taking advantage of the first time d'Aucourt was absent the entire day; that used to be the case twice a week, when he
went off for private bacchanals in the company of Desprès and the
abbot; Madame Desgranges will perhaps describe what occurred
during these outings, they lie beyond my province. The favorable
moment was soon at hand; d'Aucourt's valets, as libertine as their
master, never failed to go with him to these parties, and so I found
myself almost alone in the house. Full of impatience to put my
project into execution, I go straightway to the door of the library,
break the thin panel with a blow of my fist, rush to the drawer, find
it unlocked as I knew it would be. I remove everything it contains;
my prize amounts to not less than three thousand* louis. *I fill my
pockets, rifle other drawers; a splendid jewel case catches my eye, I
pick it up, but what was I not to find in the other drawers of that
bountiful secretary! . . . Fortunate d'Aucourt! What great good
luck for you that your imprudence was not discovered by anyone
else but me; the secretary contained enough to have had him*

*broken on the wheel, Messieurs, that is all I can tell you. Quite apart from the transparent and expressive notes addressed to him by Desprès and the abbot pertaining to their secret commerce, there was every kind of furniture needed for the performing of those infamies. . . . But I halt myself here; the boundaries you have prescribed to my depositions prevent me from saying more; Desgranges will treat the whole matter. As for myself, the theft once effected, I left at once, shuddering to think of all the dangers I had perhaps been exposing myself to by frequenting the company of such scoundrels. I crossed over to London and, as my sojourn in that city, where for six months I dwelt in the most comfortable style, offers nothing that could be of any outstanding interest to your Lordships, you will permit me to pass quickly over this part of my story. I had maintained contact with no one in Paris but Fournier; however, she advised me of the hue and cry the landowner had raised over this paltry little robbery, and I finally resolved to put an end to this blathering: I took up pen and paper and very coolly informed him that she who had happened upon his money had also discovered other things, and that if he were determined to continue to search for the culprit, I would as bravely as possible endure my fate and very certainly depose, with the same judge who would question me upon what I had done with the contents of the small drawers, a detailed statement of what I had found in the larger ones. Our man fell as silent as a tomb; and as six months later their three-partied debauchery came broadly to light and as they themselves left France for security abroad, I returned to Paris and, must I avow my misbehavior? I returned, Messieurs, as poor as I had been before dispossessing d'Aucourt, and such were my straits I was obliged to put myself back in Madame Fournier's safekeeping. As I was no more than twenty-three at the time, I did not want for adventures; I am going to ignore those exterior to my domain and recount, with your Lordships' indulgent permission, only the ones wherein I know now that you take some interest.*

*A week after my return, a barrel brimming with shit was placed in the chamber appointed for pleasures. My Adonis arrives; he proved to be a saintly ecclesiastic, but one so habituated to those pleasures, so blasé, that he was no longer capable of being stirred*

*save by the excesses I shall describe. I was naked when he entered.
For a moment he regards my buttocks, then, after having fingered
them rather brutally, he tells me to undress him and help him get
into the barrel. I remove his garments, aid him to climb in, the old
pig slides down into his element; a hole has been specially bored
for the purpose and, fifteen seconds after having immersed himself,
his prick, almost stiff, pops through the aperture; he orders me to
frig it, covered as it is with filth and horrors. I do as I am told, he
ducks his head down into the shit, splashes in shit, swallows shit,
shouts, discharges, and, clambering out, trots off to immerse himself in a bath, where I leave him in the hands of two house servants
who spend a quarter of an hour scrubbing him clean.*

*Another one appeared shortly afterward. I had shitted and
pissed into a pot a week before and had carefully preserved the mixture; this period was necessary before matters reached the stage
our latest libertine desired. He was a man of thirty-five, and my
guess was that he was connected with finance. Upon entering he
asked where the pot was; I handed it to him, he sniffed it experi-
mentally.*

*"You're perfectly certain that was done a week ago?" he
asked.*

*"Monsieur," I replied, "I am prepared to answer for its age;
you will notice the first signs of mildew there, some moldiness near
the edge."*

*"Why, indeed, it looks as if it will do very nicely," he agreed,
"it's the mold I adore, you know. Never too moldy to suit me.
Show me, if you please," he continued, "the pretty ass that shitted
what we have here."*

*I presented it.*

*"That's it," said he, "put it right there opposite me so that I
can see it while eating its creation."*

*We arrange ourselves, he samples a little tidbit, is thrilled by
the taste, plunges directly ahead, and in no time has devoured that
exquisite lunch, only interrupting his chewing to scan my bum; but
there was no other episode, he did not even draw his prick from his
breeches.*

*A month passed, another unusual fellow came to our door,
and this one would deal with none but Fournier herself. What an*

*object he selected, Great God! she had seen sixty-eight summers, an erysipelas was eating every inch of her hide, and the eight rotten teeth decorating her mouth communicated so fetid an odor it was all but impossible to speak with her at a distance of under five yards; but it was these shortcomings and nothing else that enchanted the lover with whom she was to take a tumble. Most eager to observe the contest, I run to the spy hole: the Adonis was an elderly doctor, but younger nevertheless than she. He takes her in his arms, kisses her mouth for a good fifteen minutes, then, having her present an ancient, wrinkled ass such as you see on a very old cow, he kisses and sucks it avidly. A syringe is brought in, three half bottles of liqueur too; Aesculapius' worshiper loads his syringe and pumps the healing drink into the entrails of his Iris; she receives the potion, holds it, the doctor does not cease kissing her, he licks every square inch of her body.*

*"Ah, my friend," the old lady cries at last, "I can contain myself no longer, not another second, prepare yourself, dear friend, I'm going to have to give it back."*

*Salerno's scholar kneels, from his fly pulls forth a dark, wrinkled stub of a device, which he pounds and coaxes with emphasis, Fournier settles her great ugly ass upon his mouth, pushes, the doctor imbibes, a turd or two doubtless emerge with the liquid, he gasps but it all goes down, the libertine discharges and falls backward, dead drunk. 'Twas thus this debauchee satisfied two passions at a single stroke: his wine bibbery and his lewdness.*

"One moment," said Durcet. "Those excesses always give me an erection. Desgranges," he pursued, "I fancy you possess an ass closely resembling the one Duclos has just figured; come apply it to my face."

The old procuress obeyed.

"Let it go, release it," Durcet said in a muffled voice, for he was speaking from between that pair of awe-inspiring buttocks. "Give it to me, buggress, never mind if it's not liquid, I am perfectly able to chew, and I always swallow whatever comes my way."

And the operation was concluded while the Bishop was performing a similar one with Antinoüs, Curval with Fanchon, and the Duc with Louison. But our four athletes, fully acquainted with all these extravagances and totally at their ease while committing them, performed with absolute effortlessness and even nonchalance: the four deposits were consumed without a single drop of fuck being shed in any quarter.

"Well, on with your story, Duclos, finish up for the day," the Duc said; "if we are no more tranquil than before, we are at least less impatient and better able to pay attention."

"Alas, Messieurs," our heroine answered, "I fear that the anecdote I have still to relate this evening is far too simple, too mild for the state you are in. 'Tis a pity, but no matter; its turn has come, it must keep its place." And she continued as follows:

*The hero of the adventure was an old brigadier in the King's army; he had to be stripped to the skin, then swaddled like an infant; when he was thus prepared, I had to shit while he looked on, bring him the plate and, with the tips of my fingers, feed him my turd as if it were pap. Everything is done according to prescription, our libertine swallows it all and discharges in his swaddling clothes, the while simulating a baby's cry.*

"Let us then have recourse to children," said the Duc, "since you leave us with a children's story; Fanny, my dear," he continued, "come to your old friend and shit in his mouth, and remember to suck his prick while you are about it, for it seems to have to discharge again."

"Let thy will be done," murmured the Bishop. "Come hither, Rosette; you have heard the orders given to Fanny. Then do as she."

"May the same orders apply to you," Durcet said to Hébé, who responded to his call.

"When in Rome," said the wise Curval, "do as the Romans do, my little one. Augustine, emulate your companions, cause simultaneously to flow both my fuck into your mouth and your shit into mine."

And all these things were done; upon this occasion, all those worthies came; from everywhere the sounds of farting and falling shit were to be heard, discharges too, and, much lust sated, they betook themselves to the table, their appetite was passing strong. But at the orgies, refinements were employed, the little ones were sent off to bed. Those delicious hours were spent with none but the elite fuckers, the four ladies-in-waiting, the four storytellers. Messieurs became completely drunk and performed horrors of such absolute filthiness that I should not be able to describe them without doing an injustice to the less libertine tableaux I have yet to offer my readers. Curval and Durcet were carried away unconscious, but the Duc and the Bishop, quite as cool as if nothing had happened, were perfectly able to pass the rest of the night indulging in their ordinary riot.

# THE FOURTEENTH DAY

*I*t was discovered upon that day that the weather had lent its approval to our libertines' infamous enterprises, and had removed them to an even greater distance from the probability they would be spied upon by mortal eyes; an immense blanket of snow had fallen, it filled the surrounding vale, seeming to forbid even to wild beasts access to our scoundrels' retreat; of all human beings, there was not one that existed who could dare hope to reach where they lay fast. Ah, it is not readily to be imagined how much voluptuousness, lust, fierce joy are flattered by those sureties, or what is meant when one is able to say to oneself: "I am alone here, I am at the world's end, withheld from every gaze, here no one can reach me, there is no creature that can come nigh where I am; no limits, hence, no barriers; I am free." Whereupon, thus situate, desires spring forth with an impetuosity which knows no bounds, stops at nothing, and the impunity that electrifies them most deliciously increases all their drunkenness. There, nothing exists save God and one's conscience; well, what weight may the former exert, of what account may God be in the eyes of an atheist in heart and brain? and what sway is the conscience to enjoy, what influence upon him who is so accustomed to vanquishing remorse, routing guilt, that so to do becomes for him a game, nay, a little pleasure? Luckless flock delivered to the murderous tooth of such villains; how would you have trembled had you not still been in ignorance of what lay in store for you!

That day was a festival, the second week had ended, the second marriage was to be celebrated; Messieurs were in a glad humor and

412

thought not but to frolic on that holiday. The marriage to take place was that of Narcisse and Hébé, but, cruel fate! it was also decreed that the bride and groom were both doomed to be punished that same evening; and thus, from the warm embrace of hymeneal pleasures they were to move directly to the more bitter lessons taught in this school, how unkind! Little Narcisse, who was not a dull fellow, remarked this irony, but Messieurs none the less proceeded to the usual ceremonies. The Bishop officiated, the couple was conjoined in very holy matrimony, and they were permitted to do to each other, before the public's eyes, all they wanted to do; but, who would have believed it? the order was of a too liberal scope, or too well understood, and the little husband, who had an aptitude for learning, perfectly delighted with the prospect before him but unable to introduce himself into his pretty wife, was however about to deflower her with his fingers, and would have, had he been given his way. Firm hands intervened just in time, and the Duc, making off with Hébé, thigh-fucked her on the spot, while the Bishop did likewise with Narcisse.

Dinner came next, the newly-wedded couple were admitted to the feast, and as they had been given and commanded prodigiously to eat, both upon leaving the table shitted handsomely, one for Durcet's benefit, the other for Curval's, who, after having swallowed those little products of childhood, smacked their lips and declared 'twas delicious.

Coffee was served by Augustine, Fanny, Céladon, and Zéphyr. The Duc bade Augustine frig Zéphyr, and the latter shit in the nobleman's mouth at the same time he discharged; the operation was a stunning success, so much so that the Bishop wanted to duplicate it with Céladon; Fanny attended to the frigging, and the little fellow received orders to shit in Monseigneur's mouth the moment he felt his fuck flow. But the young operatives succeeded less brilliantly than had their companions: Céladon was never able to coordinate his shitting with his discharge; however, as this exercise was merely a test of skill, and as the regulations made no mention of the subjects being obliged to excel in it, no punishment was inflicted upon him.

Durcet gleaned shit from Augustine, and the Bishop, firmly erect, had Fanny suck him while she shat in his mouth; he he dis-

charged, and as his crisis was violent, he brutalized Fanny somewhat but, unhappily, failed to find adequate grounds for having
her punished, great as was his apparent wish to arrange something
for her. A greater tease than the Bishop never lived; no sooner
would he finish discharging than he would wish for nothing better
than to see his pleasure-object gone to the devil; everyone was
familiar with his character, and the little girls, the wives, and the
little boys dreaded nothing as much as helping him to be rid of his
fuck.

The midday nap over, they passed into the auditorium, the
company distributed itself, and Duclos resumed the thread of her
narrative:

*I sometimes used to go into town for parties,* said she, *and as
they were usually more lucrative, Fournier did her best to procure
as many of that kind as she could.*

*She once sent me to the home of an elderly Knight of Malta
who opened a kind of wardrobe filled with cubbyholes, each of
which housed a porcelain chamber pot containing a turd; the old
rake had made arrangements with a sister of his, abbess of one of
the most considerable convents in Paris; that obliging girl, upon his
request, every morning sent him a crate of fresh shit produced by
her prettiest little pensionnaires. He filed away each performance
according to a classifying system, and when I arrived he bade me
take down such and such a number, and it proved to be the most
venerable. I presented the pot to him.*

*"Oh yes," said he, "that belongs to a girl of sixteen, lovely as
the day. Frig me while I eat her gift."*

*The entire ceremony consisted in twiddling his device and in
dressing my bum before his eyes while he ate, then in replenishing
the pot he had just emptied. He watched me do it, wiped my asshole clean with his tongue, and discharged while sucking my anus.
After that, the wardrobe is closed and locked, I receive my pay,
and our man, whom I visited at an early hour in the morning, curls
up and goes blissfully back to sleep.*

*Another, more extraordinary in my opinion, was an elderly
monk. He enters, demands eight or ten turds from the first person
he sees, girl or boy, it's all the same to him. He mixes them into*

*a paste which he next kneads like dough, bites into the lump and, eating at least half of it, discharges into my mouth.*

*A third, and of all the men I have met in my life he aroused the greatest disgust in me, a third, I say, ordered me to open my mouth wide. I was naked, lying upon a mattress on the floor, and he was astride me; he popped his stool into my mouth and the villain then lay down beside me, ate what I spat out, and sprayed his fuck over my teats.*

"Well, well, that's a pleasant one!" cried Curval; "by Jesus, I do indeed believe I want to shit, I really must try to. Whom shall I take, Monsieur le Duc?"

"Who?" said Blangis. "By my faith, I recommend Julie, my daughter; she is right there under your hand. You are fond of her mouth, put it to use."

"Thank you for the advice," said Julie sullenly. "What have I done to have you say such things?"

"Why, since the idea upsets her," said the Duc, "and since she's a good girl, take Mademoiselle Sophie: she's healthy, pretty, and she's only fourteen, you know."

"Very well, it's to be Sophie, that's decided," said Curval, whose turbulent prick was beginning to gesticulate.

Fanchon approaches the victim, the poor little wretch's tears start to fall at once. Curval laughs lightly, brings up his great, ugly, and dirty behind, pushes it down upon that charming visage, and gives us the image of a toad about to insult a rose. He is frigged, the bomb bursts, Sophie loses not so much as a crumb, and the crapulous magistrate's tongue and lips reclaim what he has launched; he swallows it all in just four mouthfuls while his prick is being rubbed upon the belly of the poor little creature who, the operation once over, vomits her very guts out, and directly upon the nose of Durcet who has come up posthaste to miss nothing, and who is frigging himself while being covered.

"Off you go, Duclos!" said Curval. "On with your tales, and rejoice at the effect of your discourses; do they not carry the day?"

And therewith Duclos resumed, warmed to the very cockles of her heart by the staggering success which had greeted her anecdote.

*The man with whom I held correspondence directly after the one whose example has just seduced you,* said Duclos, *insisted that the woman he was presented have indigestion; in consequence, Fournier, who had given me no foreknowledge of the thing, had me, during dinner, swallow a certain laxative drug which softened what my bowels contained, indeed rendered it fluid, as if my stool had become transformed into the effect of an enema. Our man arrives and after several preliminary kisses bestowed upon the object of his whole veneration, which, by now, was becoming painfully inflated by gases, I beseech him to start without further delay; the injection is ready to escape, I grasp his prick, he pants, swallows everything, asks for still more; I furnish him with a second deluge, it is soon followed by a third, and the libertine's anchovy finally spits upon my fingers the unequivocal evidence of the sensation he has received.*

*The next day I treated with a personage whose baroque mania will perhaps find some worshipers amongst yourselves, Messieurs. First of all, he was installed in the room next to the one in which we ordinarily operated and in whose wall was that hole so conveniently placed for observations. He was left alone to arrange himself; a second actor awaited me in the adjoining chamber: he was a cab driver we had picked up at random and who was fully apprised of the situation; as I was too, our cast knew the various roles to perfection. It was a question of having the Phaëthon shit squarely opposite the hole, so that the libertine hidden on the other side of the partition would miss nothing involved in the spectacle. I catch the turd upon a plate, see to it that it lands intact, spread the driver's buttocks, press around his anus, I neglect nothing that can make shitting comfortable; as soon as my man has done all he has to do, I snatch up his prick and get him to discharge over the shit, and all that well within sight of our observer; finally, the package ready, I dash into the other room.*

*"Here you are, take it quickly, Monsieur,"* I exclaim, *"it's nice and warm."*

*There is no necessity to repeat the invitation; he grasps the dish, offers me his prick, which I frig, and the rascal bolts everything I tender him while he exhales his fuck in tune with my diligent hand's elastic movements.*

"And what was the driver's age?" Curval asked.

"About thirty," Duclos answered.

"Why, that's nothing at all," said Curval. "Durcet there will tell you whenever you like that we once knew an individual who did the same thing, and with positively the same attendant circumstances, but with a man of sixty or seventy who had to be found in the lowest sewer of misery and filth."

"And, you know," said Durcet, "it's only pretty that way." The financier's little engine had been gradually lifting its head ever since Sophie's aspersion. "I shall at any given time be happy to do it with the eldest of veterans."

"You're stiff, Durcet," said the Duc, "don't deny it, for I know you: whenever you start that nasty boasting it's because your fuck is coming to a boil. So hold, good friend; though not so seasoned in years as you might like, still, to appease your intemperance, I offer you all I have in my entrails, and I believe you will find it enough to make a meal upon."

"Ah, by God's belly!" cried Durcet, "you always serve your guests well, my dear Duc."

The Duc entering Durcet's alcove, the latter kneels down before the buttocks which are to fill him to overflowing with good cheer; the Duc grunts once, twice, a prodigy tumbles out, the banker swallows and, transported by this crapulous excess, discharges while swearing he has never tasted so much pleasure.

"Duclos," said the Duc, "come do for me what I have done for our good friend."

"My Lord," our storyteller replied, "you will recall that I did it this morning, and that you swallowed it."

"Why, yes, 'tis true," the Duc admitted. "Very well then, hither, Martaine, I must have recourse to you, for I want none of those children's asses; I feel my fuck readying to come, but, you know, it comes reluctantly, and so we need something out of the ordinary."

But Martaine's case was that of Duclos, Curval had gobbled her shit that morning.

"What! by fuck," cried the Duc, "am I then to fail to find a turd this evening?"

Whereupon Thérèse advanced and offered the dirtiest, the

broadest, and the most stinking possible of asses you, dear reader, may hope to behold.

"Well, that will do, that will do perfectly," said the Duc, assuming the posture, "and if in my present disorder this infamous ass I've got here does not produce its effect, I don't know what I'll have to resort to."

Dramatic moment: Thérèse pushes; the Duc receives! and the incense was quite as dreadful as the temple whence it emerged, but when one is as stiff as the Duc was stiff, 'tis never excess of filth one complains of. Drunk with joy, the scoundrel swallowed every ounce, and directly into Duclos' face, for she was frigging him, shot the most indubitable proof of his male vigor.

Then to table; the ensuing orgies were devoted to the distribution of justice; that week there were seven delinquents: Zelmire, Colombe, Hébé, Adonis, Adelaide, Sophie, and Narcisse; the gentle Adelaide was granted no quarter. Zelmire and Sophie also bore away a few marks of the treatment they had undergone and, without giving further particulars, since circumstances do not permit us to give them yet, everyone retired to bed, and in Morpheus' arms recovered the strength requisite to make further sacrifices to Venus.

# THE FIFTEENTH DAY

Rarely would the day following correction offer fresh signs of misbehavior. There were none upon this one, but as strict as ever in the article of permission to shit in the morning, Messieurs granted this favor to no one but Hercule, Michette, Sophie, and Desgranges, and Curval came perilously near to discharging while watching the storyteller at work. Not overmuch was accomplished at coffee, the friends were content to fondle buttocks and to suck one or two assholes; the hour sounded, everyone went promptly to establish himself in the amphitheater. Duclos faced her audience once again and addressed the company in this wise:

*There had lately come to Fournier's a little girl of twelve or thirteen, the age preferred by that singular gentleman I mentioned to you; but I truly doubt whether in a very long time he had de-bauched anything so cunning, so innocent, or so pretty. She had fair hair, was tall for her years and fit to be painted, her physi-ognomy was tender and voluptuous, her eyes the loveliest one could hope to see, and in all her charming person there was something sweet and intriguing which turned her into a very enchantress. But what was the degradation to which such a host of attractions was about to be subjected! and how shameful was the debut being prepared for them! She was the daughter of a tradesman in lingerie, purveyor to the Palace and a man of comfortable means, and his daughter surely had been destined for a happier fate than this of playing the whore; but the more the man of whom it is a question was able, by means of his perfidious seductions, to beguile his victims to their ruin, and the more thorough the depravation into which he guided them, the greater his pleasure, the fiercer his ecstasy. Little Lucile, directly after her arrival, was scheduled to satisfy the disgusting and unclean caprices of a man who, not merely content to have the most crapulous tastes, wished, still better, to inflict them upon a maid.*

*He arrives at the house: he proves to be an old notary stuffed with gold and who, together with his wealth, has all the brutality that avarice and luxury excite when combined in a seasoned spirit. The child is exhibited to him; pretty as she may be, his first reaction is disdain; he grumbles, he grits his teeth, mutters and swears, and says that it damned well seems as if one can no longer find a pretty girl in Paris; he demands, at last, whether there is proof positive she is a virgin, he is assured that, yes, the article is mint, Fournier offers to show it to him.*

*"What? look at a cunt, I? Madame Fournier! I, look at a cunt! I certainly hope you propose the thing in jest; have you noticed me spending much time considering those objects since I have been coming to you? I use them, to be sure, but in a manner which, I believe, attests no great fondness for them."*

*"Very well, Monsieur," Fournier said, "you will have to take the house's word for it: I declare that she is as much a maid as a child born five minutes ago."*

*They go upstairs together and, as you may well conceive, curious about the forthcoming tête-à-tête, I go and establish myself at the hole. Poor little Lucile was overcome by a shame only to be described by superlative expressions, hence not to be described at all, for those expressions are needed to represent the impudence, the brutality, and the ill-humor of her sixty-year-old lover.*

*"Well, what the devil are you doing there, are you a stone?" says he in a harsh voice. "Do I have to tell you to get your skirts up? I should have been looking at your ass two hours ago. . . . Don't stand there like an idiot, move."*

*"But, Monsieur, what am I to do?"*

*"Why, Jesus Christ, are such questions still asked? What are you to do? Pick up your skirts and show me that damned ass I'm paying to see."*

*Lucile obeys, trembling like a leaf, and discloses a little white ass just as darling and sweet as would be that of Venus herself.*

*"Hum . . . looks all right," mutters the brute, "bring it nearer. . . ."*

*Then, getting a firm grip upon the two buttocks and separating them forcefully:*

*"You're damned certain no one's ever done anything to you here?"*

*"Oh, Monsieur, no one has ever touched me. . . ."*

*"Very well. Now fart."*

*"But, Monsieur, I can't."*

*"Well, try, for Christ's sake, make yourself fart."*

*She struggles, frowns, squints, a little breath of aromatic wind does escape and produces a little echo upon entering the infected mouth of the old libertine, who seems delighted.*

*"Do you want to shit?" he asks.*

*"No, Monsieur."*

*"Well, I do, I've something copious to get rid of, if you're interested in the pertinent facts; so prepare yourself to satisfy this particular need of mine . . . take off your skirts."*

*They are removed.*

*"Lie down upon that sofa. Raise your thighs."*

*Lucile settles herself, the old notary arranges and poses her so that her wide-flung legs display her cunt to the fullest advantage, in which open and prominent position it may be readily employed as a chamber pot. So to use it was his heavenly intention; in order that the container respond more perfectly to what is to be demanded of it, he begins by widening it as much as possible, devoting both hands and all his strength to the task. He takes his place, pushes, a turd lands in the sanctuary Cupid himself would not have disdained having for a temple. He turns around, eyes his work, and with his fingers presses and thrusts the filthy excrement into the vagina and largely out of sight; he establishes himself astride Lucile once again, and ejects a second, then a third stool, and each is succeeded by the same ceremony of burial. Finally, having deposited his last turd, he inserts and tamps it down with such brutal zeal that the little one utters a cry, and by means of this disagreeable operation perhaps loses the precious flower, Nature's ornament, offered the child as a gift to Hymen. This was the moment at which our libertine's pleasure attained its crisis: to have filled the young and pretty cunt to overflowing with shit, to crowd it with shit and stuff it with yet more, that was his supreme delight: all the while in action, he opens his fly and draws out a species of prick, very flaccid it is, and he shakes it, and as he toils away in his disgusting manner, he manages to spatter upon the floor a few drops of thin, discolored sperm, whose loss may be credited solely to the infamies he has been performing. Having concluded his business, he takes himself off, Lucile washes, and that is that.*

*Some time later, I found myself with another individual whose mania struck me as no less unpleasant: he was an elderly magistrate at the high court. One was obliged not only to watch him shit, no, there was more to it than that: I had to help him, with my fingers, facilitate the matter's emergence by pressing, opening, agitating, compressing his anus, and when once he had been freed of his burden, I had with utmost care to clean the soiled area with my tongue.*

"Well, by God! there's a bit of taxing drudgery, I own," said the Bishop. "The four ladies you see here, and they are our wives, or our daughters, or our nieces, these ladies nevertheless have to perform that same chore every day, you know. And what the devil, I ask you, what the devil is a woman's tongue good for if not to wipe assholes? I frankly cannot think of any other use to put it to. Constance," the Bishop pursued, turning to the Duc's lovely wife, who happened to be upon his couch, "give Duclos a little demonstration of your proficiency in the thing; here you are, I'll offer you a very untidy ass, it hasn't been cleaned since this morning, I've been keeping it this way for you. Off you go, display your abilities."

And the poor creature, only too well accustomed to these horrors, executed them as a dutiful, a thoughtful wife should; ah, great God! what will not dread and thralldom produce!

"Oh, by Jesus," said Curval, presenting his ugly, beslimed asshole to the charming Aline, "she'll not be the only one to give examples of excellence. Get to work, little whore," said he to that beautiful and virtuous girl, "outdo your companion."

And the thing was accomplished.

"Why, Duclos," said the Bishop, "I think we might proceed now; we only wished to point out that your man's request had nothing of the unusual about it, and that a woman's tongue is fit for nothing if not to wipe an ass."

The amiable Duclos fell to laughing and continued:

*You will permit me, Messieurs,* said she, *to interrupt the catalogue of passions for an instant that I may apprise you of an event which has no bearing upon them; it has only to do with me, but as you have ordered me to recount the interesting episodes in my life, even when they are not related to the anthology of tastes we are compiling, I think that the following ought not be passed by in silence.*

*I had been a great while at Madame Fournier's, had long since become the first ranked according to seniority, and in her entire entourage was the girl in whom she had the greatest confidence. It was I who most often arranged the parties and received the funds. Fournier had gradually taken the place of the mother I had lost, she had aided me in time of trouble, watched over my welfare, had written faithfully to me when I had been abroad in England, upon my return had as a friend opened her house to me when, in difficult circumstances, I desired to take asylum with her once again. Twenty times over she had lent me money, and often had never asked for it back. The opportunity arrived to show my gratitude and to respond to her limitless faith in me, and you shall judge, Messieurs, with what eagerness my soul opened itself to virtue's entrance and what an easy access it had thereinto: Fournier fell ill, and her first thought was to call me to her bedside.*

*"Duclos, my child, I love you," said she, "well you know it, and I am going to prove it by the absolute trust I am about to place in you. Despite your mind, which is not a good one, I believe you incapable of wronging a friend; I am very ill, I am old, I do not know what is to become of me. But I may die soon; I have relatives who will of course be my heirs. I can at least leave them something, and want to: I have a hundred thousand francs in gold in this little coffer; take it, my child," said she, "here, I give it to you, but upon*

*condition you dispose of this money in keeping with my instructions."*

*"Oh, my dear mother," said I, stretching forth my arms to her, "I beseech you, these precautions distress me; they shall surely prove needless, but if unhappily they were to prove necessary, I take oath and swear exactly to carry out your intentions."*

*"I believe you, my child," said she, "and that is why my eyes have settled upon you; that little coffer, then, contains one hundred thousand francs in gold; I have scruples, a few scruples, my dear friend, I feel remorseful for the life I have led, the quantity of girls I have cast into crime and snatched away from God. And so I wish to do two things by means of which it is my hope the divinity will be led to deal less severely with me: I think of charity now, and of prayer. You shall take fifteen thousand francs of this money, and you shall give it to the Capuchins on the rue Saint-Honoré, so that those good fathers will say a perpetual mass for the salvation of my soul; another sum, also of fifteen thousand francs, shall be set aside, and when I have closed my eyes, you shall surrender it to the curé of the parish and beg him to distribute it amongst the poor dwelling in this quarter of the city. Charity is a very excellent thing, my child; nothing better repairs in the eyes of God the sins we have committed in this world. The poor are His children, and beloved of Him is he who gives them succor and comfort; never is God more to be pleased than by alms distributed to the needy. There lies the true way of gaining Heaven, my child! As for the remainder, immediately I am dead you shall take sixty thousand francs to one Petignon, a shoemaker's apprentice in the rue du Bouloir: this poor lad is my son, he knows nothing of his origins: he is the bastard issue of adultery. Upon dying, I want the unhappy orphan to benefit from those marks of tenderness I have never shown him while alive. Ten thousand francs are left; I beg you to keep them, my dear Duclos, keep them as a feeble token of my fondness for you, may they be some kind of recompense for the trouble you shall have to take in seeing to the distribution of the rest of my fortune. And may this little sum aid you to resolve to abandon the dreadful trade we follow, a calling wherein there is no salvation, nor any hope. For one is not a whore forever."*

*Innerly delighted to be entrusted with such a handsome sum, and thoroughly determined, for fear of becoming confused by Fournier's intricate instructions upon sharing it, to keep her fortune intact and for myself alone, I produced a flood of very artificial tears and cast myself into the old matron's arms, reiterated many oaths of fidelity, and turned all my thoughts thenceforth to devising means to prevent the cruel disappointments certain to occur were a return to sound health to bring about a change in her resolutions. The means presented itself the very next day: the doctor prescribed an emetic, and as I was in charge of nursing her, it was to me he handed the medicine, drawing my attention to the fact the package contained two doses, and warning me to be sure to administer only one at a time because, were both given her, death would be the result; were the first to have no effect, or an insufficient one, the second could be employed later, if need be. I promised the doctor to take the greatest possible care, and immediately he had turned his back, banishing from my heart all those futile sentiments which would have stopped a timorous spirit, putting to rout all remorse and all frailty, and thinking exclusively of my gold, of the sweet charm of making it mine, and of the delicious titillation one experiences every time one concerts an evil deed, the certain prognostic of the pleasure it will give, dwelling, I say, upon all that and upon nothing else, I straightway dropped both doses into a glass of water and offered the brew to my dear friend's lips; she swallowed it down without a moment's delay and thereby, just as rapidly, found the death I had sought to procure her.*

*I cannot describe to you what feelings possessed me when I saw my scheme had succeeded; each of the retchings wherewith she exhaled her life produced a truly delicious sensation throughout my entire being; thrilled, I listened to her, I watched her, I was perfectly intoxicated with joy. She stretched her arms toward me, addressed me a last farewell, I was overwhelmed with pleasurable sensations, I was already forming a thousand plans for spending the gold. I had not long to wait; Fournier expired that same afternoon; the prize belonged to me.*

"Duclos," said the Duc, "be truthful: did you frig yourself? did crime's piercingly voluptuous sensation attain your organs of pleasure?"

"Yes, my Lord, I confess it did; thanks to my prank I discharged five times before nightfall."

"It is then true," the Duc intoned in a loud and authoritative voice, "it is then true that crime has of itself such a compelling attractiveness that, unattended by any accessory activity, it may be itself suffice to inflame every passion and to hurl one into the same delirium occasioned by lubricious acts. Well, what say you?"

"Why, my Lord," Duclos answered, "I say I had my employer honorably buried, appropriated the bastard Petignon's inheritance, wasted not a penny on perpetual masses, nor did I bother to make a single charitable distribution, for, as a matter of fact, I have always beheld charity with the most authentic horror, regardless of the speeches, such as Fournier's, that I have heard pronounced in its favor. I maintain that there must be poor in this world, that Nature wishes that such there be, that she requires it, and that it is to fly in the face of her decrees to pretend to restore equilibrium, if it is disorder she wants."

"What's this!" said Durcet. "Do you then have principles, Duclos? I am very pleased to observe this in you; for, as you appear to realize, any relief given to misfortune, any gesture that lightens the load of the distressed, is a real crime against the natural order. The inequality she has created in our persons proves that this discordance pleases Nature, since 'twas she established it, and since she wishes that it exist in fortunes as well as in bodies. And as the weak may always redress matters by means of theft, the strong are equally allowed to restore inequality, or protect it, by refusing to give aid to the wretched. The universe would cease on the spot to subsist were there to be an exact similarity amongst all beings; 'tis of this disparity there is born the order which preserves, contains, directs everything. One must therefore take great care not to disturb it; moreover, in believing it is a good thing I do for this miserable class of men, I do much ill to another, for indigence is the nursery to which the wealthy and powerful repair in quest of the objects their lust or cruelty needs; I deprive the rich man of that branch of pleasure when, by raising up the downtrodden, I inhibit this class from yielding to him. And thus my charities have done nothing but put one part of humankind very modestly in my debt and done prodigious harm to the other. Hence, I regard charity not only as something evil in itself, but, what is more, I consider it a crime against Nature who, having first made differences apparent to our eyes, has certainly never intended ideas of eliminating them to occupy our heads. And so, far from giving alms to the poor, consoling the widow, succoring the orphan, if it is according to Nature's true intentions I wish to act, not only do I leave these wretches in the state Nature put them into, but I even lend Nature a strong right arm and aid her by prolonging this state and vigorously opposing any efforts they make to change it, and to this end I believe any means may be allowed."

"What!" cried the Duc, "even stealing from and ruining them?"

"Oh my, yes," the financier replied, "even augmenting their number, since this class serves another, and since, by increasing the size of the one, though I may do it a modicum of harm, I shall perform a great service for the other."

"That, my friends, is a very harsh system indeed," said Curval. "Haven't you heard tell of the sweet pleasures of doing good unto others?"

"Abusive pleasures!" Durcet answered at once. "That delight you allude to is nothing like the one I recommend; the first is illusory, a fiction; the second is authentic, real; the first is founded upon vile prejudices, the second upon reason; the first, through the agency of pride, the most false of all our sensations, may provide the heart with a brief instant's titillation; the other is a veritable mental pleasure-taking, and it inflames every other passion by the very fact it runs counter to common opinions. In a word, one of them gets this prick of mine stiff," Durcet concluded, "and I feel practically nothing from the other."

"But must the one criterion for judging everything be our feelings?" asked the Bishop.

"The only one, my friend," said Durcet; "our senses, nothing else, must guide all our actions in life, because only their voice is truly imperious."

"But God knows how many thousand crimes may be the result of such a doctrine," the Bishop observed.

"God knows, yes, and do you suppose that matters?" Durcet demanded; "for it is enjoyable, isn't it? Crime is a natural mode, a manner whereby Nature stirs man, makes him to move. Why would you not have me let myself be moved by Nature in this direction as well as in the direction of virtue? Nature needs virtuous acts, and vicious ones too; I serve Nature as well by performing the one as when I commit the other. But we have entered into a discussion which could lead us far; suppertime is approaching, and Duclos has still ground to cover before completing her task. Go on, charming girl, pursue your way, and believe me when I say you have just acknowledged an act and a doctrine which make you deserving of our eternal esteem and of that of every philosopher."

*My first idea when once my good patron had been inhumed was to assume the direction of her house and to maintain it on the same footing she had found so profitable. I announced this project to my colleagues, and they all, Eugénie above the rest, for she was my best beloved, they all, I say, promised to regard me as their new mother. I was not too young to pretend to the title, being then nearly thirty and possessed of all the intelligence and good sense one must have to govern a convent. And so it is, Messieurs, that I shall conclude the story of my adventures not as a public whore, but as an abbess, pretty enough and still youthful enough sometimes, indeed often, to treat directly with our clients; and treat with them I did: I shall in the sequel take care to notify you each time I took personal charge of the problem at hand. All Fournier's customers remained to me, I knew the secret of acquiring additional ones: my apartments were kept very neat and clean, and an excessive submissiveness inculcated in my girls, whom I selected with discrimination, hugely flattered my libertines' caprices.*

*The first purchaser to arrive was an old treasurer of the Exchequer, a former friend of the departed Fournier; I gave him little Lucile, over whom he waxed very enthusiastic. His habitual mania, quite as filthy as disagreeable for his partner, consisted in shitting upon his Dulcinea's face, of smearing his excrement over all her features, and then of kissing her in this state, and of sucking her. Out of friendship for me, Lucile allowed the old satyr to have his way very completely with her, and he discharged upon her belly as he lay kissing and licking his disgusting performance.*

*Not long afterward, we had another; Eugénie was also as-*

signed to cope with him. He had a barrel full of shit trundled in, plunged the naked girl into it, and licked every inch of her body, swallowing what he removed, and not finishing until he had rendered her as clean as she had been prior to her immersion. That one was a celebrated lawyer, a rich man and a very well-known one; he possessed, for the enjoyment of women, none but the most modest qualities, which lack he remedied by this species of libertinage he had lovingly cultivated all his life.

The Marquis de R***, one of Fournier's oldest clients, came shortly after her death to express his sorrow upon learning that she was no more; he also assured me he would patronize the house just as faithfully as before and, to convince me of his devotion, wanted to see Eugénie that same evening. This old rake's passion consisted in first bestowing prodigious kisses upon the girl's mouth; he swallowed all the saliva it were possible to drain from her, then kissed her buttocks for a quarter of an hour, called for farts, and finally demanded the major thing. After it had been done, he kept the turd in his mouth and, making the girl bend down over him, he had her embrace him with one hand and frig him with the other; and while he was tasting the pleasure of this masturbation and tickling her beshitted asshole, the girl had to eat the turd she had deposited in his mouth. Although he was prepared to pay very well, he used to find exceedingly few girls who were willing to cooperate in this little abomination, and that is why the Marquis would come regularly to me: he was as eager to remain one of my clients as I was to have him make frequent visits to my establishment. . . .

At this point the Duc, very hot indeed, said that as the supper hour was hard upon them, he would like, before going to table, to execute the last-cited fantasy. And this is how he went about it: he had Sophie come to him, received her turd in his mouth, then obliged Zélamir to run up and eat Sophie's creation. This idiosyncrasy might perhaps have been a delight for anyone else but a child like Zélamir; as yet insufficiently mature, hence unable to appreciate the delicious, he manifested disgust only, and seemed about to misbehave. But the Duc threatened him with everything his anger might produce were the boy to hesitate another instant; the boy obeyed. The stunt struck the others as so engaging that each of them imitated it, more or less, for Durcet held that favors had to be parceled out fairly; was it just, he asked, for the little boys to eat the girls' shit while the girls went hungry? no, surely not, and consequently he had Zéphyr shit in his mouth and ordered up Augustine to eat the marmalade, which that lovely and interesting girl promptly did, her repast being as promptly succeeded by racking vomitings.

Curval imitated this variation and received his dear Adonis' turd, which Michette consumed, not without a duplication of Augustine's histrionics; as for the Bishop, he was content to emulate his brother, and had the delicate Zelmire excrete a confiture Céladon was induced to gobble up. Accompanying all this were certain unmistakable signs of repugnance which, of course, were of the greatest interest to libertines in whose view the torments they inflict are unexcelled for inspiring satisfaction. The Bishop and the Duc discharged, the two others either could not, or would not, and all four went in to supper, where Duclos' action was the object of the loftiest encomiums.

"A very intelligent creature," observed the Duc, whose regard for the storyteller could not have been more profound. "Intelligent, I say, to have sensed that gratitude is nonsense, an hallucination, and that ties of fondness or of any other sort ought never either to make us pause or even to suspend the effects of crime, because the object which has served us can claim no right to our heart's generosity; that object employs itself only in our behalf, its mere presence humiliates a stout soul, and one must either hate or be rid of it."

"Very true," said Durcet, "so true that you'll never see a man of any wit seek to make others grateful to him. Fully certain that benevolence creates nothing but enemies, he practices only the arts his wisdom approves for his safety."

"One moment," interrupted the Bishop. "It is not at giving you pleasure he who serves you is laboring, but he is rather striving simply to gain an ascendancy over you by putting you in his debt. Well, I ask, what does such a scheme deserve? He does not say, as he serves you: I serve you because I wish to do good for you. No, he simply says: I put you under obligation in order to lower you and to raise myself above you."

"These reflections seem to me," said Durcet, "abundantly to prove how abusive are the services usually rendered, and how absurd is the practice of good. But, they will tell you, one does good for its own sake and for one's own; 'tis all very well for them whose weakness of spirit permits them to enjoy such little delights, but they who are revolted by them, as are we, great God! would be great fools to bother over such tepid stuff."

This doctrine having fired their imaginations, Messieurs drank a great deal, and the orgies were celebrated with vivacity and *brio*. Our like-thinking libertines sent the children to bed, chose to spend a part of the night tippling with no one but the four elders and the four storytellers, and in their company to vie with one another in infamies and atrocities. As amongst these twelve individuals there was not one who was not worthy of the noose, the rack, and probably the wheel, I leave it to the reader to picture what was said and done. For from words they passed to deeds, the Duc got hot again, and I don't know just why it happened or how, but they say Thérèse bore the marks of his affection for weeks. However all that may be, let us allow our actors to move from these bacchanals to the chaste bed of the wife that had been prepared for each of the four, and let us see what transpired at the castle on the morrow.

# THE SIXTEENTH DAY

*O*ur heroes rose as bright and fresh as if they had just arrived from confession; but upon close inspection, one might have noticed that the Duc was beginning to tire a little. Blame for this could have been bestowed upon Duclos; there is no question but that the girl had entirely mastered the art of procuring him delight and that, according to his own words, his discharges were lubricious with no one else, which would corroborate the idea that these matters depend solely upon caprice, upon idiosyncrasy, and that age, looks, virtue, and all the rest have nothing whatever to do with the problem, that it all boils down to a certain tactfulness which is much more often found possessed by beauties in the autumn of life than by those others of no experience whom the springtide yet crowns with all her show.

There was as well another creature in the company who was beginning to make herself very amiable and to attract considerable attention; we are referring to Julie. She was already announcing signs of imagination, debauchery, and of libertinage. Astute enough to sense that she stood in need of protection, clever enough to caress those very persons for whom perhaps she did not at heart have a very great fondness, she contrived to become Duclos' friend, this in order to try to achieve some favor in the eyes of her father who, she was well aware, could, if he chose, exert a great influence upon the others. Every time her turn came to lie with the Duc, she would adopt Duclos' techniques and emulate them so successfully, give proof of such skill, so much consideration, that the Duc was always sure of obtaining delicious discharges whenever he used

432

those two creatures to procure them. Nevertheless, his enthusiasm for his daughter was waning prodigiously, and perhaps without Duclos' assistance, for the narrator consistently spoke well in her behalf, she would never have been able to occupy a place in his good graces. Her husband, Curval, was roughly of the same mind regarding her, and although, by means of her impure mouth and kisses, she still managed to wheedle a few discharges from him, disgust was dangerously near to becoming his predominating attitude toward her: one might even have said that the fires of his hostility were fanned by her impudicious caresses. Durcet held her in no esteem, she had not made him discharge more than twice since the adventures at Silling had started. And so it seemed that no one but the Bishop remained to her, and he indeed was fond of her libertine jargon, and judged hers to be the world's finest ass; and it is certain that Nature had furnished her with one as lovely as that which had been given to Venus. She hence made the most of that part, for she wished absolutely to please at whatever the price; as she felt an extreme need for a protector, she sought to cultivate Duclos.

At the chapel appeared that day no more than three persons: Hébé, Constance, Martaine; no one had been found at fault that morning. After the three subjects had ridded themselves of their freight, Durcet was taken by an impulse to be delivered of his. The Duc, who since early morning had been fluttering and buzzing about the financier's behind, seized the opportunity to satisfy himself and, sending away everyone but Constance, whom they kept as an aide, they encloseted themselves in the chapel. The Duc was appeased by the generous mouthful of shit he had from Durcet; these gentlemen, however, did not limit themselves to that prelude, and afterward Constance reported to the Bishop that they had performed infamies for a good thirty minutes. But what is one to expect? they had been friends, as I have said, since childhood, and since then had never ceased reminding one another of their schoolboy pleasures. As for Constance, she served no great purpose during this tête-à-tête; she wiped asses, sucked and frigged a few pricks, and that was about all.

They retired to the salon, the four friends conversed there for a while, and the midday meal was announced. It was, as usual, splendid and libertine and, after some lewd fingerings and bawdy colling, and a few scandalous remarks which spiced their lascivious byplay, they returned to the salon where Zéphyr and Hyacinthe, Michette and Colombe were waiting to serve coffee. The Duc thigh-fucked Michette, and Curval, Hyacinthe; Durcet fetched shit out of Colombe, and the Bishop dropped some in Zéphyr's mouth; Curval, recollecting one of the passions Duclos had related the day before, was moved to shit in Colombe's cunt; old Thérèse, who was supervising the day's quartet, placed Colombe in a suitable posture, and Curval performed. But as he produced colossal turds, proportioned by the immense quantity of victuals wherewith he stuffed himself every day, almost all of his creation spilled upon the floor and it was, so to speak, only superficially he beshitified that pretty little virgin cunt which had not, one would have thought, been intended by Nature to be used for such disagreeable pleasures.

Deliciously frigged by Zéphyr, the Bishop yielded his fuck philosophically, joining, to the delights he was feeling, that other offered by the wonderful spectacle being enacted about him. He was furious, he scolded Zéphyr, he scolded Curval, he fumed and grumbled at everyone. He was given a large glass of elixir whereby they hoped his faculties would be restored, Michette and Colombe settled him upon a sofa for his nap and stood by him while he slept. He woke amply refreshed and, in order to give him additional strength, Colombe sucked him for a moment or two; his engine responded by showing some positive signs of life, and they went next into the auditorium. The Bishop had Julie on his couch; as he was rather fond of her, the sight of her improved his mood. The Duc had Aline; Durcet, Constance; the Président, his daughter. Everything being ready, the lovely Duclos installed herself upon her throne and began thus:

*There is nothing more untrue than to say money acquired through crime brings no happiness. No greater error, I assure you; my house prospered; never had so many clients come there during Fournier's administration. It was then an idea occurred to me, a rather cruel idea, I admit, but one which, I dare flatter myself in believing, will not be altogether displeasing to your Lordships. It seemed to me that when one had not done unto another the good*

*one ought to have done him, there existed a certain wicked volup-*
*tuousness in doing him ill, and my perfidious imagination suggested*
*a little libertine mischief at the expense of that same Petignon, my*
*benefactress' son, and the individual to whom I had been charged*
*to surrender a fortune which, doubtless, would have proven very*
*welcome to that wretch, and which I had already begun to squander*
*upon trifles. The occasion arrived in this way: the poor shoemaker,*
*married to a girl of his own class and sort, had, as the unique fruit*
*of this unfortunate marriage, a daughter of about twelve; I had*
*been told that, together with all the lovely features of childhood,*
*she possessed all the attributes of the most tender beauty. This*
*child, then being brought up humbly but nevertheless as carefully*
*as the parents' indigence could permit, for she was the joy and light*
*of their life, this child, I say, struck me as a capture well worth*
*making.*

*Petignon had never come to the house, he knew nothing of the*
*legal rights that were his; immediately after Fournier had men-*
*tioned him to me, my first move was to obtain information about*
*him and those around him, and thus I learned that he possessed a*
*treasure in his house. At about the same time the Comte de*
*Mesanges came to me; a famous libertine of whose profession*
*Desgranges will doubtless have at least one occasion to speak, the*
*Comte requested me to provide him with a maid of no more than*
*thirteen at whatever the price. I don't know what he wanted with*
*the article, for he passed for a man with very rigorous scruples*
*when it was a question of women, but his proposal was simple*
*enough: after having, with the help of experts, established her*
*virginity, he said he would buy her from me for a fixed sum and,*
*from this moment on, she would be his, he would be her master,*
*and, he added, the child would be removed, perhaps permanently,*
*from France.*

*As the Comte was one of my habitués—you shall see him*
*enter upon the scene very soon—I set everything in motion in an*
*effort to satisfy him; Petignon's little daughter seemed to me exactly*
*what he needed. But how was I to get my hands upon her? The*
*child never left the house, it was there she received her education;*
*so carefully was she supervised, so circumspectly that I began to*
*despair of the prize. Nor was I able to employ that masterful*

*debaucher of girls I mentioned some time ago; he was away from the city, and the Comte was urging me to hurry. And so I could find only one means, and this means could not have been better designed to serve the secret little wickedness which was impelling me to commit this crime, for the crime was aggravated by it. I resolved to embroil husband and wife in some kind of difficulty, to strive to get both of them imprisoned, and in this way removing some of the obstacles between the child and myself, I fancied I would encounter no trouble in luring her into the snare. Wherewith I consulted one of my friends, a skilled barrister whom I trusted and who was capable of anything; I put him on the scent, he went directly to work: he compiled information, made inquiries, located creditors, aroused them, supported their claims, in brief, it took less than a week to lodge husband and wife behind bars. From then on everything was easy; an adroit scout accosted the little girl, who had been abandoned to the care of some poor neighbors, she was led to me. Her appearance perfectly matched the reports I had received: she had a sweet, a soft, a fair skin, the roundest little ornaments, charms perfectly shaped. . . . In a word, it were difficult to find a prettier child.*

*As she cost me, all told, about twenty* louis, *and as the Comte wished to pay a flat price for her and, having once bought her outright, wished neither to hear another word about the transaction nor have further dealings with anyone, I let her go for one hundred* louis; *it being essential to my interests that no one get wind of my part in the thing, I was content with a net profit of sixty* louis, *giving my attorney another twenty to create just that kind of stir which would prevent her parents from having news of their daughter for a long time. But news did reach them; the girl's disappearance was impossible to conceal. The neighbors who had been guilty of negligence excused themselves as best they were able, and as for the poor shoemaker and his wife, my man-of-law managed matters so well that they were never able to remedy the accident, for both of them died in jail some eleven years after I had made off with my prey. I reaped a twofold advantage from that little mishap, since it simultaneously assured me undisputed ownership of the child I was negotiating to sell and also assured me 60,000 francs for my trouble. As for the child, the Comte was satisfied with her; never did he encounter any difficulties, never did I, no, not a word was said, and it is more than likely Madame Desgranges will finish her story; I know no more about it. But it is high time to return to my own adventures, and to the daily events which may offer you the voluptuous details we have listed.*

"Oh by God!" Curval broke in, "I adore your prudence— there is something in your method which bespeaks a meditated villainy, an orderliness which pleases me more than I can say. And as for that rascality of having given the final stroke to a victim you had until then only scratched . . . ah, that seems to me a refinement of infamy which deserves a place amongst our own masterpieces."

"I wonder, however," said Durcet, "whether I might not have done worse, for, after all, those parents could have obtained their release from jail: there are God knows how many fools in the world who think of nothing but helping such people. Those eleven years during which they lingered on meant worry for you."

"Monsieur," Duclos answered him, "when one does not enjoy the influence you have in society, when for one's little pranks one is forced to employ second-rate allies, caution often becomes very necessary, and at such times one dares not do all one would like."

"True, true," said the Duc, "she was unable to go any further."
And the amiable creature took up the thread of her narrative.

*Dreadful it is, my Lords,* said that accomplished girl, *to have still to relate turpitudes in kind like to those I have been speaking about for several days; but you have required that I cite everything which might bear an even faint resemblance to this great genre of abomination, and insisted too that I suppress nothing. But three more examples of these filthy atrocities and we shall then continue on to other fantasies.*

*The first I propose to mention is that of an elderly administrator of the demesne, a man of I should say three score and six. He would have the woman remove all her clothes and, after having fondled her buttocks with less delicacy than brutality, he would promptly order her to shit on the floor before his eyes, in the middle of the room. When he had relished this prospect, he would*

*in his turn step up and lay his own turd next to hers, then, com-
bining them with his hands, he would oblige the girl to get down
on all fours and eat the hash, and while eating she was to present
her behind, which she was to have brought to the party in a most
maculated state. While the ceremony was in progress he would
manualize himself, and used to discharge as soon as the last bite
had vanished. There were few girls, as your Lordships may readily
believe, who would consent to submit themselves to such vile use,
but all the same the administrator had to have them youthful and
healthy. . . . Well, I used somehow to find what he needed, for
everything is to be found in Paris; however, the merchandise came
dear.*

*The second example of the three I have left to cite of this
species also required what might be termed a furious docility on
the girl's part; but as this libertine wished her to be extremely
young, I had less trouble supplying him: children lend themselves
to these games more readily than do mature women. I located a
pretty little shopgirl of twelve or thirteen for the gentleman whom
we are about to see in action; he arrives, has the girl take off only
the clothing that covers her from the waist down; he toys with her
behind for a brief moment, gets her to fart a little, then gives himself four or five copious enemas which, subsequently, he obliges his
little partner to receive into her mouth and to swallow as the cas-
cade tumbles out of his rectum. Meanwhile, as he was seated astride
her chest, he employed one hand to frig a rather thick device and
with the other he kneaded and pinched her mons veneris and, in
order that he might do it all as he wished, he had to have a completely hairless cunt to work with. This individual wanted to continue on even after his sixth explosion, for his discharge was not yet
achieved. The little girl, convulsed with vomiting, managed to
articulate her disinclination to proceed, she begged to be spared,
he laughed at her, introduced a seventh draught, expelled it, and
his fuck finally did indeed flow.*

*An elderly banker provides us with the last example of these
unclean horrors—or rather the last example of a man for whom
they were the principal element, for I must warn you that we shall
have repeated occasion to behold them as accessories to the main
endeavor. He had to have a handsome woman, but one aged from*

*forty to forty-five and with an extremely flabby pair of breasts. Immediately they were encloseted together he would have her remove all she was wearing from the waist up, and having brutally handled her teats, would cry: "These damned cow dugs! what good are such tripes, eh? What are they for if not to wipe my ass upon?" Next he would squeeze them, twist them, wring them, twine them together, tug them, pound them, spit upon them, kick and trample them, all the while saying, what a damned infamous thing is a flabby tit, he could not imagine what Nature had intended these bags of skin for, why had Nature spoiled and dishonored woman's body with these things? etc. After all these preposterous remarks he would remove every stitch of his clothing. My God, what a body! how am I to describe it to your Lordships! 'Twas no more than a disgusting ulcer, a running sore, pus seemed to cover him from head to toe, I could smell his infected odor even in the adjacent room from which I was observing the ritual; such was the relic which, however, the woman had to suck.*

"Suck?" said the Duc.

*Yes, Messieurs,* Duclos affirmed, *suck from top to bottom, every square inch of his body had to be sucked, the tongue was to neglect nothing, to explore it all; I had forewarned the girl, but apparently in vain. She'd not expected this; for upon catching sight of that ambulatory corpse she shrank away in horror.*

*"What's this, bitch?" says he, "do I disgust you? Why, that's a pity, for you're going to have to suck me, your tongue is going to have to lick every part of my body. Come now! Stop playing the shy little girl; others have done the job, see to it that you do it as well as they. That's enough, I tell you, no nonsense."*

*Ah, they speak true when they say that with money one can accomplish anything; the poor creature I had given him was in the extremest misery, and here was a chance to earn two* louis: *she did everything she was told, and the podagrous old scoundrel, thrilled by the sensation of a tongue straying softly over his hideous body and sweetening the bitter pungency devouring him, frigged himself voluptuously during the entire operation. When it had been completed, and completed, as you may well suppose, despite the horrible revulsion of the luckless woman, when it was done, I say, he had her lie down upon the floor on her back, he got astride her, shitted all over her bubs, and squeezing his performance between them, he used them, first one, then the other, to wipe his ass. But with what regards his discharge, I saw not so much as a hint, and some time later I learned that it required several such operations before he could be induced to part with his liquor; and as he was a man who seldom twice visited the same place, I saw no more of him and, to tell the truth, was by no means sorry.*

"Upon my soul," the Duc observed, "I find the conclusion of that man's operation very reasonable indeed, and I too have never been able to believe that teats were intended for anything but bum-wipes."

"One may be certain," said Curval, who at the moment was rather brutally handling those belonging to the sweet and tender Aline, "one may be certain indeed that a tit is a very infamous object. I never catch sight of one without being plunged straightway into a rage. Upon seeing these things I experience a certain disgust, a certain repugnance assails me . . . only a cunt has a worse and more decided effect upon me."

And so saying, he flung himself into his closet, dragging Aline by the breast and calling out to Sophie and Zelmire, his quatrain's two girls, and Fanchon to follow him. One cannot be sure of precisely what he did, but a loud scream, clearly a woman's, was heard by the others in the auditorium, and shortly afterward came the bellowings that usually indicated the Président had discharged. He returned, Aline was weeping and held a kerchief over her breast, and as these events rarely created any stir, or, at best, a few chuckles, Duclos went on with her story at once.

*Several days later I myself took care, said she, of an old monk whose mania, more wearying to the hand, was rather less revolting to the stomach. He presented me with a great ugly behind covered with skin as tough as bull's hide and as wrinkled as a dried leaf; the task here was to knead his ass, to handle it, drub and thump it, squeeze it with all my strength, but when I reached the hole, nothing I did seemed sufficiently violent: I had to catch up the skin, rub*

*it, pinch it, roll it between my fingers, use my nails, and it was
thanks only to the vigor of my ministrations his fuck finally
emerged. He attended to his own frigging while I abused his bum
and vent, and I was not even obliged to show him my ankles. But
that man must have made a very fierce and old habit of those
manipulations, for his behind, although slack and hanging, was
nevertheless upholstered by a skin as horny and as thick as leather.*

*The next day, doubtless having spoken highly of me and my
dexterity to his friends in the monastery, he sent one of his brethren
upon whose ass one had to bestow slaps, indeed blows of the hand,
and stout ones at that; but this new ecclesiastic, more of a libertine
and an examiner, preceded his rite by a meticulous inspection of his
woman's buttocks, and my ass was kissed, nuzzled, tongued ten or
twelve times over, the intervals being filled by blows aimed at his.
When his hide had taken a scarlet hue, his prick got bravely up,
and I can certify that it was one of the noblest engines I had
palmed and fingered until that day. He put it into my hand,
recommending that I frig it while continuing to slap him with the
other.*

"Unless I am gravely mistaken," said the Bishop, "we have
finally reached the article of passive fustigation."

"Yes, Monseigneur," replied Duclos, "we have, and as my
task for today has been fulfilled, you will consent to allow me to
postpone until tomorrow the beginning of fustigatory tastes; we
shall devote several soirees to dealing with them."

As nearly half an hour remained before supper, Durcet said
that, to stimulate his appetite, he wished to give his entrails a few
rinses; his announcement made something of an impression upon
the women, who began to tremble; but sentence had been decreed,
there was no revoking it. Thérèse, his servant that day, assured him
she introduced the tube with wonderful skill; from the assertion
she passed to the proof, and as soon as the little financier felt his
bowels loaded, he singled out Rosette, beckoned her to him, and
bade her open her mouth. There was some balking, a few complaints and a word or two of pleading, but the capital thing was
obedience and, sure enough, the poor little girl swallowed two erup-
tions, having been granted the option of regurgitating them after-

ward. And regurgitate them she did, and soon. Happily, the supper bell sounded, for the financier was getting ready to begin again. But the prospect of a meal changed the disposition of their Lordships' minds, they went to taste different pleasures. A few turds were lodged on a few bubs at the orgies, and a great deal of shit was gleaned from asses; within the assembly's full view, the Duc consumed Duclos' turd, while that splendid girl sucked him, and while the bawdy fellow's hands roamed here and there, his fuck came out in a thick spray; Curval having imitated him with Champville, the friends began to speak of retiring for the night.

# THE SEVENTEENTH DAY

*T*he terrible antipathy the Président had for Constance was manifest in daily outbursts: he had spent the night with her, having made a bilateral arrangement with Durcet, to whom he returned her the following morning with the most bitter complaints about her behavior.

"Since because of her condition," said he, "the society seems loath to expose her to the customary punishments for fear she be brought to bed before the time we have appointed to pluck her fruit, at least, by Jesus," said he, "we should find some means or other to punish the whore when she chooses to play the fool."

Ah, but what is that spirit of evil that inhabits libertines? Some glimmer of it may be obtained by analyzing Constance's prodigious fault. O reader, what do you suppose it was had waked Curval's wrath? Even worse than you may have dreamt: she had most unfortunately turned her front toward her master when he had called for her behind, ah yes, and such sins are not to be forgiven. But the worst part of her error was her denial of the fact; she declared, and there seemed some basis to her contention, that the Président was calumniating her, that he was seeking naught but her downfall, that she never lay with him but he would invent some such untruth; but as the law was precise and formal on this point, and as women's speeches were given no credence whatever in that society, but one question remained posed: how in future was this female to be chastised without risking the spoilage of the fruit ripening in her? It was decided that for each misdemeanor she would be obliged to eat a turd and, consequently, Curval insisted

443

that she begin there and then. Approbation greeted his demand. They were at the time breakfasting in the girls' quarters, word was dispatched, Constance was summoned, the Président shitted in the center of the room, and she was enjoined to approach his creation on hands and knees and to devour what the cruel man had just wrought. She cast herself upon her knees, yes, but in this posture begged pardon, and her solicitations went unheeded; Nature had put bronze in those breasts where hearts are commonly to be found. Nothing more entertaining than the grimaces and affected airs to which the poor woman resorted before capitulating, and God knows how amused Messieurs were by the scene. At last, however, decisive action had to be taken, Constance's very soul seemed to burst before she was half done, but it had all to be done nevertheless, and every ounce disappeared from the tiles on the floor.

Excited by what he was witnessing, each of our friends, while watching, had himself frigged by a small girl; Curval, singularly aroused by the operation and benefiting from the wondrous skill of Augustine's enchanted fingers, feeling himself nigh to overflowing, called to Constance, who had scarcely finished eating her mournful breakfast.

"Hither, come to me, whore," said he, "after having bolted some fish one needs a little sauce, good white sauce. Come get a mouthful."

Well, there was no escaping that ordeal either, and Curval, who, while operating, was having Augustine shit, opened the sluices and let fly into the mouth of the Duc's miserable wife, and at the same time swallowed the fresh and delicate little turd the interesting Augustine had hatched for him.

The inspection tours were conducted, Durcet found shit in Sophie's chamber pot. The young lady sought to excuse her error by maintaining that she had been suffering from indigestion.

"Not at all," Durcet observed as expertly he handled the turd, "that is not true: indigestion produces diarrhea, soup, my dear, and this article looks very sound to me."

And straightway taking up his baneful notebook, he wrote down the name of that charming creature, who did her best to hide her tears and refrained, at Durcet's request, from deploring her situation. Everyone else had abided by the regulations, but in the boys' chamber, Zélamir, who had shitted the previous evening during the orgies and who had been told not to wipe his little bum, had tidied it up none the less, disobeying orders. These were crimes of the first magnitude: Zélamir's name was inscribed. Notwithstanding the boy's delinquency, Durcet kissed his ass and had himself sucked for a brief moment, then Messieurs passed on to the chapel, where they beheld the shitting of two subaltern fuckers, Aline, Fanny, Thérèse, and Champville. The Duc received Fanny's performance in his mouth, and he ate it, the Bishop's mouth caught the two fuckers' turds, one of which the prelate devoured, Durcet made Champville's his own, and the Président, despite his discharge, gulped down Aline's with all the avidity he had exhibited while consuming what Augustine had done for him.

Constance's scene had heated the company's imagination, for it had been a long time since Messieurs had indulged themselves in such extravagances so early in the morning. Dinner conversation dealt with moral science. The Duc declared he could not understand why in France the law smote so heavily against libertinage, since libertinage, by keeping the citizens busy, kept them clear of cabals and plots and revolutions; the Bishop observed that, no, the laws did not exactly aim at the suppression of libertinage, but at its excesses. Whereupon the latter were analyzed, and the Duc proved that there was nothing dangerous in excess, no excess which could justly arouse the government's suspicion, and that, these facts being clear, the official attitude was not only cruel but absurd; what other word was there to describe bringing artillery to bear upon mosquitoes?

From remarks they progressed to effects, the Duc, half-drunk, abandoned himself in Zéphyr's arms, and for thirty long minutes sucked that lovely child's mouth while Hercule, exploiting the situation, buried his enormous engine in the Duc's anus. Blangis was all complacency, and without stirring, without the flicker of an eyelash, went on with his kissing as, virtually without noticing it, he changed sex. His companions all gave themselves over to other infamies, and then they sallied forth to coffee. As they had just played a multitude of silly little pranks, the atmosphere was calm, and this was perhaps the one coffee hour during the entire four months' outing when no fuck was shed. Duclos was already upon the tribune, awaiting the company; when everyone had taken his place, she addressed her auditors in this wise:

*I had recently suffered a loss in my house, and it had a deep effect upon me in every sense. Eugénie, whom I loved with a passion and who, thanks to her most extraordinary complaisance in whatever was connected with the possibility of earning me money, had been especially useful to me, Eugénie, I say, had just been spirited away. It happened in the strangest fashion: a domestic, having first paid the price settled upon, came to conduct her, so he said, to a supper that was to be held outside the city; her participation in the affair would be worth seven or eight louis. I was not at the house at the time the transaction took place, for I should never have allowed her to leave with someone I didn't know, but the domestic applied directly to her and she agreed to go. . . . I have never seen her since.*

"Nor shall you ever again," said Desgranges. "The party proposed was her last one, and it will be my agreeable task to add the denouement to that lovely girl's history."

"Great God!" cried Duclos. "She was so beautiful, that girl . . . only twenty, her face was so sweet, she was so delicate. . . ."

"And, one might add, her body was the most superb in Paris," Desgranges said. "All those charms conspired to her undoing, but go on with what you were saying, let's not become mired down in circumstances."

*Lucile was the girl who took her place,* Duclos continued, *both in my heart and in my bed, but not in the household's activities, for she had not by any means Eugénie's submissive temper nor her great understanding.*

*All the same, it was to her hands I entrusted, not long afterward, that certain Benedictine prior who used to pay me a visit now and again, and who had in past times been wont to frolic with Eugénie. After the good father had warmed her cunt with his tongue and thoroughly sucked her mouth, the major phase of the process began: Lucile took the whip and plied it lightly over his prick and balls, and he discharged from a limp machine; the gentle rubbing, the mere application of the lash produced his orgasm. His greatest pleasure used to consist in watching the girl slash with her whip at the drops of fuck as they spattered from his prick.*

*The next day, I myself took charge of a gentleman upon whose bare behind one had to lay one hundred carefully counted whip strokes; before his beating he prepared himself by kissing one's behind and while being lashed he frigged himself.*

*A third, with whom I had dealings some time later, had even heavier demands to satisfy; he also gilded each detail with additional ceremony: I received notice of his intended arrival a week in advance, and during that time I had to avoid washing any part of my body, and above all was to spare my cunt, my ass, my mouth; and furthermore, as soon as I learned he was to come, I selected three cat-o'-nine-tails and immersed them in a pot full of mixed urine and shit, and kept the whips soaking there until he presented himself. He was an elderly collector of the salt tax, a man of considerable means, a widower, without children, and he treated himself to such parties all the time. The first thing that interested him was to determine whether I had scrupulously abstained from ablutions, as he had enjoined me; I assured him I had followed his instructions to the letter; he wished proof, and began by applying a kiss to my lips. This experience must have convinced him, for he then suggested we go up to the room, and I realized that had he, upon kissing me, discovered I had cleansed my mouth in any way at all, he would not have wished to continue with the party. We go up together, as I say, he regards the whips steeping in the pot, then, bidding me undress, he sets to sniffing every part of my body, above all the orifices he had expressly forbidden me to wash; as I had honored his prescription in perfect faith and in every article, he doubtless discovered the aroma he desired to be there, for I saw him grow restless, appear anxious to be off, and heard him exclaim: "Ah, by fuck, that's what I want, that's just what I want!" I proceeded to fondle his ass: it was sheathed in what positively resembled boiled leather in color, texture, and toughness. After having spent a minute caressing, handling, poking about those gnarled, storm-beaten hindquarters, I seized a cat-o'-nine-tails and, without drying it, I gave him ten stinging cuts, putting all my strength into the blows; but this beginning produced not a tremor,*

*he not only remained impassive, but my blows put not so much as
the faintest scratch upon that unshakable citadel. Having opened
with this prologue, I sank three of my fingers into his anus, took
firm hold, and began to rattle him with might and main, but our
man was insensible to the same degree here as elsewhere; my
struggles failed to be acknowledged by so much as a sigh. These
two initial ceremonies completed, his turn came to act; I lay belly
down upon the bed, he knelt, spread my buttocks, and alternately
shot his pilgrim tongue into this hole and into the other, and they,
one may be sure, were, in keeping with his instructions, not entirely
unaromatic. After he had done considerable sucking, I took up
another whip, laid on a second time and socratized him again, he
knelt as before and returned to his licking, and so it went, each of
us doing his part at least fifteen times over. Finally, giving me
further instructions and bidding me guide my movements in con-
sonance with the state of his prick, which I was to observe carefully
but which I was not to touch, when next he knelt I unleashed my
turd. It shot squarely into his face, he fell back, exclaimed that I
was an insolent creature, and discharged while frigging himself
and while uttering cries that might have been heard in the street
had I not taken the precaution of drawing the shutters. But the
turd fell to the floor, he did naught but stare at and smell it, neither
putting it in his mouth nor even touching it; he had received at
least two hundred lashes, and I may assure you . . . his body bore
not a trace of what it had sustained, his horny ass, fortified by
years of rude usage, betrayed not the least mark.*

"Well, by God's bum button!" chortled the Duc, "there's an
ass, Président, worth as much as the curiosity you drag about."

"Oh yes, yes," said Curval, a stammer in his voice, for Aline
was frigging him, "yes indeed, that fellow seems to have both my
buttocks and my tastes, for, you know, I am infinitely opposed to
the use of the bidet, but I prefer a longer abstinence: I usually set
the period at a minimum of three months."

"Président, your prick's stiff," the Duc said.

"Do you think so?" Curval replied. "Faith, you'd best consult
Aline here, she'll be able to tell you what's what, as for myself, you
know, I'm so accustomed to that particular state of affairs that I

rarely notice when it ends or when it begins. There is only one thing I can tell you with complete confidence, and that is that at this very moment I'd hugely like to have my hands upon a very impure whore; I'd like her to present me with a bucketful of shit, fill a bowl to above the rim, I'd like her ass to stink from shit, I'd like her cunt to smell like a beach covered with dead fish. But hold! Thérèse, O thou whose filth is as old as the hills, thou who since baptism hast not wiped thine ass, and whose infamous cunt breeds a pestilence three leagues on every side, come bring all that to my nose's delectation, I beg thee, and to that put a fine wet turd, if 'twould please thee."

Thérèse approaches, with foul and evil charms, with parts disgusting and withered and wounded she rubs the magistrate's face, upon his nose she excretes the desired turd, Aline does frig amain, the libertine discharges, and Duclos therewith resumes the story she has to tell.

*An elderly rascal, who used to receive a new girl every day for the operation I am going to describe, besought one of my friends to persuade me to visit him, and at the same time I was given information about the ceremony regularly performed at the lecher's home. I arrive, he examines me with a phlegmatic glance, the kind of glance one encounters among habitual libertines, and which in an instant arrives at an infallible estimate of the object under scrutiny.*

*"I have been told you have a fine ass," said he in a drawling tone, "and as for the past sixty years I have had a decided weakness for fine cheeks, I should like to see whether there is any foundation to your reputation . . . lift your skirts."*

*That last phrase, energetically spoken, sufficed as an order; not only did I offer a view of the treasure, but I moved it as near as possible to his connoisseur's nose. At first I stand erect, then little by little I bend forward and exhibit the object of his devotion in every form and aspect most apt to please him. With each movement, I feel the old scoundrel's hands wander over the surface, scouting the terrain, probing the geography, sometimes creating a more consolidated effect, sometimes attempting to give it a more generous cast, compressing here, broadening there.*

"*The hole is ample, very ample,*" *says he,* "*appearances attest a furious sodomistical prostitution.*"

"*Alas, Monsieur,*" *I concede,* "*we are living in an age when men are so capricious that in order to please them, one must indeed be prepared for virtually anything, and consent to it all.*"

*Whereupon I feel his mouth glue itself hermetically to my asshole, and his tongue strive to penetrate into the chasm; I seize my opportunity, as I have been advised, and profiting from my situation, slide out, directly upon his probing tongue, the warmest, most humid, densest eructation. The maneuver displeases him not at all, but on the other hand does little to animate him; finally, after I have unleashed half a dozen winds, he gets to his feet, leads me to his bed, and points to an earthenware crock in which four cat-o'-nine-tails are marinating. Above the crock hang several whips suspended from gilded hooks.*

"*Arm yourself,*" *murmurs the roué,* "*take a cat-o'-nine-tails and one of those other weapons, here is my ass. As you observe, it is dry, lean, and exceedingly well seasoned. Touch it.*"

*I do so; he continues:*

"*You notice,*" *says he,* "*that it's old, toughened by severe treatment, and it's not to be warmed save by the most incredibly excessive attacks. I am going to keep myself in this posture,*" *and while speaking he stretched out upon the bed and rested his knees on the floor.* "*Employ those instruments, first one, then the other, now the cat-o'-nine-tails, now the whip. This is going to take a little time, but you will receive an unequivocal sign when the climax approaches. As soon as you see something out of the ordinary happening to this ass of mine, hold yourself in readiness to imitate what you see it doing; we will then exchange places, I shall kneel down before your splendid buttocks, you shall do what you shall have observed me do, and I shall discharge. But above all do not become impatient; I warn you once again: this business is not to be accomplished in haste.*"

*I begin, I alternate weapons in accordance with his prescription. But, my God! what nonchalance, what stoicism! I was drenched in sweat; that my strokes be more freely applied he had suggested I roll my sleeves to above the elbow. Three-quarters of an hour went by and I was still beating him, putting every ounce of strength into my blows, sometimes tearing at his stubborn flesh with the cat-o'-nine-tails, sometimes with the steel-tipped thongs, three-quarters of an hour, I say, and it seemed as if I had got nowhere. Still, silent, our lecher was as quiet as death; one might say he was mutely savoring the interior stirrings of delight quickened by this ordeal, but there was no outward sign of pleasure, not a single indication of pleasure's influence even upon his skin. I proceeded. By and by I heard a clock strike two and realized I had been at work three whole hours; then all of a sudden I see his rump rise, his buttocks part, I slash and send my thongs whistling between certain crevices; a turd emerges, falls, I whip away, my blows send the shit flying to the floor.*

*"Courage," I say to him, "we're within sight of port."*

*And then my man gets up in a rage; his prick, hard and in fierce revolt, is glued to his belly.*

*"Do what I did," says he, "imitate me, I need nothing now but shit and you'll have my fuck."*

*I promptly adopt the position he has just abandoned, he kneels as he said he would, and into his mouth I lay an egg which I have been holding in store for him for three days. As he receives it his fuck leaps, and he flings himself backward, shouting with joy, but without swallowing, and indeed without keeping the turd in his mouth for more than a second. In conclusion let me say, Messieurs, that, your Lordships excepted, for you are without doubt superior examples of this species, I have seen few men convulse more frantically, few who have manifested a more trenchant delight; he came nigh to swooning as he gave vent to his fuck. That séance was worth two* louis.

*But no sooner did I return to the house than I found Lucile come to grips with another old chap who, without having laid a finger upon her, without any preliminaries, had simply ordered her to fustigate him from the small of the back to just above the knees; Lucile was using a cat-o'-nine-tails soaked in vinegar, was endowing her blows with all the force she could muster, and this individual ended his ritual by having her suck him. The girl knelt before him when he gave her the signal and, adjusting his old weary balls so that they dangled upon her teats, she took the flabby engine in her mouth whereinto the chastened sinner hastened to weep for his transgressions.*

And Duclos having therewith put a period to what she had to relate that day, and the supper hour not yet having arrived, Messieurs delivered themselves of a few smutty comments while waiting.

"You must be done up, Président," gibed the Duc. "I've seen you discharge twice today, and you're hardly accustomed to such feats of liberality."

"Let's wager on a third," replied Curval, who was pawing Duclos' buttocks.

"Why, certainly, as much as you like and as often," the Duc returned.

"And I ask for only one condition," Curval said, "and that is to be allowed to do whatever I like."

"Oh, I'm afraid not," the Duc answered, "for you know very well that there are certain things we have mutually promised not to do before the appointed time indicated on our schedules: having ourselves fucked was one of them—before proceeding to that we were, according to prior agreement, to wait until some example of that passion were cited to us, but by your common request, gentlemen, we ceded on that point and suspended the restriction. There are many other pleasures and modes of taking them we ought to have forbidden ourselves until the moment they were embodied in story, and which we have instead tolerated, provided the experiments are conducted in privacy—in, that is to say, either our closets or our bedchambers. You, Président, surrendered yourself to one with Aline just a short while ago; did she utter that piercing scream for no reason at all? and has she no motive for keeping her breast covered now? Very well then, choose from amongst those mysterious modes, or from one of those we permit in public, and I'll wager one hundred *louis* you'll not be able to derive your third from one of those legitimate sources."

The Président then asked whether he might be allowed to repair to the boudoir at the end of the corridor and to take along the subjects he deemed necessary to success; his request was granted, although it was stipulated that Duclos would have to be witness to the goings on, and that her word would be accepted upon the existence of the discharge or upon Curval's failure to produce it.

"Agreed," said the Président, "I accept the conditions."

And by way of a preliminary, he had Duclos give him five hundred lashes within view of the assembly; that accomplished, he led away his dear and devoted friend Constance, in whose behalf his colleagues besought Curval to do nothing which might damage her pregnancy; the Président also took with him his daughter Adelaide, Augustine, Zelmire, Céladon, Zéphyr, Thérèse, Fanchon, Champville, Desgranges, Duclos, of course, and three fuckers besides.

"Why fuck my eyes!" exclaimed the Duc, "there was nothing in the bargain that said he could recruit an army."

But the Bishop and Durcet took the Président's side in the matter of manpower and firmly reminded Blangis that the terms of the wager included no limitation upon numbers. The Président led his band away, and at the end of thirty minutes, an interval the Bishop, Durcet, and the Duc, with the few subjects remaining to them, did not pass in holy orison, thirty minutes later, I say, Constance and Zelmire returned in tears, and the Président reappeared soon afterward with the rest of his force; Duclos then related the mighty things he had done, paid homage to his vigor, and certified that in all fairness and justice he merited the crown of myrtle. The reader will kindly allow us to suppress the text of Duclos' report, for the architecture of our novel bids us conceal the precise circumstances of what transpired in that remote boudoir; but Curval had won his wager, and that, we consider, is the essential point.

"These hundred *louis*," he remarked upon receiving them from the Duc, "will be useful in paying a fine which, I fear, shall soon be levied upon me."

And here is still another thing the explanation of which we pray the reader will permit us to postpone until the appropriate moment arrives; for the time being he need but observe how that rascal Curval would anticipate his misdeeds well in advance, and how, with unruffled calm, he would accept the fact that they would bring down upon him certain and merited punishment, a fatal necessity he faced unflinchingly and with a proud smile.

Between that time and the opening of the next day's narrations absolutely nothing out of the ordinary transpired, and therefore we propose to conduct the reader to the auditorium at once.

# THE EIGHTEENTH DAY

*B*eautiful, radiant, bejeweled, grown more brilliant with each passing day, Duclos thus started the eighteenth session's stories:

*A tall and stoutly constructed creature named Justine had just been added to my entourage; she was twenty-five, five feet six inches tall, with the husky arms and solid legs of a barmaid, but her features were fine all the same, her skin was clear and smooth, and she had as splendid a body as one might wish. As my establishment used to be swarming with a crowd of those old rakehells who are incapable of experiencing the faintest pleasure save when heated by the lash or torture, I thought that a pensionnaire like Justine, furnished as she was with the forearm of a blacksmith, could be nothing but a very real asset. The day following her arrival, I decided to put her fustigatory talents to the test; I had been given to understand she wielded a whip with prodigious skill, and hence matched her against an old commissar of the quarter whom she was to flog from chest to shin and then, on the other side, from the middle of his back to his calves. The operation over with, the libertine simply hoisted the girl's skirts and planted his load upon her buttocks. Justine comported herself like a true heroine of Cythera, and our good old martyr avowed to me afterward that I had got my hands on a treasure, and that in all his days no one had ever whipped him as that rascal had.*

*To demonstrate how much I counted upon her contribution to our little community, a few days later I arranged a meeting be-*

455

*tween Justine and an old veteran of many a campaign on the fields of love; he required a round thousand strokes all over his body, he would have no part of himself spared, and when he was afire and nicely bloodied, the girl had to piss into her cupped hand and smear her urine over those areas of his body which looked to be the most seriously molested. This lotion rubbed on, the heavy labor had to be begun again, then he would discharge, the girl would carefully collect his fuck, once again using her cupped hand, and she would give him a second massage, this time employing the balm wrung from his prick. Another triumph for my new colleague, and every succeeding day brought her further and more impassioned acclaim; but it was impossible to exercise her arm on the champion who presented himself this time.*

*This extraordinary man would have nothing of the feminine but womanish dress: the wearer of the costume had to be a man; in other words, the roué wanted to be spanked by a man got up as a girl. And what was the instrument she had to use on him? Don't think for a moment he was content with a birch ferule or even a cat, no, he demanded a bundle of osier switches wherewith very barbarously one had to tear his buttocks. Actually, this particular affair seeming to have somewhat of the flavor of sodomy, I felt I ought not become too deeply involved in it; but as he was one of Fournier's former and most reliable clients, a man who had been truly attached to our house in fair weather and in foul, and who, furthermore, might, thanks to his position, be able to render us some service, I raised no objections and, having prettily disguised a young lad of eighteen who sometimes availed us of his services and who had a very attractive face, I presented him, armed with a handful of switches, to his opponent.*

*And a very entertaining contest it was—you may well imagine how eager I was to observe it. He began with a careful study of his pretended maiden, and having found him, evidently, much to his liking, he opened with five or six kisses upon the youth's mouth: those kisses would have looked peculiar from three miles away; next, he exhibited his cheeks, and in all his behavior and words seeming to take the young man for a girl, he told him to fondle his buttocks and knead them just a little rigorously; the lad, whom I had told exactly what to expect, did everything asked of him.*

*"Well, let's be off," said the bawd, "ply those switches, spare not to strike hard."*

*The youth catches up the bundle of withes and therewith, swinging right merrily, lays fifty slashing blows upon a pair of buttocks which seem only to thirst for more; already definitely marked by those two score and ten stripes, the libertine hurls himself upon his masculine flagellatrice, draws up her petticoats, one hand verifies her sex, the other fervently clutches her buttocks, he knows not which altar to bow down before first, the ass finally captures his primary attentions, he glues his mouth to its hole, much ardor in his expression. Ah, what a difference between the worship Nature is said to prescribe and that other which is said to outrage her! O God of certain justice, were this truly an outrage, would the homage be paid with such great emotion? Never was woman's ass kissed as was that lad's; three or four times over his lover's tongue entirely disappeared into the anus; returning to his former position at last, "O dear child," cried he, "resume your operation."*

*Further flagellation ensued, but as it was livelier, the patient met this new assault with far more courage and intrepidity. Blood makes its appearance, another stroke brings his prick bounding up, and he engages the young object of his transports to seize it without an instant's delay. While the latter manipulates him, he wishes to render the youth the same service, lifts up the boy's skirts again, but it's a prick he's now gone in quest of; he touches it, grasps, shakes, pulls it, and soon introduces it into his mouth. After these initial caresses, he calls for a third round of blows and receives a storm of them. This latest experience puts him in a perfect tumult; he flings his Adonis upon the bed, lies down upon him, simultaneously toys with his own prick and his companion's, then presses one upon the other, glues his lips to the boy's mouth and, having succeeded in warming him by means of these caresses, he procures him the divine pleasure at the same moment he is overwhelmed himself: both discharge in harmony. Enchanted by the scene, our libertine sought to placate my risen indignation, and at last coaxed a promise from me to arrange for further delights in the same kind, both with that young fellow and with any others I could find for him. I attempted to work at his conversion, I assured him I had some charming girls who would be happy to flog him and who*

*could do so quite as well; no, said he, none of that, he would not
so much as look at what I had to offer him.*

"Oh, I can readily believe it," said the Bishop. "When one
has a decided taste for men, there's no changing, the difference
between boy and girl is so extreme that one's not apt to be tempted
to try what is patently inferior."

"Monseigneur," said the Président, "you have broached a
thesis which merits a two-hour dissertation."

"And which will always conclude by giving further support to
my contention," said the Bishop, "because the fact that a boy is
superior to a girl is beyond doubt or dispute."

"Beyond contradiction too," Curval agreed, "but nevertheless
one might still inform you that a few objections have been here and
there raised to your doctrine and that, for a certain order of
pleasures, such as Martaine and Desgranges shall discuss, a girl is
to be preferred to a boy."

"That I deny," said the Bishop with emphasis, "and even for
such pleasures as you allude to the boy is worth more than the girl.
Consider the problem from the point of view of evil, evil almost
always being pleasure's true and major charm; considered thus,
the crime must appear greater when perpetrated upon a being of
your identical sort than when inflicted upon one which is not, and
this once established, the delight automatically doubles."

"Yes," said Curval, "but that despotism, that empire, that
delirium born of the abuse of one's power over the weak. . . ."

"But the same is no less true in the other case," the Bishop
insisted. "If the victim is yours, thoroughly in your power, that
supremacy which when using women you think better established
than when using men, is based upon pure prejudice, upon nothing,
and results merely from the custom whereby females are more
ordinarily submitted to your caprices than are males. But give up
that popular superstition for a moment, view the thing equitably
and, provided the man is bound absolutely by your chains and by
the same authority you exert over women, you will obtain the idea
of a greater crime; your lubricity ought hence to increase at least
twofold."

"I am of the Bishop's mind," Durcet joined in, "and once it is certain that sovereignty is fully established, I believe the abuse of power more delicious when exercised at the expense of one's peer than at a woman's."

"Gentlemen," said the Duc, "I should greatly prefer you to postpone your discussions until mealtime. I believe these hours have been reserved for listening to the narrations, and it would seem to me proper were you to refrain from employing them upon philosophical exchanges."

"He is right," said Curval. "Go on with your story, Duclos."

And that agreeable directress of Cytherean sport plunged again into the matter she had to relate.

*Another elderly man,* said she, *this one a clerk at parliament, paid me a call one morning, and as during Fournier's administration he had been accustomed to dealing exclusively with me, tradition bade him solicit an interview with me now. Our conference consisted in slapping his face with gradually increasing force, and in frigging him the while; that is to say, one had at first to slap him gently, then, as his prick assumed consistency, one slowly augmented the force of one's blows, and finally a series of truly boneshattering cuffs would provoke his ejaculation. I had so well apprehended the precise nature of his eccentricity that my twentieth slap brought his fuck springing out.*

"The twentieth, you say? Why, by Jesus," exclaimed the Bishop, "my prick would have gone dead limp by the third."

"There you are, my friend," the Duc declared, "to each his own peculiar mania, we ought never blame nor wonder at another's; tolerance, I say. Say on, Duclos, give us one more and have done."

*My last example for the evening,* said Duclos, *originally was told to me by one of my friends; she had been living for two years with a man whose prick never stiffened until one had first bestowed a score of fillips upon his nose and tweaked it, pulled his ears till they bled, and bitten his buttocks, chewed his prick, nipped his balls. Aroused by these potent preliminary titillations, his prick would shoot aloft like a stallion's, and while swearing like a demon he'd*

*almost always discharge upon the visage of the girl at whose hands*
*he had been receiving this exhilarating treatment.*

Of all that had been recounted during that afternoon's sitting,
only the masculine fustigations had affected their Lordships' brains
which, now passing hot, were only cooled after prolonged use of
the fantasy which had fired their enthusiasm; thus it was the Duc
had Hercule flog him until blood seeped from his pores, Durcet
employed Invictus to the same effect, the Bishop made use of
Antinoüs, and Bum-Cleaver ministered to Curval. The Bishop, who
had done nothing that day, did finally discharge at the orgies, they
say, while eating the turd Zélamir had been preparing for forty-
eight hours. And then they went to bed.

# THE NINETEENTH DAY

*T*hat morning, after having made some observations upon the shit the subjects were producing for lubricious purposes, the friends decided that the society ought to try something Duclos had spoken of in her narrations : I am referring to the suppression of bread and soup from all the tables save Messieurs'. These two articles were withdrawn, and replaced by twice the former quantity of fowl and game. They hoped to remark some improvement, and in less than a week an essential difference in the community's excrements was indeed perceived: they were more mellow, softer, dissolved more readily, had an infinitely more subtle flavor, and the friends discovered that d'Aucourt's advice to Duclos had been that of a consummate libertine thoroughly penetrated with an appreciation of such matters. It was pointed out, however, that this new diet might have some effect upon breaths:

"Well, what does that matter?" asked Curval, to whom the Duc had addressed his objection; "'tis very faulty reasoning to maintain that, to give pleasure, a woman's mouth or a youth's must be absolutely clean and sweet smelling. Setting aside all idiosyncrasy for a moment, I most willingly grant you that he who requires stinking breath and a foul mouth is moved by depravation only, but for your part you must grant me that a mouth entirely bereft of odor gives not the slightest pleasure when kissed. There must always be some kind of spice to the thing, some flavor there, for where's the joy if it's not stung alive? the joy's asleep, I say, and it's only waked by a little filth. However clean may be the mouth, the lover who sucks it assuredly does an unclean thing, and there

461

is no doubt at all in his mind that it is that very uncleanness that pleases him. Give a somewhat greater degree of strength to the impulse and you'll want that mouth to be impure. If it fall short of smelling of rot or the cadaver, well, be patient, the taste will develop, but that it have nothing but an odor of milk and honey or infancy, that, I tell you, is insufferable. And so the diet we're going to subject them to will, at the worst, lead not at all to corruption, but only to a certain alteration, and that is all that's necessary."

The morning searches brought nothing to light . . . the youngsters were keeping strict watch over their conduct. No one requested toilet permission, and the company sat down at table. Adelaide, one of the servants at the meal, having been enjoined by Durcet to fart in a champagne glass, and having been unable to comply, was directly entered in the fatal book by her unfeeling husband who, since the beginning of the week, had been continually endeavoring to find her at fault.

Coffee came next; it was handed round by Cupidon, Giton, Michette, and Sophie. The Duc thigh-fucked Sophie, and while so doing had her shit upon his hand; the nobleman took that pretty little packet and smeared it over his face, the Bishop did precisely the same thing with Giton and Curval with Michette, but as for Durcet, he popped his little device into Cupidon's mouth as that charming boy squeezed out his turd. There were, notwithstanding, no discharges and, having risen from their nap, Messieurs went to hear Duclos.

*A man we had never seen previously,* said that amiable whore, *came to the house and proposed a rather unusual ceremony: he wished to be tied to one side of a stepladder; we secured his thighs and waist to the third rung and, raising his arms above his head, tied his wrists to the uppermost step. He was naked. Once firmly bound, he had to be exposed to the most ferocious beating, clubbed with the cat's handle when the knots at the tips of the cords were worn out. He was naked, I repeat, there was no need to lay a finger upon him, nor did he even touch himself, but after having received a savage pounding his monstrous instrument rose like a rocket, it was seen to sway and bounce between the ladder's rungs, hovering like a pendulum and, soon after, impetuously launch its fuck into the middle of the room. He was unbound, he paid, and that was all.*

*The following day he sent us one of his friends whose buttocks and thighs, member and balls had to be pricked with a golden needle. Not until he was covered with blood did he discharge. I handled that commission myself, and as he constantly shouted to me to thrust deeper, I had almost to bury the needle in his glans before seeing his fuck squirt into my palm. As he unleashed it, he thrust his face against mine, sucked my mouth prodigiously, and that was all there was to it.*

*A third—and he too was an acquaintance of his two predecessors—ordered me to flail every bit of his body with nettles. I soon had him streaming blood, he eyed himself in a mirror, and it was not before he saw his body reduced to a scarlet shambles that he let fly his fuck, without touching anything, fondling anything, without requiring anything else of me.*

*Those excesses entertained me hugely, I took a secret delight in participating in them; and all my whimsical clients were equally delighted with me. It was at about the period of those three scenes that a Danish nobleman, having been sent to me for pleasure parties of a very different character, which others have been designated to discuss, had the imprudence to arrive at my establishment with ten thousand francs in diamonds, as much in other gems, and five hundred louis in cash. The prize was too handsome to be allowed to get away; between the two of us, Lucile and I managed to rob the Dane of his last sou. He thought to lodge a complaint, but as I used to pay a heavy bribe to the police, and as in those days one did just about whatever one pleased with gold, the gentleman was ordered to put a stop to his wailing, and his belongings became mine, or rather most of them did, for, in order to assure myself of clear title to that treasure, I had to yield a few precious stones to the minions of the law. Never have I committed a theft, and I would have you remark this interesting fact, without encountering some stroke of good fortune the next day; this latest windfall was a new client, but one of those daily clients one may truly consider a brothel's bread and butter.*

*This individual was an old courtier who, weary of the homages he used unendingly to receive in the palaces of kings, liked to visit whores and enjoy a change of role. He wanted to start with me; very well, said I, and we began without further ado. I had to make him recite his lessons and recite his little speeches, and every time* he made a mistake, he had to get down on his knees and receive, sometimes on his knuckles, sometimes on his behind, vigorous blows of a leathern ferule such as the regents use in schoolrooms. It was also my task to keep a sharp eye out for signs of emotion; once the fire had been lit, I would snatch up his prick and shake it skillfully, scolding him all the while, calling him a little libertine, a very scurvy fellow, a worry to His Majesty, and other childish names which would cause him to come very voluptuously. The identical ceremony was to be executed five times each week at my establishment, but always with a different and properly instructed girl, and for this service I received a stipend of twenty-five louis per month. I knew so many women in Paris I had no trouble promising him what he asked and keeping my word; I had that charming pupil in my house for a decade, toward the end of which period he decided to pack his bags and go off to pursue his studies in hell.

However, I too was aging with the passing years, and although I had the kind of face which retains its beauty, I was beginning to notice that my visitors were men more and more often conveyed to me by whim and accident. I still had some staunch and dependable suitors even at thirty-six, and the rest of the adventures in which I took a hand belong to the period between that time and my fortieth year.

Though thirty-six years old, as I say, the libertine, whose mania I am going to relate in closing today's session, would have nothing to do with anyone else. He was an abbot of sixty or thereabouts, for I received no one but gentlemen of a certain age, and every woman who would like to seek her fortune in our trade will doubtless see fit to impose the same rules barring irresponsible youth from her house. The holy man arrives, and as soon as we are closeted together he begs to see my bum.

"Ah, yes, there's the world's finest ass," he says admiringly. "But, unfortunately, that is not the apparatus which is to provide me with the pittance I intend to consume. Here, take hold," says he, putting his buttocks into my hands, "that's the source whence all good things do come. . . . Be so kind as to help me shit."

I bring up a porcelain pot and place it upon my knees, the abbot backs toward me, stoops, I press his anus, pry it open, and, to be brief, agitate it in every way I think likely to hasten his evacuation. It takes place, an enormous turd fills the bowl, I offer *it to its author, he seizes it, precipitates himself upon it, devours it, and discharges after fifteen minutes of the most violent flogging which I administer upon the same behind that shortly before laid such a splendid egg for his breakfast. He swallowed it all; he had so nicely judged the situation that his sperm did not appear until the last mouthful vanished. All the while I plied my whip, I excited him with a steady stream of comments such as: "Well, then, little rascal, what's this?" and, "Why, here's a nasty little chap, can you really eat shit that way?" and, "I'll teach you, you funny little whoreson bastard; perform such disgraceful things, will you!"*

*And it was by dint of these actions and speeches that the libertine attained the summit of joy.*

At this point, Curval was moved to give the company a before-supper demonstration in fact of what Duclos had described in words. He summoned Fanchon, she extracted shit from him, and the libertine devoured it while the old sorceress drubbed him with all the strength of her skinny but sinewed arm. That lubric exhibition having inspired his confreres, they began hunting for shit wherever any might be found, and then Curval, who had not discharged, mixed the rest of his turd with Thérèse's, whom he had excrete without further ado.

The Bishop, accustomed to making use of his brother's delights, did the same thing with Duclos, the Duc with Marie, little Durcet with Louison. It was atrocious, why, it was unthinkable to employ such decrepit old horrors when such pretty objects stood ready at one's beck and call; but, oh how well 'tis known, satiety is born in the arms of abundance, and when in the very thick of voluptuous delights one takes an even keener pleasure in torments.

These unclean stunts over and done with, and the doing having cost only one discharge, and 'twas the Bishop who produced it, the friends went to table. Having involved themselves in a series of foul activities, they thought best not to change horses in midstream, and for the orgies would have only the four old duennas and the four storytellers; everyone else was packed off to bed. Their Lordships said so many things, did so many more, that all four came like geysers, and our libertine quartet did not retire until overcome with drink and exhaustion.

# THE TWENTIETH DAY

*S*omething very humorous indeed had occurred the night before: absolutely drunk, the Duc, instead of gaining his bedchamber, had installed himself in young Sophie's bed, and despite
all the child could say, for she knew perfectly well what he was
doing violated the rules, he would not be budged, and continued
with great heat to maintain he was damned well where he belonged,
namely, in his bed with Aline, who was listed as his wife for the
night. But as he was allowed certain privileges with Aline which
were still forbidden with the little girls, when he sought to put
Sophie in the posture that favored the amusements of his choice,
and when the poor child, to whom no one had as yet ever done such
a thing, felt the massive head of the Duc's prick hammer at her
young behind's narrow gate and contrive to batter a thoroughfare,
the poor little creature fell to uttering dreadful screeches, and,
leaping up, fled naked about the room. The Duc followed hard on
her heels, swearing like a demon, still mistaking her for Aline.
"Buggress!" he roared, "dost think it the first time?" And fancying he has overtaken her and has her at last, he falls upon Zelmire's
bed, thinking it his own, and embraces that little girl, supposing
Aline has decided to behave reasonably. The same proceedings
with Zelmire as a moment ago with Sophie, because the Duc most
decidedly wishes to attain his objective; but immediately Zelmire
perceives what he is about, she imitates her companion and dupli-
cates her resistance, pronounces a terrible scream, and leaps away.

However, Sophie, the first to take to flight, collects her wits
and, seeing full well that there is but one way to put an end to this

466

*quid pro quo,* sets off in search of light and some cool-headed individual capable of restoring order, and consequently she thinks to look for Duclos. But Duclos had behaved like a pig at the orgies and got herself blind drunk, Sophie comes upon her stretched out unconscious in the middle of the Duc's bed, and fails absolutely to bring her to her senses. Desperate, knowing not to whom under such circumstances she may apply, hearing all her comrades calling for help, she gathers up courage and enters Durcet's apartment; the financier is lying with his daughter, Constance, and Sophie blurts out what has been happening. Constance at any rate did rise from the bed, despite the efforts the drunken Durcet made to restrain her by saying he wanted to discharge; she took a candle and accompanied Sophie to the girls' chamber: she discovered the poor little dears, all in their nightgowns, clustered in the center of the room, and the Duc pursuing now one of them, now another, still persuaded he was dealing with no one but Aline, whom he swore was become a witch that night and had many shapes. Constance finally showed him his error, and entreating him to allow her to guide him back to his room, where, she assured him, he would find a very submissive Aline only too eager to do all he chose to demand of her, the Duc who, thoroughly besotted and acting as always in the very best of faith, really had no other design than to plant his staff in Aline's ass, let himself be taken to her; that lovely girl was there to greet him, and he went to bed; Constance withdrew from the room, and calm was restored generally.

They laughed very heartily all the next day over that nocturnal adventure, and the Duc declared that if, by great misfortune, he were in such a case to happen all accidentally to obliterate a maidenhead, he would not, so it seemed to him, be liable or justly subject to a fine because, intoxicated, he could not be held accountable for his actions; but, oh no, the others assured him, he was mistaken in that, he would indeed have to pay.

They breakfasted amidst their sultanas as usual, and all the little girls avowed they'd been furiously afraid. Not one, however, was found at fault despite the night's alarms; similarly, everything was in order in the boys' quarters, and coffee, like dinner, offering nothing extraordinary, they passed into the auditorium where

Duclos, entirely set to rights after the previous evening's riot, amused the company with the following five episodes:

It was once again I, Messieurs, who went on the stage in the play I am about to describe to you. The other person in the drama was a medical man; the doctor's first act was to examine my buttocks, and as he came to the conclusion they were superb, he spent more than an hour doing nothing but kissing them. He at last confessed his little foibles: they were all connected with shit and shitting, as I had surmised, and knowing what was expected of me, I adopted the appropriate posture. I filled the white porcelain pot I used to employ for this sort of enterprise. Immediately he is the master of my turd, he raises it to his mouth and begins tucking it away; he has no sooner taken a bite than I pick up a bull's pizzle— that was the instrument wherewith I was to caress his bum—I shout threats and imprecations at him, then strike, scold him for the dreadful things he is wont to do, the infamous things, and without heeding me, the libertine swallows the last mouthful, discharges, and is off with the speed of light, having tossed a louis onto the table.

Shortly afterward another came to the house, and I entrusted him to Lucile, who had truly to struggle to make him discharge. He had first of all to be sure the turd that was to be served up to him originated with an old beggar woman, and to convince him, I had to have the old crone operate before his own eyes. I gave him a venerable dame of seventy, covered with ulcers and wens and other signs of erysipelas, and whose last tooth had fallen from her gums fifteen years before. "Good, that's excellent," said he, "precisely the sort I need." Then, enclosing himself with Lucile and the turd, that equally skillful, complacent, and determined girl had to excite him to the point at which he would eat that very mature lump. He sniffed it, stared at it, even touched it, but that was all, he could not seem to make himself go further. Whereupon Lucile, having to resort to something more persuasive than rhetoric, thrust the fire tongs into the fire and, drawing them out red-hot, announced she proposed to burn his buttocks if he did not obey her on the spot and eat his luncheon. Our man trembles, has another try: the same disgust, he recoils. As good as her word, Lucile *lowers his breeches and, bringing to light an ass of very evil aspect and scarred all over, discolored and withered by operations in this same kind, she deftly singes his cheeks. The lecher swears, Lucile applies her iron again, now scorches and finally produces a very definite and sufficiently profound burn in the middle of his ass; pain screws him up to resolution at last, he bites off a mouthful, additional burnings excite him further, and little by little the work is completed. The downing of the last nibble of shit coincided with his discharge, and I have seen exceedingly few as violent; he emitted loud cries and screams, howled like a wolf and rolled on the floor; I thought he had been seized by a frenzy or an attack of epilepsy. Delighted with the patient understanding he had encountered in our house, the libertine promised to be my regular customer, provided I would give him the same girl but a different old woman each time.*

*"The more repulsive the source," said he, "the better you'll be paid for the yield. You have simply no idea," he added, "to what lengths my depravity carries me; I hardly dare acknowledge it to myself."*

*Upon his recommendation, one of his friends visited us the next day, and this individual's depravity carried him, in my opinion, a great deal further, for instead of a relatively mild branding, he had to be soundly beaten with red-hot tongs, and the author of the turd offered him had to be the oldest, filthiest, most disgusting thief we could find. A degenerate old valet of eighty, whom we had had in the house for ages, pleased him wonderfully well for his operation, and, rolling his eyes, smacking his lips, he gobbled up the old devil's turd while it was still warm and while the good Justine, using tongs heated to such a temperature they could hardly be held, thrashed his bum. And she was furthermore obliged to snatch up great bits of his flesh with the instrument, and all but roast them.*

*Another had his buttocks, belly, balls, and prick stabbed with a heavy cobbler's awl, and all this with more or less the same circumstances, that is to say, until he would eat a turd I presented to him in a chamber pot. He was not, however, curious about the turd's origins.*

*Messieurs, it is not easy to imagine to what lengths men are driven in the delirium of their inflamed imaginations. Have I not*

*beheld one who, acting according to the same principles, required
me to shower bone-breaking blows of a cane upon him as he ate a
turd which, before his own eyes, he had us fish up out of the depths
of the house's privy? and his perfidious discharge did not flow into
my mouth until he had devoured the last spoonful of that foul
muck.*

"Well, you know, everything's imaginable and even possible,"
said Curval as he pensively fondled Desgranges' buttocks. "I am
convinced one can go still further than that."

"Further?" said the Duc who at that moment was mauling the
bare behind of Adelaide, his wife for the day. "And what the devil
would you have one do?"

"Worse!" replied Curval, something of a hiss in his voice. "It
seems to me one never sufficiently exploits the possible."

"I entirely agree with the Président," spoke up Durcet, then
in the act of embuggering Antinoüs, "and I have the feeling my
mind is capable of further improvements upon all those piggish
stunts."

"I think I know what Durcet means," said the Bishop who,
for the time being, was idle, or who rather had not yet begun to
operate.

"Well, what the devil does he mean?" the Duc demanded to
know.

Whereupon the Bishop stood up and went to Durcet's alcove;
the two men whispered together, the Bishop then moved on to
where Curval was, and the latter said, "That's it, exactly!" And
then the Bishop spoke in the Duc's ear.

"By fuck!" His Highness exclaimed, "I'd never have thought
of that one."

As these gentlemen said no more that might shed light on the
thing, we have no way of knowing just what Durcet did mean or
what the Duc declared he would never have thought of. And even
were it that we knew, I believe we would be well advised to keep
knowledge of the thing strictly to ourselves, at least in the interest
of modesty, for there are an infinite number of things one ought
merely to indicate, prudent circumspection requires that one keep
a bridle on one's tongue; there are such things, are there not, as

chaste ears? one may now and again encounter them, and I am absolutely convinced the reader has already had occasion to be grateful for the discretion we have employed in his regard; the further he reads on, the more secure shall be our claim to his sincerest praise upon this head, why, yes, we feel we may almost assure him of it even at this early stage. Well, whatever one may say, each one has his own soul to save, and of what punishment, both in this world and in the next, is he not deserving who all immoderately were to be pleased to divulge all the caprices, all the whims and tastes, all the clandestine horrors whereunto men are subject when their fancy is free and afire? 'twould be to reveal secrets which ought to be sunk in obscurity for humanity's sake, 'twould be to undertake the general corruption of manners and to precipitate his brethren in Jesus Christ into all the extravagances such tableaux might feature in very lively color and profusion; and God, Who seeth even unto the depths of our hearts, this puissant God Who hath made heaven and earth and Who must one day judge us, God alone knoweth whether we have any desire to hear ourselves reproached by Him for such crimes.

Messieurs put the finishing touches on several horrors they had begun; Curval, to cite one example, had Desgranges shit, the others occupied themselves with either that same distraction, or with some others not much more improving, and their Lordships then went to supper. At the orgies, Duclos having overheard the friends discussing the new diet we alluded to earlier, whose purpose was to render shit more abundant and more delicate, at the orgies, I say, Duclos noted that she was truly astonished to find connoisseurs like themselves unaware of the true secret whereby turds are made both very abundant and very tasty. Questioned about the measures which ought to be adopted, she said that there was but one: the subject should be given a mild indigestion; there was no need to make him eat what he did not like or what was unwholesome, but, by obliging him to eat hurriedly and between meals, the desired results could be obtained at once. The experiment was performed that same evening: Fanny was waked—no one had paid any attention to her, and she had gone to bed after supper—she was immediately required to eat four large plain cakes, and the next morning she furnished one of the biggest and most beautiful turds they had been able to procure from her up until that time. Duclos' suggested system was therefore approved, although they upheld their decision to do away with bread; Duclos said they were well advised to be rid of it; the fruits produced by her method, said she, would only be the better. From that time on not a day passed but they'd gently upset those pretty youngsters' digestions in one way or another, and the results were simply beyond anything you could imagine. I mention this in passing so that, should any amateur be disposed to make use of the formula, he may be firmly persuaded there is none superior.

The remainder of the evening having brought nothing extraordinary, everyone retired in order to be freshly rested for the following day's wedding: the brilliant match to be made was destined to unite Colombe and Zélamir, and this ceremony was to be the basis for celebrating the third week's festival.

# THE TWENTY-FIRST DAY

$\mathcal{P}$reparations for that ceremony were started early in the morning; they were of the usual sort but, and I have no idea whether or not it was by a stroke of chance, the inspection uncovered signs of the young bride's misbehavior. Durcet declared he had found shit in her chamber pot; she denied having put it there, asserting that, to cause her to be punished, the duenna had come and done the thing during the night, and that the governesses often planted such evidence when they wished to embroil the children in difficulties. Well, she defended herself very eloquently and to no purpose whatever, for she was not carefully heard, and as her little husband-to-be was already on the list, the prospect of correcting both of them was the cause of great amusement.

Nevertheless, the young bride and groom, once the mass had been said, were conducted with much pomp to the salon where the ceremony was to be completed before mealtime; they were both of the same age, and the little girl was delivered naked to her husband, who was permitted to do with her whatever he wanted. Is there any voice so compelling as example's? And where if not in Silling were it possible to receive very bad examples and the most contagious ones? The young man sped like an arrow to its mark, hopped upon his little wife, and as his prick was greatly stiff, although not yet capable of a discharge, he would inevitably have got his spear in her . . . but mild as would have been the damage done her, the source of all Messieurs' glory lay in preventing anything from harming the tender flower they wished alone to pluck. And so it was the Bishop checked the lad's impetuous career, and

473

profiting from his erection, straightway thrust into his ass the very
pretty and already very well-formed engine wherewith Zélamir
was about to plumb his young spouse. What a disappointment for
that young man, and what a discrepancy between the old Bishop's
slack-sprung vent and the strait and tidy cunt of a little thirteen-
year-old virgin! But Zélamir was having to deal with people who
were deaf to common-sense arguments.

Curval laid hands on Colombe and thigh-fucked her from in
front while licking her eyes, her mouth, her nostrils, in a word, her
entire face. Meanwhile, he must surely have been rendered some
kind of service, for he discharged, and Curval was not a man to
lose his fuck over silly trifles.

They dined, the wedded couple appeared at the meal and
again in the salon for coffee, which that day was served by the very
cream of the subjects, by, I wish to say, Augustine, Zelmire,
Adonis, and Zéphyr. Curval wished to stiffen afresh, had absolutely
to have some shit, and Augustine shot him as fine an artifact as it
were in human power to create. The Duc had himself sucked by
Zelmire, Durcet by Colombe, the Bishop by Adonis. The last
named shitted into Durcet's mouth after having dispatched the
Bishop. But no sign of fuck; it was becoming rare, they had failed
to exercise any restraint at the outset of the holiday, and as they
realized the extreme need of seed they would have toward the
end, Messieurs were growing more frugal. They went next to the
auditorium where the majestic Duclos, invited to display her ass
before starting, exposed that matchless ensemble most libertinely
to the eyes of the assembly, and then began to speak:

*Here is still another trait of my character, Messieurs,* said
that sublime woman; *after having made you well enough acquainted
with it, you will be so kind as to judge what I intend to omit from
what I am going to tell you . . . and you will, I trust, dispense
me from having to say more about myself.*

*Lucile's mother had just fallen into a state of the most
wretched poverty, and it was only by the most extraordinary stroke
of chance that this charming girl, who had received no news at all
of her mother since having fled her house, now learned of her
extreme distress: one of our street scouts—hard in pursuit of some*

*young girl for a client who shared the tastes and designs of the Marquis de Mesanges, for a client, that is to say, who was eager to make an outright and final purchase—one of our scouts came in to report to me, as I was lying in bed with Lucile, that she had chanced upon a little fifteen-year-old, without question a maid, extremely pretty, and, she said, closely resembling Mademoiselle Lucile; yes, she went on, they were like two peas in a pod, but this little girl she'd found was in such bedraggled condition that she'd have to be kept and fattened for several days before she'd be fit to market. And thereupon she gave a description of the aged woman with whom the child had been discovered, and of the frightful indigence wherein that mother lay; from certain traits, details of age and appearance, from all she heard concerning the daughter, Lucile had a secret feeling the persons being discussed might well be her own mother and sister. She knew she had left home when the latter was still very young, hence it was hard to be sure of the thing, and she asked my permission to go and verify her suspicions.*

*At this point my infernal mind conceived a little horror; its effect was to set my body afire. Telling the street scout to leave the room, and being unable to resist the fury raging in my blood, I began by entreating Lucile to frig me. Then, halting halfway through the operation:*

*"Why do you want to go to see that old woman?" I asked Lucile; "what do you propose to do?"*

*"Why, but don't you see," said Lucile, whose heart was still undeveloped, "there are certain things that one is expected to do . . . I ought to help her if I can, and above all if she turns out to be my mother."*

*"Idiot," I muttered, thrusting her away from me, "go sacrifice alone to your disgusting popular prejudices, and for not daring to brave them, go lose the most incredibly fine opportunity to irritate your senses by a horror that would make you discharge for a decade."*

*Bewildered by my words, Lucile stared at me, and I saw I had to explain this philosophy to her, for she apparently had not the vaguest understanding of it. I therefore did lecture her, I made her comprehend the vileness, the baseness of the ties wherewith* they seek to bind us to the author of our days; I demonstrated to her that for having carried us in her womb, instead of deserving some gratitude, a mother merits naught but hate, since 'twas for her pleasure alone and at the risk of exposing us to all the ills and sorrows the world holds in store for us that she brought us into the light, with the sole object of satisfying her brutal lubricity. To this I added roughly everything one might deem helpful in supporting the doctrine which sane right-thinking dictates, and which the heart urges when it is not cluttered up with stupidities imbibed in the nursery.

"And what matters it to you," I added, "whether that creature be happy or wretched? Does her situation have anything to do with yours? does it affect you? Get rid of those demeaning ties whose absurdity I've just proven to you, and thereby entirely isolating this creature, sundering her utterly from yourself, you will not only recognize that her misfortune must be a matter of indifference to you, but that it might even be exceedingly voluptuous to worsen her plight. For, after all, you do owe her your hatred, that has been made clear, and thus you would be taking your revenge: you would be performing what fools term an evil deed, and you know the immense influence crime exerts upon the senses. And so here are two sources of pleasure in the outrages I'd like to have you inflict upon her: both the sweet delights of vengeance, and those one always tastes whenever one does evil."

Whether it was that I employed a greater eloquence in exhorting Lucile than I do in recounting the fact to you now, or whether it was because her already very libertine and very corrupt spirit instantly notified her heart of the voluptuous promise contained in my principles, she tasted them, and I saw her lovely cheeks flush in response to that libertine flame which never fails to appear every time one violates some prohibition, abolishes some restraint.

"All right," she murmured, "what are we to do?"

"Amuse ourselves with her," said I, "and make some money at the same time; as for pleasure, you can be sure to have some if you adopt my principles. And as for the money, the same thing applies, for I can make use of both your old gray-haired mother *and your young sister; I'll arrange two different parties which will prove very lucrative."*

Lucile accepts, I frig her the better to excite her to commit the crime, and we turn all our thoughts to devising plans. Let me first undertake to outline the first of them, since it deserves to be included in the category of passions I have to discuss, although I shall have to alter the exact chronology in order to fit it into the sequence of events, and when I shall have informed you of this first part of my scheme, I shall enlighten you upon the second.

There was a man, well placed in society and exceedingly wealthy, exceedingly influential and having a disorder of the mind which surpasses all that words are able to convey; as I was acquainted with him only as the Comte, you will allow me, however well advised of his full name I may be, simply to designate him by his title. The Comte was somewhat above thirty-five years of age, and all his passions had reached their maximum strength; he had neither faith nor law, no god and no religion, and was above all else endowed, like yourselves, Messieurs, with an invincible horror of what is called the charitable sentiment; he used to say that to understand this impulse was totally beyond his powers, and that he would not for an instant assent to the notion that one dare outrage Nature to the point of upsetting the order she had imposed when she created different classes of individuals; the very idea of elevating one such class through the bestowing of alms or aid, and thus of overthrowing another, the idea of devoting sums of money, not upon agreeable things which might afford one pleasure, but rather upon these absurd and revolting relief enterprises, all this he considered an insult to his intelligence or a mystery his intelligence could not possibly grasp. Thoroughly instilled, nay, penetrated though he was with these opinions, he reasoned still further; not only did he derive the keenest delight from refusing aid to the needy, but he ameliorated what was already an ecstasy by outrageously persecuting the humble and injured. One of his higher pleasures, for example, consisted in having meticulous searches made of those dark, shadowy regions where starving indigence gnaws whatever crust it has earned by terrible toil, and sprinkles tears upon its meager portion. He would stiffen at the thought of going abroad not only to enjoy the bitterness of

*those tears, but even . . . but even to aggravate their cause and, if
'twere possible, to snatch away the wretched substance that kept
the damned yet amongst the living. And this taste of his was no
whim, no light fantasy, 'twas a fury; he used to say that he knew
no more piercing delight, nothing that could more successfully
arouse him, inflame his soul, than these excesses I speak of. Nor
was this rage of his, he one day assured me, the fruit of depravation; no, he had been possessed by this mania since his youngest
years, and his heart, perpetually toughened against misery's plain-
tive accents, had never conceived any gentler, milder feelings for it.*

*As it is of the greatest importance you be familiar with the
subject, you must first of all know that the same man had three
different passions: the one I am going to relate to you, another,
which Martaine will explain to you later when she refers to this
same personage, and a third, yet more atrocious, which Desgranges
will doubtless reserve for the end of her contribution as doubtless one of the most impressive upon her list. But we'll begin with
the one on mine.*

*Straightway I had informed the Comte of the nest of misery
I had discovered for him, of the inhabitants of that nest, he was
transported with joy. But it so happened that business intimately
connected with his fortune and having an important bearing upon
his advancement, which he took much care not to neglect, in that
he held them vital to his misconduct, business, I say, was going to
occupy all his attention for the next two weeks, and as he did
not want to let the little girl slip through his fingers, he preferred
sacrificing the pleasure the first scene promised him, and to be
certain of enjoying the second. And so he ordered me to have the
child kidnaped at whatever cost, but without delay, and to have
her deposited at the address he indicated to me. And in order to
keep you in suspense no longer, my Lords, that address was
Madame Desgranges', for she was the agent who furnished him
with material for his third class of secret parties. And now to return to the objects of all our maneuvering.*

*So far, we had done little but locate Lucile's mother, both to
set the stage for the recognition scene between mother and daughter and to study the problems associated with the kidnaping of
the little girl. Lucile, well coached in her part, only greeted her*

mother in order to insult her, to say that it was thanks to her she
had been hurled into libertinage, and to these she added a thousand
other similarly unkind remarks, which broke the poor woman's
heart and ruined the pleasure of rediscovering her daughter. During this first interview, I thought I glimpsed the appropriate way
to talk with the woman, and pointed out to her that, having rescued
her elder child from an impure existence, I was willing to do as
much for the younger one. But the stratagem did not succeed, the
poor wretch fell to weeping and said that nothing in the world
would induce her to part with the one treasure she had left, that
the little girl was her one resource, she herself was old, infirm,
that the child cared for her, and that to be deprived of her would
be to lose life itself. At this juncture, Messieurs, I must confess,
and I do so with shame, that I felt a faint stirring in the depths
of my heart; it advised me that my voluptuous pleasure was bound
only to be increased by the horrible refinements I was about to
give to my meditated crime, and having informed the old lady that
shortly thereafter her daughter would come to pay her a visit with
a man of great influence, who could perhaps render her great
services, we left, and I bent all my efforts to employing the lures
and devices I usually relied upon to snare game. I had carefully
examined the little girl, she was worth my going to some trouble:
fifteen years of age, a pretty figure, a very lovely skin, and very
pretty features. She arrived three days later, and after having
examined every part of her body and found nothing but what was
very charming, dimpled, and very neat despite the poor nourishment she had for so long had to put up with, I passed her along
to Madame Desgranges: this transaction marked the beginning of
our commercial relations.

His private affairs attended to, our Comte reappeared; Lucile
conducts him to her mother's home, and 'tis at this point begins
the scene I wish to describe. The old mother was found in bed,
the room was without heat although we were then in the midst
of a bitterly cold winter; beside her bed sat a wooden crock containing milk. The Comte pissed into the crock as soon as he had
entered. To prevent any possible trouble, and in order to feel himself the undisputed master of the fort, the Comte had posted two
of his minions, a pair of strapping lads, on the stairway, and they

*were to offer a stubborn obstacle to any undesirable coming up
or going down.*

"*My dear old buggress,*" *intoned the Comte,* "*we have come
here with your daughter, you see her there, and a damned pretty
whore she is, upon my soul; we have come here, I say, to relieve
what ails you, wretched old leper that you are, but before we can
help you, you must tell us what's amiss. Well, go on, speak,*" *he
said, seating himself and beginning to palpate Lucile's buttocks,*
"*go on, I say, itemize your sufferings.*"

"*Alas!*" *said the good woman,* "*you come with that vixen not
to help me but to insult me.*"

"*Vixen? How's this,*" *said the Comte,* "*you dare use insults
with your daughter? By God,*" *he went on, rising to his feet and
dragging the old thing from her litter,* "*get out of that bed, get
down on your knees, and ask to be forgiven for the language you
have just employed.*"

*There was no way to resist.*

"*And you, Lucile, lift your skirts and have your mother kiss
your cheeks, and I am damned certain she wants nothing more
than to kiss them, eager as she must be for some kind of reconciliation.*"

*The insolent Lucile rubs her ass upon the seamed and wrinkled
visage of her dear old mother; overwhelming her with a tirade of
playful epithets, the Comte permits the poor woman to crawl back
into bed, and then resumes the conversation.* "*I tell you once
again,*" *he says,* "*that if you recite all your troubles to me, I'll take
the best care of you.*"

*The woe-ridden are credulous; and they love to lament. The
old woman made them privy to all her sufferings, and complained
especially, with great bitterness, of the theft of her daughter; she
sharply accused Lucile of having had a hand in it and of knowing
where the child presently was, since the lady with whom she had
come a little while ago had proposed to take her under her wing;
that was the basis for her supposition (and there was considerable
logic in the way she argued) that this same lady had taken her
away. Meanwhile, the Comte, directly facing Lucile's ass, for by
this time he had got her to step out of her skirts, the Comte, I say,
now and again kissing that handsome ass and frigging himself un-*

*interruptedly, listened, put questions to her, requested details, and regulated all the titillations of his perfidious lust according to the old woman's replies. But when she said that the absence of her daughter, thanks to whose work she was procured her wherewithal, was going to lead her gradually but inexorably to the grave, since she had nothing and for four days had been kept barely alive by that small quantity of milk he had just spoiled:*

*"Why, then, bitch," said the Comte, aiming his prick at the old creature and continuing to explore Lucile's buttocks, "why, then go ahead and croak, you foul old whore, do you suppose the world will be any worse off without you?"*

*And as he concluded his question he loosed his sperm.*

*"Were that to happen," he observed, "I believe I'd have only one regret, and that would be not having myself hastened the event."*

*But there was more to it than that, the Comte was not the sort of a man to be appeased by a mere discharge; Lucile, fully aware of the role she was to play, now that he had been relieved, busied herself preventing the old woman from noticing what he was about, and the Comte, rummaging through every corner of the room, came upon a silver goblet, the last vestige of the material well-being that had once upon a time been this poor wretch's; he put the goblet in his pocket. This fresh outrage having put new hardness into his prick, he again dragged the old woman from her bed, stripped her naked, and bade Lucile frig him upon the matron's withered old frame. Once again nothing could be done to stop him, and the villain darted his fuck over that ancient flesh, redoubled his insults, and said that the poor wretch could rest perfectly assured he was not yet done with her, and that she would soon have news of himself and of her little girl who, he wished to have her know, was in his power. He then proceeded to that last discharge, his transports of lust were ignited by the horrors wherewith his perfidious imagination was already in a ferment, by the ruin of the entire family he was contemplating, and he left. But in order not to have to return to this affair, hear, Messieurs, how I surpassed myself in villainy. Seeing that he might have confidence in me, the Comte informed me of the second scene he was preparing for the benefit of the old woman and her little daughter; he told me he wanted the child brought to him without delay and, as he wanted to reunite the whole family, he wished to have me cede Lucile to him too, for he had been deeply moved by her lovely ass; he made no effort to conceal that his purpose was to ruin Lucile as well as her ass, together with her mother and sister.*

*I loved Lucile. But I loved money even more. He offered me an unheard-of price for these three creatures, I agreed to everything. Four days later, Lucile, her little sister and her aged mother were brought together; Madame Desgranges will tell you about that meeting. As for your faithful Duclos, she continues and resumes the thread of her story this anecdote has interrupted; indeed, she wonders whether she ought not have recited it at some later time, for, esteeming it a very stirring episode, she considers it would have proven a fitting climax to her contribution.*

"One moment," said Durcet, "I cannot hear such stories without being affected, their influence upon me would be difficult to describe. I have been restraining my fuck since the middle of the tale, kindly allow me to unburden myself now."

And he dashed into his closet with Michette, Zélamir, Cupidon, Fanny, Thérèse, and Adelaide; several minutes later his shouts began to ring out, and soon after the uproar started, Adelaide emerged in tears, saying that all this made her very unhappy, and wondering why they had to excite her husband with such dreadful stories; she who told them, Adelaide declared, not others, ought by rights to be the victim. During the interim the Duc and the Bishop had not wasted an instant, but the manner in which they operated belonging to the class of procedures circumstances compel us still to mask from the reader's view, we beg him to suffer the curtain to remain down, and to allow us to move on to the four tales Duclos had yet to relate before bringing this twenty-first meeting of the assembly to a close.

*A week after Lucile's departure, I handled a rascal blessed with a rather curious mania. Warned several days in advance of his intended arrival, I had let a great number of turds accumulate in my one-holed chair, and I had induced one of my young ladies to add a few more to the collection. Our man appeared costumed* as a Savoyard rustic; 'twas in the morning, he swept out my room, removed the pot from beneath the chair, and went out to empty it (this emptying, I might note in parentheses, took a considerable length of time); when he returned he showed me how carefully he'd cleaned it out and asked for his payment. But, and this of course was all stipulated in our prior arrangement, instead of giving him a coin, I seize the broom and fall to belaboring him with the handle.

"Your payment, villain?" I cry, "why, here's what you deserve."

And I bestow at least a dozen blows upon him. He seeks to escape me, I pursue him, and the libertine, whose critical moment has arrived, discharges all the way down the stairs, bawling out at the top of his voice that they're cracking his skull, that they want to kill him, and that he's got himself into the house of a scoundrel, she's not by any means the honest woman he at first took her for, etc.

Another carried, in a small pocket case, a little knotty stick which he kept for an unusual purpose; he wanted me to insert the stick into his urethral canal, and, having plunged it in to a depth of three inches, to rattle it with utmost vigor, and with my other hand to pull back his foreskin and frig his poor device. At the very instant he discharged, one had to pull out the stick, raise one's skirts in front, and he would discharge upon one's mound.

Six months later I had to do with an abbot who wanted me to take a burning candle and direct the drops of molten tallow so that they fell upon his penis and balls; it required nothing more than the sensation this ceremony produced to bring about his discharge. His machine required no touching, but it remained limp throughout; before they would yield fuck, his genitals had to be given such a heavy coating of wax that toward the end there was no recognizing this strange object as a part of the human anatomy.

That ecclesiastic had a friend who loved nothing so much as to offer his bum to be perforated by a multitude of gold pins, and when thus decorated, his hindquarter far more resembling a pincushion than an ordinary ass, he would sit down, the better to savor the effect he cherished, and, presenting one's very wide-

*spread buttocks to him, he would twiddle his member and dis-
charge into one's vent.*

"Durcet," said the Duc, "I should very much like to see that
sweet chubby ass of yours studded all over with golden pins, ah
yes, I'm persuaded 'twould thus appear more interesting than
ever."

"Your Grace," quoth the financier, "you know that for forty
years it has been my glory and my honor to imitate you in all
things; I but ask you to have the kindness to set me an example,
and you have my word that I will follow it."

"God's loin-scum!" exclaimed the good Curval, who had not
until now been heard from, "by His sacred seed, I do declare that
story about Lucile has made me stiff! I've held my peace, but my
head's been at work none the less. Look here," said he, exhibiting
his prick standing high, "see whether I do not say true. I've a
furious impatience to hear the denouement of the story of those
three buggresses; I have the highest hope they'll meet one another
in a common grave."

"Softly there, softly," said the Duc, "let's not anticipate
events. Were you not stiff, Monsieur le Président, you'd not be in
such a hurry to hear talk of wheels and gibbets. You resemble a
great many other of Justice's servitors, whose pricks, they say,
rise up every time they pronounce the sentence of death."

"Never mind the magistrature," Curval replied, "the fact
remains that I am enchanted by Duclos' doings, that I find her
a charming girl, and that her story of the Comte has put me in
a dreadful state, and in this state, I say, I could be easily persuaded
to go abroad, stop a carriage on the highway, and rob its occupants."

"Ah, Président, take care," said the Bishop; "keep a hand
upon yourself, my dear fellow, else we'll cease to be in safety here.
One such slip, and the least we could expect would be the noose
for all of us."

"The noose? Ah, the noose, yes . . . but not for us. However,
I don't for a minute deny I'd myself gladly condemn these young
ladies here to be hanged, and especially Madame la Duchesse,
who's lying like a cow upon my sofa and who, merely because she's

got a spoonful of modified fuck in the womb, fancies no one dares touch her any more."

"Oh," said Constance, " 'tis surely not with you I count upon being respected because of my state. Your loathing for pregnant women is only too notorious."

"A prodigious loathing, isn't it?" said Curval with a chuckle, "why, indeed it is prodigious."

And, transported by enthusiasm, he was, I believe, on the verge of committing some sacrilege against that superb belly, when Duclos intervened.

"Come, Sire, come with me," said she; "since 'tis I who have caused the hurt, I'd like to repair it."

And together they passed into the secluded boudoir, followed by Augustine, Hébé, Cupidon, and Thérèse. It was not long before the Président's braying resounded through the castle, and despite all Duclos' attentions, little Hébé returned weeping from the hurly-burly; there was even more to it than tears, but we dare not yet disclose just what it was had set her to trembling. A little patience, friend reader, and we shall soon hide nothing from your inquisitive gaze.

And now Curval himself returns, grumbling between his teeth and swearing that all those dratted laws prevent a man from discharging at his ease, etc.; their Lordships sit down at table. After supper they withdrew to mete out punishment for the misbehavior that had accrued during the week, but the guilty were not that evening in great number: only Sophie, Colombe, Adelaide, and Zélamir merited correction, and received it. Durcet, who since the beginning of the evening had waxed very hot, and who had been particularly inspired by Adelaide, granted her no quarter; Sophie, whom they had detected shedding tears during the story of the Comte, was punished for that misdemeanor as well as for her former one, and the Duc and Curval, we understand, treated the day's little newlyweds, Zélamir and Colombe, with a severity that almost bordered upon barbarity.

The Duc and Curval, in splendid form and singularly wrought up, said they had no wish to retire, and having had a quantity of beverages fetched in, they passed the night drinking with the four storytellers and Julie, whose libertinage, increasing every day, gave her the air of a very amiable creature who deserved to be ranked among those objects for whom Messieurs had some regard. The following morning, while making his rounds, Durcet found all seven of them dead drunk. The naked girl was discovered lodged between her father and her husband and in a posture which gave evidence of neither virtue nor decency in libertinage; it was plain enough to the financier that (to hold the reader in suspense no longer) they had both enjoyed her simultaneously. Duclos, who, from all appearances, had functioned as an instrument to this crime, lay sprawled near the compact trio, and the others were strewn in a confused heap in the corner opposite the fire, which someone had taken care to keep burning throughout the night.

# THE TWENTY-SECOND DAY

$\mathcal{A}$s a result of these all-night bacchanals, exceedingly little was accomplished on the twenty-second day of November; half the customary exercises were forgot, at dinner Messieurs appeared to be in a daze, and it was not until coffee they began to come somewhat to their senses. The coffee was served them by Rosette and Sophie, Zélamir and Giton. In an effort to return to his usual old self, Curval had Giton shit, and the Duc swallowed Rosette's turd; the Bishop had himself sucked by Sophie, Durcet by Zélamir, but no one discharged. They moved dutifully into the auditorium; the matchless Duclos, weak and queasy after the preceding day's excesses, took her place with drooping eyelids, and her tales were so brief, they contained so few episodes, were recounted so listlessly, that we have taken it upon ourselves to supply them, and in the reader's behalf to clarify the somewhat confused speech she made to our friends.

In keeping with prescription, she recounted five passions: the first was that of a man who used to have his ass frigged with a tin dildo priorly charged with warm water, the which liquid was pumped into his fundament at the same instant he ejaculated; nothing else was required to obtain that effect, he needed no one else's ministry.

The second man had the same mania, but was wont to use a far greater number of instruments; initially, he called for a very minute one, then gradually increased the caliber, ascending the scale by small fractions of an inch until he reached a weapon with the dimensions of a veritable fieldpiece, and only discharged upon receiving a torrent from its muzzle.

Far more of the mysterious was required to please the third one's palate: at the outset of the game, he had an enormous instrument introduced into his ass, then it was withdrawn, he would shit, would eat what he had just rendered, and next he had to be flogged. The flogging administered, it was time to reinsert the formidable device in his rectum, then once again it was removed, and now it was the whore's turn to shit, and after that she picked up the whip again and lashed him while he munched what she had done; a third time, yes, a third time the instrument was driven home, and that, plus the girl's turd he finished eating, was sufficient to complete his happiness.

In her fourth tale, Duclos made mention of a man who would have all his joints bound with strings; in order to make his discharge even more delicious, his neck itself was compressed, and, half choking, he would shoot his fuck squarely at the whore's asshole.

And in her fifth, she referred to that individual who used to tie a slender cord tightly to his glans; the girl, naked, would pass the other end of the cord between her thighs, and walk away from him, drawing the cord taut and offering the patient a full view of her ass; he would then discharge.

Truly exhausted after having fulfilled her task, the storyteller begged leave to retire, and she was allowed to. A few moments were devoted to uttering smutty comments upon this and that, and then the four libertines went to supper, but everyone felt the effects of our two principal actors' disorderliness. At the orgies they were also as prudent and restrained as 'twere possible for such debauchees to be, and the entire household went more or less quietly to bed.

# THE TWENTY-THIRD DAY

"*B*ut how is it possible to shout and roar the way you do when you discharge?" the Duc demanded of Curval upon bidding him good morning on the 23rd. "Why the devil must you scream that way? I've never seen such violent discharges."

"Why, by God," Curval replied, "is it for you, whom one can hear a league away, to address such a reproach to a modest man like myself? Those little murmurs you hear, my good friend, are caused by my extremely sensitive nervous system; the objects which excite our passions create such a lively commotion in the electrically charged fluid that flows in our nerves, the shock received by the animal spirits composing this fluid is of such a degree of violence, that the entire mechanism is rattled by these effects, and one is just as powerless to suppress one's cries when overwhelmed by the terrible blows imparted by pleasure, as one would be when assailed by the powerful emotions of pain."

"Well, you define the thing very well, Président, but what was the delicate object that could have produced such a vibration in your animal spirits?"

"I was very energetically sucking Adonis' prick, his mouth, and his asshole, for I was cast down with despair at not being able to do more to my couch companion; all the while I made the best of my hard situation, Antinoüs, seconded by your dear daughter Julie, labored, each in his own way, to evacuate the liquor whose eventual outpouring occasioned the musical sounds which, you say, struck your ears."

489

"And it all worked so well that now, today," said the Duc, "you're as weak as a baby."

"No, your Grace, not at all," Curval declared; "deign but to observe my career, my motions today, and but do me the honor of judging my style and vehemence in sport, and you shall see me conduct myself quite as ever, and assuredly as well as you yourself."

They were at this point in the conversation when Durcet arrived to say breakfast was being served. They passed into the girls' quarters, where those eight charming little houris were distributing cups of coffee and hot water; the Duc therewith demanded to know of Durcet, the month's steward and presiding officer, why was it the coffee was being served with water?

"You'll have it with milk whenever you wish," said the financier. "Would you prefer it thus now?"

The Duc said that yes, he would.

"Augustine, my dear," Durcet said, "a little milk in Monsieur le Duc's cup, if you please."

Thereupon the little girl, prepared for any eventuality, placed Blangis' cup beneath her ass, and through her anus squeezed three or four spoonfuls of milk, very clear and perfectly fresh. This cunning feat produced much pleasant laughter, everyone requested milk in his coffee. All the asses were charged in the same way Augustine's was: 'twas an agreeable little surprise the month's director of games had thought to give his colleagues. Fanny poured some into the Bishop's cup, Zelmire into Curval's, and Michette into the financier's; the friends took a second round of coffee, and the four other girls performed over these new cups the same ceremony their comrades had over the first cups; and so on and on; the whole thing entertained their Lordships immoderately. It heated the Bishop's brain; he affirmed he wanted something beside milk, and the lovely Sophie stepped forth to satisfy him. Although all eight definitely wished to shit, they had been strongly urged to exercise self-restraint while dispensing the milk, and this first time to yield absolutely nothing else.

Next, they paid the little boys a good-morning visit; Curval induced Zélamir to shit for him, the Duc applauded what Giton brought to light. Two subaltern fuckers, Constance, and Rosette provided the spectacle in the chapel latrine. Rosette was one of those upon whom the old formula for promoting indigestion had been tried out; at coffee, she had had the world's worst time keeping her milk free of foreign ingredients, and now, seated upon the throne, she released the most superb turd you could hope to lay eyes upon. Duclos was congratulated, they said her system was a resounding success, and from then on they used it every day; never once did it fail them. The conversation at dinner was enlivened by the breakfast's pleasantry, and a number of other things of the same kind were invented and proposed; we shall perhaps have occasion to mention them in the sequel.

After-dinner coffee was served by four subjects of the same age: to wit, Zelmire, Augustine, Zéphyr, and Adonis. The Duc thigh-fucked Augustine while tickling her anus with his thumb, Curval did the same thing with Zelmire, but may or may not have used his thumb, his hand was not in clear view; the Bishop toiled between Zéphyr's tightly squeezed legs, and the financier fucked Adonis' mouth. Augustine announced that she was all ready to shit, how would they like her to do a little shit? The poor dear could not wait another moment, she too had been exposed to the indigestion-producing experiments. Curval beckoned her to him, opened his mouth, and the delightful little girl dropped a monstrous turd into it; the Président gobbled it up in a trice, not without unleashing a veritable stream of fuck into Fanchon's hands.

"There you are," he said to the Duc, "you see that nighttime merriment has no damaging effect upon the following day's pleasures; you're lagging behind, Monsieur le Duc."

"I'll not be behind for long," said the latter, to whom Zelmire, inspired by an urge no less imperious, was rendering the same service Augustine had a moment before rendered Curval. And, yes, as he pronounces those words, the Duc topples over, utters piercing shrieks, swallows shit, and discharges like a madman.

"Enough of this," said the stern, austere voice of the Bishop, moderation's exponent; "at least two of us must preserve our strength for the stories."

Durcet, who, unlike the Duc and Curval, had no surfeit of fuck to fling carelessly about, assented wholeheartedly, and after the shortest possible nap, they installed themselves in the auditorium, where, in the following terms, the spellbinding Duclos resumed her brilliant and lascivious history:

*Why is it, Messieurs,* the radiant creature inquired, *that in this world there are men whose hearts have been so numbed, whose sentiments of honor and delicacy have been so deadened, that one sees them pleased and amused by what degrades and soils them? One is even led to suppose their joy can be mined nowhere save from the depths of opprobrium, that, for such men, delight cannot exist elsewhere save in what brings them into consort with dishonor and infamy. To what I am going now to recount to you, my Lords, to the various instances I shall lay before you in order to prove my assertion, do not reply, saying that 'tis physical sensation which is the foundation of these subsequent pleasures; I know, to be sure, physical sensation is involved herein, but be perfectly certain that it does not exist in some sort save thanks to the powerful support given it by moral sensation, and be sure as well that, were you to provide these individuals with the same physical sensation and to omit to join to it all that the moral may yield, you'd fail entirely to stir them.*

*There very often came to me a man of whose name and quality I was ignorant, but who, however, I knew most certainly to be a man of circumstance. The kind of woman with whom I married him made no difference at all: beautiful or ugly, old or young, it was all the same to him; his partner had only to play her role competently, and that role was as follows: ordinarily, he would come to the house in the morning, he would enter, as though by accident, into a room where a girl lay upon a bed, her skirts raised to above her waist and in the attitude of a woman frigging herself. Immediately his entrance was noticed, the woman, as if surprised, would spring from the bed.*

*"What are you doing here, villain?"* she would ask very crossly; *"who gave you permission to disturb me?"*

*He would beg forgiveness, his apologies would go unheeded, and all the while showering him with a renewed deluge of the harshest and most biting invectives, she would fall to giving him furious kicks upon the posterior, and she would become all the more certain of her aim as the patient, far from dodging or shield-*

*ing his behind, would unfailingly turn himself and present the target within easy range, although looking for all the world as if he wished only to escape this punishment and flee the room. The kicking is redoubled, he cries to be spared, blows and curses are the only replies he receives, and as soon as he feels he is sufficiently excited, he promptly draws his prick from his breeches, which he has hitherto kept tightly buttoned, and lightly giving his device three or four flicks of the wrist, he discharges while rushing away under an unremitting storm of kicks and abuses.*

*A second personage, either tougher or more accustomed to this sort of exercise, would not enter the lists save with a street porter or some other stout rascal willing to sweat for his hire. The libertine enters furtively while his opponent is busily counting his money; the churl cries thief; whereupon the hard language and blows begin. Whereas with the former debauchee, the blows were scattered somewhat over his body, this one, keeping his breeches down about his ankles, wishes to receive everything squarely in the center of his unclothed bum, and that bum has to be buffeted by a good heavy boot, amply studded with hobnails and well coated with mud. At the moment he felt himself about to discharge, our gentleman ceased to parry the blows; planted firmly in the middle of the room, his breeches still lowered, and agitating his prick with all his strength, he braved his enemy's assaults, and, at this crucial juncture, dared him do his worst, insulting him in his own turn, and swearing he was about to die of pleasure. The more vile, the more lowly the man I found for this stalwart libertine, the more scurvy his antagonist, the heavier and the more filthy his boot, the more overpowering would be my client's ecstasy; I had to employ the same tact and discrimination in selecting his assailant that I would have had to devote to embellishing and beautifying another man's woman.*

*A third wished to find himself in what in a whorehouse is called the harem, at the same instant two other men, paid so to do and on hand for no other purpose, began a dispute. Both would turn upon our libertine, he would ask to be spared, would throw himself upon his knees, would not be listened to, and one of the two champions would directly snatch up a cane and fall to belaboring him all the while he crept to the entrance of another room where he would take refuge. There he would be received by a girl, she would console him, caress him as one might a child who has come to be comforted, she would raise her skirts, display her ass, and the libertine, all smiles, would spray his fuck upon it.*

*A fourth required the same preliminaries, but as soon as the strokes of the cane began to rain down upon his back, he would frig himself within sight of all. Then this last operation would be suspended for a moment; there would, however, be no interruption in the dual attack of blows and oaths; then he'd get hot again, frig some more, and when they saw his fuck was about to fly, they'd open a window, pick him up by the waist, and fling him out; he would land upon a specially prepared dung heap after a fall of no more than six feet. And that was the critical moment; he had been morally aroused by the foregoing preliminaries, and his physical self only became so thanks to his fall; 'twas never but upon that dung heap he loosed his fuck. When one went to look from the window, he was gone; there was an obscure little door below (he had a key to it), and he'd disappear through it at once.*

*A man paid for the purpose and dressed like a rowdy would abruptly enter the chamber in which the man who furnishes us with the fifth example would be lying with a girl, kissing her ass while awaiting developments. Accosting the expectant libertine, the bully, having forced the door, would insolently ask what right he had thus to meddle with his mistress and then, laying his hand upon his sword, he would tell the usurper to defend himself. All confused, the latter would fall to his knees, ask pardon, grovel on the floor, kiss it, kiss his rival's feet too, and swear he was ready to relinquish the lady at once, for he had no desire to fight over a woman. The bully, whom his adversary's pliability rendered all the more insolent, now called his enemy a coward, a contemptible fellow, a whoreson ass-fucker, and a dog, and threatened to carve up his face with the edge of his sword. And the more ugly became the one's behavior, the more humble and fawning became the other's. Finally, after a few minutes of debate, the assailant offered to make a settlement with his enemy:*

*"I see damned well that you've got no guts at all," said he, "and so I'll let you go, but upon condition you kiss my ass."*

*"Oh, Monsieur, I'll do whatever you like," said the other,*

*enchanted by this solution, "I'd even kiss it if 'twere all beshitted,
if you wish, provided you do me no harm."*

*Sheathing his sword, the bully directly pulled down his
breeches, the libertine, only too delighted, leapt enthusiastically to
work, and while the young man let fly half a dozen farts at his
nose, the old rake, having attained the summit of ecstasy, loosed
his fuck and swooned with pleasure.*

"Every one of those excesses makes sense to me," Durcet said
in a faltering tone, for the little libertine was stiff after hearing tell
of these turpitudes. "Nothing more logical than to adore degradation and to reap delight from scorn. He who ardently loves the
things which dishonor, finds pleasure in being dishonored and must
necessarily stiffen when told that he is. Turpitude is, to certain
spirits, a very sound cause of joy. One loves to hear oneself called
what one wishes only to merit being, and it is truly impossible to
guess how far a man may go in this direction, provided he be
ashamed of nothing. 'Tis once again the story of certain sick
persons whom nothing delights like the disintegration of their
body."

" 'Tis all a question of cynicism," was Curval's deliberated
opinion, pronounced while toying with Fanchon's buttocks. "Who
is unaware that even punishment produces enthusiasms, and have
we not seen certain individuals' pricks stiffen into clubs at the same
instant they find themselves publicly disgraced? Everyone knows
the story of the brave Marquis de S*** who, when informed of
the magistrates' decision to burn him in effigy, pulled his prick
from his breeches and exclaimed: 'God be fucked, it has taken
them years to do it, but it's achieved at last; covered with opprobrium and infamy, am I? Oh, leave me, leave me, for I've got
absolutely to discharge'; and he did so in less time than it takes
to tell."

"Those are undisputed facts," the Duc commented, nodding
gravely. "But can you explain to me their cause?"

"It resides in our heart," Curval replied. "Once a man has
degraded himself, debased himself through excesses, he has imparted something of a vicious cast to his soul, and nothing can
rectify that situation. In any other case, shame would act as a

496 ❖ THE MARQUIS DE SADE

deterrent and incline him away from the vices to which his mind
advises him to surrender, but here that possibility has been eliminated altogether: 'tis the first token of shame he has obliterated,
the initial call he has definitively silenced, and from the state in
which one is when one has ceased to blush, to that other state
wherein one adores everything that causes others to blush, there
is no more, nor less, than a single step. All that before affected one
disagreeably, now encountering an otherwise prepared soul, is
metamorphosed into pleasure, and from this moment onward,
whatever recalls the new state one has adopted can henceforth only
be voluptuous."

"But what a distance one must first have ventured along the
road of vice to arrive at that point!" said the Bishop.

"Yes, yes, 'tis so," Curval acknowledged; "but little by little
one makes one's way along, and the path one treads is strewn with
flowers; one excess leads to another, the imagination, never sated,
soon brings us to our destination, and as the traveler's heart has
only hardened as he has pursued his career, immediately he reaches
his goal, that heart which of old contained some virtues, no longer
recognizes a single one. Accustomed to livelier things, it promptly
shrugs off those early impressions, those soft and unsweet, those
tasteless ones which till then had made it drunk, and as it strongly
senses that infamy and dishonor are going surely to be the consequences of its new impulsions, in order to have nothing to fear
of them, it begins by making itself familiar with them. It no sooner
caresses than it is seized with a fondness for them, because they
are of the same nature as its new conquests; and now that heart is
fixed unalterably, forever."

"And that," the Bishop observed, "is what makes mending
one's ways so difficult."

"Say rather that it is impossible, my friend. And how are the
punishments inflicted upon him you wish to reform ever to succeed,
since, with the exception of one or two privations, the state of
degradation which characterizes the situation in which you place
him when you punish him, pleases him, amuses him, delights him,
and inwardly he relishes the self that has gone so far as to merit
being treated in this way?"

"Oh, what is this glory, jest, and riddle of the world!" sighed the Duc.

"Yes, my friend, an enigma above all else," said the grave Curval. "And that perhaps is what led a very witty individual to say that better every time to fuck a man than to seek to comprehend him."

And the arrival of supper interrupting our interlocutors, they seated themselves at table without having achieved a thing during the soiree. Natheless, at dessert, Curval, his prick as hard as a demon's, declared he'd be damned if it wasn't a pucelage he wanted to pop, even if he had twenty fines to pay, and instantly laying rude hands upon Zelmire, who had been reserved for him, he was about to drag her off to the boudoir when his three colleagues, casting themselves in his path, besought him to reconsider and submit to the law he had himself prescribed; and, said they, since they too had equally powerful urges to breach the contract, but held themselves somehow in check all the same, he should imitate them, at least out of a feeling of comradeship. And as they had straightway sent word to have Julie fetched in, for Curval was fond of her, she, upon arriving, took him directly in hand, and, together with Champville and Bum-Cleaver, they all four went into the salon; the other three friends soon joined them there, for the orgies were scheduled to begin. Upon entering, they found Curval close at grips with his aides, who, adopting the most lubricious postures and providing the most libertine exhortations, finally caused him to yield up his fuck.

In the course of the orgies, Durcet had the duennas give him two or three hundred kicks in the ass; not to be outdone, his peers had the fuckers serve them identically, and before retiring for the night, no one was exempted from shedding more or less fuck, depending upon the faculties wherewith by Nature he had been endowed. Fearing some fresh return of the defloratory whim Curval had just announced, the duennas were, through precaution, assigned to sleep in the boys' and girls' chambers. But this measure was unnecessary, and Julie, who looked after the Président all night long, the following morning turned him over to the society as limp as an empty glove.

# THE TWENTY-FOURTH DAY

*P*iety is indeed a true disease of the soul. Apply whatever remedies you please, the fever will not subside, the patient never heals; finding readier entry into the souls of the woebegone and downtrodden, because to be devout consoles them for their other ills, it is far more difficult to cure in such persons than in others. Such was the case with Adelaide: the more that vista of debauchery and of libertinage unfolded before her eyes, the more she recoiled and sought sanctuary in the arms of that comfort-giving God she hoped one day would come and deliver her from the evils which, she saw only too well, her dreadful situation was going to bring down upon her head. No one had a more profound appreciation of her circumstances than she; her mind could not more clearly have foreseen everything that was necessarily to follow the fatal beginning of which already she had been a victim, however mildly; she wonderfully well understood that, as the stories grew progressively stronger, the men's use of her and of her companions, evolving sympathetically, would also grow more ferocious. All that, despite everything she was told, made her avidly seek out, as often and for as long as she could, the society of her beloved Sophie. No longer did she dare go in quest of her at night; her overseers were sharp-eyed, wary, and drastic steps had been taken to thwart any more of those escapades, but whenever she found herself free for an instant, she would fly to her soul mate, and upon this very morning of the day we are presently chronicling, having risen early from the Bishop's bed, where she had lain that night, she went into the young girls' quarters to chat

with her dear correspondent. Durcet, who because of his duties
that month used also to rise earlier than the others, found her
there and declared to her there was nothing for it, he could not
both carry out his functions and overlook this infraction of the
rules; the society would have to decide the matter according to its
pleasure. Adelaide wept, tears were her sole weapon, and she
resorted to them. The only favor she dared beg from her husband
was to try to prevent Sophie from being punished; for Sophie, she
argued, could not be guilty, since it had been she, Adelaide, who
had come looking for her, not Sophie who had gone in search of
Adelaide. Durcet said he would report the fact as he had observed
it, would disguise nothing; no one is less apt to be melted than a
punisher whose keenest interest lies in punishing. And such was
the case here, of course; was there anything prettier to punish than
Sophie? Surely not, and what cause might Durcet have for sparing
her?

Their Lordships assembled, the financier made his report.
Here was an habitual offender; the Président recollected that,
when he had been at the Palais de Justice, his ingenious confreres
used to contend that recidivism in a man proves Nature is acting
more strongly in him than education or principles; hence, by
repeated errors, he attests, so to speak, that he is not his own
master; hence, he must be doubly punished—the Président now
reasoned just as logically and with the same inspired verve that
had won him his schoolmates' admiration, and he declared that, as
he viewed the thing, one had no choice but to invoke the law and
punish the incurable Adelaide and her companion with all permis-
sible rigor. But as the law fixed the death penalty for this offense,
and as Messieurs were disposed to amuse themselves yet a little
longer with these ladies before taking the final step, they were
content to summon them, to make them kneel, and to read them
the article out of the ordinances applying to their case, drawing
their attention to the grave risk they had just run in committing
such a transgression. That done, their judges pronounced a sentence thrice as severe as the one which had been executed upon
them the previous Saturday, they were forced to swear they would
not repeat their crime, they were advised that, should the same

thing occur again, they would have to endure the extreme penalty, and their names were inscribed in the register.

Durcet's inspection added three more names to the page; two from amongst the little girls, one of the boys rounded out the morning's capture. All this was the result of the experimenting with minor indigestions; it was succeeding extremely well, but those poor children, unable to restrain themselves another moment, were beginning to tumble one after another into states of culpability: such had been the experience of Fanny and of Hébé amongst the girls, and of Hyacinthe amongst the boys. The evidence found in their pots was enormous, and Durcet frolicked about with it for a long time. Never had so many permissions been requested on any given morning, and certain subordinate personages were heard to curse Duclos for having imparted her secret. Notwithstanding the multitude of requests, leave to shit was granted only to Constance, Hercule, two second-rank fuckers, Augustine, Zéphyr, and Desgranges; they provided a few minutes' entertainment, and Messieurs sat down to dine.

"Well, now you see your mistake in allowing your daughter to receive religious instruction," Durcet said to Curval; "there's nothing to be done about her now. Those imbecilities have taken root in her head. And I told you they would, ages ago."

"In faith," said Curval, "I thought that acquaintance with them would be just one more reason she'd have for despising them, and that as she grew up she would convince herself of the stupidity of those infamous dogmas."

"What you say is all very well for reasoning minds," said the Bishop, "but one simply must not expect it to succeed with a child."

"I'm afraid we're going to be forced to resort to violent measures," said the Duc, who knew very well Adelaide could overhear him.

"Oh yes, in good time," Durcet nodded. "I can assure her that if she has no one but me for her advocate, she'll be poorly defended in court."

"Oh, I know that, Monsieur!" Adelaide stammered through her tears; "everyone is aware of your feelings toward me."

"My feelings?" protested Durcet. "But, my dear wife, I ought perhaps to begin by informing you I have never had any feelings whatsoever for a woman, and assuredly fewer for you, who belong to me, than for any other. I hate religion, as well as all those who practice it, and I warn you that, from the indifference I have in your regard, I shall pass damned quickly to the most violent aversion if you continue to revere infamous and execrable illusions, phantoms which have ever been the object of my contemptuous scorn. One must first have lost one's mind to be able to acknowledge a god, and to have gone completely mad to worship such a thing. In short, I declare to you before your father and these other gentlemen that there are no lengths to which I shall not go if I ever again find you guilty of such a sin. You should have been sent to a nunnery if you wanted to pray to your fuck-in-the-ass God; there you'd have been able to worship the bugger to your heart's content."

"Ah!" put in Adelaide, groaning, "a nun, Great God, a nun, would to heaven that I were such."

And Durcet, who at the time was sitting opposite her, annoyed by her response, hurled a silver plate at her face; it would have killed her had it struck her head, for the shock was so violent the missile bent double upon crashing against the wall.

"You're an insolent creature," Curval said to his daughter, who, to avoid the plate, had leapt between her father and Antinoüs. "You deserve to have your belly kicked in."

And driving her away from him with a blow of his fist:

"Go crawl on your knees and beg your husband's forgiveness," said he, "or we'll expose you to the severest ordeal you've ever dreamt of."

In tears, she cast herself at Durcet's feet, but he, having got a very solid erection from hurling the plate, and declaring he'd have given a thousand *louis* to have hit his mark, Durcet said that he felt an immediate, a general, and an exemplary punishment was in order; another would of course be executed on Saturday, but he proposed that this one time they do without the children's services at coffee and devote that period to amusing themselves with Adelaide. Everyone consented to the proposal; Adelaide, Louison, and Fanchon, the most wicked of the four elders and the most dreaded by the women, moved into the salon; certain considerations oblige us to draw a curtain over what transpired there. But of one thing we may be perfectly certain: our four heroes discharged during that set-to, and Adelaide was allowed to take to her bed. 'Tis for the reader to invent the combinations and scene he'd like best, and kindly consent to be conveyed, if 'twould please him to accompany us, directly to the throne room where Duclos is about to resume her narrative. All of the friends have taken their places near their wives, all, that is to say, save the Duc, who was to have Adelaide that afternoon, and who has replaced her with Augustine; everyone then being ready, Duclos begins to speak.

*One day,* said that talented orator, *while I was maintaining before one of my fellow procuresses that I had surely seen all it were possible to see of the most furious by way of passive flagellation, in that I had flogged and witnessed others flog men with thorns and the bull's pizzle:*

*"Oh, by God," my colleague answered, "you still have a great deal to see, my dear, and to persuade you that you've by no means observed the worst, I'll send one of my clients around tomorrow."*

*And having given me notice of the hour of the visit, and advised me of the ritual expected by that elderly post-office commissioner whose name, I remember, was Monsieur de Grancourt, I made full preparations and awaited our man; I was to give him my personal attention, the thing was so arranged. He arrives at the house, and after we have retired to a room together:*

*"Monsieur," I say, "I deeply regret having to make the following disclosure, but I am bound to inform you that you are a prisoner and cannot leave this place. I further regret to say that Parliament has delegated me to arrest and punish you, and the Legislature has so willed it, and I have its order in my pocket. The person who sent you to me set a trap for you, for she knew full well the implications of your coming here, and she could most assuredly have enabled you to avoid this scene. As for the rest, you know the facts in the case: 'tis not with impunity one perpetrates the black and dreadful crimes you have committed, and I consider you exceedingly fortunate to get off with so little."*

*Our man had listened with the keenest attention to my harangue, and immediately I had done, he burst into tears and fell*

down on his knees before me, imploring me to deal leniently with
him.

"*Well I know,*" said he, "*that I have greatly misbehaved. I
know I have affronted God and justice; but since 'tis you, my sweet
lady, who are appointed to chasten me, I most earnestly entreat
your indulgence in my regard.*"

"*Monsieur,*" I replied, "*I shall do my duty. How can you be
sure I am not myself being closely watched? What makes you
suppose I have it in my power to respond to your pleas for merciful compassion? Remove your clothes and adopt a docile attitude,
that is all I can say to you.*"

Grancourt obeyed; in a trice he was as naked as the palm of
your hand. But, great God! what was this body he offered to my
sight! I can only compare its skin to a ruffled taffeta. Upon that
whole body, marked everywhere, there was not a single spot which
did not bear terrible evidence of the lash.

However, into the fire I had thrust an iron scourge garnished
with pointed steel tips; I had received the weapon that morning
together with final instructions. This murderous instrument had
reached a bright-red color about the same moment Grancourt had
removed his last stitch. I snatched the scourge from the coals and,
starting to beat him with it, gently at first, then with increasing
severity, then with all my strength, and that heedless of where my
blows fell, rending him from the nape of his neck to his heels, I
had my man streaming blood in an instant.

"*You are a villain,*" I told him as I brought the scourge
whistling down upon his body, "*you're a villain and you've committed all sorts of crimes. Nothing is sacred to you, and I've lately
heard that you've poisoned your mother.*"

"*'Tis true, Madame, oh, 'tis only too true. I'm a monster, I'm
a criminal,*" said he as he frigged himself. "*There's no infamy I've
not perpetrated and am not prepared to do again. Come now,
your blows are utterly in vain, I'll never mend my ways, I find too
much delight in crime. You'd have to kill me to put a stop to my
joy; crime is my element, 'tis my life, I've lived in crime, I'll die
in it.*"

And you may well imagine how, these remarks of his inspiring
my arm and tongue, I redoubled my blows and invectives. The

word "*fuck*" *escaped his lips, however: that was the signal: I lay on with all my might and endeavor to strike his most sensitive parts. He skips, hops, jumps, and capers, he eludes me and, discharging, he scampers into a tub of warm water specially prepared to purify him after this bloody ceremonial. Ah, upon my soul, yes! I ceded to my friend the honor of having seen more of this sort of thing than I, and I believe we two were able to say at the time that we had seen more than all the rest of Paris, for our Grancourt's needs never varied, and for above twenty years he had been going every day to that woman's establishment for the same treatment.*

*Shortly afterward, that same woman arranged to have me meet another libertine whose idiosyncrasy, I fancy, will seem at least as unusual to you. The scene transpired in his little house at Roule. I am introduced into a rather obscurely lit room, where I find a man lying in bed, and, posed in the center of the room, a coffin.*

*"You see before you," our libertine said to me, "a man reclining upon his deathbed, one who would not close his eyes without rendering a last homage to the object he worships. I adore asses, and if I am to perish, I want to die while kissing one. When life shall have fled this frame, you yourself shall lift me into that coffin, draw round the shrouds, and nail down the lid. It is my design thus to die in pleasure's embrace, and at this last moment to be served by the very object of my lubricious heats. Come . . . come," he continued in a broken, weak, gasping voice, "make haste, for I am nigh to the threshold."*

*I draw near to him, turn around, I exhibit my buttocks.*

*"Ah, wondrous ass!" he cries. " 'Tis well, I am easy thus to be able to take with me to the grave the idea of a behind as pretty as that one!"*

*And he fondled it, opened it, nuzzled and kissed it just the way the healthiest man in the world might have done.*

*"Oh, indeed!" said he a moment later as he left off his task and rolled toward the wall, "well I knew 'twould not be for long I'd savor this pleasure; I do now expire, remember what I have enjoined you to do."*

*And so saying, he uttered a profound sigh, grew rigid, and*

*played his part with such skill that damn me if I didn't think he
was dead. I kept my wits about me; eager to see the end of this
droll ceremony, I wrapped him in the shroud. He had ceased to
stir, and whether it was that he knew some secret for feigning
death, or whether my imagination had been affected, he felt as
rigid and cold as a bar of iron; only his prick gave some hints of
life: it too was rigid, but not cold, and glued to his belly, and
drops of fuck seemed to come oozing from it despite his moribund
condition. Directly I have him swathed in the sheet, I take him up
in my arms, and it wasn't easy, for the way he'd become rigid
made him as heavy as a steer. I succeeded nevertheless in transporting him to the coffin. As soon as I have laid him out, I start
reciting the prayer for the dead, and finally I nail the coffin shut;
that was the critical instant for him: no sooner have I driven the
last nail home than he sets to screeching like a madman:*

*"Holy name of God, I'm coming! Get out, whore, get out,
for if I catch you, you're done for!"*

*I'm seized by fear, I dart to the stairs, upon which I meet a
tactful manservant who is thoroughly acquainted with his master's
manias and who gives me two* louis; *I proceed to the door, while
the valet hastens into the patient's bedchamber to free him from
the sealed coffin.*

"Now there's a quaint taste," said Durcet. "Well, Curval,
what do you think of that one?"

"Marvelous," the Président replied; "there you have an individual who wishes to make himself familiar with the idea of
death, and hence unafraid of it, and who to that end has found no
better means than to associate it with a libertine idea. There is
absolutely no doubt about it: that man will die fondling an ass."

"Nor any doubt," said Champville, "that he is proudly impious; I know him, and I shall have occasion to describe the use he
makes of religion's holiest mysteries."

"I don't wonder he is an unbeliever," said the Duc. "He's
clearly a man who laughs at the whole business and who wishes to
accustom himself to acting and thinking the same way during his
last minutes."

"For my part," the Bishop said, "I find something very

piquant in that passion, and I'll not hide the fact I'm stiff from hearing about it. Continue, Duclos, go on, for I have the feeling I might do something silly, and I'd prefer to leave well enough alone for the rest of the day."

*Very well,* said that splendid raconteur, *here's one less complex; 'tis the story of a man who for five years regularly applied at my door for the single pleasure of getting me to sew up his asshole. He used to stretch out belly down upon a bed, I would seat myself between his legs and, equipped with a stout needle and half a spool of heavy cobbler's thread, I'd sew his anus completely closed, and this fellow's skin in that area was so toughened and so used to needle thrusts that my operation would not draw a single drop of blood from his hide. While I worked, he would frig himself, and he used to discharge like a mule when I'd taken the last stitch. His ecstasy dissipated, I'd promptly undo my work, and that would be that.*

*Another used to have brandy rubbed over every part of his body where Nature had placed hair, then I'd put a match to those areas I'd rubbed with alcohol, and all the hair would go up in flames. He would discharge upon finding himself afire, meanwhile I'd show him my belly, my cunt, and so forth, for that fellow had the bad taste never to want to see anything but fronts.*

"But, tell me, Messieurs, did any of you know Mirecourt, today président in the upper chamber, and in those days attorney to the Crown?"

"I knew him," said Curval.

"Well, my Lord, do you know what used to be, and what I dare say still is, his passion?"

"No; and he passes, or wishes to pass, for a devout and good subject, I'd be most pleased to know."

"My Lord," Duclos said, "he likes also to be taken for an ass. . . ."

"Ah! by God! said the Duc; and turning to Curval: "what do you think of that, my friend? Damned strange taste, don't you thing, for a judge? I'll wager that once he's an ass he thinks he's going to pronounce judgment. Well, what next?" he asked of Duclos.

"Next, your Grace, one must lead him by the halter, walk him about the room for an hour, he brays, one mounts astride him, and when one's in the saddle, one whips his entire body with a switch, as if to quicken his gait. He breaks into a trot, and as he's started by now to frig himself, he soon discharges and, while he does so, makes loud noises, bucks, rears, and throws the rider."

"That, I'd say, is more diverting than lubricious. And pray tell me, Duclos," the Duc went on, "did that man ever tell you he had some comrade who shared his taste?"

"Why, indeed, he did tell me so," said the amiable Duclos, entering into the joke with a merry laugh and descending from her platform, for her day's stint was over; "Yes, Sire, he told me he had a quantity of comrades, but that not all of them would allow themselves to be mounted."

The séance had come to an end, Messieurs were disposed to perform a few stunts before supper; the Duc hugged Augustine in close embrace.

"You know," he said dreamily, frigging her clitoris and directing her to grasp his prick, "you know, I'm not at all surprised that Curval is sometimes tempted to violate the pact and pop a pucelage or two, for I feel at this very moment, for example, that I could willingly send Augustine's to the devil."

"Which one?" Curval inquired.

"Both of them, bless my soul," answered the Duc; "but one must behave oneself during this sojourn; in having thus to wait a little while for our pleasures, we make them far more delicious. Well, little girl," he continued, "show me your buttocks, perhaps 'twill change the character of my ideas. . . . Bleeding Christ! look at the little whore's ass! Curval, what do you advise me to do with this thing?"

"Put some vinegar sauce on it," said Curval.

"Mercy!" exclaimed the Duc, "what a notion. But patience, patience . . . everything will come in good time."

"My very dear brother," said the Bishop in a halting voice, "there's something in your words that smells of fuck."

"Really? For indeed I have the greatest desire to lose some."

"And what prevents you?" the Bishop wanted to know.

"Oh, many things, many things," the Duc replied. "First of all, I see no shit in the pipe, and I'd like shit, and then . . . I don't know—there are so many things I'd like. . . ."

"What?" asked Durcet just before Antinoüs' turd cascaded into his mouth.

"What?" echoed the Duc. "There's, to begin with, a little infamy I simply must perform."

And retiring to the distant boudoir with Augustine, Zélamir, Cupidon, Duclos, Desgranges, and Hercule, he was heard, a minute later, to utter ringing cries and oaths which proved the Duc had finally managed to calm his brain and soothe his balls. Little precise information exists upon what he did to Augustine, but, notwithstanding his love for her, she was seen to return in tears and, ominous sign! one of her fingers had been twisted. We deeply regret not yet to be able to explain all this to the reader, but it is quite certain that these gentlemen, on the sly and before the arrival of the day heralding open season, were giving themselves over to tricks which have not so far been embodied in story, hence to unsanctioned deeds, and in so doing they were acting in formal violation of the regulations they had sworn in honor to observe; but, you know, when an entire society commits the same faults, they are commonly pardoned. The Duc came back and was pleased to see that Durcet and the Bishop had not been wasting their time, and that Curval, in Bum-Cleaver's arms, was deliciously doing everything one may possibly do with all the voluptuous objects one may possibly assemble around oneself.

Supper was served, orgies followed as usual, the household retired to bed. Lame and aching as Adelaide was, the Duc, who was scheduled to have her by him that night, wanted her there, and as he had come from the orgies rather drunk, as was his wont, it is said that he did not deal tenderly with her. But by and large the night was passed just like all the preceding nights, that is to say, in the depths of delirium and debauchery, and fair-haired Aurora having come, as the poets say, to fling open the gates of the palace where dwelt Apollo, that god, somewhat a libertine himself, only mounted his azure chariot in order to bring light to shed upon new lecheries.

# THE TWENTY-FIFTH DAY

*H*owever, a new intrigue was quietly taking form within the impenetrable walls of the Château of Silling; but it did not have the dangerous significance that had been attributed to Adelaide's league with Sophie. This latest association was being hatched between Aline and Zelmire; those two young girls' conformity of character contributed greatly to their attachment to each other: both were mild-natured and sensitive, no more than thirty months separated them in age, they were both very childlike, very simple, very good-hearted: they had, in brief, almost all of the same virtues, and almost all the same vices, for Zelmire, sweet and tender, was also, like Aline, careless and lazy. They suited one another so admirably that, on the morning of the 25th, they were discovered in the same bed, and this is how it happened: being destined for Curval, Zelmire slept, as we know, in his bedchamber. Aline was Curval's bedwife that same night. But Curval, having returned dead drunk from the orgies, wished to sleep with no one but Invictus, and thus it fell out that these two little doves, abandoned and brought together by fortune, from dread of the cold both camped in the same bed and, in bed, 'twas maintained, their little fingers itched more than their dear little elbows.

Upon opening his eyes in the morning and seeing these two birds sharing the same nest, Curval demanded to know what they were doing there, and ordering them both to come instantly into his bed, he sniffed about just below each one's clitoris, and clearly recognized that both of them were still full of fuck. The case was grave: Messieurs did indeed wish the young ladies to be victims

509

of impudicity, but they insisted that, amongst themselves, they behave decently—oh, for what will libertinage, perpetually incon-
sistent libertinage, not insist upon!—and if they sometimes consented to permit the ladies to indulge in a little reciprocal impurity,
it all had to be both upon Messieurs' express instructions and before their eyes. And thus it was the case was brought before the
council, and the two delinquents, who neither could nor dared deny
the thing, were ordered to demonstrate what they had been up to,
and before a crowd of spectators to display just what their individual talents were. They did as they were told, with much blushing
and not a little weeping, and asked to be forgiven their mistakes.
But too attractive was the prospect of having that pretty couple
amongst the culprits to be punished the following Saturday; consequently, they were not forgiven, but were speedily included in
Durcet's book of sorrows which, incidentally, was being very agreeably filled up that week.

This chore completed, breakfast was finished, and Durcet
conducted his searches. The fatal indigestions yielded still another
miscreant: 'twas the little Michette, she'd been unable to hold the
bridge, she said they'd made her eat too much the night before,
and these were followed by a thousand other infantile excuses
which did not prevent her name from being written down. Curval,
his prick jumping like a young colt, seized the chamber pot and
devoured its contents. And then bringing his angry eyes to bear
upon her:

"Oh yes, by Jesus," said he, "yes, by the Saviour's fuck, you
shall be spanked, my little rascal, my own hand will see to that.
There are rules against shitting that way; you should at least have
given us notice; you know damned well that we are prepared to
receive shit at any hour of the day or night."

And he fondled her buttocks very vivaciously while repeating
the rules to her.

The boys were found intact, no chapel permissions were distributed to them, and Messieurs repaired to table. During the
meal, there was plentiful and penetrating discussion of Aline's
deed; they ascribed a holier-than-thou attitude to her, said she appeared a little hypocrite, and behold! here was proof of her real
temperament at last come to light.

"How now, my friend," Durcet said to the Bishop, "is one still to lay any store by appearances, above all those that girls parade?"

'Twas unanimously agreed nothing was more deceitful than a girl, and that, as they were every one of them false, they never made use of their wits save to be more skillfully false. These observations brought the table talk around to women, and the Bishop who abhorred them, gave vent to all the hatred they inspired in him. He reduced them to the state of the vilest animals, and proved their existence so perfectly useless in this world that one could extirpate them from the face of the earth without in the slightest countercarrying the designs of Nature who, having in times past very surely found the means to create without women, would find it again when only men were left.

They proceeded to coffee; it was presented them by Augustine, Michette, Hyacinthe, and Narcisse. The Bishop, one of whose greatest uncomplex pleasures was to suck little boy's pricks, had been spending a few minutes playing this game with Hyacinthe, when all of a sudden he reared back and let out, not a shout, but a bubbling noise, for his mouth was full; his exclamation was interpreted thus: "Ah, by God's balls, my friends, a pucelage! That's the first time this little rascal has discharged, I'm sure of it!" And, truth to tell, no one had so far observed Hyacinthe carry things to that point; he was indeed thought still too young to bring it off. But he was well advanced in his fourteenth year, 'tis the age when Nature customarily heaps her favors upon us, and nothing could have been more real than the victory the Bishop thought he had achieved. None the less, the others were anxious to verify the thing, and each wishing to be witness to the adventure, they drew up their chairs in a semicircle around the young man. Augustine, the most accomplished frigger in the seraglio, received permission to manualize the lad within clear sight of the assembly, and Hyacinthe was given leave to fondle and caress her in whatsoever part of her body he desired. There's no spectacle more voluptuous than that offered by a young maid of fifteen, lovely as the day, lending herself to the caresses of a boy of fourteen and provoking, by means of the most delicious pollutions, his springtide discharge.

Hyacinthe, aided perhaps by Nature, but yet more certainly by the examples he had before his nose, fondled, handled, kissed naught but his frigger's pretty little buttocks, and it required little more than an instant of this to bring color to his cheeks, to fetch two or three sighs from his lips, to induce his pretty little prick to shoot, to a distance of one yard, five or six jets of sweet fuck white as cream, which emissions happened to land on Durcet's thigh, for the banker was seated nearest the boy and was having himself frigged by Narcisse while watching the operation. The fact once indubitably established, they caressed and kissed the child rather universally, each swore he'd love to receive a small portion of that youthful sperm, and as it appeared that, at his age and for a beginning, six discharges were not too many, in that he had after all just delivered himself of two without the least difficulty, our libertines induced him to shed another in each of their mouths.

Much heated by this performance, the Duc laid hands on Augustine and frigged her clitoris with his tongue until he had elicited several solid discharges from her; full of fire and blessed with a mettlesome spirit, that little minx shot them off in short order. While the Duc was thus polluting Augustine, nothing was more engaging than to see Durcet, come up to gather symptoms of the pleasure he was not provoking, kiss that beautiful child's mouth a thousand times over, and swallow, so to speak, the voluptuousness another was causing to circulate throughout her senses. The hour was advanced, they were obliged to omit the midday nap and to pass directly into the auditorium where Duclos had been awaiting them for a long time; as soon as everyone had arranged himself, she took up the thread of her adventures and spoke as hereafter you may read:

*I have already had the honor to remark in your Lordships' presence, that it is most difficult to fathom all the tortures man invents for himself in order to find, in the degradation they produce, or the agonies, those sparks of pleasure which age or satiety have made to grow faint in him. Hard it is to credit the assertion that one such gentleman of this sort, a person of sixty years and to a singular degree jaded by all the pleasures of lubricity, used only to be able to restore his senses to life by having the flames of burning candles applied to every part of his body, and principally to the ones Nature has intended for those selfsame pleasures. He would have his thighs seared, his prick, his balls roasted, and above all else his asshole: while all this was going forward, he would be kissing an ass, and after the grievous operation had been repeated for the fifteenth or twentieth time, he would discharge while sucking the anus of the girl who'd been burning him.*

*Soon after that one, I had dealings with another who obliged me to use a horse's currycomb on him, to rub down his entire body with that instrument, quite as one does to the animal I have just named. Directly his body was all an open wound, I'd next rub him with alcohol, and this second torture would cause him abundantly to discharge upon my breasts—that was the battlefield he chose to spray with his fuck. I would kneel before him, squeeze his prick between my bubs, and he'd quietly wash them with his balls' acrid humor.*

*A third would have every hair on his ass plucked out one by one. While that lengthy operation was advancing, he would frig himself upon a warm turd I'd just done for him. Then, at the same instant a conventional dribble of fuck announced the crisis' approach, I had, to give it the necessary encouragement, to drive the point of a scissors deep enough into each of his buttocks to draw a jet of blood. His ass was a maze of wounds and scars, I was scarce able to find an open space for my two gashes; immediately the steel entered him, he'd plunge his nose into the shit, smear it upon his face, and floods of sperm would crown his ecstasy.*

*A fourth put his prick in my mouth and bade me bite it as hard as I could; in the meantime, as I chewed his poor device, I was expected to lacerate his buttocks with an iron comb whose teeth were ground to sharp points; and then, at the moment I sensed his prick ready to melt—a very faint, a barely perceptible erection would tell me so—and then, I say, I'd spread his buttocks prodigiously wide, ease them close to a burning candle I'd kept in readiness on the floor, and I'd braise his asshole with it. 'Twas the burning sensation of that candle under his anus decided his emission; I'd therewith redouble my bitings, and would soon find my mouth full.*

"One moment, if you please," said the Bishop. "Every time I hear of someone discharging into a mouth I am reminded of the good fortune I had earlier today, and my spirits are disposed to tasting further pleasures of the same sort."

Saying which, he draws Invictus near, for that champion was on duty in the Bishop's alcove that afternoon, and falls to sucking the brave fellow's prick with all the energetic lustiness of a true bugger. Fuck explodes, the prelate gobbles it up, and straightway goes to repeat the operation upon Zéphyr. The Bishop was brandishing his knobkerrie, and 'twas seldom that women would feel completely at their ease when he was in this critical state and they were near him. Unfortunately, it was his niece Aline who happened to be within range.

"What are you doing there, bitch?" he rasped; "I want men for my fun."

Aline seeks to elude him, he seizes her by the hair and, dragging her into his closet along with Zelmire and Hébé, the two girls in his quartet:

"You'll see," says he to his friends, "you'll see how I'm going to teach these wenches to slip cunts under my hand when I'm doing my best to find some pricks."

Upon his order, Fanchon accompanied the three maidens, and an instant later Aline was heard to utter very shrill cries; then came tidings of Monseigneur's discharge, reverberating howls which blended with his dear niece's dolorous accents. Everyone returned . . . Aline was weeping, squeezing and clutching her behind.

"Come show me what he did to you," said the Duc; "I love nothing better than to see traces of my distinguished brother's brutality."

Aline displayed I've no idea what, for I have never been able to discover what went on in those infernal closets, but the Duc exclaimed: "By fuck, 'tis delicious, I think I'll go off and do the same." But Curval having pointed out to him that time was growing short, and having added that he had an amusing enterprise in mind for the orgies, which scheme would demand a clear head and all his fuck, Duclos was asked to go ahead with the fifth story in

order that the sitting be brought to a proper conclusion; the storyteller therewith addressed the convocation once again:

*Belonging to that group of extraordinary individuals,* said
she, *whose mania consists in wallowing in degradation and in insulting their own dignity, was a certain judge of the circuit court
whose name was Foucolet. There's truly no believing the point to
which that fellow would carry his furor; he had to be given a
sample of almost every torture. I used to hang him, but the rope
would break just in time and he would fall upon a mattress; the
next instant, I would strap him to a St. Andrew's cross and make as
if to break his limbs with a bar, but it was only a roll of paste-
board; I used to brand him upon the shoulder, the iron I used was
warm and left a faint imprint, no more; I would flog his back
in precise imitation of the public servant who performs those noble
feats, and whilst I was doing all this I had to overwhelm him with
a stream of atrocious invectives, bitter reproaches for various
crimes, for which, during each successive operation, he would demand, a candle in his hand and wearing only his shirt, God's forgiveness and the law's, pronouncing his entreaties in a very humble
and contrite tone; finally, the meeting would be brought to a close
on my ass, where the libertine would yield up his fuck when his
head had reached the ultimate degree of distraction.*

"Well now, are you going to let me discharge in peace now
that Duclos has finished?" the Duc asked Curval.

"No, not a bit of it," the Président replied; "preserve your
fuck, I tell you I need it for the orgies."

"Oh, so you take me for your valet, do you?" the Duc exclaimed. "You take me for a worn-out bugger? Do you suppose
that the small quantity of fuck I'm going to lose in a moment will
prevent me from joining in all the infamies which are going to
pop into your head four hours from now? Come now, Président,
you know me better than that; banish your fears, I'll be fit again
for anything inside fifteen minutes, but my good and holy brother
has been pleased to give me a little example of an atrocity I'd be
grief-stricken not to execute with Adelaide, your dear and estimable daughter."

And pushing her forthwith into his closet, along with Thérèse, Colombe, and Fanny, the female elements of his quatrain, he probably did there, with them, what the Bishop had done to his niece, and discharged with the same episodes, for, as not long before they heard Aline's terrible scream, so now their ears were treated to another from the lips of Adelaide and to the bawdy Duc's yells of lust. Curval wished to learn which of the two brothers had been the better behaved; he summoned the two women, and having pored at length over their two behinds, he decided the Duc had not merely imitated, but surpassed the Bishop.

They sat down at table, and having by means of some drug or other stuffed the bowels of all the subjects, men and women, with an abundance of wind, after supper they played the game of fart-in-the-face: Messieurs, all four of them, lay back upon couches, their heads raised, and one by one the members of the household stepped up to deliver their farts into the waiting mouths. Duclos was requested to do the counting and mark down the scores; there were thirty-six farters as against only four swallowers: hence there were certain persons who received as many as one hundred and fifty farts. It had been for this rousing ceremony Curval had wanted the Duc to keep himself fit, but such precautions, as Blangis had made perfectly clear, were quite unnecessary; he was too great a friend of libertinage to allow some new excess to find him unprepared; to the contrary, any new excess always had the greatest effect upon him, his situation notwithstanding, and he did not fail to produce a second discharge thanks to the humid mistral Fanchon wafted into his mouth. As for Curval, they were Antinoüs' farts which cost him his fuck, whereas Durcet bent before the gale that swept out of Martaine's asshole, and the Bishop lost all control in the face of what Desgranges offered him. The youthful beauties' efforts, 'twill be remarked, came to naught; but is it not true that it is always the crapulous individual who best executes the infamous deed?

# THE TWENTY-SIXTH DAY

*I*n that nothing was more delicious than meting out punishments, in that nothing prepared the way for so many pleasures, and those very sorts of pleasures Messieurs had mutually promised not to taste until in the stories mention thereof should permit fullest indulgence in them, the libertines sought by every imaginable means to trip the subjects into states of delinquency, and so procure themselves the joy of chastising their hapless victims; to this end, the friends, having convoked an extraordinary assembly that morning, their purpose being to deliberate upon this problem, they added several articles to the household regulations, infraction of which was necessarily to occasion punishment. Firstly, the wives, the small boys, and the girls were expressly forbidden to fart anywhere save in the friends' mouths. Instantly they were seized by the desire to break wind, they were without delay to go and find one of the friends and administer unto him what required to be set at large; a severe afflictive penalty would be the reward for disobedience. Secondly, the use of bidets and ass-wipings of any kind were absolutely outlawed; it was generally proclaimed that all subjects without exception would hereafter never wash themselves, and never under any circumstances wipe the ass after having shitted; that, whenever an ass were found clean, upon the subject concerned would lie the burden of proving it had been licked clean by one of the friends, and that friend would have to be mentioned by name. In response to which citation, the friend would be questioned, and, being in a position to procure himself two pleasures, instead of only one, to wit: that of having cleaned the ass

517

with his tongue, and that of having punished the subject who had afforded him this first pleasure. . . . Examples of this will be provided.

Thirdly, a new ceremony was introduced: at the time of the morning coffee, at the time of their entry into the girls' quarters, and also when, after that, they passed into the boys', each of the subjects would hereafter, one by one, step forth and, in a loud and clear voice, say to each of the friends: "I don't care a fuck for God; there's shit in my ass, would you like some?" and those who should fail in an intelligible voice to pronounce both the blasphemy and the invitation, would instantly be inscribed in the dread book. The reader will readily imagine what difficulties the pious Adelaide and her young pupil Sophie had to surmount before being able to utter such infamies, and their inner struggles procured Messieurs some excellent entertainment.

The foregoing once framed in law, they turned to consider delations and decided to admit them; this barbarous means of multiplying vexations, accepted by every tyrant, was warmly embraced by these. It was decided, fourthly, that every subject who should lodge complaint against some other, would thereby earn a one-half reduction of the punishment he was to suffer for the next fault he committed. Messieurs were in no way deprived by this system, because the subject who had just accused another subject could never know the extent of the punishment a half of which, he was promised, would be suppressed; and so it was a simple matter indeed to give him precisely what one wished to give him, and still to persuade him he had got off more lightly than otherwise he might. Messieurs agreed upon and published their decision, that no delation required substantiating proof in order to be believed, and that, to be inscribed, accusation brought by anyone would suffice. The duennas' authority, furthermore, was increased, and upon the basis of their slightest complaint, whether true or false, the subject would be condemned immediately. In a word, over this small population they established all the vexation, all the injustice one could imagine, certain in the belief that the more harshly their tyranny was exercised, the greater the sum of pleasures they would derive from their privileged situation.

All this legislation composed and voted, they visited the chamber pots. Colombe was found guilty; her excuses hinged upon the food they had made her eat between meals the day before; she had, said she, been unable to resist, she was dreadfully unhappy about the whole thing, and this was the fourth successive week she had been punished. The statement was true, and she had only to blame her ass, which was the freshest, the sweetest, the best-made and most endearing little ass you could hope to see. She pointed out she'd not wiped herself, and that, she supposed, should be regarded as a point in her favor. Durcet examined her, and having indeed discovered a very thick and very broad patch of shit, he assured her that, in the light of this, she'd be treated a little less rigorously. Curval, stiff at the time, laid hands on her, and having completely cleaned her anus, he had her produce her turd and ate it while having her frig him, periodically interrupting his chewing to kiss her upon the mouth and to order her to swallow, in her turn, what of her own creation he brought to her lips. They next inspected Augustine and Sophie, who had been solemnly enjoined, after the stools they had yielded up the night before, to remain in the most impure state. Sophie's appearance conformed with her instructions, even though she had slept in the Bishop's chamber, but Augustine was as neat as a pin. Sure of her reply, she advanced proudly and said that they knew very well she had, as was her custom, lain the night in Monsieur le Duc's bedchamber, and that before going to sleep he had summoned her to his bed, where he had licked her asshole while she had frigged his prick in her mouth. When interrogated, the Duc said that he had no remembrance of the thing (although the story was completely true), that he had fallen asleep with his prick in Duclos' ass, that they could substantiate the fact. They went about the matter with all possible seriousness and gravity, they sent for Duclos who, seeing clearly what was afoot, lent her support to everything the Duc advanced, and maintained that Augustine had been called to Monsieur's bed only for a brief instant, that Monsieur had shitted into Augustine's mouth and then, upon second thought, had bade her return to the bed in order that he might eat his turd. Augustine sought to defend her thesis and dispute Duclos' contentions, but silence was imposed upon her and, although perfectly innocent, her name was written down.

Amongst the boys, whose chambers they visited next, Cupidon was found guilty; he had done the world's most gorgeous turd in his chamber pot. The Duc snatched it up and gobbled it up while the young malefactor sucked his member.

All requests for chapel permission were refused; they then went to dine. The beautiful Constance, whom they sometimes dispensed from serving at table because of her state, was however feeling fit that day, and made her appearance naked; the sight of her belly, which was beginning somewhat to swell, made Curval's head very hot; the others, seeing his treatment of the poor creature's buttocks and breasts growing rather rough—Curval's horror for her was doubling every day, that was plain—were swayed by her entreaties and their common desire to preserve her fruit, at least until a certain date, and she was allowed to absent herself from all the day's functions, save for the narrations, wherefrom she was never excused. Curval started in again with his frightful speeches about child-breeders, he declared that if he had government of the country he would borrow their law from the inhabitants of Formosa, where pregnant women under thirty are, together with their fruit, ground in a large mortar; should that law, he protested, be introduced into France, the population would still be twice what it ought be.

Coffee came next; it was presented by Sophie, Fanny, Zélamir, and Adonis, but served in a passing strange manner: 'twas in the children's mouths, one had to sip it therefrom. Sophie served hers to the Duc, Fanny Curval's, Zélamir the Bishop's, and Durcet got his out of Adonis. They extracted a mouthful, gargled it a moment, and returned it into the mouths of those who'd served them. Curval, who had risen from table in a great ferment, got stiff all over again thanks to this ceremony, and when it had been completed, he laid hands on Fanny and discharged into her mouth, ordering her to swallow the whey; the threats accompanying his instructions succeeded in making the poor wretch obey without the flutter of an eyelash. The Duc and his two other confreres collected shit or farts; having finished their nap, they all trooped in to listen to Duclos, who spoke to them in this wise:

*I will move with dispatch,* said that amiable girl, *through my last two adventures concerning these unusual men who find their delight only in the pain they are made to undergo, and then with your leave we will pass on to a different variety.*

*The first, while he had me frig him, naked and standing up, wanted floods of hot water poured down on us through an opening in the ceiling; our bodies were to be showered during the entire operation. It was quite in vain I argued that, while not sharing in this passion of his, I was nevertheless, like himself, to be a victim of it; he replied, assuring me I would suffer no hurt from the experience, and that these showers were good for one's health. I believed him and let him have his way; as this scene transpired in his house, the temperature of the water, a critical detail, was something lying beyond my control. It was indeed nearly boiling. Messieurs, there is no conceiving the pleasure he felt upon being drenched by it. As for myself, all the while operating with all possible speed, I screeched, yes, I confess it, I screeched like a drowning tomcat; my skin came peeling off, and I made myself the firm promise never to return to that man's house.*

"Ah, buggerfuck!" exclaimed the Duc, "I have the strongest inclination to give the beauteous Aline a comparable scalding."

"Your Grace," the latter replied in a humble but decided tone, "I am not a tomcat."

And the naive candor in her childlike reply having fetched a chuckle from everyone, Duclos was asked to give the second and final example of the same genre.

*It was a great deal less painful for me,* said Duclos; *I had simply to don a stout glove, then with this protected hand to take burning grit from a frying pan I'd been heating on a stove, and, my hand filled, to rub that fiery sand over my man's body, from head to toe. His body was so inured to this exercise that he seemed to be covered not with skin, but with leather. When one reached his prick, one had to seize it and massage it in a handful of that same sand; he'd be up like a shot. Then, with the other hand, I placed a small fire shovel, heated red-hot for this purpose, under his balls. This rubbing with the one hand, the consuming heat which*

522 ✤ THE MARQUIS DE SADE

rose to bake his testicles, perhaps a little touching of my two
buttocks, which I had to keep well exposed and within reach during the operation, this combination of elements melted him altogether and he discharged, being very careful to spill his seed upon
the hot shovel where, to his unutterable delight, he watched it
sizzle and evaporate in steam.

"Curval," said the Duc, "there's a man who, 'twould appear
to me, has no greater fondness than have you for population."

"It looks that way to me," Curval assented; "I make no bones
about the fact I love the idea of watching fuck burn."

"Oh, I know all the ideas fuck inspires in you," said the Duc
with a hearty laugh. "And even were the seed to ripen, the
egg to hatch, you'd perform a combustion with the same pleasure,
wouldn't you?"

"Upon my soul, I do fear I would," said Curval, as he did
I know not what to Adelaide that brought a loud scream from her
lips.

"And who the devil do you think you are dealing with,
whore?" Curval demanded of his daughter. "What are these
chirpings and squallings all about? Remember the company you are
in. Can't you see that the Duc's trying to talk to me of burning,
provoking, instilling good manners into hatched fuck, and what
are you, pray tell me, but a little something hatched out of my
balls' fuck? Duclos, I say, continue, if you please," Curval added,
"for I have the feeling this bitch's tears might make me discharge.
And I'd prefer not to."

And here we are, said our heroine, come to details which,
bringing with them characters of a more singular piquancy, will
perhaps please you more. You know of course that in Paris we
have the custom of exposing the dead before the doors of houses.
There was a particular gentleman, well placed in society, who used
to pay me twelve francs for every one of these lugubrious objects
to which, in a given evening, I could lead him; his whole delight
consisted in going up with me as near to them as possible, to the
very edge of the coffin if we were able, and once we had posted
ourselves there, I had to frig him in such wise his fuck would shoot

*out upon the coffin. We used to run from one to another, would often pay our respects to three or four in an evening; it all depended upon the number I had located for him in advance, and we performed the same operation beside each of them; he never touched anything but my behind while I toiled over his prick. He was a man of about thirty, and I had his trade for at least ten years. I'm sure that, during the period of our collaboration, I made him discharge upon more than two thousand coffins.*

"But would he not say something during the rite?" inquired the Duc. "Did he not speak either to you or to the corpse?"

"He would shower invectives upon the deceased," Duclos replied; for example: 'Here, you rascal, here, take it, you villain, you bugger, take my fuck along with you to hell.' "

"A very unusual mania, that one," Curval commented.

"My friend," said the Duc, "you can be certain that man was one of our own sort, and that he surely did not stop at that."

"You are quite right, my Lord," spoke up Martaine, "and I shall have occasion to bring that actor back upon the stage."

Taking advantage of the silence which succeeded Martaine's interjection, Duclos went on.

*Another one,* said she, *carrying a more or less similar fantasy a good deal further, wanted me to keep spies on the watch near the cemeteries and to bring in word every time there was a burial of some young girl whose death had been caused by anything but a dangerous disease—he was very emphatic upon that point. As soon as I had got wind of something suitable, and he always paid me very handsomely for those discoveries, we would set off after sundown, enter the cemetery by one means or another, and heading at once for the grave our informant had indicated, above which the earth had only recently been broken, we would both fall to work, dig down to the cadaver, and when once we'd uncovered it, I'd frig him over it while he spent his time handling it and, above all, if 'twere possible, its buttocks. If perchance, and it frequently occurred, he stiffened a second time, he'd therewith shit, and have me shit also, upon the corpse, and discharge thereupon, all the*

*while palpating whatever parts of the body he could lay his hands
on.*

"Oh, my, but that one does strike a response in me," said
Curval, "and if I have to make my confession to you here and
now, I'll assure you I've done the same thing from time to time.
To be sure, I added a few little episodes I dare say our rules
prevent me from describing at this point. Be that as it may, my
prick's got monstrously fat; spread your thighs, Adelaide. . . ."

And I've not the faintest idea what happened next; all we
know is that the couch groaned beneath its burden, unmistakable
sounds of a discharge pealed from the Président's niche, and I am
led to suppose that, very simply and very virtuously, his honor the
judge had just committed incest.

"Président," the Duc called over, "I'll wager you thought she
was dead."

"Why, indeed, that's true," said Curval, "else how in the
world could I have discharged?"

And hearing not another word from the several alcoves,
Duclos brought that evening's stories to a close with the following
one:

*Lest I leave you, Messieurs, with dark images and sad
thoughts, I am going to conclude the soiree with the story of the
Duc de Bonnefort's passion. That young lord, whom I amused five
or six times, and who used frequently to see one of my close friends
for the same operation, required a woman, armed with a dildo, to
frig herself naked in his presence—to frig herself, I say, both before and behind and to keep it up for three hours without a moment's interruption. He has a clock there to guide you, and if you
drop the work before having completed the third hour, no payment
for you. He sits opposite you, he observes you, makes you turn
this way, that way, some other way, exhorts you to ply the dildo
more energetically, he would have you go out of your mind with
pleasure, and if indeed transported by the effects of the operation,
you should really swoon away with delight, 'tis very certain you
will hasten his. But if you keep your head, at the precise instant*

*the clock strikes the third hour, up he gets, approaches you, and discharges in your face.*

"Truly," quoth the Bishop, "I fail to understand, Duclos, why you didn't prefer to leave us with those other images and thoughts rather than with this innocuous picture. They had some spice to them, some color, and excited us powerfully, whereas here we have some sort of milksop business which, now that the session is over, leaves us with nothing at all in our heads."

"No, she did the right thing, insofar as I'm concerned," said Julie, who was lying with Durcet, "and I give her my warmest thanks. We'll all be allowed to go to bed more peacefully now that they don't have all those frightful ideas in their heads."

"Ah, lovely Julie, you may be very gravely mistaken," said Durcet, "for I never remember anything but the earlier one when the later one displeases me; you doubt my word? why, then pray have the kindness to follow me."

And, together with Sophie and Michette, Durcet fled into his closet to discharge I don't know how, but none the less in a manner which must not have suited Sophie, for she uttered a piercing scream and emerged from the sanctuary as red as a cockscomb.

"Well," drawled the Duc, "you surely could not have wanted to confuse her with a corpse for that stunt; for you've just made her give out the most furious sign of life."

"She was afraid, that's all," Durcet explained; "ask her what I did to her and make her tell you in a whisper."

He sent Sophie to speak to the Duc.

"Ah," said the latter aloud, "there's nothing in that either to warrant screams, or, for that matter, a discharge."

And because the supper call sounded, they suspended their conversation and their pleasures in order to go and enjoy those of the table. The orgies were celebrated rather quietly, and Messieurs retired to bed in good order; not one of them had even the appearance of being drunk; and that was extremely unusual.

# THE TWENTY-SEVENTH DAY

*T*he denunciations, authorized on the previous day, began early that morning; the sultanas, having remarked that, save for Rosette, they were all listed for correction, decided that all eight of themselves ought to be included in the game and promptly went to level accusations against her. They reported she had spent the whole night farting, and as this was really only a teasing they were giving her, she had the entire harem against whom to pit her denials; her name was straightway inscribed. Everything else moved along splendidly and, except for Sophie and Zelmire, who stuttered just a little, the friends were thrilled by the new compliment they had from these brazen little hussies: "God's fuck, I've an assful of shit, wouldst care for some?" And, as a matter of fact, there was shit everywhere to be had indeed, for, from fear of some temptation to wash, the governesses had removed every pot, every receptacle, every towel, and all water. The diet of meat but no bread was beginning to warm all those little unwashed mouths, Messieurs noticed that there was already a very appreciable difference in the little girls' breaths.

"Damn my eyes!" exclaimed Curval as he withdrew his tongue from Augustine's gullet; "that now signifies at least something; kissing this one makes me stiff."

Everyone agreed there had been a distinct improvement.

As there was nothing new or out of the ordinary until coffee, we are going to transport the reader directly to the salon. Coffee was served by Sophie, Zelmire, Giton, and Narcisse. The Duc said he was perfectly sure Sophie was the sort of girl who could discharge; the experiment, in his view, had absolutely to be made. He asked Durcet to keep a close eye on her and, laying her upon a divan, he simultaneously polluted the edges of her vagina, her clitoris, and her asshole, at first with his fingers, next with his tongue; and Nature triumphed: after fifteen minutes of this, the lovely girl became uneasy, troubled, she flushed crimson, she sighed, she panted, Durcet drew Curval's and the Bishop's attention to all these manifestations, for 'twas they who'd doubted her discharging capacities; the Duc suggested that, since he had always been confident of them, it was for the others to convince themselves, and so they all fell to imbibing that young fuck, and the little rascal's cunt left all their lips moist. The Duc could not resist the experiment's lubricious appeal; he got up and, squatting over the child, discharged upon her half-opened fur, then used his fingers to work as much as possible of his seed into the interior of her cunt. His head inspired by what he was watching, Curval seized the little one and demanded something other than fuck of her; she tendered her cunning little ass, the Président glued his mouth to it, the intelligent reader will have no trouble guessing what he received therefrom. Zelmire was meanwhile amusing the Bishop: she first frigged, then sucked his fundament. And all that while, Curval was having himself frigged by Narcisse, whose ass he kissed ardently. However, no one but the Duc lost his fuck; Duclos had announced some pretty stories for that afternoon which, she promised, would outdo what she had served up the day before, and Messieurs were disposed to save their forces for the auditorium. The hour having come, they passed to their alcoves, and that interesting girl expressed herself in the following manner:

*A man of whose circumstances and existence I had not previously known anything,* she said, *and about whom I was later to learn only a little, and, therefore, a man about whom I can give you no better than an imperfect portrait, sent me a note, and in it besought me to come to his house, in the rue Blanche-du-Rempart, at nine o'clock in the evening. I had no reason to be suspicious, his note said; although I had no acquaintance of him, I could be certain that neither would I have cause to complain were I to come as he bade me do. Two* louis *accompanied the letter, and despite my usual cautiousness, which ought certainly to have opposed my accepting the invitation of a man of whom I knew nothing, despite all that, I took the risk, trusting to I know not what intuition which, in a very low voice, told me I had nothing to fear. And so I went; and I arrived at the given address. I am greeted by a valet who informs me that I am to undress entirely, for, he explains, it is only if I am naked that he can introduce me into his master's apartment; I execute the order, and directly he sees me in the state desired, he takes me by the hand, and having led me through several intervening chambers, finally knocks upon a door. It opens, I enter, the valet withdraws, the door closes again; but, with what regards the amount of light in the room, there was precious little difference between that place and the inside of a hat, neither light nor air penetrated into that room from any opening whatever. No sooner am I in than a naked man comes up to me and seizes me without a word; I keep my wits about me, persuaded that the whole thing surely boiled down to nothing more than a little fuck to be shed by one means or another; that job once over with, I say to myself, I'll be quits with this whole nocturnal ceremony. And so I waste not a moment placing my hand upon his groin, with the intention of draining the venom from the monster as rapidly as possible. I discover a very large prick, very hard and also very rebellious, but scarcely have I touched it than my fingers are forced away: my opponent seems not to want me to find out anything about him; I am edged toward a stool and made to sit down. The unknown libertine plumps himself down near me, and grasping my tits one after the other, he squeezes and wrings them so violently that I protest that he is hurting me. Wherewith his brutalities cease, he leads me to an elevated sofa, and has me stretch out flat upon it; then seating himself between my parted legs, he falls to doing to my buttocks what he has just left off doing to my breasts: he palpates and squeezes them with unparalleled violence, he spreads them, compresses them again, kneads them, mauls, kisses, and bites them, he sucks my asshole, and as these reiterated attacks were less dangerous on that side than they might have been on the other, I held my peace and put up no resistance, and as I let him toil over my hindquarters I wondered what could be the purpose of this mysteriousness when, after all, the things he was doing were perfectly ordinary. I was trying to guess what he was driving at when all of a sudden my man began to utter bloodcurdling shrieks:*

"*Run for it, you damned whore, run for it, I tell you,*" *he shouted,* "*get out of here, bitch, for I'm discharging and won't be held responsible for your life!*"

*As you may readily imagine, my first movement was to leap to my feet; I spied a feeble glimmer of light—it was coming through the doorway I had entered—I dashed toward it—ran into the valet who had received me at the door—flung myself into his arms.... He gave me back my clothes, also gave me two* louis, *I left the place at once, very pleased to have got off so cheaply.*

"And you had excellent cause to congratulate yourself," said Martaine, "for what you were exposed to was merely a diminutive version of his ordinary passion. I shall present the man to you again, Messieurs," that worldly dame continued, "but in a more dangerous aspect."

"I expect my characterization of him will be even darker," said Desgranges, "and I wish to join Madame Martaine in assuring you that you were exceedingly fortunate to have had to put up with no more than you did, for the same gentleman has far more unusual passions."

"But let us wait and hear his entire story before arguing the point," the Duc suggested, "and, Duclos, make haste to tell us another so as to remove from our minds the image of an individual who will unfailingly arouse us if we dwell any longer on him."

*The libertine with whom next I came into contact,* Duclos went on, *wished to have a woman who had a very handsome bust, and as that is one of my beauties, after having exposed it to his scrutiny, he preferred me to any of my girls. But what use did that wretched libertine design to make of both my breasts and my face? He had me lie down, entirely naked, upon a divan, straddled my chest, desposited his prick between my dugs, ordered me to squeeze them together as tightly as I was able, and after a brief career, the wicked fellow inundated them with fuck while expec-*

*torating at least twenty mouthfuls of thick spittle, all of which landed on my face.*

"Well," grumbled Adelaide, in whose face the Duc had just been spitting, "I fail to see any necessity for imitating that infamy. Are you done now?" she continued as she wiped her face. But the Duc had not discharged.

"I'll finish when it suits my convenience, sweet child," the Duc replied to her; "bear well in mind that, alive though you may be, you are only so in order to obey and to let be done to you what we please. Proceed with your story, Duclos, for I might do something worse and, adoring this beautiful creature as I do," he said, resorting to a bit of persiflage, "I'd hardly wish entirely to outrage her."

*I know not, Messieurs, Duclos said as she resumed her discourse, whether you have ever heard tell of the Commander de Saint-Elme's passion. He had a gaming house where all who came to risk their money were deftly fleeced; but the most extraordinary part of it all was that cheating his visitors used to make the Commander's prick stiffen: every time he'd pick someone's pocket he'd discharge in his breeches, and a woman with whom I used to be on the very best terms, and whom he had been keeping for a long time, once told me that sometimes the thing would heat him to such a point that he would be obliged to go to her to seek some relief from the ardor devouring him. He did not confine himself to robbing customers at roulette; every other kind of theft was just as attractive in his eyes, and no article was safe when he was in the vicinity. Were he to dine at your table, he would make off with the silverware; when he entered your study, he'd pilfer your jewels; if near your pocket, he'd appropriate your snuffbox or your handkerchief. Everything was subject to seizure: he took a keen interest in anything provided he could get his hands on it, and everything gave him a stout erection, and would even cause him to discharge once he had made it his own.*

*But in that eccentricity of his he was certainly less outstanding than the parliamentary judge with whom I had to cope shortly after my arrival at Fournier's establishment, and whom I had as a client for many years: his being a rather ticklish case, he would deal with no one but me.*

*The jurisconsult had a little apartment, which he rented the year round, looking out upon the place de Grève; an old servant lived as a caretaker in the apartment, and her only duties were these two: to keep the premises in good order and to send word to her employer whenever preparations for an execution were visible upon the square. The judge would immediately get in touch with me, tell me to hold myself in readiness; he would disguise himself and come to fetch me in a cab, and we would repair to his little apartment.*

*In the salon the casement window was placed in such a manner it commanded a direct view of, and was situated near, the scaffold; we would post ourselves there, the judge and I, behind a lattice-work screen upon one of whose horizontal slats he rested an excellent pair of opera glasses, and while waiting for the patient to make his appearance, Themis' wise henchman would amuse himself upon a bed which had been drawn close to the window; while waiting, I say, he would kiss my ass, an episode which, by the by, pleased him enormously. Finally, the crowd's hubbub would announce the victim's arrival, the man of the gown would return to his place at the window and would have me take mine beside him, with the injunction to frig his prick gently, proportioning my strokes to the progress of the execution he was about to watch, in such sort that the sperm would not escape until the moment the patient rendered up his soul unto God. Everything was arranged, the criminal mounted upon the platform, the jurist contemplated him; the nearer the patient approached to death, the more furious became the villain's prick in my hands. The axe was raised, the axe was brought down, 'twas the instant he discharged: "Ah, gentle Jesus!" he'd say, "double-fucked Christ! How I'd like to be the executioner myself, and how much better than that I'd swing the blade!"*

*Moreover, his pleasures' impressions would be measured by the method of execution, a hanging produced in him little more than an exceedingly mild sensation, a man being broken on the wheel threw him into a delirium, but were the criminal to be either burned alive or quartered, my client would swoon away from pleasure. Man or woman, it made no difference to him.*

*"I dare say," he once remarked, "that only a pregnant woman would have a stronger effect upon me, and, unfortunately, the thing cannot be brought about."*

*"But, your honor," I said to him upon another occasion, "through your public function you have cooperated in the destruction of this luckless victim."*

*"Assuredly, yes," he replied, "and that precisely is what creates all the diversion for me; I have been judging for a good thirty years and have never pronounced any but the death sentence."*

*"And do you suppose," I said, "that you have not, if only a little, to reproach yourself for the death of these people, which so resembles murder?"*

*"Splendid," he murmured; "must one, however, look at the matter so closely?"*

*"But in society such a thing is called a horror," I protested.*

*"Oh," said he, "one has got to learn how to make the best of the horror; there is in horror matter to produce an erection, you see, and the reason therefor is quite simple: this thing, however frightful you wish to imagine it, ceases to be horrible for you immediately it acquires the power to make you discharge; it is, hence, no longer horrible save in the eyes of others, but who is to assure me that the opinion of others, almost always erroneous or faulty in every other connection, is not equally so in this instance? There is nothing," he pursued, "either fundamentally good, nor anything fundamentally evil; everything is relative, relative to our point of view, that is to say, to our manners, to our opinions, to our prejudices. This point once established, it is extremely possible that something, perfectly indifferent in itself, may indeed be distasteful in your eyes, but may be most delicious in mine; and immediately I find it pleasing, immediately I find it amusing, regardless of our inability to agree in assigning a character to it, should I not be a fool to deprive myself of it merely because you condemn it? Come, come, my dear Duclos, a man's life is something of such slight importance that one may sport with it as much as one likes, just as*

one might with a cat's life or with that of a dog; 'tis up to the feeble and weak to defend themselves, they have virtually the same weapons we possess. And since you are so scrupulous," my man added, "my stars! what would you think of the fantasy of one of my friends!"

And, with your Lordships' leave, I shall terminate the evening by giving, as my fifth story, the account of the taste the judge related to me.

This philosophical jurist told me that his friend would deal only with women scheduled to be executed. The nearer the moment that they are delivered to him borders on the moment they are going to perish, the better he pays for them. But he insists that the conference be held after they have been notified of their sentence. Thanks to his position in society within easy reach of this sort of prize, he never lets one slip through his fingers and," my informant went on, "I have seen him pay up to one hundred louis for this kind of tête-à-tête. However, he does not carnally enjoy them, or rather he requires nothing of them but that they exhibit their buttocks and shit before his eyes; for taste of shit, he maintains, there is nothing to equal what one gets from a woman who has just heard the death penalty pronounced against her. He will go to any lengths to obtain these private interviews, and of course, as you may well suppose, he does not wish to be known by the victim. He sometimes passes himself off as the confessor, or at other times as a friend of the family, and his proposals are always fortified by the promise that, if they indulge his little whimsies, he may very possibly be able to be of help to them.

"And when he has finished, when he has satisfied himself, by what, my dear Duclos," said the judge, "do you fancy he concludes his operation? Just as do I, my worthy friend; he reserves his fuck for the climax, and releases it at last when before his delighted gaze the condemned person expires."

"Ah, that's true villainy," I told him.

"Villainy?" he interrupted. "My dear child, all that's mere verbiage, prattle. Nothing's villainous if it causes an erection, and the single crime that exists in this world is to refuse oneself anything that might produce a discharge."

"And so it was he refused himself nothing," said Martaine; "Madame Desgranges and I shall have, or so I hope, occasion to entertain the company with several lubricious and criminal anecdotes relating to the same personage."

"Excellent," said Curval, "for there's a man I'm already hugely fond of. That's just the way one should reason about one's pleasures, and his philosophy pleases me infinitely. It is truly incredible the way man, already restricted in all his amusements, in all his faculties, seeks further to narrow the scope of his existence through his contemptible prejudices. For example, it is not commonly suspected what limitations he who has raised up murder as a crime has imposed upon all his delights; he has deprived himself of a hundred joys, each more delicious than the other, by daring to adopt the odious illusion which founds that particular nonsense. What the devil difference can it make to Nature whether there are one, ten, twenty, five hundred more or fewer human beings on earth? Conquerors, heroes, tyrants—do they inhibit themselves by that absurd law? Do you hear them saying that we ought not do unto others that which unto ourselves we would not have done? Forsooth, my friends, I tell you frankly that I tremble, I groan when I hear fools dare to tell me that such is the law of Nature, etc. . . . Merciful Heaven! all athirst for crimes and murders, 'tis to see to it they are committed, to inspire them Nature has wrought her law, and the one commandment she graves deep in our hearts is to satisfy ourselves at no matter whose expense. But patience; I shall perhaps soon have a better occasion to expand upon these questions, I have made the profoundest study of them, and, in communicating my conclusions to you, I hope to convince you, as convinced am I, that the single way of serving Nature is blindly to respond to her desires, of whatever kind they may be, because, for the sake of maintaining the divine balance she has struck universally, vice being quite as necessary to the general scheme as virtue, she is wont to urge us to do this, now to do that, depending upon what is at the moment necessary to her design. Yes, my friends, I shall someday discuss all that before you, but for the moment I must be still, for I have fuck that needs spilling, that devilish fellow at the executions has made my poor balls swell dreadfully."

And the Président departed for the boudoir at the end of the corridor, with him went Desgranges and Fanchon, his two dear friends, for they were as great scoundrels as he; and with him also went Aline, Sophie, Hébé, Antinoüs, and Zéphyr. I have little definite information upon what the libertine took it into his head to do in the midst of those seven persons, but his absence was prolonged and he was heard to shout: "Come, damn it, turn this way, do you hear? But that's not what I told you to do" and other ill-humored remarks interspersed with oaths to which he was known to be greatly addicted while enacting scenes of debauchery; the women finally returned, their faces very red, their hair very untidy, and with the air of having been furiously mauled and pawed in every sense. Meanwhile, the Duc and his two friends had scarcely been marking time, but of their number only the Bishop had discharged, and in a manner so extraordinary that we had better say nothing about it at present.

They went to the supper table, where Curval philosophized a little more, for, with that man, passions had not the least influence upon doctrines; firm in his principles, he was just as much an atheist, an iconoclast, a criminal after having shed his fuck as when, before, he had been in a lubricious ferment, and that precisely is how all wise, level-headed people should be. Never ought fuck be allowed to dictate or affect one's principles; 'tis for one's principles to regulate one's manner of shedding it. And whether one is stiff, or whether one is not, one's philosophy, acting independently of the passions, should always remain the same.

The amusement at the orgies consisted in a verification which had not until then been undertaken, but which was interesting none the less: Messieurs were moved to decide who amongst the boys, who amongst the girls had the most beautiful ass. And so, first of all, they had the eight boys form a line: they were standing erect ... yes, but, on the other hand, they were made to bend forward just a little, for that is the only way properly to judge an ass. The examination was both very long and very severe, opinions clashed, opinions were reversed, rectified, each ass was inspected fifteen times, and the apple was generally accorded to Zéphyr; it was unanimously agreed that it was physically impossible to find anything more perfect, better molded, better cleft.

Next they turned to the girls, who adopted the same posture. Deliberation was at first very slow, very prolonged, it proved all but impossible to decide from amongst Augustine, Zelmire, and Sophie. Augustine, taller, better made than the other two, would doubtless have triumphed had the jury been composed of painters; but libertines call rather for grace than exactitude, for fullness sooner than regularity. There was in her disfavor a shade too much of the slender and of the delicate; the two other contestants offered a carnation so fresh, so healthy, so plump, buttocks so fair and so round, a back whose line descended so voluptuously, that Augustine was eliminated from further consideration. But how were they to decide between the two who remained? After ten rounds of balloting, opinion was still equally divided.

At last, Zelmire won the prize; the two charming winners were assembled, were kissed, handled, frigged for the rest of the evening, Zelmire was ordered to frig Zéphyr who, discharging like a musket, afforded, in the throes of pleasure, the most entrancing spectacle; then, in his turn, he frigged the young lady who all but fainted away in his arms, and all these scenes, of unspeakable lubricity, brought about the loss of the Duc's fuck and of his brother's, but only mildly stirred Curval and Durcet, who agreed that what they needed were scenes far less Arcadian, far less ethereal if their weary old souls were to be cheered, and that all these winsome frolickings were only good for youngsters. They went to bed, and Curval, plunged into the thick of fresh infamies, compensated himself for the tender pastorals he had been obliged to witness.

# THE TWENTY-EIGHTH DAY

'Twas a wedding day, and the turn of Cupidon and Rosette to be united in holy matrimony, and by still another fateful combination of accidents, both were listed for punishment that evening. As no one was found at fault that morning, that entire part of the day was devoted to the wedding ceremony, and when it was over, the newlyweds were brought into the salon to see what they would do together. The mysteries of Venus were, as we know, often celebrated in these children's presence; although none of them had so far taken an active part in them, they were well enough grounded in the theory of the thing to be able to execute about everything that there is to do. Cupidon, his prick very rigidly aloft, insinuated his little peg between Rosette's thighs, and she lent herself to his maneuvers with all the candor of the most thorough innocence; the young lad was managing so nicely that he was probably well on the way to success when the Bishop, taking him in his arms, had put in himself what, I fancy, the child would greatly have liked to put into his little wife; all the while he perforated the Bishop's ample hole, he regarded her with eyes which declared his regrets, but she was herself soon occupied: the Duc thigh-fucked her. Curval stepped up in the lewdest fashion to fondle the ass of the Bishop's little fucker, and as that pretty little ass was found, in keeping with instructions, in the desired state, he licked it and began to stiffen. Durcet was up to the same tricks with the little girl the Duc was holding with her chest pressed to his.

However, no one discharged, and Messieurs went in to dine;

537

the young bride and groom, who had been admitted to the table, also appeared to serve coffee, together with Augustine and Zélamir. And the voluptuous Augustine, deeply distressed over not having won the prize for beauty the night before, had, as though sulking, left her hair in just that kind of disarray which rendered her a thousand times more intriguing to see. Curval was stirred by the sight, and, examining her buttocks:

"I fail to understand how it happened that this little rascal did not win the palm," said he, "for devil take me if in all the world there exists a finer ass than this one here."

So saying, he pried it open, and inquired of Augustine whether she were ready to do her old friend a great kindness. "Oh, yes," she replied, "a very great one indeed, for I really have to get rid of what I have there." Curval rests her upon a sofa and, kneeling before that radiant behind, he devours its turd in a flash.

"Sacred name of God," says he, licking his lips, turning toward his colleagues, and pointing to the prick straining against his abdomen, "I'm in a state for furiously undertaking something or other."

"And what would it be?" asked the Duc, who was very fond of making the Président utter horrors when he was in that particular state.

"What?" said Curval. "Why, whatever infamy you wish to propose, even were it to dismember Nature and unhinge the universe."

"Come along now," said Durcet, upon seeing him cast furious glances in the direction of Augustine, "come along, let's go listen to Duclos, it's story time. I'm persuaded," he went on, addressing the others, "that if he gets the bit in his teeth, that poor little duckling is going to spend a trying quarter of an hour."

"Oh, yes!" said the inflamed Président, "a very trying one, I can vouch for that."

"Curval," said the Duc, whose prick was nodding in the air like a vengeful lance, and who had just finished eliciting some shit from Rosette, "let the others entrust the harem to the two of us, and two hours from now we'll have turned in a capital performance."

Durcet and the Bishop, at the moment calmer than their co-proprietors, each took one of them by the arm, and it was thus, that is to say, breeches about their ankles and pricks aloft, that those libertines made their solemn entrance into the auditorium, where the assembly was already gathered and ready to hear Duclos' latest offerings; she, having anticipated, from those two gentlemen's state, that she would soon be interrupted, began in these terms:

*A nobleman at the court, aged about thirty-five, came and asked me for one of the prettiest girls I could lay my hands on. He said nothing to indicate his favorite mania, and to satisfy any need he might have, I gave him a young dressmaker who had never yet attended a party and who was incontestably one of the loveliest creatures France could boast. I introduce them to each other and, curious to observe what is about to transpire, I quickly repair to my post at the spy hole.*

*"Now where in the devil has Madame Duclos been," he opened by saying, "to find an ugly chit like yourself? Has she been raking over someone's dung heap? You must have been servicing a couple of soldiers when they came to fetch you here."*

*And the young lady, blushing to the ears with shame, for she had been forewarned of nothing, was at a loss to know what tack to take.*

*"Well, get your clothes off then," the courtier continued. "My God, but you're a clumsy slut! I've seen ugly whores in my life, but never one the likes of you, nor so stupid. Well, then? Are we going to be able to get this over with today? Ah, yes, there's that body they've been praising to the skies. Sacred Mother, what are those dugs! you'd think they'd been grafted from an old cow."*

*And he fell to handling them brutally.*

*"And this belly! What could have caused those wrinkles? You surely haven't whelped twenty children at your age?"*

*"Not one, Monsieur, I assure you."*

*"Oh, I see, not one, eh! That's how all these bitches talk; listen to them a while and they'll be trying to convince you they're all virgins. . . . Well, move about, will you, turn around . . . infamous ass you've got dragging there. Flabby, disgusting buttocks—I understand now why they described you as unusual. It*

*must have taken a lot of kicks in the ass to have arranged things this way."*

*And you will allow me, Messieurs, to remind you that the ass he was referring to was as beautiful an ass as one could find anywhere. Be that as it may, the girl began to grow upset; I could almost make out the flutterings of her little heart, and I saw her lovely eyes become worried, then misty. And the more troubled she became, the more energetically the scoundrel sought to mortify her. I cannot possibly remember all the ungenerous things he said to her; one would not dare say anything more stinging, more biting, to the vilest, most infamous of creatures. Finally, a lump welled up in her throat and her tears began to flow; 'twas for this last development the libertine, who had been polluting himself with might and main, had reserved the bouquet of his litanies. 'Tis impossible, once again, to render for you all the horrible observations he made upon her skin, her figure, her features, the sickening odor he declared she exhaled, how he criticized her bearing, her mind; in brief, he hunted up everything, he invented everything to humiliate her pride, and discharged all over her while vomiting atrocities a street sweeper would never dare utter. This scene had a most amusing outcome: the girl seemed to have taken it as a lesson, and it prompted her to take an oath; she swore never again to expose herself to such an adventure, and a week later I learned she had entered a convent for the rest of her life. I related this to the young man, who found it all prodigiously funny, and who later asked me for someone else to convert.*

*Another,* Duclos continued, *requested me to find him extremely sensitive girls who were awaiting news of an event whose unfavorable outcome might cause them an access of profoundest grief. I had unending difficulty finding anything to answer this description, and it was virtually impossible to pawn off a makeshift upon the connoisseur. He knew what he was about, had been playing the game for ages, and one glance was sufficient to tell him whether the blow he was to strike would reach the mark. And so I made no effort to deceive him, and managed somehow always to get him girls who were in the mental state he desired. I one day produced a maid who was expecting word from Dijon of a young man she idolized and whose name was Valcourt. I presented the girl to the libertine.*

*"Where do you come from, Mademoiselle?"* he asked her in a decent and respectful tone.

*"From Dijon, Monsieur."*

*"From Dijon? Why, that's a strange coincidence, for I have just this instant had a letter from Dijon containing tidings which have sore distressed me."*

*"And what is the trouble?"* the girl asked with great interest; *"I know everyone in the town, this news you have heard may be of some importance to me."*

*"Oh, not at all,"* our man replied, *"it relates only to me; it has to do with the death of a young man—I was keenly fond of him, he had just married a girl whom my brother, who also lives in Dijon, had found for him, a girl to whom he was passionately attached, and the day after the wedding, he suddenly died."*

*"His name, Monsieur, if you please?"*

*"His name was Valcourt; he was originally from Paris,"* and the libertine named the street and the number at which Valcourt had lived. *"You cannot possibly have known him, though."*

But the young girl had collapsed in a faint.

*Therewith our libertine, beside himself with delight, muttered a string of oaths, unbuttoned his breeches, and set to frigging himself upon her supine body. "Ah, by Christ! that's what I want. Make haste now, hurry,"* he said to himself, *"the buttocks, I only need the buttocks to discharge."*

*And turning her over, and pulling up her skirts, he darts seven or eight jets of fuck upon the motionless girl's ass, and then takes himself off without a thought either for the consequences of what he has said, or for what will become of the unhappy creature.*

"And did she croak as a result?" inquired Curval, who was being fucked at a great rate.

"No," Duclos admitted, "but she fell ill and lay six weeks at death's door."

"Very fine stunt, oh my, yes!" said the Duc. "But," that scoundrel went on, "I should have preferred it had your man chosen the period of her menstruation for his disclosure."

"Yes," Curval said, "quite. But, Monsieur le Duc, tell us all the truth: your prick's in the air, I can sense it from here: you would have preferred that she drop dead on the spot."

"Well, have it your own way," called back the Duc. "Since you'd wish it so, I consent, for, you know, I've not many scruples over a girl's death."

"Durcet," said the Bishop, "if you don't send those two rascals out to discharge, there'll be a merry to-do this evening."

"Ah, by the Almighty's balls," Curval shouted toward the Bishop's niche, "you're afraid for your flock. But what difference would two more or two less make? Well, Monsieur le Duc, you've heard Monseigneur the Bishop's suggestion, let's go to the boudoir, but we'll go together, for it's all too evident these other gentlemen wish to avoid a scandal tonight."

No sooner said than done; and our two libertines had themselves followed by Zelmire, Augustine, Sophie, Colombe, Cupidon, Narcisse, Zélamir, Adonis, escorted by Bum-Cleaver, Invictus, Thérèse, Fanchon, Constance, and Julie. A brief interval ensued, then two or three women's screams were heard, then the bellowings of our two lechers, who were disgorging their fuck simultaneously. Augustine reappeared dabbing at her bleeding nose, Adelaide's breast was covered by a scarf. As for Julie, always libertine enough and clever enough to get through any ordeal unscathed, she was laughing like one in hysterics and saying that had it not been for her they'd never have been able to discharge. The rest of the troupe returned; Zélamir and Adonis still had their buttocks smeared with fuck. Having assured their confreres they had conducted themselves with all possible decency and modesty, that they might have nothing to be reproached for, and that now, perfectly calm, they were in a fit state to listen, Messieurs gave Duclos the signal to proceed and she did so in the following terms:

*I sincerely regret Monsieur de Curval's precipitate haste to relieve his needs,* said that superb creature, *for I had two pregnant-woman stories to tell him, and they would perhaps have afforded him some real pleasure. I know his taste for the fruit-laden, and I am certain that, had he a flicker of warmth left in his bowels, these two tales would divert him.*

"Tell them all the same," said Curval. "You are aware, I trust, that fucking has not the least effect upon my sentiments, and that the moment when I am most infatuated with evil is always the moment after I have performed it."

*Very well*, said Duclos, *I have seen a man whose mania was straitly connected with observing a woman give birth; he would frig himself when seeing her labor pains begin, and used to discharge squarely upon the infant's head directly it hove into view.*

*A second would perch a seven-month-pregnant woman upon an isolated pedestal at least fifteen feet high. She was obliged to keep her balance, and her mind on what she was about, for if by mischance she were to have grown dizzy, she and her issue would have been definitively ruined. The libertine I speak of, very little affected by the situation of the poor creature he paid for her acrobatic skill, kept her where she was until he had discharged, and frigged himself before her while exclaiming: "Ah, the lovely statue, the beautiful ornament, the empress upon her dais!"*

"Well, Curval, you'd have shaken that column, wouldn't you, eh?" said the Duc.

"Ah, not at all, you're mistaken; I have too much respect for Nature and her works. Is not the most interesting of them all the propagation of our species? is it not a kind of miracle we ought to adore incessantly, and ought we not to have the warmest interest in those who perform it? For my part, I never see a pregnant woman without being melted; think for a moment what a marvelous thing is a woman who, just like an oven, can make a little snot hatch deep in her vagina. Is there anything more beautiful, anything quite as fetching as that? Constance, dear girl, come hither, I beseech you, come let me kiss the sanctuary wherein, at this very moment, such a profound mystery is in progress."

And as he found her right there in his alcove, he was not long searching after the temple he wished to minister to. But there is reason to suppose Constance took a somewhat different view of his intentions, or, at least, that she only half believed his professions, for an instant later she was heard to vent a scream which bore no relationship at all to the consequences of a reverence or an homage. Then silence closed again; observing that all lay quiet, Duclos concluded her narrations with the following little tale:

*I knew a man,* said she, *whose passion consisted in hearing children wail and cry; he had to have a mother with a child of no more than three or four. He required this mother to give her offspring a sound thrashing; it had to be done before him, and when the little creature, aroused by this treatment, began to bawl, the mother had next to catch hold of the rogue's prick and frig it industriously, directing the glans at the child, in whose face he would discharge when the little one was singing his loudest.*

"Now, I wager," the Bishop said to Curval, "that fellow was no more a friend of increase than you are."

"I dare say not," Curval conceded. "He must be, according to the argument of a lady reputed to possess a great fund of wit, he must be, I say, a great scoundrel; for, in keeping with the development of her thought, any man who loves neither animals, nor children, nor swollen-bellied women, is a monster fit to be put on the rack. Well, by that agreeable old fool's judgment, my case is heard and decided and writ off the agenda," said the Président, "for I certainly have no affection for any one of those three things."

And as it was late, and as interruptions had consumed a sizable portion of the séance, they went straight to supper. At table, they debated the following questions: what need has man for sensibility? and is it or is it not useful to his happiness? Curval proved that it was nothing if not dangerous, and that it was the first sentiment, this one of human kindness, one had to extirpate from children, by early making them grow accustomed to the most ferocious spectacles. Each of them having differently approached the problem, by many and long detours they all finally ended up agreeing with Curval. Supper over, the Duc and he were of the opinion the women and youngsters should be sent to bed, and they proposed the orgies be made an entirely masculine tournament; everyone concurred, the idea was adopted, Messieurs enchambered themselves with the eight fuckers and spent almost all the night having themselves fucked and drinking liqueurs. They stumbled to bed two hours before dawn, and the morrow brought with it both events and stories the reader will perhaps find entertaining if he will give himself the trouble to read what follows.

# THE TWENTY-NINTH DAY

*T*here is a proverb—and what splendid things proverbs are —there is one, I say, which maintains that the appetite is restored by eating. This proverb, coarse, nay, vulgar though it be, has none the less a very extensive significance: to wit, that, by dint of performing horrors, one's desire to commit additional ones is whetted, and that the more of them one commits, the more of them one desires.

Well, such exactly was the case with our insatiable libertines. Through unpardonable harshness, through a detestable refinement of debauchery, they, as we know, had condemned their wives to render them the vilest and most unclean services upon their emergence from the privy. They were not content with that, and on the 29th of November they proclaimed a new law (which appeared to have been inspired by the previous night's sodomistical libertinage), a new law, I say, which ruled that, as of the 1st of December, those wives would serve as the only pots to their masters' needs, and that the said needs, both the greater and the lesser, would never be executed anywhere save in their wives' mouths; that whenever Messieurs were moved to satisfy these fundamental urges, they would be followed about by four sultanas who would, once the urge had been satisfied, render them the service which heretofore the wives had rendered them and which the said wives would hereafter be unable to render them, since they were going to have graver employment; that the four officiating sultanas would be Colombe for Curval, Hébé for the Duc, Rosette for the Bishop, and Michette for Durcet; and that the least error or failure committed

545

in the course of either of these operations, whether in the course of that involving the wives or in that other involving the four little girls, would be punished with prodigious severity.

The poor women had no sooner learned of this new regulation than they wept and wrung their hands, unfortunately, it was all but in vain. It was however ordained that each wife would serve her husband, and Aline the Bishop, and that for this one operation Messieurs would not be allowed to exchange them. Two of the duennas were ordered to take turns presenting themselves for the same service, and the time for their rendering it was unalterably fixed at the hour Messieurs would depart the evening orgies; it was decided that Messieurs would at all times proceed to this ritual in each other's company, that while the elders were operating, the four sultanas, while waiting to give the service required of them, would make conspicuous display of their asses, and that the elders would move from one anus to the next, to press it, open it, and encourage it generally to function. This regulation promulgated, the friends proceeded that morning to administer the punishments which had not been distributed the night before because of the decision to perform the orgies with the assistance of men only.

The operation was undertaken in the sultanas' quarters; they were all eight taken care of, and after them came Adelaide, Aline, and Cupidon, who also were included upon the fatal list; the ceremony, with the details and all the protocol observed under such circumstances, dragged on for nearly four hours, at the end of which their Lordships descended to dinner, their heads swimming, especially Curval's head, for he, prodigiously cherishing these exercises, never took part in them without the most definite erection. As for the Duc, he had discharged in the thick of the fray, and so had Durcet. This latter, who was beginning to develop a very mischievous libertine testiness toward his dear wife Adelaide, was unable to discipline her without shudders of pleasure which ultimately loosened his seed.

Dinner was, as usual, followed by coffee; Messieurs, disposed to have some neat little asses on hand, had appointed Zéphyr and Giton to serve the cups, and to these two might have added a large number of others; but there was not one sultana whose ass was in anything like an appropriate state. In accordance with schedule, the coffee-serving team was rounded out by Colombe and Michette. Curval, examining Colombe's ass, the bedaubed condition whereof, in part the Président's own work, generated some singular desires in him, thrust his prick between her thighs from behind, while so doing fondling her buttocks vivaciously; now and again, as it moved to and fro, his engine, as if through maladdress, nudged up against the dear little hole he would have given a kingdom to perforate. For a moment he studied it attentively.

"O sacred God," he said, turning to his friends, "I'll pay the society two hundred *louis* on the spot for leave to fuck this ass."

Reason prevailed, however, he kept a grip upon himself and did not even discharge. But the Bishop had Zéphyr discharge into his mouth and yielded up his own sanctified fuck as he swallowed that delicious child's; Durcet had himself kicked in the ass by Giton, then had Giton shit, and remained chaste. Messieurs removed to the auditorium, where each father, by an arrangement which was encountered rather frequently, had his daughter on his couch beside him; breeches lowered, they listened to our talented storyteller's five tales.

*It seemed as though, since the day I had so exactly executed Fournier's pious will, happiness smiled ever more warmly upon my house,* said that distinguished whore. *Never had I had so many wealthy acquaintances.*

*The Benedictine prior, among my most faithful clients, one day came to tell me that, having heard of a quite remarkable fantasy and having subsequently observed it performed by one of his friends who was wild about it, he had a powerful desire to enact it himself, and hence he asked me for a girl well fledged with hair. I gave him a big creature of twenty-eight years who had veritable thickets both under the arms and upon her mound. "Splendid," said the prior upon beholding the goods, "that's just what I need." And as he and I were very closely attached to each other, as we had taken many a gay tumble together, he made no objections when I requested leave to watch him at work. He had the girl undress and half recline upon a couch, her arms extended above her head, and, armed with a sharp pair of scissors he set to cropping the hair beneath her arms. Once he had clipped away every bit of it, he*

turned to her mound, and barbered it also, but so thoroughly that
when he was done one would never have believed the least vestige
of hair had ever grown on any of the areas he had worked over.
The job done, he kissed the parts he'd shorn and spurted his fuck
upon that hairless mound, in a perfect ecstasy over the fruit of
his labor.

Another required a doubtless much more bizarre ceremony:
I am thinking now of the Duc de Florville; I was advised to bring
him one of the most beautiful women I could find. A manservant
welcomed us at the Duc's mansion, and we entered by a side door.

"We will now prepare this attractive creature," the valet
said to me; "for there are several adjustments to be made in order
that she be in a state to amuse my Lord the Duc . . . come with
me."

By way of detours and corridors equally somber and immense,
we finally reached a lugubrious suite of rooms, lighted only by six
tapers placed on the floor around a mattress covered with black
satin; the entire room was hung in funereal stuffs, and the sight,
as we entered, woke the worst apprehensions in us.

"Calm your fears," said our guide, "you will not suffer the
least hurt; but be ready for anything," he added, speaking to the
girl, "and above all see to it that you do everything I tell you."

He had her remove all her clothes, loosened her coiffure, and
indicated she was to leave her hair, which was superb, to hang free.
Next, he bade her lie down upon the mattress surrounded by tall
candles, enjoined her to feign death and to be exceedingly careful,
throughout the whole of the scene to follow, neither to stir nor
breathe more deeply than she had to.

"For if unhappily my master, who is going to imagine you are
really dead, perceives you are only pretending, he'll be furious, will
leave you at once, and surely will not pay you a sou."

Directly he had placed the girl upon the pallet in the attitude
of a corpse, he had her twist her mouth in such a way as to give
the impression of pain, her eyes too were to suggest she had died
in agony; he scattered her tresses over her naked breast, lay a
dagger beside her, and near her heart smeared chicken's blood,
painting a wound the size of one's hand.

"I repeat to you," he said to the girl, "be not afraid, you have *nothing to say, nothing to do, you have simply to remain absolutely still and to draw your breath at the moments when you see he is farthest from you. And now, Madame," the valet said to me, "we may withdraw from the room. Come with me, please; that you not be worried about your girl, I am going to place you where you will be able to hear and watch the entire scene."*

*We quit the room, leaving the girl, who was not without her misgivings, but whom the manservant's speeches had reassured somewhat. He conducts me to a small chamber adjoining the apartment where the mystery is to be celebrated, and through a crack between two panels, over which the black material was hung, I could hear everything. To see was still easier, for the material was only crepe, I could distinguish objects on the other side quite as clearly as if I had been in the room itself.*

*The valet drew the cord that rang a bell, that was the signal, and a few minutes later we saw a tall, thin, wasted man of about sixty enter upon the stage. Beneath a loose-flowing dressing robe of India taffeta he was completely naked. He halted upon coming through the doorway; I had best tell you now that the Duc, supposing he was absolutely alone, had not the faintest idea his actions were being observed.*

*"Ah, what a beautiful corpse!" he exclaimed at once. "Death . . . 'tis beautiful to behold. . . . But, my God, what's this!" said he upon catching sight of the blood, the knife. "It must have been an assassin . . . only a moment ago . . . ah, Great God, how stiff he must be now, the person who did that."*

*And, frigging himself:*

*"How I would have loved to see him strike the blow!"*

*And fondling the corpse, moving his hand over its belly:*

*"Pregnant? . . . No, apparently not. What a pity."*

*And continuing to explore with his hands:*

*"Superb flesh! It's still warm . . . a lovely breast."*

*Wherewith he bent over her and kissed her mouth with incredible emotion:*

*"Still drooling," he said; "how I adore this saliva!"*

*And once again he drove his tongue almost into her gullet; no one could possibly have played the role more convincingly than did that girl, she lay stock-still, and whenever the Duc drew near she*

*ceased entirely to breathe. Finally, he rolled her over upon her
stomach:*

"*I must have a look at this lovely ass,*" *he murmured.*

*And after having scanned it:*

"*Jesus Christ! What matchless buttocks!*"

*And then he opened them, kissed them, and we distinctly saw
him place his tongue in that cunning little hole.*

"*Oh, upon my word!*" *he cried, sweating with admiration,
"this is certainly one of the most superb corpses I have ever seen
in my life; happy he who took this girl's life, oh, enviable person,
what pleasure he must have known!*"

*The very idea made him discharge; he was lying beside her,
squeezing her, his thighs glued against her buttocks, and he discharged upon her asshole, giving out unbelievable signs of pleasure,
and, as he yielded his sperm, crying like a demon:*

"*Ah fuck, fuck, ah good God, if only I had killed her, if only
I had been the one!*"

*Thus the operation ended, the libertine rose and disappeared;
we entered the room to resurrect our brave little friend. She was
exhausted, unable to budge: constraint, fright, everything had
numbed her senses, she was about ready in all earnestness to become the character she had just personified so expertly. We departed with four* louis *the valet gave us; as you may well imagine,
he doubtless surrendered no more than half of our pay.*

"Ye living gods!" cried Curval, "now that is a passion! To
say the least, the thing has flavor, aroma."

"I'm as stiff as a mule," said the Duc; "I'll stake my fortune
on it, that fellow had other tricks up his sleeve."

"Right you are, my Lord," said Martaine; "he now and again
employed a greater realism. I think Madame Desgranges and I
have evidence to prove it to you."

"And what the devil are you going to do while waiting?"
Curval asked the Duc.

"Don't disturb me, don't disturb me," the Duc shouted, "I'm
fucking my daughter, I'm pretending she's dead."

"Rascal," Curval rejoined, "that makes two crimes in your
head."

"Ah, by fuck," said the Duc, "would that they were more real. . . ."

And his impure seed burst into Julie's vagina.

"Well now, Duclos, what comes next? Go on with your stories," said he as soon as he had finished his affair, "go on, my dear friend, don't allow the Président to discharge, for I can hear him over there effecting an incestuous connection with his daughter; the funny little fellow is working up some evil ideas in his head; his parents have made me his tutor, they expect me to keep an eye on his behavior and I'd be distressed were it to become perverted."

"Too late," said Curval, "too late, old man, I'm discharging; ah, Christ be doublefucked, 'tis a pretty death."

And while encunting Adelaide, the scoundrel fancied to himself, as had the Duc, that he was fucking his murdered daughter; O incredible distraction of the mind of a libertine, who can naught hear, naught see, but he would imitate it that instant!

"Duclos, you must indeed continue," said the Bishop, "else I'll be seduced by those bawdy fellows' example, and in my present state I might carry things a good deal further than they."

*Some time after that last adventure I went alone to the home of another libertine,* said Duclos, *whose mania, more humiliating perhaps, was not however so saturnine. He receives me in a drawing room whose floor was covered with a very handsome rug. He bids me remove all I am wearing and then, having me get down on my hands and knees:*

*"Let's see," says he, stroking and patting the heads of two great Danes lying on either side of his chair, "let's see whether you are as nimble and quick as my dogs. Ready? Go get it!"*

*And with that he tosses some large roasted chestnuts on the floor; speaking to me as if I were an animal, he says:*

*"Go fetch them!"*

*I run on all fours after a chestnut, thinking it best to play the game with good humor and enter into the spirit of his eccentricity; I run along, I say, and endeavor to bring back the chestnuts, but the two dogs, also springing forward, outrun me, seize the chestnuts, and take them back to their master.*

*"Well, you're clearly in need of some practice before you'll*

be in good form," said the gentleman; "it's not, by chance, that you are afraid my dogs might bite you? Don't worry yourself about them, my dear, they'll do you no harm, but inwardly, you know, they'll look down upon you if they see that you're a clumsy creature. So let's try again—try harder. Here's your chance to get even . . . bring it back!"

Another chestnut thrown, another victory carried off by the dogs, another defeat for me; well, to make a long story short, the game lasted two hours, during which I managed to get the chestnut only once and to bring it back in my mouth to him who had thrown it. But whether triumphant or bested, never did the dogs do me any harm; on the contrary, they seemed to be having a good time playing and to be amused by me, quite as though I were a dog too.

"That's enough," said the gentleman. "You've worked hard enough; it's time to eat."

He rang, a servant entered.

"Bring some food for my animals," he said.

And a moment later the servant returned, carrying an ebony feeding trough which was filled with a kind of very delicate chopped meat. He set the trough on the floor.

"Very well," my gentleman said to me, "get down and eat with my dogs, and try to put on a better show while eating than you did while playing."

There was nothing for me to reply; I had to obey. Still on all fours, I plunged my head into the trough; the trough was very clean, the food very good, I fell to munching away beside the dogs, which very politely moved over, leaving me peacefully to my share. And that was the critical instant for our libertine; the humiliation of a woman, the degradation to which he reduced her, wonderfully stimulated his spirits.

"Oh, the buggress!" said he, frigging himself assiduously, "the tramp, look at her there, gorging herself with the dogs, that's how one should deal with all women, and if they were to be handled thus, we'd have no more sauciness from them, ah, no! Domestic animals like those dogs, why should they not be treated in the same way? Ah! impudent bitch that you are, whore, slime, *scum!" he cried, stepping near and spraying his fuck over my bum, "buggress, I'll have you eat with my dogs."*

*And that was the end of that; our man vanished, I dressed promptly, and lying by my mantelet I found two* louis, *the current price and doubtless the one the rogue was accustomed to paying for his pleasures.*

*At this point, Messieurs,* Duclos continued, *I am obliged to retrace my steps and, by way of conclusion to the evening's narrations, to recount two adventures I had during my youth. As they are somewhat on the strong side, they would have been out of place amidst the mild escapades with which you had me start at the beginning of the month; and so I set them aside and kept them for the end of my contribution.*

*I was only sixteen at the time, and was still with Madame Guérin; I had been sent to the home of a man of unchallenged distinction, and, upon arriving there, was simply told to wait in a small antechamber, told to be at my ease, told to be sure to obey the lord who would soon be coming to sport with me; but they were careful not to tell me anything else: I'd not have had such a fright if I'd been forewarned, and our libertine would certainly not have had as much pleasure. I had been in the room for about an hour when the door opened at last. It was the master of the house himself.*

*"What the devil are you doing here," he demanded with an air of surprise, "at this time of day? . . . What about it, whore!" he cries, seizing me by the throat and all but choking the breath out of me, "what about it! Has the slut come here to rob me?"*

*He calls to someone, a trustworthy servant immediately appears.*

*"La Fleur," says his angry master, "I've got a thief here; she was hiding when I came in. Strip her and prepare to carry out the orders I give you."*

*La Fleur does as he is told, I am despoiled of my clothes in a trice, they are tossed aside as they are peeled off my body.*

*"Very well," the libertine says to his servant, "go find a sack, then sew this creature up inside it and toss her into the river."*

*The valet goes to find the sack. I leave it to you to wonder whether I did not take advantage of these few moments to cast* myself at the nobleman's feet and beg him to spare me, assuring him that it was Madame Guérin, his usual procuress, who had herself sent me to his house. But the lewd gentleman will have none of it, he grasps my two buttocks, and kneading them brutally between his fists:

"Why, fuck my eyes," says he, "I think I'll feed this pretty ass to the fish."

That was the single lubricious action he seemed inclined to permit himself, and until then he had exposed nothing which might have led me to suppose libertinage had something to do with the scene. The valet returns, bringing a sack with him; despite all my protests, and they were heated, I am dumped into it, the mouth of the sack is sewn up, and La Fleur lifts me upon his shoulders. It was then I heard the effects of our libertine's mounting crisis; he had probably begun to frig himself as soon as I had been put in the sack. At the same instant La Fleur raised me to his shoulders, the villain's fuck departed him.

"Into the river, into the river, do you hear me, La Fleur?" he said, stammering with pleasure. "Yes, into the river with her, and you'll slip a stone into the sack, so that the whore will drown all the more quickly."

And that was all he had to say, I was borne out, we went into the adjacent room where La Fleur, having ripped open the sack, returned me my clothes, gave me two louis, and also gave me some unequivocal proof of the manner, radically unlike his master's, in which he conducted himself in the pursuit of happiness; then I returned to Guérin's. I severely scolded Guérin for having sent me there so poorly prepared; to placate me, she arranged another party: it took place two days later, and I was even less well prepared for the battle I was to wage with this new foe.

More or less as in the adventure I have just related, I was to go and wait in an antechamber of the apartment belonging to a farmer-general, but this time I waited in the company of the valet who, sent thither by his master, had come to fetch me at Guérin's. To while away the time before my gentleman's arrival, the valet diverted me by bringing out and displaying several precious stones kept in a desk drawer in the room.

"Bless me," said the good pander, "were you to take one or

two of them I don't fancy it would make much difference; the old
Croesus is so damned rich I wager he doesn't even know how many
of 'em or what kind he's got here in his desk. Go right ahead, if
you like, don't bother yourself about me, I'm not the sort of fellow
to betray a little friend."

Alas! I was only too well disposed to follow this perfidious
advice; you know my predilections, I've told you about them; and
so, without his having to say another word, I put my hand upon
a little gold box worth seven or eight louis, not daring to make off
with any more valuable object. That was all that rascal of a valet
desired, and to avoid having to return to the matter later on, I
afterward learned that, had I refused to take something, he would,
without my being aware of it, have slipped a jewel or two into my
pocket. The master arrives, greets me with kindness and courtesy,
the valet leaves the room, we two remain there together. This
man, unlike the other, amused himself in a very real sense; he
scattered a profusion of kisses over my ass, had me flog him, fart
in his mouth, he put his prick in mine, and in one word had his fill
of every kind and shape of lubricity save for that sometimes sought
in the cunt; but 'twas all to no purpose, he did not discharge.
The propitious moment for that had not yet come, all this he had
been doing was secondary, preparatory; you will soon see to what
it was leading.

"Why, my stars!" he suddenly exclaimed, "it had entirely
slipped my mind. There's a domestic still waiting in the other room
for a gem I just a moment ago promised to give him for his
master. Excuse me, my dear, but I really must keep my word to
him; then we'll get back to work."

Guilty of the little larceny I'd just committed at the instiga-
tion of that accursed valet, you may well suppose that this remark
made me tremble. I thought for an instant to stop him, confess
to the theft, then I decided it would be better to play innocent and
run the risk. He opens the desk, looks through first one drawer
then the next, rummages about, and failing to find what he is after,
he darts furious glances at me.

"You, slut, you alone," says he, "apart from a valet in whom
I have entire confidence, you have been the only person to enter

this room during the past three hours; the article is missing; you
must have taken it."

"Oh, Monsieur," I say, shaking in every limb, "you may be
sure I am incapable . . ."

"Damn your eyes," he roars (now, you will remark that his
breeches were still unbuttoned, that his prick was protruding from
them, that this prick held a very vertical slope; all this, you would
suppose, ought to have enlightened me and dispelled my fears, but
I had all but lost my head, and noticed nothing), "come along,
buggress, my valuable has got to be found."

He ordered me to strip; twenty times I besought him on
bended knee to spare me the humiliation of such a search, he would
be moved by nothing, nothing melted him, he himself angrily tore
off my clothes, and as soon as I was naked, he went through my
pockets and, of course, it was not long before he came across the
box.

"Ah, you bitch!" he cried, "I need no more than that to be
convinced. So, buggress, you come to a man's house to steal from
him?"

And immediately summoning his lieutenant:

"Go bring an officer of the police at once," he said.

"Oh, Monsieur!" I cried, "have pity upon my youthful truancy,
I have been beguiled into this, 'twas not done of my own will, I
was told to . . ."

"Well," the lecherous gentleman interrupted, "you will explain
all that to the officer, for I'll be damned if I don't mean to put a
stop to all this crime."

The valet leaves again; the libertine, still wearing a blinding
erection, flings himself into an armchair and while he fumbles
about his crotch, he showers a thousand invectives upon me.

"This tramp, this monster," said he, "she comes to my house
to rob me, I who wanted to give her the reward her services deserve . . . ah, by God, we shall see."

As he utters these words a knock is heard at the door, and
I see a gendarme enter.

"Officer," says the master of the premises, "I have a thieving
wench here I wish to put in your safekeeping, and I turn her over

*to you naked, for I put her in that state in order to search her clothing; there is the girl, over there are her garments, and here is the stolen article; I urge you to have her hanged, officer, and good night to you."*

*Whereupon he reeled backward, sat down in his chair, and discharged.*

*"Yes, hang the bitch, by sweet Jesus, I want to see her hanged, officer, do you understand me? Hang her, that's all I ask of you!" he fairly screamed.*

*The pretended gendarme leads me away with my clothes and the damning box, takes me into a nearby room, removes his uniform, and reveals himself to be the same valet who received me and incited me to steal; so upset had I been, I'd not recognized him hitherto.*

*"Well, well!" said he, "were you frightened?"*

*"Alas," I murmur, hardly able to speak, "out of my very wits."*

*"It's all over," he said, "and here is your money."*

*So saying, he presents me with the same box I had stolen, 'tis a gift from his master, he restores my clothes to me, hands me a glass of brandy, and escorts me back to Madame Guérin's.*

"That's an odd and pleasant mania," the Bishop observed; "the major part of it can be extracted for use in other connections. My one criticism is that it contains an excess of delicacy; you know, of course, that I don't greatly favor mixing fine feelings with libertinage. Leave that element out of it, I say, and from that story one may learn the infallible method of preventing a whore from complaining, regardless of the iniquitous ways one might be disposed to take with her. One has only to proffer the bait, draw her into the trap, and when you've caught her red-handed, why then you are at liberty to do what you wish with her, there's nothing more to fear, she won't dare emit a peep for fear either of being accused or the object of your recriminations."

"It is indeed," said Curval, "and I am sure that had I been in that gentleman's place, I would have permitted myself to go somewhat further, and you, my dear Duclos, might not have got off so lightly."

The stories having been long that evening, the supper hour arrived before Messieurs had the opportunity to indulge in any frolicking. They thus repaired to table firmly resolved to make the most of the period following the meal. It was then that, having assembled the entire household, they decided to determine which of the little girls and boys could be justifiably ranked as mature men and women. To establish the critical facts, Messieurs thought best to frig everyone of the one sex and of the other about whom they had any doubts, or rather suspicions; amongst the women, they were sure of Augustine, Fanny, and Zelmire: these three charming little creatures, aged between fourteen and fifteen, all discharged in response to the lightest touch; Hébé and Michette, each being only twelve, were hardly worth considering, and so it was simply a question of experimenting with Sophie, Colombe, and Rosette, the first of whom was fourteen, the latter two being thirteen years old.

Amongst the boys, it was a matter of common knowledge that Zéphyr, Adonis, and Céladon shot their fuck like grown men; Giton and Narcisse were too young to bother putting through their paces; the abilities of Zélamir, Cupidon, and Hyacinthe remained to be ascertained. The friends formed a circle about a pile of well-stuffed pillows arranged on the floor, Champville and Duclos were nominated for the pollutions; one, owing to her qualities as a tribade, was to act as the young girls' fricatrice, the other, absolute mistress of the art of frigging the male member, was to pollute the three little lads. They entered the ring formed by the friends' chairs and filled with pillows, and there Sophie, Colombe, Rosette, Zélamir, Cupidon, and Hyacinthe were turned over to Champville and Duclos; and each friend, the better to appreciate the spectacle, took a child between his thighs: the Duc appropriated Augustine, Curval had Zelmire to do his bidding, Durcet entrusted himself to Zéphyr's skill, the Bishop favored Adonis to supply his needs.

The ceremony began with the boys; Duclos, her breasts and ass uncovered, her sleeve rolled to the elbow, mobilized all her many talents and set to polluting each of those delicious Ganymedes one after the other. The human hand could not possibly have wandered and tugged, squeezed and patted more voluptuously; her wrist, her fingers flew with a deftness . . . her movements were of a delicacy and of a willfulness . . . she offered those little boys her mouth, her breast, her ass, made all of herself available with such art that there could be no question but that they who were not finally to discharge had not yet the power to do so. Zélamir and Cupidon hardened, but all Duclos' lore, all her agility, was quite in vain. With Hyacinthe, however, the storm burst after the sixth flick of the wrist: fuck leapt over Duclos' breast, and the child went half out of his mind while fondling her ass. Messieurs were careful to observe that throughout the entire operation it had never once occurred to the lad to touch her in front.

The girls' turn came next; virtually naked, her hair very elegantly arranged and equally stylish in every other part of herself, Champville did not look thirty years old, although she was fifty if a day. The lubricity of this operation, whence, as a thoroughgoing tribade, she expected to mine the greatest pleasure, animated her large dark-brown eyes which, since her youth, had always been extremely handsome. She put at least as much verve, daring, and brilliance into her actions as Duclos had into hers, she simultaneously polluted the clitoris, the entrance to the vagina, and the asshole, but Nature developed nothing worthy of notice in Colombe and Rosette; there was not even the faintest appearance of pleasure in their expressions. But things were not thus with the beautiful Sophie: the tenth digital foray brought her fainting upon Champville's breast; little broken sighs, little panting sounds, the tender shade of crimson which sprang into her lovely cheeks, her parted lips which grew moist, everything manifested the delirium whereinto Nature had hurled her, and she was declared a woman. The Duc, his device as solid as a mace, ordered Champville to frig her a second time, and when she discharged afresh, the villain chose that moment to mix his impure fuck with that young virgin's. As for Curval, he had wrought his fell deed between Zelmire's thighs, and the two others theirs with the young boys they held locked between their legs.

The company retired for the night, and the following morning having furnished no event which deserves to be cited in this catalogue of exceptional feats, and dinner having furnished nothing, nor coffee, we shall remove at once to the auditorium, where the magnificently arrayed Duclos appears once again upon the platform, this time to end, with five new stories, the one hundred and fifty narrations which have been entrusted to her for the thirty days of the month of November.

# THE THIRTIETH DAY

*I* am not sure, *Messieurs*, said the beauteous storyteller, *whether you have heard of the caprice, quite as unusual as dangerous, for which the Comte de Lernos is celebrated, but my several liaisons with him having afforded me a thorough acquaintance of his maneuvers, and as I found them most extraordinary indeed, I believe they ought to be included amongst the delights you have ordered me to detail. The Comte de Lernos' passion is to lead into evil as many girls and married women as he is able, and apart from the books he employs to seduce them, there is truly no sort of device he will not invent to deliver them up to men; he either exploits their secret yearnings by uniting them with the object upon whom they only think longingly, or he finds them lovers if such they are lacking. He has a house devoted to nothing else, and in it all the matches he has made are tested when the individuals concerned come to grips. He unites them, guarantees them freedom from intrusion, provides them with all the facilities needed for recreation, and then goes into an adjoining chamber to enjoy the pleasure of spying upon them while they are in action. But the point to which he multiplies these disorders simply defies belief, nor would one credit an account of the immense number of obstacles he is willing to surmount in order to form these little marriages. He has associates in nearly every convent in Paris and amongst a vast quantity of married women, and this army is led by a general of such great skill that not a day passes but at least three or four little skirmishes are fought in his house. Never does he fail to watch the voluptuous jousts—without the participants suspecting*

561

*his presence—but once he has gone to take up his observation post at the hole, as he stands watch all alone, no one knows how he proceeds to his discharge, nor what its character is; nothing but the fact is known, and that is all; I thought none the less that it was worthy of being mentioned to you.*

*The fantasy of the elderly Président Desportes will perhaps prove more amusing to you. Fully informed of the etiquette observed at the home of this habitual debauchee, I arrive at his house toward ten o'clock in the morning and, perfectly naked, I present my buttocks to be kissed; he is seated in an armchair, very grave, very solemn, and the first thing I do is fart in his face. My président is irritated, he gets to his feet, seizes a bundle of switches he has close at hand, and falls to pursuing me; my first impulse is to get out of his way.*

*"Impudent hussy," says he, chasing after me all the while, "I'll teach you to come to my home to behave in this outrageous fashion."*

*I'm to flee, he's to follow on my heels; I finally gain a narrow alley, I take cover in an impregnable retreat, but, lo! there he is, he's somehow managed to get at me. The président's threats and imprecations redouble as he sees he has me trapped; he brandishes the switches, threatens to use them upon me: I creep into a corner, cower there, put on a terrified air, I shrink to the size of a mouse; this terrified, groveling attitude of mine finally awakes his fuck, and the roué squirts it over my breasts while shouting with pleasure.*

"What! Do you mean to say he didn't give you a single lick with the switches?" the Duc demanded.

"He didn't bring them within a yard of me," Duclos replied.

"A very patient individual, that one," Curval remarked; "my friends, I believe we all agree that we are somewhat less so when we have in our hands the instrument Duclos mentions."

"But you need only a small amount of patience, Messieurs," said Champville, "for I shall shortly present to you other samples of the same breed, but they'll be rather less mild tempered than Madame Duclos' président."

And Duclos, observing that silence had succeeded these comments, saw she could continue with her stories, and proceeded in the following manner:

*Soon after this adventure had befallen me, I went to the town house of the Marquis de Saint-Giraud, whose fantasy consisted in seating a naked woman upon a children's swing and having her swing to a great height, back and forth. Each time you pass by his nose, he's waiting for you, and you've got either to let fly a fart at him or expect a slap upon your ass. I did my best to satisfy him; I received several slaps, but also gave him some overpowering farts. And the Marquis having finally discharged after an hour of this monotonous and fatiguing ceremony, the swing was brought to a halt, and my audience came to an end.*

*About three years after I had become the mistress of Fournier's establishment, a man came to make an unusual proposal to me: he wished me to find libertines who would amuse themselves with his wife and daughter, the only condition being that he be hidden in a place whence he could observe everything that transpired. Not only would whatever money I might earn from their employment be mine, but, he went on, he planned to give me an additional two louis for every encounter I could arrange for them; and there was only one final condition to the bargain: for his wife's partners he wished none but men of a certain taste, and for his daughter, men addicted to another kind of whimsy: his wife's men were all to shit upon her breasts, and the procedure to be observed with his daughter involved having the men raise her skirts, broadly expose her behind in front of the hole through which he would be doing his spying, and then discharge into her mouth. He would surrender the merchandise for the said passions, but for no others. After having made this gentleman promise to accept all responsibility in the event his wife and daughter brought complaint for having been made to come to my house, I agreed to all he wanted and in my turn promised that the two ladies would be furnished in strict accordance with his instructions. He arrived with his wares the very next day: madame was a woman of thirty-six, not very pretty, but tall and majestically formed, with a great air of sweet mildness and of modesty; her daughter was fifteen years old, blond, rather inclining toward heaviness, with the most tender, most winning countenance in all the world. . . .*

*"Indeed, Monsieur," quoth his wife, "you have us do strange things. . . ."*

*"I know, my dear, I know," said the lecher, "and it mortifies me, but so it must be. Accept your lot, do as you're told, there's nothing for it, I shall not give over. And if you balk in the slightest way at the propositions and the actions we are going to submit you to —you, Madame, and you, Mademoiselle—I shall tomorrow convey you to a place I know, and it is highly unlikely you'll ever return alive from it."*

*Wherewith the wife shed a tear or two; as the man for whom I intended her was waiting, I requested her to pass without further delay into the chamber I had set aside for their bout; mademoiselle would remain in another room with one of my girls, she would be perfectly safe there and would be notified when her turn had come. At this cruel moment there were a few more tears, and it seemed clear to me that this was the first time the brutal husband had required such a thing of his wife; unhappily, her debut was arduous, for aside from the baroque taste of the individual to whom I was surrendering her, he was an imperious and brusque old libertine who would surely not treat her with any excess of courtesy or consideration.*

*"That will do, no more tears," said the husband. "Bear in mind that I am watching your conduct, and that if you do not give ample satisfaction to the thoughtful gentleman who is going to take you in hand, I will come in myself and force you to do his bidding."*

*She enters the arena, the husband and I go into the neighboring room from which we are to watch it all. It is difficult to imagine the point to which this old scoundrel's imagination was excited by contemplating his miserable wife being made a victim of some stranger's brutality; he was thrilled by each thing she was forced to do; that poor humiliated woman's modesty and candor beneath the atrocious assaults of the libertine engaged to exercise her, composed a delicious spectacle for her husband. But when he saw her thrown brutally to the floor, and when the old ape to whom I had delivered her shit upon her chest, and her husband saw the tears, beheld the horrified shudders of his wife as she first heard proposed and then saw this infamy executed, he could restrain himself no longer, and the hand with which I was frigging him was straightway soaked with fuck. This first scene ended at last, and if it had afforded him pleasure, it was as nothing compared to the climax produced by the second. It was only with great difficulty, and above all with numerous and grave threats, that we succeeded in getting the young lady to enter the ring; she had witnessed her mother's tears but knew nothing of what had been done to her. The poor little girl raised all kinds of objections; we finally helped her make up her mind. The man to whom I turned her over was fully instructed of all that was required to be done: he was one of my regular clients whom I delighted with this windfall and who, to express his gratitude, consented to all I prescribed.*

*"Oh, the lovely ass!" cried the libertine father once his daughter's stud displayed her entirely naked. "Oh, sacred Jesus, what adorable buttocks!"*

*"Gracious!" I exclaimed, "am I to take it that this is the first time you have set eyes on them?"*

*"Yes, indeed it is," said he, "I required this expedient to enjoy the spectacle; but if 'tis the first time I see that superb ass, you may rest assured it shall not be the last."*

*I frigged him at a lively pace, he grew ecstatic; but when he saw the appalling things that young virgin was being forced to submit to, when he saw a consummate libertine's hands straying over that extraordinary body which had never before suffered such fondlings, when he saw her compelled to sink to her knees, open her mouth, when he saw a fat prick introduced into it, and saw that engine discharge inside, he tottered backward and, swearing like one possessed, shouting that he'd never in his life tasted any pleasure as keen as this, he left certain proof of his statements between my fingers. Their adventure had drawn to a conclusion, the two poor women retreated, weeping abundant tears, and the husband, but too enthusiastic over the drama they had enacted for him, doubtless found the means to persuade them to provide him with additional performances, for I received that family at my house for more than six years and, always following the orders the husband gave me, I made those two unlucky creatures acquainted with*

*practically all the different passions I have mentioned in the course*
*of my thirty days of storytelling; there were, to be sure, ten or*
*twelve of the passions they had no opportunity to satisfy, because*
*we did not practice them in my house.*

"Oh, yes," said Curval, "there are many ways to prostitute a
wife and a daughter. As if these bitches were made for anything
else! Are they not born for our pleasures, and from that moment
onward, must they not satisfy them at no matter what price? I've
had a quantity of wives," said the Président, "and three or four
daughters of whom, thank God, I've only one left, and if I'm
not mistaken Monsieur le Duc is fucking Mademoiselle Adelaide
at this very instant; but had any one of those creatures ever balked
at being prostituted, in any of the numerous manners of prostitution I regularly submitted them to, may I be damned alive or condemned never to fuck anything but cunts for the rest of my life
—which is worse—if I'd not have blown their bloody brains out."

"Président, your prick is in the air again," said the Duc;
"your fucking remarks always betray you."

"My prick in the air? No," the Président said, "but I am
on the verge of getting some shit from our dear little Sophie,
and I have high hopes her delicious turd will precipitate something.
Oh, upon my soul, even more than I'd suspected," said Curval
after he'd gobbled up the hash; "by the good God I'd like to fuck,
I believe that my prick is taking on some consistency. Who from
amongst you, Messieurs, would like to accompany me into the
boudoir?"

"I'd be honored," said Durcet, dragging along Aline, whom
he had been pawing steadily for an hour.

And our two libertines, having summoned Augustine, Fanny,
Colombe, Hébé, Zélamir, Adonis, Hyacinthe, and Cupidon, and
enlisted Julie and two duennas, Martaine and Champville, Antinoüs and Hercule, absented themselves for half an hour, at the
end of which they returned triumphant, each having yielded up
their vital liquor to the sweetest excesses of crapulence and debauchery.

"Move on," Curval said to Duclos, "give us your final tale,
dear friend. And if it manages to make this prick of mine dance

up again, you shall be able to congratulate yourself upon having wrought a miracle, for in faith, it is at least a year since I've lost so much fuck at a single sitting. On the other hand, it is true that . . ."

"Very well," the Bishop interrupted, "that will do; if we listen to you, we will hear something much worse than the passion Duclos is likely to describe to us. And so, since that would be to retreat from the stronger to the weaker, permit us to bid you be silent and to listen instead to our storyteller."

That gifted whore thereupon terminated her recitations with the following passion:

*The time has finally arrived, my Lords, to relate the passion of the Marquis de Mesanges to whom, you will recall, I sold the daughter of the unfortunate shoemaker, Petignon, who perished in jail with his wife while I enjoyed the inheritance his mother had left for him. As 'twas Lucile who satisfied him, you will allow me to place the story in her mouth.*

*"I arrive at the Marquis' mansion," that charming girl told me, "at about ten o'clock in the morning. As soon as I enter, all the doors are shut.*

*" 'What are you doing here, little bitch?' says the Marquis, all afire. 'Who gave you permission to disturb me?'*

*"And since you gave me no prior warning of what was to happen, you may readily imagine how terrified I was by this reception.*

*" 'Well, take off your clothes, be quick about it,' the Marquis continues. 'Since I've got my hands on you, whore, you'll not get out of here with your skin intact . . . indeed, you're going to perish —your last minutes have arrived.'*

*"I burst into tears, I fall down at the Marquis' feet, but nothing would bend him. And as I was not quick enough in undressing, he himself tore my clothes off, ripping them away by sheer force. But what truly petrified me was to see him throw them one after another into the fire.*

*" 'You'll have no further use for these,' he muttered, casting each article into a large grate. 'No further need for this mantelet,*

*this dress, these stockings, this bodice, no,' said he when all had been consumed, 'all you'll need now is a coffin.'*

"*And there I was, naked; the Marquis, who had never before seen me, contemplated my ass for a brief space, he uttered oaths as he fondled it, but he did not bring his lips near it.*

"*'Very well, whore,' said he, 'enough of this, you're going to follow your clothes, I'm going to bind you to those andirons; yes, by fuck, yes indeed, by sweet Jesus, I'm going to burn you alive, you bitch, I'm going to have the pleasure of inhaling the aroma of your burning flesh.'*

"*And so saying he falls half-unconscious into an armchair and discharges, darting his fuck upon the remnants of my burning clothes. He rings, a valet enters and then leads me out, and in another room I find a complete new outfit, clothes twice as fine as those he has incinerated.*"

*That is the account of it I had from Lucile; it remains now to discover whether 'twas for that or for worse he employed the girl I sold him.*

"For something far worse," said Desgranges; "I am glad you have introduced the Marquis to their Lordships, for I believe I too shall have something to say about him."

"May it be, Madame," Duclos said to Desgranges, "and you, my amiable companions," she added, speaking to her two other colleagues, "may it be that you speak with greater energy than have I, with livelier images, brighter diction, superior wit, and more persuasive eloquence. 'Tis now your turn, I have done, and I would but beseech Messieurs to have the kindness to forgive me if I have perchance bored them in any wise, for there is an almost unavoidable monotony in the recital of such anecdotes; all compounded, fitted into the same framework, they lose the luster that is theirs as independent happenings.

With these words, the superb Duclos respectfully saluted the company, bowed, and descended from her throne; she next went from alcove to alcove and was generally applauded and caressed by all the friends. Supper was served, Duclos was invited to sit at the table, a favor which had never before been accorded to a woman. Her conversation was quite as agreeable as her storytelling had been, and by way of recompense for the pleasure she had given them, Messieurs named her to be the governor-general of the two harems, and the four friends also made the promise, in an aside, that no matter what the extreme treatment to which they might expose the women in the course of the sojourn, she would always be dealt with gently, and very certainly taken back with them to Paris, where the society would amply reward her for the trouble she had gone to in order to help Messieurs procure themselves a little good cheer. She, Curval, and the Duc so completely besotted themselves at supper that they were practically incapacitated and barely managed, with the expense of much effort, to reach the orgies, which they soon left, allowing Durcet and the Bishop to carry on alone, and betook themselves to the remote boudoir; Champville, Antinoüs, Bum-Cleaver, Thérèse, and Louison accompanied them, and one may be perfectly confident that they uttered and had done to them at least as many horrors and infamies as, at their end, their two more sober friends were able to invent.

Everyone repaired to his bed at two in the morning, and 'twas thus the month of November ended, thus came to a close the first phase of this lubricious and interesting holiday, for whose second part we will not keep the public waiting if to our consideration it has kindly received what we have chronicled so far.

# MISTAKES I HAVE MADE[3]

I have been too explicit, not sufficiently reticent, about the chapel activities at the beginning; must not elaborate upon them until after the stories in which they are mentioned.

Said too much about active and passive sodomy; conceal that until the stories have discussed it.

I was wrong to have made Duclos react strongly to the death of her sister; that doesn't sort with the rest of her character; change it.

If I said Aline was a virgin upon arrival at the château, that was an error: she isn't, and could not be. The Bishop has depucelated her in every sector.

And not having been able to reread all this, there must be a swarm of other mistakes.

When later I put the text in final order, I must be particularly careful to have a notebook beside me at all times; I'll have to put down very exact mention of each happening and each portrait as I write it; otherwise, I'll get horribly confused because of the multitude of characters.

For the Second Part, begin with the assumption Augustine and Zéphyr are already sleeping in the Duc's bedchamber in the First Part; likewise Adonis and Zelmire in Curval's, Hyacinthe and Fanny in Durcet's, Céladon and Sophie in the Bishop's, even though none of them has been deflowered yet.

[3] As Sade notes, the speed with which he wrote the final draft of *The 120 Days*, and because he was unable to reread and correct his manuscript, resulted in a number of minor discrepancies in dates, characters, and situations, which the careful reader will doubtless discover. None the less, given the large cast of characters, and the complexity of rules and procedures, his accuracy of detail is remarkable.—*Tr.*

# PART THE SECOND

THE 150 COMPLEX PASSIONS, OR THOSE BE-
LONGING TO THE SECOND CLASS, COMPOS-
ING THE THIRTY-ONE DAYS OF DECEM-
BER SPENT IN HEARING THE NARRATIONS
OF MADAME CHAMPVILLE; INTERSPERSED
AMONGST WHICH ARE THE SCANDALOUS
DOINGS AT THE CHÂTEAU DURING THAT
MONTH; ALL BEING SET DOWN IN THE FORM
OF A JOURNAL.
(*DRAFT*)

THE 1ST OF DECEMBER: Champville assumes the task of story-telling and relates the one hundred and fifty following tales (the number of each precedes the tale).

1. *Won't depucelate any save those aged between three and seven, but only cuntishly. 'Tis he who deflowers Champville at the age of five.*

2. *He ties a girl of nine in a curled-up position and depucelates her from behind.*

3. *He wishes to rape a girl of twelve or thirteen, and depucelates her while holding a pistol against her heart.*

4. *He likes to frig a man upon a maiden's cunt, he uses the fuck for pomade, and next encunts the maid while she is held by the man.*

5. *He wishes to depucelate three girls in succession, one in the cradle, one at the age of five, the other at seven.*

THE 2ND. 6. *He'll not depucelate anyone who is not between nine years old and thirteen. His prick is enormous; four women are needed to hold the virgin. The same individual Martaine speaks of, who only embuggers three-year-olds, the same hell-inspired individual.*

7. *He has his valet depucelate the maid, aged ten to twelve, before his eyes, and during the operation touches them nowhere save upon the ass. He now fondles the girl's, now the valet's. Discharges upon the valet's ass.*

8. *He wishes to depucelate a girl destined to be married the following day.*

573

9. *He wishes the marriage to be performed, and to depucelate the bride at some time between the hour of the mass and the moment the couple retires to bed.*

10. *He would have his valet, a very ingenious personage, go about marrying girls left and right and bring them to his master, who therewith fucks them, and next sells them to procuresses.*

THE 3RD. 11. *He must be provided with two sisters; he depucelates them.*

12. *He marries the girl, depucelates her, but 'tis all a fraud, the marriage is a fraud, once he's fucked her, he leaves her.*

13. *He will only fuck a maid, and then only immediately after another man has deflowered her while he has watched. He must have her cunt muddied up with sperm.*

14. *This one depucelates with an artificial engine, very large, and, without introducing himself, discharges upon the hole he has cleared.*

15. *He will have none but maids of rank and distinction and pays for them in accordance with their wealth. This individual proves to be the Duc, who will admit having depucelated more than fifteen hundred of them over a period of thirty years.*

THE 4TH. 16. *He forces a brother to fuck his sister in his presence, then fucks her afterward; he obliges both to shit beforehand.*

17. *He forces a father to fuck his daughter after he has himself had her maidenhead.*

18. *He brings his nine-year-old daughter to the brothel, and while she is held by a procuress, depucelates her. He has had twelve daughters; has had all twelve maidenheads.*

19. *Must have virgins between the ages of thirty and forty to fuck.*

20. *He will depucelate no one but nuns, and spends immense sums of money to get them; he fucks several.*

'Tis the evening of the 4th of December, at the orgies, the Duc depucelates Fanny, who is held by the four governesses and ministered by Duclos. He fucks her twice in a row, she faints, the second time he fucks her while she is unconscious.

THE 5TH. To celebrate the fifth week's festival, Hyacinthe and Fanny are joined in matrimony, the marriage is consummated very publicly.

21. *He would have the mother hold her daughter, he first fucks the mother, then depucelates the daughter while she is held by the mother. The same one Desgranges mentions on the 20th of February.*

22. *He likes adultery only; one must locate women for him who are generally known to be virtuous and well behaved, he makes them disgusted with their husbands.*

23. *He enjoys having the husband come himself to prostitute his wife and hold her while he fucks her. (Messieurs imitate that passion forthwith.)*

24. *He places a married woman upon a bed, encunts her while that woman's daughter, suspended above, presents him with her cunt to be licked; the next instant he effects a reversal and encunts the daughter while kissing the mother's asshole. When he has done licking the daughter's cunt, he has her piss; then he kisses the mother's asshole and has her shit.*

25. *He has four daughters, legitimate and wedded; he wishes to fuck all four: he makes all four of them conceive and bear children so as someday to have the pleasure of depucelating the children he has had by his daughters and whom their husbands suppose to be their own.*

Apropos of which the Duc recounts—but his anecdote cannot be numbered amongst the stories because, Messieurs being unable to duplicate it, it does not compose a passion—the Duc recounts, I say, that he once knew a man who fucked three children he had by his mother, amongst whom there was a daughter whom he had marry his son, so that in fucking her he fucked his sister, his daughter and his daughter-in-law, and thus he also constrained his son to fuck his own sister and mother-in-law. Curval recounts another unusual history, that of a brother and a sister who reached an agreement whereby each would surrender his children to the other: the sister had a boy and a girl, so did the brother. They mixed the pudding in such wise that sometimes they fucked their nephews, sometimes their own children, and sometimes their first cousins, or else the brothers and sister would fuck while the father and mother, that is to say, the brother and sister, fucked one another also.

That evening, Fanny is surrendered cuntwardly to the assembly, but as the Bishop and Monsieur Durcet do not fuck cunts, she is only fucked by Curval and the Duc. Henceforth, she wears a small ribbon aslant, like a baldric, and after the loss of both her pucelages she will wear a very wide pink ribbon.

THE 6TH. 26. *He has himself frigged while a woman is being frigged about the clitoris, and he wishes to discharge at the same time the girl does, but he discharges upon the buttocks of the man who frigs the girl.*

27. *He kisses the asshole of one girl while a second girl frigs his ass and a third girl his prick; they then exchange tasks, so that, when all is said and done, each of the three has her ass kissed, each frigs his prick, each frigs his ass. Farts are required of them all.*

28. *He licks the cunt of one girl while fucking a second in the mouth and while his asshole is being licked by a third; then exchange of positions as above. The cunts must discharge, he swallows their balm.*

29. *He sucks a beshitted ass, has a tongue frig his own beshitted asshole, and frigs himself upon a beshitted ass; the three girls then exchange positions.*

30. *He has two girls frigged before his eyes, and alternately fucks the friggeresses from the rear, but in the cunt, while they continue with their sapphotizings.*

Zéphyr and Cupidon are upon that day discovered in the act of frigging each other, but they have not yet had recourse to reciprocal embuggery; they are punished. Fanny is much encunted at the orgies.

THE 7TH. 31. *He would have an older girl introduce a younger girl to bad habits; the older must frig her, give her wicked advice, and end up by holding her while he fucks her, whether virgin or not.*

32. *He calls for four women; he fucks two of them orally, two cuntwardly, taking great care not to insert his prick in a mouth until after having first had it in a cunt. While all this is going on, he is closely followed by a fifth woman, who throughout frigs his asshole with a dildo.*

33. *This libertine requires a dozen women, six young, six old and, if 'tis possible, six of them should be mothers and the other six their daughters. He pumps out their cunts, asses and mouths; when applying his lips to the cunt, he wants copious urine; when at the mouth, much saliva; when at the ass, abundant farts.*

34. *He employs eight women to frig him; each of the eight must be situated in a different posture. (This had better be illustrated by a drawing.)*

35. *Wishes to have three men and three women fucking each other in divers attitudes.*

THE 8TH. 36. *He forms twelve groups of two girls each; they are so arranged only their asses are visible to him; all the rest of their bodies must be concealed from his sight. He frigs himself while studying all those buttocks.*

37. *He has six couples simultaneously frig themselves in a room paneled with mirrors; each couple is composed of two girls frigging each other in various and equally lubricious postures. He is in the middle of the room, he regards both the couples and their reflections, and discharges in the middle of it all, having been frigged by an old woman. He has kissed the buttocks of every participant in this drama.*

38. *He has four streetwalkers besot themselves with wine and then fight with each other while he looks on; and when they are thoroughly drunk, they one after another vomit into his mouth. He favors the oldest and ugliest women possible.*

39. *He has a girl shit in his mouth, but does not eat her turd, and while the first girl is in action, a second sucks his prick and frigs his ass; while discharging, he shits into the hand of the girl who is socratizing him. The girls exchange places.*

40. *He has a man shit into his mouth and eats while a little boy frigs him, then the man frigs him and he has the boy shit.*

That evening, at the orgies, Curval depucelates Michette, in front: she is held by the four duennas and ministered by Duclos; this arrangement is the conventional one and is observed upon all occasions; therefore we will not allude to it again.

THE 9TH. 41. *He fucks one girl in her mouth just after having shitted into the same receptacle; a second girl is lying on top of the first, with the first girl's head between her thighs, and upon the face of the second girl a third girl drops a turd, and he, while thus fucking his own turd in the first girl's mouth, eats the shit deposited by the third girl upon the second girl's face, and then they alternate roles, in such wise that each girl enacts all three of them.*

42. *Thirty girls pass through his hands during a given day, and he has them all shit into his mouth, consumes the turds of the*

*three or four prettiest. He repeats this party five times a week, which means that he sees 7800 girls a year. When Champville first encounters him, he is seventy years old and has been in business for fifty.*

43. *He sees twelve girls every morning and swallows their dozen turds; he sees them all at the same time.*

44. *He places himself in a bathtub; thirty women come up one after another and piss and shit into it till it is full; he discharges while paddling about in all that.*

45. *He shits in the presence of four women, requires them to watch and indeed help deliver him of his turd; next, he wishes them to divide it into equal parts and eat it; then each woman does a turd of her own. He mixes them and swallows the entire batter, but his shit-furnishers have got to be women of at least sixty.*

That evening Michette's cunt is put at the disposal of the assembly: thereafter she wears the little sash.

THE 10TH. 46. *He has girls A and B shit. Then he forces B to eat A's turd, and A to eat B's. Then both A and B shit a second time; he eats both their turds.*

47. *He requires a mother and her three daughters, and he eats the girls' shit upon the mother's ass, and the mother's shit upon one daughter's ass.*

48. *He obliges a daughter to shit into her mother's mouth and to wipe her ass with her mother's teats; next, he eats the turd in the mother's mouth, and afterward has the mother shit into her daughter's mouth, whence, as before, he eats the turd.*

(It would perhaps be advisable to substitute a son and a mother, in order to create a contrast with 47.)

49. *He wishes a father to eat his son's turd, then he eats the father's.*

50. *He would have the brother shit in his sister's cunt, and he eats the turd; the sister then must shit in her brother's mouth. He eats this second turd, too.*

THE 11TH. 51. *Champville announces she is now going to speak of impieties, and makes mention of a man who wishes the whore, while frigging him, to pronounce dreadful blasphemies; in his turn he utters terrible ones. His amusement during their dialogue consists in kissing her ass; he does no more than that.*

52. *He would have a girl come with him to a church, and frig him there, especially at the time the holy sacrament is exposed. He situates himself as near to the altar as possible, and fondles her ass while she performs her task.*

53. *He goes to confession for the sole purpose of making his confessor's prick rise aloft; he lists a quantity of infamous misdeeds, and frigs himself in the confessional all the while he speaks.*

54. *He wishes the girl to go and make her confession, then fucks her orally the moment she emerges from the confessional.*

55. *He fucks a whore throughout a mass being said in his private chapel, and discharges when the Host is raised.*

That evening, the Duc depucelates Sophie cuntwardly, and while doing so blasphemes considerably.

THE 12TH. 56. *He buys a confessor, who yields him his place; thus he is able to hear the young* pensionnaires' *confessions and to give them the worst possible advice while pardoning them their sins.*

57. *He would have his daughter go to confess to a monk he has previously bribed, and he is placed where he can overhear everything; but the monk demands that the penitent keep her skirts raised high while she catalogues her faults, and her ass posted within plain sight of the father: thus he is able to hear his daughter's confession and contemplate her ass at the same time.*

58. *Has mass celebrated for completely naked whores; while observing the spectacle, he frigs his prick upon another girl's ass.*

59. *He has his wife go to confess to a monk he has bought: the monk seduces the wife and fucks her in front of her husband, who is hidden. If the wife refuses, he emerges from hiding and helps the monk force her.*

On that day they celebrate the sixth week's festival with the marriage of Céladon and Sophie, which union is consummated, and in the evening Sophie's cunt is put generally to use, and she dons the sash. Because of this event only four passions are recounted on the 12th.

THE 13TH. 60. *Fucks whores on the altar at the same moment mass is about to be said; they have their naked asses on the sacred stone.*

61. *He has a naked girl sit astride and bend forward over a large crucifix; he fucks her cunt from behind while she is thus crouched down in such wise the head of Christ frigs her clitoris.*

62. *He farts and has the whore fart in the chalice, he pisses thereinto and has her piss thereinto, he shits thereinto and has her shit thereinto, and finally he discharges into the chalice.*

63. *He has a small boy shit upon the paten, and he eats this while the boy sucks him.*

64. *He has two girls shit upon a crucifix, he shits thereupon when they have finished, and he is frigged against the three turds covering the idol's face.*

THE 14TH. 65. *He breaks up a crucifix, smashes several images of the Virgin and of the Eternal Father, shits upon the debris and burns the whole mess. The same man has the mania of bringing a whore to hear the sermon and of having himself frigged while listening to the word of God.*

66. *He takes communion and, the wafer still in his mouth, has four whores shit upon it.*

67. *He has her go to communion and fucks her in the mouth when she returns.*

68. *He interrupts a priest in the midst of saying mass in his private chapel, interrupts him, I say, in order to frig himself into the chalice, obliges the whore to frig the priest thereinto, and forces the latter to quaff the mead.*

70.[4] *He intervenes directly the Host is consecrated and forces the priest to fuck the whore with the Host.*

Upon this day Augustine and Zelmire are found frigging together; they are both rigorously punished.

THE 15TH. 71. *He has the girl fart upon the Host, himself farts thereupon, and then swallows the Host while fucking the whore.*

72. *The same man who had himself nailed into a coffin— Duclos mentioned him—compels the whore to shit upon the Host; he also shits upon it and flings the whole affair into a privy.*

73. *Frigs the whore's clitoris with the Host, has her discharge upon it, then buries it in her cunt and fucks her, discharging upon it in his turn.*

74. *Chops it up with a knife and has the crumbs rammed into his asshole.*

75. *Has himself frigged and then discharges upon the Host and finally, when he is restored to perfect calm and after his fuck has flowed, feeds biscuit and all to a dog.*

The same evening, the Bishop consecrates a Host and Curval destroys Hébé's maidenhead with it, he drives it into her cunt and

---

[4] Passion Number 69 omitted by Sade.—*Tr.*

discharges thereupon. Several others are consecrated, and the already depucelated sultanas are all fucked with Hosts.

THE 16TH. Profanation, Champville announces, lately the principal element in her stories, will from now on be no more than accessory, and what, to borrow the brothel term, are known as little ceremonies are going to provide the main ingredient in the following complex passions. She asks her auditors to remember that everything connected with that will be presented merely as secondary matter, but that the difference subsisting between her stories and the examples Duclos has given, is that Duclos always pictured a man with one woman, whereas she, Champville, will always show several women administering to a single man.

76. *He has himself flogged by one girl during mass, he fucks a second girl orally, and he discharges when the Host is elevated.*

77. *He has two women gently flog his ass with a martinet; each woman bestows ten stripes, alternating them with asshole friggery.*

78. *He has himself whipped by four different girls while farts are being launched into his mouth: the girls take turns, so that each will have had a chance both to whip and to fart.*

79. *He has himself whipped by his wife while he fucks his daughter, next by his daughter while he fucks his wife; this is the same individual Duclos spoke of, the same man who prostituted his wife and daughter in her whorehouse.*

80. *He has himself whipped simultaneously by two girls, one flogs the front of him, the other his rear, and when at last he has been well stimulated, he fucks one of them while the other plies the lash, then the second while the first flogs him.*

That same evening Hébé's cunt is made available to the public, and she wears the little sash, not being entitled to the large one until she has lost both her pucelages.

THE 17TH. 81. *He has himself flogged while kissing a boy's ass and while fucking a girl in the mouth, then he fucks the boy in the mouth while kissing the girl's asshole, the while constantly receiving the lash from another girl, then he has the boy flog him, orally fucks the whore who'd been whipping him, and then has himself flogged by the girl whose ass he had been kissing.*

82. *He has himself whipped by an old woman, fucks an old man in the mouth, and has the daughter of this aged couple shit into his own mouth, then changes so that, ultimately, everyone takes his turn in each role.*

83. *He has himself whipped while frigging himself and while discharging upon a crucifix propped up by a girl's buttocks.*

84. *He has himself whipped while fucking a whore from the rear, using his prick to tamp a Host into her fundament.*

85. *He passes an entire brothel in review; he receives the lash from all the whores while kissing the madame's asshole and receiving therefrom into his mouth both wind and rain and hailstones.*

THE 18TH. 86. *He has himself whipped by teams of cab drivers and chimney sweeps who pass two at a time, one plying the lash, the other farting in his mouth; he employs ten or twelve in a morning.*

87. *He has himself held by three girls, he gets down on hands and knees, a fourth girl mounts astride him and thrashes him; each member of the quartet takes her turn mounting and flogging him.*

88. *Naked, he puts himself in the midst of six girls; he is conscience-stricken, asks to be forgiven, casts himself down upon his knees. Each girl decrees a penance, and he is given one hundred strokes for each penance he refuses to do: 'tis the girl he refuses who whips him. Well, these penances are all exceedingly unpleasant: one would like to shit into his mouth; another have him lick up*

her spittle from the floor; a third is menstruating and would have him lick her cunt clean; the fourth hasn't washed her feet, will he kindly lick between her toes; the fifth has snot awaiting his tongue, etc.

89. *Fifteen girls arrive in teams of three: one whips him, one sucks him, the other shits; then she who shitted, whips; she who sucked, shits; she who whipped, sucks. And so he proceeds till he has had done with all fifteen; he sees nothing, heeds nothing, is wild with joy: a procuress is in charge of the game. He renews this party six times each week.*

(This one is truly charming and has my infinite recommendation; the thing has got to move very briskly along, each girl must bestow twenty-five strokes of the whip, and it is between whippings that the first sucks and the third shits. If you would prefer fifty strokes from each girl, that will total up to seven hundred fifty, a very agreeable figure, not by any means excessive.)

90. *Twenty-five whores soften up his ass with a quantity of slaps and fondlings; he is not sent away until his ass has become completely insensible.*

That evening the Duc is flogged while culling Zelmire's forward maidenhead.

THE 19TH. 91. *He has himself tried by a jury of six whores; each knows the role she is to play. He is sentenced to be hanged. And hanged he is; but the cord snaps: 'tis the instant he discharges. (Relate this to similar ones Duclos described.)*

92. *He arranges six old women in a semicircle; while three young whores lash him, the six crones spit in his face.*

93. *A girl frigs his asshole with the handle of a cat-o'-nine-tails, a second girl whips his thighs and prick from the front; 'tis thus he is made eventually to discharge over the tits of the whipper posted before him.*

94. *Two women flay him with bulls' pizzles while a third, kneeling before him, causes him to discharge upon her breasts.*

She recounts only four that day because of the marriage of Zelmire and Adonis which marks the seventh week's conclusion, and which is consummated, Zelmire having been depucelated, with what regards the cunt, the night before.

THE 20TH. 95. *He struggles with six women, the cuts of whose whips he pretends to wish to avoid; he strives to snatch the whips from their hands, but they are too strong for him and fustigate him none the less. He is naked.*

96. *He runs the gantlet between two ranks each of twelve girls who are wielding switches; he is whipped all about the body and discharges after the ninth race.*

97. *He has the soles of his feet whipped, then his prick, then his thighs while, as he lies upon a couch, three women successively mount astride him and shit in his mouth.*

98. *Three girls alternately flog him, one with a martinet, one with a bull's pizzle, the other with a cat-o'-nine-tails. A fourth, kneeling before him and whose asshole the lecher's lackey is frigging, sucks the master's prick while frigging the lackey's, which he has discharge upon his sucker's buttocks.*

99. *He is amidst six girls: one pricks him with a needle, the second uses pincers on him, the third burns him, the fourth bites him, the fifth scratches him, the sixth flagellates him. All that everywhere upon his body, indiscriminately. He discharges in the thick of this activity.*

That evening Zelmire, depucelated on the 18th of December, is surrendered cuntwardly to the assembly—to, that is to say, Curval and the Duc, who alone of the four friends fuck cunts. Once Curval has fucked Zelmire, his hatred for Adelaide and Constance redoubles; he wishes to have Constance minister to Zelmire.

THE 21ST. 100. *He has himself frigged by his lackey while the girl, naked, balances upon a narrow pedestal; all the while he is being frigged, she may neither budge nor lose her equilibrium.*

101. *He has the procuress frig him while he fondles her buttocks; and meanwhile, between her fingers, the girl holds a very short candle which she must not drop until the roué has spat out his fuck; he is very careful not to discharge before the girl's fingers have been seared.*

102. *He sups at an immense table; for light, he has six burning candles, each inserted in the ass of a naked girl lying upon the dining table.*

103. *While he takes his supper he has a girl kneel on sharp pebbles, and if in the course of the entire meal she stirs, she is not paid. Above her are two tilted candles whence hot tallow spills upon her bare back and breasts. She need but make the slightest movement and she is packed off without being paid a* sou.

104. *He obliges her to remain four days in a very narrow iron cage, wherein she can neither sit nor lie down; he feeds her through the bars. He is the one Desgranges will mention in connection with the turkey's ballet.*

That same evening, Curval depucelates Colombe's cunt.

THE 22ND. 105. *He wraps a girl and a cat in a large blanket, has her stand and dance about; the cat bites, scratches her as she falls to the floor; but, come what may, she must skip and leap, and continue her antics until the man discharges.*

106. *He massages a woman with a certain substance which causes her skin to itch so violently that she scratches herself till her blood flows; he watches her at work, frigging himself the while.*

107. *He gives a woman a potion to drink, it halts her menstruating, and thus he makes her run the risk of grave illness.*

108. *He makes her swallow a medicine intended for horses, it causes her horrible gripes and colics; he watches her suffer and shit all day long.*

109. *He rubs a naked girl with honey, then binds her to a column and releases upon her a swarm of large flies.*

That same evening, Colombe's cunt is put at the free disposition of the company.

THE 23RD. 110. *He places the girl upon a pivot which revolves with prodigious speed. She is naked and bound and turns until he discharges.*

111. *He keeps a girl suspended head downward until he discharges.*

112. *Makes her swallow a heavy dose of emetic, persuades her she has been poisoned, and frigs himself while watching her vomit.*

113. *Kneads and mauls her breasts until they are entirely black and blue.*

114. *Kneads and maltreats her ass for three hours; he repeats this rite for nine days in succession.*

THE 24TH. 115. *He has a girl climb a tall ladder until she is at least twenty feet above the ground, at which point a rung cracks and she falls, but upon mattresses prepared in advance; he walks up to her and discharges upon her body the very moment she lands, and sometimes he chooses this instant to fuck her.*

116. *He slaps a girl's face with all his strength and discharges while so doing; he is seated in a comfortable chair and the girl is upon her knees, facing him.*

117. *Beats her knuckles with hickory ferrules.*

118. *Powerful slaps upon her buttocks until her behind is scarlet.*

119. *Inserts the nozzle of a bellows in her asshole; he inflates her.*

120. *He introduces an enema of almost boiling water into her bowels, then amuses himself observing her writhe, and discharges upon her ass.*

That evening, Aline's ass is soundly slapped by the four colleagues, who keep it up until her ass is crimson; a duenna holds her by the shoulders. A few slaps are bestowed upon Augustine's ass, too.

THE 25TH. 121. *He has some pious women recruited for his pleasure, beats them with a crucifix and rosaries, and then has each of them pose as a statue of the Virgin upon an altar, but pose in a cramped position from which they are not to budge. They must remain thus throughout an exceedingly long mass; when at last the Elevation occurs, each woman is to shit upon the Host.*

122. *Has her run naked about a garden at night, the season is winter, the weather freezing; here and there are stretched cords upon which she trips and falls.*

123. *When she has removed all her clothes, he casts her, as if by accident, into a vat of nearly boiling water and prevents her from climbing out until he has first discharged upon her body.*

124. *Naked, on a wintry day she is secured to a post in the middle of a garden and there she remains until she has repeated five Pater Nosters and five Hail Marys, or until he has yielded his fuck, which another girl excites to flow as he contemplates the spectacle.*

125. *He spreads a powerful glue upon the rim of a privy seat and sends the girl in to shit; directly she sits down, her ass is caught fast. Meanwhile, from the other side a small charcoal brazier is introduced beneath her ass. Scorched, she leaps up, leaving an almost perfect circle of skin behind her.*

That evening profane tricks are played at the expense of Adelaide and Sophie, the two believers, and the Duc depucelates Augustine, of whom he has been passionately fond for weeks; thrice he discharges into her cunt. And that same evening the idea enters his head to have her run naked through the courtyard, dreadful though the weather be. He proposes the idea with great energy and in forceful language, but his confreres regretfully reject it, saying that Augustine is very pretty and that the program calls for her further use; and, the Bishop points out, she still has not been depucelated aft. The Duc offers to pay two hundred *louis* into the common fund if the society will allow him to take her down into the cellars at once; he is again refused. He wishes at least that she have her ass spanked; she receives twenty-five blows from each friend. But the Duc applies his with his fist and discharges a fourth time between the eighteenth and nineteenth. He requisitions her for his bed and that night encunts her thrice again.

THE 26TH. 126. *He gets the girl thoroughly drunk, she lies down to sleep. While asleep, her bed is raised. Toward the middle of the night, she reaches down for her chamber pot; not finding it within reach, she gropes further and tumbles out upon a mattress; the man awaits her there and fucks her as soon as she has fallen.*

127. *He has her run naked about the garden, he follows after her, brandishing a cabman's whip, but only threatens her with it. She is obliged to run until she falls from weariness; at which instant he springs upon her and fucks her.*

128. *He bestows one hundred strokes, ten at a time, with a martinet of black silk; between each series of blows, he kisses the girl's ass with great fervor.*

129. *He flogs her with a cat-o'-nine-tails whose thongs have been steeped in brandy, and does not discharge until the girl's blood is flowing. Then he discharges upon her buttocks.*

Champville recounts only four passions on the 26th of December because it is the day of the eighth week's festival. It is celebrated by the marriage of Zéphyr and Augustine, both of whom belong to the Duc and lie at night in his chamber; but prior to the ceremony, His Grace would have Curval flog the boy while he, Blangis, flogs the girl; and 'tis done. Each receives a hundred lashes, but the Duc, more than ever aroused by Augustine because she has made him discharge frequently, lays on very emphatically and is content with nothing short of much blood.

In connection with that evening's entertainments, we must fully explain the character of the Saturday punishments—how they are meted out and how many lashes are distributed. You might draw up a list itemizing the crimes and, to the right, the appropriate number of lashes.

THE 27TH. 130. *He likes to whip none but little girls between the ages of five and seven, and always finds a pretext so as to make it appear as if he were punishing them*

131. *A woman comes to confess to him, he is a priest; she recites all her sins, and by way of penance, he gives her five hundred lashes.*

132. *He receives four women and gives each six hundred lashes.*

133. *He has the same ceremony performed in his presence by two valets, one relieving the other when his arm is fatigued by the whipping; twenty women are dealt with, each merits six hundred strokes: the women are not bound. He frigs himself while the work is in progress.*

134. *He flogs only boys aged from fourteen to sixteen, and he has them discharge into his mouth afterward. Each is warmed by one hundred lashes; he always sees two at a sitting.*

Augustine's cunt is surrendered that evening; Curval encunts her twice and, like the Duc, wishes to whip her when he has had done with her. Both gentlemen fall upon that charming girl like ravenous beasts; they propose a contribution of four hundred *louis* to the common fund in exchange for permission to take her in hand together that same evening; their offer is rejected.

THE 28TH. 135. *He has a naked girl enter a chamber; whereupon two men fall upon her and each whips one of her buttocks until it is raw. She is bound. When 'tis over, he frigs the men's pricks upon the whore's bleeding ass, and frigs himself thereupon also.*

136. *She is bound hand and foot to the wall. Facing her, and also attached to the wall, is a blade of steel adjusted to the height of her belly. If she strives to avoid a blow, it is forward she must lunge; she cuts herself. If she wishes to avoid the blade, she must fling herself backward toward the lash.*

137. *He flogs a girl, giving her one hundred lashes the first day, two hundred the second, four hundred the third, etc., etc., and ceases on the ninth day.*

138. *He has the whore descend on all fours, climbs upon her back and faces her buttocks; he squeezes his legs tight about her ribs. Once in the saddle, he brings his lash down upon her ass and curls the thongs round to her cunt, and as for this operation he employs a martinet, he has no trouble directing his blows so that they carry into the vagina's interior, and that is just what he does.*

139. *He must have a pregnant woman, he has her bend backward over a cylinder which supports her back. Her head, on the other side of the cylinder, rests upon the seat of a chair and is secured to it; her hair is strewn about, her legs tied as far apart as possible and her swollen belly appears stretched exceedingly taut; her cunt fairly yawns in his face. 'Tis upon her belly he beats a tattoo, and when his whip has brought a profusion of blood into sight, he walks round to the other side of the cylinder and discharges upon her face.*

N.B.—According to my notes, the adoptions do not occur until after defloration, hence say that the Duc adopts Augustine at this point. Verify whether or not this is true, and whether the adoption of the four sultanas does not occur at the very beginning, and whether at the beginning it is not said that they sleep in the bedrooms of the friends who have adopted them.

That evening, the Duc repudiates Constance, who therewith falls into the greatest discredit; however, they treat her with some consideration, because of her pregnancy, in connection with which Messieurs have certain plans. Augustine now passes for the Duc's wife, and hereafter performs none but a wife's functions upon the sofa and in the chapel. Constance descends in rank to below that of the governesses.

THE 29TH. 140. *He works exclusively with girls of fifteen, and he flogs them with sting nettles and holly until they are bleeding; his taste in asses is highly developed, he is not easy to please.*

141. *Flogs only with a bull's pizzle, continuing until the buttocks are in tatters; he uses four women one after another.*

142. *Flogs only with steel-tipped martinets, discharges only when blood is flowing generally.*

143. *The same man of whom Desgranges will speak on the 20th of February requires pregnant women; he flogs with a bull-whip, by means of which he is able to remove respectable chunks of flesh from the buttocks; from time to time he aims a blow or two at her belly.*

Rosette is flogged that evening, and Curval has her forward maidenhead. The intrigue between Hercule and Julie is brought to light; she has been having herself fucked. When scolded for her misbehavior, she replies libertinely; she is therewith whipped extraordinarily. Then, because Messieurs are fond of her, and also of Hercule, who has given yeoman service so far, they are pardoned and frolicked with.

THE 30TH. 144. *He places a candle at a certain height. Attached to the middle finger of her right hand is a piece of bread soaked in wax and set afire; if she does not make haste, she'll be burned. Her task is, with this bit of ignited bread, to light the other candle set high upon the shelf; she is obliged to leap in order to reach it; the libertine, armed with a leathern-thonged whip, lashes her with all his strength, to encourage her to leap higher and to light the candle more quickly. If she succeeds, there's an end to the game; if not, she is flogged till she falls unconscious.*

145. *He flogs first his wife, then his daughter, and prostitutes them at the brothel in order to have them whipped while he looks on, but this is not the same man of whom we have already spoken.*

146. *Whips with a cat-o'-nine-tails, from the nape of the neck to the calves of the legs; the girl is bound, he excoriates her entire back.*

147. *Whips breasts only; he insists that they be exceedingly large. And pays twice the sum when the woman is pregnant.*

Rosette's cunt is delivered up to the society that evening; after Curval and the Duc have thoroughly fucked it, they and their colleagues thoroughly whip it. She is down on her hands and knees; Messieurs take care to drive the martinet's steel tips well up into her.

THE 31ST. 148. *He whips the face only, using a bundle of dry switches; he must have charming faces. Desgranges will refer to him on the 7th of February.*

149. *Using switches, he impartially lashes the entire body, sparing nothing, face, cunt, and breasts included.*

150. *Gives two hundreds blows of the bull's pizzle, these being distributed evenly up and down the backs of lads aged from sixteen to twenty.*

151. *He is in a room, four girls arouse and flog him; when at last he is all afire, he leaps upon a fifth girl, who is naked and awaiting him in the next room and, wielding a bull's pizzle, he assails whatever of her he can reach, maintaining the hail of blows until he discharges; but in order that his ejaculation arrive sooner*

*and the patient suffer less, he is not sent into the second room until*
*his discharge is imminent.*

(Find out why there is one too many.)

Champville is applauded, the same honors are bestowed upon
her that were given Duclos, and that evening both storytellers dine
with Messieurs. Later, at the orgies, Adelaide, Aline, Augustine,
and Zelmire are condemned to be whipped with switches all over
the body save upon the breasts, but as the friends are to sport
with them for another two months, they are treated circumspectly.

# PART THE THIRD

THE 150 CRIMINAL PASSIONS, OR THOSE BE-
LONGING TO THE THIRD CLASS, COMPOSING
THE THIRTY-ONE DAYS OF JANUARY PASSED
IN HEARING THE NARRATIONS OF MAD-
AME MARTAINE; INTERSPERSED AMONGST
WHICH ARE THE SCANDALOUS DOINGS AT
THE CHÂTEAU DURING THAT MONTH;
ALL BEING SET DOWN IN THE FORM OF A
JOURNAL.
(*DRAFT*)

THE 1ST OF JANUARY. 1. *He loves nothing but to have himself embuggered, and he is never able to find too thick a prick. But, says Martaine, she'll not lay much emphasis upon this passion which is too simple a taste and one wherewith her auditors are far too well acquainted.*

2. *He wishes to depucelate none but little girls between the ages of three and seven, in the bum. This is the man who had her pucelage in this manner: she was four years old, the ordeal caused her to fall ill, her mother implored this man to give aid, money. But his heart was of flint. . . .*
*And this man is the same one of whom Duclos spoke on the 29th of November; the same again who appears in Champville's story of the 2nd of December. He has a prick of colossal proportions, he is enormously rich. He depucelates two little girls every day: one of them in the cunt, in the morning, as Champville related on the 2nd of December, the other in the bum, in the afternoon; and he has a quantity of other passions as well. Four women held Martaine when he embuggered her. His discharge lasts six minutes, and he bellows like a bull while it is in progress. His simple, straightforward, and adroit method of threading her needle, even though she was a young thing of four; describe all that.*

3. *Her mother sells the pucelage of Martaine's older brother to a man who sodomizes boys only, and who would have them exactly seven years old.*

599

4. *She is now thirteen, her brother fifteen; they go to the home of a man who constrains the brother to fuck his sister, and who alternately fucks now the boy's ass, now the girl's, while they are in each other's clutches.*

Martaine proudly describes her ass; Messieurs request her to display it, she exhibits it from the platform.

*The man she has just spoken of, she continues, is the same person who figured in Duclos' story of the 21st of November, the Comte, and who will appear in Desgranges' of the 24th of February.*

5. *He has himself fucked while embuggering the brother and sister; the same personage Desgranges will refer to on the 24th of February.*

That same evening, the Duc depucelates the bum of Hébé, who is a mere twelve. The operation succeeds only at the price of infinite trouble: she is held by the four duennas and administered by Duclos and Champville. And as there is to be a festival on the morrow, in order that things run smoothly then, Hébé's ass is also, on the evening of the 1st of January, surrendered to the society, and all four friends take full advantage of it. She is carried away unconscious; has been buggered seven times.

(Martaine must not say that she has a uterine deformity; that would be false.)

THE 2ND. 6. *He has four girls fart in his mouth all the while he embuggers a fifth, then he changes girls. All rotate: all fart, all are embuggered; he does not discharge until he has finished with the fifth ass.*

7. *Amuses himself with three small boys: embuggers and has each of them shit, puts all three to each task, and frigs the boy who is inactive.*

8. *He fucks the sister in the mouth while having her brother shit into his mouth, then he reverses their roles, and during both exercises he is embuggered.*

9. *He embuggers none but girls of fifteen, but only after having, by way of preliminary, flogged them with all his strength.*

10. *For an hour he pinches and molests her buttocks and asshole, then embuggers her while she is flogged with exceeding violence.*

The ninth week's festival is celebrated upon that day: Hercule weds Hébé and fucks her cuntwardly. Curval and the Duc take turns sodomizing first the husband, then the wife.

THE 3RD. 11. *He embuggers only during mass, and discharges at the moment of the Elevation of the Host.*

12. *He embuggers only while kicking a crucifix about in the dust; the girl must treat it with like contempt.*

13. *The man who amused himself with Eugénie on Duclos' eleventh day has the girl shit, wipes the well-beshitted ass; he possesses an outsized prick, and embuggers, ploughing into the asshole behind a consecrated Host.*

14. *Embuggers a youth, has a second youth embugger him, both ploughing, as above, behind a protective Host; upon the nape of the neck of the boy he is embuggering rests another Host, and a third youth shits thereupon. He discharges thus, without changing position, but while uttering fearful blasphemies.*

15. *He embuggers the priest while the latter is in the act of saying mass, and when the priest has performed the consecration, the fucker withdraws for a moment; profiting from this brief interval, the priest buries the Host in his ass, the fucker returns straightway to work and re-embuggers him, tamping in the wafer.*

That evening, Curval, with a Host depucelates in the bum the young and charming Zélamir. And Antinoüs fucks the Président with another Host; while fucking, the Président's tongue pushes a third into Fanchon's asshole.

THE 4TH. 16. *He likes to embugger none but very aged women while they are being lashed.*

17. *Embuggers only very aged men while being fucked.*

18. *Has a regular intrigue with his son.*

19. *Will embugger none but monsters, or blackamoors, or deformed persons.*

20. *In order to combine incest, adultery, sodomy and sacrilege, he embuggers his married daughter with a Host.*

That evening the four friends avail themselves of Zélamir's ass.

THE 5TH. 21. *He has two men alternately fuck and flagellate him while he embuggers a young boy and while an old man sheds a turd into his mouth. He eats the turd.*

22. *Two men take turns fucking him, one in the mouth, the other in the ass; this exercise must last no less than three hours by the clock. He swallows the fuck emanating from him who fucks him in the mouth.*

23. *He has himself fucked by ten men, whom he pays so much by the discharge; during a given day he withstands as many as twenty-four without himself discharging.*

24. *For the purposes of ass-fuckery, he prostitutes his wife, his daughter, and his sister, and watches the proceedings.*

25. *He employs eight men at a time: one in his mouth, one in his ass, one beneath his left testicle, one beneath his right; he frigs two others, each with one hand, he lodges a seventh between his thighs and the eighth frigs himself upon his face.*

That evening, the Duc deflowers Michette's ass and causes her frightful pain.

THE 6TH. 26. *He has an elderly man embuggered in his presence; several times over the prick is removed from that ancient asshole, it is placed in the mouth of the examiner, who sucks it, then sucks the old man's prick, sucks his asshole, and penetrates it while he who has been fucking the old man now embuggers the lecher, and is lashed by the lecher's governess. For the lecher is still a young man.*

27. *He vigorously constricts the neck of the fifteen-year-old girl he is embuggering—choking her neck has the effect of tightening her anus; meanwhile, he is flogged with a bull's pizzle.*

28. *He has large spheres of quicksilver inserted into his bowels. These spheres rise up in his entrails, then descend, and during the excessive titillation caused thereby, he sucks pricks, swallows fuck, has shit out of whores' asses, bolts turds. This ecstasy lasts a good two hours.*

29. *He would have himself embuggered by the father while he sodomizes that father's son and daughter.*

Michette's ass is surrendered to the company that evening. Durcet selects Martaine for his bedroom companion, following the precedent established by the Duc, who has Duclos, and by Curval, who has Fanchon; Martaine has begun to exert upon Durcet much the same lubricious influence Duclos exerts upon Blangis.

THE 7TH. 30. *He fucks a turkey whose head is gripped between the legs of a girl lying on her belly—while in action he looks quite as if he were embuggering the girl. While he is at work he is being sodomized, and the moment he discharges, the girl cuts the turkey's throat.*

31. *He fucks a goat from behind while being flogged; the goat conceives and gives birth to a monster. Monster though it be, he embuggers it.*

32. *He embuggers bucks.*

33. *Wishes to see a woman discharge after having been frigged by a dog; and he shoots the dog dead while its head is between the woman's thighs. But he does not harm the woman.*

34. *Embuggers a swan after having popped a Host up into its ass; then strangles the bird upon discharging.*

This same evening, the Bishop embuggers Cupidon for the first time.

THE 8TH. 35. *He has himself placed in a specially prepared wickerwork structure provided with an opening at one end; against this opening he places his asshole after having anointed it with mare's fuck. The structure he is in represents a mare's body and is covered with horsehide. A genuine horse is fetched in, mounts the artificial mare, embuggers him and meanwhile he fucks a pretty white bitch he has with him in the basket.*

36. *He fucks a cow, it conceives and gives birth to a monster which, shortly thereafter, he fucks.*

37. *In a similar basket he places a woman who receives a bull's member in her cunt. He watches this entertaining spectacle.*

38. *He has a tamed serpent which he introduces into his anus; while being thus sodomized, he embuggers a cat in a basket. Firmly contained therein, the animal can do him no harm.*

39. *He fucks a she-ass while having himself embuggered by an ass.* (For this delight an elaborate machine is indispensable. We will give a description of it elsewhere.)

That evening, Cupidon's ass is presented to the society.

THE 9TH. 40. *He fucks the nostrils of a goat which meanwhile is licking his balls; and during this exercise, he is alternately flogged and has his asshole licked.*

41. *He embuggers a sheep while a dog licks his asshole.*

42. *He embuggers a dog whose head is cut off while he discharges.*

43. *He obliges a whore to frig a donkey, he is fucked while observing this spectacle.*

44. *He fucks a monkey's asshole, the animal is enclosed in a basket; while being sodomized, the monkey is tormented in order that its anus will constrict about the libertine's member.*

That evening, the tenth week's festival is celebrated by the marriage of Bum-Cleaver and Michette; the union is consummated, 'tis a dolorous experience for the bride.

THE 10TH. Martaine announces that she is going to move on to another passion, and that the whip, of central importance in Champville's contributions of December, will enjoy only a secondary one in hers.

45. *The procuress is obliged to find him girls guilty of some felony or other; he arrives, frightens them, says that they are going certainly to be arrested but that he will take it upon himself to protect them provided they will submit to a violent fustigation, and, afraid as they are, they let themselves be whipped till they bleed.*

46. *Has a woman with beautiful hair brought to him, saying he simply wishes to examine her hair; but he cuts it off very traitorously and discharges upon seeing her melt into tears and bewail her misfortune, at which he laughs immoderately.*

47. *With all sorts of attendant ceremonies, she enters a dark room. She sees no one there, but overhears a conversation regarding her—give details of this conversation—which is of a nature to frighten her nearly to death. Finally, she receives a deluge of slaps and blows without knowing whence they come; she hears the cries accompanying a discharge, then is taken out of the room.*

48. *She enters a kind of subterranean sepulcher which is lit by nothing but a few oil lamps; they reveal all the horror of the*

*place. After a moment, during which she is able to observe every-*
*thing, all the lamps are extinguished, a horrible series of screams*
*and the rattlings of chains are heard, she collapses in a swoon; if*
*she does not faint, the noises are multiplied until finally she does*
*fall unconscious from terror. Once unconscious, a man swoops*
*down upon her and embuggers her, then abandons her, and valets*
*later come to her rescue; he must have very young and very in-*
*experienced girls. Novices, if possible.*

49. *She enters a similar place, but provide a few details to*
*distinguish it from the sepulcher above. She is stripped, thrust*
*naked into a coffin, the coffin's lid is nailed down, and the rhythm*
*of the hammer driving the nails finally excites the man's discharge.*

That afternoon, Zelmire was taken down to the cellars we
have previously mentioned, which had been prepared in the manner
we have just described. The four friends are there, naked and
equipped with weapons; Zelmire swoons, and while she is unconscious, Curval depucelates her bum. The Président has been seized
by the very same sentiments of love (mixed with lubric rage) for
this girl that the Duc has for Augustine.

THE 11TH. 50. *The same Duc de Florville, of whom Duclos*
*spoke on the 29th of November, and of whom Desgranges, in her*
*fifth story, will speak on the 26th of February, wishes to have the*
*corpse of a beautiful and recently murdered girl placed upon a bed*
*covered with black satin; he fondles the body, explores its every*
*nook and cranny, and embuggers it.*

51. *Another individual requires two corpses, those of a boy*
*and of a girl, and he embuggers the youth's dead body while kiss-*
*ing the buttocks of the girl's and driving his tongue into its anus.*

52. *He receives the girl in a small room filled with most con-*
*vincing wax representations of dead bodies, they are all pierced in*
*various ways. He recommends that the girl make her choice, say-*
*ing he intends to kill her in whatever way she prefers, inviting her*
*to choose the corpse whose wounds please her most.*

53. *He binds her to an authentic corpse, knee to knee, mouth to mouth, and flogs her until the back of her body is covered with blood.*

Zelmire's ass is made the evening's treat, but before being served up, she is subjected to a trial, and she is advised that she will be killed that night; she believes what she is told but, instead of dispatching her, Messieurs are content each to give her a hundred lashes after having generously embuggered her, and Curval takes her to bed with him. She is further embuggered all night.

THE 12TH. 54. *The girl must be menstruating. She arrives at his home, a valet conducts her to a room in the cellar where the libertine stands awaiting her, but he is near a kind of reservoir of icy water, more than twelve feet across and eight deep; it is concealed in such a way the girl does not notice it. She approaches the man, he topples her into it, and discharges the instant he hears the splash; she is pulled back out at once, but as she is menstruating, severe disability is the very frequent result of her adventure.*

55. *He lowers her into a very deep well and shouts down after her that he is about to fill it with large stones; he flings in a few clods of earth to frighten her, and discharges into the well, his seed landing on the naked whore's head.*

56. *He has a pregnant woman brought to him and terrifies her with threats and words, flogs her, continuing his ill-treatment of her until she either has a miscarriage there and then, or will surely have one when she returns home. If she disgorges her fruit while under his roof, she receives double payment.*

57. *He locks her into a black dungeon, surrounded by cats, rats, and mice; he gives her to understand she has been put there for the rest of her life, and every day he goes to her door, frigs himself, and banters with her.*

58. *He inserts sheafs of straw in her ass, ignites them, and watches her buttocks sizzle as the straw burns short.*

That evening, Curval announces he will take Zelmire to be his wife, and does indeed publicly marry her. The Bishop officiates at the wedding, the Président repudiates Julie who therewith falls into the greatest discredit, but her libertinage speaks strongly in her favor and the Bishop is disposed to protect her somewhat until the time shall arrive for him to declare himself entirely for her— he will so declare himself later on.

More clearly than ever before, upon this particular evening his associates notice Durcet's teasing hatred for Adelaide; he torments her, vexes her, she wails and is melancholy. And her father, the Président, does not by any means give her his support.

THE 13TH. 59. *He attaches a girl to a St. Andrew's cross suspended in the air, and whips her with all his might, flaying her entire back. After which, he unties her and casts her out through a window, but mattresses are there to lighten her fall, upon hearing which he discharges. Give further details of the scene in order to justify his reaction.*

60. *He has her swallow a drug which unhinges her imagination and causes her to see horrible things in the room. She fancies the room is being flooded, sees the water rise, climbs upon a chair, but still the water mounts, reaches her, and she is told that she has no alternative but to leap in and swim; she plunges, but falls upon the stone floor and injures herself badly. 'Tis at this point the libertine discharges; previously, he has taken much pleasure in kissing her ass.*

61. *He holds her suspended by a rope that runs up through a pulley affixed to the top of a tower; he stands at a window, she hangs directly outside and opposite him. He frigs himself and threatens to sever the rope as he discharges. While all this is afoot he is being flogged, and earlier he induced the whore to shit for him.*

62. *She is held by four slender cords, each attached to one of her limbs. She is held thus in a very cruel and painful position; a trap door is opened beneath her and a charcoal brazier, very hot,*

is discovered to her view: if the cords break, she falls thereupon. The roué meddles with the cords, strains them, cuts one while discharging. Sometimes he suspends the girl in the same attitude, places a weight upon her belly, then suddenly jerks all four cords, pulling her up, and in so doing rupturing her stomach and tearing her muscles. She remains where she is until he discharges.

63. *He binds her to a low stool; suspended a foot above her head is a dagger whose point is filed needle sharp; the dagger hangs by a hair—if the hair snaps, the dagger drives into her skull. The libertine frigs himself while watching his victim's anxious contortions. An hour later, he frees her and bloodies her buttocks with light jabs of the same dagger which, he would like to have her remark, pricks very nicely; he discharges upon her blood-soaked ass.*

That evening, the Bishop depucelates Colombe's bum, and after his discharge lashes her with a whip, for he cannot bear to have a girl cause him to discharge.

THE 14TH. 64. *He embuggers a young novice who knows nothing of the ways of the world, and as he discharges, he fires two pistol shots very close to her ear. The powder singes her hair.*

65. *He makes her sit down in an armchair balanced on springs; her weight releases a number of springs connected to iron rings which bind her tightly to the chair. Certain levers and gears advance twenty daggers until their points graze her skin; the man frigs himself, the while explaining that the least movement of the chair will cause her to be stabbed. He sprays his fuck upon her, in so doing touching the chair very delicately with his foot.*

66. *A bascule carries her down into a small crypt hung in black and furnished with a prie-dieu, a coffin, and an assortment of death's heads. She sees six specters armed with clubs, swords, pistols, sabers, poignards, and lances, and each is about to pierce her in a different place. Overcome by fear, she sways, is about to fall; the man enters, catches her in his arms, and flogs her until he*

*is weary, then discharges as he embuggers her. If she is unconscious at the time he enters, and this is frequently the case, his lash restores her to her senses.*

67. *She enters a room in a tower, in its center she sees a large charcoal brazier; upon a table, poison and a dirk; she is allowed to choose the manner whereby she is to perish. It generally happens that she elects poison. 'Tis a variety of opiate which plunges her into a profound drowsiness; while the spell lasts, the libertine embuggers her. He is the same personage Duclos cited on the 27th of November and of whom Desgranges will say more on the 6th of February.*

68. *The same gentleman who will figure in Desgranges' story of the 16th of February goes through the entire ceremony of preparing to decapitate the girl; just as the blow falls, a rope suddenly snatches the girl's body away, the axe-blade sinks three inches into the block. If the rope does not drag the girl away, she dies. He discharges while bringing down the axe. But prior to this, he has embuggered her as she lies with her neck upon the block.*

Colombe's ass is plumbed by the society that evening, and Messieurs pretend to cut off her head. They are accomplished actors.

THE 15TH. 69. *He slips a noose around the whore's throat and hangs her. Her feet rest upon a stool, a cord is tied to one leg of the stool, he sits in an armchair, watching and having the whore's daughter frig him. When he discharges, he pulls the cord, the whore hangs, he leaves, valets enter and cut the whore down. A leech lets some blood from one of her veins and she returns to life, but these attentions are given her without the libertine's knowledge. He goes off to bed with the whore's daughter and sodomizes her all night long, while doing so telling her he has hanged her mother. Have Martaine say that Desgranges will refer to him again.*

70. *He holds the girl by the ears and walks her around the room, discharging as he parades with her.*

71. *He pinches the girl's body, nipping her everywhere save upon the breast, till she turns black and blue.*

72. *He pinches her breasts, molests them, and kneads them until they are completely bruised.*

73. *He writes letters and words upon her breasts, working with a needle which has a poisoned tip; her breasts become infected, and she suffers excruciatingly.*

74. *Drives between one and two thousand pins into her breasts, and discharges when he has covered them.*

More libertine with every passing day, Julie is discovered frigging herself with Champville. The Bishop affords her additional protection and thereafter admits her into his bedchamber, as the Duc has Duclos, Durcet Martaine, and Curval Fanchon. Julie confesses that at the time of her repudiation, having been condemned to sleep in the stables with the other animals, she appealed to Champville and was taken into her chamber; they have been bedding together ever since.

THE 16TH. 75. *He buries large hatpins in the girl's flesh, dotting her entire body, her nipples included; he discharges after having driven home the last pin. Desgranges will return to the same enthusiast in her fourth story of the 27th of February.*

76. *He gives her a great deal to drink, then sews up her cunt and asshole; he leaves her thus sealed up till he remarks she is nigh to collapsing from the need to piss and shit, two activities which are impossible in the state she is in; or else he waits until the weight of the shit and the pressure of the piss finally break the stitches.*

77. *Four gentlemen enter the room and cuff the girl, strike and kick her until she falls. When she is down, all four mutually frig one another and discharge.*

78. *She is deprived of air, then given air, then 'tis taken away again. She is lodged within a pneumatic machine.*

To celebrate the end of the eleventh week, the wedding of Colombe and Antinoüs takes place that day, and is consummated. The Duc, who has been indulging in some prodigious cunt-fuckery with Augustine, has been seized by a lubricious fury: he has had Duclos hold her, and has given her three hundred lashes distributed between the middle of her back and her calves, and, after that, has embuggered Duclos while kissing Augustine's flogged ass. Directly after having molested her, he does some foolish things, for his head is completely giddy: he has her sit beside him at table, will touch no food save what he has out of her mouth, dotes upon her, and does a thousand other things, all very illogical and very libertine. But he and his confreres are men of that strange turn of character.

THE 17TH. 79. *He binds the girl belly down upon a dining table and eats a piping hot omelette served upon her buttocks. He uses an exceedingly sharp fork.*

80. *He immobilizes her head above a grill, lights a brisk fire, and roasts her until she loses consciousness, embuggering her steadily.*

81. *He gently toasts the skin of her breasts and buttocks, proceeding very gradually, and using sulphur-tipped matches.*

82. *He uses candles and extinguishes them again and again by snuffing them out in her cunt, her asshole, and upon her nipples.*

83. *With a match he sears her eyelids; this prevents her from sleeping soundly that night, for she cannot close her eyes.*

That evening, the Duc depucelates Giton, who finds the experience discomfiting, for the Duc is enormous, fucks with great brutality, and Giton is, after all, only twelve.

THE 18TH. 84. *Pointing a pistol at her heart, he obliges her to chew and swallow a live coal, and then he washes out her cunt with aqua fortis.*

85. *He has her dance the* olivettes. *Naked, she is to dance round four pillars; but the only path her naked feet can tread is studded with shards of broken glass and bits of sharp metal and pointed tacks and nails; by each pillar stands a man, a bundle of switches in his hand, and he lashes whichever side of her body she offers every time she passes by him. She is thus obliged to run a certain number of turns around, it all depending upon whether she is more or less attractive. The most beautiful are harried the most.*

86. *He strikes her violently in the face until the blows of his fist bring blood from her nose, and he continues yet a while longer, the blood notwithstanding; he discharges and mixes his fuck with the blood she has lost.*

87. *Employing very well-heated tongs, he pinches her flesh, and mainly her buttocks, her mons veneris and her breasts. Desgranges will have more to say about this personage.*

88. *Upon various parts of her naked, reclining body, especially the more sensitive areas, he places little mounds of gunpowder, then sets fire to them.*

Giton's ass is made public property that evening, and after this ceremony, he is flogged by Curval, the Duc, and the Bishop, who have fucked him.

THE 19TH. 89. *He inserts a cylinder of gunpowder in her cunt, removes the cylinder, leaves the powder there; he puts a match to the charge and ejaculates upon seeing the flames dart forth. Earlier, he has kissed her ass.*

90. *He soaks her everywhere from head to foot with brandy, brings a match near and entertains himself with the spectacle of this poor girl all covered with flames. Then he discharges. He repeats the same operation two or three times.*

91. *He gives her bowels a rinsing with boiling oil.*

92. *He introduces a red-hot iron into her anus, another into her cunt, after having thoroughly whipped the latter.*

93. *He likes to trample upon a pregnant woman until she aborts. Prior to this he whips her.*

That same evening, Curval depucelates Sophie's bum, but this ordeal succeeds another: she has first been given one hundred lashes by each of the friends and is streaming blood. Directly Curval has discharged into her ass, he offers to pay the society five hundred *louis* for permission to take her down to the cellars that very evening and to be given a free hand with her. Curval's request is rejected, he re-embuggers her, and upon emerging from her ass after this second discharge, he gives her a kick which sends her sprawling upon a mattress fifteen feet away. He revenges himself upon Zelmire, whom he flogs till his arm aches.

THE 20TH. 94. *He appears to be caressing the girl who is frigging him, she suspects nothing; but at the moment he discharges, he seizes her head and batters it against the wall. The blow is so strong and so unexpected that she usually falls unconscious.*

95. *They are four libertines assembled; they judge a girl and, ultimately disagreeing upon what punishment to inflict, decide to sentence her individually. All in all, she receives one hundred strokes of the whip; each juror metes out twenty-five of them: the first flogs her from the back to the loins, the second from the loins to the calves, the third from the neck to the navel, breasts included, the fourth from the belly to the shins.*

96. *Using a pin, he pricks each of her eyes, each nipple, and her clitoris.*

97. *He drops molten sealing wax upon her buttocks, into her cunt, and upon her breasts.*

98. *He opens the veins in one arm and bleeds her until she faints.*

Curval suggests they bleed Constance because of her pregnancy; and bled she is, until she collapses, 'tis Durcet who acts as her leech. That evening, Messieurs avail themselves of Sophie's ass, and the Duc proposes she be bled also, it could not possibly do her any harm, no, on the contrary, they might make a nice pudding of her blood for tomorrow's luncheon. His idea is acclaimed, Curval now plays the leech, Duclos frigs him while he operates, and he wishes to make the puncture at the same moment his fuck departs his balls; and he makes a generous puncture, but his blade finds the vein none the less. Despite it all, Sophie has pleased the Bishop, who adopts her for his wife, repudiating Aline, who falls into the greatest discredit.

THE 21ST. 99. *He bleeds both of her arms and would have her remain standing while her blood flows; now and again he stops the bleeding and flogs her, then he opens the wounds again, and this continues until she collapses. He only discharges when she faints. Earlier in the game he had her shit for him.*

100. *He bleeds her from all four of her limbs and from her jugular vein too, and frigs himself while watching the five fountains of blood.*

101. *He lightly scarifies her flesh, concentrating upon her buttocks, but neglecting her breasts.*

102. *He scarifies her vigorously, cutting deep, devoting particular attention to her breasts and especially to her nipples, and to the environs of her asshole when he turns his attentions to her behind. Next, he cauterizes the wounds with a red-hot iron.*

103. *He is bound hand and foot, as if he were a wild beast, and he is draped in a tiger's skin. When thus readied, he is excited, irritated, whipped, beaten, his ass is frigged; opposite him is a plump young girl, naked and tied by her feet to the floor, by her neck to the ceiling, in such wise she cannot stir. When the roué is all a-sweat, his captors free him, he leaps upon the girl, bites her everywhere and above all her clitoris and her nipples, which he generally manages to remove with his teeth. He roars and cries like a ferocious animal, and discharges while shrieking. The girl must shit, he eats her turd upon the floor.*

That evening, the Bishop depucelates Narcisse; he is surrendered to the society the same evening, so that the festival of the 23rd will not be disturbed. Before embuggering him, the Duc has him shit into his mouth and render him, together with the turd, his predecessors' fuck. And then, after having sodomized the lad, Blangis scourges him.

THE 22ND. 104. *He pulls out her teeth and scratches her gums with needles. Sometimes he heats the needles.*

105. *He breaks one of her fingers, several upon occasion.*

106. *Employing a heavy hammer, he flattens one of her feet.*

107. *He removes a hand, sawing through the wrist.*

108. *While discharging, he batters in her front teeth with a hammer. He is very fond of sucking her mouth before proceeding to the major phase of his operation.*

The Duc depucelates Rosette in the rear that evening, and the same instant his prick sounds her ass, Curval extracts one of the little girl's teeth—this in order that she may experience two terrible pains at the same time. So that the morrow's festival not be disturbed, her ass is made generally available that same evening. When Curval has discharged thereinto (and he is the last of the four to do so), he sends the child spinning with a blow of his fist.

THE 23RD. Because of the holiday, only four are related.

109. *He amputates one foot.*

110. *He breaks one of her arms as he embuggers her.*

111. *Using a crowbar, he breaks a bone in her leg and embuggers her after doing so.*

112. *He ties her to a stepladder, her limbs being attached in a peculiar manner, a cord is tied to the ladder; he pulls the cord, the ladder falls. Sometimes she breaks one limb, sometimes another.*

Upon that day Invictus was married to Rosette; their wedding celebrated the twelfth week's festival. That evening, Rosette is bled after she has been fucked, and Aline is likewise bled after Hercule has fucked her; both are bled in such a way their blood spurts upon our libertine's thighs and pricks. Messieurs frig themselves while looking on, and discharge when both have fainted.

THE 24TH. 113. *He cuts off one of her ears. (See to it that you specify what these persons do by way of a prelude to their major stunt.)*

114. *He slits her lips and nostrils.*

115. *After having sucked and bitten it, he pierces her tongue with a hot iron.*

116. *He tears several nails from her fingers, and also from her toes.*

117. *He cuts off one of her fingers at the last joint.*

And, upon close questioning, the storyteller having said that, provided the wound is dressed at once, such a mutilation has no undesirable aftereffects, Durcet straightway cuts the end off one of Adelaide's fingers, for his lewd jesting and teasing have been increasingly directed against her. His practical joke fetches a discharge from him, his flow of fuck is accompanied by unheard-of transports.

That same evening, Curval depucelates Augustine's ass, even though she is now the Duc's wife. Her anguish, her sufferings. Curval rages against her afterward; he conspires with the Duc to take her down to the cellars without further delay, and they tell Durcet that if they are granted permission to carry out the expedition, they in their turn will allow him to dispatch Adelaide at once, but the Bishop delivers an impassioned sermon to those truants, and obtains the promise that they will restrain themselves yet a little longer for the sake of their own pleasure. Curval and the Duc hence limit themselves to giving Augustine a ferocious whipping. Both lash her at once.

THE 25TH. 118. *He distills fifteen or twenty drops of molten lead into her mouth and burns her gums with aqua fortis.*

119. *After having had her lick his beshitted ass with her tongue, he snips off the end of that same tongue, then, when once she is mutilated, he embuggers her.*

120. *He employs a machine involving a hollow steel bit which bores holes in the flesh and which, when removed, takes with it a round chunk of flesh which is as long as the drill has penetrated; the machine bores on automatically if not withdrawn.*

121. *He transforms a boy of ten or twelve into a eunuch.*

122. *With a pair of pliers isolating and raising each nipple, he cuts off the same with a pair of scissors.*

That same evening, Augustine's ass is made generally available. While embuggering her, Curval had wished to kiss Constance's breast, and upon discharging, he made off with a nipple in his teeth, but as her wound was treated and bandaged at once, Messieurs assured one another that the accident would have no harmful effect upon the child in her womb. Curval says to his colleagues, in answer to their pleasantries upon his mounting rage against Constance, that he has no control over the fury she inspires in him.

When in his turn the Duc embuggers Augustine, his own powerful feelings for that beautiful girl are exhaled with incomparable violence: had the others not kept an eye upon him, he would have injured her, either while mauling her breasts or squeezing her neck with all his strength as he discharged. Once again he asks the society to put her in his power, but he is requested to wait for Desgranges' narrations. His brother entreats him to be patient and abstain until he himself sets an example by dispatching Aline; haste, the Bishop points out, makes waste; and why spoil the latter part of the holiday by upsetting a schedule admirably designed to guarantee them a daily fare of moderation, wherein only happiness lies? However, the Duc will not listen to reason, he cannot any longer hold himself in check, and so, since he absolutely must torture the lovely girl, he is allowed to inflict a light wound upon her arm. He executes it upon the fleshy part of her left forearm, sucks blood from the cut he has made, and discharges; Augustine is so skillfully patched up that four days later no trace of the Duc's teeth marks is to be seen.

THE 26TH. 123. *He breaks a bottle of thin glass against the face of the girl, who is bound and unable to protect herself; before doing so, he sucked her mouth with great vigor and sucked her tongue also.*

124. *He tears off both her legs, ties one of her hands behind her back, puts a little stick into her free hand, and invites her to defend herself. Then he attacks her, wielding his sword with great vigor and dexterity, wounds her here and there, and finally discharges upon her wounds.*

125. *He stretches her upon a St. Andrew's cross, goes through the ceremony of breaking her, strains but does not dislocate three of her limbs, but does definitely break the fourth, either an arm or a leg.*

126. *Pistol in hand, he has her stand facing to the right and lets fly with a charge which grazes her two breasts; he aims to shoot away one of her little nipples.*

127. *He has her crouch down twenty feet away and present her buttocks; he shoots a bullet up her ass.*

That same evening, the Bishop depucelates Fanny's bum.

THE 27TH. 128. *The same man of whom Desgranges will speak on the 24th of February flogs a pregnant woman upon the belly until she miscarries; she must lay the egg in his presence, and he lashes her till she does.*

129. *He very tidily castrates a young lad of sixteen or seventeen after having embuggered and whipped him.*

130. *He must have a maiden brought to him, he slices off her clitoris with a razor, then deflowers her with a cylinder of heated iron, driving the device home with hammer blows.*

131. *This personage performs an abortion when the woman's pregnancy has entered its eighth month. He forces her to drink a certain brew which brings the child out dead in a trice. Upon other occasions, this libertine by his art causes the child to be born from the mother's asshole. But the child emerges dead, and the woman's life is gravely imperiled.*

132. *He severs an arm.*

That evening, Fanny's ass is made generally available, Durcet rescues her from a torture his colleagues had been preparing for her; he takes her to be his wife, has the Bishop perform the marriage, and repudiates Adelaide, who is submitted to the torture originally readied for Fanny. It is however a paltry business after all: the Duc embuggers her while Durcet breaks her finger.

THE 28TH. 133. *He cuts off both hands at the wrist and cauterizes the wounds with a hot iron.*

134. *He removes the tongue, cutting it at the roots, and cauterizes it with a hot iron.*

135. *He amputates one leg, usually having someone else cut it off while he embuggers her.*

136. *He extracts all her teeth, replacing each one with a red-hot nail, which he secures in place with a hammer; he does this directly after having fucked the woman in the mouth.*

137. *He removes one eye.*

Julie is roundly whipped by everyone that evening and all her fingers are pricked with a needle. This latter operation takes place while the Bishop, who is passing fond of her, embuggers her.

THE 29TH. 138. *Allowing molten sealing wax to flow thereupon, he blinds and ultimately dissolves first one eye, then the other.*

139. *He neatly slices off one breast, then cauterizes the wound with a hot iron. Desgranges will here interject that 'tis this same man who made off with the nipple she is missing, and that she is positively certain he ate it after having cooked it upon a griddle.*

140. *He amputates both buttocks after having flogged and embuggered her. It is believed that he too eats the meat.*

141. *He shaves off both her ears.*

142. *Clips off all the extremities, to wit: ten fingers, ten toes, two nipples, one clitoris and the end of the tongue.*

That evening, Aline, after a vigorous whipping given her by the four friends and an embuggery the Bishop performs for the last time, is condemned to have a finger on either hand and a toe on either foot cut off by each friend. Thus she loses a total of eight parts.

THE 30TH. 143. *He carves away several chunks of flesh, selecting them from divers areas upon her body; he has them roasted and obliges her to eat them with him. Desgranges will mention the same man on the 8th and 17th of February.*

144. *He cuts off a young boy's four limbs, embuggers the trunk, feeds him well and allows him so to live; as the arms and legs were not severed too close to the body, the boy lives for quite a while. And the surgeon embuggers him steadily for approximately a year.*

145. *He chains one of the girl's hands and secures the chain to the wall; he leaves her thus, without food. Near her is a large knife, and just beyond her reach sits an excellent meal: if she wishes to eat, she has but to cut through her forearm; otherwise, she dies of starvation. Prior to this he has embuggered her. He observes her through a window.*

146. *He manacles both mother and daughter; in order that they both survive, one has got to get to the food placed not far away: survival, that is, means that one must sacrifice a hand. He amuses himself listening to them discuss their dilemma, and argue about who is to resolve it.*

She recounts only four stories, for that evening the thirteenth week's festival is to take place. During it, the Duc, acting in the capacity of a woman, is married to Hercule, who is to be the husband; acting now as a man, the Duc takes Zéphyr to be his wife. The young bardash who, as the reader is aware, possesses the prettiest ass amongst the eight boys, is dressed as a girl, and so clad appears as beautiful as the goddess of love. The ceremony is consecrated by the Bishop and transpires within the sight of the entire household. The dear little Zéphyr surrenders his virginal bum to the Duc, who finds all his pleasure therein, but much trouble making a successful entry; Zéphyr is rather badly torn, and bleeds profusely. Hercule fucks the Duc throughout this operation.

THE 31ST. 147. *He plucks out both her eyes and leaves her locked in a room, saying that she has before her what she needs to eat, that she has but to get up and search for it. But in order to reach the food she must cross a broad plate of iron, which, of course, she cannot see, and which is kept heated to a very high temperature. Situated at a window, he amuses himself watching how she manages: will she burn herself, or will she prefer to perish from hunger? She has been, previously, very soundly whipped.*

148. *He subjects her to the rope torture; this consists in having one's four limbs tied to ropes, then one is raised high in the air and suddenly dropped from a considerable height, then raised, then dropped; each fall dislocates and sometimes breaks the limbs, because one never quite falls to the ground, the ropes halting one just a short distance above it.*

149. *He inflicts upon her a quantity of deep wounds into which he pours boiling pitch and molten lead.*

150. *The moment after she gives birth to a child, he binds her hand and foot, and ties her child not far away from her. The infant wails, she is unable to get to it. And thus she must watch it expire. Then he steps up and lashes the mother, aiming his whip-strokes at her cunt and managing the thing so that the interior of her vagina is well tickled. He himself is usually the child's father.*

151. *He gives her copiously to drink, then sews up her cunt, her asshole and her mouth as well, and leaves her thus until the water bursts through its conduits, or until she dies.*

(Determine why there is one too many; if one is to be deleted, suppress the last, for I believe I have already used it.)

That same evening, Messieurs avail themselves of Zéphyr's ass, and Adelaide is condemned to a rude fustigation, after which a hot iron is brought very close to the interior of her vagina, to her armpits, and she is slightly scorched beneath each nipple. She endures it all like a heroine and frequently invokes God. This further arouses her persecutors.

# PART THE FOURTH

THE 150 MURDEROUS PASSIONS, OR THOSE
BELONGING TO THE FOURTH CLASS, COM-
POSING THE TWENTY-EIGHT DAYS OF FEB-
RUARY SPENT IN HEARING THE NARRATIONS
OF MADAME DESGRANGES; INTERSPERSED
AMONGST WHICH ARE THE SCANDALOUS
DOINGS AT THE CHÂTEAU DURING THAT
MONTH; ALL BEING SET DOWN IN THE FORM
OF A JOURNAL.
(*DRAFT*)

Begin by giving a full description of the new situation which exists in February; there has been a radical change in the appearance of things. The four original wives have been repudiated, but the Bishop has extended his protection to Julie, whom he keeps near him as a kind of servant to wait upon him; Duclos has been allowed to share her quarters with Constance, whose fruit Messieurs are eager to keep from spoiling; Aline and Adelaide have been driven out of house and home and now sleep amongst the animals intended for their Lordships' table. The sultanas Augustine, Zelmire, Fanny, and Sophie have replaced the wives and now fulfill all their functions, to wit: as wipers in the chapel, as waitresses at the meals, as couch companions, as Messieurs' bed companions at night. Apart from the fucker, who changes from day to day, Messieurs have:

The Duc: Augustine, Zéphyr, and Duclos in his bed, together with his fucker; he sleeps surrounded by the four of them, and Marie occupies a sofa in his bedchamber;

Curval: the Président likewise sleeps amidst Adonis, Zelmire, a fucker, and Fanchon; his room is otherwise empty;

Durcet sleeps amidst Hyacinthe, Fanny, a fucker, and Martaine (*check the foregoing*), and he has Louison lie upon a neighboring divan.

The Bishop sleeps amidst Céladon, Sophie, a fucker, and Julie; Thérèse sleeps upon the divan.

Which reveals that each of the little ménages, Zéphyr and Augustine, Adonis and Zelmire, Hyacinthe and Fanny, Céladon and Sophie, all of whom are married, belong, husband and wife, to a single master. Only four little girls remain in the girls' harem, and four in the boys'. Champville sleeps in the girls' quarters, Desgranges in the boys' quarters. Aline is in the stable, as we pointed out, and Constance is in Duclos' room, but alone there since Duclos spends every night in the Duc's bed.

627

Dinner is always served by the four sultanas (by, that is to say, the four new wives), and supper by the remaining four sultanas; a quatrain always serves coffee; but the quatrains formerly allocated to each niche in the auditorium are now reduced in number to one boy and one girl.

The reader will recall our mention of the pillars in the auditorium; at the beginning of each séance, Aline is attached to one of them, Adelaide to the other, their buttocks facing out toward the alcoves, and near each pillar is a little table covered with assorted punitive instruments; and so it is the two women are at all times ready to receive the lash. Constance has permission to sit with the storytellers. Each duenna keeps close to her couple, and Julie, completely unclothed, wanders from couch to couch, taking orders and executing them upon the spot. As always, one fucker per couch.

Such is the situation when Desgranges begins her narrations. The friends have also ruled, in a special decree, that, during this month, Aline, Adelaide, Augustine, and Zelmire shall be surrendered to Messieurs' brutal passions, and that Messieurs are at liberty, upon the prescribed day, either to immolate them privately or to invite whichever of their friends they please to witness the sacrifice; and that with what regards Constance, she shall be employed for the celebration of the final week, a full explanation of which shall be given in due time and place. Should the Duc and Curval, who by this arrangement are to be made widowers, be disposed to take another wife to care for their needs until the end of the holiday, they shall be able to do so by making a selection from amongst the four remaining sultanas. But the pillars will remain ungarnished when the two women who garnish them now shall have been bidden a last farewell.

Desgranges starts, and after having reminded her auditors that henceforth the tales shall be those of an exclusively murderous character, she says that she will be careful, as their Lordships have enjoined her to be, to enter into the most minute details, and above all to indicate with what ordinary caprices these libertine assassins preface their more serious exercises; thus, their Lordships will be able to perceive and judge their relationships and associations, and to see how an example of simple libertinage, rectified and elaborated by an unmannerly and unprincipled individual, may lead straight to murder, and to what kind of murder. Then she begins.

THE 1ST OF FEBRUARY. 1. *He used to enjoy amusing himself with a beggarwoman who had not had a bit to eat in three days, and his second passion is to leave a woman to die of hunger in a dungeon; he keeps a close watch upon her and frigs himself while examining her, but does not discharge until the day she perishes.*

2. *He maintains her in her prison cell, toying with her for a long season, gradually diminishing her daily portion of food; beforehand, he has her shit, and eats her turd upon a platter.*

3. *He formerly liked to suck the mouth and swallow its saliva; in recent days he has developed the passion of immuring a woman in a dungeon with food to last no more than a fortnight; on the thirtieth day, he enters her prison and frigs himself upon the corpse.*

4. *First, he would have her piss, then he would slowly destroy her by preventing her from drinking although feeding her all she wanted to eat.*

5. *He would flog, then later kill the woman by depriving her of sleep.*

That same evening, Michette, after having eaten a big supper, is hung head downward until she has vomited everything upon Curval, who stands frigging himself beneath her and eating the manna that descends from on high.

THE 2ND. 6. *His first passion was to have her shit into his mouth, and he would eat it as it emerged; nowadays he feeds her a diet of worthless bread and cheap wine. A month on this fare and she starves to death.*

7. *He was once a great cunt-fucker; now he gives the woman a venereal distemper by injection, but of such virulence she croaks in very short order.*

8. *As a youth, he was fond of receiving vomit in his mouth, now, by means of a certain decoction, he gives her a deathly fever which results in her speedy demise.*

9. *He was once wont to gather shit from assholes, presently injects an enema containing toxic ingredients dissolved in boiling water or aqua fortis.*

10. *Once a famous fustigator, today he binds a woman to a pivot upon which she uninterruptedly revolves until dead.*

That evening, an enema of boiling water is given to Rosette the moment after the Duc has finished embuggering her.

THE 3RD. 11. *He used to like to slap the whore's face; as a mature man, he twists her head around until it faces backward. When so adjusted, one may simultaneously look at her face and at her buttocks.*

12. *Addicted to bestiality as a youngster, he now likes to have a girl depucelated by a stallion while he looks on. She ordinarily dies.*

13. *Once an ass-fucker, he now buries the girl up to her waist and maintains her thus till the lower half of her body rots.*

14. *Previously, he was wont to frig her clitoris, and he still does so, but more vigorously, employing one of his servants to keep at the work until the girl expires.*

15. *Gradually perfecting his passion over the years, a fustigator now flogs every part of a woman's body until she perishes.*

That evening, the Duc would have Augustine, endowed with an unusually sensitive clitoris, frigged thereupon by Duclos and Champville, who relieve each other at the post and continue the task until the little lady falls unconscious.

THE 4TH. 16. *His earlier passion was to squeeze the whore's neck, in later years he would tie the girl by the neck. Before her sits a sumptuous meal, but to reach it she must strangle; otherwise she dies of hunger.*

17. *The same man who slew Duclos' sister and whose taste is to subject the flesh to a prolonged mauling, abuses the breasts and buttocks with such furious violence that his treatment of the whore proves fatal to her.*

18. *The man Martaine mentioned on the 20th of January, he who formerly adored bleeding women, now kills them by dint of repeated bloodlettings.*

19. *He whose passion in times past was to make a naked woman run until she dropped from exhaustion, in this age of unbridled libertinage shuts her up in a steaming bathhouse where she dies of asphyxiation.*

20. *He whom Duclos cited earlier, the gentleman who liked to be wrapped in swaddling clothes and fed whoreshit in a spoon rather than pap, swathes a girl so tightly in baby's blankets that he kills her.*

Shortly before the company moved into the auditorium that afternoon, Curval was found embuggering one of the scullery maids. He pays the fine; the girl is ordered to reappear at the evening's orgies, where the Duc and the Bishop embugger her in their turn, and she receives two hundred lashes from the hand of each of them. She's a strapping country girl, twenty-five, in satisfactory health, and has a fine ass.

THE 5TH. 21. *His first passion is for bestiality, his second is to sew the girl into an untanned donkey's skin, her head protruding; he feeds and cares for her until the animal's skin shrinks and crushes her to death.*

22. *He of whom Martaine spoke on the 15th of January and who liked to hang a girl for his amusement, currently amuses himself by hanging her by her feet until the blood rushing to her head kills her.*

23. *Duclos' libertine of the 27th of November who liked to besot his whore, today inserts a funnel into her mouth and floods her with liquids till she dies therefrom.*

24. *Once he was wont to mistreat nipples, but has progressed since then and now buckles a sort of small iron pot over each breast and lowers her over a stove; the iron heats, and she is allowed to perish thus in frightful pain.*

25. *His whole delight used to consist in watching a woman swim, but he now casts her into a pond and fishes her out half-drowned, then hangs her by the feet to encourage the water to drain out of her. Once she has returned to her senses, into the pond she goes again, and so on and so forth, till she gives up the ghost.*

Upon that day and at the same hour, another kitchen servant is found being embuggered, this time by the Duc; he pays the fine, the servant is summoned to the orgies, where everyone cavorts with her, Durcet making good use of her mouth, the others of her bum, and even of her cunt, for she is a virgin, and she is condemned to receive two hundred lashes from each of her employers. She is a girl of eighteen, tall and well made, her hair is auburn in color, and she owns a very fair ass.

That same evening, Curval utters the opinion that it is a matter of extreme urgency that Constance be bled again on account of her pregnancy; the Duc embuggers her, and Curval bleeds her while Augustine frigs his prick against Zelmire's buttocks and while someone else fucks Zelmire. Upon discharging, he executes the puncture; his aim is true.

THE 6TH. 26. *As a young man he used to kick a woman in the ass, tumbling her into a brazier, whence she would emerge before suffering excessively. He has lately refined this stunt, now obliges a girl to stand upright between two blazing fires: one cooks her in front, the other behind; and there she remains until the fat on her body melts.*

Desgranges announces that she is going to describe murders which, bringing on a prompt death, cause very little suffering.

27. *In former times he would impede respiration by constricting the neck with his hands or by blocking the nose and mouth, but these days he deposits the whore between four mattresses and she suffocates.*

28. *He of whom Martaine said a few words and who used to allow his victim a choice from among three manners of dying* (see the 14th of January) *has of late begun to blow out the whore's brains, denying her any say in the matter; he embuggers, and upon discharging, pulls the trigger.*

29. *The man Champville referred to on the 22nd of December as the libertine who made the girl dance with the cat, presently flings the whore from the top of a tower. She lands on sharp gravel. He discharges upon hearing her land.*

30. *That gentleman who liked to throttle his partner while embuggering her, and whom Martaine described on the 6th of January, has advanced to the stage at which, as he embuggers her, he slips a black silk cord about her neck and strangles her while discharging; this delight, says Desgranges, is one of the most exquisite a libertine can procure himself.*

Upon that day, Messieurs celebrate the festival of the fourteenth week, and, in the guise of a woman, Curval becomes Bum-Cleaver's wife, and, as a man, takes Adonis to be his helpmeet; 'tis not till then that child is depucelated, and the event occurs very publicly, while Bum-Cleaver is fucking the Président.

Messieurs besot themselves at supper. And they flog Zelmire and Augustine about the loins, the buttocks, the thighs, the belly, the cunt, and the groin, then Curval has Zelmire fucked by Adonis, his new wife, and embuggers both of them one after the other.

THE 7TH. 31. *He once liked to fuck a drowsy woman; he does much better now: he kills her with a strong dose of opium and encunts her during her death-sleep.*

32. *The same roué she referred to very recently, and who subjects the whore to a series of duckings, has still another passion: tying a stone to her neck, he drowns the woman.*

33. *Whereas once he was content to slap her face, now he carries matters further: he pours molten lead into her ear while she is asleep.*

34. *He was fond of whipping her face; Champville spoke of him on the 30th of December (verify that); but now he dispatches the girl with a quick hammer blow upon the temple.*

35. *This libertine would previously allow a candle to burn out in a woman's anus; today, he attaches her to a lightning rod during a thunderstorm and awaits a fortuitous stroke.*

36. *A sometime fustigator. He has her bend over with her behind facing the muzzle of a small piece of artillery. The ball enters her ass.*

That day 'tis the Bishop they discover with his prick lodged in the third kitchen servant's asshole. He pays the fine, the Duc and Curval embugger and cunt-fuck her, for she is also a virgin, then she is given a total of eight hundred stripes, two hundred by each friend. She is Swiss, nineteen, very fair of skin, very plump, and has a splendid ass. The cooks complain and say that the service will not be able to continue any longer if Messieurs go on fussing about with the help, and the society agrees to a truce extending until March.

Rosette loses a finger that evening, and the wound is cauterized with fire. She is sandwiched between Curval and the Duc during the operation: one fucks her ass, the other her cunt. Adonis' ass is made generally available that same evening; and so it is that the Duc cunt-fucks one servant and Rosette at the orgies and ass-fucks the same servant, ass-fucks Rosette too, and Adonis. He is tired.

THE 8TH. 37. *His whole delight once lay in beating a woman's entire body with a bull's pizzle; 'twas to him Martaine alluded as the man who strained all four of his victim's limbs on the rack and broke but one of them. He likes now thoroughly to break the woman on the wheel, but he chokes her to death when he has finished exercising her.*

38. *Martaine's gentleman who would feign a decapitation and have the woman snatched from beneath the blade at the last moment, now severs her head in all good faith. He discharges as the blow falls. He frigs himself.*

39. *Martaine's libertine of the 30th of January who was wont to perform an extensive scarification, now consigns his victims to perish in dungeons.*

40. *He used to be a whipper of pregnant women's bellies, has latterly perfected that by causing an enormous weight to fall on the pregnant woman's belly, thereby crushing her and her fruit at one stroke.*

41. *Formerly, he was known to be fond of the sight of a girl's bare neck, which he would squeeze and molest somewhat; that mild passion has been replaced by the insertion of a pin in a certain spot upon the woman's neck. The pin kills her at once.*

42. *At the beginning he would gently burn various parts of the body with a candle flame, more recently he has begun to hurl women into a glowing furnace where they are consumed instantly.*

Durcet, his prick very stiff and who during the storytelling has ventured forth twice to flog Adelaide awaiting him at her pillar, proposes to lay her lengthwise in the fire, and after she has had sufficient time to quake over an idea Messieurs would be nothing loath to put into execution, they burn her nipples for the sake of their convenience; Durcet, her husband, burns one, her father, Curval, burns the other. This exciting operation causes both to discharge.

THE 9TH. 43. *In his young years a pin-pricker, he has got himself a more formidable weapon: discharges while thrice driving a dagger into the woman's heart.*

44. *He used to adore burning gunpowder in the cunt, but has since improved his passion: he attaches a slender but attractive girl to a large rocket, the fuse is ignited, the rocket ascends, then returns to earth with the girl still attached.*

45. *The same personage who put gunpowder in all the orifices of a woman's body, now wedges cartridges into them; they explode simultaneously, sending the members flying in every direction.*

46. *First passion: he enjoyed secreting an emetic in the girl's food, unbeknownst to her; his second passion: he mixes a certain powder with her snuff, or sprinkles it on some flowers, she inhales and straightway falls dead.*

47. *First passion: he would flog her breasts and neck; refinement thereof: he aims a blow of a crowbar at her throat, it fells her forever.*

48. *Duclos spoke of him on the 27th of November, Martaine on the 14th of January* (verify the dates): *the whore enters and shits before the rake, he scolds her; brandishing a whip, he pursues her, she thinks to take refuge in a loft. A door opens, she spies a little stairway, believes she will be safe, rushes up the steps, but one of them gives way and she plunges into a large vat of boiling water; she dies, scalded, drowned, asphyxiated. His tastes are previously to have the woman shit and to lash her while she is doing so.*

Curval had solicited and obtained shit from Zelmire that morning; now, directly the aforementioned tale is concluded, the Duc demands further shit from her. She cannot produce any; she is promptly condemned to have her ass pricked with a golden needle until it is covered with blood; in that it is the Duc whose interests have suffered as a result of her refusal, he is the one who recovers damages.

Curval requests shit of Zéphyr; the latter replies, saying that the Duc had him shit that morning. This the Duc denies, Duclos is called to give evidence, she supports Blangis' contention even though it is false. Consequently, Curval has the right to punish Zéphyr, despite the fact he is the Duc's bardash, just as the Duc has punished Zelmire, who is Curval's wife. The Président flogs Zéphyr until the lad streams blood, then tweaks his nose six times; the tweaks fetch forth more blood, and that makes the Duc roar with laughter.

THE 10TH. Desgranges says that she is now going to discuss murders of imposture and duplicity in which the manner is of principal significance; that is to say, the murder itself is merely incidental. Wherewith, says she, poisonings will be presented first.

49. *A man whose caprice consisted in bum-fuckery and in no other kind, now envenoms all his wives; he is presently on his twenty-second. Never does he fuck them save in the ass, nor have they ever been deflowered otherwise.*

50. *A bugger invites a number of friends to a banquet, and with each succeeding course a few of them are stricken with stomach cramps which prove fatal.*

51. *Duclos spoke of him on the 26th of November, Martaine on the 10th of January; he is a bugger, pretends that it is relief he is giving the poor, distributes food, but 'tis poisoned.*

52. *A treacherous bugger regularly employs a drug which, sprinkled on the ground, very wonderfully kills whosoever walks thereupon; he sprinkles it about rather frequently, and over wide areas.*

53. *A bugger, equally skilled in alchemy, uses another substance which causes death after inconceivable torture; the death throes last a good two weeks, and no doctor has ever been able to diagnose or treat the ailment. He takes the keenest pleasure in paying you a visit while you are in the toils.*

54. *A sodomizer of men and women makes use of yet another powder which deprives you of your senses and renders you as if dead. And such you are believed to be, you are buried, and full of despair, you die in your coffin, into which you have no sooner been placed than you regain consciousness. He endeavors to find the exact place you have been buried, to place an ear to the ground and listen for a few screams; if indeed he hears your cries, 'tis enough to make him swoon with pleasure. He thuswise slew part of his family.*

While joking and making merry that evening, Messieurs give Julie a powder concealed in her food, which causes her frightful cramps; they advise her that she is poisoned, she believes it, she wails, is beside herself. While watching her convulsions, the Duc has Augustine frig him directly opposite Julie. Augustine has the great misfortune of allowing the prepuce to slip back over the Duc's glans, and that is something which displeases the Duc extremely: he was just about to discharge, the girl's carelessness prevents it. He declares he is going to cut off one of that buggress' fingers and, as good as his word, does so, slicing a digit from the hand that failed him, and while cutting, he has his daughter Julie, still persuaded she is poisoned, crawl up to him and complete his discharge. Julie is cured that same evening.

THE 11TH. 55. *A consummate bugger would frequently dine at the home of friends or acquaintances and would never fail to poison the individual his host cherished most dearly amongst all living creatures. He employed a powder which finally slew after causing two days of atrocious agony.*

56. *An erstwhile breast-abuser has perfected his passion: he poisons infants being suckled by their nurses.*

57. *He once used to love to receive back into his mouth milk enemas he had injected into his partner's rectum; his later passion: he administers toxic injections which kill while causing horrible spasms and colics.*

58. *A crafty bugger of whom she will have occasion to say more on the 13th and the 26th, used to love to set fire to poor-houses, and would always see to it that a quantity of persons were consumed, above all children.*

59. *Another bugger liked to cause women to die in childbirth; he would come to pay his respects, bringing along a powder whose odor would cause spasms and convulsions ending in death.*

60. *The man to whom Duclos referred during her twenty-eighth evening enjoys watching a woman bear a child; he murders it immediately it emerges from the womb and within full view of the mother, and does so while feigning to caress it.*

That evening, Adelaide is first dealt a hundred lashes by each friend, and then, when she is well bloodied, shit is demanded of her; she gave some that morning to Curval, who swears 'tis not so. Consequently, they burn her two breasts, the palm of each hand, spill drops of molten sealing wax upon her thighs and belly, fill her navel therewith, burn her pubic hair after having doused it with cognac. The Duc attempts to pick a quarrel with Zelmire, and the Président severs a finger from each of her hands. Augustine is scourged about the cunt and asshole.

THE 12TH. Messieurs assemble in the morning and decide that the four governesses, who are no longer of much use to the society and whose functions the four storytellers shall henceforth be perfectly able to carry out, may just as well provide the society with a little amusement; Messieurs therefore decree that the elders shall be martyrized one after another, the first sacrifice being scheduled for the evening of that same day. The four storytellers are invited to replace the elders; they accept upon condition they shall suffer no illtreatment. Messieurs promise to subject them to none.

61. *The three friends, d'Aucourt, the abbot, and Desprès, of whom Duclos spoke on the 12th of November, are now living abroad and still enjoying each other's company, and this is one of their common passions: they require a woman whose pregnancy is in its eighth or begun its ninth month, they open her belly, snatch out the child, burn it before the mother's eyes, and in its place substitute a package containing sulphur and quicksilver, which they set afire, then stitch the belly up again, leaving the mother thus to perish in the midst of incredible agonies, while they look on and have themselves frigged by the girl they have with them.* (Verify the girl's name.)

62. *He was fond of depucelating, has gradually broadened his scope of activity: he has a great number of children by several women, then, when they reach the age of five or six, he depucelates them, boys and girls alike, and directly he has fucked them, throws them into a blazing oven. Or he sometimes throws them in at the same moment he discharges.*

63. *The man Duclos mentioned on the 27th of November, Martaine on the 15th of January, and she herself on the 5th of February, whose taste was to play at hanging, to see hanged, etc., this same fellow, I say, hides some of his personal effects in his domestics' wardrobes and declares he has been robbed. He strives to have his servants hanged, and if he succeeds goes to watch the spectacle; if not, he locks them in a room and strangles them to death. While operating, he discharges.*

64. *An inveterate shit-lover, he of whom Duclos spoke on the 14th of November, has a specially prepared commode at his home; he engages his intended victim to sit down upon it, and once the victim is seated, the seat buckles, gives way, and precipitates the sitter into a very deep ditch filled with shit, in which environment she is left to die.*

65. *A man to whom Martaine made reference and who would amuse himself watching a girl fall from a ladder, has perfected his passion thus* (but find out which man) :

*He situates the girl upon a little trestle on the edge of a deep ditch filled with water; on the farther side of it is a wall which seems to be all the more inviting, what for the ladder leaning against it. But to reach the ladder she must cross the moat, and she becomes all the more willing to spring into the water as the fire burning behind the trestle moves gradually closer to her. If she hesitates too long, the fire will reach her, consume her, and as she does not know how to swim, she will be drowned if she plunges into the water. While she is considering what to do, the fire approaches, and she finally elects to struggle with a different element and endeavor to get to the wall. It frequently happens that she drowns; if so, the game is over. But if by good fortune she reaches the other bank and then the ladder, and starts to climb it, toward the top there is a rung which breaks beneath her weight and she drops into a hole covered over with a thin layer of earth, and the hole contains a bed of live coals upon which she perishes. Hard by the scene, the libertine observes it with the keenest interest, frigging himself industriously.*

66. *The same man Duclos spoke of on the 29th of November, the same who bumwise depucelated Martaine when a little girl of*

*five, and also the same with whom Desgranges announces she will conclude her narrations* (the hell episode), *this individual, I say, embuggers the prettiest girl of sixteen or eighteen the procuress can find for him. Sensing his crisis about to arrive, he releases a spring, upon the bare and completely unadorned neck of the girl descends a machine furnished with steel teeth; the machine begins to move laterally and gradually saws through the pinioned neck while the libertine occupies himself with completing his discharge. Which always takes a very long time.*

That very evening Messieurs discover the intrigue involving Augustine and one of the subaltern fuckers; he has not yet fucked her, but to attain his ends has suggested that they both escape from the castle, and he has outlined to her a very easy way to do so. Augustine confesses that she was about to grant him what he sought from her in order to save herself from a place where she believes her life to be in danger. 'Tis Fanchon who discovers and reports everything. The traitorous quadrumvirate leap upon the fucker without warning, bind him hand and foot, and take him down to the cellars, where the Duc embuggers him with extreme vigor and without pomade, while the Président saws through his neck and the other two apply red-hot irons to all parts of his body.

This scene transpires directly after dinner is over and hence coffee is omitted that day; the work completed, everyone repairs to the auditorium as usual, then to supper, and amongst themselves Messieurs debate whether, in return for having disclosed the conspiracy, they ought not accord Fanchon a reprieve, for their decision that morning was to maltreat her the same evening. The Bishop declares himself against sparing her, and says that it would be unworthy of them to yield to the sentiment of gratitude, and that, for his part, he will always be seen to favor any decision likely to afford the society one pleasure more, just as he will always vote against any motion apt to deprive it of a pleasure. And so, after having punished Augustine for lending herself to the subversive scheme, first by obliging her to watch her lover's execution, then by embuggering her and making her believe her head would be cut off as well, next by actually pulling out two of her teeth, an operation performed by the Duc while Curval was embuggering that beautiful girl, finally by giving her a sound whipping, after all that, I say, Fanchon is led into the arena, made to shit, given a hundred lashes by each of the friends, and then the Duc deftly shaves off her left nipple. She raises a storm, criticizing their behavior toward her and describing it as unjust. "Were it just," says the Duc, wiping his razor, "it would surely fail to give us an erection." Whereupon they dress the old whore's wounds, eager to preserve her for further ordeals.

Their Lordships perceive that indeed there had been faint but definite rebellious stirrings amongst the subaltern fuckers; the prompt sacrifice of one of them has, however, thoroughly quelled their murmurs. Like Fanchon, the three other duennas are divested of all responsibility, removed from office, and replaced by the four storytellers and Julie. They tremble, do the old dames; but by what shifts are they to escape their fate?

THE 13TH. 67. *A great connoisseur of the ass, he declares his love for a girl and, having arranged a boating party, lures her upon the water in a small boat, the which has been prepared for the outing, springs a leak, founders; the girl is drowned. He sometimes pursues his objective by different means: will, for example, lead a girl out upon a high balcony, have her lean upon the railing, which gives way; and once again the girl dies.*

68. *A man, while making his apprenticeship in life, was content first to whip and then to embugger; now, having reached a mature age, entices the girl to enter a specially prepared room; a trap door yields beneath her step, she falls into a cellar where the rake awaits her; he plunges a knife into her breasts, her cunt, and into her asshole as she lies stunned by her fall. Next, he casts her, dead or still alive, into another cellar, over which a stone drops into place; she tumbles upon a heap of other corpses, and she expires in a great fit if life has not already departed her sore-beset frame. And he is very careful to administer delicate stabs, for he would prefer that she live a little and finally perish in the cellar mentioned latterly. Prior to all this, he of course embuggers and flogs her and discharges; 'tis coolly and with utmost method he proceeds to her undoing.*

69. *A bugger has the girl mount astride an untamed, unbroken horse which unseats her, drags her along a rocky terrain, and finally pitches her over a precipice.*

70. *Martaine's hero of the 18th of January whose juvenile passion was to distribute little mounds of gunpowder upon the girl's body, has made significant progress. He lays the girl in a special bed; when properly tucked in, the bed gives way, dropping her into a large brazier of live coals, but she is able to scramble out of it; however, he is standing by and, as she repeats her attempts to escape the fire, he drives her back, wielding a pitchfork and with it aiming stout blows at her belly.*

71. *The gentleman she mentioned on the 11th, who likes to burn down poorhouses, endeavors to lure a beggar, whether a man or a woman, from out of one and into his own home, upon the pretense of bestowing charity; he embuggers his victim, then breaks his back and leaves him thus discomfited to die in a dungeon.*

72. *He who was wont to defenestrate a woman, hurling her upon a dung heap, the same man of whom Martaine spoke, by way of second passion executes the following one: he allows the girl to sleep in a room she is acquainted with and whose window she knows to be not far above the ground; she is given opium, when in a deep slumber she is conveyed to another chamber, identical with the first but having a window high above the ground which, on this side of the house, is strewn with sharp rocks. Next, the libertine enters where she lies sleeping, makes a dreadful noise, terrifies her; she is informed that she is about to die. Knowing the drop from the window to the ground to be short, she leaps through it, but falls thirty feet and lands upon the murderous rocks, killing herself. No one has so much as laid a finger upon her.*

In the character of a woman, that great histrionic, the Bishop, marries Antinoüs, whose role is that of a husband, and also weds Céladon, whom he takes to be his wife, and 'tis that evening the child is embuggered for the first time.

This ceremony celebrates the festival of the fifteenth week; to complete the holiday, the prelate wishes to expose Aline to some

severe vexations, for his libertine rage against her has been quietly
but steadily mounting: she is hanged, then quickly cut down, but
while seeing her however briefly aloft, everyone discharges. Durcet
opens her veins, this treatment restores her to life; the next day
she appears none the worse for wear, but suspension has added an
inch to her height; she relates what she experienced during the
ordeal. The Bishop, for whom everything is an occasion of jollity
and everyone the object of game that day, cuts one of old Louison's
nipples clean off her breast; whereupon the other two duennas see
very clearly what their fate is to be.

THE 14TH. 73. *A man whose simple taste was to flog a girl,
perfects it by every day removing morsels of flesh the size of a pea
from the girl's body, but her wounds are not dressed, and thus she
perishes over a low fire, as it were.*

Desgranges announces that she will now deal with exceedingly
painful murders wherein 'tis the extreme cruelty which comprises
the main element; Messieurs more strongly than ever urge her to
furnish abundant details.

74. *He who was fond of letting blood daily relieves his victim of a half ounce of it, continuing till she is dead. Messieurs greet
this example with hearty applause.*

75. *He who was wont to prick the ass with many pins every
day administers a more or less superficial gash with a poignard.
The blood is stanched, but the wound is not treated, neither does
it mend, and thus 'tis a slow death she dies. A fustigator (75)
quietly and slowly saws off all four limbs, one after the other.*

76. *The Marquis de Mesanges, of whom Duclos spoke in connection with the shoemaker Petignon's daughter, bought by the
Marquis from Duclos, and whose first passion was to undergo four
hours of flogging without discharging, for a second passion places
a little girl in the hands of a giant fellow who holds the child by the
head over a large charcoal brazier which burns her very slowly;
the victims must be virgins.*

77. *His first passion: little by little to burn the breasts and buttocks with the flame of a match; his second: over every part of the girl's body to plant a forest of sulphur-coated slivers, which he lights one by one. He watches her die in this way.*

"Nor is there any more painful way to die," observes the Duc, who then confesses to having surrendered himself to this infamous pastime, and to having discharged vigorously thanks to it. They say that the patient lives six hours, sometimes eight.

Céladon's ass is made generally available that evening; the Duc and Curval indulge themselves heavily. Constance's pregnancy is still on the Président's mind; he suggests that she be bled, and bleeds her himself while discharging in Céladon's ass, then he lops off one of Thérèse's nipples while embuggering Zelmire, and the Duc sodomizes the duenna during the amputation.

THE 15TH. 78. *Once beguiled by the charms of a mouth to suck and saliva to swallow, he is now of sterner stuff: every day he inserts a funnel into the girl's mouth and pours a small dose of molten lead down her throat; she gives up the ghost on the ninth day.*

79. *First a finger-twister, he currently breaks all her limbs, tears out her tongue, gouges out her eyes, and leaves her thus to live, diminishing her sustenance day by day.*

80. *A perpetrator of sacrilege, the second one Martaine mentioned on the 3rd of January, he secures a beautiful youth to a tall cross, binding him with cords and leaving him there as food for ravens.*

81. *An armpit-sniffer and -fucker, to whom Duclos alluded, binds a woman hand and foot and hangs her by a rope looped under her arms; he goes every day to prick some part of her body so that the blood will attract flies; her death is by slow degrees.*

82. *A passionate admirer of asses rectifies his worship: he now seals a girl in an underground cave where she has food to last*

*three days; before leaving her, he inflicts several wounds upon her body, thuswise to render her death more painful. He wishes to have them virgins and spends a week embracing their asses before organizing their destruction.*

83. *Formerly he loved to fuck very youthful mouths and asses; his later improvement consists in snatching out the heart of a living girl, widening the space that organ occupied, fucking the warm hole, replacing the heart in that pool of blood and fuck, sewing up the wound, and leaving the girl to her fate, without help of any kind. In which case the wait is not long.*

Still wroth with the lovely Constance, Curval maintains that there is no reason under the sun why one cannot successfully bear a child even though one has a broken limb, and therefore they fracture that unlucky creature's arm the same evening. Durcet slices off one of Marie's nipples after she has been well warmed by the lash and made copiously to shit.

THE 16TH. 84. *A fustigator refines his passion: he learns and then practices the art of gently removing flesh from bones; he then extracts the marrow, usually by sucking it out, and pours molten lead into the cavity.*

At this point the Duc loudly exclaims that he'll not fuck another ass while he lives if that isn't the very ordeal he has had in mind for his beloved Augustine; that poor girl, whom Blangis has been embuggering for some time, utters cries and sheds a torrent of tears. And as thanks to her misbehavior she interferes with his discharge and frustrates it effectively, he withdraws, takes hold of his engine in one hand, and while with the other he gives her a dozen slaps which resound through that wing of the castle, he manages his discharge very satisfactorily by himself.

85. *A bugger uses an ingenious machine to chop the girl into small pieces: this is a Chinese torture.*

86. *Weary of his early fondness for girls' pucelages, his latest passion is to impale a girl upon the point of a sharp pickaxe intro-*

*duced into her cunt; there she sits, as if upon a horse, he ties a cannon ball to each of her legs, the pick works deeper, and she is left to her own devices and a slow death.*

87. *A fustigator flays the girl thrice over; he soaks her fourth layer of skin with a devouring escharotic which brings about death accompanied by hideous agonies.*

88. *His first passion was to sever a finger; his second is to pluck up some flesh with a pair of red-hot tongs, to cut off the flesh with a pair of scissors, then to burn the wound. He is quite apt to spend as long as four or five days whittling away a girl's body piecemeal, and she ordinarily dies while the cruel operation is still advancing.*

Sophie and Céladon have been found amusing themselves together and are punished that evening; both are whipped over their entire bodies by the Bishop, whose chattels they are. Sophie loses two fingers to the shears, Céladon as many; but he recovers very quickly. The Bishop is no less eager to use them in his pleasures, however they be maimed.

Fanchon returns to the center of the stage. After having been beaten with a bull's pizzle, the soles of her feet are burned, each thigh, before and behind, is burned also, her forehead too, and each hand as well, and Messieurs extract all her remaining teeth. The Duc's prick is almost continually wedged into her ass throughout this lengthy operation.

Mention that it has been prescribed by law that a subject's buttocks shall be left intact until the day the said subject reaches the end of his career.

THE 17TH. 89. *Martaine's gentleman of the 30th of January and the same one she herself described on the 5th of February, pares away a girl's breasts and buttocks, eats them, and upon her wounds puts plasters which so violently burn the flesh that they are her undoing. He also forces her to eat her own flesh, which he has had grilled.*

90. *A bugger cooks up a little girl in a double boiler.*

91. *A bugger: he has her roasted alive on a spit directly after embuggering her.*

92. *A man whose initial passion was to hăve little girls and boys embuggered in his presence by massive and ponderous pricks, impales the girl, a spear in her ass, and leaves her thus to die while he studies her contortions.*

93. *Another bugger: attaches a woman to a wheel, it is then set in motion and, without having done her any previous harm, he allows her to die a very pretty death.*

That evening, the Bishop, his spirits in a great ferment, wishes to have Aline tormented, his rage against her has reached its fever pitch. She makes her appearance naked, he has her shit and embuggers her, then, without discharging, he withdraws in a towering fury from that enchanting ass and injects a rinse of boiling water into it, obliging her to squirt it out at once, while it is still boiling hot, upon Thérèse's face. After that, Messieurs hack off all the fingers and toes Aline has left, break both her arms and burn them with red-hot pokers. She is next flogged, beaten, and slapped, then the Bishop, still further aroused, cuts off one of her nipples, and discharges.

Wherewith they transfer their attentions to Thérèse, the interior of her vagina is seared, her nostrils, tongue, feet, and hands are all burned too; then she is given six hundred lashes with a bull's pizzle. Out come the rest of her teeth, fire is introduced into her throat. A witness to these harsh proceedings, Augustine falls to weeping; the Duc lashes her belly and cunt until he has drawn a suitable amount of blood therefrom.

THE 18TH. 94. *A flesh-scarifier in his early days, his adult entertainment consists in quartering girls by bending four saplings, attaching an arm or leg to each, and releasing the trees, which spring back erect.*

95. *A fustigator suspends her from a machine which lowers a girl into and immediately lifts her out of a fire, then repeats the operation until there is very little left of the patient.*

96. *He once loved to extinguish candles by snuffing them out upon flesh; today, he envelopes her in sulphur and uses her for a torch, being careful to prevent the fumes from choking her.*

97. *A sodomist: rips the intestines from a young boy and a young girl, puts the boy's into the girl, inserts the girl's into the boy's body, stitches up the incisions, ties them back to back to a pillar which supports them both, and he watches them perish.*

98. *A man who was fond of inflicting light burns, improves his passion: he now roasts his victim upon a grill, turning him over and over again.*

Michette is, that evening, exposed to the libertines' fury; all four begin by whipping her, then each tears out one of her teeth, they cut off four fingers (each friend amputates one), her thighs are burned in four places, two in front and two behind, the Duc manhandles one of her breasts until it is truly unrecognizable, sodomizing Giton in the meantime.

Louison is next on the bill of fare; she is made to shit, she is given eight hundred strokes with the bull's pizzle, she is divested of all her teeth, her tongue is burned, as is her asshole, her vagina, and her remaining nipple, and so are six places upon her thighs.

When everyone has retired to bed for the night, the Bishop goes in search of his brother, they wake Desgranges and Duclos, and the four of them take Aline down into the cellars; the Bishop embuggers her, the Duc embuggers her, they pronounce the death sentence, and by means of excessive torments which last until daybreak, they execute it. Upon returning, they exchange words of unqualified praise for these two storytellers and advise their colleagues to undertake no serious projects without their help.

THE 19TH. 99. *He places the woman so that the base of her spine bears upon the sharpened head of a tall post, her four limbs are held in the air only by light cords; the effects of her suffering make the lecher laugh incontinently, the torture is frightful.*

100. *A man who used to enjoy cutting small steaks from the girl's rump has become absolutely a butcher: he has the girl sand-*

*wiched between two heavy planks, then slowly and carefully sawed in two.*

101. *An embuggerer of both sexes has brother and sister fetched in; he declares to the brother that he is about to die a horrible death, and shows the young man all the deployed tackle he proposes to use; however, the libertine continues, he will save the brother's life if he will fuck his sister and strangle her at once. The young man agrees, and while he fucks his sister, the libertine embuggers now one of them, now the other. Then the brother, fearing for his life, deprives his sister of hers, and the moment he completes that operation, both he and his dead sister tumble through a trap door into a capacious charcoal brazier, wherein the libertine watches them be consumed.*

102. *A bugger compels a father to fuck his daughter in his presence. Next, the father holds the daughter, the bugger sodomizes her; after which he informs the father that the girl absolutely has to perish, but that he has the alternatives of killing her himself by strangling her, which will cause her little suffering, or, in that other case, if he prefers not to kill his daughter, then he, the libertine, will do the work, but the father shall have to witness it all, and his child's agonies will be atrocious.*

*Rather than see her undergo frightful tortures, the father decides to kill his daughter with a noose of black silk, but while he is preparing to dispatch her, he is seized, bound, and before his eyes his child is flayed alive, then rolled upon burning iron nails, then cast into a brazier, and the father is strangled; this, says the libertine, is to teach him a lesson not to be so eager to choke the life out of his own children, for 'tis barbaric. Afterward, he is dumped into the same brazier wherein his daughter perished.*

103. *A great devotee of asses and of the lash brings together mother and daughter. He tells the girl that he is going to kill her mother if she, the girl, does not consent to the sacrifice of both her hands; the little one agrees, they are severed at the wrist. Whereupon these two creatures are separated; a rope suspended from the ceiling is slipped around the girl's neck, she stands upon a stool; another cord runs from the stool into the next room and the mother*

*is requested to hold the end. She is then invited to tug on the cord: she pulls it without knowing what she is doing, she is led directly into the first room to contemplate her work, and during that moment of her keenest distress, she is smitten down by a saber blow aimed at her head from behind.*

Jealous of the pleasure the two brothers had the night before, Durcet, that evening, is moved to suggest that they vex Adelaide, whose turn, he assures the society, is soon to come. And so Curval, her father, and Durcet, her husband, worry her thighs with white-hot tongs while the Duc's unlubricated member sounds her ass. The tip of her tongue is pierced, the ends of both her ears are shorn away, with the aid of instruments Messieurs dispossess her of four teeth, and then she is given a savage whipping. That same evening, the Bishop bleeds Sophie while her dearly beloved friend, Adelaide, watches the blood issue from the child's veins; the fountains are kept turned on until Sophie loses consciousness; as he bleeds her, the Bishop embuggers her, remaining in her ass throughout the operation.

While Curval is sodomizing him, Narcisse loses a pair of fingers, then Marie is hailed into court, red-hot irons are thrust into her cunt and asshole, more irons are applied to six places upon her thighs, upon her clitoris, her tongue, upon her one remaining breast, and out come the remainder of her teeth.

THE 20TH. 104. *Champville's of the 5th of December, the man who was wont to have the mother prostitute her son and hold him while he embuggered the lad, improves his taste by bringing the mother and son together. He tells the mother that he is about to kill her, but will spare her if she will murder her son. In case she refuses to do so, he slits the boy's throat before the woman's eyes. Or if she consents: then she is bound to her son's dead body and left quietly to meditate and finally to die.*

105. *A very incestuous personage assembles two sisters after having embuggered both of them; he binds them to a machine, each has a knife in her hand: the machine is set in motion, the girls are brought suddenly together and mutually kill each other.*

106. *Another devotee of incest requires a mother and her four children. They are locked into a room; he observes them through a small barred window. He gives them nothing to eat in order to study the effects of famine upon this woman, and to discover which of her children she will eat first.*

107. *Champville's of the 29th of December, who liked to flog pregnant women, calls for a mother and daughter, both of whom must be gravid: they are tied to a pair of steel plates one set above the other; the women face one another; the machine starts, the jaws of the vise close with great speed and power, the two women are ground to dust, together with their fruit.*

108. *A very buggerish gentleman entertains himself in the following manner: he assembles lover and mistress:*
*"There is in all the world but one person who stands in the way of your happiness," says he, taking the lover aside; "I am going to put that individual in your power."*
*And he leads him into an obscurely lit chamber containing a bed; upon it someone lies asleep. Greatly aroused, the young man takes dagger in hand and stabs his enemy. When he has had done, he is permitted to recognize his mistress' dead body: 'twas she he slew; he kills himself in despair, or if he does not, the libertine kills him with a shot from a rifle, fired at a distance, not daring to enter the room with the furious young man who still has a weapon in his hand. Previously, he fucked the youth and his beloved too, they singly yielded to him in the hope he would help them and bring them together, it is after having enjoyed them he rids the world of them.*

In celebration of the sixteenth week, Durcet, as a woman, marries Invictus, who enacts a masculine role; and as a man he takes Hyacinthe to be his wife; the ceremonies are performed that evening and, by way of festivity, Durcet wishes to torment Fanny, his feminine wife. Consequently, her arms are burned, so are her thighs in six separate places, two teeth are extracted from her mouth, she is flogged; Hyacinthe, who loves her and who is her husband thanks to the voluptuous arrangements hitherto described, Hyacinthe, I say, is obliged to shit into Fanny's mouth, and she to eat the turd.

The Duc pulls out one of Augustine's teeth and immediately afterward fucks her in the mouth. Fanchon reappears, she is bled, and while blood flows from her arm, her arm is broken; next, they remove her toenails and sever the fingers from both her hands.

THE 21ST. She announces that the following examples are of buggers who wish to commit exclusively masculine murders.

109. *He buries the muzzle of a shotgun in the boy's ass, the weapon is loaded with buckshot and he has just finished fucking the lad. He pulls the trigger; the gun and his prick discharge simultaneously.*

110. *He obliges the lad to watch his mistress being mutilated, and to eat her flesh, principally her buttocks, breasts, and heart. He has the option of eating these meats, or of dying of hunger. As soon as he has devoured them, if 'tis that he elects to do, the libertine inflicts several deep wounds upon him and leaves him thus to bleed to death; if he abstains from eating, he then starves to death.*

111. *He tears off the youth's testicles and, a short while later, serves them up to him in a ragout, then, in place of the stolen treasure, substitutes spheres of quicksilver and fills his voided scrotum with sulphur a-plenty, which cause such violent suffering that the patient succumbs. During his agony, the libertine embuggers him and increases the boy's trouble by burning him here, there and everywhere with sulphur-impregnated slivers, and by scratching, picking, and further burning these wounds.*

112. *He drives a long spike through the victim's asshole and thus nails him to a slender pole, and leaves him to sigh away his last hours, or days.*

113. *He embuggers, and whilst sodomizing, opens the cranium, removes the brain, and fills the cavity with molten lead.*

Vigorously fustigated beforehand, Hyacinthe's ass is made generally available that evening. Narcisse is presented to the assembly: off come his balls with a snip of the scissors. Adelaide is summoned forth, a red-hot fire shovel is brushed over the rear of her thighs, they burn her clitoris, pierce her tongue, lash her breasts with cruel instruments, cut off the two little buttons on her breasts, break both her arms, carve away her remaining fingers, tear the hair from her cunt, tear a handful of hair from her head, pull out six of her teeth. Thus discomfited, she causes Messieurs to discharge every one save the Duc who, his livid prick straining upward, demands leave to exercise Thérèse all alone. Leave so to do is accorded him; using a pocketknife, he pries out all her nails and, as he proceeds, burns her fingers with a candle, then he fractures one of her arms, and still he does not discharge; very wroth, he leaps upon Augustine, encunts her and tears out one of her teeth as he spills his seed into her womb.

THE 22ND. 114. *He breaks a young boy on the rack, then affixes him to a wheel upon which he is left to expire: upon the wheel he is turned in such a way as to expose his buttocks, and the scoundrel, his tormentor, has his table set beneath the wheel, and dines there every day until the patient is no more.*

115. *He flays a young boy, rubs his body with honey, and invites the flies to the feast.*

116. *He slices off his prick and breasts, nails one of his feet to a post, one of his hands to another post, and thus he is left to expire with however little dignity.*

117. *The same man who had made Duclos take supper with his dogs, owns a lion too, and, arming a boy with a light stick, introduces the youngster into the lion's cage. The boy's defense only further arouses the animal; the libertine watches the contest and discharges when the loser is completely devoured.*

118. *Clothed in a mare's skin, his asshole smeared with mare's fuck, a small boy is surrendered to an excited horse. The libertine observes their struggles and the boy's death.*

Giton is subjected to tortures that evening: the Duc, Curval, Hercule, and Bum-Cleaver penetrate his ass ungreased. He is whipped very lustily, Messieurs extract four of his teeth, cut off four of his fingers (as always, each friend has a share in the despoiling of the victim), and Durcet crushes one of his balls between thumb and forefinger. All four gentlemen soundly flog Augustine. Her glorious ass is soon washed in blood, the Duc embuggers her while Curval severs one of her fingers, then Curval marches into the breach while the Duc six times sears her thighs with a hot iron; Blangis snips away yet another finger the same instant his colleague discharges, and despite all this rough treatment, she spends the night, a stormy one, in the Duc's bed. Marie sustains a broken arm, her fingernails are drawn out, her fingers burned.

That same night, Durcet and Curval, seconded by Desgranges and Duclos, accompany Adelaide to the cellars. Curval gives her a farewell embuggering, then they cause her to die in the throes of terrible sufferings, which you will give in full detail.

THE 23RD. 119. *He places a young boy in a machine which stretches him, dislocating his bones; he is meticulously and thoroughly broken, then removed from the machine, given a chance to recover his breath, exposed to the process again; and so it continues for several days, until the patient's death.*

120. *He has a pretty girl pollute and fatigue a young boy; he is drained very dry indeed, but still the girl toils over him, he is given no nourishment, and eventually dies in horrible convulsions.*

121. *In the space of a single day, he performs four operations upon the young man: a gallstone removal, a trepanning, the excision of a fistula in the eye, of one in the anus. He knows just enough about surgery to botch all four operations; then he abandons the patient, giving him no further help and watching him expire.*

122. *After having sheared off the boy's prick and balls, using a red-hot iron he hollows out a cunt in the place formerly occupied by his genitals; the iron makes the hole and cauterizes simul-*

*taneously: he fucks the patient's new orifice and strangles him with his hands upon discharging.*

123. *He massages him with a currycomb; when he has generally abraded his flesh in this fashion, he rubs him with alcohol, ignites it, resumes his combing, rubs again with alcohol, relights the torch, proceeding in this wise till death makes further care unnecessary.*

That same evening, Narcisse's turn arrives to be vexed; fire is applied to his thighs and little prick, then Messieurs crush his two balls.

They turn again to Augustine upon the recommendation of the Duc, whose spiteful attitude toward her seems only to have worsened; they burn her thighs and armpits, a very hot bar of iron is rammed into her cunt. She faints, the Duc waxes all the more furious, he shears off one of her nipples, drinks her blood, breaks both her arms, and tears out her cunt hair, all her teeth, and cuts off every finger left on her hands, cauterizing the wounds with fire. And once again 'tis in his bed she sleeps, or rather lies, that night, for if one is to believe Duclos, he fucks her fore and aft the whole night long, repeatedly telling her that the day about to dawn will be her last.

Louison appears, they break one of her arms, burn her tongue, her clitoris, tear out all her nails, and burn the tips of her bleeding fingers. Curval sodomizes her in this state and, in his rage, twists and manhandles one of Zelmire's breasts while discharging. Not content with those abuses, he catches hold of her again and whips her until he cannot lift his arm.

THE 24TH. 124. *The same man Martaine referred to on the 1st of January wishes to embugger the father while his two children observe, and as he discharges, he stabs one child to death with one hand, and with his other strangles the second.*

125. *His first passion was to flog the bellies of pregnant women; his second is to assemble six of them whose pregnancy has reached the end of the eight month: he ties them back to back, their*

*bellies prominently thrust forward: he splits open the belly of the first, perforates the belly of the second with dagger thrusts, gives a hundred kicks to the third's, a hundred blows of a club deflates the belly of the fourth, he burns the fifth's, applies a rasp to the sixth's, and then, using a truncheon upon her belly, he finishes off whichever amongst them has survived her treatment.*

Curval interrupts the narrations with some furious scene or other, this passion having had a great effect upon his mind.

126. *The seducer mentioned by Duclos assembles two women. Says he to the first: "Deny God and religion if you wish to live," but his valet has whispered to her, telling her to say nothing, for if she does, she shall surely be killed, but by keeping silent she shall have nothing to fear. Hence, she is mute; he blows out her brains, murmuring, "There's one for God." He calls the second; struck by the example of the first and remembering what she has been told before entering the room, that she has no choice but to renounce belief in God and religion if she is to save herself, she assents to all he proposes: he blows out her brains: "And there's another for the Devil." The villain plays that little game every week.*

127. *He is a great bugger and he is fond of giving dances, but the ceiling in the salon is of a special order, it collapses as soon as the room is filled, and nearly everyone perishes. Were he to remain living in the same city for any length of time, he would be detected, but he moves frequently; he is eventually found out, but only after having given his fiftieth dance.*

128. *Martaine's of the 27th of January, whose taste is to promote abortions, establishes three pregnant women in three cruel postures, composing an artistic group. Thus situated, they give birth while he looks on, then he ties each infant to its mother's neck until the little creature either dies or is eaten, for the libertine keeps the women just where they are and gives them no food. The same personage has yet another passion: he has two women whelp in his presence, blindfolds them, and after having himself identified the infants by some mark, he puts them side by side and bids each woman go and recover each her own offspring; if the ladies are not*

*mistaken, he permits their young to live, but if they are in error, he
carves up the children with a saber.*

Narcisse is presented at the evening orgies. While the Bishop
sodomizes the little fellow, Durcet relieves him of his remaining
digits and inserts a red-hot needle into his urethral canal. They bid
Giton step forth, he is kicked about, 'tis a lively game of ball they
play with him, three of the friends fracture one of his legs while
the Duc embuggers him.

Zelmire's turn: they roast her clitoris, sear her tongue, bake
her gums, extract four of her teeth, burn her thighs in six places
before and behind, snip away her nipples, unfinger both her hands,
and when she is thus prepared to afford pleasure, Curval embuggers
her. But he does not discharge.

Up steps Fanchon. Their attentions cost her an eye.

Escorted by Desgranges and Duclos, the Duc and Curval make
a journey to the cellars with Augustine in the course of that night;
her ass has been preserved in excellent condition, 'tis now lashed to
tatters, then the two brothers alternately embugger her, but guard
their seed, and then the Duc gives her fifty-eight wounds in the
buttocks, pours boiling oil into each gash. He drives a hot iron into
her cunt, another into her ass, and fucks her wounded charms, his
prick sheathed in a sealskin condom which worsens the already
lamentable state of her privities. That accomplished, the flesh is
peeled away from the bones of her arms and legs, which bones are
sawed in several different places, then her nerves are laid bare in
four adjacent places, the nerve ends are tied to a short stick which,
like a tourniquet, is twisted, thus drawing forth the aforesaid
nerves, which are very delicate parts of the human anatomy and,
which, when mistreated, cause the patient to suffer much. Augustine's agonies are unheard-of.

She is given some respite and allowed to recruit her strength,
then Messieurs resume work, but this time, as the nerves are pulled
into sight, they are scraped with the blade of a knife. The friends
complete that operation and now move elsewhere; a hole is bored
in her throat, her tongue is drawn back, down, and passed through
it, 'tis a comical effect, they broil her remaining breast, then, clutching a scalpel, the Duc thrusts his hand into her cunt and cuts

through the partition dividing the anus from the vagina; he throws aside the scalpel, reintroduces his hand, and rummaging about in her entrails, forces her to shit through her cunt, another amusing stunt; then, availing himself of the same entrance, he reaches up and tears open her stomach. Next, they concentrate upon her visage: cut away her ears, burn her nasal passages, blind her eyes with molten sealing wax, girdle her cranium, hang her by the hair, attach heavy stones to her feet, and allow her to drop: the top of the skull remains dangling.

She was still breathing when she fell, and the Duc encunted her in this sorry state; he discharged and came away only the more enraged. They split her belly, opened her, and applied fire to her entrails; scalpel in hand, the Président burrows in her chest and harasses her heart, puncturing it in several places. 'Twas only then her soul fled her body; at the age of fifteen years and eight months thus perished one of the most heavenly creatures ever formed by Nature's skillful hand. Etc. Her eulogy.

THE 25TH. That morning, the Duc takes Colombe to be his wife and hereafter she performs all a wife's functions.

129. *A great connoisseur of the ass and a man mightily fond thereof, he embuggers the mistress while the lover looks on, then the lover while his mistress watches, then he nails the lover over the mistress' body and leaves them to expire, mouth to mouth.*

Such will be the end of Céladon and Sophie, who are in love, and Messieurs interrupt the storyteller to oblige Céladon himself to spread a little hot sealing wax on his dear Sophie's thighs; while obeying instructions, he collapses: while lying unconscious, he is embuggered by the Bishop.

130. *He who was wont to amuse himself by throwing a girl into water and pulling her out, has as his second passion that of casting seven or eight whores into a pond and watching them thrash about, for they are poor swimmers. He tenders them an iron pike, but it is heated red hot; still they cling to it, but he thrusts them*

*away, and that they the more certainly perish, he has amputated
one limb from each of them before throwing them in.*

131. *His earlier caprice was to cause vomiting; his improvement thereof is, by using a secret means, to spread the plague
throughout an entire province: he has brought about the death of
a truly incredible number of people. He also poisons wells and
streams.*

132. *Fond of employing the whip, he has three pregnant
women locked in an iron cage, and with them he imprisons their
three children; a fire is lit beneath the cage, its occupants caper and
dance more and more in earnest as the floor heats; the women take
the children in their arms, and finally fall and die in this manner.*

(That one belongs somewhere further above; move it to its proper
place.)

133. *'Twas he who pricked with an awl; more of a man today,
he seals a pregnant woman in a chest whose interior is studded with
sharp nails; he then has the chest rolled and dragged through the
garden.*

These tales of pregnant women being chastised have proven
as woeful to Constance's ears as they have delighted Curval's; she
sees only too well what the future holds in store for her. As her
fatal hour is drawing nigh, Messieurs are of the opinion her vexations may be inaugurated: her thighs are burned in six places, molten wax is allowed to trickle upon her navel, and her breasts are
teased with pins.

Giton appears, a burning needle is run through his little member, his little balls are stabbed, four of his teeth are extracted.

Then comes Zelmire, whose death is not far off; deep into her
cunt runs a red-hot poker, six wounds are inflicted upon her breasts,
a dozen upon her thighs, needles are driven far into her navel, each
friend bestows twenty strong blows upon her face. They forcibly
remove four of her teeth, her eye is pricked, she is whipped, she is
embuggered. While in the act of sodomizing her, Curval, her
husband, gives her intelligence of her death, scheduled for the

morrow; she declares she is not sorry to learn the tidings, for 'twill put a period to her sorrows.

Rosette steps forward; four teeth are jerked from her mouth, each of her shoulders is branded, her thighs and calves are gashed and hacked; she is then embuggered while several hands worry her breasts.

And now Thérèse advances; out comes an eye, a hundred blows of the bull's pizzle rain down upon her scrawny back.

THE 26TH. 134. *A bugger takes his stand at the foot of a tower; the earth about him is studded with sharpened steel rods pointing upward; his associates pitch several children of both sexes from the top of the tower. He has previously embuggered them, and now enjoys seeing them impaled a second time. 'Tis, he considers, very thrilling to be splashed by their blood.*

135. *The same personage she cited on the 11th and 13th of February, whose tastes ran to instigating combustions, also delights in binding six pregnant women to bundles of inflammable materials; these he sets afire, and if his victims undertake to save themselves, he awaits them, pitchfork in hand, skewers them and hurls them back into the blaze. However, when half-roasted, the floor gives way and they spill into a large vat of boiling oil, wherein they finally perish.*

136. *He is the nobleman Duclos spoke of, who has no fondness for the poor and who bought Lucile, her mother, and her sister, and whom Desgranges has also cited* (verify this) ; *another of his passions is to assemble a family of beggars over a mine and to watch those luckless creatures blown to bits.*

137. *A notorious sodomist, in order to combine that crime with those of incest, murder, rape, sacrilege, and adultery, first inserts a Host in his ass, then has himself embuggered by his own son, rapes his married daughter, and kills his niece.*

138. *Greatly partisan to asses, he strangles a mother while embuggering her; when she is dead, he turns her over and cuntfucks her corpse. While discharging, he kills her daughter with a*

*knife, slashing her breasts, then he buggers the girl even though she is dead; then apparently convinced there is still some life in his victims, and fancying they are yet capable of suffering, he hurls the cadavers into a fire and discharges as he watches them burn. Duclos spoke of this wealthy individual on the 29th of November: 'twas he who liked to see the girl lying on the pallet covered with black satin; he is also the same man who figured in Martaine's first tale of the 11th of January.*

The evening's program begins with Narcisse. One of his hands is lopped off.

Giton loses a hand too.

The interior of Michette's cunt is burned, the same treatment is given Rosette's, and then both girls are burned upon the body and breasts. But Curval, who has lost control of himself, violates the society's charter and cleaves an entire breast from Rosette's chest, all the while embuggering Michette.

Thérèse makes a further appearance; she receives two hundred blows of the bull's pizzle and loses her other eye.

Curval goes in search of the Duc that night when all is still and, accompanied by Desgranges and Duclos, those two champions take Zelmire down to the cellars where the most refined tortures are put to use upon her: they are all much more painful, more severe than the others employed upon Augustine, and the two men are still hard at work by the time breakfast arrives the following morning. That enchanting girl dies at the age of fifteen years and two months. 'Twas she who could boast the most beautiful ass in the harem of little girls. And thus deprived of a wife, the Président weds Hébé the next day.

THE 27TH. The seventeenth and last week's festival is postponed until the morrow, in order that the holiday may coincide with the end of the narrations; Desgranges recounts the following passions:

139. *A man Martaine described on the 12th of January, the one who set off fireworks in the woman's ass, has, for his second,*

*this other passion: he ties two pregnant women together so that they form a ball and fires them from a large mortar.*

140. *He was a scratcher and scab picker; he now places two pregnant women in a room and obliges them to fight with knives (he observes them from a safe position); they are naked, he threatens them with a gun he keeps trained upon them, and promises to shoot them dead if they begin to dally and falter. If they kill each other, why, that is precisely what he wishes, if not, sword in hand, he rushes into the arena and, after killing one, he disembowels the other and burns her entrails with aqua fortis, or with pieces of red-hot metal.*

141. *A man who once liked to flog pregnant women's bellies has reformed: he presently binds a pregnant girl to a wheel and beneath it, fixed in a chair and unable to move, sits the girl's mother, her head flung back, her mouth open and ready to receive all the ordures and rubbish which flow out of the corpse, and the infant, too, if the girl gives birth to it.*

142. *Martaine's of the 16th of January, whose joy was to prick asses, attaches a girl to a machine studded with sharp iron points; he fucks her as she lies upon that bed, with every blow of his loins he drives her upon the nails, then he turns her over and fucks her asswise, that she may also be punctured on the other side. When he has finished that phase of the operation, he lays a second plank above her, and it is likewise provided with nails; the planks are brought together by means of bolts, thus dies the patient, crushed and stabbed in a multitude of places. The pressing is carried out gradually, she is given ample opportunity to savor her pain.*

143. *A fustigator stretches a pregnant woman out upon a table; he nails her thereto, first driving a fiery nail into each eye, one into her mouth, another into either breast, then he burns her clitoris and nipples with a taper, and slowly saws her knees halfway through, breaks her legs, and ends by hammering a red-hot spike, of enormous size, into her navel: it undoes both mother and child. He likes to have her ready to give birth.*

Messieurs whip Julie and Duclos that evening, but from amusement, since they are both amongst the inhabitants of Silling who shall transfer their residence to Paris: nevertheless, Julie's thighs are burned in two places, and she is depilated.

Sentenced to die the next day but unaware of her impending fate, Constance appears; her nipples are scorched, molten wax is allowed to trickle down over her belly, she yields four teeth, Messieurs prick the white of her eyes with needles.

Narcisse, also due to be immolated on the 28th of February, enters upon the stage; he loses an eye and four teeth.

Giton, Michette, and Rosette, destined to accompany Constance to the grave, each surrenders an eye and four teeth, Rosette her two nipples to the knife and six chunks of flesh, some of them carved from her arms, some from her thighs; all her fingers are neatly severed, and hot irons are introduced into her cunt and bum. Both Curval and the Duc discharge twice.

Up steps Louison; she weathers a storm of one hundred blows of the bull's pizzle; Messieurs pluck out one of her eyes and, most cynically, bid her swallow it. Down it goes.

THE 28TH. 144. *A bugger: has two girls brought to him, they are fast friends, he ties them mouth to mouth, and by their side sits an excellent meal; but they cannot get to it, and he watches them bite and eat each other when hunger begins to exert its influence upon them.*

145. *A man who as a boy was wont to flog pregnant women, now shuts six of this sort into a round cage formed by large iron hoops: they are all facing one another. Little by little, the hoops contract, little by little they are brought together, slowly they are flattened, gradually all six are crushed, their fruit crushed too. But prior to this he has cut a buttock and a breast from each and fashioned six collars therefrom: each woman wears one as you might a fur tippet.*

146. *Another pregnant-woman beater binds two of these objects each to the end of a long tilting pole; a clever machine, into which the other ends of the poles are inserted, bumps and bangs the women against each other. These repeated collisions are their*

*mutual undoing, and he discharges. He makes every effort to procure himself a mother and daughter, or two sisters.*

147. *That Comte of whom Duclos spoke at length, and to whom Desgranges alluded once before on the 26th, he who purchased Lucile, Lucile's mother, and Lucile's little sister, of whom Martaine also spoke in her fourth tale on the 1st of January, this Comte, I say, has another passion still: 'tis to suspend three women over three holes. The first woman hangs by her tongue, beneath her is a very deep well; the second hangs from her breasts, underneath her lies a charcoal brazier; the scalp of the third has been loosened, she hangs by her hair over a pit studded with pointed iron rods. When the weight of their bodies causes these women to fall free— when the scalp is torn from the head of the third, when the breasts of the second tear loose from her torso, when the tongue of the first is torn from her mouth—they only escape one difficulty in order to encounter a new one. Whenever possible, he suspends three pregnant women, or three women from the same family; such was his unkind use of Lucile, her sister, and her mother.*

148. *The last passion.*

(But why the last? Where are the other two? They were all there in the original outline.)

*Desgranges recounts the last passion:*

*The nobleman who indulges in this final passion we shall designate as the infernal caprice or, more simply, as the hell passion, has been cited four times: by Duclos in the last story she told on the 29th of November; by Champville, when referring to a personage who depucelates nine-year-olds only; by Martaine, as he who depucelates three-year-olds in the bum; by Desgranges who mentioned him in an earlier connection* (establish that connection more precisely). *He is a man of some forty years, enormous in stature and furnished with the member of a stallion: his prick is very near to nine inches in circumference and a foot in overall length; he is exceedingly wealthy, a very powerful lord, very harsh, very cruel, his heart is of stone. He has a house on the outskirts of Paris which he uses for no purpose other than the gratification of this passion.*

*The surroundings wherein he savors his delight is a spacious*

*room, simply decked, but padded everywhere, the floor covered
with mattresses; upon entering the room one sees a single long casement window, the room has no other opening save for the door;
that window looks down upon an underground cellar, twenty feet
below the salon where he busies himself, and looking out, one sees
the mattresses which break the fall of the girls he flings down into
the cellar, a description whereof we shall give shortly. He requires
fifteen girls for this party; their ages must be between fifteen and
seventeen, neither more, nor less; he employs six procuresses in
Paris, as well as twelve in the provinces, and they are to spare no
efforts, no expense to find him everything of the most charming that
may possibly be found of that age, and as it is collected, the material
is sent to a country convent over which he has absolute control, and
there, in that nursery, the girls ripen, and from it he selects the
fifteen objects for his debauch, which is regularly executed every
fortnight.*

*That evening before the ceremony begins, he personally exam-
ines the said material, the least defect in which warrants its rejection; he insists that his creatures be perfect models of beauty.
Escorted by a procuress, they arrive at the house and are lodged in
a room adjacent to the pleasure-salon. They are first exhibited to
him in this adjoining chamber, all fifteen are naked. He touches,
feels, fondles, experiments with them, he scrutinizes them, sucks
their mouths, and one after the other has them all shit into his
mouth. But he does not swallow.*

*This initial operation performed with dreadful seriousness, he
brands each upon the shoulder, imprinting a number in her flesh; it
is to indicate the order in which he will receive them. That done,
he goes alone into the salon, where he remains for a brief space: no
one knows what he does in this moment of solitude. Then he knocks.
Girl Number 1 is cast into his lair. And she is properly cast into it:
the procuress flings her toward him, he catches her in his arms, she
is naked. He shuts the door, takes up switches and begins to flail
her ass; after that he sodomizes her with his gigantic prick. Never
does he need any help. He does not discharge. His prick retires,
still rock-hard; he seizes the switches again and returns to lashing
the girl's back, the front and back of her thighs, then he lays her
down again and deflowers her cunt; next, he goes back to beating*

her, now upon the breasts, both of which he seizes and grinds and kneads with all his strength, and he is a strong man. And now he picks up an awl and six times stabs her body, driving his point once into each bruised breast.

After all that has been done, he opens the casement window, places the girl in the middle of the room, standing erect, at attention, facing the window; he stands behind her and, when all is ready, gives her a kick in the ass of such startling violence that she flies across the room, crashes against the windowsill, topples over it, and vanishes into the cellar. But before launching her, he slips a ribbon around her neck, thereby to signify which torture, according to his best belief, will be most suitable for that particular patient, which torture will prove most voluptuous to inflict upon her, and his acuity and judgment in these matters, his tact and discrimination are truly wonderful.

And thus the girls pass one by one through his hands, the identical ceremony awaits them all, and thus he makes away with thirty maidenheads in a given day, and performs those heroic feats unscathed: not a drop of fuck does he lose. The subterranean apartment into which the girls tumble is furnished with fifteen different assortments of frightful torture machines, and an executioner, wearing the mask and emblems of a demon, wearing also the colors of his specialty, presides over each apparatus. The ribbon placed about the girl's neck corresponds in color with the torture to which she has been condemned, and directly she falls into the pit, the appropriate executioner steps forward, having recognized his victim, and drags her to the machine of which he has charge, but the tortures do not begin until the fifteenth has entered the gallery and been claimed by her demon. As soon as the entire complement has descended, our man, by now in a furious state after having depucelated thirty orifices without discharging, our man, I say, makes his entrance into the infernal repair; he is practically naked, his prick is glued against his belly. Everything is ready, all the tortures are in motion, and they proceed simultaneously, amidst much noise.

The first torture engine is a wheel upon which the girl is strapped and which, rotating uninterruptedly, bears against an outer circle studded with razors which everywhere scratch and tear *and slice the unfortunate victim, but as the blades do not bite deep, only superficially, she turns for at least two hours before dying.*

*The second: the girl lies two inches above a red-hot iron plate which slowly melts her.*

*Third: she is attached by the waist to a piece of burning iron, and all her limbs are twisted and frightfully dislocated.*

*Fourth: the four limbs attached each to a spring which slowly moves away, gradually stretching her arms and legs until they are detached and the trunk falls into a brazier.*

*Fifth: a red-hot cast-iron bell is placed over her head, but the bonnet is several sizes too large, the iron does not touch her, but her brain slowly melts, her head is slowly grilled.*

*Sixth: she is chained inside an iron tub of boiling oil.*

*Seventh: she is held standing before a machine which, six times a minute, shoots a small dart into her body, and each time into a different place; the machine does not stop until she is entirely feathered.*

*Eighth: her feet anchored in a furnace, a mass of lead very gradually descends upon her head, thrusting her further into the oven.*

*Ninth: her executioner continually pricks her with a red-hot iron goad; she is bound before him, he thus meticulously works over every inch of her body.*

*Tenth: she is chained to a pillar underneath a large glass dome, twenty famished reptiles devour her alive.*

*Eleventh: a cannon ball attached to each foot, she is suspended by one hand, and if she falls, 'tis into a furnace.*

*Twelfth: a hook is driven through her mouth; thus she hangs, a deluge of burning pitch incessantly pouring over her body.*

*Thirteenth: the nerves are pulled from her flesh and tied to cords which draw them further, and meanwhile burning nails are driven into her body.*

*Fourteenth: alternately torn with tongs and whipped upon her cunt and ass with martinets whose steel tips are heated red hot, and from time to time scratched with burning iron rakes.*

*Fifteenth: she is poisoned by a drug which burns and rends her entrails, which hurls her into frightful convulsions, causes her to utter hideous screams, and insures her death; but it is slow, and she is the last to succumb. This is one of the most terrible of the ordeals.*

The villain walks about the torture chamber as soon as he arrives there, spends fifteen minutes contemplating each operation while swearing like one of the damned and overwhelming the patient with unmentionable invectives. When toward the end he can bear no more of it and his fuck, captive for so long, is ready to escape him, he falls into a comfortable armchair whence he can observe the entire spectacle, two of the demons approach him, display their asses and frig him, and he squirts his seed while pronouncing shouts so stentorian that they rise above and totally blot out the din his fifteen patients are producing. And now he gets to his feet and leaves the gallery, the coup de grâce is given the girls who are not yet dead, their bodies are buried, and there's an end to it until the next fortnight comes round.

Wherewith Desgranges terminates her contribution; she is congratulated, toasted, acclaimed, etc. . . .

Upon the morning of that day there had been the most ominous preparations for the great holiday Messieurs were meditating. Curval, detesting Constance as he does, had been cunt-fucking her at a very early hour and while fucking her had imparted grave news to her. Coffee was served by the five victims, to wit: Constance, Narcisse, Giton, Michette, and Rosette. Horrid things were perpetrated in the salon; during the recitations the reader has just perused, the quatrains Messieurs had been able to arrange had been composed of naked children. And as soon as Desgranges had brought her narrations to a term, Fanny had been marched to the fore: her remaining fingers and toes had been hacked off, and Curval had embuggered her without pomade, so had the Duc, so had the four first-rank fuckers.

Sophie was led into the center of the stage; Céladon, her lover, had been obliged to burn the interior of her cunt, all her fingers had been severed, her four limbs bled, her right ear had been torn away, her left eye gouged out. Céladon had been constrained to lend his assistance in all these operations, and his least frown or lowest murmur was rewarded by a flogging with an iron-tipped martinet. Supper had come next, the meal had been voluptuous, Messieurs drank naught but sparkling champagne and liqueurs.

The torturing was arranged for the orgy hour; as the friends sat at dessert, word was brought to them that everything was in readiness, they descended and found the cellars agreeably festooned and very properly furnished. Constance lay upon a kind of mausoleum, the four children decorated its corners. As their asses were still in excellent condition, Messieurs were able to take considerable pleasure in molesting them; then at last the heavier work was begun: while embuggering Giton, Curval himself opened Constance's belly and tore out the fruit, already well-ripened and clearly of the masculine sex; then the society continued, inflicting tortures upon those five victims. Their sufferings were long, cruel, and various.


Upon THE 1ST DAY OF MARCH, remarking that the snows have not yet melted, Messieurs decide to dispatch the rest of the subjects one by one. Messieurs devise new arrangements whereby to keep their bedchambers staffed, and agree to give a green ribbon to everyone whom they propose to take back with them to France; the green favor is bestowed, however, upon condition the recipient is willing to lend a hand with the destruction of the other victims. Nothing is said to the six women in the kitchen; Messieurs decide to do away with the three scullery maids, who are well worth toying over, but to spare the cooks, because of their considerable talents. And so a list is drawn up; 'tis found that, to date, the following creatures had already been sacrificed:

Wives: Aline, Adelaide, and Constance . . . . . . . . . . .  3
Sultanas: Augustine, Michette, Rosette,
    and Zelmire . . . . . . . . . . . . . . . . . . . . . . . . . . . .  4
Bardashes: Giton and Narcisse . . . . . . . . . . . . . . . . .  2
Fuckers: one subaltern . . . . . . . . . . . . . . . . . . . . . . . .  1
            Total . . . . . . . . . . . . . . . . . . 10

The new ménages are arranged:

The Duc takes unto himself, or under his protection:
    Hercule, Duclos, one cook . . . . . . . . . . . . . . . .  4
Curval takes: Bum-Cleaver, Champville, one cook . . .  4
Durcet takes: Invictus, Martaine, one cook . . . . . . .  4
And the Bishop: Antinoüs, Desgranges, Julie . . . . . .  4
            Total . . . . . . . . . . . . . . . . . . 16

Messieurs decide that, upon a given signal, and with the aid of the four fuckers and the four storytellers, but not the cooks whom they do not wish to employ for these purposes, they will seize all the others, making use of the most treacherous possible means and when their victims least expect it; they will lay hands upon all the others, I say, save for the three scullions, who will not be seized until later on; it is further decided that the upstairs chambers will be converted into four prisons, that the three subaltern fuckers, manacled, will be lodged in the strongest of these prisons; Fanny, Colombe, Sophie, and Hébé in the second; Céladon, Zélamir, Cupidon, Zéphyr, Adonis, and Hyacinthe in the third; and the four elders in the fourth; that one subject will be dispatched every day; and that when the hour arrives to arrest the three scullions, they will be locked into whichever of the prisons happens to be empty.

These agreements once reached, Messieurs appoint each storyteller the warden of one prison. And whenever they please, Messieurs will amuse themselves with these victims, either in their prison or in one of the larger rooms, or in their Lordships' bed-chambers, depending upon Messieurs' individual preference. And so, as we have just indicated, one subject is dispatched daily, in the following order:

On the 1st of March: Fanchon.
On the 2nd: Louison.
On the 3rd: Thérèse.
On the 4th: Marie.
On the 5th: Fanny.
On the 6th and the 7th: Sophie and Céladon together, for they are lovers, and they perish nailed one to the other, as we have hitherto explained.
On the 8th: one subaltern fucker.
On the 9th: Hébé.
On the 10th: another subaltern fucker.
On the 11th: Colombe.
On the 12th: the last of the subaltern fuckers.
On the 13th: Zélamir.
On the 14th: Cupidon.
On the 15th: Zéphyr.
On the 16th: Adonis.
On the 17th: Hyacinthe.

On the morning of the 18th, Messieurs and their cohorts seize the three scullions, lock them in the prison formerly occupied by the elders, and dispatch one upon that day,

A second upon the 19th.

And the last upon the 20th.

Total . . . . . . . . . . . . . . 20

The following recapitulation lists the inhabitants of the Château of Silling during that memorable winter:

Masters . . . . . . . . . . . . . . . . . . . . . . . . . . . . . 4
Elders . . . . . . . . . . . . . . . . . . . . . . . . . . . . . 4
Kitchen staff . . . . . . . . . . . . . . . . . . . . . . . 6
Storytellers . . . . . . . . . . . . . . . . . . . . . . . . 4
Fuckers . . . . . . . . . . . . . . . . . . . . . . . . . . . 8
Little boys . . . . . . . . . . . . . . . . . . . . . . . . . 8
Wives . . . . . . . . . . . . . . . . . . . . . . . . . . . . 4
Little girls . . . . . . . . . . . . . . . . . . . . . . . . . 8

Total . . . . . . . . . . . . . . 46

Whereof thirty were immolated and sixteen returned to Paris.

### FINAL ASSESSMENT

Massacred prior to the 1st of March,
    in the course of the orgies . . . . . . . . . . 10
Massacred after the 1st of March . . . . . . 20
Survived and came back . . . . . . . . . . . . . 16

Total . . . . . . . . . . . . . . 46

With what regards the tortures and deaths of the last twenty subjects, and life such as it was in the household until the day of departure, you will give details at your leisure and where you see fit, you will say, first of all, that thirteen of the sixteen survivors (three of whom were cooks) took all their meals together; sprinkle in whatever tortures you like.

# NOTES

Under no circumstances deviate from this plan, everything has been worked out, the entirety several times re-examined with the greatest care and thoroughness.

Detail the departure. And throughout the whole, introduce a quantity of moral dissertation and diatribe, above all at the suppers.

When you produce the final version, keep a notebook; in it you will place the names of all the principal characters and the names of all those who play important roles, such as they who have several passions and who will appear several times in the romance, as, for example, the hell libertine; leave a wide margin beside their names and, as you recopy, fill it with everything you come across that has any bearing upon them; this note is very essential, it is the sole way to keep your work clear of obscurities and to avoid repetitions.

Edulcorate Part the First, it is much too strong; things develop too rapidly and too far in it, it cannot possibly be too soft, mild, feeble, subdued. Above all, never have the four friends do anything until it has first been recounted. You have not been sufficiently scrupulous in that connection.

In Part the First, say that the man who mouth-fucks the little girl prostituted by her father is the same man, of whom she has already spoken, who fucks with a dirty prick.

Do not forget to place somewhere in December the scene of the little girls serving supper, squirting liqueurs from their asses into Messieurs' glasses; you announced such a scene but failed to include it in the plan.

## SUPPLEMENTARY TORTURES

—By means of a hollow tube, a mouse is introduced into her cunt, the tube is withdrawn, the cunt sewn up, and the animal, unable to get out, devours her entrails.

—She is made to swallow a snake which in similar wise feeds upon her entrails.

673

## ADDENDA

In general, describe Curval and the Duc as two hot-blooded and imperious scoundrels, 'tis thus you conceived of them in the plan and in Part the First, and figure the Bishop as a cool, reasoning and tough-minded villain. As for Durcet, he must be mischievous, a teaser, false, traitorous, perfidious. In accordance with which, have them do everything that conforms with such characters.

Carefully recapitulate all the names and the qualities of all the personages your storytellers mention; this to avoid repetition.

Upon one page in your notebook of characters draw the plan of the château, room by room, and in the blank space next to this page, itemize all the things done in each room.

*This entire great roll was begun the 22nd of October, 1785, and finished in thirty-seven days.*

# The Marquis de Sade

# Part Four

# Theater

# Oxtiern, or The Misfortunes of Libertinage
## (1800)

$\mathcal{S}$ade was particularly attached to the theater, and there is good reason to believe that the author of Justine and The 120 Days would have given up a great deal in exchange for success as a dramatist. Among his earliest writings is the one-act play in prose Le Philosophe soi-disant, which is contained in his manuscript of early works, Œuvres diverses. It was probably this play which Sade had performed in 1772, on the private stage he had installed in his La Coste château.

Sixteen years later, in his list of works-to-date drawn up in the Bastille—the Catalogue raisonné of 1788—Sade placed the two manuscript volumes of his theatrical works, comprising some thirty-five acts of various plays, a comic opera, and a ballet, at the head of his proud list. Following his release from the Monarchy's dungeons, on Good Friday of 1790, Sade concentrated much of his energy upon trying to peddle his plays and get them performed. On the 3rd of August, 1790, the Théâtre-Italien accepted his one-act verse play, Le Suborneur, which went into rehearsal the following January and had its première on the 5th of March, 1792. The Journal des théâtres of the 10th of March relates what transpired at this first performance:

> On Monday, the 5th of March, this theater [Le Théâtre-Italien] attempted to present a one-act comedy in verse, Le Suborneur. During the first scene,

*murmurs arose. . . . During the second scene, the noise
increased; during the third, it reached its highest pitch;
during the fourth, the actors left the stage. What was
the reason for all this? We have no idea; we were
unable even to hear what the commotion was all about.
During the intermission, we saw patriots donning the
red bonnet with the tip pointing forward, like the
Phrygian* corno. *One of those who was thus coifed
said in a loud voice that henceforth this red bonnet
would be the signal, in public places, round which
patriots should rally, and especially in the theaters,
where the aristocracy would be ceaselessly combated
by the friends of liberty. . . ."*[1]

*Thus ended the first performance of a Sade play. On
the 17th of August, 1790, just two weeks after* Le Suborneur
*had been accepted by* Le Théâtre-Italien, *Sade gave a reading of his free-verse play,* Le Boudoir ou le Mari crédule
*at the Comédie-Française. Although it was ultimately re-
jected by one vote, the committee which had heard it agreed
to a second reading, providing the author made certain
changes. A month later, Sade's five-act comedy in free verse,*
Le Misanthrope par amour ou Sophie et Desfrancs *was
"unanimously accepted" by the Comédie-Française, though
it was never performed. Within the next few months several
more of Sade's plays were "accepted" by various theaters,*[2]
*but only one more was ever publicly presented: that is the
play we include in the following pages,* Le Comte Oxtiern
ou les Effets du libertinage, *the première of which took place
on the 22nd of October, 1791, at* Le Théâtre Molière *on*

---

[1] Cited in Lely, *op. cit.,* Vol. II, pp. 394–395.

[2] In letters to Gaufridy, Sade relates that *Le Jaloux corrigé ou l'Ecole
des Coquettes*—which is apparently another title for the play earlier rejected by the Comédie-Française, *Le Boudoir ou le Mari crédule*—was
accepted by Le Théâtre-Italien; that *Le Criminel par vertu* had been taken
by Le Théâtre du Palais-Royal; and that his *Azélis* was accepted by Le
Théâtre de la rue de Bondy. As Sade was to learn, however, there could
be many a slip between the acceptance and the performance.

the rue Saint-Martin. Of this, Sade wrote elatedly to his steward Gaufridy a few days later:

> I have at last appeared in public, my dear lawyer. Last Saturday, the 22nd, a play of mine was presented, the success of which, thanks to certain cliques, hirelings, and the women I insulted, was somewhat mixed. It will be staged again on the 29th, with some changes. Pray for me; we shall see. Adieu.[3]

The second performance, however, was postponed until the 4th of November, and at the curtain the audience called for the author, who appeared to take a bow. Two days later Le Moniteur reviewed the play, and after giving a résumé of its plot, judged it thus:

> The play is interesting in itself and for its vigor; but the character of Oxtiern is a revolting atrocity. He is a worse villain, a creature more dispicable, than Lovelace, with none of his more endearing qualities.
>
> A slight incident threatened to disturb the second performance. At the start of the second act, a member of the audience, either discontent or malicious, but in any case wholly lacking in tact, shouted "Lower the curtain!" . . . The stage hand made the mistake of following this isolated command and lowered the curtain more than half way. Whereupon many other members of the audience, after having obliged him to raise it again, cried: "Throw him out!", referring to the person who had caused the original disturbance. Whence resulted some degree of dissension among the audience. A tiny minority hissed and whistled, for which the author was more than compensated by the hearty applause of the majority. They called for him after the performance: it was Monsieur de Sade.[4]

---

[3] Pierre Bourdin: *Correspondance inédite du marquis de Sade, de ses proches et de ses familiers.* Paris, Librairie de France, 1929, p. 298.

[4] Guillaume Apollinaire: *L'Œuvre du Marquis de Sade. Pages choisies.* Paris, Bibliothèque des Curieux, 1912, pp. 41–42.

Sade was learning that the Revolution, which had delivered him from the dungeons of a Monarchy he had every reason to detest, was far from ready to receive him, a ci-devant, unreservedly. In a letter to Gaufridy shortly after the second performance of Oxtiern, Sade noted:

> The frightful disturbance which it [Oxtiern] occasioned is the reason the play is not being repeated under the same title, and the reason why I have postponed further performances. The members of the audience were at each other's throats. The guards, and the commissaire, were obliged to remain in a state of constant readiness each time it was played. I preferred to suspend it. We shall put it on again this winter.[5]

Actually, it was not until eight years later that Oxtiern was performed again, under a slightly different title,[6] on the stage of the Société dramatique at Versailles, with Sade himself playing the role of Fabrice. The same year—Year VIII of the Republic—Sade had the play printed by the Versailles bookseller Blaisot.

What of Sade the playwright? It is an understatement to maintain that, were his seventeen plays[7] all that history had bequeathed us of his writings, Sade would hardly have a claim to immortality. The force, and indeed the essential worth, of Sade's works varies directly in proportion to their clandestine nature. The more open and public they are, the more conventional they become. The dramatic works, being most public, suffer most from conventionality and from what appears to be Sade's inherent timidity when faced with the dramatic form. What makes Sade of interest is his absolute refusal to compromise, his determination to carry his convictions to their ultimate conclusions. In the theater this was virtually impossible. While he could still treat the same themes that abound in his fic-

---

[5] Lely, op. cit., Vol. II, p. 389.

[6] Which was: Oxtiern ou les Malheurs du libertinage.

[7] Or eighteen, if one counts the early Le Philosophe soi-disant, which Sade did not include in his Catalogue raisonné.

tion, and portray virtue overwhelmed by vice, both character and dialogue had greatly to be diluted and tempered. That Sade was fully capable of writing brilliant, biting, and often witty dialogue is unquestionable—one need only turn to his Dialogue between a Priest and a Dying Man, for example, or to Philosophy in the Bedroom. Or, more simply, one need but compare the dialogues and characterization in the novella Ernestine, from which Oxtiern was drawn.

Ernestine was written while Sade was a prisoner in the Bastille and, as noted, was first published in 1800 as one of the eleven stories contained in Les Crimes de l'Amour. Comparing the story and the play, Maurice Heine observed:

> The denouement of the story is at once more somber and richer in meaning than the play. Ernestine's lover is not only imprisoned but sentenced to death and, though innocent, is executed on a scaffold erected before Oxtiern's windows, at the very moment when he is violating Ernestine. Later there ensues a duel between Ernestine and her father, both of whom believe they are fighting Oxtiern. In this duel, Ernestine is mortally wounded. Her father at length obtains justice; Oxtiern is granted a reprieve, upon condition that he be forever banished to the mines, there to perform hard labor.[8]

Both these situations are typically Sadean. In the first —a "pleasure" recounted in The 120 Days—the hero-villain contrives to coincide the moment of his own pleasure with that of his rival's execution. In the second, he arranges to have two of virtue's pawns mistakenly engage each other in mortal combat, the outcome of which cannot help but be tragic for the combatants, and therefore a source of pleasure to him.

Though Lely does not rank Ernestine with Eugénie de Franval and Florville and Courval—which he considers the two masterpieces of Les Crimes de l'Amour

---

[8] Cited in Lely, op. cit., Vol. II, p. 390.

—in some respects it is the superior work. Each of the three principal characters—and even the two villains, Oxtiern and Madame Scholtz—are finely-drawn personages, not of pure black or white but of varying shades of gray. Colonel Sanders, a well-meaning man who has the best interests of his daughter at heart, is none the less weak and vacillating, susceptible to the blandishments of a scoundrel such as Oxtiern. Ernestine herself, though essentially a good and virtuous girl, is far from as steadfast as Justine, and allows her head to be turned by the dazzle of wealth and the temptation of high estate. And in the worthy Herman, Ernestine's betrothed, Sade has painted a splendid portrait of a man who, by the oppressive nature of his goodness and his stifling lack of imagination, helps drive Ernestine into Oxtiern's careful trap. In this tale, Sade has given the characters a psychological basis for their acts. Oxtiern, as Sadean man, is still very much the manipulator of their fate, but his three victims—Ernestine, Colonel Sanders, and Herman—are more than mere pawns, or the incarnations of a principle: they are, to a far greater degree than most of Sade's characters, responsible for their own fate.

# Oxtiern

## OR

## THE MISFORTUNES OF LIBERTINAGE

PROSE DRAMA IN THREE ACTS

by D.-A.-F. S.

Staged at the *Théâtre de Molière*, in Paris, in 1791;
and at Versailles, on the stage of the *Société Dramatique*,
on 22 *Frimaire*, Year 8 of the Republic.

---

Woe unto scoundrels whom remorse does not check!

*Oxtiern,* Act Three, Scene III

---

VERSAILLES

Published by Blaizot, Bookseller, rue Satory

---

YEAR EIGHT

# *Act One*

*The setting for the first two acts is the sitting room of an inn, which opens into several private rooms; on one side of the stage is a writing table, with an armchair near the table.*

## SCENE I

### FABRICE, CASIMIR.

FABRICE.

Monsieur Casimir, do you think these chambers will be suitable for the young lady your master is bringing here with him today?

CASIMIR.

I do indeed, Monsieur Fabrice. Is there a room close by for Amélie, her maid, and another bedroom for Mademoiselle Ernestine?

FABRICE.

Yes, there are two bedrooms adjoining this room; one key locks all three. They will be quite comfortable here, I can assure you. . . . 'Tis a quiet district . . . the rooms face the garden: they will not hear the least sound of the other travelers.

CASIMIR.

Excellent! (*Taking Fabrice aside, and with an air of mystery.*) Monsieur Fabrice?

FABRICE.

Yes, what is it?

CASIMIR.

A most extraordinary man, my master, you must confess. You have known him since he was a young man.

FABRICE.

I've known Oxtiern for a long time; and 'tis for that reason I would venture to say there's no man in all the provinces of Sweden more dangerous than he.

CASIMIR.

Yes; but he pays well.

FABRICE.

And therefore is all the more to be feared: there is nothing so pernicious as gold in the hands of wicked men. . . . Who can resist him who possesses the surest means of corruption? . . . My friend, if I had my way I would see to it that the world's wealth was controlled by honest and decent people. . . . But, pray tell me, what is this latest adventure all about?

CASIMIR.

A charming girl! . . . Ah! Monsieur Fabrice, more's the pity. Great God! you mean you allowed it! Is't possible for such a creature to be the pawn of deceit and debauchery!

FABRICE, *much surprised.*

What do you mean? Has the crime already been committed?

CASIMIR.

It has, Monsieur Fabrice, it has. . . . And yet she's the daughter of Colonel Falkenheim, the grand nephew of Charles XII's favorite. He has abducted her . . . and dishonored her. I tell you, Monsieur Fabrice, the poor girl is lost!

FABRICE, *as above.*

He hasn't married her? 'Tis a virtuous girl he is bringing here, a girl he has seduced, deceived, and ravished? . . . Casimir, fly to your master in all haste; tell him the inn is full . . . say I cannot receive him. I have already had more than my share of the liberties he thinks he can take when he's beneath my roof—since he does me the honor of considering me his protégé. I greatly prefer to forgo a nobleman's protection when the sole result, as it usually turns out, is my complicity in his licentious ways. (*He exits.*)

CASIMIR, *running after him to stop him.*
One moment, my friend, one moment. You would lose everything, and no wrong would be righted. Open your house to him, offer him your hospitality, and if the occasion presents itself, try secretly to render the lady some service. (*What follows must be stressed.*) Stockholm is but a league away . . . 'tis not late. . . . They will be retiring early . . . they are in need of rest. You have friends in the capital. . . . Do you understand my words, Monsieur Fabrice?

FABRICE, *after a moment's reflection.*
Friends! . . . yes, I do have friends; but there are other means . . . surer means, which I trust may prove successful. Tell me now . . .
(*We hear the sound of the Count's carriage.*)

CASIMIR.
Let us save our words for later. . . . I hear a carriage coming. . . . I shall meet you shortly in your room, and there shall instruct you in greater detail. . . . What a frightful din! No question, 'tis the Count: should vice be permitted to strut so boldly?

FABRICE.
I only wish your Count would go and lodge with the devil! 'Tis a terrible trade to be an innkeeper and obliged to open your doors to all kinds of people. . . . 'Tis the only aspect of my profession I find distasteful.

# SCENE II

### FABRICE, CASIMIR, CHARLES.

CHARLES, *to Fabrice.*
Monsieur, two ladies sent by Count Oxtiern have just arrived and desire lodgings. The Count himself will be here shortly. He and his friend Monsieur Derbac have stopped off a short distance from here, and have sent instructions to offer the ladies your best chambers. There are, in truth, more than twenty guards escorting the carriage.

FABRICE, *curtly*.

All right, I shall receive them; 'tis here they will lodge. . . . Not a word, Casimir; and when the occasion arises, let us try and help the poor girl: the rewards are such, my friend, that we should never waste the least opportunity to perform a good deed whenever we can. . . . Come with me, Charles.

# SCENE III

CASIMIR, *alone*.

A worthy man! 'Tis there, none the less, one finds virtue. . . . In an anonymous creature . . . without any background or breeding. While those born to wealth often have naught to offer—their riches notwithstanding—save corruption and a whole host of vices. . . . But why did the Count not come with Ernestine? . . . Ah! he is doubtless off hatching some plot with Derbac, that most worthy accomplice of his debaucheries. But Derbac, less dissolute than the Count, will perhaps raise some objections to this latest and vilest adventure.

# SCENE IV

CASIMIR, FABRICE, ERNESTINE, AMELIE.

FABRICE, *to Ernestine*.

I trust, Mademoiselle, you will find these lodgings comfortable. I have been at great pains to ready them for you, as the Count has instructed me to, and as Mademoiselle deserves.

ERNESTINE, *in deep despair*.

Thank you, Monsieur, thank you. 'Tis much too good for me; the most profound solitude, 'tis that and only that would really suit me.

FABRICE.

Since Mademoiselle wishes to be alone, I shall withdraw and attend to other matters which may help make my lodgings more bearable for her.

CASIMIR, *to Ernestine.*

Shall I bring the Count to Mademoiselle's chambers when he arrives?

ERNESTINE.

Is he not the lord and master of them?... The master of my entire existence?... Leave us, Monsieur, pray do. We wish to be alone.

# SCENE V

ERNESTINE, AMELIE.

AMELIE.

This melancholy state of mind wherein I find you worries me, Mademoiselle. How pleased I'd be to see you rest a while.

ERNESTINE.

Rest?... I rest? Great God, no!... Oh, no!... there can be no further rest upon this earth for poor Ernestine.

AMELIE.

What! You mean to say the barbarous author of your misfortunes can do nothing to make amends?

ERNESTINE.

For such cruel desecrations there can never be amends, Amélie. Reflect for a moment how the man, resorting to the most arrant roguery, abducted me from my family ... from my lover ... from everything I hold dear in this world. And were you aware that he had this man, this worthy Herman whom I love, cast into irons? He has founded his case upon false accusations, resorted to the worst kind of calumnies, made use of informers and traitors. 'Tis they who have brought the poor man low; base gold, and Oxtiern's crimes, have led to his undoing. Herman is a prisoner ... perhaps he has already been sentenced ... and 'tis upon the very chains of the man I love that this cowardly Oxtiern has come to sacrifice his wretched victim.

AMELIE.

Ah, Mademoiselle, your words make me tremble!

ERNESTINE, *in despair.*

What hope is there for me?... What have I to look forward to? Great God! What recourse is left to me?

AMELIE.

But what of your father?...

ERNESTINE.

You know that my father had been absent from Stockholm for some time when Oxtiern, resorting to cruel deceit, invited me to his house, pretending that, were I to come, I would be helping my lover's cause and obtain not only his release but perhaps his hand as well; Oxtiern's brother, the Senator, was to be there and could use his influence to help poor Herman, or so he declared. 'Twas a venture which, for me, was as guilty as 'twas foolhardy, I realize now. How could I ever have dreamt of a betrothal without my father's consent? Heaven has punished me dearly for it. . . . Do you know whom I discovered there, instead of the protector I was expecting? Oxtiern, ravenous Oxtiern, a dagger in his hand, offering me the choice of death or dishonor, nor did he even give me the opportunity to make a choice. Had that choice been mine, Amélie, I swear I would not have hesitated for a single moment; the most frightful torments would have been for me sweeter than the loathsome deeds that perverted man had prepared for me; frightful bonds prevented me from defending myself. . . . The scoundrel!... and, as a crowning blow, Heaven has seen fit to let me live . . . the sun still casts its rays upon me, and I am lost! (*She slumps into the chair which is near the table.*)

AMELIE, *in tears, taking her mistress' hands.*

O Mademoiselle! most miserable of women, please do not despair!... Your father has already been apprised of your departure; do you think he will waste a minute before flying to your defense?

ERNESTINE.

'Tis not he I expect to avenge me and punish him who has tortured me.

AMELIE.

And what if the Count were to keep his word? He spoke, or so I was given to understand, of cherished ties, eternal bonds. . . .

ERNESTINE.

And even were Oxtiern to desire them, could I ever consent to spend my life in the arms of a man I loathe? . . . a man who has done me the most grievous wrong? Can you marry a man by whom you have been debased? . . . Can you ever learn to love what you deem to be beneath contempt? Ah, Amélie, I am lost, irrevocably lost. . . . All that remain for me are sorrow and tears; my only hope is in death: one does not recover from the loss of one's honor. . . . From any other hurt, but never from that!

AMELIE, *glancing around her.*

Mademoiselle, there is no one here; who stands in our way, or stops us from fleeing? from going to beg the Court for its protection, a protection you not only merit but which it is your bounden duty to claim?

ERNESTINE, *proudly.*

Were Oxtiern a thousand leagues away, I would do everything in my power to shorten the distance between us, nor would I lift a finger to flee. The traitor has dishonored me; I must avenge myself. I shall not fly to any corruption-ridden Court to ask for a protection which would be denied me; you have no inkling, Amélie, to what extent wealth and influence debase the souls of those who dwell in that house of horror! Monsters! I perhaps would be merely one further morsel for their dreadful desires!

# SCENE VI

### THE ABOVE, AND FABRICE.

FABRICE, *seemingly sad, but with an interested air.*

The Count has sent word that an important affair has detained him not far from here, but that he will be here shortly. Is there anything Mademoiselle desires meanwhile?

ERNESTINE, *pointing to the room she thinks is hers.*

This is my room, is it not, Monsieur?

FABRICE, *as before.*

It is, Mademoiselle.

ERNESTINE.

Then I should like to retire to it. . . . Come, Amélie, come and let us ponder the important plans before us, plans which alone are capable of giving your poor mistress any respite from her torments.

## SCENE VII

FABRICE, *alone*.

Casimir was quite right, this girl is beautiful, she is charming. . . . Ah! Monsieur le Comte, how guilty you are to have been the instrument of this young lady's destruction; should she, who so deserves to be the object of your affection, be turned into the object of your villainy and brutality? But here he comes; not another word. Traitors cannot bear the truth; they, more than any other kind, are receptive to flattery, and consciously desire it; even they find crime so repulsive that, in order to steel themselves to the necessity of being evil, they like to be thought of, and constantly painted, as paragons of virtue.

## SCENE VIII

FABRICE, COUNT OXTIERN.

OXTIERN.

How can I ever thank you, my dear Fabrice! Your friendship, your affection of long standing, are ever more clearly in evidence. Words cannot express my gratitude.

FABRICE, *with a straightforward and affectionate air*.

A trifle more candor, Monsieur, and a trifle less gratitude. Pray spare me any gratitude which would be purchased at the cost of an ill deed, 'twould debase me. Be frank with me, Monsieur: who is the young lady you have brought here, and what do you intend to do with her?

OXTIERN, *quickly interrupting*.

My intentions are honorable, Monsieur. Ernestine is a seemly young lady, whom I am not keeping here by force. Perhaps I did allow myself to be carried away by an excess of love, and hasten the day which will join us forever; but she must be my wife, and indeed she will, my friend. Would I dare to consider her otherwise, and would I bring her here, 'neath your roof, if such was not my intention?

FABRICE.

'Tis not the story people have been telling, Monsieur. Still, I must believe you. If you are deceiving me, however, I shall no longer be able to offer you my hospitality.

OXTIERN.

Given the virtuous motives which prompt them, Fabrice, I forgive you your suspicions. But set your mind at ease, my friend, let me say it again. My plans are as pure as she who inspires them in me.

FABRICE.

You are a noble lord, Count, I know. But please be convinced of this: that the moment your conduct renders you base in my eyes, I shall cease to regard you as anything but a man all the more contemptible because he was born to be honest; and, having been blessed, more than most men, with marks of distinction which ought to be deserving of esteem and respect, such a man is, at the same time, all the more guilty for not having profited from them.

OXTIERN.

Fabrice, why all this concern? What have I done to deserve such suspicion?

FABRICE.

Nothing yet, or so I am willing to believe. . . . Where do you plan to take this girl?

OXTIERN.

To my estate near Norrköping, and there I shall marry her the moment we arrive.

FABRICE.

Why is her father not with her?

OXTIERN.

He was not in Stockholm when she left; and the force of my love did not allow me to tarry over formalities . . . with which I thought I could easily dispense: how strict you are, my friend ... I have never seen you so stern before.

FABRICE.

'Tis not a matter of being stern, Monsieur, 'tis a matter of justice; would you, were you a father, consent to see your daughter abducted?

OXTIERN.

I would not like to have her dishonored; but will Ernestine be dishonored when I marry her?


SCENE IX

THE ABOVE, AMELIE.

AMELIE.

Gentlemen, Mademoiselle requests that you move to another room; she's resting at present, and would like ...

OXTIERN, *warmly.*

Please assure her, my dear Amélie, that we shall comply with her request. Is there anything in the world I desire more than the peace and happiness of my mistress?

AMELIE.

Ah! Monsieur, and yet how far she is from either!

OXTIERN, *to Fabrice, without paying any attention to what Amélie has just said.*

Come, Fabrice, I wish to finish convincing you that my soul has never entertained any principles of a sort which might afflict yours. ... Amélie, please tell Ernestine to let me know when she will receive me. (*She exits. To Fabrice.*) Come, my friend, let us go.

FABRICE, *alone.*

I shall follow shortly. ... I, the friend of that man? Oh, no, never! ... Were he to give me his entire fortune I should still not be his friend. ... Through Casimir privy to the affair, I can now be of some use to Ernestine; let us hasten to Stockholm. He is not leaving until tomorrow; I still have time. I must save this poor girl or lose my life in the attempt: honor and probity make it my bounden duty; these are the most sacred laws of my heart.

END OF ACT I

# Act Two

## SCENE I

### OXTIERN, DERBAC.

OXTIERN.

This creature is of a sensibility which is . . .

DERBAC.

Most stimulating, is it not? How charming women are whenever tears appear and endow their features with the full disorder
of sorrow. . . . You, my dear Count, are what may be termed a
thoroughly corrupt man. . . .

OXTIERN.

What do you expect, my friend? 'twas from the ways of
women that I learned all the vices wherewith I ravage them today.

DERBAC.

I assume you plan to marry her?

OXTIERN.

Can you suspect me for one moment of being so ridiculous?

DERBAC.

But once you are in your château, what excuse can you offer
Ernestine to justify your conduct? She will never allow you to live
with her as a lover with his mistress.

OXTIERN.

Oh! her intentions, her desires, her wishes are the things which
concern me least of all. My happiness, my satisfaction: there is the

698

goal, Derbac, and the goal is attained; in an adventure such as this, the moment I am happy, everyone must be happy.

DERBAC.

Ah! my friend . . . my dear Count, allow me to dispute for a moment principles as dangerous as these!

OXTIERN.

No, you would only displease me without convincing me. . . . Never forget that your fortune depends upon mine, and that what I expect you to be is an agent for furthering my plans, not a censor.

DERBAC.

I flattered myself that, considering me only as a friend, you would want my advice. . . . What you are contriving is frightful.

OXTIERN.

In your eyes, it may well be; because you are a lackey, full of Gothic prejudices . . . upon which the light of philosophy has not yet managed to direct its rays. . . . A few more years at my school, Derbac, and you will no longer pity a woman for such a peccadillo.

DERBAC.

The sweet, sensitive creature who, for our happiness even more than for her own, has been able to bestow, with such refinement, all her glory and all her felicity in her virtue, has very clear claims to our love and our protection, when scoundrels despoil it.

OXTIERN.

Ah! you're moralizing, Derbac!

DERBAC.

And what if I am? Let us dwell solely upon the dangers to you; do you not see any dangers to yourself in this affair? . . . The Colonel, the Colonel's son . . . or young Herman, whom this charming girl loves so tenderly: do you fear nothing from any of these people?

OXTIERN.

The Colonel is old, he will not put up much of a fight . . . in fact he won't fight at all. . . . His son will never get to me; I'm having him followed; (*In a low voice.*) if he even ventures close to my estate, my friend, he's as good as dead. (*Aloud.*) As for Herman, the chains in which I have him languishing are not of a sort to be broken. I had the foresight to implicate him in an important affair, from which he will not be able to disentangle himself without a considerable fortune, which he is far from possessing. It cost me a pretty penny . . . false witnesses . . . corrupt judges; I defy him to extricate himself from it. . . .

DERBAC.

And what of the law, my friend, what of the law?

OXTIERN.

I have never known the law to resist the power of gold.

DERBAC.

And what of the voice within, wherein virtue has always been able to claim its due? . . . I mean your conscience.

OXTIERN.

Clear . . . perfectly unperturbed.

DERBAC.

But the Court, my dear Count, that Court of which you are the proud adornment and delight. . . . What if the Court were to learn of your conduct?

OXTIERN.

That is the only thing I fear from this furious girl; she threatened me, which is why I must keep a close watch on her. Remember to give orders that everything be in readiness tomorrow at dawn; I wish to get away from Stockholm as soon as possible. Fabrice is turning virtuous, and we are still too close to the capital for me not to have some qualms about such a knave's remorse; I know nothing more terrible or more humiliating than the necessity to treat such rascals with consideration whenever one has need of them. 'Tis the obligation of crime; but, Good God, my friend, 'tis the torment of pride; to convert Fabrice, I have dispatched my valet as an influence upon him. And would you believe it? Casimir himself is not as solid as I had thought; you have no idea, my friend, of the effect a girl's tears can have upon all these weak and vacillating souls.

DERBAC.

Fortunately for humanity, there are only a few as perverted as yours!

OXTIERN.

Because I have worked at it, my friend; I have witnessed much, experienced much; if you had any idea whither a surfeit of experience can lead one!

DERBAC.

I hear some noise from Ernestine's quarters. . . . Here comes Amélie. I'll wager they want you. . . . Lucky creature!

OXTIERN.

I've already told you: the only way to a woman's heart is along the path of torment. I know none other as sure.


## SCENE II

### THE ABOVE, AMELIE.

AMELIE, *to the Count.*

Mademoiselle Ernestine would like to join you in this room, Monsieur, to speak to you for a few minutes, if you have nothing more pressing.

OXTIERN.

Can there be anything more sacred . . . what am I saying, anything dearer to me than conversing with your lovely mistress? Amélie, tell her I await her with love . . . with a lover's impatience.

AMELIE, *surprise mingled with anger.*

You, Monsieur?

OXTIERN.

Yes, I. Do my sentiments surprise you?

AMELIE.

Oh, no, Monsieur, assuredly not; nothing any longer surprises me about you. Mademoiselle will be here shortly, I shall tell her you're expecting her.

## SCENE III

### OXTIERN, DERBAC.

DERBAC.

That girl knows you, my friend, and I can read on her face the expressions which reveal to me every movement of her mistress' soul.

OXTIERN.

How can one tremble because of the movements of a woman's soul? Poor Derbac, your fears make me laugh. . . . Off with you now, go see to the preparations for our journey; remember that we are still not in port, that we must reach it, and reach it safely.

DERBAC.

I dread the reefs more than you do, and I still suspect that this business is far from finished.

OXTIERN.

Fear not. (*Touching his forehead.*) There are, in here, more ruses than were needed to set all Europe aflame; given which, judge whether I should be concerned over one little intrigue.

DERBAC, *vehemently.*

Ah, my dear Count . . . adieu . . . since you want from me neither reproaches nor counsel, then perhaps you shall not have me long as a friend. (*He exits.*)

## SCENE IV

### OXTIERN, *alone.*

I pity all these people; a mere nothing upsets them and chills their ardor; I reveal my soul to none of them. . . . Let us keep up the pretense with Ernestine. . . . Angelic child . . . There are times when the sentiments you inspire in me threaten to weaken my resolution . . . moments when, instead of betraying you as I should, I can think only of adoring you. Ah! no faltering now; Ernestine has been used too ill not to be feared, and if I redeem her I am lost.

## SCENE V

### OXTIERN, ERNESTINE.

#### ERNESTINE.

However painful it is for me to appear before you, Monsieur, whatever humiliation I may feel in your presence, it is none the less necessary for me to ask you, following the horrible deed you have perpetrated, what satisfaction your probity can offer me.

#### OXTIERN.

Is it my probity that should be questioned, Ernestine, when 'tis my heart that you hold captive . . . a heart that is wholly yours?

#### ERNESTINE.

I trust you do not imagine that this gift can assure my happiness. . . . What reason can you have for proposing it to me? . . . How, after the baseness wherein you have wallowed, can you think that savage heart worthy of me?

#### OXTIERN.

I am grieved by your reproaches, all the more so since I confess I merit them. . . . Ah! do not punish so cruelly the failings of love!

#### ERNESTINE.

Of love! . . . You? O God! if this is what love inspires, let my heart be forever free from any feeling so capable of defiling man! . . . No, Monsieur, that is in no wise love; that is not the comforting sentiment, the basis for all good works . . . ; would it counsel crimes?

#### OXTIERN.

My conduct was reprehensible, I must confess; but I adored you, and I had a rival.

#### ERNESTINE, *firmly*.

Monster, what have you done to this rival?

#### OXTIERN.

'Tis not I who determined his fate.

ERNESTINE.

You alone stole him from me; you alone must return him to me.

OXTIERN.

'Twas not my hand that deprived you of him, Ernestine. The laws were evoked and applied, and under them Herman has been sent to prison. All I can do is use my influence to render the harshness of his chains more bearable.

ERNESTINE.

What! 'Twas you who forged them! How can I so deceive myself that now I stoop to ask that you break them! . . . Begone, I want nothing from you. . . . I, offer you the chance to do something generous? . . . the means wherewith to blot your horrors from my mind? . . . You see, Oxtiern, I am losing my mind. . . . All right, what do you intend to do with your victim? . . . Tell me, where are you taking me? . . .

OXTIERN.

I offer you, Ernestine, both my hand and my heart.

ERNESTINE.

Enchain myself to my torturer? . . . Never, never!

OXTIERN.

'Tis not as though there were another choice; is there?

ERNESTINE.

Ah, indeed there is. . . . Have you failed to divine it, Monsieur? Have you forgotten that I still have a father? . . . And a brother? (*With great pride.*) Have you forgotten that I still live and breathe?

OXTIERN.

All these cruel courses would serve no end; they would only result in bloodshed and would in no wise restore your honor. Only he whom you accuse of having taken it from you can return it to you. Consent to be his wife, and all is forgotten.

ERNESTINE, *as emphatically as possible.*

Traitor, what match can you propose to me now that you have dishonored me? I would remain caught forever between opprobrium

and humiliation, a constant prey to grief and tears, trying to captivate my husband in ties he shall have formed solely out of duty.
Tell me, Oxtiern, what moments of peace or contentment can I look
forward to upon this earth? hate and despair on the one hand, constraint and remorse on the other. For us, the marriage tapers would
be lighted from the torches of the Furies, serpents would form the
bonds between us, and death would be our only salvation.

OXTIERN, *casting himself at Ernestine's knees.*
If this be so, then—since 'tis I alone who deserve it—strike,
Ernestine, here is my heart; with your hands, spill this guilty blood,
which is no longer worthy to sustain a creature barbarous enough
to have misjudged you so cruelly.

ERNESTINE, *repelling him even more forcefully.*
Then let it be spilled without wetting the ground; otherwise,
'twould cause crimes to sprout up.

OXTIERN.
What is't then you want, Ernestine, and what can I do to prove
you my love and earn your forgiveness?

ERNESTINE, *showing anger, scorn, and strength.*
Your love, never! . . . As for your repentance, that I shall believe when you break the irons wherewith, thanks to your villainy,
my lover is fettered: go and confess your plots to the judges; go
and meet the death your crimes deserve; burden the earth no more
with a weight which wearies it; the sun is less pure since for shedding light upon your days.

OXTIERN, *with controlled pride.*
Ernestine is forgetting—or am I mistaken?—the situation
wherein she finds herself?

ERNESTINE, *nobly and energetically.*
You are right, Oxtiern; were I to dwell upon it, either I would
cease to live or you would die.

OXTIERN.
When a woman believes herself to be unhappy, she should
make some slight effort to deal tactfully with him upon whom her
destiny depends.

ERNESTINE, *proudly*.

This woman depends only upon herself; she is responsible only to herself; she alone will determine her fate.

OXTIERN.

Let us pursue our route, Ernestine; tomorrow we shall reach one of my estates; there perhaps I shall succeed in mollifying and calming you.

ERNESTINE, *as above*.

No, I am going no farther; it was in spite of myself that you decoyed me here; here I must be avenged, or here I shall die.

OXTIERN.

These outbursts of a frenzied soul tire you and remedy nothing, Ernestine; I was hoping from you less hate . . . a more complete resignation.

# SCENE VI

*This scene must move at a very rapid pace.*

## THE ABOVE, AMELIE, CASIMIR.

*Each takes his master aside in one corner of the stage.*

CASIMIR, *to Oxtiern*.

Monsieur?

OXTIERN.

What is it, Casimir?

AMELIE, *entering slightly after the others*.

Mademoiselle?

ERNESTINE.

Have you come to apprise me of still further reverses?

CASIMIR, *to Oxtiern*.

An officer has just arrived at this inn.

AMELIE, *to Ernestine.*

A soldier, whom I haven't yet seen, requests most earnestly to speak with you.

OXTIERN.

Try to discover who it might be.

ERNESTINE, *to Amélie, with a show of joy.*

'Tis my father! He must have received my note, and he's arrived!

CASIMIR, *to Oxtiern.*

Monsieur, do not come out; 'tis essential you not see this man.

OXTIERN, *to Ernestine.*

Excuse me, urgent matters summon me. Is it too much to hope that when next we meet I may find you a trifle calmer?

ERNESTINE, *nobly and steadfastly.*

Yes, yes, you may count on me, Monsieur; never again will you see me in the character you must imagine mine to be. . . . You doubtless thought me beneath contempt, that much at least your conduct has proved to me; soon you will confess that I was worthy of your esteem.

OXTIERN, *exiting.*

You will always be worthy of my heart!

## SCENE VII

### ERNESTINE, AMELIE.

ERNESTINE, *very rapidly.*

Fly, Amélie, and learn who this stranger is. . . . Heavens! if 'twere my father!

AMELIE, *leaving in great haste.*

May he come and put an end to all our woes!

## SCENE VIII

ERNESTINE, *alone.*

O height of misfortune and immodesty! Between Oxtiern and myself, we offer the picture of the one and the other! I dare defy the hand of fate to place upon earth both a creature more to be pitied than I and one more shameless than he. . . . He offers me his hand to compensate for the wrongs into which his villainy has plunged me . . . were I to accept it, I should but finish the work he has so basely begun. No, no, Oxtiern, 'tis not your hand I want, 'tis your head; only your death can assuage the state to which your savagery has reduced me.

## SCENE IX

ERNESTINE, COLONEL FALKENHEIM.

ERNESTINE, *rushing toward him, then immediately backing away fearfully.*

Father . . . oh, Father! I am no longer worthy of you!

THE COLONEL.

What is this I hear?

ERNESTINE, *painfully.*

Why did you leave me, Father? baleful voyage . . . wretched event . . . The cruel man: he chose the time when you were gone . . . he deceived me; he led me to believe he could give me the happiness that you were hesitant to grant me; and, taking advantage of my weakness, he has rendered me unworthy both of you and of life itself.

THE COLONEL.

Unjust Heaven! didst Thou prolong my days only to have me witness such an abomination? The traitor must die. . . . (*He attempts to exit.*)

ERNESTINE, *stopping him.*

No, no, vengeance must be mine and mine alone, I shall attend to it myself.

THE COLONEL.

Your plans alarm me!

ERNESTINE, *rapidly*.

Do not try to unravel them, they are just and right . . . proud as the soul you bequeathed me. . . . I shall discover them to you when the time is ripe. Have you seen him, Father? Did he dare present himself to you?

THE COLONEL.

He was careful not to; a single glance from me would have reduced him to nothing.

ERNESTINE.

You learned of my flight through my note?

THE COLONEL.

'Twas your note that hastened my steps hither.

ERNESTINE, *rapidly*.

Oh! Father, have you ever doubted me for a moment?

THE COLONEL.

Never; but you left no protectors behind.

ERNESTINE.

Do the poor and downtrodden ever have any defenders? Oxtiern is rich, he is influential; we were virtuous and poor. . . . Oh yes, Father, oh yes, he had to be right. . . . And poor Herman, have you any news of him?

THE COLONEL.

I heard tell of a bankruptcy in which he was implicated; this wretched affair, so I have been informed, will cost a small fortune to settle, and we have none.

ERNESTINE, *aside*.

Oxtiern, Oxtiern, so this is how you take revenge upon a rival!

THE COLONEL.

If only I had consented to your marriage! My cruel refusals are the cause of everything!

ERNESTINE.

You deemed them just; is that not all I require to make me
erase from my mind the ill they have done me? Who better than
the author of our days can judge what is best for us? . . . Forgive
me, Father, I beg of you to withdraw for a moment, I haven't a
minute to lose. At dawn we're leaving for the Count's château,
and tomorrow I shall perhaps be enchained forever unless I succeed
in freeing myself today. . . . Keep away from Oxtiern, avoid seeing
him. . . . Fabrice, the innkeeper, seems to me a worthy man. Ask
him to conceal you, and leave the rest to me.

THE COLONEL, *worried*.

Fabrice was not here when I arrived; I was told he had gone
to Stockholm on important business, but that he was expected back
before tomorrow morning.

ERNESTINE, *perturbed*.

Fabrice gone! . . . Could I have been mistaken? Gone to
Stockholm? What business can he have there? Could the Count
have sent him? He's known him for a long time! . . . With what
new bond am I about to be shackled? Everything takes me unawares! Everything terrifies me!

THE COLONEL, *with a display of nobility and strength*.

Don't worry, Ernestine, your father will not desert you again;
dear, unhappy child, either we shall emerge triumphant together
or we shall be destroyed in each other's arms. Adieu; let Amélie
keep me informed if you should have the slightest need of me. And
remember that the scion of Charles XII's favorite is perforce a man
born to sustain the honor and glory of his family.


# SCENE X

ERNESTINE, *alone*.

There is but a single means whereby to satisfy me, Oxtiern:
'tis that you must spill my blood, or that I must shed yours to the
last drop. . . . Now, let us pen a note. (*She sits at the table and
reads aloud as she writes:*) "A decent man does not outrage a

virtuous girl with impunity; you know the rules of honor, abide by them; the opponent I offer you is full worthy to engage you in a duel; it will take place in the garden of this hostelry, with swords the choice of weapons; rendezvous this evening at eleven at the appointed spot; a young man clothed in white will appear before you; attack him stoutly, he will respond in like measure; bear in mind that one of you must die, Oxtiern; be as brave as you have been base; upon this condition alone shall Ernestine forgive you. Adieu." (*She seals her note, then rings.*)

## SCENE XI

### ERNESTINE, AMELIE.

AMELIE, *hurrying in.*
May I be of service, Mademoiselle?

ERNESTINE, *rapidly.*
Go take this note to the Count. . . . Take care that he does not see my father. . . . Hold, I'm going to retire. Go fetch the Colonel, bring him to this room and have him wait here while you are delivering my note; this errand, Amélie, is as important as it is secret; mind you not to overlook the slightest detail. (*She exits.*)

## SCENE XII

### AMELIE, *alone.*

This note worries me; her expression when she gave it to me; the manner in which she has held forth to me about her brother upon occasion in the past; I'll warrant she's asking him to come here, that she'll have him challenge the Count to a duel. . . . I must warn the Colonel . . . they are his children. I should never forgive myself for concealing from him what I suspect. Good Lord, what unhappiness the base maneuvers of a scoundrel can cause! (*She starts to exit and meets the Colonel.*)

## SCENE XIII

### AMELIE, THE COLONEL.

AMELIE.

Oh! Monsieur, your daughter begs you to remain for a short time in this room while I take this message to Count Oxtiern.

THE COLONEL.

What does it say?

AMELIE.

I don't know; but it must be a matter of great importance, for Mademoiselle enjoined me to give it my most urgent attention.

THE COLONEL.

And you have no notion what it contains?

AMELIE.

Excuse me, I think it's about a duel; Monsieur your son . . . Mademoiselle your daughter . . . Count Oxtiern . . .

THE COLONEL.

My son? Pray be more explicit, I don't understand you.

AMELIE, *eagerly*.

Monsieur, I'll wager that Mademoiselle, your daughter, is summoning your son to seek revenge; that by this note she is challenging the Count to a duel, with your son as the Count's opponent. . . . Oh! Monsieur, is there not some other way to punish such a crime, without risking your son's life?

THE COLONEL.

There are doubtless other ways . . . most assuredly there are. No matter . . . go and deliver this note. Do as your mistress has prescribed, and count upon me to take care of the rest in proper manner. (*Calling her back impatiently.*) Amélie, if my son should arrive, should it be learned he is anywhere near this inn, make certain he speaks to no one. Have him brought to me immediately. On this point, give the strictest orders.

AMELIE, *exiting*.

Yes, Monsieur, I shall, of that you can be sure. I understand the full importance of your instructions.

## SCENE XIV

THE COLONEL, *alone*.

My son will not fight a duel; 'tis up to me alone to clear this stain. . . . Oh, daughter, daughter, your defense is my concern, no one else's. . . . I shall test my courage with this hateful man, and we shall see whether this hand, trained in combat . . . guided by the more justified cry for revenge, will be steadied by the God who is the protector of honor! Let us go apprise the Count of these resolutions, but let us keep them a secret from my daughter. . . . I want her to learn of the duel only by my victory. Yes, my victory is certain; 'tis a monster I am going to punish, and Providence is too wise to allow Virtue to be crushed beneath the perfidious assaults of vice and villainy.

END OF ACT II

# Act Three

*The stage represents the garden of the hostelry. Throughout the act, the light slowly fades, so that, at the denouement, the stage is enveloped in total darkness.*

## SCENE I

OXTIERN, DERBAC.
*At the start of this scene, the delivery is prolonged and mysterious.*

DERBAC.

I asked you to step down here into the garden, my dear Count, in order to converse with you more privily. There are all sorts of agitation in this house; and since the arrival of Colonel Falkenheim, Ernestine has locked herself in her room and refuses to see anyone; Amélie is everywhere at once; and Casimir, who is following every move, informs me of the most extraordinary things.

OXTIERN.

What is it you suspect then?

DERBAC.

I suspect nothing, my friend, I know everything. Begin by reading this note, if the little daylight remaining allows you to. Amélie was supposed to deliver it to you; not finding you, she left it with Casimir, with instructions that it be given to you with all possible haste: I took it from your valet's hands . . . and I read it.

714

OXTIERN, *casting his eye over the note,*
*pauses at the following words:*

"The opponent I offer you is full worthy to engage you in a duel. . . ." Do you know who this opponent is?

DERBAC.

I think I can guess.

OXTIERN.

Who is it then?

DERBAC.

Ernestine herself.

OXTIERN.

Ernestine?

DERBAC.

I'm quite certain.

OXTIERN.

What proof of this absurdity do you have?

DERBAC.

I saw the manservant of the inn carrying with his own two hands the white raiment to which the note refers. He was taking it to Amélie, who was supposed to give it to Ernestine. And 'tis in this guise she will come to do battle with you herself.

OXTIERN.

'Tis inconceivable, such a plan, motivated by rage . . . and by despair. We must avenge ourselves for it, and nothing could be easier.

DERBAC.

But the Colonel who is here . . .

OXTIERN.

Even were there ten colonels, this creature is plotting to kill me, and I must forestall her. I refuse to fight a duel with her, I would only kill her, and I want her to live . . . to live to rue the day she plotted my downfall. If she thwarts my plans, I am lost. She will cast herself at the feet of the King, and disgrace me; all my wealth and possessions, my position, my influence, will be wiped out, everything. Therefore, I have no choice but to . . . Take a look, Derbac, at who is walking toward us through this thicket.

DERBAC.

'Tis Casimir.

(*The light gradually fades.*)

## SCENE II

### THE ABOVE, CASIMIR.

CASIMIR.

Colonel Falkenheim has just ordered me to deliver this note to you without delay, Count.

OXTIERN.

Give it to me. (*He reads it quickly; then, signaling to Casimir to leave them, he goes over to Derbac and, mysteriously, says.*) My friend, 'tis a challenge from Ernestine's father. Knowing that his daughter is arming her brother against me, he does not wish to yield to anyone the honor of so necessary a revenge. He is coming down to this garden and requests that I await him here, to engage him in a duel. You see, you were mistaken; Ernestine's brother must have slipped into the inn unbeknownst to us: 'tis he the opponent she has picked for me, and the white garb was to serve him as a disguise. (*Waxing more and more wild, and increasingly emphatic.*) Embrace me, my friends; we were looking for means to rid ourselves of this girl, and now fate offers us an unparalleled opportunity. (*More coldly.*) Casimir, go and tell the Colonel that I await him. By then it will be dark. . . . Tell him I shall be dressed in white; that he should attack without consideration the person he sees in the shadows, clothed in this garb.

CASIMIR, *trying to calm his master.*

Monsieur, Monsieur.

OXTIERN.

Quiet, you knavish lout; if it makes you tremble, then begone with you!

CASIMIR.

I shall do as you say. The Colonel shall be informed that his enemy, clothed in white, will appear at the appointed time and place. (*Aside.*) I only hope Fabrice returns before a crime so horrible is committed. (*Approaching.*) Monsieur, if you would permit me to say one word.

DERBAC.

Speak up, my friend, tell us what you know.

CASIMIR.

The white garment is not for Ernestine's brother; I am certain her brother has not entered the house. I have kept a close lookout on every new arrival, and I swear to you that this young man, whom I know perfectly well, was not among them; this garment is for Ernestine, of that you can be sure; the servant of the house, who, thanks to your gold, has been won to our side, was sent to fetch it somewhere in the neighborhood. And 'tis to Ernestine herself they are supposed to give it.

DERBAC, *very emphatically*.

That clarifies everything. You see what the plan is, Oxtiern: Ernestine, to conceal her plans from her father, told the Colonel that she was counting on her brother to redress her wrongs; the Colonel believed her; he doesn't want his son to fight a duel, and is coming in his stead.

OXTIERN, *very keenly*.

And will Ernestine also come?

DERBAC.

It would seem likely.

OXTIERN.

And will she come dressed in white?

CASIMIR.

That much is certain, Monsieur.

DERBAC, *with a cry of horror*.

What! you intend to have the girl murdered by her own father!

OXTIERN.

Quiet! Don't you see, my friends, 'tis fate that has come to offer me these means of punishment; and you oppose my taking advantage of them?

DERBAC.

The crime is execrable; it revolts me.

OXTIERN.

'Tis useful for my tranquillity.


# SCENE III

## OXTIERN, DERBAC.

OXTIERN.

I'm losing patience with that valet. He lacks steadfastness of purpose. These imbeciles have no principles. Anything that deviates even slightly from the beaten paths of vice or villainy amazes them; the thought of remorse terrifies them.

DERBAC, *sharply*.

Woe unto scoundrels whom remorse does not check! woe unto you if you persist in your plans; never was a crime more foul conceived, even in hell.

OXTIERN.

I agree, but it serves my purpose. . . . Did this proud creature not plot my downfall?

DERBAC.

She engaged you in a duel; she was risking her own life.

OXTIERN.

Playing the heroine . . . I dislike any show of pride in a woman.

DERBAC, *with considerable feeling*.

Ah! is the creature who most deserves our respect not entitled to display any pride?

OXTIERN.

Ah, there you go moralizing again; the minute I turn my back on you, you begin to lose your grip, and 'tis all I can do to bring you round again. . . . Come now, Derbac, a little backbone; lest Casimir fail to carry out my orders as he should, I want you to carry them out as well; the Colonel will be here shortly; tell him to throw himself ardently at the enemy whom he will see advancing toward him clothed in white: it will be his daughter. . . . Do you understand, Derbac? and I shall be avenged. (*He exits.*)

## SCENE IV

DERBAC, *alone.*

No, I cannot bring myself to serve such a loathsome deed; let Casimir be responsible for it, and let us not become involved in this horror. I want to leave this man's company. . . . I shall revert to my former poverty, from which his influence rescued me, and 'tis greatly to be regretted, no doubt; but 'tis better than the misfortune of further corrupting myself at his unworthy school; the lack of fortune frightens me less than does crime: suffer as he may, the honest man finds solace in his heart. . . . (*He exits as soon as he sees someone coming.*)

## SCENE V

THE COLONEL, *groping his way in the shadows.*

'Tis here the duel is supposed to take place. I thought he had preceded me; he will doubtless be here shortly. . . . O you unhappy person, what are you going to do? . . . The cruel laws of honor, how unfair you are! Why must the offended party risk life and limb, when 'tis the aggressor who is guilty? . . . Ah, let him kill me, slice me to shreds, I cannot survive my disgrace! (*He trembles.*) I think I hear him coming . . . and why is it that the approach of this opponent gives rise to feelings I cannot control? yet I have never known fear; the desire for vengeance troubles me and prevents me from distinguishing the real source of the impressions to which I am prey: the night is growing so dark I shall be hard put to recognize the color of the clothing I was told he would be wearing. (*What follows is said very softly, and above all so that Ernestine cannot hear it.*) 'Tis he; let us attack him in silence and not noise the duel abroad. (*He draws his sword and falls upon Ernestine, who is dressed in man's clothing, of the color referred to before. Scarcely has the duel begun when we hear two pistol shots off-stage, one of which is Herman's and the other the Count's; Herman rushes in, having just killed Oxtiern. Fabrice dashes in a moment later.*)

## SCENE VI

### THE COLONEL, ERNESTINE, HERMAN, FABRICE.

*The rhythm of this scene is extremely rapid.*

HERMAN, *still off-stage.*
Die, traitor, Ernestine is avenged. (*Flying to separate the duelists.*) Merciful Heaven, stop! Do you realize whose blood you were about to spill? Wretched father! don't you know your own daughter?

ERNESTINE, *discarding her sword.*
Oh, God! (*She throws herself in her father's arms.*)

THE COLONEL.
Dear, unhappy child!

FABRICE, *entering and with great feeling.*
Your troubles are over, Colonel. No sooner had I learned of the Count's wicked schemes than I flew to Stockholm, freed your young friend from the chains wherein Oxtiern had held him captive: you see to what use he has put his first moments of freedom.

HERMAN.
The coward; his defeat has cost me but little; 'tis so easy to triumph over a traitor. Having emerged victorious, I hastened hither, Monsieur, to apprise you of the crimes of which, despite

yourselves, he was making you the instrument, and to ask you for the hand of this beloved girl, which I still covet and which, I dare flatter myself, I now deserve.

*The Colonel makes a gesture half of approbation, half of sorrow.*

ERNESTINE, *to Herman.*

Can I still hope for such happiness?

HERMAN, *to Ernestine, tenderly.*

Ah! could the crimes of a villain such as Oxtiern wither Nature's most beautiful handiwork?

THE COLONEL.

Oh! Fabrice, my debt to you is great. How can I ever repay you?...

FABRICE.

By your friendship, my friends, 'tis what I am due. I put my money to the best use possible. . . . To punish crime and reward virtue. . . . Let someone tell me whether 'twere possible to invest it at a higher rate of interest! . . .

END OF THE THIRD AND FINAL ACT

# Ernestine, A Swedish Tale (1788)

# Ernestine,
## A Swedish Tale

After Italy, England, and Russia, few countries in Europe seem to me as intriguing as Sweden. But if my imagination was burning to see the celebrated countries whence came, in times past, such legendary heroes as Alaric, Attila, and Theodoric —in short all those heroes who, followed by countless numbers of soldiers, did proper obeisance to the imperial eagle whose wings were aspiring to embrace the world, those heroes who caused the Romans to tremble at the very gates of their mighty capital—if indeed my soul was consumed with a burning desire to visit the country of Gustavus Vasa, of Christina, and of Charles XII . . . all three of whom owe their fame to very different sources, since the first is renowned for that quality—rare and much to be desired in a sovereign—of a philosophic turn of mind, for that estimable prudence which rides roughshod over any religious systems whenever they impinge upon the authority of the government to which they are presumed to be subservient, and upon the happiness of the people, which is the sole object of legislation;[1] the second for that nobility of soul which causes one to prefer solitude and a love of literature to the vainglory of the throne; and the third for those heroic virtues which make him forever deserving of the surname Alexander—if, I say, I was prompted by all these various objects of my admiration, fancy then how much more ar-

---

[1] Gustavus Vasa, having seen that the Roman clergy, by nature despotic and seditious, was encroaching upon Royal authority, and that by its ordinary vexations was ruining the people whenever restraints were not placed upon it, introduced Protestantism into Sweden, after having restored to the people the great wealth and lands which the priests had taken from them.

dent was my desire to become acquainted with and admire this
wise, virtuous, sober, and magnanimous people whom we may
properly term the model of the North.

'Twas with this in mind that I left Paris the 20th of July,
1774, and after having traveled through Holland, Westphalia, and
Denmark, I arrived in Sweden toward the middle of the following
year.

After I had spent some three months in Stockholm, my curiosity was directed toward those famous mines about which I had read
so much and wherein I imagined I might encounter some adventures
similar to those related by the Abbé Prévost in the first volume of
his anecdotes. And indeed I did . . . but how different were the
adventures I encountered! . . .

Accordingly, I repaired to Uppsala, a city situated on the
Fyris River, which divides that town in two. Long the capital of
Sweden, Uppsala is still today, after Stockholm, the second most
important city of that country. After spending three weeks there,
I continued on to Falun, the ancient cradle of the Scythians, the
customs and dress of which the present-day inhabitants of Dale-
carlia still retain. As I reached the outskirts of Falun, I came to
the Taperg mine, one of the most imposing in all Sweden.

These mines, long the most precious natural resource of the
State, ultimately fell beneath the yoke of the English, because of
debts contracted by the mine owners with the English, a nation
which stands forever ready to serve those whom she fancies she
may one day be in a position to dominate and engulf, after having
upset their balance of trade or having whittled away their strength
by dint of usurious loans.

Once at Taperg, my imagination was filled with these thoughts
just prior to my descent into these subterranean depths, wherein
the luxury and the avarice of a handful of men was capable of
dominating so many others.

Only recently returned from Italy, I was under the impression that these quarries doubtless resembled the Catacombs of
Rome or Naples. I was mistaken. Though situated far deeper in
the bowels of the earth, I was to discover there a solitude less
terrifying.

At Uppsala I had been provided with a highly cultivated man

to act as my guide, a man well versed in letters and with a knowledge both profound and broad. Fortunately for me, Falkeneim (for
that was his name) spoke impeccable German and English, the only
languages in common use in the North, through which I was able to
communicate with him. We found that we both preferred the former language, and settled upon it; conversation on all subjects was
thus no problem for us, and 'twas easy for me to learn from his lips
the tale that I shall shortly relate.

With the aid of a basket and a pulley and rope—an apparatus
so designed that the descent could be made without the slightest
danger—we reached the bottom of that mine, and in the twinkling
of an eye found ourselves some hundred and twenty fathoms beneath the surface of the earth. 'Twas with considerable amazement
that I saw in these depths a veritable subterranean city: streets,
houses, churches, inns, much hustle and bustle, work being performed, police, judges: in short, everything the most civilized city
of Europe might offer.

After having surveyed these singular dwellings, we went into a
tavern, where Falkeneim was able to order from the innkeeper all
that we needed to quench our thirst and satisfy our hunger: a beer
of excellent quality, dried fish, and a kind of Swedish bread commonly used in rural areas made of the bark of pine and birch trees,
mixed with straw, some wild roots, and kneaded together with oat-
meal. Does one need any more to satisfy one's veritable needs? The
philosopher who travels the ways and byways of the world in search
of knowledge must learn to adapt himself to every time and clime,
to every custom and religion, to all kinds of lodging and food,
and leave to the indolent voluptuary of the capital his prejudices
. . . his luxury . . . that shameless luxury which, never satisfied by
real needs, daily creates factitious ones, to the detriment of one's
health and fortune.

We were just finishing our frugal meal when one of the mine
workers, dressed in a blue jacket and breeches, his head covered
with an inadequate and ill-fitting blond wig, came over and greeted
Falkeneim in Swedish. Out of deference to me, my guide having
answered him in German, the prisoner (for such he was) forthwith
began to converse in that language. This poor wretch, seeing that I
was the sole reason for their conversing in German, and thinking to

728 THE MARQUIS DE SADE

discern my nationality, paid me a compliment in French, which he spoke to perfection, then turned back to Falkeneim and asked him if he had any news from Stockholm. He spoke of the King, mentioned several persons of the Court, and did so with an ease and assurance that caused me to study him more attentively. He asked Falkeneim whether he deemed it possible that he might one day be pardoned, to which my guide replied negatively, shaking his head with a show of regret.

The prisoner immediately departed, his eyes filled with chagrin, after having refused to share our food or drink, despite our insistence. A moment later he returned and asked Falkeneim whether he might entrust him with a letter that he would hasten to write. My companion promised to do whatever the prisoner desired, and the latter withdrew a second time.

As soon as he was outside:

"Who is that man?" I asked Falkeneim.

"One of the foremost noblemen of all Sweden," he replied.

"Your words amaze me!"

"He is fortunate indeed to be here. Our sovereign's leniency in his behalf might be likened to the generosity of Augustus with what regards Cinna. That man you just saw is Count Oxtiern, one of the Senators most ardently against the King during the Revolution of 1772.[2] After peace had been restored, he was further guilty of unparalleled crimes. After he had been tried and found guilty by the laws of the land, the King, remembering the hate that Oxtiern had evinced against him, summoned him and said: 'Count Oxtiern, the judges have decreed your death ... 'twas not so many years ago you decreed my banishment from the land; 'tis for this reason I intend to spare your life: I wish to show you that the heart of him whom you deemed unworthy of the throne was none the less not utterly without virtue.' Oxtiern fell at Gustavus' feet, a torrent of tears issuing from his eyes. 'I should have preferred to pardon you completely,' said the King, helping Oxtiern to his feet, 'but the enormity of your acts made this impossible. I am sending you to the mines. I do not claim you will be happy there, but at least you

_____

[2] It is worth while recalling that in this Revolution the King had cast his lot with the popular party, and that the Senators were against the King and the people.

will be alive. You may go.' Thus Oxtiern was brought to this place; 'tis he you have just seen. Come now, let us be going," added Falkeneim, " 'tis growing late. We shall fetch his letter on our way out."

"Oh, Monsieur," I then said to my guide, "were it necessary to spend a full week here, you have piqued my curiosity uncommonly; I refuse to leave these entrails of the earth so long as you have not revealed to me the reasons which have brought this poor wretch hither. Though a criminal, he has a most interesting face; why, the man is not a day over forty! I should like to see him set free. He might turn over a new leaf, and lead an honest life."

"Oxtiern, honest? Never . . . never . . ."

"For pity's sake, Monsieur, satisfy my curiosity!"

"All right, I shall," Falkeneim replied. "Besides, that will give him time to write his letters. I shall send word to him that he need not hasten. Come, let us repair to this back room, where we will be less disturbed than here next to the street. . . . Still, I am most reluctant to discover these things to you, 'twill erase from your heart any feeling of pity the villain may have aroused in you. I should prefer that you remain in ignorance, and that he thus lose none of your good will toward him."

"Monsieur," I said to Falkeneim, "the failings of man teach me to know him better; my sole purpose in traveling is to study. The further he has deviated from the barriers which Nature or man-made laws have imposed upon him, the more interesting is he as a subject of study, the more worthy to be examined and the more deserving of my compassion. Virtue needs naught but worship, its career is one of happiness . . . it could not be otherwise, a thousand arms open to receive its disciples if ever adversity overtakes them. But no one opens his arms to the guilty person. . . . People blush to be in his presence, are embarrassed to offer him their tears, as though terrified of contagion; he is banished from every heart: pride impels us to heap abuse upon him whom we ought to succor out of a feeling of humanity. Therefore, Monsieur, when can we find a mortal more interesting than he who, from the pinnacle of fame and fortune, has suddenly fallen into the pit of misfortune, who, born to greatness, experiences naught but the pangs of disappointment, of disgrace . . . who is henceforth surrounded by naught save the calamities of poverty, and whose heart is filled with the shafts of remorse or the serpents of despair? Such a man, my dear friend, is full worthy of my pity. I shall not add my voice to those fools who say: 'He has no one to blame but himself,' nor shall I join the chorus of hardhearted souls who, to justify their induration, cry out: 'Why, the man is all too guilty.' Eh! What does it matter to me what bounds he has exceeded, what rules or laws he has scorned, what he has done! He is a man, and therefore weak . . . he is a criminal, he is miserable, he has my pity. . . . Speak up, Falkeneim, pray do, I am burning to hear what you have to tell."

And my worthy friend related to me the following tale in these terms:

In the early years of the present century, a German nobleman, Roman Catholic by religion, was obliged to flee his own country over a matter which is far from being a discredit to him. Knowing that, although we have abjured our papistic errors, the Roman religion was none the less tolerated in our provinces, he came to Stockholm. A young and handsome man, with a strong bent for the military and eager for a taste of glory, he caught the fancy of Charles XII and had the honor of accompanying him on several of his expeditions. He took part in the unfortunate battle of Poltava, remained with the King in his refuge at Bendery, shared his imprisonment in the Turkish dungeons, and returned with him to Sweden. When in 1718 our country lost this hero beneath the walls of Fredrikshald, in Norway, Sanders ('tis the name of the man of whom I am speaking) had by this time attained the rank of colonel in our armies, and 'twas in this capacity he retired from service and went to live in Norrköping, a commercial city fifteen leagues from Stockholm, situated on the canal which, in the province of Ostergöt-land, joins Lake Vättern to the Baltic Sea. There Sanders married and had a son, whom the later Kings Frederick I and Adolphus-Frederick accepted into their service as his father had been accepted before him. Through his own merit, the young man advanced in the King's service until, like his father, he attained the rank of colonel. Although still a young man, he retired to Norrköping, his birthplace, and there he married the daughter of a rather impecunious merchant. This worthy lady died twelve years later, after having given birth to a daughter, Ernestine, who is the subject of the present tale.

The story opens three years ago, at which time Sanders must have been about forty-two. His daughter was then sixteen, and was very rightly judged to be one of the most beautiful creatures ever to grace our fair land. She was tall, a perfect model for an artist's brush; noble and proud in bearing, she had black eyes as beautiful as they were lively, extremely long hair of the same color, which as you know is exceedingly rare in our part of the world. In spite of her dark hair and eyes, she had the most beautiful, the most alabaster skin. People found that she somewhat resembled our beautiful Countess de Sparre, the illustrious friend of our learned Christina, and 'tis indeed true.

Young Mademoiselle Sanders had not reached the age of sixteen without her heart already having made a choice. Having often heard her mother complain how cruel it was for a young wife who adored her husband to be constantly separated from him by the duties of a State to which he owes total allegiance and which detains him now in one city, now in another, Ernestine, with her father's approval, had decided to marry a young man, Herman by name, who was of the same religion as she and who intended to enter the world of commerce. Herman's training for that profession was presently taking place in the offices of M. Scholtz, the most famous merchant in Norrköping and one of the richest in all Sweden.

Herman was the scion of a merchant family. But he had lost his parents while he was still very young, and his father, upon his deathbed, had commended him to his former associate Scholtz. Thus he shared their dwelling, and having been found deserving of their full confidence by his seriousness of purpose and his diligence, Herman had been placed in charge of the business' funds and books, although he was not yet twenty-two. 'Twas at this juncture that the head of the business died, leaving no heirs. Herman henceforth found himself dependent upon Scholtz's widow, an arrogant and haughty woman who, in spite of all her husband's instructions, seemed firmly resolved to get rid of the young man if he did not straightway accept the plans she had in mind for him.

Herman was a perfect match for Ernestine, as handsome as

she was beautiful, adoring her as much as she loved him; there was also little doubt that the widow Scholtz was not blind to his qualities and that she, still attractive at forty, was enamored of him. But Herman, whose heart was taken, made not the slightest move to respond to his patroness' prepossession, and although he strongly suspected her feelings toward him, he wisely feigned to be unaware of them.

Ernestine Sanders, however, was alarmed by Madame Scholtz's passion; she knew her to be a bold and enterprising woman, jealous and hot-tempered; a rival such as she worried her prodigiously. Furthermore, she herself was far from being as good a match for Herman as was Madame Scholtz: her father had no dowry to offer her, and although her mother had left her a modest inheritance, how could she pretend to compete with the impressive fortune that Madame Scholtz could offer her young treasurer?

Colonel Sanders approved of his daughter's choice; as she was his only child, he adored her, and he knew that Herman possessed some wealth, that he was intelligent, was a young man of high principles, and that, furthermore, he had won Ernestine's heart; thus he had no intention of raising the least objection to so suitable a match. But fate does not always will what is best. It seems, in fact, to take pleasure in unsettling the best-laid plans of men, in order that from these inconstancies they may derive lessons and so learn never to count upon anything in this world, whose most certain laws are instability and disorder.

"Herman," the widow said one day to Ernestine's lover,[3] "by now you have had sufficient training in the world of commerce to make a decision concerning your future. The money your parents left you has, thanks to my husband and me, increased in value more than enough to allow you to live comfortably. Set up your own establishment, my friend, I soon plan to retire. We can reconcile our accounts at the first possible occasion."

"Whatever you wish, Madame," said Herman. "You are aware of my honesty and disinterest. I am as little concerned about

<hr>

[3] Though Sade uses the terms *amant* and *amante* in referring to Herman and Ernestine, it is obvious their relationship is platonic and pristine. In translating, we have none the less used both "lover" and "paramour"; they should, however, be understood as Sade intended them.—*Tr.*

my money which is in your hands as you must be about your money which I control in managing your affairs."

"But Herman, have you no plans to establish your own business?"

"I am still young, Madame."

"All the more reason for some sensible and impressionable young woman to judge you an attractive match. I am certain you must already have someone in mind whom you assuredly would make happy."

"I wish to have a greater fortune before I reach such a stage."

"A woman would help you to amass it."

"When I marry, I want my fortune already made, so that I can devote my full attention to my wife and children."

"You mean to say there is no woman in the world who has caught your fancy?"

"There is one whom I revere as I would my own mother, to whom my services are dedicated as long as she vouchsafes to accept them."

" 'Tis not to these sentiments I am referring, my friend. I am grateful for them, but 'tis not upon such that a marriage is founded. Herman, I wish to know whether you have found anyone with whom you would like to share your life?"

"No, Madame."

"In that case why do you spend all your time at the Sanders'? What keeps constantly enticing you back to that man's house? He is a military man, you are a merchant. You should spend more time frequenting persons of your own profession, my friend, and forget those who are not."

"Madame knows that I am Catholic. The Colonel is too. Thus we often meet to pray together . . . to visit together those chapels which are open to us."

"I have never held your religion against you, although I do not share your belief, and indeed am perfectly convinced of the uselessness of all that nonsense, of whatever persuasion. You must confess, Herman, that I have never interfered with you on that score."

"Well, Madame, that is why—for religion—that I sometimes call upon the Colonel."

"Herman, there is another reason for these frequent visits, something you are hiding from me: you love Ernestine, that mere wisp of a child who, to my mind, has neither wit nor beauty but who, to hear the townsfolk talk, is one of the wonders of all Sweden. . . . Yes, Herman, you love her . . . you love her, I say, and I know it."

"Mademoiselle Ernestine Sanders thinks well of me, I believe, Madame. But her birth . . . her station . . . Were you aware, Madame, that her grandfather, Colonel Sanders, was a close friend of Charles XII, and originally a high-ranking nobleman from Westphalia?"

"I was."

"Well, then, Madame, would she make a suitable match for me?"

"I assure you most emphatically, Herman, that I think she would not. What you need is a mature woman, one who would attend to your fortune and give it her constant attention; a woman, in one word, of my age and position."

Herman blushed and turned away. . . . As at that point tea was served, the conversation was interrupted, and Herman, after luncheon was over, returned to his occupations.

"Oh! my dear Ernestine," said Herman the following day to Sanders' daughter, " 'tis all too true that that cruel woman has designs upon me, of that there can no longer be any doubt. You are aware of her temper, her moods, her jealousy, and her influence in the town.[4] Ernestine, I fear the worst."

And as the Colonel entered at this point, they informed him of their apprehensions.

Sanders was a former soldier, a man of exceeding good sense who preferred not to create any trouble for himself in the town, and clearly perceiving that the protection he was granting Herman was going to draw down upon him the wrath both of Madame Scholtz and of all her friends, he thought it best to advise the youths to surrender to circumstance. He attempted to make Herman see that the widow upon whom he was dependent would, in fact,

---

[4] Norrköping is a wholly commercial city. Consequently, a woman such as Madame Scholtz, in a town of this kind, would, as the head of one of the most prosperous businesses in Sweden, wield considerable influence.

make a far better match for him than Ernestine, and that, at his age, he should value far more a fat purse than a pretty face.

"'Tis not that I refuse you my daughter's hand, my boy," quoth the Colonel. "I know you and I esteem you. You have won the heart of her whom you adore, and I have no desire to create any obstacles to your happiness; but I am as much loath to prepare something you may live to regret. You are both young; at your age you are blind to all save love, you fancy that love is all you need to live. You are mistaken; without wealth love wilts and withers away, and the choice one makes when prompted by love alone is oft a poor one, which is soon followed by remorse."

"Father," said Ernestine, casting herself at Sanders' feet, "respected author of my days, I beseech you not to deprive me of the hope that my beloved Herman will one day be mine. Since I was a child you have promised me his hand. That thought is my only source of joy and pleasure; to deprive me of it will surely send me to my grave. My heart has been captured by him, secure in the knowledge that you approved of my sentiments. In Herman's love for me he will find all the necessary courage to resist the blandishments of Madame Scholtz. . . . O Father! do not abandon us!"

"Get up, my child," the Colonel said. "I love you . . . I adore you . . . since you can only be happy with Herman, and since you both love one another, set your minds at rest, you will never have any save Herman for husband. . . . And in fact, he owes that woman nothing. His honesty . . . his zeal, have more than repaid the gratitude he owes her; he is under no obligation to sacrifice his life in order to please her. . . . But we must manage things so that there is no falling out with anyone. . . ."

"Monsieur," said Herman, clasping the Colonel in his arms, "you who have granted me the right to call you Father, how can I ever repay you for the promises which you have just made me from the depths of your heart? Yes, I shall be worthy of the gift you are giving me. My every thought and act will be but for you and your beloved daughter. . . . I shall be the pillar and the companion of your declining years. . . . Father, fear not . . . we shall not make any enemies for ourselves, there is no contractual agreement between Madame Scholtz and me. When I present her with a proper accounting of her funds, and reclaim from her merely what she owes me, what can she say?"

"Ah! my boy, you do not know the hearts of those you intend to confront," the Colonel resumed, prey to a kind of concern he was unable to master. "There is no crime on the face of the earth to which a wicked woman will not stoop when 'tis a question of revenging herself for the charms a lover has spurned. That wretched woman will cause the poisonous effects of her wrath to rain down upon us all, and 'twill not be the roses of happiness you will reap, but the dark cypresses of mourning."

Ernestine and the man she loved spent the rest of the day calming her father's fears, allaying his apprehensions, and assuring him of their future happiness, which they painted for him in gentle hues. Nothing is as persuasive as the eloquence of lovers; theirs is a logic of the heart that the mind's logic can never equal.

Herman dined with his tender friends and left them at an early hour, his soul full to overflowing with hope and joy.

Approximately three months passed in this manner, without the widow ever raising the subject again, and without Herman daring to take the initiative and propose a settlement and separation. The Colonel gave the young man to understand that there was nothing disadvantageous in these delays. Ernestine was young, and her father did not in the least object to adding to the modest dowry which was already hers, in the form of a certain inheritance she could expect to receive from the widow Plorman, her aunt, a native of Stockholm who, already well along in years, might reasonably be expected to die at any moment.

But Madame Scholtz was impatient, and too clever not to detect her young bookkeeper's embarrassment; 'twas she who first broached the subject again and asked him whether he had reflected upon what they had discussed the last time they had had an opportunity to talk.

"Yes," replied Ernestine's lover, "and if 'tis a rendering of accounts and a separation that Madame is referring to, I am at her service."

"It seems to me, Herman, that was not precisely the topic we discussed."

"What was it then, Madame?"

"I asked you whether you wished to establish a business of your own, and whether you had chosen a wife who might help you run it."

"I thought I had replied that I preferred to wait till I had amassed a greater fortune before marrying."

" 'Twas what you said, Herman, but I must confess I did not believe you. And as we talk now, every expression on your face reveals the deceit in your soul."

"Ah! never has deceit besoiled my heart, Madame, and you know it well. Since childhood I have been close to you; you have vouchsafed to replace the mother I had the misfortune to lose. Have no fear that my gratitude may ever lessen or vanish."

"You speak constantly of gratitude, Herman. I should have preferred from you a sentiment more tender."

"But, Madame, can I control my . . ."

"Traitor! Is this your reward for all my loving care? Your ingratitude is most enlightening, that I can see. . . . I have been devoting myself to a monster. . . . Since I have become a widow, Herman, 'tis to your hand and heart I aspired, I can no longer conceal it. . . . The manner wherein I managed your affairs, the way I made your money grow and prosper . . . my conduct regarding you . . . even my eyes, which doubtless betrayed me . . . all this, false-hearted creature, all this, could not have failed to persuade you of my passion . . . and is this my reward? I am to be paid back with indifference and contempt? Herman, you do not know the heart of the woman you are insulting. No, you have no idea of the things whereof she is capable . . . you will learn only after it is too late. . . . Now, leave me, yes, leave me forthwith and prepare your books, Herman. I intend to do the same, and we shall go our separate ways. Yes, we shall separate. You will have no difficulty finding a roof for yourself; Sanders' house is doubtless open and waiting."

Madame Scholtz's state was such that our young lover had no difficulty perceiving that it was essential that he conceal his true feelings in order not to bring down upon the Colonel the full force of this dangerous creature's wrath and desire for vengeance. Herman therefore followed the dictum that a soft answer turneth away wrath, told his protectress that she was quite mistaken in her assumptions, and reminded her that the fact that he did not wish to marry until he had measurably increased his fortune surely belied her contention he had plans to marry the Colonel's daughter.

"My friend," Madame Scholtz replied to that, "I know your heart as though 'twere my own. I know that 'tis impossible you could have grown so distant were your heart not aflame for someone else. Although I may not be in the first flush of youth, do you think that I am still not attractive enough to find another husband? Yes, Herman, 'tis clear indeed: you would love me were it not for that creature whom I loathe, and upon whom I shall revenge myself for your indifference."

At these words Herman shuddered. Colonel Sanders, not wholly at home in his new land, and retired from service, was far from enjoying the powerful influence in Norrköping which Madame Scholtz could command. Her influence was as far-reaching as it was overwhelming, whereas the Colonel had virtually dropped out of the public eye and lost contact with those personages who, in Sweden as elsewhere in the world, hold in esteem only those who impress them by their favor or wealth; the Colonel, I say, was no longer considered as more than an ordinary individual whom influence and gold could easily crush, and Madame Scholtz, as with all scurvy souls, was not long in perceiving the truth of this situation.

Herman, therefore, made the decision to declare himself much more openly, albeit hypocritically, than he ever had done before. He cast himself at the knees of Madame Scholtz, besought her to calm her fears, reassured her that his heart contained no sentiment which could in any wise prove harmful to her from whom he had received so many blessings, and he begged her not to consider any further for the moment the idea of the separation with which she had threatened him. Realizing full well the young man's state of mind at that time, Madame Scholtz decided that this was the most she could expect; she placed all her hopes in a combination of her own charms and the beneficent effects of time, and quickly regained her composure.

Herman did not fail to inform the Colonel of this most recent conversation, and this wise and worthy man, still fearful of the possible vexations and dangerous character of Madame Scholtz, again tried to persuade the young man that he would be better off

yielding to the designs of his patroness than persisting in his desire
to marry Ernestine. But both lovers mustered every argument at
their command to remind the Colonel of the promises he had made
them and to make him pledge that he would never forswear them.

Things had been in this pass for about six months when Count
Oxtiern, this villain whom you saw in irons a short while ago in
these mines—irons to which he has been confined for more than a
year and to which he is condemned to spend the rest of his days—
Count Oxtiern, I say, was obliged to come from Stockholm to pay a
visit to Norrköping. The object of his visit was to withdraw certain
funds invested with Madame Scholtz by his father, whose fortune
the Count had just inherited. Madame Scholtz, full aware of her
visitor's importance—he was the son of a Senator and a Senator
himself—had prepared her best chambers for him, and prepared to
receive him with the full luxury that her wealth permitted.

The Count arrived, and the day following his arrival his elegant hostess gave him a sumptuous dinner, followed by a ball, to
which all the most beautiful women in town were invited. Ernestine
was not forgotten, and 'twas not without some trepidation that
Herman saw she was resolved to go. Were it possible for the Count
to see someone as beautiful as she without paying her the respects
which were due her? What did Herman not have to fear from such
a rival: assuming the worst came to pass, would Ernestine have the
strength or force of character to refuse the proffered hand of one
of the mightiest lords of Sweden? And were she to refuse, would
there not be formed against both Herman and Ernestine a league
whose chief conspirators would be the powerful Oxtiern and
Madame Scholtz? And what misfortunes might then be Herman's?
Could he, with his limited and straitened circumstances, resist the
arms of so many enemies conspiring against him?

He informed Ernestine of his apprehensions, and this worthy,
sensitive, and delicate girl, fully prepared to sacrifice such frivolous
pleasures for the sentiments which burned within her, proposed that
Herman immediately tell Madame Scholtz that he was refusing her
offer. Herman himself was rather of the same opinion. But since, in
this small circle of worthy souls, no decisions were made without
the prior consent of Sanders, they sought his advice, and found that
he was far from sharing their opinion. He maintained that to refuse

Madame Scholtz's invitation would inevitably result in a rupture
with her, that that clever woman would be quick to divine the
reasons for their refusal, and in a situation where it was above all
essential not to offend her, their proposed course of action was
bound to upset her.

At this point Ernestine dared to ask the object of her affections
what precisely it was he feared, nor did she conceal from him the
sorrow that his suspicions caused her.

"Oh, my dear friend!" said that interesting girl, clasping Herman's hands in her own, "were the most powerful personages of all
Europe present at this soiree, were they all to fall in love with your
dear Ernestine, could you for one moment doubt that all their
collective flatteries could be aught but a further homage to him
who has won her heart? Ah! fear not, Herman, she whom you have
captivated could never lose her heart to another. Were I obliged to
live with you in a state of slavery, I should prefer it to living with
another upon the throne itself; can any boon the earth has to offer
hold any meaning for me in the arms of another besides her beloved! . . . Herman, give yourself due credit: can you for one
moment fancy that my eye may perceive any mortal at this ball who
is your equal? Let my heart be the sole judge of your worth, my
friend, and you will be the most amiable of creatures, as you are
the most beloved."

Herman covered his mistress' hands with a thousand kisses, he
desisted from giving any further evidence of his fears, but they none
the less remained anchored in his heart. There dwells in the heart
of a man in love certain presentiments which are rarely mistaken.
Herman felt them, he repressed them, and the beautiful Ernestine appeared at Madame Scholtz's party like a rose in the
midst of lesser flowers. She was attired in the garb of ancient
Sweden, in the style of the ancient Scythians, her features noble and
proud, singularly heightened by that adornment, her figure delicate
and supple, infinitely better outlined beneath this free-falling, un-
pleated gown which only suggested her gentle forms, her lovely
hair cascading down in waves over the quiver slung across her back,
and with the bow held in her hand . . . all this made her look like
Love itself disguised beneath the features of fair Bellona. It was
as though each of the arrows she carried with so much grace was

destined, each time it touched the heart of someone present, to enchain it forthwith to that celestial beauty.

If Herman did not see Ernestine enter the room without a feeling of trepidation, Oxtiern, for his part, experienced an emotion so keen that for several minutes he found it impossible to utter a word. You have seen Oxtiern; he is a rather handsome fellow; but what a soul Nature has enclosed within that deceptive exterior! The Count was immensely wealthy and, only recently come into possession of his full fortune, never dreamt for a moment there could be any restraints imposed upon his impassioned desires; whatever reason and circumstance raised as obstacles in his path served only to whet the appetite of his impetuosity. As unprincipled as he was lacking in virtue, still steeped in the prejudices of a corps whose pride had led it to revolt against the King himself, Oxtiern fancied that there was nothing in the world which could act as a bridle to his passions. Now, of all the passions wherewith his ardent soul was inflamed, love was the most impetuous; but this sentiment, which in a noble soul may approximate a virtue, is bound to become the source of many a crime in a heart as corrupt as Oxtiern's.

No sooner had that dangerous man laid eyes upon our beautiful heroine than he straightway conceived the idea of seducing her. He danced with her a number of times, arranged to be seated next to her at dinner, and in short so clearly demonstrated the sentiments she inspired in him that in a trice the whole town was persuaded that she would soon become either Oxtiern's wife or his mistress.

'Tis impossible to depict the cruel state of mind which was Herman's while all this was taking place. He had gone to the ball, but seeing his beloved the center of such ardent attention, were it even conceivable for a moment that he approach her? Ernestine's sentiments for Herman had most assuredly not changed one whit; but is't possible for a young girl to protect herself against the sin of pride? Is't possible for her not to lose her head, were it even for a moment, when such public homage is paid to her? And that vanity wherewith she is flattered and which people play upon—by demonstrating to her that she can be beloved of all—does it not lessen within her the desire she previously felt to be responsive solely to the attentions of a single soul? Ernestine noticed that Herman was concerned; but Oxtiern was full of flattering attentions, the entire gathering had naught but the highest praise for her, and Ernestine, ensnared by pride, did not feel, as she should have, the sorrow she was causing her poor lover.

The Colonel was also the recipient of many marks of esteem on the part of Count Oxtiern, who singled him out especially in the course of his conversations. He offered to help the Colonel in any way he could in Stockholm and assured him that, still far too young to be retired, he should join some army corps and continue his ascent through the ranks until he had reached the high pinnacles to which his birth and talents had destined him. The Count added that he would help him in that matter as in whatsoever else he might desire at the Court, and begged him to take advantage of the offer, saying that he would consider as so many personal pleasures each of the services such a worthy gentleman would enable him to render. The ball ended at dawn, and the guests departed.

At the first opportunity the following day, Senator Oxtiern asked Madame Scholtz to give him further details concerning the young Scythian of the night before, whose ravishing image had remained fixed in his mind since he had first set eyes upon her.

"She is the most beautiful girl in all Norrköping," the merchant said, delighted to see that the Count, by thwarting Herman's love, might render her his heart. "In truth, Senator, there's not a girl in the length and breadth of the country who can compare with our Ernestine."

"Of the country!" cried the Count, "in all of Europe, Madame. . . . And what does she do . . . what thoughts fill her mind? . . . Who is in love with her . . . who adores this heavenly creature? Who is the man who would dare to vie with me for the possession of her charms?"

"I shall spare you a recital of her birth and background: you know that she is the daughter of Colonel Sanders, a worthy man, a man of quality and high birth. But what you are unaware of perhaps—and the news will grieve you, from what you say about your sentiments toward her—is that she is on the eve of marrying a young bookkeeper who works for me, with whom she is madly in love and who loves her at least as much."

"A match such as this for Ernestine!" cried the Senator. . . . "This angel, the wife of a bookkeeper! . . . 'Tis out of the question, Madame, the match must not take place; you and I must join forces to make certain it never does. 'Twould be utterly ridiculous; Ernestine was born to grace the Court with her brilliance, and I wish to present her there under my name."

"But with no fortune, Count . . . the daughter of an impoverished nobleman . . . of a soldier of fortune."

"She is the daughter of the gods themselves," said Oxtiern, beside himself, "she must dwell in their abode."

"Ah! Senator, you will drive the young man I mentioned to despair. Rare is a love as pure and strong as his . . . rare the sentiments as sincere as his for Ernestine."

"What disturbs me least in the world, Madame, is a rival of this kind. Should I, should my love, be alarmed by this inferior breed of men? I count upon your helping me discover the means whereby we get rid of him . . . send him away. And if he refuses to go of his own free will . . . Leave it to me, Madame Scholtz, leave it to me, we shall rid ourselves of this scurvy fellow."

Madame Scholtz was inwardly delighted, and far from trying to discourage the Count, she offered him only that kind of argument which is easily overcome and which, when vanquished, serves but to incite love.

But while all this was taking place at Madame Scholtz's, Herman was at the feet of his beloved Ernestine.

"See now! Was it not exactly as I said, Ernestine?" he cried, tears streaming down his face, "did I not foresee that this accursed ball would cause us untold sorrow? Each compliment he paid you, each word of praise he offered you was another dagger thrust into my wounded heart. Do you still doubt that he adores you? Has he already declared his love to you?"

"What do I care, unjust man," Ernestine replied, doing her best to calm the sole object of her affections, "what do I care about the fulsome praise this man enjoys showering upon me, so long as my heart belongs to you alone? Did you believe I was flattered by the attention he paid me?"

"Yes, Ernestine, I did believe you were, and was not mistaken.

Your eyes shone with pride at the knowledge you pleased him, all you did or said was intended for him alone."

"I resent these reproaches, Herman; coming from you they grieve me sorely. I thought you discerning enough, and possessed of sufficient tact, not to yield so easily to your fears. Very well, confess your concern to my father, and let us celebrate our marriage tomorrow, I have no objection."

Herman wasted no time taking advantage of her suggestion. He went straightway to Colonel Sanders, together with Ernestine, and throwing himself in the Colonel's arms, made him swear upon everything he held holy that Sanders would raise no further objections to the consummation of their happiness.

But pride had already wormed its way much further into Sanders' heart than into his daughter's, and in his there were fewer sentiments to counterbalance its effects. The Colonel, a man of honor and candor, was not in the least inclined to fail to keep the commitments he had made to Herman, but the thought of Oxtiern's protection dazzled him. He had been quick to remark upon his daughter's triumph over the Senator's heart. His friends had insinuated to him that, if that passion resulted in the legitimate consequences he had every right to expect it would, his fortune would inevitably be made. These thoughts had preoccupied him throughout the night; in his mind he had made plans, had indulged in fantasies wherein his ambitions were realized. The timing was, in one word, bad; in fact, Herman could not have chosen a worse moment. None the less, Sanders was careful not to refuse the young man's request; such conduct was alien to his nature. Moreover, might he not have built all his dreams upon a foundation of sand? What guarantee did he have of the reality of the fantasies wherewith he had been toying? Thus he fell back upon the selfsame reasons he had been in the habit of employing in the past: his daughter's youth; the inheritance expected from her Aunt Plorman; the fear of provoking, against both Ernestine and himself, the full fury of Madame Scholtz who, now supported by the Senator, was all the more to be feared. Moreover, would it be wisest to choose the very moment when the Count was in town? It seemed pointless to make a spectacle of oneself, and if Madame Scholtz were truly going to be upset by this match, the very moment when she found herself buttressed by the Count's favor and influence would surely be the moment when she risked to be most dangerous. Ernestine was more insistent than ever; her conscience was slightly guilty because of her conduct the evening before, and she was most anxious to prove to her friend that a chilling of her sentiments toward him could not be counted among her wrongs. The Colonel, uncertain as to the better course of action, and little accustomed to resisting his daughter's entreaties, asked merely that she await the Senator's departure, promising that he would then be the first to eliminate any remaining obstacles, even to the extent of going to see Madame Scholtz, if that became necessary, in order to calm her wrath, or to get her agreement to audit the accounts, for without a rendering of their accounts Herman could not properly effect a separation from his patroness.

Herman left without feeling fully satisfied. He none the less felt reassured concerning his mistress' sentiments, but he was consumed by a dark feeling of despair which he could not manage to dispel.

No sooner had he left the Sanderses' house than the Senator appeared. He had been brought hither by Madame Scholtz and had come, he declared, in order to pay his respects to the worthy soldier whom it had been his great privilege to encounter in the course of his visit, and at the same time requested permission to pay his respects as well to the charming Ernestine.

The Colonel and his daughter received these compliments with the becoming modesty expected of them. Madame Scholtz, concealing her rage and jealousy because she began to perceive a whole host of possible means whereby she might implement the cruel designs concealed in her heart, showered fulsome praise upon the Colonel and endless compliments upon Ernestine, and the conversation was thus as pleasant as it could be under the circumstances.

Several days passed in this manner, during which Sanders and his daughter, and the Count and Madame Scholtz, paid each other visits, dined together now at one house, now at another, all of which occurred without Herman's ever participating in any of these pleasure-parties.

During this period of several days, Oxtiern lost no opportunity to speak of his love, and it became impossible for Mademoiselle Sanders any longer to doubt that the Count was consumed with the most ardent passion for her; but Ernestine's heart had protected her, and her boundless love for Herman prevented her from falling into the trap of pride a second time; she dismissed everything, demurred to everything, appeared restrained and dreamy at all the festive occasions to which she was invited, and she never came away from any without begging her father not to take her to any others. It was too late: Sanders, who as I have said did not have the same reasons to resist the bait tendered by Oxtiern, was an easy prey. There had been a number of secret conversations among Madame Scholtz, the Senator, and the Colonel, which had succeeded finally in dazzling poor Sanders, and the artful Oxtiern, without ever compromising himself overmuch, without ever once revealing his hand, simply persuading the Colonel that sooner or later 'twas the inevitable course of fate that things would work out the way he predicted, Oxtiern, I say, had so beguiled Sanders that not only had he extracted from him the promise not to honor his commitments to Herman, but also had convinced him to forsake his solitary existence in Norrköping and come to Stockholm, in order to take advantage of the influence he promised to exert in his behalf and the favors wherewith it was his intention to shower him.

Ernestine, who in the course of all this activity had less of an opportunity to see her lover, none the less continued to write him, but as she knew he was full capable of an outburst of temper and wished to avoid any scene, she did her best to disguise all that was happening. Furthermore, she was far from reassured as to her father's weakness. Before making any false promises to Herman, she resolved to clarify the situation.

One morning she went into the Colonel's room.

"Father," she said respectfully, " 'twould appear the Senator intends to spend considerable time in Norrköping. Yet you have made a solemn promise to Herman that we would soon be wed. May I be so bold as to ask you whether you are still of the same mind? And why, pray tell, is't necessary to wait for the Count's departure before celebrating a marriage which we all desire with equal ardor?"

"Ernestine," said the Colonel, "sit down and listen to me. As long as I believed, my dear child," he went on, "that your fortune and happiness could be found with young Herman, far from standing in the way I did everything in my power, as you have seen, to hasten your wishes to a happy conclusion. But when a happier fate awaits you, Ernestine, why do you wish me to sacrifice you?"

"A happier fate, you say? If 'tis my happiness you care about, Father, never for one moment imagine that it might lie with anyone save my beloved Herman: 'tis only with him it can be assured. Never mind . . . I think I detect your plans . . . they appall me. . . . Ah! vouchsafe not to make me their victim."

"But, my child, my career depends upon these plans."

"Oh! Father, if the Count takes it upon himself to advance your fortune only at the price of obtaining my hand in marriage . . . so be it, then the honors he promises you will be yours to enjoy, that I acknowledge, but he who sells them to you will not enjoy the prize he hopes for; I shall die before yielding to him."

"Ernestine, I judged your soul more tender . . . I thought you loved your father better."

"Ah! beloved author of my days, I thought your daughter was more precious to you, that . . . Wretched voyage! . . . vile seducer! . . . We were all happy before that man appeared here . . . we were faced with but a single obstacle, which we would have overcome. So long as my father was on my side, I feared nothing; when he abandons my camp, there is naught left for me to do but die. . . ."

And the poor unhappy Ernestine, plunged into deep despair, was racked with sighs that would have moved even the hardest hearts to pity.

"Listen, my child, listen to what I have to say before you give way to such distress," said the Colonel, wiping away with a gentle caress the tears wherewith his daughter's face was covered. "The Count wishes to make me happy, and although he has not positively said to me that he would demand your hand in return, 'tis easy enough to understand that such is his sole objective. He is sure, or so he pretends, that he can reinstate me into active military service; he requests that we go to live in Stockholm, he promises us the most flattering prospects if we do, and as soon as I arrive there he per-

sonally wishes to offer me, he says, a commission of a thousand
ducats' pension for my own past services and those of my father
. . . a pension the Court, the Count hastens to add, would have
granted long ago if we had had the least friend in the capital who
would have spoken in our behalf. Ernestine . . . do you want to
forgo all these favors? Do you mean you would turn your back on
your own fortune, and upon mine?"

"No, Father," Sanders' daughter replied firmly, "no I do
not. But I ask one favor of you, and that is to put the Count to a
test which I am sure he will fail. If he is serious in his intent to
help you, as he says, and if he is honest, his friendship must be as
steadfast as it is disinterested. If he imposes conditions upon it, his
conduct is greatly to be feared: 'twould prove it is motivated by
personal feelings, 'twould from that moment onward prove 'twas
doubtless false. 'Tis no longer a friend you are involved with, but
my seducer."

"He will marry you."

"He will do no such thing. And furthermore, Father, mark
well my words: if his sentiments with what regards you are real,
they should be independent of those he may have conceived for
me. He cannot wish to please you if, in so doing, he is certain to
make me suffer. He must, if he is virtuous and sensitive, exert his
influence in your behalf as he has promised, without demanding me
in return as his reward. In order to test the true manner of his
thinking, tell him that you accept all his promises, but that you
request, as an initial show of his generosity with what regards me,
that he personally arrange for the marriage of your daughter with
the only man in the world she can ever love. If the Count is loyal,
if he is frank, if he is disinterested, he will agree; if his intention
is but to sacrifice me by serving you, then he will reveal his hand.
He has to reply to your proposition, and that proposition on your
part should not surprise him, since, you say, he has not openly
asked you for my hand. If his reply is to ask for it in return for
his good works in your behalf, then he reveals he is more interested
in serving his own ends than he is in serving yours, since he will
know I am engaged and that, despite my heart's commitment, he
will still attempt to coerce me. In which case, the man's soul is dishonest, and you should distrust his every offer, no matter in what

glowing terms he describes it. A man of honor cannot aspire to the hand of a woman whose heart he knows will never be his. 'Tis not at the expense of the daughter that he must render service to her father. The test cannot fail, I beg you to try it. . . . If it succeeds . . . I mean if we become convinced that the Count's intentions are legitimate, then we must consent to all he proposes: he will have furthered your advancement without in any wise infringing upon my felicity, and we shall all be happy. . . . We shall all be, Father, and you will have no regrets."

"Ernestine," said the Colonel, " 'tis very possible that the Count is an honest man, even though he may wish to help me only upon condition that you become his wife."

"Yes, were it not for the fact he knows I am engaged. But when you remind him of this fact, if he persists in desiring to serve you only in return for gaining his ends with what regards me, then his schemes are motivated by egoism alone, he shows himself to be wholly lacking in refinement. Consequently we must judge all his promises as extremely dubious. . . ."

And Ernestine, casting herself in the Colonel's arms:

"O Father," she cried, tears bathing her face, "grant me the test I demand, do not refuse me this one request, Father, I beseech you, do not sacrifice so cruelly a daughter whom you adore and who cannot live without you. Poor Herman would die of a broken heart, he would die hating us, I would soon follow him to the grave, and you would have lost the two souls your heart cherishes most deeply."

The Colonel loved his daughter; he was a generous and noble man. All one might reproach him for was that sort of good faith which, though it makes the honest man such an easy target for knaves, none the less reveals the full candor and frankness of a beautiful soul. He promised his daughter to do everything she asked, and the following day he spoke to the Senator.

Oxtiern, more perfidious than Mademoiselle Sanders was delicate and discriminate, and who together with Madame Scholtz had doubtless foreseen every eventuality and prepared for it, replied to the Colonel in the manner most likely to give him entire satisfaction.

"You mean you thought I was offering to help you out of my

own selfish interest, my dear fellow? I would that you knew my heart better: 'tis filled with naught but the desire to be useful to you, quite apart from any other considerations. Assuredly, I love your daughter. 'Twould serve no purpose to conceal the fact from you. But the moment she deems I am incapable of making her happy, far be it from me to exert the least pressure to dissuade her. I shall not undertake to help her tie the bonds of hymen here, as you seem to desire: 'twould be too painful to my wounded heart. If I am to be sacrificed, allow me at least the privilege of not participating in the sacrifice myself. But the marriage shall take place; I shall contribute in some way to it and delegate my authority in the matter to Madame Scholtz. Since your daughter prefers to become the wife of a bookkeeper rather than of one of the foremost senators of Sweden, let the choice be hers. Have no fears that her choice prove harmful in any wise to the services I wish to render you. I intend to leave shortly. As soon as I have put a few urgent affairs in order, a carriage of mine will come to fetch you and your daughter. You and Ernestine will come to Stockholm; Herman can follow close behind and wed her there, or, if you prefer, wait here until I have succeeded in placing you in the post I have in mind for you, which would enhance the marriage."

"Worthy man!" said Sanders, clasping the Count's hands in his own, "how grateful I am to you! The favors you vouchsafe to perform in our behalf will become all the more precious for being disinterested, and for having been done at the cost of a great personal sacrifice. . . . Ah! Senator, 'tis the ultimate degree of human generosity. In a century when virtue is so rare indeed, so noble an act should be rewarded by temples built to commemorate it."

"My friend," said the Count in reply to the Colonel's compliments, "an honest man is the first to benefit from the good he does. Are good deeds not the sustenance of his happiness?"

The Colonel wasted no time in relating to his daughter the crucial conversation he had just had with Oxtiern. Ernestine was touched to tears by it, and was completely taken in by everything he said. Noble souls are unsuspecting, and easily convince themselves of the good in others of which they see themselves capable. Herman was not quite so credulous. A few rash remarks that Madame Scholtz had let slip, doubtless because of her joy at seeing her revenge all but assured, gave rise to certain suspicions which he communicated to his mistress; this tender girl reassured him; she insinuated that a man of Oxtiern's birth and station must perforce be incapable of duplicity. . . . The innocent creature, little did she know that vice, buttressed by noble birth and high station, and emboldened by impunity, becomes all the more dangerous.

Herman said that he would like to have the matter out personally with the Count; Ernestine forbade him to resort to violence; the young man declared that such was not his intention. But essentially heeding naught but the dictates of his pride, his courage, and his love, he loaded two pistols. The following morning he slipped into the Count's bedchamber, and surprising him while he was still abed, he said to him boldly:

"Monsieur, I believe you to be a man of honor. Your name, your station, your wealth, all these persuade me that this is so. I therefore demand your word, Monsieur, your written word that you renounce all claims, the attentions you have displayed notwithstanding, to the affections of Ernestine. If you refuse, I shall expect you to accept one of these two weapons and engage me in a duel to the death."

The Senator, taken slightly aback by the compliment, began by asking Herman whether he had reflected seriously about what he was suggesting, and whether he believed a man of his high station was required to make any amends to a subaltern such as himself?

"Spare me your insults, Monsieur," Herman replied, " 'tis not to hear your invectives I have come here, but, on the contrary, to ask that you give me satisfaction for the outrage you have done me in trying to seduce my mistress. A subaltern, you say, Senator! Every man has the right to demand redress for something that has been taken from him, or for an offense he has suffered. The prejudice which makes a distinction among the classes is pure fantasy. Nature has created all men equal; there is not a single one amongst us who has not issued from his mother's womb naked and poor, not one whom she preserves or whom she annihilates differently from any other. The sole distinction among them I recognize is that which virtue confers upon them. The only man who is born to be the object of our contempt is he who uses the rights granted unto him by false conventions merely to indulge with greater impunity in vice. On your feet, Count! Were you a prince of royal blood, I would still demand from you the satisfaction which is due me. Get up, I say, and prepare to defend yourself forthwith, or I shall blow your brains out there where you lie."

"One moment, young man," said the Count, slipping on his clothes. "Sit down, and let us have breakfast before we duel. . . . Would you deny me this one request?"

"As you wish, Count," Herman replied, "but I trust that afterward you will consent to give me the satisfaction I demand. . . ."

The Count rang, breakfast was served, and the Senator, having given strict orders to be left alone with Herman, asked him, after their initial cup of coffee, whether all this had been undertaken with the knowledge and consent of Ernestine.

"Most certainly not, Senator! She is completely unaware that I am here; and, what is more, she did her best to convince me you were interested in being of service to me."

"If this be true, can you explain to me what made you act in such a rash manner?"

"The fear of being deceived, the certainty that once one has loved Ernestine 'tis impossible to conceive of giving her up. In short, the desire to have it out with you, to reach some sort of understanding with you."

"You soon will, Herman, and though I owe you naught but reproaches for the immoderation of your methods . . . though this ill-considered scheme might well have caused me to change my plans with what regards helping the Colonel's daughter, I shall none the less keep my word. . . . Yes, Herman, you shall marry Ernestine; 'tis a promise I have made, and one I shall keep. I am yielding nothing to you, young man; I am not the kind of man who need yield anything to you. 'Tis Ernestine and she alone who wins from me whatever she will, and 'tis for her happiness that I sacrifice my own!"

"Oh, noble and generous man!"

"You owe me nothing, I tell you. I have done it for Ernestine, and 'tis from her alone I would expect any show of gratitude."

"Allow me to share that gratitude, Senator, and permit me at the same time to offer a thousand excuses for my hastiness and outburst. . . . But, Monsieur, can I count upon your keeping your word, and if indeed you intend to keep it, would you refuse me the favor of putting your agreement into writing?"

"I shall indeed; I shall write whatever you like, but 'tis point-less, and these ill-founded suspicions only add to the folly you have just committed."

" 'Tis in order to reassure Ernestine."

"She is less distrustful than you; she believes me. No matter; I have no objection to writing what you ask, but upon condition it be addressed to her. To do otherwise would be in bad taste, I cannot both serve you and abase myself before you. . . ."

And taking a writing desk, the Senator penned the following lines:

*Count Oxtiern hereby promises Ernestine Sanders to allow her to make her own free choice, and to take the most op-portune measures necessary to enable her to enjoy forthwith the pleasures of hymen, no matter what the cost may be to him who adores her, whose sacrifice will soon be as certain as 'twill be horrible.*

Poor Herman, who failed completely to understand the cruel ambiguity the note contained, took it from the Count, kissed it passionately, reiterated his excuses for the rashness whereof he had been guilty, and flew to Ernestine, bearing her the sad trophies of his victory.

Mademoiselle Sanders reprimanded Herman sharply and ac-cused him of having no confidence in her. She added that, after what she had told him, Herman should never have resorted to such extreme measures with a man whose station was so far above him in life, that it was now to be feared that the Count, perhaps having yielded to Herman's demands only out of concern for his own safety, would upon reflection be subsequently impelled to take ex-treme measures of his own which might be fatal for them both and which, in any event, would doubtless prove most harmful to her father.

Herman hastened to reassure his mistress, reminded her of the promises contained in the Count's note . . . which she had also read without perceiving the ambiguity contained therein. They revealed all that had taken place to the Colonel, who disapproved of Herman's conduct even more keenly than had his daughter. None the less, they finally reconciled their differences, and our three friends, full confident that the Count would keep his word, separated feeling considerably reassured.

Meanwhile, immediately after his scene with Herman, Oxtiern had gone downstairs to Madame Scholtz's chambers, and there recounted to her everything that had happened. That wicked woman, ever more convinced by the young man's intemperate act that 'twas becoming impossible to hope that she might one day seduce him, cast her lot more completely with the Count's cause, and promised him that she would serve him until poor Herman had been completely crushed or destroyed.

"I have sure means of causing his downfall," this cruel wench declared. "I have a set of duplicate keys to his strongbox, though he is unaware of it. I must shortly redeem the sum of a hundred thousand ducats for bills of exchange due and payable to some Hamburg merchants. I can easily arrange to find him in error; at which time he will have the choice either of marrying me or of being utterly ruined."

"Were he to choose the latter," said the Count, "you shall inform me forthwith; you may be certain I shall take all necessary steps which our mutual desire for revenge requires."

Then the two villains, all too cruelly united by common interests, laid their final plans to give their perfidious schemes the full stability and baseness they desired.

Once these arrangements had been made, Oxtiern came to take his leave of the Colonel and his daughter. In her presence he restrained himself, and rather than reveal to her his love and true intentions, gave evidence of all the nobility and disinterestedness that his hypocrisy enabled him to summon forth. He repeated his generous offers to Sanders to be of service to him, and they agreed that the Colonel would keep to his plan concerning a visit to Stockholm. The Count urged that Sanders and his daughter consent to stay with him during their sojourn in the capital, but the Colonel replied that he would prefer to stay with his relative, Madame Plorman, whose fortune he was expecting his daughter to inherit. He pointed out that this token of friendship would give Ernestine an opportunity to deal tactfully with this woman, who was in a position to augment considerably her fortune. Oxtiern approved of the plan; they agreed that the voyage should be made by carriage, because Ernestine was afraid of the sea, and they took leave of one another with the most touching declarations of friendship and mutual esteem, without Herman's rash venture ever once having been mentioned in the course of their conversation.

Madame Scholtz continued her hypocritic ways with Herman. Feeling the need to conceal her true sentiments until the plot she was preparing was fully hatched, she made no mention to him of her feelings and, in contrast with the way she had previously acted, she now evinced naught but solicitous concern for and interest in him. She concealed from him the fact that she had learned of the blunder he had made in visiting the Count, and our worthy young man continued under the mistaken impression that, as the Count had not emerged from the confrontation in a very good light, he had taken pains to keep it a secret.

None the less, Herman was not unaware of the fact that the Colonel and his daughter were planning to leave Norrköping. But, full confident that his mistress' heart was wholly his, that the Colonel's friendship was steadfast, and that the Count's word was as good as gold, he had not the slightest doubt but that the first use to which Ernestine would put her influence with the Senator upon arriving in Stockholm would be to make him arrange for their immediate marriage. Sanders' daughter had constantly assured him that such was her intention, and indeed she sincerely believed her own words.

Thus several weeks went by, when one day the people of Norrköping saw a superb carriage arrive, attended by several valets, who brought with them a letter from Count Oxtiern to Colonel Sanders, and instructions to await that officer's orders relative to the voyage he was to make to Stockholm together with his daughter, for which the carriage they were accompanying was intended.

The letter announced to Sanders that, through the Senator's good offices, the widow Plorman was expecting her two relatives and had indeed prepared for them the best chambers in her house; it went on to say that she would expect them any time they might care to come, and that the Count would await that moment in

order to discover to his friend Sanders the results of the initial
efforts he had made in his behalf. With what regarded Herman,
the Senator added, he deemed it best that he be left behind to
conclude without distraction the affairs that he had yet to settle
with Madame Scholtz. Once they were concluded, and with his
fortune in order, he would be in a much better position to come and
offer his hand to the beautiful Ernestine. He further added that
everyone would benefit from this arrangement, for during this same
time the Colonel, honored with a pension and perhaps with a commission, would be even better situated to help his daughter.

This clause displeased Ernestine; it aroused some suspicions
in her, which she lost no time in communicating to her father.
The Colonel pretended that he had never conceived of Oxtiern's
plans in other terms than those outlined in his letter.

"And furthermore," Sanders continued, "how could you expect Herman to leave Norrköping before he has settled his finan-
cial affairs with Madame Scholtz?"

Ernestine shed a few tears and, still caught between her desire
not to harm her father and her love for Herman, she did not dare
to dwell upon her extreme inclination not to take advantage of the
Senator's offers until such time as her beloved Herman was free
to join them.

They had therefore to make up their minds to leave. The
Colonel invited Herman to come and dine with them the evening
of their departure, in order to bid one another a fond farewell. He
came to dinner, and their leave-taking, that painful moment of departure, did not take place without the keenest display of emotion.

"O my beloved Ernestine," said Herman, his face bathed in
tears, "I take my leave; I cannot say whether I shall ever see you
again. You are leaving me behind with a cruel enemy . . . with a
woman who disguises her true sentiments, which, I fear, are yet far
from being annihilated within her heart. To whom shall I turn for
help when this wench overwhelms me with the countless troubles
whereof she is full capable? . . . when she sees me more than ever
determined to follow you, and when I have declared to her that my
heart can never be given to anyone but you? And what about you?
Where, Great God, are you both going? To a place where you will
be dependent upon a man who has loved you, who loves you still

. . . and whose sacrifice is scarce worthy of belief. He will seduce you, Ernestine, he will dazzle you and blind you; and poor Herman, abandoned to his fate, will have naught to comfort him but his own tears."

"Herman will always have Ernestine's heart," said Mademoiselle Sanders, clasping her lover's hands in hers. "Can he ever fear that this heart, which is his alone, could ever betray him?"

"Ah! may I never lose it," said Herman, casting himself at the feet of his beautiful mistress. "May Ernestine, never yielding to the solicitations to which she is sure to be subjected, remain convinced that 'tis impossible for there ever to be on the face of the earth a man who loves her as deeply as do I!"

And the hapless young man dared to ask Ernestine to allow that he cull from her rosy-colored lips a precious kiss which might serve him as a pledge for the promises he had asked of her. The wise and worthy young daughter of Colonel Sanders, who had never before granted him so much as he was now asking, none the less deemed the circumstances were such as to allow it, and buried herself in Herman's arms. Herman, who was burning with love and desire, and succumbing to that plethora of somber joy whose sole expression is the shedding of tears, sealed his declarations of love upon the most beautiful mouth in the world, and from these self-same lips, still planted upon his, received the most delightful expressions of both love and constancy.

Yet the baleful hour of departure at last arrived. For two hearts truly in love, what difference is there between this hour and the hour of death? It seems as though, upon leaving the object one loves, one's heart literally breaks; 'tis as though our organs, as it were enchained to the cherished object whom we are leaving, wither away and die at this cruel moment. One wishes to fly away, one retraces one's steps, embraces once again, bids one last farewell, finds it impossible to make up one's mind to do so; finally compelled to leave, 'tis as though we had lost possession of our very faculties, as though the vital force which motivates our life had abandoned us, and what remains is dull and senseless, that the full meaning of existence lies but in the person from whom we are taking our leave.

The Colonel had decided that they would leave directly they had finished dinner. Ernestine cast a last look at her lover, whose face was bathed in tears; her heart literally broke within her. . . .

"O Father," she cried out, breaking into tears herself, "see the sacrifice I am making for you." And, again throwing herself into Herman's arms: "You whom I have never ceased to love," she said to him, "you whom I shall love to the very edge of the grave, receive here in the presence of my father the solemn oath which I hereby make never to belong to anyone but you. Write to me, let your thoughts be of me, never listen to anything save what I am now saying, and consider me the most vile of creatures if ever another save yourself receives either my hand or my heart."

Herman was in a state of extreme agitation. He bent to the ground and kissed the feet of her whom he worshiped. It was as though, by means of these ardent kisses, his soul which impressed them, his entire soul, was, with these fiery kisses, striving to subdue and enthrall Ernestine. . . .

"I shall never see you again . . . I shall never see you again," he murmured above the sobs wherewith he was enveloped. . . . "Father, let me follow you directly; suffer not that they take Ernestine from me or, if this is the fate to which I am condemned, alas! then plunge your sword into my heart!"

The Colonel reassured and calmed his friend, he gave him his word of honor never to stand in the way of his daughter's desires; but that love which feareth the worst can never be soothed. Seldom have two lovers taken leave of each other under such cruel circumstances; Herman sensed it only too well, and despite himself his heart was broken. But at last they had to leave. . . . Ernestine, overwhelmed with sorrow, her eyes filled with tears, climbed up beside her father into a carriage which bore her from the presence of him she loved. At that moment Herman had a vision wherein he thought he saw Death envelop with its dark wings the funereal carriage which was spiriting away from him his sweetest possession. His mournful cries rang out after her, calling Ernestine, his distraught soul sped after her, but she was gone, he could no longer see any trace of them. . . . All was gone . . . all was lost in the deep shadows of the night, and the wretched young man returned to Madame Scholtz's in such a violent state that he managed to increase even further the jealousy of this dangerous monster.

The Colonel and his daughter reached Stockholm the following day, and upon their arrival found awaiting them, at Madame Plorman's door, Senator Oxtiern, who presented his hand to Ernestine. Although it had been several years since the Colonel had seen his relative, he was none the less very warmly received. But it was easy to see that the Senator's influence had had a prodigious effect upon the welcome they had received. Ernestine was much admired and flattered. Her aunt asserted that her beautiful niece would eclipse all the beauties of the capital, and that very day arrangements were made to procure her every possible pleasure, in order to make her head swim, to make her drunk with joy, and cause her to forget her lover.

Madame Plorman's house was naturally a solitary one. This woman, already well along in years and by nature avaricious, entertained but seldom. And 'twas perhaps for this very reason that the Count, who knew her ways, was in no wise upset at the choice of dwelling the Colonel had settled upon.

Madame Plorman had living with her a young officer of the Regimental Guards, who was a degree closer to her in relationship than was Ernestine; he, consequently, had a greater claim to her inheritance. Sindersen by name, he was a decent fellow, a gallant young man, but one who quite naturally looked somewhat askance at relatives who, less closely related to Madame Plorman than he, none the less seemed to have formulated the same designs upon her fortune. This knowledge created a slight coolness between him and the Sanderses. None the less, he was all civility and urbanity with Ernestine, and knew how to disguise beneath this worldly gloss we call politeness the slightly less affectionate sentiments which held sway in his heart.

But let us leave the Colonel to get settled in his new dwelling and return to Norrköping, while Oxtiern bends his every effort to make a dazzling impression upon Ernestine, to keep her father amused, and in short to bring to a successful conclusion his treacherous schemes.

A week and a day following Ernestine's departure, the merchants from Hamburg arrived to claim the hundred thousand ducats owed them by Madame Scholtz. That sum was presumed to be safely locked in Herman's safe. But the duplicity was already done and, thanks to her duplicate set of keys, the funds were no longer there.

Madame Scholtz, who had invited the merchants to remain for dinner, straightway sent word to Herman to prepare their money, given that her guests wished to leave by boat that same evening for Stockholm. It had been some time since Herman had inspected that safe, but certain that the money was there, he confidently opened it, and almost fainted dead away when he realized that it had been robbed. He recovered his senses and ran to inform his protectress. . . .

"Oh! Madame," he cried, in a state of distraction, "we've been robbed!"

"Robbed, you say! My friend, no one has broken in here, and I can answer for the integrity of my own household."

"Yet someone must have broken in, Madame . . . it could not be otherwise, since the money is gone! And you certainly are sure of me!"

"I used to be, Herman, but when love turns the head of a boy such as you, it opens the floodgates of his heart to every kind of vice. . . . You miserable young man, beware of what you may have done. I need my money forthwith. If you are guilty, confess your error to me . . . but if you have done wrong and persist in keeping it from me, 'tis not you alone I may implicate in this fatal affair. . . . Ernestine left for Stockholm at the same time that my money disappeared . . . who can say whether she has not fled the country? . . . She precedes you . . . 'tis a premeditated theft."

"No, Madame, no, you do not for one moment believe what you are saying," Herman replied firmly. "You do not believe your own words, Madame. No thief commences his career by stealing such an enormous sum, and the major crimes in the hearts of men are always preceded by a previous display of vice. What have you seen from me till now that would lead you to believe I am capable of such embezzlement? Had I committed the theft, would I still be here in Norrköping? Has it not been more than a week since you first informed me this money would have to be paid? If indeed I had stolen it, would I have the effrontery to wait peacefully for the day of reckoning when my shame would be revealed? Is such conduct imaginable, and do you suppose I am capable of it?"

" 'Tis not for me to search out the reasons which might account for your actions when I am the party injured by your crime, Herman. I am certain of this much only, and that is that you are in charge of my safe, you alone are responsible for it, 'tis empty when I have need of the money presumed to be contained therein, the locks are in no wise tampered with, none of my people has run away. This theft, which reveals no signs of burglary from without, whereof there is not a single trace, could only be the handiwork of the person who possesses the keys. For the last time, Herman, examine your heart and conscience. I shall make up some excuse to keep the merchants here another twenty-four hours. Tomorrow my money . . . or I shall have to call upon the authorities to sort the matter out."

Herman left the room in a state of despair easier felt than described. He burst into tears and charged Heaven with the responsibility for allowing him to live only to be beset by so many misfortunes. Two choices lay open to him: to flee, or to blow out his brains . . . but no sooner had he formulated the one and the other than he put both of them out of his mind with horror. . . . Die without vindicating himself? . . . without cleansing himself of suspicions which would greatly distress Ernestine? Would she ever recover from the blow of having given her heart to a man capable of such abject conduct? Her delicate soul would never sustain such a blow, the sorrow would bring her to her grave. . . . To flee would be tantamount to admitting one's guilt; were it possible thus to provide grounds for accusing him of a crime he had never committed? Herman decided to leave the matter up to fate, and by letter to call upon the protection of the Senator and the friendship of the Colonel. He believed he could count upon the former, and felt absolutely certain of the latter. He wrote to them, recounting the terrible misfortune that had just befallen him, emphasized his innocence in a most convincing manner, and especially stressed to the Colonel how fatal such a situation might become for him, involving as it did a woman whose heart, filled with jealousy, would not pass up the opportunity to eliminate him. He urged them to advise him as to a course of action without any delay, then commended himself to the decrees of Heaven, daring to believe as a certainty that their impartiality would not allow his innocence to suffer unjustly.

You can easily imagine what a terrible night our young man spent. Early the following morning Madame Scholtz summoned him to her chambers.

"Well, my friend," she said to him with an air of graciousness and candor, "are you ready to confess your errors, and are you now of a mind to tell me what impelled you to do such a singular thing?"

"I offer myself, and surrender myself for any justification," the young man replied bravely. "I would not have remained under your roof had I been guilty of the crime whereof I am accused. You gave me the time to flee, I would have taken advantage of it."

"Perhaps you would not have gotten very far without being followed, and such a flight would have been an admission of your crime. Your flight would have proved we were dealing with an inexperienced thief; your firmness leads me to believe 'tis with a hardened thief we are involved."

"We can settle our accounts whenever you wish, Madame. Until such time as you find them in error, you have no right to treat me thus, and I have the right to request that you have more certain proof of my guilt before casting any slurs upon my integrity."

"Herman, is this what I had the right to expect from the young man whom I raised as my own child and in whom I had placed my every hope?"

" 'Tis not an answer to what I have said, Madame. That you resort to this subterfuge surprises me; in fact 'twould almost arouse certain doubts in my mind."

"Do not provoke me, Herman, do not provoke me when you ought to be doing everything within your power to move me to pity," she said, before adding warmly: "Are you not aware, cruel creature, of my sentiments toward you? Who then, this being the case, would be most inclined to conceal your misdeeds? . . . Would I try and uncover faults when I would gladly shed my own blood to extirpate those you already have? . . . Listen, Herman, I can repair the damage. I have deposited in various banks ten times more than is required to cover the missing sum. All I ask is that you confess to the theft . . . consent to marry me, and the whole affair will be forgotten."

"And, as my reward for this horrible lie, I shall be given the greatest misfortune ever to befall me?"

"The greatest misfortune ever to befall you, false-hearted boy! What! 'Tis thus you conceive of the bonds I propose, when a single word from me will seal your doom forever?"

"You are not unaware, Madame, that my heart is no longer mine to offer. Ernestine possesses it entirely. Anything which threatens to interfere with the plans we have to join our destinies can only be regarded as hideous to me."

"Ernestine? . . . Give her not another moment's thought. She is already Oxtiern's wife."

"Ernestine? . . . 'Tis utterly impossible, Madame; I have her word, and her heart. She is incapable of deceiving me."

"The whole matter was arranged in advance; the Colonel was a party to it."

"Merciful Heaven! All right! I shall find out for myself. I shall fly immediately to Stockholm . . . there I shall see Ernestine and learn from her own lips whether what you are saying is true. . . . What am I saying? Ernestine capable of betraying her lover! No, never . . . you do not know the workings of her heart, since you are capable of believing such a story. No, Madame, the sun would cease to bless us with its light before so heinous a crime could ever besoil Ernestine's heart."

And upon these words the young man made as though to dash from the house. . . . Madame Scholtz, detaining him:

"Herman, you are running off to your own ruin. Listen to me, my friend, 'tis the last time I shall speak to you. . . . Must I say it? There are six witnesses who have signed depositions against you; you were seen taking my money from the house; the use whereto you put it is also known: you distrusted Count Oxtiern. Provided with these hundred thousand ducats, you planned to abduct Ernestine and take her with you to England. . . . Judicial proceedings are already under way, I must stress that fact to you. A single word from me will stop them. . . . Here is my hand, Herman; accept it, and the whole affair is forgotten."

"A tissue of horrors and lies!" Herman cried out. "See how

glaring are the lies and inconsistencies in what you say! If, as you pretend, Ernestine is already wed to the Senator, there is no reason why I should have stolen for her sake the sums missing from your coffers; and if indeed I took that money for her, then 'tis false that she is the Count's wife. The moment you are able to lie so rashly, this whole affair stands revealed as a pure fabrication, a trap wherein your wickedness would ensnare me. But I shall find the means—or so I dare at least believe—to regain for myself the honor whereof you would strip me, and those who will remain convinced of my innocence will at the same time prove you guilty of the crimes you have hatched in order to avenge yourself for my disdain."

So saying, and thrusting aside the arm which Madame Scholtz again raised to restrain him, he immediately dashed out into the street, intending to flee to Stockholm. Poor Herman! . . . little did he realize that his chains were already forged and waiting. . . . On Madame Scholtz's doorstep, ten men seized him and dragged him ignominiously through the streets to the prison reserved for hardened criminals, while that savage creature responsible for his ruin looked on, seeming to enjoy, as she watched him being dragged away, the spectacle of misfortune wherein her unbridled rage had just engulfed this wretched young man.

"Great God!" said Herman, seeing himself cast into the abode of crime . . . and all too often of injustice, "is't possible for Heaven to invent any further sorrows wherewith to burden my heart even more? Oxtiern . . . false-hearted Oxtiern, you are the artful schemer responsible for this entire plot, and 'tis your jealousy that has brought me here; I am the victim of your own jealousy and that of your accomplices. . . . 'Tis thus that men can be plunged from one moment to the next into the utter depths of humiliation and despair! I fancied that 'twas crime alone could bring them to such a sorry pass. . . . No . . . all that is required to make them criminal is the mere shadow of suspicion; one needs but to have powerful enemies in order to be annihilated! But you, Ernestine, you whose solemn pledges still console my heart, is yours still wholly mine in this time of affliction? Is your innocence still as entire as mine? Or is't possible you are somehow implicated in this affair? . . . O Merciful Heaven! What terrible suspicions!

That I could have harbored such a thought, even for a moment, oppresses me more than all the other wrongs wherewith I am overwhelmed. Ernestine guilty! . . . Ernestine capable of having betrayed her lover! . . . Never could either fraud or deceit find any room in her sensitive soul! . . . And that tender kiss which I still cherish . . . this one, this tender kiss which I received from her, could it have been culled from lips sullied by lies? . . . No, never, beloved soul, no, it could not. . . . We are both the pawns of deceit. . . . How these monsters will try and take advantage of my situation to debase me in your eyes. . . . Heaven-sent angel, do not be deceived by the artful stratagems of evil men, and may your soul, as pure as the God by Whom it was given, be as shielded as its model from the iniquities of this world."

A silent, somber sorrow seized hold of this miserable man. As he slowly began to realize the full horror of his situation, his grief became so overwhelming that he began to struggle and thrash about in the midst of his irons. At times 'twas the thought of proving his innocence that motivated his movements; at others, 'twas to the feet of Ernestine he would run. He writhed on the floor, the vaults above his head rang out with his piercing cries. . . . He got to his feet, he hurled himself against the walls around him, striving to break them with his weight. He battered himself mercilessly against them, he was covered with blood and, falling again near the barriers which he had not even shaken, the only signs of life in his beleaguered soul were the tears and sobs and moans of despair which issued from him.

There is no situation under the sun that can be compared to that of a prisoner whose heart is aflame with love. The impossibility of communicating, of reaching an understanding or dissolving one's doubts straightway brings all the ills of this sentiment into focus in a most frightful manner; the benevolent features of a loving God are, for the prisoner, but so many vipers attacking his heart; a thousand fantasies becloud his vision; by turns anxious and calm, now credulous and the next moment filled with dread suspicion, both fearing and desiring the truth, detesting and adoring the object of his passion, believing her to be false and at the same time excusing her perfidious ways, his soul, like the waves of an angry sea, is naught but a spongelike mass which absorbs all passions and by them is consumed all the more quickly.

The authorities hastened to succor Herman. But what a baleful favor they were doing him by raising the cup of life to his grieving lips, when there remained for him within naught but the bitter lees!

Feeling the necessity to defend himself, and realizing that his overwhelming desire to see Ernestine could only be brought about by proving his innocence, he assumed his own defense. The judicial inquiry was opened, but the case was deemed too important to be heard before a lower tribunal such as that of Norrköping, and was transferred to a higher court in Stockholm. The prisoner was taken to Stockholm, where he was happy (if indeed the term is applicable to such a cruel situation) to be able to breathe the same air as his beloved Ernestine.

"I shall be in the same town as she," he said to himself before he was moved to the capital. "Perhaps I may even be able to apprise her of my fate . . . which is doubtless being concealed from her! . . . Perhaps I may even manage to see her. But regardless of what may happen, I shall be there, less vulnerable to the plots directed against me. 'Tis impossible for whatever comes in contact with Ernestine not to be purified by the proximity of her beautiful soul; the brilliance of her virtues reflects upon everything around her. . . . They are the rays of the sun which give life to the earth. . . . I have nothing to fear so long as she is near."

Poor credulous lovers, such are the fantasies which fill your hearts . . . they comfort you, 'tis a gift not lightly to be dismissed.

Let us now leave the unfortunate Herman, to see what is happening in Stockholm among those persons with whom we are concerned.

Ernestine, with her constant distractions and her continual round of festivities, had none the less not forgotten her beloved Herman; far from it. She surrendered naught but her eyes to the new spectacles with which they were trying to impress her, but her heart, still filled with her lover, had no room for anyone other than him. She would have preferred that he be present to share her pleasures, which were pale and insipid without him. She desired him, she saw him at every turn, and the loss of her illusion only made the truth of her situation all the more cruel. Poor Ernestine had not the slightest inkling of the dreadful state to which the man who occupied her thoughts with such despotic sway had been reduced. All she had received from him was one letter, written before the arrival of the merchants from Hamburg, and sure measures had been taken since then to make certain that she receive no further word from him. Whenever she expressed her concern about his silence, her father and the Senator simply blamed these delays upon the magnitude of the business affairs for which the young man was responsible, and sweet Ernestine, whose delicate soul feared the very thought of sorrow, let herself gently be lulled into believing whatever seemed to calm her troubled heart. Was she plagued by further reflections? Again they reassured her in the same manner, the Colonel in all good faith, the Senator out of sheer hypocrisy; but reassure her they did, and meanwhile, beneath her feet, the abyss was steadily being prepared.

Oxtiern was also making sure that Sanders was enjoying himself, and had arranged for him to be invited to the homes of several ministers. These marks of attention flattered the Colonel's pride; they also made him more indulgent concerning the Count's delay in keeping his word, and Oxtiern never tired of telling him that, all his efforts notwithstanding, the wheels of the Court were wont to grind slowly.

This dangerous suborner who, had he been able to attain his desired ends by some other manner than through the crimes he was contemplating, might have refrained from committing them, attempted upon occasion to revert to the language of love with her whom he was yearning to corrupt.

"There are times when I regret the efforts I am exerting in your behalf," he said one day to Ernestine. "I can feel that the power of your eyes is eroding my courage by slow degrees. My honesty compels me to keep my word and arrange for your marriage with Herman, but my heart resists. O Merciful Heaven! why does the hand of Nature both endow fair Ernestine with so many graces and implant such seeds of weakness in Oxtiern's heart? I would serve you better were you less beautiful; or perhaps I would love you less were you not so unyielding."

"Count Oxtiern," said Ernestine, much alarmed by his words,

"I thought these sentiments had long ago been put out of your mind, and I cannot conceive that you are still preoccupied with them!"

" 'Tis to give but slight credit to either of the following possibilities, and that is to believe that the impressions you provoke are any less strong than they were before, or to imagine that, when 'tis my heart that has received them, they might be less than eternal."

"Can they be reconciled with the question of honor? And did you not swear by all that is holy that you would bring me to Stockholm only in order to further my father's career and to help arrange my marriage with Herman? Was this not what you solemnly promised?"

"Herman! always Herman, Ernestine. Tell me, is there no way to make you forget this baleful name?"

"Assuredly not, Senator, 'tis a name I shall utter so long as the cherished image of him who bears it shall remain graven in my soul, and I must forewarn you that death alone could alter this situation. But Count, why do you dally so in fulfilling your promised obligations? I should soon be seeing—'tis your own words I repeat—this beloved and unique object of my love; why, therefore, is he so slow in joining us here?"

"His accounting problems with Madame Scholtz, 'tis certainly the reason for this delay which so disturbs you."

"Directly that is done, will he join us?"

"Yes . . . you will see him then, Ernestine. . . . I promise you that I shall arrange for you to see him, regardless of how much it may pain me . . . regardless of the place where you will be reunited . . . you will certainly see him. . . . And what will be my reward for these services rendered?"

"The pleasure you derive, Count, from having rendered them; for a sensitive soul, there is none greater."

"To purchase such a pleasure at the cost of the sacrifice you require is to pay it very dearly, Ernestine. Do you think there are many souls capable of such an effort?"

"The greater the effort, the more deserving I shall find you."

"Ah! how cold the epithet 'deserving' is, and how poorly it describes the sentiments I have for you!"

"But if 'tis the most you can expect to obtain from me, should it not satisfy you?"

"Never ... never!" the Count then said, casting a furious look at poor Ernestine. . . . And, immediately rising to take his leave: "You do not know the soul that you are flouting, Ernestine . . . you are blind, too blind. . . . No, you do not know that soul, you do not know to what lengths your contempt and disdain can drive it."

It is easy to imagine that these last words left Ernestine in a state of alarm. She wasted no time recounting them to the Colonel who, still completely convinced of the Senator's integrity, failed to see in them the meaning that Ernestine had sensed. The credulous Sanders, wrapped up in his ambitions, upon occasion reverted to the theme of his preferring the Count to Herman as a son-in-law. But at these times his daughter reminded him of his word, to which the frank and honest Colonel was a thrall. He yielded to Ernestine's tears and vowed to keep on reminding the Senator of the promises he had made to them both, adding that if he thought he detected the least sign of insincerity on the part of Oxtiern, he would request that the Count take her back to Norrköping.

'Twas about this same time that these two worthy souls, who were being too cruelly deceived, received some letters from Madame Scholtz, with whom they had parted on the best of terms. These letters begged them to excuse Herman for his silence, and added that he was in the best of health. But, overwhelmed with the many problems attendant upon a settling of accounts—accounts which were proving somewhat difficult to balance, doubtless attributable to the grief wherewith Herman was afflicted at being separated from the person he loved—he was obliged to borrow the hand of his benefactress in order to send news of himself to his best friends. He besought them not to be worried, and reassured them that within a week Madame Scholtz herself would bring him to Stockholm, where he would prostrate himself at the feet of his beloved Ernestine.

These missives succeeded in somewhat allaying her anxiety, but failed to reassure her completely. . . .

"It takes but a few minutes to write a letter," she said. "Why did Herman not take the trouble to write himself? He must have recognized that I would have placed greater faith in a single word from his own hand than in twenty epistles written by a woman whom we have every reason to distrust."

Sanders tried to set his daughter's mind at ease; Ernestine, who was a trusting soul, yielded momentarily to the efforts her father was making to soothe her, only to feel the grave pangs of anxiety return immediately to sear her troubled soul.

Meanwhile, the judicial inquiry into Herman's alleged crime was proceeding apace. The Senator, however, who had been in contact with the examining magistrates, had recommended that the case be treated with all possible discretion. He had demonstrated to them that if it became publicly known that the case were being investigated, Herman's accomplices—those who were in possession of the money—would cross the border into a foreign country, if indeed they had not already done so, and because of the security measures they would have taken, 'twould be impossible ever to recover the missing sum. This specious reasoning resulted in the magistrates conducting their inquiry with complete secrecy. Thus the entire proceeding took place in the very city where Ernestine and her father were living without either the one or the other ever realizing it, and without it ever being possible that any news of it was brought to their attention.

Such was more or less the state of affairs when the Colonel, for the first time in his life, found himself invited to dinner at the Minister of War's. Oxtiern was unable to escort him there personally; he had, he said, some twenty people himself that evening, but he gave Sanders to understand that he was responsible for that favor and, when he implied as much, urged the Colonel not to turn down the invitation. The Colonel had not the slightest desire to be remiss, although there was a question in his mind as to whether this perfidious dinner would really contribute to his happiness. He dressed as impeccably as he knew how, commended his daughter to the care of Madame Plorman, and set off for the Minister's mansion.

He had not been gone an hour when Ernestine saw Madame Scholtz appear in her quarters. The greetings were brief.

"Let us waste not a minute," the merchant said to her, "but hasten together to Count Oxtiern's. I have just brought Herman thither, and have come here as quickly as I could to inform you that your protector and your lover both await you with equal impatience."

"Herman?"

"None other."

"Why did he not accompany you here?"

"He had some initial business with the Count, no doubt some obligation he felt compelled to pay him. The Senator, who loves you, is sacrificing himself for this young man; does Herman not owe him his eternal gratitude? . . . And would he not be remiss if he failed to express it? . . . But you see how both of them have sent me flying to fetch you. . . . 'Tis the day when sacrifices are to be offered, Mademoiselle," Madame Scholtz pursued, casting a hypocritical glance at Ernestine. "Come and see them consummated!"

That miserable girl, torn between the urgent desire to fly to where they told her Herman was waiting and the fear of acting rashly in consenting to go to the Count's while her father was away, could not make up her mind what to do. And as Madame Scholtz was still urging her to come, Ernestine thought it prudent in such a situation to ask Madame Plorman for her advice, and to request that she be accompanied either by the widow herself or by her cousin Sindersen. But Sindersen was not at home, and when she consulted Madame Plorman the widow replied by saying that the Senator's house enjoyed too high a reputation for a girl to have the slightest fear about going there alone. She added that her niece must be familiar with the house, since she had been there several times with her father and, what was more, the moment Ernestine went there accompanied by a lady of the age and high station of Madame Scholtz, there was certainly no danger. She said further that she would be only too happy to join them were it not for the fact that for the past ten years painful infirmities of a most horrible nature had restricted her to the confines of her own home, from which it had been impossible to venture forth into public.

"But you are running no risk at all, my dear niece," Madame Plorman went on. "Go where you wish without feeling the slightest qualm. I shall inform the Colonel the moment he returns, so that he may come and fetch you straightway."

Ernestine, delighted to hear advice which agreed so completely with her own views, wasted no time climbing into Madame

Scholtz's carriage, and they soon arrived at the Senator's house, to find him awaiting their arrival at the door of his mansion.

"Come hither, my charming Ernestine," he said, offering her his hand, "come and revel in your triumph, enjoy my sacrifice and that of Madame Scholtz, come and prove to yourself that in the souls of sensitive creatures the virtue of generosity perforce must prevail over any other sentiment. . . ."

Ernestine could no longer control herself; her heart was pounding with impatience, and if the anticipation of happiness made her more beautiful, then she was doubtless at this moment more worthy than ever to receive the homage of the entire universe. . . . And yet there were certain things that alarmed her and acted as a damper upon the sweet emotion wherewith she was consumed. Although it was still broad daylight, not a single valet was to be seen anywhere in the house, wherein a lugubrious silence reigned. Not a word was to be heard, and as she moved from room to room the doors closed carefully behind her. The deeper they penetrated into the house, the darker it grew, and these precautionary measures so terrified Ernestine that she was on the verge of fainting by the time they reached the room wherein she was to be received. She at length arrived in this chamber, a rather spacious salon which overlooked the public square. But the windows which looked upon the square were tightly closed; only one of the rear windows of the room was slightly ajar, through which a few rays of sunlight filtered through the lowered blinds, and when Ernestine entered the room it was completely empty. The poor girl was scarcely breathing: realizing none the less that her safety depended upon her courage, she maintained her *sang-froid* and said:

"Monsieur, what is the meaning of this solitude, and of this dreadful silence? . . . The doors which are carefully closed behind us, these windows closely shuttered so that scarcely a ray of light can get through them: all these measures have been taken with the express purpose of frightening me: where is Herman?"

"Sit down, Ernestine," said the Senator, taking a seat between her and Madame Scholtz. "Remain calm and listen to what I have to say. A great many things have happened, my dear girl, since you left Norrköping. The man to whom you have given your heart has unfortunately proven that he is unworthy of your gift."

"O Merciful Heaven! You frighten me!"

"Your Herman is a scoundrel, Ernestine. What remains to be determined is whether you are in any way involved in the theft of a considerable sum of money which he stole from Madame Scholtz. You are under suspicion."

"Count," said Ernestine, getting to her feet with as much nobility as steadfastness of purpose, "your artifice is discovered. I can see that I have acted rashly . . . I am as good as lost . . . I have fallen into the hands of my two worst enemies . . . I am completely at the mercy of those who have plotted my destruction. . . ." And, falling to her knees: "Almighty God," she cried out, "I have now no longer anyone but Thee as my protector; do not, I beseech Thee, abandon innocence to the dangerous hands of crime and cunning!"

"Ernestine," said Madame Scholtz, raising her from her kneeling position and forcing her in spite of herself into the same chair in which she had been sitting, " 'tis not a question of praying here to God, 'tis a question of replying. The Senator is in no wise misrepresenting the matter to you. Your Herman has stolen a hundred thousand ducats from me, and he was within an ace of coming to fetch you away when, fortunately, the entire affair was brought to light. Herman was arrested, but the money has still not been found, and he steadfastly denies having misappropriated the funds. 'Tis this which has led us to believe that the money is already in your hands. Meanwhile the whole affair is shaping up badly: there are several witnesses who have testified against him; several citizens of Norrköping have admitted having seen him leave my house under cover of night carrying some sacks beneath his coat. The crime has been proven beyond the shadow of a doubt, and your lover is now in the hands of justice."

*Ernestine*—Herman guilty! Herman suspected of having committed a crime! And you believed it, Monsieur? . . . You allowed yourself to believe it?

*The Count*—Ernestine, we have neither the time to discuss this matter nor the time to think of anything save remedying the situation as quickly as possible. Rather than mention it to you to no purpose or grieve you senselessly, I wished to have the entire story before resorting to the scheme wherein you see me involved today. At present you are merely under the cloud of suspicion, 'tis

for this reason I wished to spare you the humiliations of imprisonment. I owed it to your father, and to you, and I have fulfilled that
obligation. But as for Herman, he is guilty. . . . No, my dear girl,
'tis even worse than that, and I tell you this with fear and trembling:
he has been sentenced. . . .

*Ernestine* (blanching)—Sentenced! . . . Herman sentenced!
. . . The very paragon of innocence! . . . O Merciful Heaven!

"The whole affair can be put right, Ernestine," the Senator
hastened to resume, supporting her in his arms, "the whole affair
can be put right, I say. . . . All I ask is that you resist my passion no
longer; grant me, here and now, the favors I demand of you, and
I shall hasten directly to the magistrates. . . . They are within a
stone's throw of here," he said, pointing to the public square, "they
are assembled to conclude this cruel affair. . . . I shall fly out there
to them . . . I shall take them the hundred thousand ducats and
testify that the error was mine, whilst Madame Scholtz will withdraw all complaints against him and at the same time swear that
'twas but an error in the bookkeeping due to the reconciliation of
accounts between Herman and herself, wherein the missing sum
was posted twice. In one word, I shall save your lover . . . and that
is not all: I shall furthermore keep the promise I made you, and
within a week I shall see to it that you become his wife. . . . Make
up your mind, Ernestine, and above all waste not a moment, for
time is precious. . . . Bear in mind the sum I shall be sacrificing . . .
the crime whereof you may stand accused . . . the dreadful situation
of Herman . . . the happiness which at last will be yours, if only
you consent to satisfy my desire."

*Ernestine*—I, you would have me consent to such infamies!
You would have me redeem, at such a price, a crime whereof neither
Herman nor I were ever guilty!

*The Count*—Ernestine, you are in my power; the thing you
fear can come to pass without your surrender. I am therefore doing
more for you than I should by rendering to you him whom you
love, upon condition you grant me a favor I can obtain without that
clause. . . . Time is of the essence. In one hour 'twill be too late
. . . in one hour Herman will be dead, and you will not be the less
dishonored. . . . Reflect well upon this: your refusal will result in
your lover's death, without having saved your modesty, whilst the

sacrifice of that selfsame modesty—the high regard in which 'tis held is imaginary—will result in the reprieve of him you hold so dear—what am I saying?—will straightway restore him to your waiting arms. . . . Credulous and falsely virtuous girl . . . if you hesitate between two such choices, you were guilty of a reprehensible weakness, nay, worse yet, of a most certain crime. By granting what I ask, you will lose naught but an illusory asset. . . . By refusing, you will be guilty of sending a man to his death, and that man whom you will have sacrificed is the one you love most in the world. . . . Make up your mind, Ernestine, make up your mind; I shall give you no more than five minutes.

*Ernestine*—I have already made up my mind, Monsieur. 'Tis out of the question to commit one crime in order to prevent another. I know my betrothed well enough to be certain he would prefer his own death to my dishonor, all the more so because he would not marry me after I had been debased. Were I to consent to your demands, therefore, I would render myself guilty without making him any happier, and my guilt would not have saved him, since he assuredly would not survive such an excess of horror and calumny. Therefore let me leave, Monsieur, and refrain from making yourself more criminal than I suspect you already to be. . . . I shall go and die beside my lover; I shall share his dreadful fate, but at least I shall die worthy of him, and I prefer to die virtuous than to live in ignominy. . . .

Then the Count became furious. . . .

"You expect to leave this house!" he said, fuming with rage and love, "you expect to escape me before I have satisfied my desire! 'Tis an empty hope; do not delude yourself, you wild creature. . . . Thunderbolts will strike the earth and wipe it out before I shall ever set you free, before you have quenched the flame wherewith I am devoured," he said, taking the poor girl in his arms. . . .

Ernestine tried to defend herself . . . but in vain. . . . Oxtiern was a madman, whose wild schemes make one's blood run cold. . . .

"Wait!" said Madame Scholtz, "wait one moment. Perhaps her reluctance stems from her doubts."

"Perhaps it does," said the Senator, "we must convince her."

And taking Ernestine by the hand, he dragged her toward the

windows which looked out onto the public square, and hurriedly opened the blinds.

"There, treacherous creature," he said to her, "see your Herman and his gallows."

And indeed, there on the square stood the bloody theater, and poor Herman, on the threshold of losing his life thereon, appeared with a confessor at the foot of the scaffold. Ernestine recognized him . . . she attempted to cry out . . . tried to throw herself out the window . . . she felt her entire body growing weak . . . all her senses began to fail her, and she collapsed.

At this point Oxtiern rushed to accomplish his perfidious designs. . . . He seized the poor unconscious creature and, without being the least bit frightened by the condition she was in, he dared to consummate his crime, he dared utilize, to satisfy his uncontrollable rage, that respectable creature whom Heaven had abandoned and unjustly allowed to be subjected to the most horrible frenzy of his passion. Ernestine was dishonored without ever recovering consciousness; at the same moment, Oxtiern's unfortunate rival submitted to the blade of justice: Herman was no more.

After they had ministered to her, Ernestine at length opened her eyes. The first word she uttered was Herman; her first wish was for a dagger. . . . She rose to her feet, went back to that terrible window which was still partly open, and tried to cast herself out of it, but they restrained her bodily. She asked for her lover, was told that he was alive no longer and that she alone was responsible for his death. . . . She shuddered . . . her mind became unhinged . . . disjointed phrases tumbled from her lips . . . sobs punctuated the words . . . 'twas only the tears which refused to flow. . . . Only after all this did she perceive that she had just been made Oxtiern's victim . . . she cast a furious look at him.

"So 'tis you, scoundrel," she said, " 'tis you who in one fell swoop have ravished my honor and deprived me of my lover!"

"Ernestine, there is no wrong that cannot be made right," said the Count.

"Of that I am sure," said Ernestine, "and no doubt it will. And now am I free to go? Has your rage been appeased?"

"Senator!" cried Madame Scholtz, "do not let this girl leave here. . . . She will be the undoing of us both What do we care about this creature's life? Let us straightway cut it short and spend the rest of our days in peace."

"No," said the Count. "Ernestine realizes that to lodge a complaint against us would serve no purpose. She has lost her betrothed, but she can still see to it that her father's fortune is made. Let her not breathe a word, and happiness can still be hers."

"Complaints, Senator, I lodge complaints? . . . Madame suspects that I might be tempted to institute an action against you? No, no . . . There are certain kinds of offenses for which a woman does not lodge any complaint . . . she cannot without debasing herself, and the avowals, which would be all too embarrassing to her, would offend her modesty far more than the redress she would receive to satisfy her revenge were ever worth. Let me go, Senator, let me leave this place, and you may count upon my discretion."

"Ernestine, I intend to let you go. . . . And let me remind you once again: your fate is in your own hands."

"I know that full well," responded Ernestine proudly, " 'tis they will insure it."

"How unwise of you!" Madame Scholtz exclaimed. "Oh! Count, I would never have agreed to be your accomplice had I suspected you were capable of such weakness!"

"Ernestine will not betray us," said the Count. "She knows I love her still. . . . She knows that the reward for her silence can be marriage."

"Ah! have no fear, have no fear," said Ernestine, getting into the carriage which awaited her. "I care far too much about redeeming my honor to resort to such base methods. . . . You will be pleased by those I choose, my dear Count. They will do honor to us both. Adieu."

Ernestine's carriage started off. . . . Her way home took her through the middle of the public square whereon her lover had just perished; she had to fight her way through the crowd which had just finished feasting its eyes upon the terrible spectacle. Her courage alone sustained her; her resolution lent her strength, and at last she arrived home.

Her father returned at the same moment; Oxtiern had artfully arranged for the Colonel to be detained the length of time required for the consummation of his crime. . . . He saw his daughter pale and distraught . . . her hair in disarray; but she was none the less dry-eyed, her countenance was proud, and her words firm.

"May I speak to you privately, Father?" she said. "I have something I must tell you."

"Daughter, you frighten me. . . . What has happened? You have been out while I was away. . . . I have heard rumors concerning the execution of a young man from Norrköping. I hurried home in a state of deep distress . . . greatly disturbed. Tell me all you know . . . the icy hand of death grips my heart."

"Listen to me, Father . . . restrain your tears" (and, casting herself into the Colonel's arms): "We were not born to know happiness, Father. There are certain persons whom Nature creates solely to drift from one misfortune to the next throughout the short span of their days here on earth. Not all of us can hope to experience an equal share of happiness; on this score we must submit to the will of Heaven. But at least you still have your daughter, she will be a source of help to you in your old age, a rod and staff to comfort you. . . . The poor young man from Norrköping about whom you have just heard is none other than Herman; he has just perished on the gallows before my very eyes. . . . Yes, Father, before my eyes. . . . They wanted me to witness the execution . . . and I did. Herman died the victim of Madame Scholtz's insane jealousy and Oxtiern's mad rage. . . . 'Tis not all I have to tell, Father: would that the loss of my lover were all I had to discover to you; but, alas, I have suffered an even crueler one. . . . Your daughter has been returned to you dishonored . . . Oxtiern . . . while one of his victims was being sacrificed beneath the executioner's blade, was despoiling the other."

Sanders, in a state of fury, rose to his feet:

"I have heard enough," he said. "My duty is clear. The son of that worthy friend of Charles XII needs no one to tell him how to deal with a traitor. Within the hour either I shall be dead or your honor will be avenged."

"No, Father, I beseech you," said Ernestine, restraining the Colonel from leaving. "I demand, in the name of all you hold most dear, that you not seek this revenge yourself. If I had the misfortune to lose you, can you imagine the horror of my fate? Left alone, with no one to look to for support . . . an easy mark for the foul schemes of these monsters; do you think they would waste any time sacrificing me in turn? . . . You must live for me, Father, for your dear daughter who, in the depths of her despair, has no one but you to turn to for help or consolation . . . has only your hands wherewith to wipe away her tears. . . . Listen to my plan; it requires but a minor sacrifice, which may even prove to be superfluous if my cousin Sindersen is a man of feeling. The fear that my aunt may show a preference for me in her will is the sole reason for the slight coolness that has existed between us. I intend to dispel his fears and sign a statement renouncing my share of her inheritance; I shall win him over to our cause. He is young, he is courageous, he is a soldier like yourself. He will go and find Oxtiern and will cleanse my wrong with the blood of this traitor. And as we demand satisfaction, if he succumbs I shall no longer restrain your arm, and you in your turn will go seek out the Senator and avenge at once both your daughter's honor and the death of him she loved. By so doing, the scoundrel who deceived me will have two enemies against him rather than one; and for one such as he, the more enemies the better!"

"But Daughter, Sindersen is very young for a foe such as Oxtiern."

"Have no fears, Father, traitors are always cowards, victory will not be difficult. . . . Ah! may it be given to me to see him thus vanquished! . . . In any case, I demand that this plan be followed . . . you owe it to me, Father . . . the wrong I have suffered gives me that right. I beseech you to grant me this one request. . . . 'Tis at your feet I request it."

"If 'tis what you want, then I consent to it," said the Colonel, helping his daughter to her feet, "and the argument that makes me yield to your wishes is the certainty of increasing the number of enemies, as you say, arrayed against the person who dishonored you."

Ernestine kissed her father and hurried off to find her cousin. She returned in a short time.

"Sindersen agrees and is ready, Father," she said to the Colonel. "But because of his aunt he most earnestly entreats you not to breathe a word of this to Madame Plorman, who could never forgive herself for having advised me to go to the Count's house, which she did in all good faith. Sindersen is therefore of the opinion that all this must be kept from Madame Plorman; he will avoid meeting you till the affair is concluded, and you will do the same with him."

"Agreed," said the Colonel, "let him fly forth and seek revenge . . . I shall be but a step or two behind. . . ."

All grew calm. . . . Ernestine retired for the night, apparently quite calm. The following morning at an early hour Count Oxtiern received a letter in an unknown hand which consisted merely of the following words:

*A heinous crime cannot be committed with impunity; an odious injustice cannot go unavenged; a decent girl cannot be dishonored without the tempter, or him who is responsible for the crime, paying with his life. At ten o'clock tonight an officer dressed in a red uniform will be strolling near the port, a sword beneath his arm, awaiting your arrival. If you fail to meet him there, this same officer will come to your house the following day and there will blow your brains out.*

The letter was delivered by a servant out of livery, and since he had been instructed to return with a reply, he came back with this same note, on the back of which was penned simply these four words: *I shall be there.*

But the false-hearted Oxtiern was too intrigued to learn what had transpired at Madame Plorman's house since Ernestine's return not to have employed every means his fortune could command to obtain that information. He learned who the officer dressed in red was to be; he learned too that the Colonel had instructed his personal valet to prepare for him an English uniform, as he intended to don a disguise to follow him to whom the task of avenging his daughter had been entrusted, so that the avenger would not recognize him. And, in the unlikely event that he were defeated in the duel, he, the Colonel, would take up the cudgels on the spot. 'Twas more than enough for Oxtiern to use in order to devise a new and terrible plot.

Night fell, and 'twas an unusually dark one; Ernestine sent word to her father that Sindersen would leave in an hour and, given her state of distress, asked his permission to retire for the night. The Colonel, only too pleased to be alone, bid his daughter good night and made preparations to follow him who had sworn to avenge her honor. He left the house. . . . He was unaware of the uniform Sindersen would be wearing. Ernestine had not showed him the challenge; in order to maintain the aura of secrecy the young man had requested, and in order not to arouse his daughter's suspicions, he had refrained from asking any questions. He was not concerned about the details; he knew where the duel was scheduled to take place, and he headed toward the port, certain that he would have no difficulty in recognizing his nephew. He arrived at the appointed spot and, seeing no one appear, kept on walking. Just then a stranger accosted him, bearing no weapons, and with his hat held low.

"Monsieur," said this man to him, "are you not Colonel Sanders?"

"I am."

"Then prepare to defend yourself. Sindersen has betrayed you, he has no intention of engaging the Count in a duel. But this last-named gentleman is not far off, and 'tis against you alone he intends to duel."

"God be praised!" said the Colonel with a shout of joy, "nothing could please me more."

"One word of caution, if you don't mind, Monsieur," resumed the stranger. "Do not say a word; this spot is not very safe. The Senator has many friends. The slightest sound from you might bring them running to stop the duel. . . . He prefers that it not be stopped, and desires to offer you full satisfaction. . . . Therefore say nothing and launch an all-out assault upon the officer dressed in red whom you will see advancing toward you from that direction."

"Good," said the Colonel, "and now withdraw with all dispatch. I am burning to cross swords. . . ."

The stranger withdrew, Sanders circled twice again the designated site until at last he saw lurking in the shadows an officer dressed in red who was walking proudly toward him. He had no doubt 'twas Oxtiern, and Sanders lunged at him with drawn sword, saying not a word for fear of being separated. The officer put up a stout defense—also without uttering a sound—and displayed exceptional bravery. At length his valor yielded to the Colonel's vigorous assaults, and the poor creature fell, mortally wounded, to the dust. At that moment a cry escaped the lips of the Colonel's opponent—'twas a woman's cry, a baleful cry that pierced the Colonel's heart. . . . He approached the fallen fighter . . . and perceived features far different from the masculine traits of the person he thought he was dueling. . . . Merciful Heaven! . . . 'Twas his own daughter . . . 'twas she, brave Ernestine, who wished to avenge her own honor or die in the attempt and who, bathed in her own blood, lay dying, a victim of her father's sword.

"O dreadful day for me!" the Colonel cried. . . . "Ernestine, 'tis you I have slain! What a horrible mistake! . . . Who is responsible for it? . . ."

"Father," said Ernestine in a weak voice, clasping the Colonel in her arms, "I did not recognize you. Forgive me, Father, for having taken arms against you. Can you forgive me?"

"Great God! when 'tis my hand has brought you to death's door! O my dear soul, with how many envenomed blows does Heaven intend to strike us at once?"

"This whole scheme is once again the handiwork of perfidious Oxtiern. . . . A stranger accosted me and, saying he was by Oxtiern dispatched, told me to remain completely silent, in order that the duel not be stopped. He further advised me that, upon seeing a man dressed in the uniform you are wearing, I should draw my sword and attack, for 'twould be the Count. . . . I believed his words; it was an act of purest perfidy! . . . I am dying . . . but at least I have the comfort of dying in your arms, 'tis the gentlest, sweetest death I could hope to have after all the afflictions wherewith I have just been overwhelmed. Embrace me, Father, and receive your poor Ernestine's last farewell."

With these words the ill-fated girl breathed her last. Sanders bathed her with his tears. . . . But the desire for revenge helps allay sorrow's hurt. . . . He left his daughter's blood-stained body to fly and seek redress from the law . . . determined to die or bring Oxtiern to justice. . . . 'Tis only in a court of law he decided he could hope to make his appeal. . . . To deal further with a villain of Oxtiern's stature was out of the question: the Count would sooner have him murdered than consent to cross swords with him in equal combat. Still covered with his daughter's blood, the Colonel prostrated himself before the magistrates, discovered to them the frightful chain of circumstances wherewith he had been beset and revealed the full extent of the Count's infamies. . . . They were moved by his recital, concerned by what he said; nor did he fail above all to prove to them how complete, in the case of Herman, had been the miscarriage of justice, because of the stratagems of the same traitor against whom he was lodging his complaint. . . . He was promised retribution.

Despite the immense influence the Senator prided himself upon enjoying, he was arrested that same night. Believing himself as safe as he was certain of the outcome of his criminal designs—or perhaps having been wrongly informed by his spies—he was lying peacefully coupled in the arms of Madame Scholtz, celebrating with her the ghastly manner in which they had taken their revenge. They were both taken away and cast into prison. The judicial inquiry was held with utter rigor . . . no shadow of influence was allowed to intrude upon it. The two guilty parties contradicted each other's testimony . . . the one and the other mutually convicted themselves. . . . The memory of Herman was rehabilitated. Madame Scholtz was sentenced to pay for the horror of her crimes on the selfsame gallows whereon she had caused the innocent Herman to perish.

The Senator was sentenced to suffer the same fate. But the King tempered the harsh verdict by pardoning him, to the extent of banishing the Count for life to the depths of the mines.

From the guilty parties' possessions, the King offered the Colonel a pension of ten thousand ducats, and raised him to the rank of General in his service. But Sanders refused both offers.

"Sire," he said to the monarch, "you are too generous. For if these favors are being granted as a reward for my services to the Crown, then they are far too magnanimous, I do not deserve them. . . . And if they are offered as payment for the losses I have suffered, they are insufficient. Sire, the wounds inflicted upon one's heart cannot be healed either with gold or by the bestowal of honors. . . . I beseech therefore Your Majesty to grant me a certain time alone with my despair. In a short while I shall solicit from Your Highness the only favor that may seem befitting to me."

"This then, Monsieur," Falkeneim broke in, "is the essence of the story you asked me to relate. I only regret that we are under the obligation to see this Oxtiern again; he can only be an object of horror in your eyes."

"No one is more understanding than I, Monsieur," I replied, "when 'tis a question of the errors into which we are led by our constitutions. I look upon evildoers, in the midst of honest and upright people, as those irregularities which Nature mingles in amongst the beauties wherewith she adorns the universe. But this man Oxtiern you have described, and especially Madame Scholtz, abuse the right which men's weaknesses must obtain from philosophers. 'Tis impossible that crime be carried to any greater lengths. In the conduct of the one as of the other, there are acts which make one's blood run cold. To ravish that hapless girl while her lover is being put to the sword . . . then to have her murdered by her own father . . . these are subtle refinements of horror which cause one to be ashamed to be a man, when one is unfortunate enough to have to share this title with such monstrous villains."

Scarcely had I uttered these words than Oxtiern appeared, bearing his letter. He was too clever and perceptive a man not to detect upon my face that I had just been made privy to his adventures. . . . He looked at me.

"Monsieur," he said, in French, "have pity upon me. Immense wealth . . . a powerful family . . . influence: these are the sirens who lured me to my doom. Educated by misfortune, I have learned the meaning of remorse, and I can now live among my fellow men without terrifying or harming them."

These words from the ill-fated Count were accompanied by a flow of tears, which I could not bring myself to share. My guide took his letter, repeated his offer to be of service, and we were preparing to leave when we saw a crowd of people in the street moving toward us. . . . We stopped; Oxtiern was still with us. Slowly we were able to distinguish among the crowd two men who were conversing heatedly and who, upon seeing us, straightway headed in our direction. Oxtiern recognized both personages.

"O Heaven!" he exclaimed, "what is this? . . . Colonel Sanders brought hither by the director of the mine! . . . Yes, 'tis our pastor coming, bringing the Colonel toward us. . . . What! you mean this implacable enemy has come to find me even unto the bowels of the earth!... Does this mean my cruel punishment does not suffice to satisfy him!..."

Oxtiern was still giving utterance to these thoughts when the Colonel accosted him with these words, as soon as he had reached his side:

"You are free, Monsieur," he said to him, "and 'tis to the man in the world whom you have most grievously offended that your pardon is due.... Here it is, Senator, from my own hand. The King offered me commissions, honors; I refused them all. The only favor I requested was your freedom, and my request has been granted. You are free to follow me."

"O most generous of men!" Oxtiern cried, "is it possible?... I, free?... and free thanks to you?... you who, were you to take my life, would still not punish me as I deserve to be?"

"I was certain that such would be your reaction," said the Colonel. "That is why I imagined there would no longer be any risk involved in restoring to you a gift which 'twould be impossible that you further abuse.... Moreover, does your suffering in any wise ease my own? Can your sorrows make me happy? Can your detention pay for the blood your barbarous acts have spilled? If I deemed 'twere so, I would be as cruel as you, and as unjust. Does casting a man into prison compensate society for the wrongs he has done it?... Such a man must be set free, if amends are to be made, and if he is freed there is none who would fail to make them, there is not a single man alive who would not prefer doing good to the necessity of living in chains. When, amongst some nations, despotism denies this truth or when, amongst others, the rigor of the law prevents it, the heart of the honest man confirms it.... Go then, Count, leave these depths; I say it again, you are a free man...."

Oxtiern tried to embrace his benefactor.

"Monsieur," Sanders said to him coldly, pushing him away. "Save your gratitude; nor do I want you to be grateful to me for something I have done for myself alone.... Let us leave this place forthwith; I am more eager than you to see you beyond the confines of this mine, in order to explain everything to you."

Sanders, seeing us with Oxtiern and having learned who we

were, invited us to ascend to the surface with him and the Count;
we accepted. Oxtiern went with the Colonel to complete certain
formalities required before he could be set free; our sidearms were
returned to us, and we ascended to the surface.

"Gentlemen," Sanders said to us as soon as we were outside,
"I would be grateful if you would act as my witnesses in what yet
remains for me to discover to Count Oxtiern. You have seen that
I did not tell him everything back there in the mine; there were too
many bystanders. . . ."

And as we were still walking while we talked, we soon found
ourselves in the vicinity of a hedge which completely concealed us
from any prying eyes. Then the Colonel seized the Count by the
collar:

"Senator," he said to him. . . . "I expect you now to give me
satisfaction; I trust you are brave enough not to refuse me this
demand and intelligent enough to realize that the most cogent
reason I had for acting in this manner was the hope of slitting your
throat or having mine slit by you."

Falkeneim attempted to intervene and separate the two op-
ponents.

"Monsieur," the Colonel said to him testily, "you are not
unaware of the outrages I have suffered at the hand of this man.
My dear departed daughter's spirit cries out for blood: one of
us will not leave this spot alive. Gustavus is privy to the plan; when
he granted me the privilege of setting this wretch free, he voiced
no objections to it. Therefore, Monsieur, I beg you not to interfere."

And the Colonel, removing his coat, straightway drew his
sword. . . . Oxtiern drew his as well, but scarcely had they crossed
swords than the Count, seizing the end of his own and taking the
point of the Colonel's in his left hand, offered him the handle of
his weapon and, dropping to one knee:

"Gentlemen," he said, glancing at us, "I ask you both to be
my witnesses; I want you to know that I do not deserve the honor
of fighting a duel with this worthy man, but that I place my life
in his hands, and ask only that he take it from me. . . . Here is my
sword, Colonel, take it, 'tis yours. And here is my heart; thrust your
own sword into it, I shall help direct it to its mark. Do not hesitate;

'tis not a request I make, but a demand. Deliver this earth forthwith of a monster who has too long besoiled it."

Taken aback by Oxtiern's movement, Sanders cried out to him to defend himself.

"I shall not, and if you refuse to put this sword I am now holding to use," Oxtiern firmly declared, directing the tip of Sanders' sword to his bare breast, "if you refuse to use this sword to put an end to all my days, I swear to you, Colonel, that I shall use it to gouge out my eyes."

"Count, blood must be shed . . . it must, I say, blood must be shed."

"I know," said Oxtiern, "and 'tis for this reason I bare my breast to you. Thrust your sword into it . . . 'tis from this breast alone that blood must flow."

"But 'tis not thuswise I wish to act," Sanders responded, still trying to wrest his sword from Oxtiern's grasp, "but upon the field of honor I wish to punish you for all your villainies."

"I am unworthy to meet you on any field of honor, Colonel Sanders," Oxtiern retorted, "and since you refuse to satisfy your honor as 'tis only meet you should, I shall therefore spare you the trouble. . . ."

So saying, he fell upon the Colonel's sword, which he was still gripping in his hand, and from his entrails there spurted a stream of blood. But the Colonel, quickly withdrawing his sword:

" 'Tis enough, Count," he exclaimed. . . . "Your blood has been shed, my honor is appeased. . . . May Heaven complete your punishment; I have no desire to act as your executioner."

"Let us then embrace, Monsieur," said Oxtiern, who was losing considerable blood.

"No," said Sanders. "I can forgive you for your crimes, but ask not that I be your friend."

We hastened to bind the Count's wound, the kindhearted Sanders lending a hand.

"Now go," he then said to the Senator. "Go and take advantage of the freedom I have rendered you. Try, if 'tis possible for you, to atone by a few good deeds for all the crimes whereof you have been guilty. Otherwise I shall spread the word throughout the length and breadth of Sweden of the crime whereof I was guilty in setting free a monster of which the country had already been delivered. Gentlemen," Sanders went on, turning to Falkeneim and me, "I have provided for all contingencies; the carriage which is waiting at the inn where we are now going was brought thither for Oxtiern alone, but it can take you both as well. My horses await me elsewhere; I bid you adieu. I ask that you swear to me by all that is holy that you will give the King a fair account of what you have just seen."

Oxtiern wanted once again to cast himself into the arms of his liberator; he begged him to reconsider and be friends, and besought him to come and share both his dwelling and his fortune.

"Monsieur," said the Colonel, pushing him away a second time, "I have already told you I cannot accept from you either your friendship or your gifts. But what I still demand from you is virtue; do not make me regret what I have done. . . . You tell me that you want to console me for the sorrows I have known; the surest method of doing so is to alter your conduct. In my retreat, each time I hear tell of a good deed you have done, a little of the sorrow wherewith my soul is graven will perhaps be effaced. If you resume your infamous ways, every crime you commit will conjure before my eyes the image of her who, through your perfidious plot, died by my hand, and you will plunge me into despair. Adieu . . . 'tis time to take leave, Oxtiern. And may we never meet again. . . ."

Upon these words, the Colonel turned and left. . . . Oxtiern, in tears, made as if to follow him, scarce able to move from his wound; we restrained him and practically carried him, for he was nigh to unconscious, to the waiting carriage, which soon brought us to Stockholm.

The poor man hovered for a month between life and death; at the end of this period, he invited us to accompany him to see the King, who asked us for a detailed account of all that had transpired.

"Oxtiern," said Gustavus to the Senator, "you see how crime humiliates man, and how it debases him. . . . Your rank . . . your wealth . . . your noble birth, all gave you a higher station in life than Sanders. But his virtue alone places him above you, on a station you will never attain. Take full advantage of the great favor he has done you, Oxtiern, a favor to which I gave my prior consent. . . . After a lesson such as this, resolve either to mete out your own punishment before word reaches me of any new crimes you commit or to make certain you will never again stoop so low as to commit any."

The Count cast himself at the feet of his sovereign and swore to him that his conduct would henceforth be irreproachable.

He was as good as his word: a thousand good deeds, one more magnanimous and edifying than the other, atoned for his former errors in the eyes of all Sweden. And his example demonstrated to that wise nation that 'tis not always by the paths of tyranny, or through ghastly vengeance, that man is restrained from evil or brought back to the path of good.

Sanders had returned to Norrköping, and there he ended his career, leading a solitary life burdened daily by the tears he shed over the loss of his unfortunate and ill-fated daughter, a life cheered by naught but the news received each day filled with encomiums concerning him whose chains he had broken.

"O Virtue," he would sometimes exclaim, "perhaps 'twas essential that all these things happen thus in order to bring Oxtiern back to thy temple! If that be true, then my heart takes comfort in the thought, for I alone have suffered from the crimes he committed, whilst his good deeds redound to the benefit of all."

# *Bibliography*

## I. WORKS PUBLISHED DURING THE AUTHOR'S LIFETIME

### LITERARY WORKS

1. *Justine, ou les Malheurs de la Vertu. En Hollande, Chez les Libraires associés* [Paris, Girouard], 1791. Two volumes, 8vo. Frontispiece by Chéry. During Sade's lifetime, there were six further printings between the initial publication and 1801. Sade's re-arrest that year put an end to the reprintings. These subsequent editions were:
   1) *En Hollande* [Paris, Girouard], 1791. Two volumes, 12-mo. Certain copies of this edition include twelve erotic engravings.
   2) *A Londres* [Paris, Cazin], 1792. Two volumes, 18 mo. Frontispiece and five engravings.
   3) *Troisième* [fourth] *édition corrigée et augmentée. Philadelphie* [Paris], 1794. Two volumes, 18mo. Frontispiece and five engravings.
   4) *A Londres* [Paris], 1797. Four volumes, 18mo. Further augmented edition. Six erotic engravings.
   5) *En Hollande* [Paris], 1800. Four volumes, 16mo. Presented as the *Troisième édition corrigée et augmentée,* this is actually a reprint of the original edition.

792 ❧ THE MARQUIS DE SADE

6)  *En Hollande* [Paris], 1801. Four volumes, 16mo. Also presented as the *Troisième édition corrigée et augmentée*, this was a reprinting of the 1800 edition.[1]

2.  *Aline et Valcour, ou le Roman philosophique. Ecrit à la Bastille un an avant la Révolution de France. Orné de quatorze gravures. Par le citoyen S\*\*\*. A Paris, chez Girouard, Libraire, rue du Bout-du-Monde, n° 47, 1793.* Eight volumes, 18mo.
    There are actually three different editions of this work, bearing different dates and, in some instances, containing sixteen rather than twelve engravings. Sade announced[2] the book would appear at Easter of 1791, but the instability of the times and the death of Girouard beneath the guillotine in 1794 kept the book from appearing until 1795, which date should be taken as the date of reference of the original edition.

3.  *La Philosophie dans le boudoir. Ouvrage posthume de l'auteur de "Justine." A Londres, aux dépens de la Compagnie, MDCCXCV.* Two volumes, 18mo. Frontispiece and four erotic engravings.

4.  *La Nouvelle Justine, ou les Malheurs de la Vertu. Ouvrage orné d'un frontispice et de quarante sujets gravés avec soin. En Hollande* [Paris], 1797. Four volumes, 18mo. These four volumes comprise the first part of the definitive edition of this work, of which the second part, in six volumes, bears the title:

5.  *La Nouvelle Justine, ou les Malheurs de la Vertu, suivie de l'Histoire de Juliette, sa soeur [ou les Prospérités du vice.] Ouvrage orné d'un frontispice et de cent sujets gravés avec soin. En Hollande* [Paris], 1797.

6.  *Oxtiern, ou les malheurs du libertinage, drame en trois actes et en prose par D.-A.-F. S. Représenté au Théâtre Molière,*

---

[1] See the *"Bibliographie des Œuvres de Sade"* drawn up by Robert Valençay in *Les Infortunes de la Vertu,* Paris, Les Editions du Point du Jour, 1946.
[2] In a letter of March 6, 1791.

*à Paris, en 1791; et à Versailles, sur celui de la Société Dramatique, le 22 frimaire, l'an 8 de la République. A Versailles, chez Blaizot, Libraire, rue Satory. An huitième* [1800]. One volume, 8vo, 48 pages.

7. *Les Crimes de l'Amour, Nouvelles héroïques et tragiques; précédées d'une Idée sur les romans et ornées de gravures, par D.-A.-F. Sade, auteur d' "Aline et Valcour." A Paris, chez Massé, éditeur-propriétaire, rue Helvétius n° 580.* An VIII [1800]. Four volumes, 12mo. Four frontispieces. This work contains eleven stories, as follows:
   Vol. I—*Juliette et Raunai, ou la Conspiration d'Amboise, nouvelle historique; La Double Epreuve.*
   Vol. II—*Miss Henriette Stralson, ou les Effets du désespoir, nouvelle anglaise; Faxelange, ou les Torts de l'ambition; Florville et Couvral, ou le Fatalisme.*
   Vol. III—*Rodrigue, ou la Tour enchantée, conte allégorique; Laurence et Antonio, nouvelle italienne; Ernestine, nouvelle suédoise.*
   Vol. IV—*Dorgeville, ou le Criminel par Vertu; la Comtesse de Sancerre, ou la Rivale de sa fille, anecdote de la Cour de Bourgogne; Eugénie de Franval.*

8. *L'Auteur de "Les Crimes de l'Amour" à Villeterque, folliculaire. Paris, Massé, an XI* [1803]. 12 mo, 20 pages.

9. *La Marquise de Gange. Paris, Béchet, Libraire, quai des Augustins, n° 63, 1813.* Two volumes, 12mo.

POLITICAL PAMPHLETS

1. *Adresse d'un citoyen de Paris, au roi des Français.* Paris, Girouard, no date [1791]. 8vo, 8 pages.

2. *Section des Piques. Observations présentées à l'Assemblée administrative des hôpitaux. 28 octobre 1792. De l'Impri-*

*merie de la Section des Piques, rue Saint-Fiacre, n° 2.,* 8vo, 4 pages.

3.  *Section des Piques. Idée sur le mode de la sanction des Loix; par un citoyen de cette Section. De l'Imprimerie de la rue Saint-Fiacre n° 2, 2 novembre 1792.* 8vo, 16 pages.

4.  *Pétition des Sections de Paris à la Convention nationale. De l'imprimerie de la Section des Piques.* No date [1793]. 8vo, 4 pages.

5.  *Section des Piques. Extraits des Régistres des délibérations de l'Assemblée générale et permanente de la Section des Piques. De l'Imprimerie de la Section des Piques, 1793.* 8vo, 8 pages.

6.  *La Section des Piques à ses Frères et Amis de la Société de la Liberté et de l'Egalité, à Saintes, département de la Charente-Inférieure. De l'Imprimerie de la Section des Piques, 1793.* 8vo, 4 pages.

7.  *Section des Piques. Discours prononcé par la Section des Piques, aux mânes de Marat et de Le Pelletier, par Sade, citoyen de cette section et membre de la Société populaire. De l'Imprimerie de la Section des Piques, 1793.* 8vo, 8 pages.

8.  *Pétition de la Section des Piques, aux représentans du peuple français. De l'Imprimerie de la Section des Piques, 1793.* 8vo, 8 pages.

## II. PRINCIPAL POSTHUMOUS PUBLICATIONS

1.  *Dorci ou la Bizarrerie du sort, conte inédit par le marquis de Sade, publié sur le manuscrit avec une notice sur l'auteur* [signed A. F. (Anatole France)]. Paris, Charavay frères, éditeurs, 1881. 16mo, 64 pages.

2. *Historiettes, Contes et fabliaux de Donatien-Alphonse-François, marquis de Sade, publiés pour la première fois sur les manuscrits autographes inédits par Maurice Heine. A Paris, pour les membres de la Société du Roman Philosophique, 1926.* 4to, 340 pages.
Contains the following works: HISTORIETTES—*Le Serpent; La Saillie gasconne; L'Heureuse Feinte; Le M. . . puni; L'Evêque embourbé; Le Revenant; Les Harangueurs provençaux; Attrapez-moi toujours de même; L'Epoux complaisant; Aventure incompréhensible; La Fleur de châtaignier.* CONTES ET FABLIAUX—*L'Instituteur philosophe; La Prude, ou la Rencontre imprévue; Emilie de Tourville, ou la Cruauté fraternelle; Augustine de Villeblanche, ou le Stratagème de l'amour; Soit fait ainsi qu'il est requis; Le Président mystifié; La Marquise de Thélème, ou les Effets du libertinage; Le Talion; Le Cocu de lui-même, ou le Raccommodement imprévu; Il y a place pour deux; L'Epoux corrigé; le Mari prêtre, conte provençal; La Châtelaine de Longueville, ou la Femme vengée; Les Filous.* APPENDICE—*Les Dangers de la bienfaisance (Dorci).*

3. *Dialogue entre un prêtre et un moribond, par Donatien-Alphonse-François, marquis de Sade, publié pour la première fois sur le manuscrit autographe inédit, avec un avant-propos et des notes par Maurice Heine.* [Paris], Stendhal et Compagnie, 1926. Small 4to, 62 pages.

4. *Correspondance inédite du Marquis de Sade, de ses proches et de ses familiers, publiée avec une introduction, des annales et des notes par Paul Bourdin.* Paris, Librairie de France, 1929. Small 4to, 452 pages.

5. *Marquis de Sade. Les Infortunes de la Vertu. Texte établi sur le manuscrit original autographe et publié pour la première fois avec une introduction par Maurice Heine.* Paris, Editions Fourcade, 1930. 8vo, 206 pages.

6. *Les 120 Journées de Sodome, ou l'Ecole du libertinage, par le marquis de Sade. Edition critique établie sur le manuscrit*

original autographe par Maurice Heine. A Paris, par S. et
C., aux dépens des Bibliophiles souscripteurs, 1931–1935.
Three volumes, 4to, 500 pages (uninterrupted pagination
throughout the three volumes).[3]

7. Marquis de Sade. L'Aigle, Mademoiselle. . . , Lettres publiées pour la première fois sur les manuscrits autographes
inédits avec une Préface et un Commentaire par Gilbert Lely.
Paris, Les Editions Georges Artigues, 1949. One volume,
16mo, 222 pages.

8. Marquis de Sade. Histoire secrète d'Isabelle de Bavière,
reine de France. Publiée pour la première fois sur le manuscrit
autographe inédit avec un avant-propos par Gilbert Lely.
Paris, Librairie Gallimard, 1953. One volume, 16mo, 336
pages.

9. Marquis de Sade. Le Carillon de Vincennes. Lettres inédites
publiées avec des notes par Gilbert Lely. Paris, "Arcanes,"
1953. One volume, 16mo, 106 pages.

10. Marquis de Sade. Cahiers personnels (1803–04). Publiés
pour la première fois sur les manuscrits autographes inédits
avec une préface et des notes par Gilbert Lely. Paris, Corréa,
1953. One volume, 12mo, 130 pages.

11. Marquis de Sade. Monsieur le 6. Lettres inédites (1778–
1784) publiées et annotées par Georges Daumas. Preface de
Gilbert Lely. Paris, Julliard, 1954. One volume, 16mo, 288
pages.

12. Marquis de Sade. Cent onze Notes pour La Nouvelle
Justine. Collection "Le Terrain vague," no. IV. [Paris,
1956.] Small 4to, 158 pages (unnumbered).

---

[3] An earlier edition of The 120 Days, edited by Dr. Eugen Dühren, was published
in 1904. The version is so riddled with errors, however, that Maurice Heine's 1931–
1935 edition must rightly figure as the original edition of this work.

## III. PRINCIPAL UNPUBLISHED MANUSCRIPTS

1. *Œuvres diverses (1764–1769).* Contains the one-act play *Le Philosophe soi-disant;* the epistolary work *Voyage de Hollande;* various letters, couplets, etc. Until the discovery of this notebook, Sade's earliest writing was thought to date from 1782.

2. *Les Jumelles ou le Choix difficile.* Two-act comedy in verse.

3. *Le Prévaricateur ou le Magistrat du temps passé.* Five-act comedy in verse.

4. *Jeanne Laisné, ou le Siège de Beauvais.* Five-act tragedy in verse.

5. *L'Ecole des jaloux ou la Folle Epreuve.* One-act comedy in *vers libres.*

6. *Le Misanthrope par amour ou Sophie et Desfrancs.* Five-act comedy in *vers libres.*

7. *Le Capricieux, ou l'Homme inégal.* Five-act comedy in verse.

8. *Les Antiquaires.* One-act comedy in prose.

9. *Henriette et Saint-Clair, ou la Force du Sang.* Prose drama in five acts.

10. *Franchise et Trahison.* Prose drama in three acts.

11. *Fanny, ou les Effets du désespoir.* Prose drama in three acts.

12. *La Tour mysterieuse. Opéra-comique* in one act.

13. *L'Union des arts ou les Ruses de l'amour.* A play in alexandrines, prose and *vers libres.* In the *Catalogue raisonné* of 1788, this work was to comprise six parts and a final *Divertissement.* In the extant manuscript, the *Divertissement* and one play, *La Fille malheureuse,* are missing.

14. *Les Fêtes de l'amitié.* Two acts incorporating prose, verse, and vaudeville.

15. *Adélaïde de Brunswick, princesse de Saxe, événement du XI*ᵉ
    *siècle.* Novel.


## IV. PRINCIPAL UNPUBLISHED MANUSCRIPTS EITHER DESTROYED OR NOT RECOVERED[4]

1. *L'Egarement de l'infortune.* Three-act prose drama.

2. *Tancrède.* One-act lyric play in alexandrine verse with music
   interspersed.

3. *La Fille malheureuse.* One-act comedy in prose.

4. *La Fine Mouche.* Tale.

5. *L'Heureux Echange.* Tale.

6. *La Force du Sang.* Tale.

7. *Les Inconvénients de la pitié.* Tale (first draft).

8. *Les Reliques.* Tale.

9. *Le Curé de Prato.* Tale.

10. *La Marquise de Thélème.* Tale (first draft).

11. *Le Portefeuille d'un homme de lettres.* Of this projected
    four-volume work, there exists eleven *historiettes* published
    by Maurice Heine, an *avertissement*, the *Voyage de Hollande*
    previously cited, and various fragments.

12. *La Liste du Suisse. Historiette.*

13. *La Messe trop chère. Historiette.*

14. *L'Honnête Ivrogne. Historiette.*

15. *N'y allez jamais sans lumière. Historiette.*

---

[4] Numbers 1 through 17 represent works mentioned in the 1788 *Catalogue raisonné;*
numbers 18 through 20 are works seized at Sade's publisher, Massé, on 15 *Ventôse,
An IX;* number 21 is the projected ten-volume work burned at the *Préfecture de
Police* after Sade's death.

16. *La justice vénitienne. Historiette.*

17. *Adélaïde de Miramas, ou le Fanatisme protestan. Historiette.*

18. *Les Délassements du libertin, ou la Neuvaine de Cythère.*

19. *Les Caprices, ou un peu de tout.* Political work.

20. *Les Conversations du château de Charmelle.* The first draft of *Les Journées de Florbelle.*

21. *Les Journées de Florbelle, ou la Nature dévoilée, suivies des Mémoires de l'abbé de Modose et des Aventures d'Emilie de Volnange servant de preuves aux assertions, ouvrage orné de deux cents gravures.* This immense work, contained in over a hundred notebooks, according to Lely's estimate, was burned by the police at the request and in the presence of Sade's son, Donatien-Claude-Armand.